A Legend for a Girl

Rosemary Delnavine

© 2017 Rosemary Delnavine
All rights reserved.

ISBN: 154505844X
ISBN 13: 9781545058442

PROLOGUE

It is bright morning in Alaska, where a wild animal is going to eat Elinore Crum's father for breakfast. Hector Crum has gone to bathe in a river and, showing his usual disregard for social constraint, has crashed naked through the undergrowth onto the very spot where *Ursus arctos horribilis* has scooped salmon out of those waters forever.

Later, belongings in his nearby tent will enable passing hunters to put a name to the bits that the bear left behind, but no one will ever really know why his running off to embrace the world should have ended in Alaska. Could it be the untamed vastness of the country? Hector's loud complaint has always been that wee, strait-laced Scotland, overrun with philistines and clerics, offers poor soil for nourishing visionaries such as he. No record exists of his progressive art and dense, allusive poetry having inspired Alaskan gold miners and fur trappers. Straw men, fisher kings, Icarus as metaphor and rough beasts slouching across the page are understandably less compelling, less galvanizing of the Alaskan mind than *ursus* of some local species padding straight across one's own backyard. Still, we can assume that, unlike certain jaded cognoscenti in Hector's homeland, hospitable Alaskans have never spat "Derivative!" at him along with their tobacco juice.

Hector will leave behind a wife, Melba, who has dwelt in a different untamed vastness far longer than he has been in Alaska. It is the region created by her youth, beauty and feckless self-absorption, the latter two being extreme. He will also leave behind a child, Elinore; a cottage; and an inheritance that now resembles a truckle of Stilton hollowed into crumbs by the kind of long-handled silver spoon that Hector has always believed to be his birthright. He is the spiritual child of another era, poor man. It has been desperately hard for him to shoulder his responsibilities: to live, in Scotland some decades before the millennium, the kind of life that would have been perfectly normal and natural in the Florence or Biarritz of generations earlier. Now he is in the wrong place at the ultimate wrong time. No bachelor dilettante ever encountered man-eaters in the *piazza* or on the *plage*.

Nevertheless, Hector Crum's end is worthy of the best kind of nineteenth-century melodrama. Perhaps, then, it can be said that he has lived the right way all along, to succeed in dying with such anachronistic panache. And is this end really a tragedy for his little family? Under the circumstances, it is a blessing that they will be spared the expense of a funeral, not to mention the strain of exchanging platitudes, the enforced contact with relations on both sides who quickly and long ago consigned Hector and Melba to yet another kind of wilderness: the one where embarrassing relations of good families must live out their lives.

Hector's story will end within seconds. Melba's story belongs to a different writer, a talented plumber of the depths of self-anointed celebrity. Lacking in those skills, I can only strive humbly to do Melba justice for as long as she appears in the following pages.

Elinore's story is the one I can tell. You, the reader, can decide whether it is tragedy or comedy. After all, you are skilled in making exactly the same judgment of your own lives, day after day. Or will you find that this story is something else altogether, something nameless that lies between?

1

The news of Hector's demise eventually reached his home in Scotland. Never had a piece of news been at once so delicious to the consumers of local gossip and so well nurtured by circumstance that it could extend itself every week in fascinating new detail. Melba, keenly aware that such an opportunity for melodrama was passing rare, excelled in her interpretation of the tragically young widow. It was not so difficult. A black velvet pillbox hat with a perky bow did not cost a great deal, and she knew how to perch it on the back of her head in exactly the manner of that other famous widow. She wore black gloves too. She was very correct. This was not so difficult either, since her respectable upbringing and private education were barely behind her. But, like snow off a dyke, these attributes soon slid off her. Her widow's weeds suddenly incorporated a lustrous black fur cape whose buttery gold satin lining flashed now and then like a scandalous secret, a nod and a wink to a different future altogether, as Melba walked around being gracious on high heels. The talk was of family money coming to the widow's rescue; her wardrobe was evidence of that, for lack of any other. Perhaps it was the foil of all that black, but she did seem to become more ravishingly gorgeous with every week of mourning. Decency began to be affronted by finery and the bloom of youth. Family aid was right and proper, but this use of it was not. She could at least have kept some pallor, went the thinking. The contrast was made all the more pointed by the presence of that wee ragamuffin Elinore, who remained a perennial affront to respectable notions of child rearing. Then spring came and Melba threw aside Mrs Kennedy and all that compelling dignity in favour of dresses that vied with herbaceous borders. And anyway, Mrs Kennedy was now Mrs Onassis.

Young Elinore Crum found that becoming fatherless was not, for her, the terrible event that she had read about in stories, Hector having already dimmed considerably in her mind. At first, his permanent disappearance changed little but the duration and nature of noise in the cottage, the wild veerings from conjugal detestation to passion and back again having ceased. He had been absent more and more as she was growing up, no doubt practising how to run away. Indeed, she had grown to call him Hector instead of Daddy, because he was so markedly unlike any other example of a Daddy in her world.

That world was Criven, a village so close to England that it was barely in Scotland. It lay cupped in a sheltered spot by a river, ignored by tourists because it was unremarkable, rather in the way that an unassuming person elderly enough to have experienced two world wars might be overlooked. Over and around the long Borders hills, innumerable figures – lords and reivers, Covenanters and cattle-rustlers, shepherds, farmers, moss-troopers and many others – had marauded, pillaged, traded, driven their stock and hunted for centuries. But Criven was now a benign place. It had a river with a ruined pack-bridge over rippling shallows that offered excellent paddling and all a child needed to build and rebuild many dams. The hunting was now done with nets attached to bamboo canes, for minnows, or for foxes if one had a good enough pony and a hunt membership. A library van visited regularly (although not nearly often enough to satisfy Elinore Crum). The school was small, for primary classes only; local mothers made the school dinners five days a week and none of the teachers was a bully. Every child who expected an invitation to a birthday party duly received one.

Remnants of other times were everywhere. Close to Elinore's home, a ruined chapel, even older than the grassy, humpbacked bridge, crumbled amid ivy and brambles. One gable end held a plaque showing fragments of Latin and contorted heraldic creatures in relief. Elinore would stand and gaze up at this, hopeful that the serpents and dragons might unwind and speak to her, but the only hissing and roaring she ever heard was that of the wind.

Trees were more congenial. They were always expressing themselves, and Elinore regarded them as secondary inhabitants of the village. The avenue of beeches leading to the church greeted her in the manner of a whispering assembly of refined, upright ladies. They evoked the maids of honour at the Queen's coronation, and the throng of peeresses whose upraised arms had branched whitely as they removed and then replaced their coronets at the moment of crowning. Elinore happened to know rather a lot about that resounding occasion. She had long ago given up belief in God, after one too many dubious claims about the sky's holding capacity for live winged persons and endless dead ones, but her veneration of the Royal Family was absolute. Accounts of their doings were to her what reports of the latest dieting trend or hem height were to Melba. Buckingham Palace and Balmoral were not only real and on the map, but also completely comprehensible as a form of heaven. She owned a few sacred books that proved this with colour plates.

Eleanor's home, the only one she could remember, was a cottage shrouded in Virginia creeper. In front was a neglected rockery; behind, a piece of sloping lawn that was good for a few somersaults and little else. Elinore felt about her home as Ratty, Mole and Mr Badger felt about each of theirs. It was almost two hundred years old, with small, leaky windows set deep in sandstone walls.

This thick masonry had muffled the racket made by Hector and Melba when they quarrelled day in, day out about everything and nothing and money in particular. Such was their devotion to quarrelling and very occasionally to each other that they had tended to forget all about the child they possessed. Elinore always had holey socks, hand-me-down jumpers that were too short in the arms, and hair that ought to have been washed the previous week. She never had party dresses, a coat with velvet cuffs and collar, and winter boots with fur inside, as shown off by her friends at the village school. Meals were erratic, to say the least, and Elinore often went to bed with a grumbling tummy. Her mother's distaste for cooking and the humbler kinds of shopping practically ensured it. Dieting and the shape of her own figure held great fascination for Melba Crum, whereas Elinore did not. Together, the Crum parents had been so taken up with their visions of the contrary lives that each one desired, and with the immediate work of making the present life miserable for each other, that Elinore had been left largely untended; to hang as she grew, in the words of other mothers in the village.

In winter, when the disorder and skimpy housekeeping at the Crum cottage increased all its discomforts and deficiencies as a place of retreat from weather, Elinore sidled as often as she could into the homes of her school friends. She hung around their tinselly Christmas trees, their gas fires whooshing out warmth at the flick of a switch, and their television sets. In all seasons, she ate vicariously through kitchen aromas and the sight of tables set neatly and abundantly. Often, she filled her tummy at the insistence of someone else's mother. Her manners were exceptional. This had much to do with her diligent study of Miss Agnes Pound's *Book of Charm & Essential Etiquette*, copyright 1937, which she had found under a table at the church jumble sale. She knew how to clasp her hands behind her back and stand silently in places that attracted her intense curiosity but into which she had not actually been invited. No one at a farm, the back premises of a shop, a neighbour's garden or the church when ladies were decorating it for a seasonal festival ever had reason to turn her away. On the contrary, sometimes she was offered a little job to draw her in; after all, was not Elinore Crum an obvious unfortunate in the clutches of two ne'er-do-wells who were better at giving themselves airs and graces than keeping a bairn fed and clothed? Sometimes her watchful politeness and interest in learning odd things (why are tea chests called tea chests, what happens if the lamb can't get out of the ewe, why are peanuts called that if they aren't green, do hounds actually eat up the fox when they catch it, and similar enquiries into the nature of the immediate universe) resulted in unlooked-for gifts from people she did not know well enough to call friends, and who were decidedly not friends of her parents. (Hector and Melba did not have *friends*: their sole function was to be fodder for talk.) Sometimes these gifts landed on her at critical moments, almost as if someone were watching over her – not that she harboured any such idea.

After Hector, the next man in Elinore's life was called Bank Manager. She never met him, but her mother did, frequently. It was rather like having a father again, for Bank Manager always put Melba in a bad mood, just as Hector had done. But really, it was better to have Bank Manager as the man of the house instead of Hector, because Bank Manager never came to her house and slammed doors or broke crockery or demanded that she stay perfectly quiet for hours on end because someone called the Muse was visiting.

One afternoon, however, Elinore arrived home from school to find a To Let sign affixed to a post stuck in the middle of the rockery. Melba was in her bedroom, taking clothes out of the wardrobe and piling them on the bed.

"Mummy! What's happening to our house?"

Melba affected an air of unconcern, flapped a hand at Elinore as if at an insect and began to sort the clothes into piles.

"Oh, no need to work yourself up. We aren't going to Alaska! Only to Edinburgh."

"Why do we have to go anywhere? This is *my* place," Elinore said, her voice rising.

"Well, it certainly is not mine," declared Melba. "The Bank Manager and I have decided it's time for a new life. I need to be seen to make the most of myself and this place is all cows and sheep and ancient colonels in dreadful tweeds. And we need to replace Hector. Do you not think you could do with a new father? An improved one?"

"No!" shouted Elinore. "I *do not* need one. You can get one if you want. Get Mr Finnie at the manse. He's very nice and he hasn't got a wife, he's all alone in the world."

"Good gracious, Elinore! Don't open your mouth about things you don't understand. A *minister*? For *me*? God save me."

"But his house is too big for him. He could come and live here and we –"

"*Stop* this shouting immediately. You're taking after Hector and my nerves won't stand it. We are going to Edinburgh whether you like it or not. Everyone says that I ought to be a star. I'll be a sensation, yes, quite quickly, and Edinburgh will be grateful. You too."

Ah, Melba – already long since famous for her airs and a few wavering graces. The Bank Manager's reasons for urging the poor widow to put a tenant in her cottage and move to the city, where lots of ladies went out to work, were not quite in tune with Melba's plans for taking Scotland's capital by storm. She regarded herself as a businessman would a surefire investment generating guaranteed, age-defying dividends; a sort of endlessly renewing bank account. Indeed, she *was* exceptionally beautiful, with rosy lips, huge sapphire eyes and lots of wavy blondeness that did not come out of a bottle, as she took care to remind everyone. Imbued with the haste and fragmentary attention that she allotted to everything except dressing and applying makeup, her local appearances gave the impression that she was a *Vogue* model who had just remembered a necessity – tea, stamps, a pound of mince – while en route to studios full of avid lenses. Retired colonels might be well below her attention, but still, their Land Rovers usually doddered to a stop at the sight of her. As for Elinore, she took it for granted that everyone must admire and adore her mother, for was not Melba the only beautiful lady in Criven, the only special person, the only one who resembled film stars from America and real princesses?

Now Melba suddenly seemed to notice Elinore's appearance and relate it to her aims.

"What a tatterdemalion you are, child! Certainly no credit to me in that state. We can't afford to frighten off any likely new Hector. You'll have to smarten up and stay that way."

Elinore sat down on the floor, crossed her legs and her arms and glowered so hard that she almost crossed her eyebrows.

"I will not leave my home!" she stated.

"But you are not in any way useful, Elinore. How can I expect a tenant to look after you? Furniture is one thing – they'll pay more for tables and chairs – but you do nothing to furnish a room."

Melba spoke in the bell-like tones of the beautiful ladies whom Elinore worshipped, and which did not issue from any other mouth in Criven. She was a Sassenach, clear and decisive. Elinore gaped at her, aghast.

"Aren't we taking the furniture with us? My bed? My bookcase?"

Melba flapped her hand again, shooing off this notion.

"*We* have no need of furniture. We're going to live with the Caltrops, who have a big enough house. They say it's their Christian duty to help family members in distress, even if I am only a third or fourth cousin by marriage, thrice removed – I *think* that's what they said I was. Anyway, you must be very nice and grateful to them."

"No!" shrieked Elinore. She leapt up and stamped one foot very hard and then the other one, and clenched her fists into balls. "I will *not* be nice and I will *not* go! I will stay in my bedroom!"

She picked up a giant swansdown powder puff from Melba's dressing table and threw it at her before running to her own room and slamming the door. She hurled herself onto the bed and stared at the bookcase on the opposite wall for a long moment.

Elinore did not own nearly as many books as she wished. She wished for an entire library. Meanwhile, she thought her old bookcase and all the books that she did own looked very fine together. The bookcase had occupied its place on the end wall of her bedroom for as long as she could recall. It was a piece of campaign furniture: three teak shelves, four brass rods and a most colourful history. It murmured foreign names to itself at night, and sometimes Elinore would hear or read a nugget of history and wonder why this general or that battle sounded familiar.

Now she addressed the bookcase in a whisper.

"She says we're going away and she says you have to stay behind with *strangers*. And the bed too. They won't dust you properly. They won't put a nice posy on your top shelf. She said we'll be living in Edinburgh. In someone else's house. *With* them. It's horrible!" The whisper became a wail. "I *have* to stay and look after you."

Elinore curled herself up on the bed, sniffling angrily. It was an Edwardian three-quarters bed, a size that up-to-date households no longer considered useful or desirable. Unlike the bookcase, it had feminine lines. Marquetry garlands decorated the mahogany headboard and footboard. With age, the two ends had come to lean towards each other, and now the middle seemed to sag even more, as if dispirited by this news of departure.

Much later, when the only sounds were a fox's bark from over the river and tiny scratchings of mice within the walls of the cottage, the bookcase and the bed discussed this development in their lives.

"I shall miss her sorely," rasped the bookcase. "Her solicitous ministrations have indeed ensured my comfort. I am not as firm as I once was, y'know. Extremes of dryness and damp take their toll on the joints."

"I do understand," said the bed. "If we are to remain up here, ignored by connoisseurs, no one will take care of us after she is gone. No one will ever take all the books from your shelves every Sunday to let you breathe!"

"Quite possibly not. And equally, it is possible that they will stuff me with paperback romances in *lurid* covers" – little groans and tremors – "and overburden me with piles of forgotten newsprint, ingraining me with dust and printer's ink. Newspapers make me look *so* unkempt. Or they will stuff me with popular magazines. They are even heavier and will flop over my edges just the same. I have been content of late, but I tell you, such treatment will make me yearn for the rectitude of military life."

The bed sighed. "Well, we were both abandoned here before. It might turn out well again. As for the child, I wonder where exactly she will be taking up residence. It *is* fanciful, I know, but I should like to go too and have a view from a different window. A larger one."

"Oh, it will be a fine house in Edinburgh," said the bookcase. "One might almost smell it from here – parcel gilt, no doubt, bits of ormolu, a general worthiness pervading every room. The French have a word for it. Life is refined in Edinburgh. As a somewhat contused and abraded campaign piece, I should not fit in, even if I were to be smuggled in. I cannot speak for you, of course, dear Bed."

"She might *not* go."

"But she might well have to, my dear. Let us face the unpalatable fact that we three are creatures of the corner. It is our fate to be left in corners because we are worn and far from modish; it is hers to be lodged in one, so to speak, until she is much older. My heyday of necessity, when I did my bit to preserve a serving officer's sanity, is gone forever. Hers has not begun, chiefly because she is not old enough to marry. I am sure her mother will want to marry again as soon as she can. She must already have a scheme of some kind, and this move will be part of it."

The bed sighed again. "How little have the aspirations of women changed since the days of my joinery! I fear it is as good as done. A *fait accompli*. We are to be left and she is to be taken away. *Force majeure*. She has been the perfect occupant for me: lightweight and singular. Oh, how I dread change! It is a terrible strain on all parts. And naturally I do not expect to be dusted and polished in the future any more than you do, Bookcase. Moreover, my inlaid parts are delicate work that could loosen and fall out with rough treatment. They might put *children* in me. It is too, too distressing to contemplate."

"Well, *she* is a child," responded the bookcase. "They are not all bad. We must put a good front on it. Even, ahem, boys might not be that bad." He did miss male company keenly.

"But *she* has never once bounced on me," said the bed. "*She* is an altogether different sort of child."

2

The intentions of a bear, a woman and a bank manager had crossed in the dimension known as Fate. For Elinore, the result was ancient, grey-black Edinburgh and an end to the liberty of neglect she had enjoyed in Criven.

On the dreadful (for Elinore) day of departure from Criven, all her books were in one cardboard box and all her clothing in two others; a bag held miscellaneous treasures and necessities, such as her pencils, a tiny set of watercolour paints, old conkers, a pony's shoe, one horn of a bullock, and the magazine pictures that had been stuck to her bedroom walls. She sat squashed into the back seat of a large car belonging to Mr Fairgrieve, the local garage owner, while Melba was arrayed prettily in front with two hatboxes on her lap and one at her feet. Mr Fairgrieve himself was in the driver's seat, uneasily checking his rear-view mirror. Apart from Elinore and her own meagre belongings, the back seat and the very back, where the Fairgrieve dogs normally lolled, were completely filled with Melba's suitcases and a decrepit green cabin trunk.

Mr Fairgrieve had not *really* offered to convey the Crums to Edinburgh; at least, he could not recall making any such outright offer. Enough of Melba's charm had dripped onto him, however, to blur the distinction between his need to go to the city on business that day and Melba's need to get there without any effort or expense. Furthermore, Melba had simply parked Hector's chugging, stalling, rusted Morris Minor outside his garage and handed him the keys. Its slow, inexorable dying had infuriated her for years, but it did *go*, as she informed him brightly, and would no doubt go much better in his hands or someone else's if he cared to sell it. Melba had already mentally transported herself to Edinburgh. She was sailing around in taxis, always en route to restaurants, nightclubs and other highly public venues (improved transportation that allowed her to alight in cool grace being another element of her master plan for acquiring a new and better Hector). With such a pleasant vision in place, she could be serene at this moment, despite the Fairgrieve dog hairs all over the car and dog smell emanating from Mr Fairgrieve's tweeds. Of course, he *would* be wearing tweeds, thought Melba. Country life – ugh! But no more, no more.

They drove to a part of Edinburgh that lay south of the city and east of the hills spreading hazily at the very edge. The streets of sandstone villas all looked alike to Elinore. She was not used to seeing so many tall hedges, as if each house had tendencies to fortification, but she was relieved to see plenty of trees and glimpses of large, well-maintained gardens. She had always wanted a nice, big garden with a lawn that did not slope awkwardly like the one she had left behind in Criven. Mr Fairgrieve was driving slowly and peering at house numbers. He stopped at No. 17 Dunallan Crescent. A flat-sided, flat-topped laurel hedge rose high behind a low wall with metal stumps in it, where railings had been sawn off to feed a wartime hunger for iron. The hedge obscured the house, and the double gates at the end of the short tarmacked drive were closed.

Melba scrambled out of the car, fluffed her skirt and hair and disappeared towards the house. Mr Fairgrieve opened the gates and backed the car into the drive. Elinore remained hunched in her seat. If she stayed exactly where she was, perhaps time would roll backwards and take her with it, unnoticed, as Mr Fairgrieve drove away to Criven and then she would be back where she belonged.

But he was opening the car door on her side and saying surely she'd like to stretch her legs now while he started unloading the baggage. And there was Melba, accompanied by a heavyset woman who, to Elinore, looked old but far from grandmotherly.

"Elinore, come on, get out and introduce yourself."

It was a mild spring day, and Mrs Caltrop had come only from the front door, but nevertheless she was wearing a hat. From under its squashy, mushroom-coloured felt, her hair sprang out like fibres from an old Brillo pad. Her cheeks bore two round spots of fierce red and behind her spectacles her small eyes were the bright, hard blue of painted china. Her lips were fleshy and also very red, and, as they stretched into a sort of smile at Elinore, big white teeth gleamed between them. Elinore thought at once of certain animals at Edinburgh Zoo, the kind that needed to eat a lot of meat twice a day. Gingerly, she took the Caltrop hand that was extended to her. It felt hot and rough.

Mrs Caltrop's effort at smiling vanished at the sight of suitcases and boxes piling up on her drive. Her shrub-like eyebrows went up and the fleshy mouth formed an O of consternation.

"Dear me, what a lot you are bringing into this house! I suppose you want to see where you will be putting it all. Follow me."

Melba gripped Elinore's shoulder as they walked behind Mrs Caltrop and hissed, "Be *nice!*"

Elinore glowered.

Through a vestibule they went, into a tenebrous panelled hall, where Mrs Caltrop hung up the mushroom hat on an ornate mirrored hall stand, and up the stairs to a landing wainscotted in the same dark wood as below. She opened a door and gestured into the room beyond.

"I have to say, the wardrobe in here has always been ample enough for guests in the past."

Melba clasped her hands at the level of her heart and smiled, but only for two seconds. Then she was frowning and her eyes were darting all around the room. Two single beds, two bedside tables, two lamps. A dressing table and stool, a wash-hand basin with a mirror above it and a lidded wicker laundry basket below. A fireplace with a one-bar electric fire in the scoured grate. And a wardrobe that was a fraction bigger than the one she had left in Criven. Carpeting was confined to a central square in shades of pea soup, porridge and egg, which was small enough to leave a three-foot perimeter of bottle-green linoleum. The wallpaper displayed bunches of something resembling primroses, but in ochres, beiges and the same greens as the flooring. At the window, beige brocade over heavy net curtains kept daylight at bay.

"Yes, de-*light*ful, perfectly lovely, quite – comfortable."

"Thank you." Mrs Caltrop inclined her head in gracious acknowledgement. "Our guests always sleep well in this room."

"Oh, I hope we shan't be putting anybody out by taking up this room."

"It is our Christian duty to give shelter in the hour of need, as I have said. We do have another spare room."

"I'll just run down and tell Mr Fairgrieve to bring up the things. Coats and dresses, you know – not good to leave them packed like sardines!"

She cast a dazzling smile at Mrs Caltrop and ran downstairs. Elinore stood staring, hands clenched into fists in the pockets of her anorak. Was she really expected to share that room with Melba? Her bedroom in the cottage at Criven was tiny, slope-ceilinged and damp, but it had been indisputably hers; the private territory of her dreams, the stories she read and made up, and the companionship of her bed and bookcase.

But no, Mrs Caltrop was beckoning her along the landing. Through a closed door they went, then two steps down into a short, low-ceilinged corridor with three doors on one side. Mrs Caltrop opened the first.

"Your room. It would have been less work to have you both in the one, but we could not go moving furniture around, could we?"

The last occupant of this room had been a skivvy of sorts, long, long ago. Furniture amounted to a narrow iron bedstead; a tiny bedside table; a chair; a utility-era chest of drawers; and a small, hexagonal table on bamboo legs, one of which did not touch the floor at all, perhaps in revulsion at the linoleum, which was the same bottle-green as in Melba's room. The walls had last been painted cream or white a generation or two ago, and they were now yellowed, the corners greyed as if rubbed with dust. The cotton curtains also appeared to have been made long ago; sunlight and annual boiling in washing soda had wilted their sprigged flowers into faint, bluish-green shadows. A candlewick bedspread in the colour and texture of rice pudding covered the bed. A small wood-framed mirror was propped against the wall on top of the chest of drawers. Two framed prints hung over the bed and a small fireplace (its grate empty of even a one-bar electric fire) respectively. Their vivid, acidic colours shouted in this room. No doubt that was the Caltropian intention, since each portrayed Jesus with a host of adoring children in a garden where palm trees mingled confusingly with pines and igloos stood by minarets. Elinore stared at this interior, trying to comprehend it as part of her life now, and her insides churned.

"May I please use the bathroom?" she asked.

Without speaking, Mrs Caltrop waved Elinore out of the room and opened the last of the three doors in the short, low corridor.

"Your bathroom," she said, and then turned on her heel, adding as she went, "You may go downstairs after you have washed your hands." When she reached the door to the main landing, she closed it firmly, as if underlining the desirability of keeping Elinore separate from the rest of the house.

Elinore went into the bathroom and closed the door. The linoleum in here was a dulled hell-fire red. Daylight from a single skylight fell on this and gave the damp-streaked walls and tongue-and-groove wainscoting a pinkish cast, but no version of this hue had ever been less suggestive of warmth in Elinore's brief experience. A claw-foot bathtub stood opposite the door; a wash-hand basin was under the skylight; and a toilet with a wooden seat and lid squatted below a tank with a pull-chain. All the white enamel was stained wherever it had metal fittings. Two thin towels hung on a rail. A cork bathmat, fragmenting at its corners, lay by the bath. The smell of Domestos, which Elinore loathed, hung in the air.

Mr Fairgrieve was about to depart. Melba, fussing over the baggage pile in her room, had already forgotten about service kindly rendered, but Elinore shadowed him to his car. An emissary of the normal, of Criven, that is to say, was disappearing. Thirty minutes of Mrs Caltrop and her dwelling had made Elinore ready to leap into the passenger seat and refuse to be moved. But then what?

She agonized and fidgeted. Mr Fairgrieve fastened his seat belt. Then he pulled out of the glove compartment a small package wrapped in crumpled Christmas paper.

"Nearly forgot this. Julie says to tell you it's just right for keeping under your pillow." He winked at Elinore and lowered his voice. "Careful, now! That woman is no fan of Radio One."

His car disappeared down Dunallan Crescent and Elinore plopped onto the front step, commanding herself to be angry and nothing less. Instinct warned against appearing as a small, vulnerable animal within sight of Mrs Caltrop's sharp eyes and large teeth. The gift from her friend Julie Fairgrieve was a perfect distraction, and Julie had enclosed a card. It showed a doleful dog, with collar and trailing leash, lying head on paws by an open door. Curlicued script across the top of the card spelled out "Thinking of you!"

> *Dear Elinore,*
>
> *I got my Dad to put new batteries in this. It is called a tranny. I hope you like it! I remembered you said you didn't have one. My new one is much bigger and red in colour with silver nobs!! I hope you are very excited by Edinburgh. If you come to Criven in the summer I MIGHT have a pony.*

I am very excited about THAT!!! And you can also ride it. Promise, promise, promise!

I hope you are happy in the new house. We will all miss you at school and me most of all because you helped me with my spelling and everything else!!!!

Love from,
Julie F.
XXXXXXXXX

Elinore had never dreamed of owning her own transistor radio. Deciding to go up to her room and hide this treasure immediately, she pushed it under her sweater and crossed her arms over her chest. Mr Fairgrieve's "Careful, now!" was echoing in her ears.

Mrs Caltrop was talking to Melba in the hall.

"You will have had luncheon, of course. When Kenneth comes home from his church meeting, we will have afternoon tea as usual at three. High tea is at half-past six *prompt*. Kenneth always listens to the six o'clock news first and we never disturb that."

"Yes, of course," muttered Melba. "I mean, of course *not*, we do not, would not."

Elinore's insides lurched again: she had forgotten that a second Caltrop lived here too. But she was relieved to hear mention of tea. In the topsy-turvy haste of leaving Criven, she had eaten a ham sandwich and half a tin of baked beans, cold. She went on up the stairs to her room. By the time Mr Caltrop made his appearance, she was ravenous and becoming almost as bad-tempered as Melba over the sad job of unpacking. It was such an insult to her books to be homeless, bereft of her dear friend the bookcase.

A booming complaint was the first sign that Kenneth Caltrop had arrived.

"Roberta! The gates are open. Both of them. Wide open! Are my bedding plants safe?"

Some muttering from Mrs Caltrop.

"Well, well, no doubt you will set our guests straight with the rules of the house. And where are they now?"

Melba pushed Elinore ahead of her down the stairs. A very tall man was staring up from the gloom of the hall. Meagre strands of white hair lay plastered across his otherwise bald, shiny head, and gold-rimmed spectacles gleamed faintly. He was far from wide, but the bulky, outmoded cut of his suit made him look bigger than he was.

"So, Melba and Elinore! I was just telling the kirk meeting what a fine thing it is to share our strength and comforts with you as you walk through your vale of tears without Hector. Yes, Hector – terrible, terrible indeed!"

Mr Caltrop shook his head dolefully. It was unclear whether he was ascribing terribleness to Hector's delinquencies as a father or to Hector's fate as bear food. Suddenly he bent and angled himself like a question mark while shooting out a long arm to tickle Elinore under her chin.

"But *you* will be a good wee girl indeed, will you not?"

Elinore jumped backwards, stumbled on the stairs and scrambled to put two steps between herself and this second dreadful Caltrop.

"*Do* excuse her, *such* shyness at that age, you know!" said Melba.

"A *virtue* in the eyes of the Lord," said Mrs Caltrop. "Forwardness in a child is a danger – the top of a slippery slope." She pursed her fleshy lips and stared at Elinore.

Mr Caltrop rubbed his hands together vigorously.

"Now, Roberta, let us have some tea and then we will all be properly acquainted. That kirk business leaves one with a rare thirst from all the talking."

They sat in the morning room, eating hard scones and digestive biscuits, watery jam, (possibly raspberry) and thin slices of orange cheese with dry whitish bits at the edges. After Mr Caltrop had scooped up his two scones, four biscuits, dollops of jam and butter, and eight slices of cheese, and Mrs Caltrop had taken exactly half that amount for herself, the remainders looked strangely untouchable, as if their meagreness signified a right to remain on the plate and far from a child's mouth; as an offering, perhaps. Mrs Caltrop's eyes slid from food to Elinore to Melba to Elinore to food. Elinore tried to remember Miss Agnes Pound's instructions for taking things from plates and leaving the rest in the name of politeness, but all she could think of was how famished she was and how horrible *everything* was. Mutiny began to stir in her belly in concert with the usual rumbles.

"We use the dining-room for church social occasions, and for the annual general meeting of my committee – my retired missionaries' welfare committee, that is." Mrs Caltrop looked immensely self-satisfied as she said this. "The sitting room," she continued, "is not used – except after funerals. Does she play?"

"What?" said Melba.

"Does the child take music lessons? No? Very good, she will have no need to create dust in there by using the piano. We must keep Mrs Wattie's work down. Fine furnishings take a great deal of keeping up. I will show you the rest of the house after tea."

"Who is Mrs Wattie?" asked Elinore, immediately apprehensive about a third adult in this place.

"Our twice-weekly woman. Every Tuesday and Friday, and extra when we have a spring and autumn turn-out."

"Our treasure!" boomed Mr Caltrop.

"Indeed," said Mrs Caltrop. "Now, Melba, in front of Mrs Wattie and in front of the young" (a pointed glance at Elinore) "we are Mr and Mrs Caltrop, although you may call us Kenneth and Roberta at other times."

"Goodness!" said Melba. "My poor little memory will never be up to that. But I can call you Mr and Mrs C. *all* the time, and then no one's nose will be out of joint, will it?"

Both Caltrops looked nonplussed at this exercise of initiative. Mrs Caltrop cleared her throat.

"I see. Now, to continue with Mrs Wattie. Considering all the extra work of a child in the house, a little weekly contribution to her would be quite in order."

"Oh. Yes. Little contributions. We did agree – I remember *that*! – that I would pay no rent. I will only be working part-time, you know. I do believe a dramatic career takes just as much keeping up as your fine house!"

"Rent? Indeed, no, it would not be Christian of us to ask for rent!" Mr Caltrop looked offended that he might be perceived as deficient in his Christianity. "As Roberta says, a contribution here and there – yes, here and there, since Mrs Wattie is not the only pillar of our, heh-heh, *wee castle* – would be most appreciated. But oh dear no, we couldn't be asking for *rent*, for your widow's farthings in your hour of need!"

Mrs Caltrop went to a writing desk in a corner and brought two sheets of paper back to the table.

"I thought it would be a kindness to write down for you our modest expectations. One copy for each of you. I suggest you and Elinore look at them every morning and every night, when you say your prayers. You are unlikely to forget anything if you make it part of your routine."

"I don't know any prayers," said Elinore. "We never say them."

Mr Caltrop's eating ceased abruptly. Both Caltrops looked at each other in consternation, and the red carnations on Mrs Caltrop's cheeks darkened and spread.

"You naughty girl!" cried Melba. "That is a silly, silly – you *do* know prayers, you went to Sunday school."

"But I stopped – "

"Yes, yes, you did stop, *we* stopped saying our prayers at home when we heard about Hector. It was the shock! A *bear*! I am sure God will forgive us this lapse under the circumstances. Elinore is still shocked. Her memory is deranged. It has sent my careful upbringing of her *completely* out of her mind!"

"We must get her into Sunday School without delay!" exclaimed Mr Caltrop.

"God has certainly brought you both to the right home," said Mrs Caltrop, whose china-blue eyes were now as fierce as the red on her face. She rose again and took a small book from one of the glassed-in shelves on either side of the fireplace. "Elinore, I trust you *do* know how to respect books. I wish you to take this and learn from it. If you read it twice a day, preferably kneeling by your bed, you will soon make good these dangerous deficiencies into which you have been tempted by sadness and despair. And Mr Caltrop and I will help you accomplish this, believe me!"

Counting silently, Elinore kept her hands in her lap and her eyes on her plate as Mrs Caltrop held out the book. One, two, three, four . . . Melba half-rose from her chair and almost screamed, "How terribly kind of you, Mrs C.!" She leant across, took the proffered book and slammed it down by Elinore's plate. "Now, what was it that you wanted *me* to look at?" She glanced at the handwritten pages. "*So* helpful. It must have taken you hours and hours! Such clarity. You must be a marvellous committee member and all the other ladies surely adore you!"

"Committee *Chair*, actually," said Mrs Caltrop, "if you mean my committee for the retired missionaries. But thank you, yes, I do serve on several others."

Mr Caltrop persisted with the notion that a form of higher education was still necessary for both Crums.

"Now, Melba, as a widow you need to be gathered into the fold of our congregation. The Sunday School will do wonders for guiding wee Elinore – take the strain off you – and the ladies of the kirk will keep you busy with all their good works, and not just on Sundays! They will make your heart blithe again even as you cherish the fond memory of poor Hector for all time."

Melba's eyes narrowed. "Oh, ree-aally . . ." was the only reply she gave. Elinore looked up, alert. She knew that sound, that look.

Together they had been the prelude to loud and furious attacks on Hector with ammunition that was not always verbal, or to equally loud denunciations of anything getting in the way of Melba's latest fervent desire, whatever that might be. She held her breath and waited. The only sound in the room was the chink of china and the gurgle of tea pouring into a cup. If Melba exploded and threw crockery at the Caltrops, surely she and Elinore would be banished from No. 17 Dunallan Crescent, and then they could go back to Criven; perhaps not to the cottage, but *someone* might give them a home – yes, Mr Finnie, in his big, empty manse, Mr Finnie who was religious because he had to be, being a minister, but who was nevertheless very nice and nothing, *nothing* like this petrifying pair of –

"But of course, you'll be keeping yourself busy with making a living, Melba. Do tell us about your new job. In Thistle Street, you said?"

Melba's eyes expanded to their normal width and she exhaled. "Yes, Mrs C. From noon until closing all week and all day on Saturdays at Grisella's Gowns. I've been a good customer, and when Grisella found out that I wanted to work in Edinburgh she offered me the job on the spot."

"My, the Lord was looking after you and no mistake," chuckled Mr Caltrop.

"Well, *actually*, it is because *I* have been looking after my figure – unless the Lord has had a hand in that too!" Melba laughed. Mrs Caltrop glared. Elinore slumped in her chair as her dream of Criven Manse evaporated. "They know I can model any of their gowns. If a gentleman calls in to buy one as a surprise for his wife, that can be a great help. The male imagination, you know – or lack of, shall we say?" Melba beamed at Mr Caltrop, who seemed at a loss for words.

Mrs Caltrop was frowning. "Afternoons and Saturdays? Who is to keep the child in order if no one is here when she returns from school? And the doors – she would need a key! This is a serious responsibility."

"And the front gates, the garden – the dogs! Indeed, a responsibility!" cried Mr Caltrop, clearly much exercised by this prospect.

"But I love dogs," said Elinore. "I can take them for walks. I did that at home with my friends' dogs. Where are your dogs?"

"We – do – *not* have dogs," replied Mrs Caltrop. Her teeth appeared to be clenched. "But there are dogs in Dunallan Crescent and beyond, and if they get into the garden they make an appalling mess. Everywhere. And nowadays there is always the danger of juvenile delinquents running loose. The gates *must* be kept closed. I have made that very clear on my list. Melba, please hand back those pages. Mr Caltrop and I will discuss the matter of a key and so on, and I will add the appropriate items of guidance. Clarity will be lacking otherwise."

"And clarity *is* next to godliness," said Melba. "Or should that be charity?"

"No, Mummy, you are wrong, it's *cleanliness*." Elinore felt pride in her command of general knowledge, especially since she had come to understand in Criven that she was far from godly.

Mrs Caltrop suddenly got up from the table and started clearing the tea things onto a huge wooden tray with silver handles. Her lips were a straight line and her frown might have been graven in stone.

"Please follow me. We will look at the rest of the house, and the garden, not that you will have much business in either part."

3

Let us look at the Caltrops and tease out their subtleties, their parts known to God, perhaps, but not to Melba and Elinore Crum.

Although her devotion to Christian service suggests a lineage of missionaries, Roberta Caltrop comes from an Indian Civil Service family. Until she was sent home to school, she grew up in India. She does not seem to have got over that or the final sending home in 1947. The Caltrops' imposing sandstone villa, with its upper and lower bay windows, its morning room, butler's pantry, tradesman's entrance, domestics' quarters (now Elinore's) and general structure of a hierarchy with many unseen busy hands at the bottom, is stuffed with mementoes. Every room displays a veritable bazaar of hammered silver and intricately etched brass bric-a-brac. The solid mahogany furnishings that are usually to be found lowering brownly in such Scottish residences must here compete with fidgety ogee-legged tables inlaid with mother of pearl, numerous cane chairs and stools, and little decorative bookcases too small for anything bigger than a psalter or prayer book or school Bible. Every houseplant sits in a big brass pot atop a teetering stand that writhes with leafy life of the fretted sandalwood or teak variety.

The zeal that her forebears exercised in the administration of Indian affairs is in Roberta concentrated mainly on the church and congregation to which she and Kenneth belong. But this alone is so very much smaller, so painfully *lesser* than an Indian province or even a lowly district! Roberta is relentless in her nosing for opportunity to do more, and for the deferential respect that should accompany that. The days of the heaven-born are behind her, but Roberta Caltrop believes that she can regain a different kind of height under the small pale sun of Edinburgh.

Kenneth Caltrop's family was cut from the same template. But he was a delicate child, too much so for India, and consequently he has never lived anywhere but No. 17 Dunallan Crescent. He has always attended one church: the same one that his mother first took him to in the age of knickerbockers. The deeply engrained circumscription of his thought processes is therefore too obvious to require further description.

Then there is the afterlife. Housing Melba and Elinore Crum is a sort of premium payable on insurance for the *right* kind of afterlife: the celestial equivalent of Simla in the summer, not the low, scorching plains. The Crums represent an especially rich opportunity. The family connection, however distant, exists and God would frown if it were not honoured. The cruel loss of a husband and father; the obvious need to support the dangerously beautiful widow lest she fall into frivolity and worse; and the hints of a sullen, independent nature in the child – the firm taking in hand of all this will ensure a greatly satisfying dividend when God's paying-out arrives.

The Crums followed Mrs Caltrop around her house. "The domestic offices first," she said, leading them to the kitchen. Its walls were a varnished butterscotch yellow, like marine paintwork, and the wooden cupboards were hospital green. Limp, possibly ancient woven rugs lay at precise points on the stone-flagged floor. The butler's pantry between kitchen and dining room was made a gloomy slit by more tall cupboards in the same dark wood as the hall panelling. In the other direction was a scullery, the back door to the garden, a small room containing gardening things, and a dark, Domestos-reeking lavatory with tank, chain and mahogany fittings.

Mrs Caltrop opened the back door and led them to a steep, grass-covered mound at the very end of the garden, by the high wall that separated No. 17 from its rear neighbours.

"*Do not* climb or play on that," she commanded, bending slightly to stare directly at Elinore. "It is an Anderson shelter and very, very unsafe. Do you know what it was for?"

"No," said Elinore.

"People went in there during the war, when bombs were falling. They said their prayers and their home was saved."

"But you said it wasn't safe to go in. And it's so little! I wouldn't go in if bombs were falling, I would stay in the house."

"That is beside the point – please pay attention." The gimlet look flicked up accusingly to Melba at this evidence of forwardness and then down to Elinore. "You must never set foot *on* it, do you hear? The rest of the lawn is good enough for playing with your dolls and so forth. But not on wash days – you must not upset Mrs Wattie by going on the drying green on wash days." She pointed to a washing line propped by poles.

"I *don't* play with dolls! They're stupid and anyway I don't *have* any!" Elinore was offended and her voice rose. Melba's hand clenched her shoulder again.

"Elinore is such a *reader*, you know! It keeps her quiet for whole days. And her drawing and painting – yes, I guarantee she'll be happy to stay out here with her books and paint set for hours on end."

"Dear me, another artist in the family? I trust that she will get *that* out of her system while still young," said Mrs Caltrop. She appraised Elinore. "I must say, I cannot see any resemblance to Hector, or to you, Melba. She does not have the Crum features *at all*."

It was true. Melba's tender, shining, blue-eyed blondeness came from her family, and Hector's rugged, square-jawed, blue-eyed blondness from his. Elinore's thick, dark hair was the opposite of their silky golden locks; it defied prettiness and all currently fashionable treatments for little girls' hair, and had only ever been parted and pulled to either side by two clips (one was never strong enough). Her skin was neither pearly-pink in tone like Melba's, nor Nordic like Hector's; it was ivory, with a distinct undertone of olive despite the rosiness of her cheeks, the result of day after day of cold, fresh, country air. Her eyes were green, above high, distinct cheekbones that were certainly not a Crum feature.

Melba's hand tightened on Elinore's pointy shoulder blades. "Yes, well, but she is a very good, quiet girl. She takes after all that is best in the family. *Both* sides," she ended forcefully.

Mrs Caltrop's nostrils flared in expression of distaste. She sighed and then waved her arm to indicate the garden as a whole. "The flowerbeds are *strictly* off limits. They are Mr Caltrop's concern. We have a man for the mowing and heavy digging."

They returned indoors, to be allowed a peek at the sitting room and dining room; both were sufficiently dark and oppressive, ideal, in fact, for a funeral wake on a chill, wet, blustery day in the better part of Edinburgh. Then upstairs, to the main bathroom first. Mrs Caltrop showed Melba a short red line on the inner side of the bathtub.

"The waterline," she pronounced, tapping the line firmly. "We do not bathe in deeper water."

Elinore peered at this novelty. She had not investigated the inside of her own bathtub, but presumably the same line would be there too. She saw two lines, a fainter one below Mrs Caltrop's finger.

"What is the other line for?" she asked.

"That was our wartime waterline – five inches. We are now at seven and a half inches. *Highly* economical."

Elinore looked doubtful. "Mummy likes deep baths," she said. "I don't think the bubbles work very well if you don't have enough water. She likes to have bubbles all around her head because they smell nice."

Silence. The expressions on the faces of both Mrs Caltrop and Melba became identical, and Elinore thought how odd it was that both turned bright red at once. Then she winced as Melba's hand clamped once again on her shoulder. "Oww! Stop hurting me!"

"*How – very – sensible!*" said Melba through gritted teeth, over her shoulder to Mrs Caltrop as she steered Elinore rapidly out of the bathroom and into her own clothes-strewn bedroom. With not quite a slam, the door closed on Elinore. She could hear the voices of the two women as they went around the landing, opening doors, and down the passage to her own bedroom. She threw herself on the bed, sprawling over Melba's garments (where was she going to *put* them all?) and staring at the fringed, fly-spotted silk lampshade hanging from the precise centre of the ceiling. She was angry. If only the Caltrops could vanish into the maw of a bear. Several bears, preferably, just to make sure, for they would definitely be gristly, stringy old meat. A tiring meal for one bear, and Elinore wanted not a shred left over.

Picturing the death agonies of the Caltrops made her feel better, although she was still angry. She began to sing, very softly.

"Two Cal-trops, two Cal-trops. See how they run! See how they run!"

She stopped and considered. The end of the Caltrops could not come quickly enough for her liking, and the closest bears would be in Edinburgh Zoo.

"They got cut up by the zoo keeper, who fed them both to the big black bears.

Did you ever see such a sight in your life, as two Caltrops?"

She felt very pleased with this and continued to sing it, a little more loudly each time, while lying like a starfish on the bed, until Melba rushed into the room and closed the door with another not-quite slam.

"You bad, bad girl!" she cried. "You *must* be nice. You must mind your manners and stop being rude whenever you open your mouth. The Caltrops are our *saviours!*"

Saviours. A Bible word, now in the mouth of her mother of all people. Everything was turning upside down in this nasty, perplexing house.

"I *am* nice!" said Elinore fiercely. "These people are *not* nice, I hate them and I want to go back to Criven."

Through the heavy panelled door, Mr Caltrop's voice could be heard faintly, calling for his wife. Elinore stuck her fingers in her ears, waggled them and summoned the loudest, rudest raspberry she could blow in his direction. Then she ran out of Melba's room, taking care to give the door a proper slam, and along the passage to her own miserable quarters.

Now she was very angry. A crime had been, was still being, committed. By whom and against what or whom, she was not sure, but certainly something had been stolen, perhaps even murdered, and it had nothing to do with a hungry bear in Alaska. She stood by the window and considered her lot while staring down at the manicured lawn with the dangerous mound, the prim flowerbeds and the walls that separated No. 17 from its neighbours. The flowers probably needed permission to grow here.

A cat appeared, strolling into the scene along the top of one wall. He was bright ginger with white patches on his face, and so large that his sides appeared to flop over the edge as he settled down for a rest and a wash. He was the only sign of independent life that Elinore had so far encountered in this place, and she thought of going out to introduce herself.

Suddenly Mr Caltrop leapt into view, holding a broom like a lance and shouting at the cat. It vanished. Mr Caltrop stood shouting and waving his broom-lance for a few seconds more. Cruelty to animals, thought Elinore, which means they are evil, which means I am right about them and Mummy is all wrong.

She decided to befriend the cat at the earliest opportunity, and this idea led her to another; a cheering, enlivening one. Why not be a secret agent, under the very noses of the Caltrops? They were enemy. Escape and victory would take time, but sabotage and other secret doings could be plotted immediately, ready for enactment whenever opportunity arose. The televisions of her friends in Criven had introduced her to the world of spies and agents, notably to the dashing men from U.N.C.L.E., and she had always found the characters who slunk, shot and sleuthed across those screens to be highly appealing. It seemed to be a fascinating career, especially for a lady. Yes! She would be Agent Solo and she could start right now. First of all, she needed a notebook, for making secret plans that would be impenetrable to decode if seized by Caltrops.

Her drawing and writing things were on top of the chest of drawers. Beside them lay a book and sheet of lined paper that had not been there earlier. Mrs Caltrop must have been in her room; Elinore resented that. She had left for Elinore the book of prayers and the list, the written guidance that together would keep her from straying off the path of heavenly love at No. 17 Dunallan Crescent.

1. CONSUMPTION OF FOOD
(i) All food in the refrigerator and pantry is subject to planning of meals by Mrs Caltrop, and the preparation thereof by Mrs Caltrop and/or Mrs Wattie. It is not to be eaten except as part of a formal meal; to wit, breakfast, luncheon, afternoon tea and high tea.
(ii) The domestic quarters are out of bounds to Elinore unless an adult is present.

2. USE OF BATHROOMS
Baths are to be taken only after consultation, to ensure
(i) fair distribution of hot water; and
(ii) that no inconvenience may be caused to any other party desirous of using the bathroom.
(iii) Baths are never to exceed 7½ inches in depth.
(iv) Ten minutes is considered an appropriate maximum duration of bathing time.

3. HOUSEKEEPING
(i) Mrs Wattie must not be impeded or distracted in her tasks, which shall be performed on Tuesdays and Fridays between the hours of 10 o'clock and 3 o'clock.

(ii) Rooms are to be dusted and tidied by their occupants, except for the floors, which shall be vacuumed and damp-mopped by Mrs Wattie (see 3(i) concerning impedimenta).

4. USE OF MORNING ROOM
The table in the morning room may be used for homework and letter-writing when not required for meals as noted in 1(i) above. All paraphernalia pertaining to such activities must be cleared entirely away no less than ten minutes before the start of any meal.

5. USE OF GARDEN
(i) The Anderson Shelter is not a plaything. It is STRICLY out of bounds.
(ii) The gates to No. 17 must be kept closed at all times, to prevent destruction of the garden by trespassing animals and juveniles.
(iii) Do not feed birds.
(iv) The washing-line props are not playthings. Do not interfere with them.
(v) Do not trespass on the drying-green when Mrs Wattie is using it.
(vi) Do not pick flowers under any circumstances.

6. USE OF TELEPHONE
Please request the use of the telephone in the morning room (this house does not contain any other telephone).
(i) Calls must be logged by date and duration to the nearest half-minute, and the appropriate sum paid weekly.
(ii) No calls should be made beyond Edinburgh without use of the Advise Duration of Call Service via the operator.

7. VISITORS
(i) Visitors are permitted only after prior discussion with Mrs Caltrop. Evening visitors are not permitted. Visitors are not

permitted on Tuesdays and Fridays during the hours when Mrs Wattie is present.
(ii) Doctors are an exception.

8. SCHOOL FRIENDS
School friends are permitted to accompany Elinore up to the front door. They are not permitted indoors on any account.

9. ACCESS TO HOUSE
(i) Under no circumstances is Elinore permitted to be left alone in this house.
(ii) She will not be provided with a house key.
(iii) In the rare event that no one can be present upon her return from school, she must remain at a friend's house until someone has returned home.
(iv) She will eat school dinners in term. To be discussed: midday feeding during holidays.

4

Within twenty-four hours, Rules 9 (i), (ii), (iii) and (iv) became immediately applicable. After breakfast, Mrs Caltrop handed another piece of paper to Elinore, containing the Caltrops' address and telephone number and directions for reaching Aikendean Primary School on foot. Melba was oblivious of the moment when Elinore left No. 17 for another enforced plunge into the unknown. She was due to start work at Grisella's Gowns at noon, and her whole being was attuned to the moment when she would arrive there as a resplendent new star with no hint of Criven in her trail.

The distance that Elinore walked was not far, but it quickly took her into a neighbourhood that was as different as a white bread jammy piece from the egg and watercress sandwich of Dunallan Crescent. The bombs that missed No. 17 had fallen on this area, and much of it had been cleared and rebuilt. For the first time in her life, Elinore walked past the base of residential tower blocks; she could not imagine living in one, so far from the ground and looking at trees from the wrong end. The inhabitants must have developed special survival skills, she surmised, like creatures in the Arctic or the Sahara. But still, she felt sorry for any children who had to be stuck up there. Open spaces surrounded the towers, barren tracts where Criven's darting minnows and bounding lambs would be as alien as Martians. Litter flourished abundantly instead.

Aikendean Primary School was a pre-war remnant on the far edge of this strange new world. It filled an elevated, triangular space where two streets divided. It was Victorian and had a tarmacked playground; these two features were the only ones that related it to Criven School in Elinore's mind. This school reared up in front of her like a dark, becalmed ship, a prison hulk perhaps. She climbed a flight of steps to the playground and looked for a main entrance, determined to get inside and find a teacher before she attracted close attention from the knots of loitering pupils. Their loudness made her nervous.

But a bell rang suddenly, and her plan changed as the knots formed themselves into separate lines of boys and girls. Elinore hung back until she was the very last girl to enter. Then she was in a cloakroom leading onto a long corridor with open doors on either side; a great deal of noise came from each door, including the shouts of exasperated grown-ups. The doors slammed shut one by one. No teacher was in sight. Elinore walked along the corridor until she came to a staircase and (she assumed) a teacher: a woman running down the wide stone stairs with a sheaf of papers in her hand.

"Excuse me, I am new. Could you please tell me where to go?" she enquired in her best Agnes Pound manner.

"What? Where's your mother?"

"She has to go to work."

"Ach, same old story," muttered the woman, who was the school secretary. "How old are you? What class were you in before?"

Elinore was hustled upstairs to an office, where the bit of paper with her address written on it came in useful, and hustled down again. The secretary opened a door, pushed Elinore inside and announced, "A new one for you, Miss Blaikie."

Twenty-nine pairs of eyes bored into Elinore with a special local blend of curiosity and latent hostility to the new.

"But I've had no notice of that!" exclaimed Miss Blaikie indignantly, but the secretary was already gone. "Where on earth have you come from? What's your name?"

Elinore repeated the necessary facts while Miss Blaikie stood with hands on hips, her eyes running up and down this two-legged intrusion as if it were showing symptoms of an unpleasant malady. Then she sighed and pointed to an empty seat by the far wall, below three tall, narrow windows.

"Sit there. We'll sort out your books and jotters later. Just be quiet and pay attention for now."

The windows were set so high that children could only see clouds when they lifted their eyes from the scarred, pitted old desks. No nature table like the one in Criven School existed here, but organisms were surely growing anyway, sprouting in stale air that was thick with the odour of old apple cores, old milk and clothes that were none too clean. Elinore did exactly as she was told. Her first day was extremely boring, but this did allow her some mental space to continue planning undercover actions as Agent Solo in the very headquarters of the Caltrop Organisation, which was, of course, bent on world domination.

A boy told her that she was sitting in Dougie McCallum's seat. He was off sick, *really* sick, so sick he might not be back, and Elinore would get his germs if she weren't careful. Carefully, Elinore rubbed her skirt, her sleeves, her cardigan against the desk, trusting that any acquired germs would keep their potency until she could transfer them to vulnerable Caltrop surfaces.

At midday, she realised that Melba had not thought to give her any money for school dinner. But, after Miss Blaikie discovered this while ticking off names and taking in coins, she ate anyway. "Bring twice that sum tomorrow or pay for the week in advance," instructed Miss Blaikie. The food was not nearly as good as that cooked by the dinner ladies at Criven School, but it was far more plentiful than any that had appeared so far on the Caltrop table. Elinore was happy to eat the mince with bits of carrot and onion, mashed potatoes and mushy peas, followed by a jam-and-soggy-pastry pudding with a choice of runny custard or a snow-white fluffy substance called Angel Creme Topping, with no relation to cream.

By the time she was retracing her morning route back to Dunallan Crescent, Elinore's feelings were a mixture of homesickness for Criven, relief that she had got through her first day at this airless, dreary new school and pleasure at the notion that she was carrying something nasty destined for the Caltrops. She completed the rest of the week in the same fashion. Her initial nervousness remained, however, simmering away, heated by wariness. The children in her class all seemed bigger and louder than her peers in Criven, and they joked and yelled about things she did not know or fully understand. The girls seemed older than their years, already entranced by teenage fashions and pop idols, and they sorted themselves into little flocks according to who was in or out with whom. She was not invited to be excited about The Jackson Five with them, and doing the Funky Chicken was out of the question. In the Caltrop house, entertainment came solely from the wireless, and anyway Top of the Pops would have been proscribed as an emission of the devil. In class, she did what Miss Blaikie expected, but refrained from putting her hand up too often, because any answers that she volunteered were always at least partly correct, and that was guaranteed to attract the wrong sort of attention.

Every morning and afternoon, she saw girls and boys who were en route to and from other schools, and who all wore uniforms. They looked interesting, and she determined to investigate, but not immediately. The uniforms made her shy. Despite Melba's earlier complaint that Elinore's appearance would hinder the hunt for a new Hector, she had made virtually no effort to improve it. Elinore wanted to look smart and clever like those other children, all hurrying in a different direction from her.

Elinore's first Saturday at No. 17 was a wet one from dawn to dusk. She had wanted to get out and explore, and rain would not have stopped her in Criven, but the streets looked unfriendly under the ceaseless downpour. She explored the range of her transistor radio instead, and discovered Radio Four. Suddenly, she could listen to plays, discussions between individuals called experts or critics, factual programmes about history and science, and (best of all on a wet Saturday) comedy shows – everything that Mr Caltrop did not listen to on the wireless downstairs, in other words. With the BBC and her books, and Agent Solo's action plans, she was able to amuse herself in her room. Both Caltrops coughed rather a lot that day, and she had strong hopes for the effectiveness of Dougie McCallum's germs.

By Saturday evening, the Caltrops had not sickened. This was unfortunate, for their zealous intent to enfold the Crums within their church had not abated. To Elinore's surprise, Melba agreed that it would be *most* interesting to meet so many new people, and asked at what time they should be ready the next morning. After tea, she told Elinore to bring her clothes into the main bathroom, where the light was best, to be inspected.

"*Why* are you are such a messy child? Look at the state of these. This blouse and this skirt will have to do, and you must polish your shoes and find a pair of socks that match and don't fall down. Good heavens! This cardigan is all rubbed away in the elbows and full of holes. How could that possibly have happened?"

"I want a school uniform."

"Your school does not have a uniform."

"Why can't I go to a school with a uniform?"

"Because I cannot afford a uniform, let alone school fees. When we find a new Hector, all that will change."

"Why do we have to go to church? You *hate* church. And I *hate* Sunday school. I want to stay here and paint or go out and explore or – "

"We are going because the rules say you can't stay here alone, and I need to be seen. Pews are public places. The right man might well be sitting in church tomorrow. A widower, perhaps, a lonely gentleman with a large house and no one to cheer him up."

"Mr Finnie was lonely in the manse at Criven. I *told* you! You could have married him and not moved me into this horrible, disgusting, *evil* house." Elinore's voice rose and echoed in the bathroom, which was essentially a larger, white-walled and less dingy version of her own, with a tall, frosted-glass window instead of a small skylight.

"Quiet! That man Finnie is as poor as a church mouse. If you don't stop arguing with me, you'll be sent away to boarding school as soon as I can possibly afford it."

"I want to go right now. They have uniforms at boarding schools."

"I will gladly send you if you will just cooperate in helping me find the means. Now go and see to your shoes and socks. You can use my polish, but don't you dare get it on anything but shoes."

On her way out, Elinore saw a long piece of flat leather hanging on the wall, and asked Melba what it might be.

"A strop for sharpening razors and punishing bad girls who make trouble for their good, kind mamas," replied Melba. "It will happen to you if you continue being obstructive to our wellbeing."

Sunday morning brought glorious June sunshine. Melba chose to wear a short (very short) A-line shift in a swirling floral pattern of near-psychedelic vibrancy. To complete this church-going outfit, she added a little jacket in Schiaparelli's shocking-pink; tall high-heeled boots in a stretchy white open-weave fabric; a butcher's boy cap in white cotton with little gold buttons to right and left of the brim; and white gloves. Gold hoop earrings dangled from her ears and a pink bag swung on a long gold chain from her shoulder. Divine!

The Caltrops did not think so.

Mrs Caltrop had on a lumpy tweed suit resembling under-stirred, over-cooked porridge. A blouse was fastened tightly at her throat with a brooch, a miniature targe; on her head was a version of the mushroom hat, this time in the blue of a disappointed sky, which was skewered by a hatpin in the shape of a jagged silver thistle. On her arm hung a large handbag in the hide of some reptile. Her lace-up shoes were black and so were her gloves. Mr Caltrop wore his usual bad, boxy suit and a hat. They had been stamping around impatiently in the hallway, and as Melba tripped down the staircase their jaws descended in unison with each step she took.

"I say – I say – " spluttered Mr Caltrop.

"Melba," said Mrs Caltrop, "am I correct in saying that you are wearing what is known as a *mini* dress?"

"I am indeed, Mrs C! How clever of you to know. It will gladden hearts, don't you think? Now, where is Elinore? I told her to wait down here for me. Elinore! Come this instant!"

Elinore could not come, because she was in her bathroom, holding the front of her blouse under cold running water. She had been ready to leave long, long before Melba; so long in fact that doodling flowers while listening to her transistor radio had evolved into an urge to paint them. Melba's dress had inspired her. The table with the uneven legs was not helpful, however. It jiggled and rocked and somehow managed to empty the water jar – by then tinted a deep purple – over her front.

She heard Melba's distant command and grabbed a towel to sop up water from the fabric. Putting the blouse on wet felt horrid. When she looked down at herself, she saw that her socks were splashed too. She rolled them down to conceal that, put on her cardigan and ran to the stairs. She was quite proud of the shine she had raised on her shoes, but exasperated with her freshly-washed hair; it had frizzed out horizontally on either of side of her head and doubled its volume.

"Oh, wretched, *wretched* child!" screeched Melba. "How *dare* you appear looking like that? You will have to stay behind, I cannot possibly be seen with you."

"Out of the question!" cried Mrs Caltrop. "Rule 9 – it shall not be broken. You must stay with her, Melba. And we must leave immediately. Never once in twenty-odd years have we been late for church."

"Indeed, indeed, never. Never once!" boomed Mr Caltrop, visibly perturbed.

"*Stay?* Stay *here* after all this effort? I ree-aa-lly don't think so . . ." Elinore saw her mother hoist the familiar storm signals and waited, fascinated. The red spots on Mrs Caltrop's cheeks were large and vivid.

The telephone rang.

Mrs Caltrop seized the receiver, spoke her usual grim greeting and listened, frowning. Sound leaked from the receiver, but Elinore could not tell whether it was the voice of a man or a woman.

"Yes, Mrs Crum is here at this very moment. Yes, her child is with her. They reside here at present. Who is calling? Oh, really. Yes. Yes – it was a long time ago but I do recall. Today? This morning? *Now?* We are on our way to church, and we cannot possibly delay – but . . ." Mrs Caltrop exhaled and straightened her shoulders. "Melba and the child will stay behind to await you here. No. 17 Dunallan Crescent. Yes. They will be *delighted*. Goodbye."

A look of triumph suffused Mrs Caltrop's face as she turned to Melba.

"That was Arabella Cheyne. From poor Hector's father's mother's side, but I cannot possibly explain ancestry at this moment. She is going to call on you since she happens to be passing through Edinburgh. The good Lord clearly wishes you to have as much family support as possible in your tribulations. But *we* are expected to do our duty in church as usual, and we must go now."

She clutched her husband's arm and steered him very quickly towards the front door. As soon as it closed behind them, it opened again and Mrs Caltrop thrust her head around it.

"Do not use the kitchen. Do not offer Arabella cups of tea and the like. She will take you out for luncheon."

The door closed. Melba sat down on the stairs and heaved a great sigh. "Ohhh, the trials I face . . ." She turned around to look at Elinore, who had also sat herself down. "Put on another blouse. Sunday lunch is still a public occasion and you will *not* disgrace me."

"I don't have another blouse. The other one got too small. But I've got a shirt for gym, somewhere. I think I do. Who is Arabella Cheyne?"

"I haven't the slightest clue. Put on the gym shirt. And take some water and flatten that frightful hair. And pull up your socks! You are without doubt as infuriating as your father."

Melba got up and went into the morning room, to throw herself into an armchair (carefully, without creasing her dress and jacket) in the manner of a cruelly burdened mother. Elinore did as she was told. The worn, crumpled Aertex gym shirt she unearthed was now far too short and would not stay tucked into the waistband of her skirt. To all of Criven, she had been just that wee skinnymalink, but lately the skinnymalink's thin limbs and torso had been growing longer and fuller by the week, it seemed, much to Melba's annoyance. It signified unavoidable expenditure. Elinore buttoned her cardigan over the shirt from top to bottom. She did her best to remove the purple splashes from her socks, but whatever made socks stay up on legs had vanished from this pair. Then she picked up her paintbrush and carried on creating. If only I had much bigger sheets of paper, she thought, I could stick up my own pictures over those Jesus ones. She turned on her radio, and turned it up a little (the Caltrops were out of the house!), and a little more. Radio One's Junior Choice programme was on: *"'ello darlin'!"* She felt content enough to hum along with the songs. *"In the summertime when the weather is hot / You can stretch right up and touch the sky..."* The disc jockey was endlessly cheerful, sunlight was poking into her room and she did not have to sit in Sunday school wearing a wet blouse. *"Everything is beau-uuuu-ti-ful..."*

Here was a new idea to ponder: that good things might possibly arise from being bad, or at least from being judged bad by everyone else in this house. If she had not decided to paint, the water jar would not have upset itself over her front, and they would all have left the house promptly, before that telephone call from a lady who was now coming to take them out to lunch. This lady might or might not be Caltropian, but the prospect of going out for lunch was definitely appealing. They might have missed that altogether through never knowing that someone had rung! It was high time for an inventor to invent a machine for answering the telephone, thought Elinore: a Telephone Secretary Robot. Futuristic gadgets brought secret agents to mind, and her tasks as Agent Solo. How was she going to subdue the Caltrops before the postponed threat of Sunday school became reality next weekend?

In the company of Ed "Stewpot" Stewart and with her creative energies thus engaged, Elinore did not hear the doorbell ring, or Melba's shout from downstairs. She jumped when Melba barged into the room and yanked Elinore from her chair.

"Now you're being rude by ignoring our visitor! Out, out, hurry up – we're going to lunch in a hotel."

Standing in the hall was a tall, upright woman. She wore a loose silk jacket embroidered in floral profusion from collar to hem. She had deep strawberry-blonde hair, roughly pinned up, and her skin was very pale in contrast, the same paleness as in the pearl earrings that swung like miniature pears when she moved her head. Her blue-grey eyes were penetrating, and altogether she had an air of authority. Whether that was the least of it, whether her teeth were as fierce as Mrs Caltrop's, Elinore could not tell, because she was looking Elinore up and down without the trace of a smile, over a long, straight nose that would have sat well on a marble statue. Something familiar about her waved at the back of Elinore's mind, but she could not put a name to it.

The woman held out her hand and said, "Elinore. I'm Arabella. I hope you're hungry. We are going straight to lunch." Rings glinted and bracelets shone; she wore several of each.

"Thank you very much. I am always hungry," Elinore said.

"Nonsense!" said Melba, rolling her eyes. "Anyone would think you were being starved."

Arabella merely nodded as if Elinore's reply had been quite fitting, and said, "Good. Let's be off, then. My taxi is waiting outside."

Melba was rummaging in her bag. "One moment! I have no lipstick." She ran upstairs.

Arabella stuck her hands in the pockets of her jacket and meandered around the hallway, looking at this and that artefact from British India. The door to the morning room was open and she moved towards it.

"Hmmm," she murmured, as she paused in the doorway, looking into the Caltrops' sanctum. "A *lair*. Is this where they go to ground, those Caltrops? I'm quite sure this is where they sit and scoff chocolates every night."

"We never get chocolate here," said Elinore.

"*You* will never get chocolate here," said Arabella, "but I can assure you that several fancy boxes of chocolate are hidden behind the two doors on the left." She pointed to a pair of cupboard doors by the fireplace. "I have no desire to nose around in the Caltrops' lair, but you might like to take a look sometime."

Surprised, Elinore looked sideways at her, and then realised where she had seen that long-nosed, milk-white, regal profile before. Straight from illustrations of British history, it was Queen Elizabeth I. Executions! Heart of a lion! Mortal enemy of Mary Queen of Scots! Heads rolling – not as many as her father, King Henry VIII, had sent flying from necks, but still . . .

"And I suspect you'll find biscuits in there too – ginger snaps, rich tea, Jaffa cakes, that sort of thing," continued Arabella. "Make sure you take one or two from each open package. They will notice a missing chocolate without fail, but not biscuits. But do be careful. You wouldn't want to be a secret agent caught by the Caltrops."

Elinore's mouth opened in shock, but she could not think of anything sensible to say. Instead, she thought she might have done something wrong by not curtseying when Arabella had greeted her. It seemed appropriate for this possible reincarnation.

Arabella turned on her heel and went to the foot of the stairs. "Melba!" she called. "We'll see you in the taxi. Hurry up, we're famished!"

Without waiting for any response, she strode off down the drive to a taxi waiting at the kerb. Elinore dithered on the doorstep and then ran after her. She almost skipped. Someone else – *Melba!* – was being told to hurry up for a change.

"Do excuse my memory, Arabella, but I simply cannot recall you. Were you at my wedding?" asked Melba, as soon as they were all seated in the taxi.

"No," said Arabella, "I generally avoid weddings." She looked out of the taxi window.

"Oh."

Arabella observed the passing houses for a few silent moments. Elinore tried to study her without appearing to stare. Even in the back of a taxi, Arabella appeared luminous, like a light bulb. She was not exactly beautiful, and under the embroidered coat her green dress was quite plain, but she was far more striking than Melba. This was almost shocking to Elinore, who had always thought that no one (except the Queen and some film stars she had seen in old *Life* magazines) could outshine Melba. Still looking out of the window, Arabella spoke again.

"Family trees are an awful headache. My grandmother was a Mordaunt, and her sister married a Crum. Something like that."

"Oh." Hector's family members had interested Melba only insofar as their relation to money that Hector might or might not inherit.

"But now and then they have their uses," added Arabella. "They can be grapevines. That's how I heard that you were here in Edinburgh."

"Oh. And – have you come far? Roberta Caltrop said you were only passing through."

"I'm on my way to friends in Northumberland for a week, or a fortnight – or longer. I always stop in Edinburgh for some shopping."

"Oh – shopping!" Melba was back on solid conversational ground. "Do you need a gown? Grisella's in Thistle Street has an exclusive selection. I'm there, you know, just until I start on the, ah, entertainment side of things – or strictly theatrical, I haven't quite decided yet. Grisella can fit *any* figure, you know." She stared at Arabella's feet in their plain, flat-heeled tan shoes as if they signified the kind of body that would challenge even a Grisella.

"Grisella, Grisella . . ." Arabella gazed out of the window again, thinking. "Wasn't she Grizel Mutch before her husband died and left her pots of money? Enough to become *refeened*, at any rate. No, a gown is not a priority on this occasion, but thermal underwear is, even though it's June. And some boxes of Edinburgh Rock. Have you tasted it yet, Elinore?"

"No," said Elinore, who had never heard of Edinburgh Rock. "Is it a sweetie?"

"It is tooth-rot. But the Caltrops might be partial to it – see if they have any." Very deliberately and still unsmiling, Arabella winked at Elinore. "I'm only buying it for visiting Americans."

"Americans! Will they be staying with you?" enquired Melba, for whom America held equal fascination with shopping.

"No, they are guests of the people I'll be visiting. They went to Edinburgh once – the Americans – and became mildly addicted to Edinburgh Rock. So I'm told. I don't know them personally."

"Oh, I see . . . Well, how nice that you can take a holiday at this time of the year."

"*Holiday* is not part of my vocabulary. Unless it applies to time that other people take off. I'm going down there because my friends need a lot of help with their house. They need my specialty."

"I see. Do you – decorate?"

"Some people might call my work that, but only the completely ignorant. Look, we're here. The Balmerinoch Hotel. I never stay anywhere else now when I'm in Edinburgh."

Halfway down a sandstone terrace, the Balmerinoch appeared to be entirely typical of the scores of such small hotels, once private houses, that can be found in Edinburgh. Melba was out of the taxi and at the door before Arabella or Elinore; it was a public place, more or less, and so the opportunity to make a fine entrance must not be wasted. She sailed through the vestibule and stopped dead, causing Elinore to bump into her.

"There must be a mistake," said Melba. "We can't be eating anything *here*. Oh!" A few coils of wood shavings had fallen straight down through the air onto her head and shoulders. Two belligerent male voices drifted down too, from the first-floor landing.

"No, no, that's nae guid at a', and ye ken it, ye young skiver. Get going with that plane again!"

"But I've been at it all bluidy mornin' – what're you after, perfection?"

"Aye! An' one mair swear out o' yous an' ye're fired! An' clean up this floor too – it's a disgrace, man!"

Many more shavings then showered onto Melba, who lifted her hands in terrible distress and jumped sideways, knocking against a pile of wooden crates. *"Oh, oh!* What is this place? Why are we here?"

Elinore did not know what to make of the place either, but it was a bright, refreshing surprise to her eyes after the overall brownish dimness at No. 17. The hall and all visible spaces leading off it were painted white, and sunlight from a large skylight in the roof poured down three or four storeys to where she stood. The stone stairs and the flagstones of the hall were uncovered, except for little piles and sprinklings of sawdust. Long planks were stacked against one wall and a tool bag sat halfway up the stairs. The only suggestion of hotel reception came from several chairs (covered with dust-sheets) and an antique table on which stood a lamp in the shape of a gold urn (with a towel over its shade), a telephone, a ledger and an enormous, ornate Chinese vase filled with flowers. Red and blue dragons snarled and writhed all over the vase and a mass of chrysanthemums and dahlias in varying shades of red erupted out of it. Elinore thought it was magnificent. The cushiony, vivid reds were so *alive* in that vase – just like the dragons – and especially against all that white. They seemed more alive than anything growing in Mr Caltrop's flowerbeds.

Arabella smiled for the first time, showing perfectly normal teeth.

"This way. Welcome to the grand passion of my dear friend Clova Balmerinoch. Her great *mission*." She walked ahead of them into a dazzling white, sun-filled dining room dotted with round tables that were all set. Large, bright canvases of indeterminate subject matter hung on every wall. Otherwise, the room was empty.

"Mission?" said Melba plaintively. "I do hope this place has nothing to do with Roberta Caltrop's retired missionaries, or dying missionaries, or whatever they are. If it's a joke, I don't care for it." She shot a venomous look at Arabella while flicking particles of wood from her clothes.

Arabella's smile widened and her eyes gleamed. She pulled out a chair at a table in the centre of the room and said, "Sit, Melba." The last time Elinore had heard that command in exactly that tone was in Criven, when Mrs Cameron was training one of her Labrador puppies. "Do you need smelling salts or will your nerves hold up? I assure you, the Balmerinoch Hotel couldn't be further from the Caltrop's mausoleum for the living. Don't mind the carpenters. Everyone is working overtime to get the place finished before the Festival. You're privileged to witness the dawn of something revolutionary in Edinburgh!"

Melba did not appear to feel honoured by this privilege. "I can't believe anyone would stay in a half-finished barn of a place like this. It certainly isn't up to *my* standards."

"And what are your standards, Melba?" asked Arabella pleasantly, still smiling. Without waiting for an answer, she carried on.

"Clova is on a mission to liberate Scotland from bad, predictable food and dispiriting interiors which, combined, tend to result in the Scottish hotel of this day and age. You won't find any tinned fruit salad here, or tough slabs of gammon topped with rings of tinned pineapple, or scampi in a basket or vegetables murdered by long boiling. Or peach Melba – sorry! She does serve chips, but not with everything. Nor will you find acres of fusty carpet in hideous swirling patterns whose main functions are to conceal dirt and induce biliousness in sensitive types like me. You will not be expected to dine amid a blue fug of nicotine. Smokers can only light up in the smoking room, and I hear she's going to keep some bedrooms for non-smokers only. Clova is years, *decades* ahead of her time, you know."

"Well – I've always liked the smell of a fine cigar," muttered Melba.

"Really? In your hair and on those clothes? You surprise me, Melba. But look, here's Clova herself. She'd be most interested in your opinions of her endeavour."

If Arabella had been somewhat forbidding at first sight to Elinore, Clova Balmerinoch was downright alarming. In a starched, spotless white lab coat, she was taller even than Arabella. Her dark hair was pulled straight back into a bun, her glasses black-framed, her lipstick scarlet and she was not smiling. She carried a clipboard with many sheets of paper on it. To Elinore, this was Nana Mouskouri crossed with a scientist. Quite possibly a mad scientist, like the ones on television. What on earth might come out of this woman's kitchen?

"Excellent timing," Clova declared by way of greeting. "You can enjoy the exhibition before the crush. We have quite a number of luncheon reservations today."

"Oh, yes, I forgot to tell my guests that bit," said Arabella. "The Balmerinoch is also a gallery. Who is this?" She waved a hand at the surrounding canvases.

"Diego Balthazaar – one of my discoveries. The opening is next week."

"Never heard of him. But Melba here might know the name. Her late husband, Hector Crum, did a bit of painting – am I right, Melba? And this is Elinore Crum."

"Delighted to welcome you," said Clova, with a little forward inclination of her upper body, but still no smile. "Now I must rush off. I have some foraging to do. Anna will be along in two ticks to take your order. Goodbye!" She marched out, shouted something to the workmen upstairs and disappeared.

"Does this place have a loo that works?" asked Melba.

"Past the desk in the hall, first right, follow the signs," said Arabella. Melba left the room, still brushing off real and imagined sawdust.

Arabella clasped her hands in front of her, sat back and looked at Elinore. Her eyes had that penetrating quality again. "At some point, my dear Elinore, you and I will have a practical and intelligent conversation. Grown-ups do go on and on, but *you* are my reason for barging in and introducing myself. Nothing else would induce me to go near the Caltrops."

"Me?" said Elinore, bemused. "What for? I'm only nine, well, *almost* ten. I'm not –" She stopped, not sure which deficiencies were the ones that disqualified her from high-level conversation. She was nervous of disappointing Queen Arabella.

"Good afternoon, may I take your orders?"

A girl in a black skirt, white blouse and crisp white apron had appeared at their table, silently, from some entrance that Elinore had not noticed. Her blonde hair was pulled straight back into a bun, and she wore bright pink lipstick and flat black pumps. She looked like a ballet dancer and moved like one too, and was extremely polite. Elinore was impressed and a little awed. This was surely a creature in whose veins ran the blood of Miss Agnes Pound.

The menu was full of intriguing choices, but Elinore chose tomato soup, roast beef with roast potatoes and Yorkshire pudding: favourites that she had enjoyed in Criven, but rarely, and never once courtesy of her mother. Melba managed to return to the dining room at just the moment when two interesting-looking gentlemen with expensive briefcases arrived, and there was a pretty display of manners and preening as they insisted that Melba precede them. She sat down and so did they, in a far corner. She tossed her blonde hair and looked several times in their direction, but they only had eyes for documents they had laid out on the table. Then she went into a sulk and picked a bread roll into tiny little bits. The room did not yet contain any other men who might score highly on the New Hector scale, and Arabella's attention was on Elinore.

"So, you are *almost* ten – when will you definitely be ten?"

"June the 30th."

"Ah. Would you like to repeat this little outing then, as a birthday lunch?"

"Yes, please! I like this hotel. I'd like to live in it."

"I'll pass that on to Clova. It's exactly what she needs to hear."

"I like her name too. I'd like to have the name of a plant."

"Actually, it's Clov-*a*. Her second name, but she hates her first name, which is – hmm, I forget. Just what she wants."

"That's like me," said Elinore, intrigued. "I hate my first name too. It's horrible."

"Elinore, do not exaggerate," snapped Melba. "It is a perfectly good family name, from Hector's side. You were too young to decide that you *hated* it, but you would never answer to it."

"Very sensible, I'd do exactly the same," said Arabella. "And what is that other name, may I ask?"

"Ermine," said Elinore.

Arabella said nothing at all for several seconds. She lifted her water glass and drank. She turned to stare at Melba and raised her eyebrows. Then she said very quietly, "Really. Now we know." Melba blushed. Elinore had never seen that happen before. Melba blushed a bit more and a bit more after that, until she suddenly rose and almost ran out of the dining room.

"The Balmerinoch ladies' loo must be up to your mother's standards after all," said Arabella. "Now, what do you know about Edinburgh? What have you seen so far?"

"Nothing," replied Elinore. "I went once with Hector – maybe I went twice – but I don't remember anything. It was a long time ago. He didn't show me any places. Mummy used to come here for dresses and things, but I always stayed at home. I haven't been anywhere except school." She described her walking route to Aikenhead Primary, and a little of what that was like.

Arabella grimaced. "Dear me, how time disappears in all the wrong ways when one is young. We must add sightseeing to your birthday lunch, then. I'll send you a note as soon as I know exactly when I'll be back in Edinburgh."

"Where do you live?" asked Elinore.

"In the Highlands, in an old house on top of a hill. A draughty place, but the view is beyond description. I'm very fond of it."

Just then, two or three groups of people entered the dining room all at once. Elinore spotted a girl of her own age, with her brother, their parents, one elderly lady and a set of grandparents; the relationship was obvious. The girl had long, wavy brown hair held by a white bandeau. Her short, straight dress was sky blue with a white Peter Pan collar and white sleeves, and patterned all over with big white daisies and leafy tendrils. A waitress – another Anna in appearance, except with a brunette ponytail – led them to a reserved table in the bay of the window. They were clearly happy to be there, and interested in their surroundings, especially the mother, who was looking around at all the canvases on the wall. Elinore was intrigued. She stared and stared, suddenly wanting to join them, whoever they were. She also wanted a dress just like that, and she wanted to be wearing it right there and then.

The brown-haired girl turned and looked straight at Elinore, as if such avid curiosity had sent feelers across the dining room. Elinore blushed and hunched low in her chair, dropping her eyes. Why did life not offer a menu to young people, so that they could choose to wear the right kind of clothes before they ever landed in the world? It was very annoying to be stuck with a lopsided skirt whose pleats had lost their crispness while on the body of the previous owner, whose waistband had to be fastened with a safety pin, and a wreck of a cardigan over an old gym shirt.

Her discomfiture worsened. As soon as the family had given the waitress their orders, the girl and her mother got up and walked around the room together, arm in arm, examining each painting closely. Or rather, the mother did. The girl looked at everything and everyone else too, including Elinore, who dropped her head and was thankful for her seat at a centre table yards away from the walls. Arabella looked at Elinore; her eyes narrowed and her mouth tightened. She signalled to Anna and said something, and then Elinore found a dessert menu being placed carefully in front of her.

"The puddings here are *scrumptious*," said Arabella. "I shall have the honey and lemon soufflé."

Melba reappeared at that moment and picked up the dessert menu. She made a moué and laid it down again. "Awful fattening things."

"Fine," said Arabella. "I will order in your stead and Elinore can take some pudding home with her. Something chocolatey, perhaps, or fruity – Florentines are always lovely. Elinore, please choose something that Melba would never eat."

Elinore complied, glad to have a reason for keeping her head down without being rude to Queen Arabella. She wanted to linger in this bright, interesting room; she wanted to get up and look at all the paintings too. But she did not want to do any of that in front of the girl in the dress that *she* wanted to wear, whose gaze she would be relieved to escape.

5

They returned to Dunallan Crescent by taxi, a convenience much praised by Arabella.

"A horde of black beetles, always ready to scurry around at my bidding."

"Don't you drive?" asked Melba. "How will you go down to Northumberland?"

"I have two vehicles. I might get halfway to Edinburgh in either one of them, but that would kill it or me. And if I'm driving, I can't read or put my feet up, so it's a waste of time over long distances. I'll hire a car for Northumberland. It used to be a simple journey by train, very pleasant, until that man Beeching cut the Waverley Route. He should be reincarnated as an earthworm, in the garden of a boy who likes to chop up living things."

Elinore knew about Dr Beeching. He was the Man from the Government who had decreed that the railway station nearest to Criven should be closed in the name of efficiency. He was still very much alive, but, as far as people in the Borders were concerned, he had already consigned himself to a low pit of hell and the mythology of devils. Arabella's judgement of him was enchanting. It also evoked the all-powerful Elizabeth Tudor and increased Elinore's suspicions of reincarnation. The sun came through the taxi window and tinged Arabella's hair with red; the way she looked down her long nose at a person, and the paleness of her skin – it all added up. When Arabella spoke next, it was to Elinore, who could not tell if she had received a request or a command.

"Elinore, you mentioned the books you brought with you. I'd like to see them. And you can show me around the rest of your, ah, home."

"It isn't my *home*. My real home is in Criven. We're just staying here until Mummy finds a new Hector."

It was such an obvious explanation to give Arabella, especially since Melba herself never ceased repeating it. Elinore could not understand, therefore, why Melba turned scarlet for the second time in one day and was clearly fuming at her, if silently. Arabella merely said, "Hmm," and looked out of the taxi window.

The Caltrops had returned from church by the time the taxi drew up at No. 17. Mrs Caltrop did not exactly welcome Arabella into her home; she stood in the hall with arms folded. Neither did Arabella extend her own hand. She tilted her head ever so slightly back, looked down her nose at Mrs Caltrop and said, as if surprised to see her there in her own hall, "Oh, Roberta – hello. How many years has it been? You're just as bonny as ever. Excuse me while I dash up to see Elinore's books." And she ran up the stairs after Elinore.

Mrs Caltrop said, "In *my* house –", added something else under her breath, and started up the stairs too, but suddenly came down again and went into the morning room.

Arabella looked carefully at every single book.

"An interesting, diverse collection. I'm particularly impressed to see Agnes Pound's *Book of Charm & Essential Etiquette*. Did you know she had a finishing school in London? My mother was always threatening to send me there. She was convinced I was unmarriageable and that Agnes Pound was the cure for it. Your books would be much happier in a bookcase, I feel. I wonder if the Caltrops have a spare one."

"I have a bookcase in Criven," said Elinore. "It looked after all my books. And I have a nice bed there . . ." She trailed off, not knowing whether she felt furious or mournful, and her brows drew together.

"I see. Well, the furniture in this room is certainly not nice. That table is a troublemaker if I ever saw one."

Then she peered at the two framed pictures on the wall, and sighed. "Appallingly didactic tastes, that Roberta. What would you like to see up there instead?"

"Old ones. Like the pictures in some of my books. Ones from different countries, like Holland. And I like snow pictures with sheep."

"Definite tastes, I see," said Arabella. "I like snow scenes too, but this bedroom in winter might put you off them for life. Paul Gauguin and Raoul Dufy would be good in December – do you know those artists?"

"No."

"But you might *not* be here in December. We'll deal with this dismal decor one step at a time."

Arabella plucked each print from the wall and tucked them both under one arm.

"Tell Roberta – only if she notices they're gone – that I recognised the rarity of these nasty cheap prints – leave out that bit – and I've taken them away to be valued by an art expert. Now, what's behind these other doors?"

Scrutinising Elinore's bathroom, she said only one word: "Ugh." Then she went to the third door in the corridor and tried the knob.

"It's locked all the time," said Elinore.

"Yes, it would be, wouldn't it? It's where the Caltrops keep their ghastly secrets. Find a key in another lock and see if it works. I'd do it myself, but now I have to be on my way. Tea will *not* be on offer here, so no point in waiting around for an invitation."

"Elinore, stop that scowling, and sit up straight. You are at a table, not a trough."

At teatime that evening, Melba and Mrs Caltrop appeared to have found common cause in the denigration of Arabella, which Elinore thought was a great injustice. She slumped, scowled and shouted at both of them in her head.

"Dreadful, bossy woman with not an ounce of fashion sense. Plain white face – obviously, she's never even heard of rouge. Completely out of date, like the rest of her. Those flat shoes! No one has been seen in things like that since 1965. I swear I could smell mothballs. And she was *so* nasty about Grisella, who is a dear friend of mine."

"The makings of a black sheep are always visible in the young if one knows what to look for," pronounced Mrs Caltrop, sending a sideways scowl at Elinore, who scowled back. "I predicted Arabella's dangerous future many years ago. We can only be glad that the Lord has placed her far enough away not to be a bad influence on *this* child."

"She is not far away! She's coming here for my birthday!" cried Elinore.

Mrs Caltrop folded her arms like a boxer facing his opponent. "I will not have my home turned into a way station for that godless creature. Precisely what date are we referring to?"

"June 30th – no, June 29th," said Melba.

"You're wrong, my birthday is on the 30th. And we're going back to that hotel where they have lots of really, *really* nice *proper* food!" Reckless truth-telling beckoned Elinore, and she longed to slide right into it.

"Be quiet, you nasty girl!" shrilled Melba.

"Good," said Mrs Caltrop. "This is not a house for *celebrations*. I have no doubt that Arabella would make a party here, given the slightest encouragement. The rumours I have heard . . ." She shuddered.

"Yes, indeed, indeed, quite the talk," added Mr Caltrop, who all this time had been engrossed in the usual silent, rapid filling of his plate that preceded the noisier filling of his mouth.

※

The Edinburgh nights were lengthening towards midsummer's eve, and Elinore's bedroom was still washed in a pale glow, diffused by the threadbare curtains, long after she was sent to bed. She was glad not to have the two Jesus pictures staring at her any more. She knew that she was nothing like the children they had portrayed, all shining with goodness and happiness. She was a secret agent.

She was tired, but unable to fall asleep. Questions were mushrooming in her head. Why had Melba got so red and flustered over that silly name, Ermine? Why had Arabella wanted to meet *her* above all? Could Arabella possibly be related to Queen Elizabeth I? Elinore marshalled all the features of Elizabeth that she could remember from books and lined them up against Arabella. Masses of coppery hair; white skin; loads of jewels – especially pearls; knew Latin, Greek, French and Italian; heart of a lion (verification required for these last two); cousin to Mary, Queen of Scots, whose head she cut off (could Mrs Caltrop's head be a substitute?); daughter of King Henry VIII, who cut off *so* many heads. Since Elinore's exposure to her relations on either side of the family had been minimal, she had only a few faint recollections and could not assess the fearsomeness of any Cheyne. But Arabella was not the slightest bit impressed by Melba, and that alone made her imperial, for Melba was beautiful and the queen of any realm in which she found herself, was she not? Elinore decided that Arabella was most likely very good at saying and doing exactly as she liked, and being naughty in the process, while also being strict about laws and things like that. She had taken the two pictures – stolen them, really – but Elinore could not imagine her pilfering sweeties or anything else, large or small. If she wanted jewels, she would just go to the very best jeweller's shop and not bother trying to be a cat thief.

She was grateful for Arabella's interest in her books. A few were on the table, another few on the chest of drawers, but most of them were housed in the cardboard box that had carried them from Criven. They looked miserable, thought Elinore, like poor homeless orphans. Her bookcase was probably miserable too, and pining for her.

In a humble, irreligious way, Elinore sent up a prayer, to whom or what she could not name. She asked for the safekeeping of the bookcase, and kind treatment with respect for its age. Then she did the same for the bed. She fell asleep wondering why on earth she had done such a thing, for surely it was pointless, although she could not associate it with the detestable volume of prayers that Mrs Caltrop had left in her room. She had touched that only once, when she put it in the bottom drawer, below what passed for her winter clothes.

By the same hour exactly one week later, promise had sprouted in Elinore's unwished for, unwelcome new life. The letter appeared first. On the Saturday morning, Mrs Caltrop held an envelope by the tips of her fingers as she laid the post on the breakfast table.

"Elinore, this is addressed to you. It is from Arabella. I recognise her unrefined scrawl."

Melba craned to look. "Thick paper and an engraved crest. She must be staying in a very expensive hotel, one of those country house places. Or a fat farm. I could tell right away that she'd lost her figure – that's why she was flapping around in that jacket."

Mrs Caltrop sniffed and flared her nostrils in censure. She and Melba were still chewing over Arabella's deficiencies of character. "Her extravagant tastes are notorious in the family. It is a miracle to me that she did not fall into destitution years ago."

"Perhaps the Lord lent a helping hand," suggested Melba, with a crafty smile.

"She isn't at a hotel. She said she was going to stay with friends," said Elinore, who was holding the letter under the table, on her lap, clutching it against possible extraction by Caltrop bad magic.

"And who are they? Did she give a name?" demanded Mrs Caltrop.

"Not once," said Melba.

"Well, then – she has stolen the writing paper from an hotel, so that she can send it to people whom she wants to impress." Mrs Caltrop sounded immensely satisfied with this verdict.

Melba was still on the trail. "On the other hand, it does sound awfully like an assignation. If she *is* at a hotel, she is absolutely not alone. In hiding from some poor betrayed wife – I'd lay money on it."

Mrs Caltrop looked scandalised. "*Please!* Pas devant les enfants."

Finishing her meagre portion of toast and one boiled egg, Elinore went to her room to open the letter. The crest on the reverse of the envelope was repeated on the head of the writing paper, above an engraved address: Castle Welkinlaw, Northumberland. The letter was dated June 16th.

> *Dear Elinore,*
>
> *Please expect me at 9 o'clock on the morning of Saturday 25th. The calendar dictates that we must celebrate your birthday five days early – or do you wish to play truant on Thursday 30th? I am more than happy to assist in that, but my advanced age compels me to point out that certain individuals would object strenuously, and are quite likely to inform the authorities. If you are not too busy on the Sunday, we can make another excursion.*
>
> *I think you would enjoy Welkinlaw very much. It has many rooms that no one has used for years and years, and they are all stuffed. I have a <u>great</u> deal of work ahead of me.*

> *Do you have anything to report about the fancy chocolates?***
>
> *Yours most sincerely,*
> *Arabella Cheyne*
> *PS* ***Ditto Chamber of Ghastly Secrets.*

Excitement flared in Elinore. She studied the Welkinlaw crest again and decided to keep to herself – she could not say why – the knowledge that Arabella really was staying with friends in a castle. Once she had confirmed certain essentials – did Arabella go to bed in a turret, did Welkinlaw possess a deep moat, a clanking portcullis, a working drawbridge, dungeons, a ghost or all of the foregoing? – she might deign to enlighten Melba and the Caltrops.

So taken up was she by the prospect of the following Saturday that she temporarily forgot that the next day would be a Sunday; the dreaded regular kind, revolving around going to church with the Caltrops instead of lunch in a hotel with a reincarnated queen who was also showing signs of being a highly experienced secret agent. Her tummy jumped like a startled pony, therefore, when Mrs Caltrop, over a supper of dry white fish, boiled cabbage and potatoes, cleared her throat and announced that tomorrow was Sunday and she had something to say about it.

"Mr Caltrop and I feel that you need some quiet time with the child, Melba. Just the two of you. We do not expect you to attend church with us."

Melba looked puzzled and her nose wrinkled, as if a dish even more distasteful than overcooked fish and bleached cabbage had been slid in front of her. She started to say something, changed her mind and switched on a winsome, gladsome smile instead.

"How understanding, Mrs C.! Yes, you are right, that is precious time."

As soon as the Caltrops had marched off down Dunallan Crescent the next morning, Melba told Elinore that she could do whatever she wanted as long as she, Melba, was not disturbed in her occupation of the bathroom.

"Can I go out?"

"Yes, go, and stay away for a long time because you won't be able to get in while I'm still busy with my hair and manicure. The Caltrops will have a terrible fit if they come home and find any door unlocked, as you very well know. You will only lose my key if I give it to you."

An idea struck Elinore. This was her chance to search for chocolates in the lair of the Caltrops. She had never been alone in there before for any stretch of time.

It was a beautiful morning, but the morning room did not know it. The bay window was swathed in the same draperies as Melba's room, mounting the same defence against daylight. Two wing-chairs sat by the fireplace; again, a scoured, whitened hearth, but with a much larger heater standing in it than in Melba's room. By each chair were a footstool and a small table with shelves for newspapers and magazines, and a standard lamp. The dining table was covered in a fringed paisley cloth that was overlaid with a linen one at mealtimes; below the fringe, bulbous mahogany legs echoed a high, heavily carved mahogany sideboard. Four balloon-back chairs were ranged at the table, and another four against the dado. The walls were painted a fleshy pink-tinged magnolia. Two large gilded frames held murky oil paintings of Highland vistas that were oddly alike; only the numbers of shaggy cattle and their kilted herders differed much. The other framed pictures were all sepia photographs of India. Glass-fronted bookshelves reached the ceiling on either side of the fireplace; the cupboards that Arabella had indicated were at their base.

Elinore crept – not knowing why she crept – towards the cupboard doors on the left. They had keyholes, but no keys. She pulled each brass handle gently, and less gently when nothing happened. The doors were locked. She tried the right-hand cupboard, with the same result. It was proof, surely, that the Caltrops were hiding something. For now, she was satisfied with that discovery. She wanted to be outside, not hunting for a small key hidden in any one of a hundred or more places in this curio-laden shrine to India.

As she walked out of the gates and along the pavement, a large ginger cat popped out of a laurel hedge and trotted ahead of her; she recognised it as the one that had outraged Mr Caltrop. "Puss, puss!" she called, eager to stroke warm, living fur. The cat turned, paused and lay down as she approached, clearly expecting to receive just that kind of attention. He was a handsome creature, if very fat.

"I'm sorry, but I can't amuse you all day," said Elinore after a minute or two of stroking and tickling under the cat's chin. She stood up and the cat sprang up, winding itself around her legs. He was purring loudly. She set off again, and the cat kept pace with her to the end of Dunallan Crescent and around a corner, as far as the second house in this unfamiliar street. This property had railings and low shrubs instead of a monstrous laurel hedge. Just then, the front door opened and closed, and Elinore saw a girl coming down the drive, swinging a wicker shopping basket. The ginger cat ran to her immediately, and she lifted him up, laid her cheek on his fur and murmured something.

She was the brown-haired girl Elinore had seen a week ago in the Balmerinoch Hotel. Elinore's curiosity ignited and she could only stand and stare. The girl wore a yellow jumper, light corduroy trousers, and white sandshoes. If she had offered any kind of greeting to Elinore at that moment, Elinore would have leapt into instant acquaintance. But the girl merely buried her face deeper in the cat's fur until only her eyes showed above it, returning Elinore's stare.

Elinore flushed. She walked on down the street as quickly as she could without breaking into a run, wanting to reach the next corner and disappear. She chastised her imagination. Why would an immaculate, up-to-date girl like that make friends with one who looked like Elinore? Elinore's dark green sweater, with the usual complement of pills, holes and trailing bits of wool, was unseasonal in both colour and weight, and too small for her; half the length of her forearms stuck out. Under it was the old, too short Aertex gym shirt. Her faded blue cotton trousers stopped above her anklebones and had a tear along the seam of one leg. She had long desired a pair of snowy white sandshoes, but last year's scuffed brown sandals were all she had for a morning like this. And her hair was not sleek and neat in a white bandeau.

Embarrassment made her feel sick. In the distance, she saw some shops. Hoping for distraction in their windows, even though they would be closed on a Sunday, she marched towards them. The streets were quiet. An elderly lady looked up from tending her flowers and said with a smile, "My, it's a fine morning, isn't it?" Then she bent over again without another glance, which made Elinore feel slightly less of an oddity. None of the other few passers-by seemed to notice her at all.

The row of shops and estate agencies lined the ground floor of an impressive red sandstone building that housed many flats in a further four storeys. On the corner was a newsagent-cum-grocers, the only business that was open. Elinore went straight to a charity shop whose window displayed several dresses for girls and women, books, record albums, a gilded porcelain tea service on a tray and a scatter of bric-a-brac. A girl's dress, a plain navy shift with a sailor collar, attracted her immediately. A full-skirted white dress with black polka dots and a red belt looked as if it might fit her too; it could be the party dress she had yet to own. She must try to inveigle Melba along here, or find a way to earn pocket money. A sign was stuck on the door: *Open from 10:00 – 3:00, Monday to Saturday. Volunteers welcome.*

A jingling doorbell made her look over at the corner shop. The girl in the yellow jumper came out. Her wicker basket hung from one arm and she held a copy of *Princess Tina* in that hand. She paused, folded the comic open and set off on a different route from that along which Elinore had fled. She went slowly because she was reading and also dipping her free hand into the basket every so often to bring something to her mouth. Elinore's eyes followed her until she turned a corner.

Elinore had an idea. Her secret agent skills could operate here too. This made her feel bold and clever, which was so much a better feeling than embarrassment that she did not hesitate. She entered the corner shop and went straight to the counter, where a small, brown, bespectacled man was arranging fresh rolls in a tray. He wore a collar and tie and a khaki warehouse coat that had been ironed, possibly even starched.

"Good morning to you, miss," he said. "What can I get for you?"

Elinore had never been called 'miss' in all her life, and this courtesy emboldened her further.

"Please, can you tell me the name of the girl who came in here? She had a yellow jumper. I think she's a friend of mine from another place."

"Oh, that is Susanna. We know her very well. She is a friend of my daughter Usha and they go to the same school." The small man looked and sounded as if this were a great pleasure in his life. "So, was Susanna your friend at another school?"

"No. She just looked like her. Thank you very much for telling me." Elinore turned to leave, but paused in front of a rack of comics. What a luxury to have a brand-new *Princess Tina* every week, instead of random old issues passed on by other people, which had been her lot in Criven.

"Susanna buys her comics here every weekend," said the man. "If you would like us to keep one or two for you every week too, that would be very simple."

The bead curtain behind the counter jiggled and parted and a girl appeared, carrying a satchel. She wore a blue plaid dress and, like the shopkeeper, had an ironed-and-starched neatness about her. Elinore was fixated by her hair, which hung over the front of one shoulder in a thick, shining black plait that almost touched her elbow. With such hair, one could have a different exotic look every single day. The girl smiled tentatively at Elinore.

"Ah, Usha – this young lady thought she knew Susanna. I was telling her how the two of you are such good friends. Are you going to your tutor now?"

"Yes. Then I'll be home for lunch."

"Very good," he said, and the two girls left the shop at the same time.

Elinore had no intention of walking away from this fruitful situation. She stood there waiting for it to develop further, smiling at the friend of the intriguing Susanna.

"Which way are you going?" asked Usha.

"Oh – I don't know. I was just exploring. I'm new here."

"You might get lost. Where do you live?"

"Dunallan Crescent."

"I know where it is. I've got a friend who lives near there. If you come with me, I can show you her street, so you don't get lost."

"Yes, please!" Elinore smiled widely in gratitude. They set off in silence. Then Elinore remembered Agnes Pound on one's responsibility for making small talk with shy people.

"Do you go to a tutor every Sunday?"

"Yes. For mathematics."

"Gosh." This sounded very unpleasant to Elinore, who was poor at numbers. "Where do you go to school?"

"The Ina Blackadder School for Girls. Where do you go?"

"Aikenhead Primary School."

"Oh. I don't know where that is."

Silence. Then Usha surprised her. "What do you like doing at the weekend?"

Elinore did not answer for a moment. Her world had become arid yet complex, restrictive yet full of things to explore if only she could, and ruled by Caltrops; over everything lay her homesickness. Tales of her present life would be boring at best, and at worst would put this nice girl right off. Instead, she began to describe four seasons of pastimes in Criven. Their pace slowed to a dawdle and Elinore became aware that Usha was raptly attentive. Suddenly Usha stopped, and her hand flew to her mouth in consternation. "We've gone right past my tutor's house! It's back there – the one with the green door. I'll be late. Can you wait for me? Just one hour? Please! I want to hear more!" Then she ran off.

Agent Solo stood on the pavement, amazed and gratified. Being bad – telling fibs, even, and to a nice, helpful gentleman! – had once again produced extraordinary results. She ran back to note the number of the house with the green door, and then a little farther until she found the street name on a sign. It was easy to lose track in these alien rows. Although the bay-windowed terraced houses were large and comfortable with pretty front gardens, in their long, long rows they reminded her of the tall, unnatural towers on the way to school; almost the same sort of thing, she felt, only laid flat on the ground. Then she meandered on, making for a sunlit stretch of trees in the distance, and feeling very happy until it struck her that she had no means of knowing when the hour would be up. She had never owned a wristwatch. Sitting in deep, chilly shadow on the tutor's doorstep would be the only sure way to be on time. This was not appealing. She walked towards the greenery as quickly as she could. When she saw it was a churchyard, she looked up in sudden hope: yes, a steeple, and on the stone face below it – *yes*, a clock! The hands stood at quarter past eleven.

Highly pleased with herself, Agent Solo decided that her resourcefulness deserved a rest in the sun for the next half hour. She settled her back against a gravestone within sight of the clock and began to make a daisy chain. For the first time since arriving in Edinburgh, she relaxed. The sun was lovely, the trees rustled and she could hear a bee. She could also hear singing from within the church, but when it was time for the congregation to come out, any of the gravestones would conceal a small secret agent, and everyone would be distracted by thoughts of Sunday lunch.

꧁

"Surprise!" cried Elinore, dangling a very long daisy chain in front of Usha, who squeaked with pleasure and put it around her neck. She touched it as if it were filigreed silver.

"I've never made one," she confessed. "But I love flowers and things. I want to be a scientist and work with plants."

They ambled along back to the shop, and Usha asked for more stories about Criven. "You are so lucky," she said, which was a novelty to Elinore's ears. "I wish I lived in your village. It sounds like a place in a book. Sometimes we go for a drive outside Edinburgh, and I don't want to come home. But we never really go anywhere. Daddy is in the shop every day and Mummy doesn't drive the car."

"I want to go home all the time."

"How long do you have to stay here?"

"I don't know. Until my mother finds a new man to marry."

Usha looked startled. She giggled and covered her mouth, and then she said, "But what if he doesn't want to go back to your village? What if he wants to stay here? What if he wants to go away with your mother to the ends of the earth?"

This grim prospect had never occurred to Elinore. She pushed it down at once. "I'll run away."

"Gosh, that's *brave*," Usha said admiringly. "You could run here and hide." They had reached the shop and she pointed to the sign above the door. "See? V. K. Patel. That's our name. If you run away and get lost, just ask how to get to Patel's in MacAlpine Place."

It was time to part. "Can you come back next weekend?" asked Usha.

"I don't think so. I'm going out with someone. I think she's a kind of aunt."

Usha took out a notepad from her satchel and wrote down a number for Elinore. "You could phone and tell me. We could go to Susanna's if you want. I'll tell her I met you."

Usha had forgotten to point out the street where the unknown friend lived, but Elinore made her way back to Dunallan Crescent easily. She ran and skipped along for a bit, out of sheer pleasure and excitement over her adventure, but tarmac was no substitute for grass and she soon gave that up.

She was not late for lunch and so no one showed any interest in where she had been; she would not have revealed it anyway. The fatty mutton and boiled carrots made her feel nauseous, but her attention was on a matter of burning importance. How to buy at least one of the two dresses in the charity shop window? How to make sure no one else bought them before she could even try them on? After lunch, she sat cross-legged on the entirely daisy-free lawn and set off down the old, old road of sartorial improvement for the purpose of acceptance by one's peers and advancement of one's social status. In Elinore's case, this began with the blank pages left in her arithmetic jotter from Criven School and two lists: Important Things to Do and Important Things to Get.

※

On Monday morning, she realised that it was the second last week of school before summer holidays. Sports day would take place on the Wednesday; the location was a playing field that lay close to Dunallan Crescent. Miss Blaikie instructed her class loudly and repeatedly on the preparations. Pupils would change into their gym clothes at the noon break and walk in crocodiles to the playing field, shepherded by teachers. They could go straight home after every race had been run. Parents were welcome to come along and help. Shortly after hearing this, Elinore conceived a plan for Agent Solo. It required a new, unpractised level of deception: entirely warranted, she felt, given the positive, socially rewarding results of previous badness.

Wednesday was a dull, cool day. By noon, rain still threatened and the Aikenhead pupils wore coats and anoraks over their shorts and shirts, which made Elinore happy because her gym clothes were barely wearable. As her class crocodile formed two by two, she deliberately chose Darlene Bell as her partner and kept her back until they were at the very end. Darlene was an outcast who was good at only two things: tittering at everything she heard, however inappropriate that response might be, and faithfully repeating the last thing that someone might have told her directly. She was delighted to have Elinore take her arm and guide her, seeing nothing amiss in being held slightly back so that a widening gap grew between them and the others.

They reached the entrance to the playing field, where the crocodiles instantly disintegrated into a mass of running, whooping children and running, shouting teachers. Elinore sprang into action – or rather, she clutched her stomach and gasped.

"Aaaagghh!" she moaned in best *Princess Tina* speech balloon fashion, pulling Darlene to a halt. "My tummy! I'm *sick*. I have to get home."

Darlene stood with her mouth open. Elinore doubled over. "Tell Miss Blaikie I went home because I was sick. My house is over there – see?"

She pointed in the general direction of No. 17. Darlene nodded and tittered.

"Ohh, I have to go right now. I need the bathroom. You go on."

Elinore gave Darlene a push in the right direction and, as fast as she could while bent over, ran off until she could turn out of sight. Then she ran and ran until she reached MacAlpine Place.

When Elinore entered the charity shop, she was flushed and very hot, having had to run in a coat while carrying her satchel and a gym bag containing her school clothes. Two grey-haired ladies standing behind the counter looked alarmed.

"Please can I try on the navy-blue dress in the window?" Elinore asked as normally as she could. She wanted to flop on the floor and lean against the wall – horrible, hard tarmac! – but Agent Solo had to be tough.

"Why, yes, dearie – but do you not need a glass of water? Are you feeling bad?" asked one of the ladies.

"I'm fine! I was just running. But I would like a glass of water. Thank you very much." Elinore straightened herself up. One lady bustled off to the back of the shop while the other one took the navy dress out of the window. "A pretty thing," she commented, patting the crisp white sailor collar with its blue lines and pointing to a tiny anchor embroidered on either corner at the back. A white ribbon was tied loosely at the neck and navy buttons ran up the front.

Elinore drank her glass of water in one go, and went into a curtained-off changing space with a mirror. She had never done this before, and it felt grown-up. "Come out when you're ready and show yourself off!" called one of the ladies. The dress was just a little big for her, but Elinore was happy: it meant that she would have longer to wear it. She pulled aside the curtain and the ladies clapped.

"Now, isn't that fine," said one. "Suits you to a T," said the other. "Are you looking for a special dress, for a party maybe?"

"Um, yes. I need a party dress and just – a dress. Just for going out." She stroked the fabric, unsure if that was the right way to describe the purpose of a dress. Then she remembered that she was going out in three days' time. "I'm going to the Balmerinoch Hotel soon for my birthday. I mean, my birthday's on another day but I want a dress for going to the hotel."

The ladies were all a-twitter.

"The Balmerinoch? Oh, my. I read about that place in The Scotsman just the other day. Very fine indeed!"

"For a birthday treat too! Yes, you'll need to look your best for that."

One of them turned to a rack and began searching. "Now we know what you're like in that, we'll find you some more." The first she pulled out was the black and white polka dot one. Elinore lit up inside like a Christmas tree. She went behind the curtain with three more dresses. This was like Christmas on the outside too, or rather, like one of her imagined versions. Then her inner Christmas lights dimmed as she remembered that she had no money for one dress, let alone three or four. In the end, the polka dot one did not fit her well and she did not like the other three as much as the navy one; its cloth had the weight and silky smoothness of some of Melba's extravagances.

After the dresses, Elinore's own clothes felt coarse and ugly. She laid the navy one on the counter, not knowing what to do next. Two words popped into her head: pocket money. They were only words. The reality had always been what other children talked about. Pocket money was the province and indulgence of benign fathers who were always there to dispense it, along with a modicum of interest in the happiness of their offspring. Still, she knew a little about the process: pocket money appeared only on certain days of the week and never before.

"Well, dearie, do you want to take it now, or do you want to think about it?"

"Oh no! I mean, I *don't* want to think about it. But I don't have my pocket money yet."

The two ladies exchanged a glance and one nodded.

"And maybe you'll get some early birthday money too, with the usual," the other lady said. "Would you like us to put it by for you until Friday closing – och, let's make it Saturday. Can you come in the forenoon?"

"*Yes!*" said Elinore, so loudly that she startled even herself. "I mean, yes, please, and thank you very, very much indeed."

The ladies' mouths twitched. They busied themselves with the dress, a bag and a note stating Elinore's name and the words "HOLD until Saturday 25th – noon." As they did so, rain started falling heavily and the shop front was soon streaming. Elinore knew she would be drenched by the time she reached Dunallan Crescent, but that was of no concern. She had secured the dress for two and a half days. She plunged into the downpour while the ladies were still talking about finding an old umbrella for her, and once again ran and ran.

6

That Wednesday evening, Melba arrived at No. 17 a good hour later than usual. She was not only soaked but also limping slightly, and one of her shins was grazed. Elinore was very surprised to see that all this and the downpour had not put her in a villainous temper. She was merely preoccupied. Mrs Caltrop, however, was annoyed that two wet people had dripped all over the floors that Mrs Wattie had cleaned only the previous day. Why had they not entered through the back door?

"Was that in the rules, Mrs C.?" asked Melba.

"It is common sense!" snapped Mrs Caltrop, the red flowers blooming quickly on her cheeks.

"But I have no key for the back door, and Elinore has no key at all."

"*That* is the function of a doorbell."

"Oh, well . . ." Melba said, and yawned. "Do excuse me. I must lie down. I was run off my feet today and my poor knee is frightfully sore." She smiled, but only to herself, and limped from the tea table.

"Too much haste these days, oh, yes indeed," intoned Mr Caltrop, shaking his head. "Too many accidents where man or woman is too busy to keep to the right and careful ways of life. That's what

McGrigor and MacHaffie say over and over, you know, in their great work. *The Devil's Toeholds* – it's right there on the shelf."

Forgetting himself, he pointed with his fork at the bookcases, and two peas rolled off, bounced on his plate and fell onto the tablecloth. Elinore recoiled at this abandonment of etiquette.

She pushed her own portion of peas, a pork chop (which she loathed), and the inevitable boiled potato around on her plate for a moment, and then decided to strike before Melba's unusual sweetness turned sour.

"Excuse me, I'm going to see if Mummy is all right," she said.

"That food must not be wasted! I can't have this spoilt behaviour at mealtimes. If you knew what a starving child in Africa would make of that –" Mrs Caltrop was in full flow, but Elinore was already running upstairs.

Melba was not lying down at all. She was rummaging in the wardrobe and throwing garments onto the bed. It reminded Elinore of the moment when she had learned that they would be leaving Criven.

"Mummy, I need to ask you something."

"What is it? I need to concentrate right now."

"Can I have pocket money?"

"*What?* Ridiculous! How can you suggest such a thing when you know I'm working myself to exhaustion and scraping pennies together to keep us housed?"

"But why can't I have some pocket money for my birthday? Just enough for one day?" She named a sum that doubled the price of the navy dress.

"Well – one day might be possible. Ask me again in the first week of next month. Your birthday isn't until then anyway."

"That's *after* my birthday! I need it for this Saturday. I need pocket money for when I go out with Arabella."

Melba straightened up with a jerk. "What do you mean, for Saturday? Is that woman going to appear then?"

"Yes, she told me in the letter. She's taking me out for my birthday, and maybe on Sunday too."

"I see." Melba seemed oddly pleased. "Well, let me think . . ." She turned back to the wardrobe and pushed coat hangers this way and that. Elinore sat down on the floor, for the obvious places were all taken up with clothing and frilly items vital to Melba's daily life. Then she lay down flat and stared at the ceiling, which was restful. Her bursts of running and the tension of being Agent Solo in extreme action had left her tired out, and the loathsome pork chop had done nothing to replenish her. She would not move until pocket money had appeared. She studied the greyish, flaking paint on the cornice and ceiling, the obnoxious flowers on the wallpaper and the hideous shade of the ceiling light. If she had a house of her very own – in Criven, of course – things like these would all be banned. If she had a house of her very own, it would have a sitting room with walls of sunshine, and she would cook in a kitchen the colour of cucumber and young lettuce – greens so fresh as to make Peter Rabbit drool – with a snow white ceiling, doors and cupboards; her bedroom would be all the pinks and reds of old roses, and her bathroom would warm her just to look at it, even on the coldest days, because it would be ablaze in the fiery hues of nasturtiums; the entrance hall would be the colour of fresh apricots, to make visitors feel welcome –

"All right, you can have this much money for your outing with Arabella." Melba was standing over her, purse in hand. "But only on one condition! You must keep yourself busy with Arabella on both days, and you must not come back here until your bedtime. If you disobey, I will never give you any money ever again. Do you understand?"

Elinore did not understand why Melba should order her to do something that she could hardly wait to do anyway. But she said nothing and held out her hand. Melba dropped coins into it. Elinore counted them: *enough!* Even more than enough.

Thursday passed so slowly that Elinore was practically itching with impatience. Miss Blaikie said nothing about her disappearance from sports day, and gradually Elinore accepted that it had not been noticed. Darlene Bell had collided with two big boys when everyone was running in the rain, and this accident had apparently knocked all memory of Elinore's retreat right out of her head; she could only talk about her sore arm and her sore leg. Friday was the same, until the last lesson of the day. Miss Blaikie reminded them as usual to bring their school dinner money on Monday. Then she asked them to bring extra money on Wednesday for a special collection. A missionary was coming to tell the whole school about Africa, and to raise money for all the extra Bibles he needed to help the poor African children.

Elinore raised her head from the private game she was playing (how many words can one make out of 'exaggerate'?). The poor African children were often present in spirit at the Caltrop table, and unfailingly so when Elinore was in a mind to produce 'wasted food'. They seemed to have a large body of dedicated supporters who were far from shy about asking for help on their behalf. Elinore, on the other hand, was completely alone on her path of self-improvement. (Agent Solo's mission of killing off the Caltrops was so far not dependent on funding.) She sensed a possible threat to her minuscule reserve, her one day's pocket money. Melba might refuse point-blank to supply more for any reason. Miss Blaikie, however, in her short account of the forthcoming visitor to the school, had also inadvertently provided a solution.

Agent Solo went into action at teatime, as soon as Melba had once again left the table early to go upstairs and rest.

"A missionary is coming to our school on Wednesday," she began. "He's from Africa. We're going to have a talk with a slide show."

"We could do with a great deal more of that in the schools these days," said Mrs Caltrop.

Mr Caltrop nodded vigorously and slapped a hand on the tablecloth. "Now, that's an admirable thing indeed. You'll learn much about your brothers and sisters in heathen lands."

"But they aren't heathens," said Elinore. "They read the Bible and we're going to give the missionary money so he can buy more Bibles. He's going to all the schools in Edinburgh."

"It is a fine point whether they are or are not heathens, regardless of the Bible," observed Mrs Caltrop. "I have great experience in the matter. Is the school taking up a collection for this good man, then?"

"Yes. We all have to take money specially for that on Wednesday. But I don't have *any* money to give." She let out a great sigh and bowed her head.

"Well, we cannot possibly allow this household to be seen as delinquent on such occasions," declared Mrs Caltrop, for whom the act of donating to a collection plate was as public an event, and as gratifying, as any speaking role on stage would have been to Melba.

She went to the writing desk and wrote on an envelope, into which she put some coins from her purse. She sealed it and handed it to Elinore. "Ensure that the good man receives this in his hands. Do not simply drop it into the collection." Elinore read what she had written:

Donated by
Mrs Roberta Caltrop
Chair, Committee for the Welfare of Retired Missionaries
and
Mr Kenneth Caltrop
Elder, Church of Scotland
Congregation of _____

"Will he know who you are?" she enquired.

Mrs Caltrop preened. "That would not surprise me in the slightest."

"The Lord spreads word of his tireless workers as examples to all men, heathen or not," droned Mr Caltrop.

Agent Solo put the envelope in her satchel, where it kept company with the lists of Important Things to Do and Important Things to Get (for self-improvement) and another list, in a code that she was still developing, of ways and means of destabilising the Caltrop organisation. Her hard-won pocket money was safe. Satisfaction filled her again. It was a warm feeling that almost made up for being hungry most of the time; hungrier, in fact, than she had been in Criven, since no one had replaced all those mothers who had so often made her stay for tea.

When Elinore awoke early on Saturday, the Edinburgh wind was making curtains of rain blow in all directions. Immediately, she began to worry. Melba had ordered her to stay out until nearly bedtime. Arabella might become terribly bored with entertaining her on a filthy wet Edinburgh day, so bored that she would jump in one of her black beetles and run away back to that castle over the border. And she had to get to the charity shop before noon! It was worse than being Cinderella. Elinore felt responsible for all these complications and her nerves twanged every minute as nine o'clock drew closer. She did have faith that Arabella would appear, but then what? She sat on the top step of the stairs, wearing her coat and holding a tiny purse that Melba had tossed to her as a plaything years ago. It contained her pocket money.

At two minutes to nine, the doorbell rang. Mrs Caltrop said nothing at all as she opened the door to Arabella, who was wearing a man's trench coat and flat tweed cap and standing under a huge black umbrella. Elinore hurtled down the stairs.

"Good morning!" cried Arabella. "Shall we go? Goodbye, Roberta – lovely to see you again, I know you're impervious to all weather, but no need to wave us off."

Instead of a taxi, they got into Arabella's hired car. They did not move off until after Arabella had asked Elinore two important questions.

"First, what did you eat for breakfast this morning?"

"Toast with margarine on it. There was an egg, but I couldn't eat it." She had been far too keyed up. Fortunately, Mrs Caltrop enjoyed making the same boiled egg reappear in front of her over several days, and so Elinore had escaped an immediate lecture.

Arabella made a face. "Sawdust and grease, as I suspected. Second question: is there anything you particularly want to do today?"

Elinore almost cried with relief. "Please could we go to a shop near here?" she asked. "I have to get there before noon. But it doesn't open until ten o'clock."

"Perfect. You can have a proper breakfast first. I can't be dragging a malnourished child around. You'd faint in Princes Street and someone would call the authorities. The disgrace of it!"

Once again, Elinore arrived at the Balmerinoch Hotel. Passing the dining room, she saw a few guests at breakfast, but she was not to join them. Arabella led her down a passage and through a heavy, green baize-lined swing door into the kitchens. Only three or four people were in the main area, but they seemed to be busy in every part all at once. Clova stood with her back to them, in her white lab coat, operating a rumbling, crunching machine. "Mad scientist, definitely," thought Elinore. The noise stopped and Arabella said, "Clova! Don't start that thing up again."

Clova turned around. "Just trying out my new nut grinding machine." She patted it. "Fresh peanut butter now on the menu for Americans."

"Is peanut butter good for local children? We have a starving child here," said Arabella. "She's had nothing but toast and margarine."

"Margarine is axle grease. Miss Elinore Crum, I believe? Good morning." Clova held out her hand and Elinore shook it. "Glad to see you again. I need guinea pigs for my experiments. If you don't like anything, say so immediately."

Elinore felt alarmed. Disliking food might be an even worse sin in this place. Clova laid a hand on her arm.

"Now don't worry. Whatever you don't want will be gobbled up by a young man over there" – she indicated a figure heaving greengrocers' boxes around the kitchen – "who is *always* hungry."

"Can we have a pot of tea? One of your concoctions, please," said Arabella.

At one corner of the biggest table she had ever seen, Elinore and Arabella sat while Clova whisked about, apparently concocting something at the huge gas range, while sending questions and bits of her kitchen philosophy their way.

"Porridge, Elinore – how do you feel about that? It is best taken at night, I believe, especially if you have trouble sleeping. Definitely a soporific. Evening porridge is a staple at the Balmerinoch. With honey. Or yoghurt, depending on the nationality and tastes of a guest. Or both."

"I have taken my porridge at night for *years*," said Arabella, in a satisfied tone.

"Oh, but I didn't learn that from *you*," said Clova. "Now, Elinore – have you ever tasted peanut butter? Americans are flocking to my hotel already, you know. They don't all want a mixed grill for breakfast, and of course the vegetarians would die if I served that up, black pudding and all. I'm fine-tuning my vegetarian haggis at present, and you can certainly try that if you want. What are your favourite fruits? Do those people, Calvins, Calbutts, oh, Cal*trop*, thank you, do they ensure that you have at least two servings of fresh fruit daily? What – the same breakfast *every* morning? Do they *really* expect you to go to school on a miserable boiled egg? And how old will you be on this birthday? Dear me. Stunted tastes, stunted children – appalling state of affairs."

"Generally speaking or only *chez* Caltrop?" enquired Arabella.

"Both. Try this to start with, Elinore."

Elinore beheld a plate with an aromatic, bulging golden half-circle. Over its arc were fanned long pieces of buttered toast like thick, crusty rays to a rising sun, and in between each piece of toast was a sliver of cheese. It looked almost embarrassingly special, and

Elinore felt hesitant about disturbing its visual appeal. Clova and Arabella were looking expectant, however. Carefully, she applied her knife and fork.

"Oh!" The golden half-circle burst open and spilled glistening gems of red, yellow, green and brown, dotted with patches of pure white. The aroma intensified: oniony, yes, but different; peppery and – indescribable. She had no names for these unfamiliar smells, only a sudden unclear memory of bending her face very close to green, leafy plants that smelled like that. It must have been a long time ago.

Clova set down two mugs and a teapot. "This is tea that Arabella will certainly like, and you might too – but remember, you don't *have* to eat or drink *anything*."

Arabella lifted the teapot's lid and sniffed. "Peppermint, and – ?"

"Yes, peppermint, sliced lemon and a good pinch of dried rosemary. Good for the digestion. Dried the herbs myself. They're from Tom's garden, which I raid as often as I can. He says I must start paying him."

They nattered on as Elinore ate. She chewed very, very slowly and closed her eyes for a moment. When she opened them, Clova was looking intently at her. "All right?" she asked.

"I *love* it. I've never had anything like this, ever."

"Scandalous! We'll have to make up for it." Clova smiled for the very first time, with the air of a scientist confirming an expected result, and poured tea into Elinore's mug. "That's an omelette. I stuffed it with tomato, chives, garlic, bacon, sweet peppers, mushroom, cream cheese and lots of herbs. The bread is our own, baked here, and the other cheese is called Red Leicester. Forget the rain outside! A good cook always generates sunshine inside."

"Is that a pun?" asked Arabella.

"I don't know. Puns are your business," replied Clova. "I learned omelettes at the Dough School."

A *dough* school? Elinore was curious, but too intent on eating to ask questions. She ate on, slowly and seriously, aching for the plate to be a magic one that would reappear, filled with exactly the same food, in her bedroom every morning. When her plate was empty, she said her wish aloud.

"Starving child has spoken," said Arabella.

"I think *starved* is more accurate," said Clova. "It's like this. Young Callum over there is convinced he's starving. His mum cooks a full breakfast for him and he gets his dinners every day that he works here, but –" She raised her voice. "Callum! Are you hungry, by any chance?"

"Aye, I'm *starving*. This is heavy work. Have you got something for me?"

The rain was still relentless as they set off for MacAlpine Place in Arabella's hired car. Elinore's insides had never felt so full and contented. She wondered if the navy dress might fit differently as a result.

"What kind of shop are we visiting?" asked Arabella.

"A charity shop. I found a dress but I had to wait for my pocket money."

"Admirable! I applaud your thrift. Do you mind if we do more shopping afterwards? Viewing the glories of Edinburgh in this rain would be akin to spending a Sunday alone with the Caltrops."

"I'd like to do anything. Mummy said I had to stay out until bedtime anyway, and the same tomorrow."

Arabella looked at her sharply and frowned. Elinore was alarmed: had she said the wrong thing, forgotten her manners and made herself a burden?

"Well, I'm exceedingly glad to hear that because I have *lots* planned for you. But I'm curious: why do you have to stay out until that hour?"

"I don't know. She just tells me to do things."

"I see."

The two ladies behind the counter of the charity shop were not the same two whom Elinore had met earlier, but her dress was still waiting for her. Arabella examined it inside and out.

"It's a Laura Ashley. Like new. Will you try it on for me?"

Arabella lavished approval on her appearance in the dress, and then announced she was going to browse. By the time Elinore had changed back into clothes that she was now even more desperate to be rid of, Arabella had deposited on the counter a pale green vase, a blue and white china bowl, two headscarves, a necktie, a box in padded Oriental silk, a long scarf in broad stripes and a man's paisley-patterned pocket-handkerchief.

"I'm still rooting about!" Arabella called from a far corner where books were stacked on sagging shelves. "Come and see." With enough money in hand, Elinore did not hesitate. Five paperbacks went quickly to the counter. When she pulled out her tiny purse, however, Arabella said, "Absolutely *not* – put that away for another day when you're exploring on your own. May I write a cheque for all this?"

The lady who took her cheque looked at it and said, "Excuse me, I seem to know your name, but I just can't place it. Are you local?"

"Oh, no, just visiting. I live far away. But I'm sure you'll see us both again. I like to support a good cause while hunting for treasure. Goodbye!"

They stowed their finds in the car boot and drove off. Before Elinore could start on the elaborate thanks she was rehearsing in her head, Arabella said, "Well! Quite the Aladdin's cave in there. Did you see my celadon vase – the pale green one? *Very* special, very special indeed. And the haberdashery is timely for a certain gentleman's birthday. I'm *most* grateful to you for leading me there." Elinore did not know what haberdashery was, but assumed it was everything she had seen on the counter that was not meant to sit on a shelf or a lady's neck.

"But this is quite a way from Dunallan Crescent," continued Arabella. "How did you stumble upon it?"

Elinore described her exploration. She mentioned meeting Usha, but not the embarrassment of encountering Susanna. Nor did she mention her frantic dash on sports day. She could not tell whether disappearing from organised games would qualify as being enterprising or quite bad or terribly bad in Arabella's opinion. The matter of badness was becoming complicated for, every time she ventured into it, the good results were extraordinary. But Arabella had moved on from the subject of supporting charity shops.

"Now, I hope your tummy is still full with breakfast because we won't leave our next destination until we are *done*."

Arabella parked her car in a quiet spot in the city centre and announced a brief walk in the rain. They trotted along under the huge umbrella, to which other people on the pavement reacted as a highly anti-social object. Arabella liked this. "Isn't it a splendid thing? Everyone has to get out of the way!" She laughed, and Elinore saw a handsome man stopping in his tracks and turning to watch them as they hurried by. How strange, she thought, Arabella never even noticed him. How different from Melba.

Elinore knew that Edinburgh held the Palace of Holyroodhouse, where the Queen stayed now and then, and the Castle, where she did not. As for the rest of the city, her knowledge came mostly from one school outing by Criven school to the Royal Scottish Museum. The sights around her now made her feel as if she had been dropped into one of her old books. Most of the buildings were aged and impressive. Fanlights and porticos, pillars and pilasters, long sash windows, black railings, brass nameplates and bell-pulls, and so much decorative stone-carving that some of the high, blackish, smoke-darkened stone frontages might have been alive and growing.

But she had to watch her step as they hurried along the wet pavements, which were cracked and lumpy with repairs in many spots. Her shoes were too big at the sides and too wide at the heel, and they tended to flop off her feet. With all this looking down, she was startled when Arabella suddenly stopped, tipped the umbrella back and said, "Behold! One of the grandest sights in Scotland!" She flung wide the arm that was not holding the umbrella and hit a man straight across his forehead.

"*Oof!* Woman! This pavement's for all of us – have you not learnt that yet? God help us all if you drive like that."

"Oh, I *quite* agree," said Arabella. "I never drive when my brain is in the full flush of an enthusiasm. It would be disastrous." She smiled at the man, who walked away, muttering and feeling his forehead.

They were at the corner of South St David's Street and Princes Street, where the far side was empty of cliffs of buildings and all the tarmac fell away into the green slopes and hollows of the Gardens. Opposite them, on that far side of Princes Street, a soaring tower dominated the scene; Elinore had to crane her neck to find its pinnacle. The rain made it difficult to see details, but she could see a statue in the wide, open base of buttresses: a man, seated on a plinth, with a dog beside him, at the top of a flight of steps up from the street. He looked as if he were seated at home, quietly welcoming the world.

"I know who that is," Elinore told Arabella. "Sir Walter Scott. I've got one of his books, but I haven't read it yet. It's a really old one. An old lady gave it to me."

"Yes, I remember, you showed it to me. *The Heart of Midlothian.* Rather dense. It might take you a few years to get to it. But how did you know that was Sir Walter sitting there?"

"I've got a magazine with a picture of his tower. It said it was called the Scott Monument. You can climb it in the inside."

"You *can* climb it, but not today. Today you are going to explore a monument to commerce, a palace, in fact. This way!"

Arabella turned right onto Princes Street and walked a few yards to the deep-arched entrance of Jenners. From his plinth in the world's largest monument to a writer, Sir Walter Scott could contemplate the caryatids on the facade of one of the world's oldest department stores.

"First things first: we need to pee or else it will become a nuisance at the wrong moment." Arabella said this loudly enough, as they climbed Jenners' central staircase, to offend a trio of very proper Edinburgh ladies. Oh, well, thought Elinore, to whom climbing the monument sounded more exciting than being in a big shop, I suppose looking at ladies' things with Arabella will be a *bit* better than doing it with Mummy. She was curious to see what a reincarnated Tudor queen might buy here.

At the first landing, Arabella changed her mind with no explanation and stopped a passing saleslady. "Where can I find children's underwear?"

"Next floor up, madam."

"Quick, Elinore! Upstairs. We must be efficient with time or it will disappear down a rabbit hole. That happens in places like this. It is a world unto itself."

In Children's Underwear, Elinore waited, startled, while Arabella galvanized a saleslady into seizing one vest, a pair of pants and one pair of socks, and ringing them up on the cash register.

"Thank you, we will return shortly. *Now*, Elinore, to the loos!" Off they raced again, to the ladies' lavatories, where Arabella gave a bemused Elinore the bag containing the newly purchased underwear.

"Take off your old undies and put them in this bag. Put on the new ones. When you come out, drop the bag in that rubbish bin over there."

When she was inside the pristine underthings, the feel of newness and freshness, the tautness of all the elastic was so luxuriant that Elinore wriggled with delight. She barely got a "Thank you" out before Arabella asked, "Everything fits, yes? Do you feel ready for anything now?"

"Oh – yes," replied Elinore, who was rather apprehensive about what "anything" might encompass and whether Arabella had x-ray eyes.

"Excellent. We must start from the bottom up, and that is a pun, I believe."

Arabella rushed Elinore back to Children's Underwear and scooped up several more of each item. Then she pulled a list from the pocket of her trench coat and consulted it closely. She drew lines through some words and under others, and added arrows or asterisks in plenty before waving it in the air and turning into Elizabeth I again in Elinore's imagination. Something about a white horse and lots of troops . . .

"Onwards! We must look lively. We'll become Arabella and Elinore in Wonderland if we dawdle in this carpeted lotus land. Excuse me! Are girls' shoes in the Children's Wear Department or elsewhere?"

"Teen shoes and fashion shoes are in Ladies Footwear, madam." The sales assistant in black dress and pearls eyed Elinore. "But I suggest you start in Children's Footwear first. Next floor up, madam."

So began Elinore Crum's Cinderella hours, which stretched past noon. They paused in Jenners' restaurant, with apologies from Arabella because it was "not exactly the most exciting place for a birthday lunch." Elinore thought it was lovely. She was a little dazed. It appeared that she, Elinore, was being dressed as someone or something entirely new.

"Your fine Laura Ashley dress notwithstanding, I want to make sure you're covered for all occasions – oh, is that a pun? Covered – ha!" Elinore hadn't a clue what Arabella was laughing at. "*Prepared* is the word. With spares. Hmm, I like that: be prepared with spares. I *am* in good form today. Elinore, remember that. You don't want your one and only dress to wear out too quickly, do you? What if you had to go and meet the Queen at Holyrood next month?"

"*I* can't meet the Queen."

"Why not? She'll want to meet you if you do something special. Are you never, ever going to do anything special in your whole life?"

"Well – I *might*, but –"

"There you are, then. She might ask you to turn up at short notice – better be prepared with spares. Ladies-in-waiting have to carry spares for the Queen, you know. She can't carry *everything* in that handbag of hers."

The trying on and taking off and trying on all over again took ages under Arabella's critical eye. Salesladies ran around to fetch different sizes and styles, turning Elinore this way and that, tut-tutting or cooing according to whether something fitted, and generally working to make her as perfect as the mysterious Susanna. It was an experience of outrageous pleasure. But it would have been indelibly embarrassing had she been forced to exhibit herself in her old saggy pants and frayed vest, both more grey than white from careless laundering and long, long use. Arabella's list acquired not only underlinings but also additions whenever her mind was prompted in unexplained ways as she strode around. While Elinore was in the middle of trying things on, Arabella was off, casting like a hound for signs of more listed items. She did not neglect any part of Elinore's day, and came up with two nightgowns and a dressing gown in ruby red soft cotton with matching slippers. "When you make yourself warm and bright in that hideous, cold room, you are cocking a snook at the Caltrops. Remember those words, but do *not* repeat them!"

By the time Arabella finally announced that the expedition to Jenners was over, Elinore was deliriously happy. She left the building wearing a yellow sweater (*just like Susanna's!*) over a blouse patterned in tiny blue, yellow and white flowers, and a hooded anorak in navy blue with white piping. If the rain had not been falling, she could have worn her new white sandshoes (*white sandshoes!*), but the streets were still streaming and the skies still as thunderous as two Caltrops on a bad Sunday. Her feet were safe and dry in a pair of shiny yellow rain boots. Her old clothing, every piece of it, was now dispersed among Jenners' rubbish bins. Their pile of boxes and bags was being assembled into one delivery, which would be sent by taxi to the Balmerinoch within the hour. Arabella could not be bothered to fetch her car and drive around the crowded streets looking for a convenient loading spot.

Elinore had kept hold of one shopping bag, however, which she could not bear to let go. It contained large oval cakes of luxurious bath soap, wrapped in floral paper with twirly French writing all over it and exuding the scents of lemon verbena, rose, lavender and jasmine. "I regret that I can't send in the decorators to cheer up that ghastly bathroom of yours," Arabella had said, "but proper soap will do a little to dispel its workhouse atmosphere. No doubt the Caltrops use green laundry soap with carbolic for everything." She shuddered. "Now, it's time for tea at this very moment, isn't it? What do your insides say?"

"My insides are *starving*," said Elinore with glee. "That was heavy work!"

"I agree. We'll go straight to another palace, then: a palace of comfort, cakes and crumpets. Don't tell Clova I called it that or she'll throw me out of her hotel."

As they went along Princes Street to the North British Hotel, thunder rolled in the distance.

"Aahh, isn't that good," said Arabella. "A portent of change. Something is being shaken up."

Elinore looked at her in wonder. She was smiling and her face was tilted upwards. She could be a witch too, thought Elinore, a queen witch, or maybe a witch queen – was there a difference? It was too much to think about all at once. The idea of x-ray eyes alone was enormous.

7

At that very moment, in a street to the north of the North British Hotel, Melba Crum was preparing to take up a starring role. It had nothing to do with any product of Edinburgh's theatrical elite, and no influential visitor from London had spotted her immense talent from behind their mirrored sunglasses. This role would put her front and centre, however. She intended no lesser outcome.

What might be called her audition had taken place three days ago on the wet Wednesday afternoon. At Grisella's Gowns, it was the rule that two salesladies must be in the shop at all times, and so Melba never spent her breaks in the company of Joyce or Deirdre, her co-workers. But Melba was only interested in one kind of company. All around her were shops offering an ever-changing abundance of objects of desire that absorbed her fully. She tried them on her body, her feet, her fingers and wrists, and on her head. She ogled larger items intended for a domestic display of status, while her imagination zoomed forward to the time – *very soon!* – when she would be married to a new and better Hector and ensconced in a mansion with her own Mercedes at the front door, and a cleaning woman or two.

But all these treats for Melba's imagination were also tinder for her impatience. After a little taste of the Caltrops and regular employment (both insults to her constitution and sensibilities), *very soon* had still not turned into *now*. The smoke of agitation was beginning to rise from her. On that past Wednesday, when Joyce rushed in late from her break, Melba was ready to scream over the stupid woman with ten dresses in a changing room, who was going to say, "Well . . . I *reelly* don't know . . ." again, and then again.

"Here, Melba – you *have* to see this woman!" gasped Joyce, pushing a small card into Melba's hand. Her face was bright pink from something other than running and her round eyes even wider than usual, and shining. "Sorry I'm a wee bit late. The woman went on and on and I've never been so excited! Go right now – promise?" Joyce was privy to most of Melba's hopes and dreams, and vice versa, in the absence of any other intellectual stimulation within Grisella's Gowns.

A voice trailed from behind a curtain. "Well . . . I *reelly* don't know . . ." and Melba raised clenched fists and rolled her eyes. "It's that Mrs Rose again, isn't it?" whispered Joyce. "I'll see to her." She clutched Melba's arm and leaned in close. "I can afford to be nice to these old hens for a wee bit longer, 'cause I'm leaving! I got told. Your turn!" She pushed Melba away in the direction of the shop door, and said loudly to the unseen, unsure customer, "Oh, Mrs *Rose*! How *naice* to see you back again. It's Joyce here. Melba's had to go and I'll be taking care of you. Now, how many lovely frocks have you got in there with you?"

Only when she was in the street did Melba look at the card in her hand. It was pale lavender and printed with the words 'Mrs Marlock, Diviner of Destinies, Edinburgh', and a telephone number. Handwritten in blue ink was the name of a nearby tearoom and the words 'Mondays, Tuesdays, Wednesdays'. In that year of Melba's life, no one was talking about the 'information superhighway', but at that moment she was ready for the metaphysical equivalent of the M1 to speed her away from the present.

When she entered the tearoom, Melba saw nothing indicating a person who might be expected to provide useful information about the future. She stood by the door, scanning the mass of douce Edinburgh citizens with its leavening of tourists, until a waitress asked if she wanted a table to herself. When Melba spoke the name of Marlock, the waitress led her to the furthermost corner of the room where a grey-haired, meek-looking lady sat alone. She was writing in a small notebook. Tea for one and a half-eaten scone were the only items on the table.

"Excuse me, I am looking for a Mrs Marlock," said Melba, unable to accept that this dumpy, tweed-suited female could possibly envisage elements of Melba Crum's glittering destiny. She was even wearing a blue hat suspiciously like Mrs Caltrop's mushroom version.

The woman raised her unremarkable head and smiled. "Do sit down, dear. Shall we order tea? I think the tea leaves will be best for you today, especially since you're so short of time." Her accent was refined, but not in the manner of Morningside. To Melba, still half-expecting the exotic, it evoked Metroland, the stockbroker Tudor regions of her own birth, and discomfited her even more.

"Yes, I really mustn't be late back at work," she said, and then wondered how the woman knew how little time she had.

Mrs Marlock chuckled. "Oh, I shouldn't worry about that, if I were you – not today. Now, do you have any particular questions for me?" The waitress brought the tea things to their table and Mrs Marlock poured for both of them. "Or shall we simply let the leaves tell us what is most important?"

Melba suddenly felt absurd. This was such a novel sensation that she did not know what to do with it. She shook her head, added milk to her tea and drank it all as quickly as she could. Mrs Marlock scanned the bottom of the cup and said nothing at all for what to Melba seemed like five terribly long minutes. Then she sighed very, very deeply.

"Great change . . . great change." Silence. "I see a far-off place, many mountains, huge rivers. Someone following a dream, travelling far away from here into that land, crossing vast distances. I see startling news coming this way – not exactly *bad* news to those who receive it, but yes, definitely startling. I see a woman and a child, a girl, together in the same house, but not here in Edinburgh. In the country. Something about that child . . ." Melba half-rose from her chair.

"But that's *all* in the *past*! I came to find out about my future. Please – not another word about my dead husband and that bear in Alaska."

Mrs Marlock looked straight at her, the mildness of her blue-eyed gaze not changing in the slightest.

"The future is precisely what I am conveying, my dear. I can only tell you what I see, and I see only the future." She bent her head to the teacup again.

"This change is all the greater for its suddenness. And its completeness. Nothing left but memories, and even those . . ." She sighed again and looked over Melba's head towards the street outside the tearoom. "You are in a city. You feel enormous satisfaction with every single day of your new life. In fact, one might say that you are extraordinarily *lucky*. Luck seems to come your way at the drop of a hat. The immense good fortune of your life – and your beauty, my dear – will cause many people to envy you. You will never lack admirers who will be at your service, one might say. Be careful to spread some genuine good in the world while you are enjoying all these fine things. It will do something to deflect the actions of the envious."

She looked again at the tealeaves, and tapped her fingers on the table for emphasis. "*This* is important, and I do want you to pay attention." Again, she looked straight at Melba, who was by now tight-lipped with the anger of disappointment. "Twin peaks. The colour brown – the brown of, ah – yes, animal fur. A cow, definitely a cow. No, wait – a smaller animal, *considerably* smaller than a cow. A dog or even a cat – yes, that's it, a cat. Hmmm, this is confusing, for I do see the cow and the cat together. *Cats*, actually. Altogether, they – I mean the twin peaks and the cow and the cats – they *must* be treated properly if you are to allow your great desire to come to you as quickly as you wish." She sat back in her chair and looked kindly at Melba. "Forgive me if I sound like a schoolmistress, dear, but really, I can't emphasise that strongly enough – you must *pay attention*." Then she exhaled deeply and picked up the half-eaten scone. "My goodness, that was quite tiring work. It happens sometimes. The intensity of another person's feelings, you know."

The intensity of Melba's feelings sprung her out of her seat like a jack-in-the-box. She was furious: with Joyce, with this charlatan, with Hector for dying by a river in mountainous Alaska, with every single thing, large or small, that caused her immense *dis*satisfaction in this new life. Good fortune at the drop of a hat? Cows and a cat – *cats*? Cats made her sneeze and turned her eyes red and watery instantly; their hairs got onto clothing and simply stuck there forever. Utter claptrap! Her fury was instantly watered by self-pity.

"I have no idea what I owe you and I don't care!" she declared, much too loudly for a respectable tearoom. "You've taken advantage of me. A widow! *I* know what work is – more than you will ever know. Here! I shan't pay you a penny more for that pile of mumbo-jumbo." She flung a few coins onto the table and rushed from the tearoom. The other patrons looked up in surprise. It was clear to them at once – judging by her glamour and the height of her hemline – that only Melba could be in the wrong, whatever might have happened at the table in the corner. They directed their raised eyebrows and righteous mutterings in her direction, and were gratified to see her forced to struggle with the heavy door of the tearoom before rushing out.

Horrid, *tweedy* old woman, thought Melba savagely. I ought to have left at first sight of her.

In the tearoom, Mrs Marlock suddenly said aloud, to the bemusement of a passing waitress, "Coco Chanel *adores* tweed, you know." Perfectly composed, she returned to her notebook and wrote the following:

*Hey diddle-diddle,
The cat and the fiddle,
The cow jumped over the moon;
The little dog laughed
To see such sport,
And the dish ran away with the spoon.*

"Curious indeed," she murmured, and added, "More clarity, please, before you send the next seeker my way. Thank you."

Running in high heels on a setted street is very unwise. When the runner is distracted by high emotion, when rain suddenly spatters on her cheeks and trickles from her hair into her eyes, she is almost guaranteed to fall on the slippery, uneven stones.

※

Dwayne Donald McMonagle was experiencing frustration, which was bad for his blood pressure. Before the Company had sent him to Scotland, his doctor had given him the annual check-up and the usual warnings, but in a more severe tone this time. He was a big man and he was getting bigger in all the wrong places; certain test results also continued to show a steady annual increase that made his doctor wag a finger at him. Watch your stress levels, he was told; take it easy, delegate more, start thinking about retirement, don't act like you're indispensable. But the Company seemed to think he was indispensable. Only Dwayne McMonagle could sort things out in Scotland! Only he could turn every shaky, troublesome deal into a solid, smoothly running generator of profit! And hey, Dwayne, didn't you say your folks were from the old country? It'll be homecoming, then. Find some long-lost relatives and relax over the scotch – do you good! Oh, and one more thing, Dwayne: once you're done in Aberdeen, just head down to Edinburgh and check up on that greenhorn Carl. Nothing like the personal touch – right, Dwayne?

Scotland alone would have put Dwayne in a foul mood. He was sure of it. Everything was too small, too slow, too antiquated. The weather was completely unpredictable, although wetness and wind-chill were apparently constants. Hotel beds were always too short, too narrow, too hard. This poky little peewee country didn't deserve all that oil in its sea! The food was terrible, and as for half-decent service of any kind, anywhere – forget it. Fortunately, Americans would be right on top of the oil business for years to come, and maybe the Scotch would learn how to get with the times while they had the chance. That so-called restaurant for a start. Almost impossible to find – although what d'you expect with these crazy streets and no grid system, no common-sense numbered coordinates? Weren't they all bombed in the war anyhow? Why didn't they invest in some real city planning? Then Carl not showing up for lunch, and not answering his office phone – did everyone, even *secretaries*, go to sleep over lunch in this toy-town? – and the looks on those waiters' faces when he asked to make a call, okay, a couple, maybe three, from the phone in the restaurant – *jeez!*

Dwayne had had enough. He left the restaurant still hungry and still mystified over Carl's non-appearance, but in the mood only for checking out of his hotel and getting back to London right away. He'd start to feel better at Heathrow. He jammed his hat onto his head (whaddya know, it's raining again!) and barrelled along. Good thing he always wore his Stetson and his Frye boots wherever he was: you couldn't even count on *asphalt* in this place, look at these damn medieval cobble things. He glanced at his watch and mentally switched time zones, and then it hit him – *uuuhhh!*

The shock of falling all but face down made his heart jump violently. For an instant he thought it was the heart attack that his doctor had insisted was lying in wait for him. Only when he lumbered to his feet did he see that the cause was a blonde who had also tripped right in front of him while he was staring at his watch, and who was still trying to get up. She was in such distress that Dwayne dropped to his knees again and reached out a hand.

"Ma'am, are you OK? I am *real* sorry about landing on you like –"

"Yes! You should be sorry!" shrieked the blonde, who had the most amazing blue eyes Dwayne had ever seen. "You could have broken my neck! Take your hands *off* me."

None of Melba's dreams had included a very paunchy, late middle-aged American with bags under his eyes and no dress sense. Her fury was fuelled by the absence of a better knight, such as Burt Reynolds, on the rescue scene. She slapped the outstretched hand and began struggling to her feet. Then she felt the pain and saw the blood trickling from her grazed knee. Melba could not stand the sight of blood, even if it was her own. "Ohhh . . ." She stopped trying to get up and buried her head in her arms. "This is the last straw! It's all too much. I've had enough of this awful, *awful* life!"

Melba meant that she was fed up with Edinburgh and not having a Burt Reynolds to rescue her, but Dwayne interpreted her last words in the most alarming way possible. The sight of her bloody knee only deepened the connotations of greater harm. He knew he must act responsibly. His large hand ventured towards her shoulder again.

"Ma'am, I'm going to get you a cab and then we're going to take you to hospital or take you home or – or wherever." He turned to a knot of idling pedestrians who were showing interest in this little international incident. "Hey, get me a cab, will you? This lady needs help. Ma'am, you can count on me. I'm going to make sure you get where you need to be and I'm not leaving you until I'm satisfied, OK?" The hand on her shoulder gave a reassuring squeeze. The words and the touch slowed Melba's galloping self-pity to a canter and then a trot, allowing self-interest to regain control. Her circumstances demanded responsibility. She was duty-bound to spin all forms of help out for as long as possible.

"No, no – not home. Take me back to work," she sniffled, pushing her hair back from her face with a tragic gesture. "I am a widow and must support myself. I could be fired for being late." She gave a little cry, pressed some more tears from her eyes and bowed her head again. She saw that the blood on her shins was drying inconveniently fast and must be covered before it ceased to cause alarm. "Oh, my knee, my leg – do you have a handkerchief?"

A taxi pulled up and Dwayne helped Melba into it as if she were porcelain. It was a very short distance to Grisella's Gowns, but long enough for both passengers to realise that being responsible in the face of sudden mishap could be rewarding. As Melba limped into the shop, she had already reached the stage of deciding that this rather too grizzled and over the hill American made Hector look puny. He reminded her of the advertisement for Marlboro cigarettes. That cowboy in a haze of dust was definitely not the man of her dreams. But better to have been fallen on by this cowboy instead of some inconsequential little clerk in a shiny suit.

For his part, Dwayne was determined that this gorgeous female, who wore no wedding ring and did not appear to be Scotch, was not going to disappear now that he had hold of her, literally, with one arm tightly around her tiny waist and the other on her arm. He had tied his own handkerchief around her knee. Grisella and the girls flapped around and fetched a chair for Melba. Dwayne crouched down beside it, and fixed her with a solemn, responsible gaze.

"Now, ma'am, this here is my business card, so you can see I'm on the up and up. If you will do me the honour of having a drink, something to eat – whatever hits the spot – with me when you're all done today, I'll be right back here with a cab at closing time. I can't just run off and leave a beautiful lady in distress, now, can I? Not when it was *all my fault* that she got hurt." He shrugged, spread his hands and gave what he hoped was a rueful, winsome smile.

Melba sensed that she *might* be on the up and up at that moment too, although her British ears had taken a quite different, but equally positive meaning from the phrase. She nodded mutely, opened her eyes very wide (no longer brimming, unfortunately) and held Dwayne's gaze for as long as she could until her mouth trembled (that was helpful, though) from the effort of restraining a smile. For the second time in one afternoon, she accepted a small piece of printed card imbued with the power of destiny.

By the time Grisella's Gowns closed on the following Saturday, Melba was ready to wine, dine and be swept off her feet. The easiest role in the world! The role of brave, lonely widow complemented it marvellously, and so, in time, would that of brave, selfless widowed mother. She had not yet mentioned the existence of her child, the one to whom she was devoted and whose future she considered endlessly – after all, was it not her desire to do the very best by Elinore and her education that had brought the pair of them to the city? She could tell Dwayne that she had been too overcome on Wednesday to mention Elinore to him; her emotions too fragile, especially at the startling discovery that someone actually *cared* about her! Yes, she could introduce the existence of Elinore with much clutching of Dwayne's hand, swallowing and blinking back tears, dabbing of a handkerchief and making halting, whispery confessions about how terribly hard it was at times to be brave for the sake of a little one. Oh, the *aloneness* of it all! That should do it. And Dwayne McMonagle would do too, at least for now. He was *American*! That was a bonus.

She checked her handbag for the precise location of two brand-new lace-edged handkerchiefs, and came up with a tatty piece of lavender card.

"Oh, Joyce, would you like to pass this on to someone else? I shan't be seeing that woman again. I seem to be quite able to take charge of my own destiny. I do hope she hasn't led you up the wrong path with silly fantasies!"

She raised her eyebrows in kind, gracious concern, and gave Joyce a kind, gracious smile, unaware that she was talking not only to the future Joy Gillanders, darling of national children's television and wife of an ITV producer, but also to her even later incarnation as Joy Rosales, wife of a stupendously rich and internationally idolised Spanish football player.

8

Elinore Crum stands in a bedroom at the Balmerinoch Hotel, staring at bags and boxes piled on the carpet (which is a plain light grey, with not a squirl or whorl). The pile reminds her of a picture in *National Geographic* showing a volcanic island that had erupted from the sea. Astonished that she has acquired so much clothing and footwear in one afternoon, Elinore cannot recall any instructions from Miss Agnes Pound on the thanking of fairy godmothers. Arabella Cheyne, she has concluded, in addition to possibly being a reincarnated queen and a witch, is most certainly a fairy godmother.

Arabella is not standing around waiting for thanks. She pulls off her trench coat, throws it across a chair and claps her hands.

"To work! Your dresses and so forth *must* all be hung up to be happy! Some items you will take back with you tonight, and some I'll bring tomorrow, after Roberta Caltrop has found wardrobe space for them. She can find it if she tries hard enough. A little prod from me will help. I'll divide all this loot in two while you bathe."

"Bathe? Right now?"

"But of course. We're going downstairs to dinner and I don't want to be disgraced by a grubby child any more than by a starving one fainting at my feet on the streets. Besides, I can't believe that Roberta permits wallowing of any kind. You might as well splash around in my sumptuous bathroom before I return you to your cell. Off you go. Make it deep and use plenty of that stuff in the fancy green bottle."

Although she had given up on Sunday school, Elinore had heard of something called 'heaven on earth'. *This* is it, she thought, this is why Mummy likes it so much. For the very first time in her life, she was neck-deep in hot, scented water in a warm bathroom. The pale blue walls did not stream with condensation. In comparison with the shrunken, greyish, threadbare items issued by Mrs Caltrop, the pure white towels were the size of small thick carpets.

Afterwards, Elinore eagerly explored the Balmerinoch dinner menu. It was a relief to be in the company of a grown-up who, unlike Mrs Caltrop, did not subject every mouthful Elinore took to intense scrutiny. Arabella ate with gusto and encouraged her to do the same.

"I strongly recommend the Beef Stroganov after all your exertions in Jenners. It's the real thing here, a proper 19th century Russian recipe, so Clova tells me. No tinned mushroom soup or other abominations, which are adulterating Stroganovs in kitchens across the country as we speak."

Their first course was mulligatawny soup, with a Balmerinoch twist that was pure genius according to Arabella. With her last spoonful, she declared her cockles, whatever or wherever they might be, to be well and truly warmed.

"Let us discuss tomorrow. We could march around the castle and other ancient monuments, but monuments are not fleeting and neither are their pleasures. The weatherman promises sunshine, which we must seize. We'll take ourselves on a jaunt to the country."

A bell rang in Elinore's memory: a telephone bell. Tomorrow was Sunday. She had forgotten all about her promise to ring Usha, and where was that piece of paper with the Patels' number?

"Such a worried expression, Elinore! Is it the prospect of my driving? Leaving the Caltrops behind for another whole day? Missing their Sunday lunch?"

When Elinore told her about Usha, Arabella waved her hand and dismissed any problem. "She'll come with us. We'll look them up in the book and I'll talk to her parents. Didn't you tell me she loved fields and flowers? We're going to visit Tom, Clova's brother. His garden is quite out of control – your friend might like that. His house is beyond description. He lives in an old village with a ruined castle. We'll take a great big picnic, because Tom is a bad cook. In fact, he *can't* cook, the results are peculiar and possibly dangerous. He's been wanting to marry me for years, you know. I keep telling him he's confusing *wife* with *housekeeper*, and he can simply advertise for one of those. A lovely man, terribly learned, but still, he thinks my work is merely a frivolous form of housekeeping!" She waved her hand again in disdain or dismissal.

"What *do* you do?" asked Elinore. "I mean, what kind of job? Are you going to work in the castle for a long time?"

"My job has no name. I can describe a bit of what I do, but not the how or why of it. As for Welkinlaw . . ." She paused. "Let's play a bit of What's My Line – yes, I know you're too young to remember it on the wireless, but never mind. I'll tell you a few things and you give my job a name. If it's a good one, I'll order extra pudding for you to eat as a midnight snack in that cell of yours. Pretend you're at boarding school. All right?"

Elinore nodded, eyes gleaming.

"First, a little bit of philosophy – mine. My philosophy is – oh, let's borrow from Hamlet."

Arabella leaned towards Elinore and declaimed, "There are more things in heaven and earth, Horatio / Than are dreamt of in your philosophy." She sat back, looking very satisfied with this shorthand. "Even in *my* philosophy," she added. Elinore looked at her in complete puzzlement.

"Oh, dear," said Arabella. "I told you it was peculiar."

She looked around the dining room, leaned close again and said, "Magic. A sort of magic. I don't have any other explanation."

"Are you magic?"

"Good heavens, *no*. I look, I listen, I move things around a lot and often right out of the place, which clarifies the situation wonderfully, and I tell everyone else what they should be doing and how to do it, for which I am notorious." She smiled happily. "The magic is something that happens in between. I might be wrong, it might be science, but I was always bad at that at school and I'm not looking into being scientific now. It can remain as magic for the sake of convenience. The thing is, it brings about change. People are *very* resistant to change, you know, especially in their houses. And worst of all, *they pile things up!* This is a poisonous habit, Elinore – *poisonous*. Left unchecked, piles can cause terrible, untold harm."

Arabella looked deadly serious, as if she were a doctor describing a particularly virulent disease.

"As for Welkinlaw," she continued, "it's a bigger mess than usual because it's a castle, and that's why I'm spending so much time on it. Some of it is ancient, and all of it is horribly awkward to live in. It belongs to the Ansketts, dear friends of mine. They have one son and heir, who is in New York making huge amounts of money. He's fallen in love with an American girl, but it was always his intention to return to Welkinlaw and take over from his father in due course. Now he wants to bring his girlfriend, and he's talking as if he wants to marry her. But he won't come unless his parents clean up the castle first, because he says she'll turn tail at the sight of it and he'll die of a broken heart. Or something like that. I didn't think that kind of melodrama was still in vogue with the young, and perhaps his parents got a bit carried away when they were telling me – they are in a bit of a state, you understand – but that is what I'm dealing with, generally speaking. The Ansketts are ditherers. It takes them ages to agree on anything, and just when I think I've got something settled, one of them will say, what about such-and-such, and we're off again – or rather, we aren't off anywhere, we're covering old ground, which I *hate*."

She took a drink of water and once again leaned in and spoke quietly, as if what she was about to impart was only a breath away from being a secret.

"The thing is, the more stuff is removed from Welkinlaw or rearranged inside it, the clearer the heads of the Ansketts. *That* is at the bottom of everything I do, Elinore. They are getting better at making decisions, even if their dithering does make me boil over with impatience. The place is full of rubbish! It looks like a furniture repository, and it feels like a miserable, grumpy old man. Places do have personalities. A ghost or two might be happy in Welkinlaw at present, but not an American fiancée."

"What about ghosts? Do you talk to ghosts too?"

"Ghosts never bother to introduce themselves to me. A good thing too, because the last thing I need is *that* kind of reputation. I have enough on my plate with flesh and blood characters or moping buildings that want to have a bit of fun and new life and never get it. That's another source of trouble, you see: if you ignore the spirit of a place, it will become a pain in the neck *and* the bank account. Or it will simply crumble and fall apart. People subject their dwellings to such awful, dreary, unsuitable existences! They're all the same: castles, Regency flats in Bath, bungalows by the sea, villas in Tunbridge Wells. Really and truly, they want to be taken care of by the right people in the right ways and have stimulating lives."

To Elinore, this was more or less gobbledegook, with the exception of one salient point that she presented at once.

"But maybe you're helping them at the same time – the ghosts. If the house is happy, it could make a ghost happy. Don't they bother people because they were sad when they died?"

"So my house medicine could be working on ghosts too, you think, whether I care about it or not? Very perceptive. That theory alone is worth a helping of midnight pudding."

House medicine. That's a clue, thought Elinore.

"Well – I think you're a sort of Mary Poppins for houses," she said. "She made the Banks children happy, didn't she? No one was listening to them, and they wanted to have fun too. Except you can't pour medicine down a chimney with a spoonful of sugar!" She giggled and then stopped, blushing, for Arabella was laughing.

"Mary Poppins for houses! Utterly distinctive. I will adopt the title forthwith and that's two helpings of secret pudding for you. But I only use my umbrella for rain, I swear."

"And knocking people off the pavement," said Elinore.

"Of course. But not if they're old ladies. That would be shockingly bad. Elinore, I predict you will go far in the world, whatever job you decide to do."

"I think I'd like a job like yours. It must be the best in the whole world."

"I am uniquely unfitted for any other profession. I do have a few other handy skills, but that's the one that takes me away from home a lot."

"Do you live in an old house too?"

"Yes, but it's only from the days of Queen Victoria, which is like yesterday to a place like Welkinlaw. And it isn't at all grand – just a farmhouse. I'm doing it up, and I'm not even halfway through it. Perhaps you'd like to visit some time. One spare room is finished, more or less, and it's quite safe – I mean, you wouldn't fall through the floorboards in *that* room. And I think you'd like the surroundings very much, because you could roam for hours and climb to the tops of hills. You'd see deer and other creatures, all kinds of birds, children too – a few of those live nearby, all perfectly civilised and I'm sure they'd welcome you. There's a river at the foot of my hill, with lots of stony shallows where you can wade right across. It's a friendly sort of river, like a happy person who's always pleased to see you. Not like some people we know."

Elinore was silent. Criven filled her mind's eye, and once again she could not tell whether she felt mournful or angry, or both at once. It had come over her in a split second. Her brows drew together, she could feel the glower coming on, and her fists bunched in her lap. Instantly she was embarrassed at being visibly not a nice, happy friend in front of Arabella. *That* would be badness: the real thing, not merely bad behaviour. But surely she wasn't a bad *person*, not really! She would never knock old ladies off the pavement with her umbrella either. She was suddenly overwhelmed with feelings that needed sorting out. Her stomach screwed itself up. Then a squirt of panic was added to the mix: only an hour or so left before she would be back in the bleakness of No. 17 Dunallan Crescent! Only one more day before Arabella would disappear into another world altogether, a world of castles, farmhouses and rivers among hills. She must not turn into a cry-baby and spoil the time that was left, or worse, repel Arabella from taking her out in public ever again.

Arabella, observing this mighty struggle, was silent too.

Before leaving the Balmerinoch, they found the Patels' telephone number in the directory. Arabella asked Elinore to speak first because after all she, Arabella, was a complete stranger.

"What do I call you? I mean, are you my aunt?" asked Elinore.

"Yes, for this purpose I am an aunt. I don't go in for pedantic exactitude in such matters."

Mr Patel was effusively pleased to hear from Elinore and Usha was relieved. "I didn't want you to disappear! I told Susanna all about you today. Can you come back tomorrow? Susanna has to visit her grandmother, but I only have tutoring in the morning."

"Yes, I can come, but guess what, *we* can take *you* out in the car – my Aunt Arabella's car. We're going to a village in the country with a ruined castle and a beautiful garden. Do you want to come too? Arabella needs to ask your mother and father for permission."

Squeaks of delight issued from the telephone receiver, which Elinore handed to Arabella with pride. Sunday was already starting off extremely well. Her friend, her birthday outing, her – aunt.

A little later, they drove up to No. 17. A fine rain was still falling. Arabella looked at the closed gates and sighed. "Fort Caltrop . . . Would you mind jumping out and breaching these defences for me? Then we can unload everything at once." Elinore decided to leave the gates open for Arabella's convenience, in contravention of Rule 5(ii). Trespassing animals and juveniles would all be indoors keeping themselves dry at this hour, she reasoned.

Mrs Caltrop wrenched the front door open before Elinore knocked.

"It is *late!*" she hissed. "Our routine is being disturbed. What is that car doing in the drive? *What* are you bringing into the house now?"

Arabella was right behind Elinore, laden with bags. "Roberta!" she cried, in a most genial tone. "So kind of you to offer help. We *do* need it with another matter. Just let me get this upstairs first – all this lovely loot."

At the word loot, Mrs Caltrop's mouth fell open. Arabella manoeuvred past her, smiling.

They quickly deposited everything on Elinore's bed. Arabella had stripped the packaging down to essentials for transport. "Hide the puddings in a drawer," she whispered. "This room is completely unaccustomed to lovely smells, and it will betray you. Roberta's nose will twitch at once." Mrs Caltrop appeared in the doorway seconds later, her chest heaving and the red spots on her cheeks flaming like chrysanthemums.

"Your mother is out," she spat at Elinore. "She did not tell us when she would return. This is *not* an hotel!" Elinore was at a loss to know why Melba's comings and goings should cause this indignation, since she did have a key.

"Quite all right, Roberta" said Arabella smoothly. "We don't need Melba, we need you. Now, look: Elinore needs to be properly dressed for school or any occasion, and above all church, wouldn't you agree? She has very respectable new clothes from Jenners. The ones I bring tomorrow must be hung up, or they will not look respectable. Where can we do that?"

Mrs Caltrop stared with the kind of disbelief that would have been appropriate on the utterance of vile swearing.

"A *wardrobe*, Roberta," Arabella repeated. She put her hand on Elinore's shoulder, which was clad in the Laura Ashley dress. "Where is Elinore going to hang this charming item when she takes it off tonight?"

"Her mother has a large wardrobe," said Mrs Caltrop.

"Unfortunately that won't do," said Arabella. "It's stuffed, isn't it, Elinore?" Elinore nodded. "Another spare room wardrobe, perhaps? Are you expecting houseguests in the near future? Or how about the room next door to this one – shall we look right now?"

"This is an outrage! Coming into this house as if you own it and bringing in all this – this frippery. And more to come, you say. All this finery for a *child*!"

"Yes, it is a nice pile, isn't it?" said Arabella. "It's never too early to start a child off the right way when it comes to clothing and self-respect, I always say. And yes, I shall bring more tomorrow – the dresses and blouses – once we've settled where they'll hang. Next door would be most convenient for Elinore and everyone else, wouldn't you agree? I have nothing else on this evening, so I'm happy to wait while you fetch the key and let us have a peek."

Mrs Caltrop turned on her heel and went downstairs. "She's going to get the key to the chamber of ghastly secrets!" whispered Arabella with glee.

"How do you know?" whispered Elinore.

"Gut feeling. Never wrong." That was puzzling to Elinore, whose insides were in a tumult over the hostility expressed towards her. What if Mrs Caltrop came back with a carving knife?

Mrs Caltrop came back with a key. When she opened up the room, they saw bare floorboards; a few tea chests ranged against one wall; several cardboard boxes; a table like the one in Elinore's room (but with one leg completely missing); and a wardrobe like the one in Melba's room.

"Isn't that splendid!" said Arabella. "We knew you'd come up trumps, Roberta."

Mrs Caltrop opened the wardrobe and pulled out a quantity of interesting garments, all gaudy and undeniably feminine. Without a word, she carried the lot out of the room and down the corridor, trailing a mothball reek.

"Fascinating," murmured Arabella. "There's a secret in that lot – what did I tell you? We'll theorise later. This wardrobe desperately needs Mrs Mopp. I'll borrow cleaning things from the hotel tomorrow. Now, let's get everything off the bed so that you can actually get into it."

When they closed the door on the boxroom, Arabella paused, her hand still on the knob. Then she took the key out of the lock and dropped it into her shoulder bag.

"If Roberta makes a noise about the missing key, tell her you haven't a clue what happened to it. Say Arabella must have it, which is true. She's spiteful and quite capable of locking your so-called frivolous finery away to save your soul, especially if I'm not around to object."

When Elinore finally got into bed, she could not settle. Despite the drabness and wetness of the day, the evening sky still held the long light of a northern June evening. Her mind was crowded with images from the most remarkable day of her life so far. A song she had heard on Radio One, called Jumpin' Jack Flash, looped through her mental imagery in endless accompaniment. Her thoughts flashed and jumped this way and that, and three times she jumped out of bed to look at some special thing that was now indisputably hers. She looked at the books she had found in the charity shop; reading would settle her, she knew. But Mrs Caltrop clearly considered no occupant of this room to be worthy or perhaps capable of reading for pleasure (prayers were to be memorised after all, were they not?), and she had not equipped it with a bedside lamp. Elinore disliked reading under the lone bulb in the ceiling and having to get out of bed to turn it off.

Then she saw the bag of soaps. She went back to bed and spread the decorative little packages on the bedspread. The jasmine one extended an embrace, a soothing heaviness, like a big feather pillow into which she could sink and be borne aloft and away. She unwrapped it, smoothing out the paper printed in copperplate script and laying it aside carefully, for it too was a treasure, to be saved at least until she could understand French, and possibly forever. No matter how humble, every scrap from this day held magic. The smooth oval fitted her hand and jasmine, warmed and unhindered by the wrapper, enveloped her. She turned on her transistor radio and found the BBC voices that were good at putting her to sleep. They brought to her a vibrant world of places, events and barely-understood entertainments that she intended to explore in the far-off days of being grown-up. She hoped that world of her future would be full of BBC people with those calm, steady voices. They exuded qualities that were magnetic to her: good humour and courtesy, and something indefinable that she perceived as warmth, which had much to do with their absolute reliability in being there to speak to her whenever she turned on her radio, as if Elinore Crum's listening presence were known to them and appreciated. They were, collectively, an extra blanket. Jumpin' Jack Flash in her head was soon displaced by the acerbic voices of three drama critics disagreeing with each other while managing to be polite about it.

A contented tummy helped her sleep unusually well. When sunlight nudged her eyelids, she sat up in fright. Had she overslept and thrown Arabella's careful planning into disarray? Her radio, its batteries exhausted by the transmission of an entire night's worth of national culture, was emitting faint sounds that grew no louder when she turned up the volume for some indication of the time. Heart racing, she opened her bedroom door and listened. The house was silent: five o'clock had not struck and Mr Caltrop had not yet risen to begin his devotions with the BBC's Prayer for the Day.

Elinore felt it necessary to reassure herself that Saturday had not been a fairy tale. She opened the drawers of the dresser one by one and looked lovingly at their contents, patting and smoothing them. No djinn or goblin or dwarf had sneaked in during the night to carry off her clothes or her two portions of pudding. No evil queen had raised a wand against her while consulting a mirror far away in a land that was not in any atlas. That left only the Caltrops, and Agent Solo would deal with them. Happiness surged as she realised that she could now choose clothes that were exactly right for the day's activities. She took out denim jeans, a pale blue

T-shirt that reminded her of Arabella's scented bathroom at the Balmerinoch, blue socks and the yellow sweater. A pair of lace-up suede boots put her decisively in the explorer category and quite up to any ruined castle or jungly garden.

She dressed and sat cross-legged on her bed to eat apple crumble whose oatmeal topping was crunchy with chopped almonds, walnuts and cashews, and dotted with plumped-up sultanas. Someone had thought to put paper napkins in each bag, and a silver spoon engraved with a B surmounted by a thistle. Then she unwrapped the lemon verbena soap and took it to her bathroom sink, where she washed the silver spoon and the plastic container. At the Balmerinoch Hotel, bath and hand soaps rested and dried on little china dishes; Elinore felt that she was doing her beautiful lemony cake of soap an injustice by putting it down unprotected on the stained old enamel of her sink. She placed it tenderly inside the pudding container instead. Returning to her cross-legged pose on the bed, she started a new list.

Things to Find in the Charity Shop or Somewhere.

1. soap dish
2. bag with shoulder strap

The second item was essential. She needed it to hold her secret lists, a pen, pocket money and pieces of paper with important information that people such as Usha might give her.

By now, the usual morning sounds were filtering through the house. It was time to face another breakfast under the eye of Mrs Caltrop. Elinore decided to eat the boiled egg and a piece of toast, but no margarine, since two trustworthy grown-ups had condemned it as axle grease. Mrs Caltrop would be pleased to see a scraping of grease spared for another meal.

Melba did not appear at breakfast. Both Caltrops remarked on this at the beginning and end of the meal and exchanged looks and nods loaded with black significance in between. Finally, Mrs

Caltrop got up and announced that she would knock on Melba's door in case she was unwell after such a late night.

"Very wise, Roberta." said Mr Caltrop. He turned to Elinore. "It was so late that we never heard her come in! Keeping such hours is a dangerous habit in all respects. It's never far from keeping bad company. Remember, Elinore, good folk are right to see it as a worse danger for women. It's the hallmark of a fallen woman!"

So, thought Elinore, what's wrong with falling and hurting your knee? Mummy's leg might be sore.

"Yes, indeed," Mr Caltrop droned on, "and you were a fair bit late yourself last night." He wagged a finger at Elinore and produced something that might have been a coy smile in a woman but which on his face was a leer.

"Yes, and I'll be late again tonight. Mummy told me not to come back for a long time. I think she's going to be busy today. I'm going out with Arabella. We're going to a visit a man called Tom who wants to marry her."

Mr Caltrop's mouth was open and he looked deeply upset. Bits of egg were on his lower lip. Elinore thought he looked like a baby on the point of crying because he wanted more food. It was really very bad of him not to keep all his food firmly inside his mouth, and not to have swallowed it before opening that mouth in her presence. Miss Agnes Pound said that people were not fit to appear in public *at all* if they had not mastered basic table manners.

She got up, pushed her chair firmly into the table and carried her eggcup and plate to the tray on the sideboard. She, Elinore Crum, habituée of fine hotels, knew her manners.

Mrs Caltrop was still standing with her ear to Melba's closed door when Elinore went upstairs. "If you are *quite* well, then, may I remind you that this is *not* an hotel?" she was saying. Elinore heard something like a long yelp from the other side of the door. Mrs Caltrop straightened up sharply. Her lips were tightly compressed. She went downstairs without a word to Elinore, who saw no need to bother Melba since she was obviously alive and speaking.

The doorbell rang while Elinore was rearranging her books to accommodate the five new ones. A commotion of three voices started up in the hall and when Elinore went downstairs she found Mr Caltrop agitating on the doorstep. Once again, the gates to No. 17 had been opened to allow Arabella's car up to the front door; once again, the gates had been left open, but now it was morning and Mr Caltrop was not snoozing in an armchair. Arabella was carrying a large bag, a basket and a plastic bucket; she was looking at the Caltrops as though they were intent on trespassing into *her* house. Elinore ran out past them and dragged the gates closed.

"Thank you, Elinore, and good morning," said Arabella. "Shall we proceed, now that the perimeter has been secured against incursions?" She swept upstairs as if the Caltrops no longer existed, straight to the boxroom.

"Spit-spot!" she cried, grinning at Elinore and handing her the bucket. "I'm taking my Mary Poppins role seriously. Fill this halfway with warm water, please, from your bath tap. Spit-spot!"

They wiped the wardrobe clean of dust inside and out, and dried it with fresh rags. From the large bag, Arabella took wire coat hangers, scissors and a long roll of white paper. She cut paper to line the drawers at the base of the wardrobe, pronounced the job done, and then changed her mind.

"That window . . . the room must be aired if clothes are coming into it." She sloshed a wet rag over every part, removing dead flies, dust, spiders and their webs. "Wear rubber gloves at all possible times, Elinore. One can do anything with gloves on." She wrung the dirty water from the rag, repeated the wiping, dried the window with a fresh rag and opened it. Air and birdsong rushed into the room, lifting Elinore's heart even further. She did not care a whit about angry, hovering Caltrops as she and Arabella went down to carry up the remainder of her new clothes. Magic was being performed and she was at the centre of it.

Just as they were leaving No. 17, a blonde head appeared over the landing balustrade.

"Elinore! Remember your promise. No more you-know-what if you disobey me."

The head withdrew as Melba drifted on into the bathroom.

"She means I have to stay out until bedtime today or else I don't get any more pocket money ever," Elinore explained to Arabella, who was looking at her with raised eyebrows.

Arabella went to the foot of the stairs and called up loudly enough for anyone in the house to hear.

"Oh, Melba dear! Please feel free to enjoy your *entire* day without thinking once about Elinore. I'll do I all I can to keep her from pining and wanting to rush back to this bosom of homely comfort and joy. Goodbye!"

9

It might have been a limousine en route to the grandest ball of the season, the two young ladies in the back were so excitedly expectant; the Misses Crum and Patel, that is. But it was only a little hired Hillman driven by Arabella Cheyne. On the passenger seat sat a giant picnic hamper. Arabella was whetting their eager curiosity by refusing to do more than sketch their destination: village, ruined castle, house that defied description and wild, wild garden. And a man called Tom, brother to Clova Balmerinoch.

Clova had been just as uninformative when they collected the picnic hamper from the hotel.

"You're going to visit a salmagundi. If you don't know what that means, sorry, I'm under orders not to provide clues. You can have these trugs instead." She handed them two long, shallow baskets that held some folded linen towels. "Arabella will show you what to do. You are hereby appointed official herb gatherers of the Balmerinoch Hotel."

They took the coast road, and arrived at the village of Squair via spine-tingling views of Tantallon Castle and the Bass Rock. Squair was centred on a green, overlooked by another sandstone ruin. It was a very junior relation of Tantallon. No air of undying menace surrounded it, only a few tourists with cameras. Usha began sighing over the houses clustered around the green. "Oh, *sooo* pretty. It's like one of my jigsaws." Arabella turned onto a side road, driving slowly to let them peer at the houses and gardens. "*That* one – that's where I want to live forever," said Usha, pointing to a cottage covered in wisteria, clematis and honeysuckle. Elinore was attracted to a long, high sandstone wall further up the road, interrupted by pillars with something on top. Walls meant separate worlds with stories and secrets all of their own. She craned to see what kind of house the walls protected, and gasped when the car turned sharply between the pillars. She heard the crunch of gravel and saw a house that captured her heart instantly.

"Are we – here?" she asked, just to make sure.

"Yes, here we are and here it is," replied Arabella. "The Dower House of Squair."

It was far from being a chocolate-box house or one that would fit cosily into Usha's jigsaw collection entitled Britain's Best-loved Village Scenes. Two unequal wings joined in an L that was open to a gravel court in front, and rose four storeys at their highest point under crow-stepped gables. The front door, which stood wide open, was set into an angled wall joining the two wings of the L. Above it was a square stone plaque deeply carved with letters, numerals and something else, reminding Elinore of the heraldic plaque on the wall of the ruined chapel at Criven. The windows were irregular in size, shape and placement. Unlike the other houses she had seen in Squair, the exterior of the Dower House was harled, in a deep ochre blotched with lichen and streaked with rust from drainpipes and gutters. The gables were rife with moss; little clumps of rosebay willowherb waved gently from up there too, as if communicating with their siblings growing around the base of the house and all the weedy relatives sprouting in the gravel. Elinore fancied that the open front door allowed those who belonged here, past and present, to move in and out and enjoy a fine new day as they pleased. She turned her face to the sun. Far above, a westbound jet made a straight white trail but no sound. For the first time since leaving Criven, she was in an old quietness threaded with the lull of woodpigeons, the layered song of other birds and the rustling of many trees in full leaf. Usha was silent, awed to find herself suddenly in a scene whose elements she had only previously encountered in books, jigsaws and scenic calendars.

A clang of metal on stone broke the spell of their arrival, followed by loud swearing and then a tall, stoop-shouldered figure who loped around a corner of the house carrying a profuse bunch of flowers in one hand, long sprigs of greenery tucked under his arm and some tools in the other hand. Thick, curly grey hair sprang around his rather plump, pinkish face, which beamed at the sight of them. Spectacles were the only thing he showed in common with Clova, and they were different too: round ones with tortoiseshell rims. Elinore decided at once that he was an elderly, elongated cherub from one of her old paintings – well, perhaps not *elderly*, for his voice was youthful and as full of life as his messy hair.

"My *dear* ladies!" he shouted. "If only you'd arrived *late*! I'm sure I'd have got the fountain working – all in your honour! – in just one more hour. Defeated again. But see, I've brought you the makings of a floribundant spectacular – that's my latest new adjective, by the way, floribund*ant* from floribund*a*. Who will practise some feminine arts on this stuff so that it can honour our luncheon table?" He waved the flowers in front of them and Usha grabbed them. "Excellent, take this too," said Tom and handed her the greenery.

"Feminine arts my you-know-what!" snorted Arabella. "Men do flowers too, dear Tom, and some of them make an excellent business out of it."

"But that's in London, dear girl, for high society shindigs. I am just a humble bachelor, a callus-handed rude mechanical, deprived of all feminine graces that might smooth the rough edges of my hard, dim existence in a rural backwater, as you know so very –"

"Enough!" said Arabella sternly. "Here you are dishing out chores to so-called honoured guests whose names you haven't even asked. This is Elinore, my something cousin, and this is her friend Usha."

"Usssshhhaaaa . . . *what* an exquisite name! Like the wind in long dry grass. I'm so glad you could join Elinore, and I will give you a fine vase for your bouquet as soon as Arabella stops haranguing me."

Tom turned to Elinore. "Elinore, one is not supposed to say this on first greeting, but I shall: I've heard *so* much about you. Thank goodness you could come and enliven the dull solitude of my Sunday, and with a friend to boot. So much nicer than hard-hearted Arabella all by herself."

Arabella blew a loud raspberry at him and he hooted with delight. Elinore was enchanted. She glanced at Usha, who was in shy retreat. Her face was all but obscured by flowers and foliage, perhaps in alarm at two grown-ups who still had one foot each in the playground.

The sight of the giant picnic hamper elicited another hoot from Tom, and he and Arabella carried it between them as they all walked towards the house. Tom was still carrying the tools in one hand. He stopped and said to Elinore, "My dear, would you mind going around that corner and picking up the long spanner I dropped there? I might forget all about it, and I hate losing things."

"No, really?" said Arabella. "Who would ever have guessed?"

"Enough, you scold, you harpy!" said Tom, and to Elinore, "Turn right when you come into the hall, keep going down that long passage and you'll find us in the back of the house."

Elinore ran around the corner and stopped. In their brand-new desert boots, her feet itched to keep going, to run right across the overgrown lawn dotted with molehills and hurl herself into the wood that spread beyond it. She saw huge old trees, sunlight flickering through infinite shades of green, and some mossy, man-made shapes. This was no mere garden: it was the polar opposite to the Caltropian domain of strictly controlled growth and access. This was a place for running away and forgetting that Dunallan Crescent existed. She remembered her manners, picked up the spanner and ran back to the open front door of the Dower House.

The hall was pitch black to her sight and cold to her skin. Elinore stood still for a moment, letting her eyes adjust and gaining a first sense of the house, and then jumped when somewhere behind her a clock struck the hour of noon in resounding bongs. It was not a large hall, more of an anteroom to a more spacious one to her left. Dark wood panelled the walls from floor to ceiling and from them periwigged figures stared at her from the two squares and a rectangle of three murky portraits. A marble-topped table held a telephone, a khaki hat, two tweed caps, a litter of opened envelopes and a little stack of others stamped and ready to post. On one side of the table stood an upholstered chair with a high back whose seat sagged like a saucer; on the other, a tall Chinese pot holding walking and shooting sticks. A spiral stone staircase began only a short distance from Elinore's feet and wound three flights above her head; what light there was came mostly from the single square windows on each landing and a set of narrow half-glazed doors on the far side of the hall, through which she could see the garden. To her right was a long wainscotted passage; it was lit by a single tall window in a very deep embrasure, piled with yellowing newspapers, which looked onto the front court. Tom's voice came faintly from that direction, and Elinore set off towards the sound.

The passage made a right-angled turn and led her to a kitchen silted up in strata of disorder. It was the mess of desuetude that occurs in a room of work when, decade after decade and bit by bit, its appurtenances are pushed aside to make space for the new, and then never touched again except by spiders and flies; a room in which an undomesticated man has made himself comfortable; a man whose inertia at the mere mention of "kitchen" or "housework" is counterweighted by several consuming passions, the paraphernalia of which he tends to bring into and drop in this already full space. It was a dim room too, with only one square, low window. In an adjacent scullery, Elinore saw a door open to the sunshine, and she went through this, past an enormous galvanized metal sink, and out to a drying green. Tom had dragged a table and four chairs out there, where a frayed washing line hung between two rusted ornamental posts. Usha was putting the flowers and greenery in a big copper jug, and Arabella and Tom were laying out the contents of the hamper. "Marvellous, *marvellous*," he was saying, lifting a container to his nose and then lifting up the lid. Arabella slapped his hand.

"Do you like my flowers?" Usha asked Elinore.

"Yes. You're really good at that arranging," replied Elinore, adding in a lower voice, "Are you all right? Do they bother you?"

"*No!*" Elinore was surprised by Usha's vehemence. "I mean nothing's bothering me. I love this garden and I wish my mother and father could come here too."

They began to enjoy Clova's abundant picnic dishes. This was a far cry from the hardboiled eggs-floppy lettuce-tomato quarters-Heinz salad cream-and watercress sandwich version of a picnic, of which Elinore had a single dim memory. As a cold chicken pie was being cut up, a dog ambled onto the scene, stopped, sniffed the air and then trotted right up to the table and sat down by Tom.

"Ha! Meet my neighbour Boris. Lovely chap. He stays here when his owners are away, and comes to check up on me when they're not." Tom ruffled the creamy, wavy fur on the back of the dog's neck, and Boris laid his head on Tom's knee, rolling his eyes so that the whites showed. "You old ham! Look at that: never has a slice of pie received such a gaze of soulful longing."

Elinore felt her face reddening. She too had been staring at the luscious chicken pie with deep emotion. Perhaps the words in her head had shouted themselves without her hearing them: if only I could take all this food back to No. 17 and hide it in my bedroom!

"Boris has the look of a spaniel, but I'm not sure . . ." said Arabella.

"Yes, he's a Clumber spaniel. As English as they come, despite his name. He's a Boris because his owners love opera."

"I fail to see the connection," said Arabella.

"Ha! Got you, Miss Know-It-All-Cheyne. Boris *Godunov*. No? Still not connecting? They think this Boris looks like Mussorgsky, and I must say, dog and man do seem to exhibit the same follicular abundance."

Arabella blew her loudest raspberry yet at him and said, "Show-off! I bet you didn't connect either until your neighbours enlightened you."

Tom stuck out his tongue at her and wiggled his fingers above his ears. "Philistine!" he cried. Usha laughed out loud, making Elinore happy, although she was sure that Usha had as little idea as she of what these adults were being rude to each other about. But hearing that word again – "Philistine!" – in the voice of a man so markedly different from Hector Crum, had sparked in her another longing: I wish I could never go back to those Caltrops, not today, not ever, and just stay here, and maybe Mummy could meet Tom and marry him instead of looking for any more new Hectors.

The girls drank Clova's homemade lemonade. Tom and Arabella shared a bottle of cider.

"Now, I'm going to be uncouth and put my feet up on this table and relax," announced Tom. "Cider in hand, plenty of good food inside and the gorgeous Arabella Cheyne on whom I shall feast my eyes. If you young ladies wish to run off and explore, carry on. It's all yours, all safe – garden, fields, village, castle. Come back when you want different entertainment and we'll do a house tour."

Usha whispered something in Elinore's ear.

"Can you show us where the bathroom is first, please?" asked Elinore.

Tom sprang up. "This way. Who wants to use the downstairs one, and who wants to climb the stairs? Only two loos in this whole house, but they are both, um, *special*."

"I'll climb the stairs," said Elinore. "I think Usha is a bit tired. She might have to lie down."

"I am *not*! We're going to explore *everything* next!"

"And I have to show you around the whole house after that, so no, you can't be sleepy just from eating a fine lunch. That's for dogs like Boris and pathetic old chaps like me," said Tom.

"Joking, joking!" cried Elinore. "But I'm still going upstairs."

Following Tom's directions, Elinore found a long, low-ceilinged bathroom whose every wall was covered in a *trompe l'oeil* garden. On the ceiling, a formal design of wreaths and garlands radiated from the central light fixture out to the cornice. A plain, uncovered window allowed daylight to shift and play on the scene, touching it with life in an eerie way, as if by the wand of another kind of visitor. The colours were soft and aged, but the detail and sense of visual richness were captivating. Elinore's surprise at finding this magic in a bathroom of all places made her exclaim aloud, "Gosh – like a *palace*."

Her Majesty the Queen must surely have a bathroom like this in one of her several homes; it was fit for royalty and could not possibly exist only in an obscure Scottish house that had weeds growing on its outsides. Then she remembered reading that people used to do up their houses extravagantly if they were fortunate (or unfortunate – the costs could be ruinous) enough to house a travelling monarch even for a night. Perhaps the Dower House had once been on the map of a royal progress.

The bathroom fixtures were certainly regal: each ponderous piece of porcelain showed the manufacturer's full name, motto and fancy crest. What was not porcelain or chrome was solid mahogany. Elinore was struck by a notion: what might happen if she bathed in here by candlelight? Not for any reason that might encourage Melba, the bathing queen, to do the same, but rather as an experiment to see if she, Elinore Crum, could travel backwards in time. She might pull out the plug in the enormous bath and find herself whirling with the draining water down, down through generations until she reached, say, the 18th century. She decided to write down the idea later; it could be a story as well as an experiment.

This brief trip up and down stairs took her past a plethora of curiosities on the walls and on side tables, on the floors and even perched on the steps of the spiral staircase. Her questions for Tom were piling up too; she would never remember them all. If only she had that bag she wanted – a woven Greek one, perhaps, with a long, braided shoulder strap, like those casually slung across the bosoms of older girls. Then she could carry a notebook like a reporter. Not like a spy: spies had to memorise words and then eat the paper.

Usha was hopping around on the flagstones of the entrance hall, waiting for her. In the unlit little space, her teeth in her dark, grinning face seemed to be the brightest spot. Elinore liked to see her so openly excited and not covering her mouth as if apologetic for merriment.

"You'll never *guess* what was in that place!" Usha said, grabbing Elinore's arm and pointing towards the larger hall.

"You'll never guess what was upstairs!" said Elinore. "But that's for later. Let's go *out!*"

When Elinore started to run, she could not stop. The joy of being free in a grassy realm that was not only unbounded as far as she could see, but also new and tantalising, was overwhelming. She was outstripping Usha, but she could not slow down even for a few seconds. Her new boots were winged! She had to let it all out and for a long, long moment leave it all behind – cars, tarmac, Caltrops, paved garden paths, silly gates and prissy flowerbeds, the lot. She ran along the side of the house to where she had picked up the spanner and then struck off across the lumpy lawn towards the green wilderness that had beckoned earlier. A wide path went through it, with narrower ones disappearing into the tangles on either side. The stone shapes turned out to be statuary and urns on plinths, but she shot past all of them, pushing low boughs out of her way every few feet. The overgrowth had long ago blurred all formality of design, and that made her progress through the dim, dappled greenness even more wondrous. Abruptly, the main path stopped at a wrought iron gate in a high wall. The sun was full on the field that lay beyond and sloped upwards like the lawn of her old home in Criven.

Elinore turned the handle of the gate and pulled. It was heavy and very stiff, and she had to tug it past weeds and grass, but it opened enough for her body. She squeezed through and, still winged and full of fire, ran up the slope, making her legs extend as far as they could. A flock of blackface sheep started in surprise and huddled together, all staring at her. She halted below the crest and looked back. Usha was just visible on the path behind the gate. Elinore waved and shouted. "Up here!" Alarmed, the sheep bobbled off as one, and Elinore laughed at the sight, a bit of Criven; all sheep were her friends and familiars because of those she had taken for granted as part of her landscape until so recently. She threw herself down, spread-eagled under the sun.

Eventually, Usha arrived and dropped into the same pose, still panting a little. "Sorry," said Elinore. "I really needed to run."

"You're like a horse! I think I'm a dog. I have to look at everything. And I *smell* it too. It's amazing down there. Can we look all over the garden? He said there was a fountain. Is he your uncle? You're *sooo* lucky. It's like living in the Botanic Gardens, except this is a jungle, so it's more fun. If I'm really, really nice to you, will you let me come back here with you some day?" Usha giggled and covered her mouth as if she had been rather too daring.

"What's the Botanic Gardens?"

"It's in Edinburgh, and it's my favourite place – favourite *there*, I mean. I think this is my favourite place now. Susanna's mother takes us there sometimes. She's an artist. She likes looking at plants and things too, for her paintings. Do you want to come with us next time we go?"

"Yes. But I don't want to hear about Edinburgh just now. Come on! Let's go right to the top of this hill and then run all the way back down. Or we could roll down! Or somersault!"

Elinore sprang up and took off over the last few yards of the sloping field, whose boundary was marked by a fence. On the other side, the grass continued, but dropping more gently downwards into a wide, shallow prospect that was both beautiful and disturbing. At its centre was a huge, imposing, rectilinear house whose every opening was boarded up. Around it were the remains of terraces and a walled garden where one side had almost completely tumbled down. A long greenhouse was all smashed up. Two straight lines of trees revealed avenues leading to the house from west and south, and Elinore could make out the dark reddish metal of old-fashioned park fencing that also defined the avenues, and enclosed some other stretches of grass. The fences too were missing in some parts and bent out of their strict lines in others. Trees appeared to be clustered together in groves which, from this higher viewpoint, could easily be seen as varying in leaf, branch and height, bringing eye-catching colour and texture to the broad scene. Dots and splashes of bright, deep hues all around the outer terraces indicated rhododendrons. The size and vigour of trees and shrubs contrasted sharply with the lifeless look of the house and the decay and destruction surrounding it, and made the scene all the more unsettling. Far in the distance to her right, Elinore saw a hazy blueness that she interpreted as the sea and, between that and the house, a narrow strip with irregularly moving dots that glittered in the sunlight: a main road.

"Oh! What happened? The house looks blind! It's scary." Usha's hand was at her mouth again, her eyes wide.

"Well, *something* happened, and all the people went away and left it to die. Or perhaps they all got the plague and died. It's like a house in a fairy story. Poor house."

"But the garden's still alive – look at all those bushes with the lovely flowers. I think they're rhododendrons. They look as big as the ones in the Botanic Gardens."

"Let's go back to Tom's house. This place makes me feel sad."

"Me too. Maybe it's haunted."

When they reached the wrought iron gate, they decided to split up and see who could find the fountain first.

"You have to make an owl sound when you find it, or if you find anything really interesting," instructed Elinore. "To-wit-to-wit-to-*woooooo*! Really loud."

In this fashion, they darted, climbed, poked and peered over every acre of Dower House grounds. The bounds of its walled garden were intact, if crumbling, and the sun-warmed, scented profusion within made Usha ecstatic. "Oh, oh . . ." she kept repeating, fingering flower and weed alike with reverence. It was clearly a choice destination for bees too, and the air was abuzz. The fountain turned out to be at one end of this walled garden, on a square of grass that was as unkempt as all Tom's grass but still fine for lying down on. Elinore sprawled again while Usha meandered and murmured. A living fountain would have been perfection, she thought but, even without the plash of water, it was still heavenly. She lay still, basking in the red glow of sunlight through closed eyelids, until Usha said she was thirsty.

"Me too," said Elinore. "Then we can explore the castle and the village – if you feel like it."

"Yes, I *told* you, I want to see everything. I want to *stay* here."

Not as much as I want to, thought Elinore. You've got nice, smiley parents and I've got Caltrops.

Tom's feet were back on the table, and Arabella, who had put on a big floppy sunhat, was lounging in her chair with her feet on another one. But they were talking loudly and animatedly despite their pose, and waving their hands about, until they caught sight of the girls.

"What ho, explorers!" shouted Tom. "What discoveries have you made? *We* heard something never before known in my garden: a whole parliament of owls. In broad daylight!"

"We're not finished yet, and we want to ask you things, but we just came for a drink before we go to the castle," said Elinore.

"I wish we could have lemonade like this in the shop," said Usha.

"I wish it came out of a tap," said Elinore.

"Tell Clova," said Arabella. Elinore wondered if Clova was secretly an almost-magic person like Arabella.

Out and off they ran again, through the gates in the Dower House and along the road to the centre of Squair. The village was so compact and the castle so ruinous that their exploration was over in under an hour. Their most intriguing discovery was a beehive-shaped structure with a door in the bottom but no windows, only a round hole at the top that was open to the sky. All around the inner wall were tiny boxlike spaces. The only other people looking at it just then were four tourists, gesturing to each other over features of the structure and being excited about it, but not in English.

"I give up, I can't guess what it's for," said Usha.

"Me too. Let's go back and ask Tom – and about the blind house too."

"Do you think it's just blind for a while or really dead? Sometimes they put boards on the windows in Edinburgh when they make houses new again."

Elinore considered this question as they strolled along, kicking pebbles, their jumpers tied around their middles; it was now too hot for running. It was the kind of question that she herself liked to ask, but until today her world had contained no one else who could or would discuss such esoterica. Tom would inform them. He must like history, she reasoned, otherwise he wouldn't be so fond of his crumbly old house.

"I don't know. Maybe it's in between – asleep," she finally said. "It might be waiting for someone to open it up again."

"I think it could be a Sleeping Beauty house," said Usha. "And all the trees and bushes are covering it up too, just like in the story. It's waiting for a kiss from the Prince – the House Prince!"

"You can't have a *House* Prince –" Elinore began, and then stopped, remembering how she had named Arabella as a Mary Poppins for houses. "Well, all right, we can call it the Sleeping Beauty House." Then she put a question to Usha. "Do you think Tom and Arabella are mad?"

"Well – they *might* be," said Usha slowly. "I've never, ever met people like them before. They're not normal, are they? But they're very nice and I really like them. So, I think they could only be a little tiny bit mad, and not the bad kind of mad people. You have to lock up the bad kind."

"I think so too," said Elinore. "I think they're only a wee bit mad."

They found Arabella stretched out on a plaid rug on the drying green, and Tom reading to her from a newspaper; his feet were back on the table. Elinore and Usha plopped onto the grass too. Tom looked at them over his glasses and said, "Arabella, you'll have to read that review of *Beyond the Valley of the Dolls* all by yourself. Our present company is too elevated for it. How about the one on *The Railway Children* instead?"

Elinore was surprised that these two superior beings would interest themselves in entertainment that must be aimed at girls who liked Barbie dolls. It was the daftest title she had ever heard.

"Actually, we want to know about some things we saw," she said. Tom took his feet off the table and sat up, squaring his elbows as if ready for hard work. "Fire away," he said.

"What's the little round building with the hole in the top, next to the castle?"

"A doocot – a dovecot, if you're speaking English. A palace for cushie-doos. Imagine about one thousand pigeons nesting inside – did you see those little boxes all around the walls? – laying their eggs and flying in and out through the hole. That doocot is at least four hundred years old. No fridges then. But with a doocot, people could eat the pigeons and have fresh meat and eggs all through winter."

"Why couldn't they eat cows and sheep too?"

"Same reason: no fridges. They could wring the necks of a few pigeons and make a pie or a stew whenever they wanted, and that would keep until it was eaten up, but how would they preserve whole sides of beef and half a sheep and so on for months and months? And here's another reason for keeping pigeons: farmers often had to kill their livestock *before* winter set in, because they couldn't afford to feed them until spring. They didn't have all the ways and means of modern farmers. So, that little building, our beautiful doocot, was actually keeping a lot of people alive and as well-nourished as they could be in those times. The castle would have been full of people. If you keep your eyes open, you'll see lots of doocots in the Lothians, but that one's special because of its shape."

"And it isn't falling down like the castle," said Usha.

"True, it's in remarkably good condition, but it is looked after properly now. People understand that it's unique and have come to value it. Not like some sad places."

"We saw a sad place," said Elinore. "Usha thinks it's blind. Or it could be dead or asleep. But we couldn't tell, because we didn't go up close to it. It's a bit scary when houses don't have any eyes."

"Ah – the big place over the hill? That's Squair House. I'd say it's in a coma, having suffered injury and near death by demolition. The family that built it – the same lairds that built this house, descended from the castle dwellers – had to sell up after the war. Until the new owner sorts out a mountain of legal and financial complexities concerning how he got the money to buy it and his plans for its future, it will stay like that. A long story with a sad ending, as far as I can see. You'll be stuck here until tomorrow if I start telling it."

That idea stirred a commotion of approval from Elinore and Usha.

"Not on your nelly!" came a voice from the rug on the grass.

"Go back to snoring like a sow, Arabella, and stop discouraging the enthusiastic young. Do you really want to hear the life of Squair House? All right, I'll tell it as your intellects deserve, but in potted form. I know you two are terribly bright. Remember, we're talking about *people* here, not merely things out of the blue. People bring houses into being and people kill them."

He continued slowly and carefully, ticking off each point on his fingers. "Death, greed, more death. Gambling, extravagance, ambition, greed, love, snobbery, social climbing, sorrow. The Great War, deaths plural, incurable war wounds, good fortune, bad judgement, bad luck. The Great Depression, the state of British agriculture, optimism, hope, disillusion. World War II, deaths plural again, incurable war wounds of new and different kinds. Government policies on land use. Economics, alcoholics, mental instability acquired and inherited, inheritance taxes, capital gains tax, loss of Empire. And a good deal more than all that, seasoned throughout with the politics and hypocrisies of families and nations which, *au fond*, my dears, is all the same unsavoury *mélange, embrouillamini* – a *salmigondis*, I think my flour-fingered sister would call it."

That word again. Elinore had got the melancholy gist of Tom's little speech, although overall it was like a river flowing too fast to let her look at the interesting boats it was bearing along. Too many interesting things were flitting past her. She *must* get a bag to hold a notebook and pen. She could practise being a reporter then. She opened her mouth to ask for the meaning of salmagundi, but Tom was still in full flow.

"If you got in a helicopter and flew the length and breadth of Britain," he added, "you would see countless other places like Squair House. At least its roof is still on. Some owners took the roofs off so that they wouldn't have to keep paying taxes on the property. What do you think would happen to you if you were old and had to stand out in all weathers with no hat, mackintosh or umbrella, year after year?"

Elinore and Usha looked at each other and shivered. The blind house had lodged itself in their sympathies, even without the name of a single person who had lived there.

"Well done," said Arabella, still prone on the rug. "You've spared us one of your sagas. We'll be able to leave before the moon rises. But really, can two tender young minds swallow that doom-laden *potage*, let alone find it tasty? Far too heavily salted with your scholarly tendencies, I'd say. And Frenchified to boot!"

Tom groaned and got up. "I refuse to talk down to the young. Come on, you two, let's explore history without rude comments from persons lying about on the ground – the *lower orders*. Ha! That's good. To the main entrance! The house tour begins *now*."

"Did you grow up here?" asked Elinore.

"No, I grew up in another old house, in a glen to the north. But I fell in love with this place on my first visit. Some houses are magical. I'm sure *you* know that."

It was an effort to keep up with Tom: not so much because of his long stride and the way he took the winding stairs two or even three at a time, but rather his animated outpouring of detail on everything they laid eyes on, and the way he bounded from one era to another in his anecdotal linking of this house with the battered, comatose one over the hill. But, like Arabella, he missed nothing. He noticed when the house spoke to each girl in her own language. When moments of silent attraction lengthened – in front of a portrait of children wearing sashed frocks and pantaloons and holding a small dog, for example, or a musical box that opened up like a jewelled tree, or a three-hundred-year-old book, illustrated with woodcuts, open on a carved mahogany reading stand, or a magic lantern that showed silhouettes in clothes and hats that no one in cold, wet Scotland could ever have worn – at those moments he stood and smiled until they had looked and touched to their satisfaction, or joined in their excitement and awe as if he were exactly their age.

The *trompe l'oeil* bathroom did have a story firmly anchored in history.

"During the Great War," recounted Tom, "Squair House became a hospital for wounded soldiers. The two young daughters of the family – they were called Skirving – came here with their governess to live until the war ended and all the soldiers went home. Their London cousins, two girls and a little boy, were sent up to join them when Zeppelin attacks made people very nervous. London had never been bombed from the air before. This governess was very artistic, and she had a brother who was a proper artist with a reputation for country scenes. When he came to visit his sister one summer, the two of them laid out the design for the bathroom."

Usha sighed. "I like that story. I'd like to paint a garden in my bathroom, but it's too small. Maybe I could do a flowerbed!"

"But it was only an old bathroom. Why did they bother to make it so pretty?" asked Elinore. "This garden should be in the bedroom of a princess."

"Or in the study of a horticulturally-minded prince," said Tom, "Yes, a bedroom would have been a more practical choice. I do my best to keep the room aired, but dampness is very destructive. I think they painted in here because they felt they could do what they liked. The walls elsewhere would have been just as crammed with stuff then as now, and some have fixed hangings and wallpaper as you see – all original from before the time when those young ladies were cooped up here. The decoration was the idea of a governess, remember – she was still a servant, albeit a higher-up one. Servants weren't supposed to have artistic ideas above their station and start disturbing their employers' household arrangements."

He showed them the signatures: Olivia Greenlees, in a clear hand, and a jumbled one that Tom said was Quentin Greenlees. Below that, another line: *Qua perfecta anno MCMXVII.* Usha went up close. "Latin!" she exclaimed, and then mouthed the words. "I think it means – made in 1917?"

"Top marks!" said Tom. "This work was finished in the year 1917, that's the exact translation. I wish they'd noted when they started it."

Elinore was full of admiration. "Do you really know Latin?"

"No, we don't do it till next year," admitted Usha. "But I started learning the numbers for fun, and then my tutor said I should look at the words too, just to get used to them. She gave me a book."

Elinore's admiration increased despite being immediately assailed by envy.

Although the story of the painted garden contained no link with the passage of monarchs, the little downstairs lavatory that had so delighted Usha revealed a unique acquaintance with royalty. It was reached through a narrow, windowless room with rows of hooks on both long walls. On these hung scores of hats and outdoor garments, and below were boots of all kinds. Elinore disliked it because it reminded her of the cloakroom at Aikenhead Primary School, although it held no odour of forgotten snacks, sickly-sweet sticky things, and coats and anoraks that were never washed from one year to the next. This room smelled of tweed, oilskin and neatsfoot-oiled leather. Usha rushed through it and threw open the door at the end. "Abracadabra –shazzam!" she shouted in glee. Although a window let in plenty of daylight, Elinore took some moments to comprehend what was lining every inch of wall above the wainscotting.

Squares and rectangles of mostly white or cream card had been pasted onto the wall with no regard for chronology or pattern, but every individual card adhered to a certain formal template. Some were clearly menus of the grandest kind. Others had engraved lettering and dates, and a line or two handwritten in pen; nearly all bore crests or coats of arms, and many of those were royal. They were invitations that had gone out in another world, requesting the favour of the recipient's presence at balls, garden parties, dinners, weddings, christenings, house parties, soirées, levees, birthday celebrations, investitures, occasions of national or local importance and even coronations. It was a long way from Buckingham Palace, but never had Elinore been closer to her revered monarchs than in this peculiar cupboard of a room with the usual water tank high up on the wall, wooden-seated lavatory and sink stained by copper and rust.

"Dear ladies, I am *most* pleased to command you to appear in my throne room today," said Tom in a quavery falsetto. "God bless this loo and all who – who . . ." He and Usha were lost to laughter, and Elinore joined in, a little nonplussed. It felt almost like bad manners to make that kind of joke in the presence of such august communiqués. What on earth would Miss Agnes Pound have done?

"Goodness gracious," said Tom, wiping his eyes with a handkerchief. "I really ought to put up a picture of Queen Victoria on the door. In a fine gold frame! That would certainly count as taking the piss out of – oh, dear, oh dear, that's an *extraordinarily* fine pun, isn't it, but you must *not* tell Arabella or I'll be accused of ruining your delicate sensibilities. But it's all your fault! I've had so much unaccustomed entertainment and excitement in one day that it's quite gone to my head, poor solitary wretch that I am. You may tell Arabella *that* bit, of course. Come along, then! We must bash on through this house before you turn me into a giggling, gibbering idiot."

By the time she and Usha had fingered and marvelled their way through every room, Elinore had fallen deeply in love with the Dower House. The rooms echoed the overgrown walled garden in their profusion of dusty enchantments and neglected glories: carved, lacquered and gilded furnishings, silk and embroidery, paintings and tapestries, porcelain and crystal, and books – so many books that Elinore's yearning for them made her feet drag. On the ground floor was a proper library. It was a little square room whose floor-to-ceiling shelves, all filled, were in soft, pale unvarnished pine and edged with dark red leather that had been cut in scalloped strips and gilded. The mantelpiece, in the same wood, had fluted sides and garlands in relief across the top. In its centre, two tiny female figures in flowing classical draperies danced around an urn spilling flowers. Elinore ran her fingers over them. They were carved wooden figures, but they were her friends. If she spent time in this room, in that rose-pink wing chair by the window, they might just sing to her.

In a bedroom close to the top of the house, where a narrow bed had long since been given over to friable stacks of the *Illustrated London News* and *The Tatler* from decades past, Usha was captivated by brass-edged glass cases of different sizes. They held pinecones, bits of coral, shells, chunks of quartz and other semi-precious stones, leaf skeletons, bleached skulls of tiny creatures, feathers and blown shells of birds' eggs. Some items had labels: strips of paper bearing ink faded to the colour of weak tea, the careful penmanship of a long-ago boy.

"Did you find all these?" Usha asked Tom. "Are you an explorer? Some of them don't come from here. Oh – this is *special!* And so are these!" She had spotted a brass microscope. Lying next to it on the leather-topped desk were three magnifying glasses of different sizes, whose handles were respectively of antler, thick bamboo ringed in gold and ebony with a silver finial on the end.

"No, I'm far from an explorer, at least, not the intrepid kind that you mean," replied Tom. "These all belonged to a boy who came to live here and never left until he died, so he was no globetrotter either. But he collected whatever intrigued him, from when he was younger than you, and so you could say he travelled widely in that sense. The world came to his doorstep. I'm afraid I'm a bit of the same – and it can be a very untidy pleasure as you see!" He grinned and spread his arms, indicating the whole house. "But other people in that boy's family did travel and live in other countries, including your own, Usha. Some of the things they brought back are still living. Come and see."

From a window on the other side of this topmost corridor, Elinore and Usha could look right over the grounds, including trees that made up the mysterious, leafy depths through which they had run at the start of their exploration. Down there, where paths snaked this way and that, and the mossy stone figures and shapes might have come alive just as a girl ran by – who knows? – it had been all one enveloping greenness. But from high up in the house, an inexact but still visible intent could be detected in the display of tree crowns.

"The Dower House and Squair House have one important feature in common," said Tom. "The Skirving family brought trees and shrubs from all over the world – experiments, really – and they made specimen groves. They wanted to make patterns to delight and intrigue the eye from all viewpoints and, of course, to educate. Our forebears were awfully keen on educational entertainment. The gardens of Squair could be a little tour around the globe, you see."

"Well, it *is* like the Botanic Gardens, then!" said Usha in a satisfied tone.

"At Inverleith, you mean?" asked Tom. Usha nodded. "Dear me, your young brains are too fast for mine. I was going to say, the Skirvings actually gave plants to the Botanic Gardens. I don't know which ones, but they'll have records if you want to dig – oh, hell's bells, there I go, punning again. Perhaps you're a *bad* influence, both of you. I need something to drink! Do you think it's teatime yet?"

10

They returned Usha to MacAlpine Place first. With the same air of ceremony as in the morning, Mr and Mrs Patel appeared on the pavement while the girls were still getting out of the car and Arabella was checking that Usha had left nothing behind inside it. On their departure from the Dower House, Tom had handed each of them a rectangular package. Usha's was heavy; Elinore's was lighter, but she could feel a depth of softness under the brown paper. They clutched their gifts all the way home, having agreed to prolong the excitement of mystery by waiting until bedtime to unwrap them.

Mrs Patel was wearing the same emerald green and silver sari of that morning. Elinore thought it most glamorous and wanted to touch it: she had seen pictures of Indian ladies in such saris curtseying to the Queen, but she had never seen one worn before. The evening was still bright, and its light was deepening and enriching the earthly things under it. Standing there, her many gold bracelets gleaming on both arms, Mrs Patel was queenly and exotic in Elinore's eyes. A maharani perhaps, fallen from a flying carpet on the way to her Indian palace, or at least to the Ritz (the only hotel in London of which Elinore had ever heard).

The little beige Hillman seemed to have acted like a magic carpet upon Usha, who had expanded. Her eagerness to recount the marvels of her day bubbled over in a louder than usual voice; she gestured with the hand that was not clutching Tom's weighty gift to her chest, and laughed. Her mother's eyes sparkled too and she smiled at this sight, although one hand stayed hovering near her mouth. Mr Patel shook hands with Arabella and then with Elinore, and was gravely polite in his gratitude on behalf of his daughter, who, he would admit, was always asking her boring, busy father when they could go for a drive out of the city.

"Oh, no," said Arabella, "we are the grateful ones. It wouldn't have been half as much fun for any of us without Usha. Elinore really needed better company in that place than a pair of boring old things. We were able to sit and fan ourselves in the sun! I hope you'll let us carry her off again if the chance arises."

If the chance arises . . . Elinore snatched at these words. So, the day had *not* been a mirage and it *might* be repeated. Arabella could be trusted not to spout pretty, unmeant niceties. Elinore was also different now from her morning self: she had contracted. She watched Usha silently for the most part, and waved goodbye to the Patels, who remained on the pavement until the Hillman turned a corner, but then she slumped in her seat, glowering as they passed through streets whose familiarity signified return to No. 17. Arabella noticed. She said nothing that could be interpreted as jollying along by an ignorant grown-up.

"Will you send me a postcard or a letter, Elinore, and tell me what's in that parcel? I'm dying to know what Tom's plucked for you from his cabinet of curiosities – I mean the whole house, he has far too many actual cabinets to count. You've got my address at Welkinlaw. Now, may I suggest something? When you enter that dreary bastion of piety and post-imperial affectation, shortly to appear on our left" – Elinore dropped her head and hunched her shoulders even more – "those Caltrops will no doubt question you about your day. If not tonight, then tomorrow. They're very suspicious of anything I do, because they I know I set out to enjoy every day of my life *to the hilt*, and apparently that attitude doesn't sit well with God. Well, never mind. Whatever they ask, just say – no, *shout* it, you'll feel much better, believe me – just shout that you've had a perfectly *divine* day. That's it. Repeat as needed, no need for details. *Divine* will do fine! They can't object to that word, can they? Oh, and grin at them. Grin as wide as you can, like the Cheshire cat."

Elinore heaved a sigh of her own. "All right," she said. "I'll just tell Mummy what I was doing, if she wants to know." But she wondered if Melba would expect details of her day; very likely not, once it was clear that Elinore had been running around either inside the kind of house that Melba detested or outside in a tangled garden and fields full of sheep. Melba, who was looking so hard for another Hector . . . "I wish Tom was my father," Elinore muttered.

Arabella knew exactly what line Elinore's thoughts were taking.

"Why don't you tell him yourself? I'll write down his address, and you can send him your thanks. He'll be chuffed – he never gets anything like that from *me*."

Mr Caltrop opened the door when they rang. Mrs Caltrop was upstairs, he said. The idea of people being out and about at this hour of a summer evening seemed to perturb him, and he kept shaking his head and sighing, and referring to Melba's absence. That a child should have returned at night to its lodging in their home without a mother immediately on hand to keep it in line was clearly an upset. Anxiously, he stood in the hall and watched them go upstairs, as if delinquency might burst from Elinore's skinny frame and wreak its evil not only on the knick-knacks along the landing but also the entire Presbyterian order of things. He made not one word of enquiry about Elinore's day. Elinore held in reserve her assurance that it had been divine, although she was now quite eager to shout it – shout *something* – at the Caltrops.

Still holding her parcel, she asked Arabella if she would like to see its contents right now. Arabella shook her head.

"We all need something to look forward to, whether it's two hours or two weeks or two years hence. You might fall asleep with a thud after all that running around and fresh air. Or you might not. If you're restless, that's the time to sit up and open it."

Elinore remembered something important.

"I still have some secret pudding from yesterday," she whispered. "In that drawer. I could open my present and have a midnight feast at the same time."

"Just what I'd do," agreed Arabella. "Here is Tom's address." She took a notepad from her leather bag, tore off a perforated page and wrote on it. Then she looked in the bag again and took out a book of first-class stamps. "Take these. I never leave home without them. And one more thing – this phone number." She tore off a separate page and wrote down large numbers and words: Mr & Mrs Anskett, Welkinlaw. "I know it's on my letter to you, but keep this safe too, just in case. Who knows, you might want to get in touch with me quickly. If I'm not there, Henry and Marigold will know where I am and what to do. You *must* pick up the phone if you need to speak to me urgently, Elinore – is that clear? For *any* reason." Her severe tone evoked Queen Elizabeth I again and surprised Elinore. "Now, let's take a look at your fine dressing room before I go."

She marched into the boxroom next door. The window was still open, and the air felt fresh and cool. "Good," said Arabella. "If Roberta had been nosing around in here, she would have shut that window, I'd lay money on it. Asserting her territorial rights." She opened the wardrobe. "All present and correct?"

Simply looking at the neat array of her new clothes, and the new shoes lined up below them, made Elinore feel a little better. She could choose something to wear to school the next day, and she could look forward to making the right impression on the elevated Susanna when Usha introduced them next weekend. Arabella was right: a person needed things to look forward to.

Arabella patted her bag. "The key stays with me," she said in a stage whisper. Then she was gone.

Elinore felt sticky and scratchy after all her running about under the sun, and decided to have a bath. Her fine soap brought up scents and images of the Dower House's walled garden. She got into bed. It was a great pleasure not to have seen or heard Mrs Caltrop this evening. Her room was still light; she got out of bed to open the curtains a little, so that she could watch the sky turn over its colours to night. BBC voices would have been comforting at that moment, but her radio's batteries were absolutely dead. Then she got out of bed again to find her list of things to buy, because an even more pressing lack had also presented itself: writing paper and envelopes. Melba would have none, she knew, and asking a Caltrop for anything was out of the question. And she needed a nice pen to replace her single old Biro, which made blotches. She would not write important letters of thanks in pencil: how childish! She tried to remember if she had seen a chemist or a newsagent nearby, somewhere convenient that would sell these essentials. Mr Patel might have something. She would go after school the very next day, and perhaps bump into Usha. While trying to work out how long that expedition might take if she were not pelting along the streets as a truant from school sports, she fell asleep. One hand was still on the parcel, which lay beside her on the bedspread.

She dreamed that she was standing alone in front of the Walter Scott monument. The Princes Street Gardens were verdant and inviting under the bluest of skies, but not a single other person was out enjoying them. She could hear a humming, throbbing sound of no obvious origin. From his seat, Sir Walter Scott beckoned to Elinore, and she climbed the steps to join him. His dog, Maida, got onto his lap and he wrapped his stone draperies firmly around her. The knobbly, crinkly-looking stonework decoration of the monument began to scintillate and the throbbing sound increased. Then the whole monument rose straight up into the air for a long way: at least as high up as three of those towers, end on end, where people lived near Aikenhead Primary School. The monument tilted until it was horizontal, and Sir Walter's seat tilted with it, so that he was looking straight ahead in the direction of his craft's flight. So was Elinore Crum, gripping his cold, hard shoulder.

"Are you from *Thunderbirds*?" she asked. "Are we in a rescue story?"

Sir Walter shook his head. "No, child, we are not in any man's story, not even one of my own imagining. Look down, look ahead! The story spreads itself all around, and you will find your own place in it."

"Is it magic?" asked Elinore.

Sir Walter nodded. "Without question. All stories are magical." He held up the stone book he was carrying. "They unlock doors."

Then he smiled and put his finger to his lips for a moment, before spreading one arm wide and telling Elinore to "Look! Look!"

She understood what the scene below them was, although only two features, Edinburgh Castle and the village of Criven, were familiar to her eyes. They were over Scotland and moving rapidly about the country, crisscrossing it from east coast to west and back again, all the time moving northwards. The sea rolled about the land in big, frothing, blue-green waves that crashed on black rocks, and under the waves fish glimmered in immense silver shoals, each one tens of thousands strong. Snowy mountains rose in the distance; the sky darkened as they flew towards them over an undulating, riverine panorama where some parts were forested and others bare, and the air grew cold. Soon they were flying under a radiant moon and the landscape had turned to black, white and grey. Elinore felt shivery and apprehensive, but Maida jumped out of Sir Walter's cloak and licked her face and hands until she was warm again. She felt something growing inside her like a tree: an enormous, uncontainable curiosity, and excitement too.

"Are we going to land soon?"

Sir Walter smiled again. "Very soon. A little jolting, but no great or prolonged perturbations. Trust those words, child: trust them. Fear not!" He pointed to the moon with the hand that held the book. The moonlight bathed it, turning hand to flesh and stone book to crimson leather with gilt edgings and a title in two lines of gold-blocked letters. Elinore craned to read the words, but she could only make out the very first letter, a singular A. She stretched her whole body further, but some part of Sir Walter's stony figure jabbed her and she moved back sharply. Suddenly she was no longer flying but in her bed in Dunallan Crescent, and the corner of Tom's parcel was digging into the underskin of her arm.

Elinore half sat up, confused. The dream was still vivid: to slip back into its enchantment, she need only lie down and close her eyes. It was tempting, especially since Sir Walter's voice was warm and kindly, and Maida was such a friendly dog. But the room was light and she knew it was Monday morning. And an unwrapped parcel lay in front of her.

She started to unwrap it, before getting out of bed and opening the door to find out how much time she might have before the humdrum stuff of Caltrops and school began to swallow up her morning. The house was quiet save for a faint murmuring downstairs. She crept as far as the landing, and then the clock in the morning room struck the quarter hour and simultaneously a BBC voice could be heard. Mr Caltrop was up, then, setting his devotional clock as usual to the daily broadcast of spiritual words for the nation, but no one else would be; she had time.

Under the brown paper and string was a finely-woven shawl in a design that Elinore knew was called paisley. The shawl was wrapped around two framed pictures, each one about the same size as her largest book of old masterpiece paintings. Between them was a letter from Tom. The unheaded paper was soft, thin and a little crumpled on one edge, as if he had taken it from a much-used jotting pad.

Sunday 26ᵗʰ June

Dear Elinore,

My spies inform me that your birthday is only four days off. They also say that your surroundings are lamentably bleak! <u>Devoid</u> of colour & interest! These two pictures will change that – if you <u>like</u> them enough to keep them around you, that is. You should only have pictures around you that <u>you like</u>. My chief spy tells me that narrow-minded, censorious busybodies rule your lodgings (I won't call it '<u>your house</u>', because it is not & I know that you don't want it to be), & so I chose these pictures with <u>great care AND cunning!!!</u> Viz:

1) <u>In mahogany frame: one seated, upset lady, one kneeling angel.</u>

ANNUNCIATION by

LEONARDO DA VINCI & ANDREA DEL VERROCHIO

Painted in Italy circa 1472-1475.

2) <u>In gold frame:</u>

<u>17 gentlemen, 13½ horses, 2 hounds, all going downhill.</u>

THE JOURNEY OF THE MAGI by

SASSETTA (STEFANO DI GIOVANNI)

Painted in Italy circa 1433-1435.

I've heard that the aforementioned busybodies think you should stare at religious pictures in your little room. These pictures ARE RELIGIOUS! The upset lady is the Madonna/Virgin Mary, & she is annoyed because the Archangel Gabriel has appeared out of the blue to announce (hence ANNUNCIATION) that she is going to have a child. They are waving their hands at each other in the way that people do when one is trying to say something that the other does not want to hear (e.g. our dear Arabella).

> Three of the gentlemen on horseback are the Three
> Wise Men, otherwise known as Magi, following the Star
> of Bethlehem. In other words, all religious to the highest
> degree, ha-ha-HA!
> I'd enjoy telling you more about each painting, but I
> must stop here, because you are packing up to leave as I
> write! Moreover, you, Elinore the Explorer, are meant to
> discover their charms for yourself. Make them your own.
> THANK YOU for visiting and for bringing Usha with you.
> My old house has been enlivened! I earnestly hope that you
> will both return, and until then I wish you MANY HAPPY
> RETURNS of the birthday kind!!!!
>
> Yours most sincerely,
> Tom
> P.S. The shawl is a gift for you too. One of the ladies of this
> house used to wear it – very old indeed. (The shawl.) (And
> the lady.) I know you will treasure it & take greatest care of
> it! Ask Arabella for instructions on care.

Elinore sat and stared at these three offerings. A loitering angel might as well have dropped them there, so surprising were the riches of colour and imagery they brought to her room. She fingered the shawl, wanting to spread it right out and study its intricacies, but dropped it when a ragged fingernail snagged the fine wool. She picked up the Magi picture instead and peered closely at the odd, homely little figures going down a steep slope. Which ones were the wise men, why did they not ride camels, and where was the star? A peculiar scene, but she did love puzzles.

Two smallish pictures and a shawl: in size and number, a little gift compared with Arabella's largesse, but entirely its equal in uniqueness and goodheartedness. Tom's letter was a special gift too. She would read it over and over again, look up all the words she didn't know, and find out how to say the Italian names. No doubt clever Usha would be able to help.

A clock was chiming the inexorable passage of Monday morning. Elinore put Tom's letter and the shawl in the chest of drawers, where a large piece of chocolate sponge with raspberry sauce was still waiting for her. She decided it would keep a little longer. Eating it very slowly in tiny spoonfuls would be another kind of gift. She went into the boxroom to choose clothes for school.

She took out a pleated navy skirt; a white blouse with an embroidered daisy on the pocket; long navy socks; and tan lace-up shoes with brass eyelets. She added a navy cardigan and also the anorak with white piping. The sky was bright at present, but it was an Edinburgh sky after all. Then she changed her mind and exchanged the white blouse for the floral one she had worn when departing from Jenners on Saturday. The white blouse was pristine and she could not bear the thought of sullying it just yet. The Queen was unlikely to request her presence this week, but still, it would do no harm to be prepared for a surprise occasion of any degree of formality.

Once again, Melba was not present at breakfast, although various sounds and signs revealed that she had arisen. Mrs Caltrop's eyes ran around twice as busily, not only tracking every bit of food taken by Elinore but also examining every seam and button of her new clothes. Mr Caltrop sighed a lot and hunched morosely over his porridge. At the very end, just as Elinore was getting up from the table, he raised his head and asked, "Well then, was your Sabbath jaunt a fine one?"

"Oh, *yes*," replied Elinore. "It was *di-vine!*" She had not shouted it, but still, it sounded just right to her ears. Then she grinned as Arabella had instructed, and left the room. Mrs Caltrop's fleshy mouth was open, but not at all in the manner of the Cheshire cat.

On the way to school, Elinore was happy to be herself. Her new clothes were not a uniform, but still, she felt the equal of anyone from the Ina Blackadder School for Girls. Summer holidays began this week, and then she would be free to meet Usha, Susanna and possibly other uniform-wearing girls. She could explore Edinburgh. She had pocket money!

The pocket money increased by a small but useful amount when Miss Blaikie handed back one day's dinner money to her. "Only four dinners this week, Elinore. We'll be finished on Friday, remember?" Elinore had forgotten to tell Melba. It dawned on her that Melba would never remember what sum she had doled out – after all, Elinore had to ask for it every Sunday and Melba had to be reminded of the right amount every time. She put the coins back in her satchel and decided that they would come out again only as pocket money. It was common sense, not badness.

It began to rain as she turned into Dunallan Crescent, and, despite the wonderful new anorak, she decided to put off her visit to Mr Patel's shop until the next afternoon, out of concern for her new shoes.

Mrs Caltrop's usual boiled and scanty supper was even more unpalatable after the experience of Clova Balmerinoch's hearty dishes and sweet delicacies eaten under the sun at Squair. Melba appeared more or less on time. Although she was as uninterested in the events of Sunday as Elinore had expected, she was strangely focused on Elinore, who was not used to any prolonged attention from her mother, and certainly not with that air of deep, effortful thought. Whenever she looked up, there was Melba observing her, frowning. The frown was a sign of import, for Melba's one consistent exercise of self-discipline was that she never did anything that might lead to wrinkles.

Elinore forgot everyone else as soon as she had closed the door of her room. She had much to do. First, the two new pictures must go up. She wanted to see them when in bed and also be able to handle and study them easily, and so she propped them up side by side on top of the chest of drawers. Next, the shawl. She took a pair of new socks, put them over her hands and spread out the shawl. On that narrow bed, it was as big as a counterpane and its dense whorls of colour – peacock blues and greens, reds and purples on a terracotta ground – blasted defiance at the surrounding drabness. Elinore sat in the chair and looked from shawl to pictures and back again with satisfaction. She felt that she might actually have treated the room to a drop of Mary Poppins-for-Houses medicine.

Now began the real work. First, she reread Tom's letter and made a list in red pencil of words that needed looking up, including the artists' names, with a space for writing down the meaning. This was the kind of homework she truly enjoyed. She had an Oxford dictionary that had long ago lost its board covers and spine, but all its pages were intact, thanks to the three elastic bands around it. It was able to help her with every word whose meaning was hazy or unknown, and she found salmagundi in there too. Then she started writing out a rough copy of her reply to Tom, so that no crossed-out bits or other unsightly errors would mark the version that eventually ended up on proper writing paper. She was interrupted by noises. They were indistinct, but, thanks to her having lived under the same roof as Hector and Melba Crum, still identifiable as a commotion. Her mother's raised voice; a slammed door; other raised voices – and her own name, a loud, fierce summons. That was new and alarming. She jumped up.

Mrs Caltrop was at the head of the stairs, steaming.

"Elinore! *What* is the meaning of this? A strange man is on the telephone, and he is asking for *you*."

"It's Tom," said Elinore without a second's wondering. "Arabella's friend. We went to see him yesterday."

"Oh no! This is no *Tom*! He can barely speak English. He says his name is *Patel*." Mrs Caltrop's mouth twisted as if the two syllables had been little jugs of vinegar. "A *Hindu*! *What* have you been up to? Answer me!"

Elinore was dumbfounded. This was a different sort of commotion from all preceding ones in her experience, and it was dangerous because it was aimed solely at her and was completely without reason. Her first impressions of Mrs Caltrop as kin to wild flesh-eating creatures flooded her anew and set her whole being on alert.

"It might be my friend Usha's father. He's called Mr Patel."

Heavy, angry breathing was Mrs Caltrop's only response for a few seconds, before she commanded, "Come down at once and we will deal with this man. And then you can explain." She pointed to the stairs, making Elinore go first.

Elinore looked at her mother's closed bedroom door and then went downstairs. She was sure she could feel the heat of Mrs Caltrop's ravening breath on her neck. In the morning room, Mr Caltrop was on his feet, clutching a newspaper and eyeing the telephone receiver, which was lying off its hook, as if it were a snake come all the way from India to seek his wife.

"Pick that up," said Mrs Caltrop, still in officer mode.

"Hello, this is Elinore Crum speaking," said Elinore.

"Ah, Elinore! V.K. Patel here, Usha's father. I apologise most deeply for being a disturbance in your family evening."

"It's all right, you aren't disturbing anybody. Does Usha want me?"

"I am telephoning to find out the proper name and address of the gentleman who gave Usha the beautiful, valuable gift. We must thank him at once for all his kindness, but we don't know where to send the letter. Usha is very anxious that he will judge her to be rude and ungrateful if we delay, and we don't know when we are going to see you again. It is very upsetting for her. So, I said I would find where you are in the telephone directory. Usha remembered the name of the people you told her and the name of the street. And it was quite simple because there is only one of that name in the directory, you see."

"Yes, I've got Tom's address. I'll go and get it for you right now."

"Splendid!" cried Mr Patel. "Permit me to wait on this line, Elinore. I do not wish you to have to use the telephone at the expense of your kind hosts, all because of me. Please take your time!"

Elinore rushed up and down again, and read out Tom's name and address slowly and clearly, spelling out Balmerinoch, Dower and Squair. Throughout, the Caltrops remained standing as if on guard. Mr Patel asked if she wanted a word with Usha, but she declined. "But I'm coming to see her anyway – very soon," she said, not wanting to be more specific in front of the Caltrops.

"Wonderful news!" said Mr Patel, who thanked her and all over again begged leave for his disturbance before ringing off. Elinore put the receiver on the hook and turned to find herself still in the full glare of the Caltrops.

"Well?" said Mrs Caltrop.

"Well what?" said Elinore, without thinking.

"*Oh!* How *dare* you be insolent to me?"

"I'm not – I don't know what you –"

"Oh yes, you do. Consorting with Indians and their families behind our backs is bad enough, but encouraging them to telephone here at all hours – I am aghast at your waywardness, Elinore Crum. You are heading for trouble and your mother may be blind to it, but I am most certainly *not*." She moved her feet further apart, folded her arms and fixed her hard blue eyes on Elinore.

"Indeed, indeed," boomed Mr Caltrop, holding his newspaper high in front of his chest and waving it slightly as if to ward off the latent evil in Elinore Crum.

"Usha is my *friend*. She's very clever, she has a tutor and she goes to a proper school for girls, with a *uniform*. Her father is a very nice man."

"What school does this girl supposedly attend?"

"The Ina Blackadder School for Girls."

Mrs Caltrop's mouth dropped open. She closed it quickly, pressing her thick lips into a nasty, smirking line.

"And what does this *nice* Mr Patel do, to be able to buy his daughter a place at *that* school?"

"He's got a shop."

"What kind of shop?"

"Newspapers and – and things."

"Aha! You were lying about that girl, Elinore, and I knew it. The Ina Blackadder School admits only the highest class of girl and the daughters of immigrant newsagents simply do not go there. And could not pay to go there. So, you have been running around with the family of an Indian shopkeeper and you have concocted a story about it, and that is the same as lying. I will discuss this with your mother. You may go now." She waved her hand in the direction of the door.

Elinore stood still. "But I don't know what I'm doing wrong. You were living in India. Why can't I have a friend from there?" Again, Mrs Caltrop's mouth dropped open, and Elinore, seeing that she had surprised her, pressed on more loudly. "And I am *not* lying about her school! I don't tell lies, so there!" Suddenly she was very angry about all this unfairness, and the sheer nonsense of it all. Something was in the middle of it, something glaringly obvious that nevertheless kept slipping out of her mental grasp. "*You* are the bad people!" she cried. Her fists clenched, her shoulders hunched, her head dropped and she shot past the hateful pair and upstairs.

Melba was opening her door. "What *is* going on?" she demanded. "I need to talk to you about phone calls –"

"Mind your own business!" shouted Elinore, and ran on into her own room, where she slammed a door purposely for the first time in her life. She expected pursuit and punishment, at the very least an intense lecture from Melba on the need to be nice to their deeply generous hosts. She sat on the bed, her back to the door, waiting for someone to barge in and continue the unfairness. No one did. After ten minutes, she returned to the draft of her letter to Tom. She wished very much for the dog Maida – in fur and flesh, not stone – to appear, or the amiable Boris; any creature that would lean warmly against her leg as she wrote. Or perhaps an Alsatian that would guard her against all comers. Yes, that felt right – but wait! Even better would be her own devoted wolf, ready to tear out the jugular of a Caltrop who dared to scold her. Then she would get on its back and they would bound across Edinburgh and away to – where, exactly? Squair was as good a place as any; she had better get on with that letter of thanks to the one person who could be relied on to shelter her there, even with a wolf in tow.

Elinore was left alone for the rest of that evening. She remained far too angry at the Caltrops to ponder whether her behaviour towards them counted as real badness. When she went to bed, she missed the BBC voices acutely, and determined to buy batteries the next day, regardless of weather. She could wear the yellow rain boots and carry her shoes in her satchel if necessary. And she would buy writing paper and envelopes. If Mr Patel did not sell them, he could tell her where to go, and the letter to Tom would soon be done. She understood Usha's anxiety on that score, or rather she thought she did; but she was not fully acknowledging her own fear that, if she delayed the letter by too long (how long that might be, she could not guess), the beautiful day at Squair might dissolve in reality and turn out to be as fantastical as her flight in the Scott Monument.

Tuesday morning did bring rain, and a chill to the air. Elinore put on her yellow sweater and set out the rain boots. She had a plan to improve the morning. First, chocolate cake in her bedroom instead of a boiled egg in the morning room. Then, an early, speedy departure from No. 17 before anyone began to expect her at the breakfast table, and a running start on her trudge to school. No one would follow her in that rain. She liked this plan, with its sense of escape. Escape! That was a good word. She muttered it seven times over, since seven was a magic number according to certain reliable sources, and repeated that hopefully until she lost count, and anyway it was time to eat the cake.

Finally, she put into her satchel the tiny purse containing all her pocket money, Tom's letter and her list of words from it; if there was time, Usha would surely help with the Italian names. Elinore had a horror of mispronunciation. She cleaned her teeth, put on her anorak, started to put on the boots and changed her mind:

they squeaked slightly. Carrying them, she made her way to the head of the stairs. Melba's door was open, but the bathroom door was closed. The wireless sent muffled tones out from the morning room, and Mrs Caltrop was clattering crockery in the kitchen. Elinore escaped, not even pausing in the vestibule to put on her boots. It was worth slightly damp socks just to be successful. She ran, not minding the rain at all, enjoying the flash of bright, shiny yellow every time her feet moved, and the freedom to make "Escape, escape, escape!" a panted, reasonably loud incantation. Three was also a magic number and easier than seven to count while running.

At school, she kept her yellow boots on all day, because the thought of their possible theft bothered her far more than the prospect of overheated feet. In the grubby, overcrowded, cloakroom, the only boots were dull black wellingtons. She never left her satchel alone either, containing as it did all that money and the great treasure of Tom's letter. At lunchtime, she sat with a group of girls and younger boys from another class, who were too mousy to be loud and inquisitive about the yellow boots and why her satchel was between her feet or slung across her body instead of left on the floor by her desk like all the others. Being different in even the smallest ways was not helpful at Aikenhead, a lesson that Elinore had already learned. She *was* different, but she had got by. She had earned sufficient reproof from Miss Blaikie for daydreaming to keep her on the right side of those who would have ganged up on a posh wee swot. Girls who might have made trouble for her sensed that she was not in competition with them for anything – especially in her old clothes. Now it was too late in the term for anyone to be offended by the relative expense of another pupil's clothes, or whether the clothes looked like something out of *Princess Tina* or even *Jackie*. The air inside the classrooms was humid and rank; the cooped-up children, raring for their holidays to begin, were fractious and noisy; and Miss Blaikie was short-tempered. Elinore watched the big clock and felt her legs itch with desire to be out of it all.

It was still raining when they finally erupted from the school. Elinore didn't care. The satisfaction of her morning escape was giving a rosy tinge to the whole afternoon, despite the necessity of return to No. 17. When she entered Mr Patel's shop, he was busy with two ladies, but still quick to greet her as if she were another grown-up customer. She looked around and found batteries, realising that she could afford spares too. "Be prepared, carry spares!" Feeling very efficient, she took two more from the shelf, and was looking for paper when she overheard one of the ladies talking about Usha. "She'll go far, mark my words, but you have every reason to be proud of her now. She is *such* a hard worker, I hear – and my spies don't lie!" The speaker laughed and reached over the counter to pat Mr Patel's hand.

"We *are* proud. You planted our little flower in the right soil, so to speak!" All three laughed. Forgetting Miss Agnes Pound's severe condemnation of staring at others and eavesdropping on their private conversations, Elinore stood and stared.

The lady who had spoken was petite and fine-boned. Her pure white hair was swept up high under a silk headscarf that seemed large enough to make her a dress. She wore a strawberry-coloured tweed suit under a shiny white A-line raincoat with buckle fastenings, wide cuffs and collar all in black, and black leather boots with low heels. A black quilted leather bag on a gilt chain strap was hanging from her shoulder, which was only slightly stooped. It was a dashing look that both suited her and was completely at odds with her age. The other lady was heavyset and much taller, dressed respectably but not stylishly at all. She carried a wicker shopping basket, a zippered nylon bag and a handbag. A black and white striped umbrella was propped against the counter.

Mr Patel startled Elinore as she was studying this pair. "Elinore! Please come and be introduced. Lady Groule, I present Miss Elinore Crum, Usha's special friend, who took her out on the visit on Sunday. The visit to the garden that she cannot stop talking about! Elinore, I am so pleased for you to meet Lady Groule. And also Mrs Digby."

The small lady turned her whole body and returned Elinore's stare, raising pencilled eyebrows into outlandishly high arches. "Re-aaa-lly?" she said. Her eyes flicked downwards and rested on Elinore's feet. "Do tell me where you found those *divine* boots. Exactly what *I* need."

"In Jenners," said Elinore.

"Oh, good. We'll go tomorrow, Mavis."

The other lady nodded and murmured something. Lady Groule addressed Elinore again.

"I hear that you're a very good influence, Elinore Crum. Where exactly is this land of delights?"

"At Squair. We went to visit my aunt's friend who lives there."

"*Squair?*" The eyebrows arched dramatically again. "Good heavens. No one's mentioned that name for aeons. I used to dance at Squair House when I was a gel. Then it dropped off the map. The war, you know. And who is the friend of your aunt?"

"Mr Balmerinoch – Tom. He lives at the Dower House."

"Good *heavens*. Does he have a sister with a name like a weed?"

"He has a sister called Clova. C-L-O-V-A."

Lady Groule stared in wonderment. "How *extraordinary*. I knew the parents. The mother was a wild creature from Glen Clova. Who or what else are you going to surprise me with next, Elinore Crum?" She cocked her head and looked intently at Elinore.

"I don't really know anyone else yet. I'm not from Edinburgh."

Mrs Digby suddenly coughed and shot out an arm to check her watch. Lady Groule said, "Yes, quite right, Mavis, we must get along. Well, Elinore, you do know Usha in Edinburgh, and now you know me. Usha will bring you for tea one day and we can start there. Come soon!" And then, with goodbyes to Mr Patel and best wishes to Mrs Patel, they were out of the shop and Mrs Digby was unfurling the black and white striped umbrella to hold it high above Lady

Groule as they hurried down the street. Elinore had never seen anyone that old move so quickly; in the shiny white raincoat, beside Mrs Digby, and from the rear, Lady Groule made one think of a scuttling, fashionable infant.

Mr Patel came out from behind the counter, smiling hugely. "Usha will be here soon. She is meeting Mrs Patel after school to help her with some shopping. But you can be happy that you came early and met Lady Groule. Let me tell you what she did!"

But the doorbell rang and a woman came in, followed by another with a noisy little boy who wanted sweeties. Elinore went back to her own errand, and found Biros (she bought a black and a blue one), a small pad of blue Basildon Bond paper and some white envelopes of another brand. They would have to do. The shop was still busy. She drifted to the magazine shelves, and was weighing the worth of a *Princess Tina* versus even more batteries when Usha's voice breathed "Boo!" in her ear.

"How did you get in here?" demanded Elinore, who was standing next to the door.

"Up the other stairs to our flat, through the outside door."

"Gosh! You could play hide and seek all day if you've got two staircases."

"Yes, but no one ever plays it with me. It's our teatime soon: do you want to stay? Are you coming back on Saturday? I've got to show you what Tom gave me, but I'm not telling you first. It's *amazing*."

"Yes, I *am* coming on Saturday! You said I could meet Susanna. I think I have to go now. But I could stay for tea on Saturday, if your mother doesn't mind. And my holidays begin on Friday, so I could come then. I've got things to show you too. You can help me with some of it – you're so brainy!"

"Our school concert's on Friday. Come on Saturday. And Sunday! And don't be silly about staying for tea, Mummy will never mind. Mrs Berg gives us tea too."

"Who's she?"

"Susanna's mother."

"I met a lady here in your shop – a real Lady with a capital L. I don't know how to spell her last name, but it sounds like that stuff that people in stories have to eat when they're sick or really poor."

Usha looked blank.

"You know – gruel."

"Oh – *that* lady! She's my fairy godmother! Lady G-R-O-U-L-E."

"What did she do?"

"She heard me reading all to myself when I was little, when I was sitting in the shop with Daddy. And I used to do counting games and practise with the money in the till. I counted out change for her one day. So, she started asking all about me and she told Daddy that I had to go to the Ina Blackadder School. Then she got someone from the school to write to him and tell him how I could get a scholarship. That means you don't pay anything. Then Daddy and Mummy took me to the school and I had tests, and then they – the school people – said I could go to the school. And *then* – guess what she did?"

"What?"

Usha dropped her voice and her eyes shone. She took hold of Elinore's arm and whispered, "She took me to the shop that sells uniforms for all the schools in Edinburgh and she bought everything I needed! It was a lot. You have to have a summer uniform and a winter one, and all the sports things – tons of stuff! You even have to have hats and gloves! You *have* to wear them when you go out of the school."

"Gosh!" Elinore was thrown. Was her own fairy godmother-directed shopping spree a secret or a joy to be shared? She wanted her new clothes to signify who she truly was and had always been. "Like girls in school stories?" she asked instead.

"Yes! Do you read the Chalet School stories? I've got some, do you want to read them? *Please* stay for tea right now."

Elinore bit her lower lip and was silent. She knew which tea table would be welcoming and doubtless abundant; she also knew that dark clouds were now massed permanently over her head at

Dunallan Crescent. She had failed to appear at the breakfast table. Perhaps it would be safer to keep her bad actions to only one a day. It would be like leaving space for running between the lightning bolts that would inevitably rip out of the thunderclouds and straight down towards her.

"No, I can't," she said finally. "But I'll see you on Saturday. I have to go now. Ooops, I forgot! I have to pay for these. I'm writing to Tom too." She took her finds to the counter and waited for Mr Patel to finish commiserating with an elderly gentleman over the nation's woes, in which striking workers, collapsing industry, decimal currency and the very idea of joining something called the European Economic Community figured largely and evilly.

Usha giggled. "It's all right, we wouldn't call the police if you forgot and took them away. We know you're not like *some people*. They come in here and think they can steal because they're posh."

Elinore stared at her, disbelieving. "You mean posh like Lady Groule?"

"All kinds of posh. Ladies who put things in their baskets and inside their coats. Dad gets very upset. It's bad for his heart."

Elinore was silent again. That was incomprehensible badness. When she paid for her own purchases, Mr Patel put them in a paper bag and fretted over his neglect to maintain stock of blue Basildon Bond envelopes. "Wait!" cried Usha. She ran through the back of the shop and upstairs. Elinore went back to the comics until Usha reappeared and thrust a few of the right kind of matching envelopes at Elinore. "Daddy, you can give Elinore her money back for those other envelopes. No, let me! How much?" She went straight to the till. "Here you are, madam, and thank you kindly for your custom. We'll see you again soon!"

Elinore was laughing as she left the shop, and the corners of her mouth stayed upturned as far as the first corner. The rain was nothing, and neither was a hungry tummy. Then she became concerned with donning Agent Solo's cloak of super-alertness and checking her invisible armour for re-entry into the Caltrops' force field.

On the path between No. 17's garden gate and its front door, she hesitated, remembering the previous week's unpleasantness over wet floors. She was supposed to use the back door on such days. Then the front door opened and Melba flew out, putting up an umbrella as she went.

"*There* you are, where have you been dawdling? The taxi will be here any moment."

"What for?"

"Really, Elinore – you must take your head out of the clouds! We are going out for tea, and I told you at breakfast."

"No, you didn't, because I didn't have any breakfast. I just went to school."

"Oh. Well, it *is* still your fault for not paying attention, because you ran off last night when I tried to tell you then, after someone rang to invite us."

"I don't know anything about that either. What someone? Is it Arabella?"

Melba grabbed Elinore's arm and pulled her back to the street, where a taxi had drawn up. She did not speak until they were under way and after she had flounced about a bit, arranging her clothes to avoid creases, checking her lipstick in a compact mirror, and scrutinising Elinore for a long moment. To Elinore, her mother's air was strange and jumpy, like that of a nervous pony, and she thought it might be a good thing to be very attentive, at least until Agent Solo had figured out what intrigue was afoot.

"Why are you wearing those violent yellow boots? And *why* must you go about with that dreadful mop on your head? I did speak to you about it already. You must *brush* your hair. Your appearance reflects on me, Elinore. I *cannot* seem to get that across to you!"

"But my hair always goes like that in the rain. I can't help it. And I'm wearing my rain boots *because* it's raining, so there. And a lady, a *real* one with a capital L, told me she wanted ones just like that. And she looked like a picture in one of your fashion magazines. So *there!*" She folded her arms, slumped back in her seat, stuck the yellow boots out in front of her as far as she could and glared furiously at them. Melba was silent except for the rapid tapping of a lacquered fingernail on the edge of the taxi window. Elinore realized that her mother was indeed nervous. How extraordinary!

"Mummy, where are we going? Why are you kidnapping me like this?"

"We are going to have tea with a very, very, nice, kind, generous, lovely –" Melba drew a sharp breath – "friend. Who wants to meet you. Right now."

11

Elinore Crum sits at tea in a grand hotel, wearing fine new clothes and bright yellow boots that are the envy of a Lady. Arrayed before her are exquisite cakes and pastries, immaculate sandwiches and a cheese plate proffering four of Elinore's great favourites alongside the cheddar and such: Carr's water biscuits, Jacob's cream crackers, digestive biscuits and Bath Olivers. On her left, her ever-fashionable mother dispenses tea from a silver service and what she presumes to be *bons mots* from her beautiful painted mouth, while basking in the sidelong looks of other tea-sippers. On Elinore's right sits a manly assemblage of brand names: Frye, Stetson, Levi's, Rolex, Ray-Ban Aviator and enough Aramis to challenge the waves of Ô de Lancôme rolling out at the merest rustle or shift of limb by Melba. Many sidelong glances are being directed at him too, so that all around this charming scene hangs the breath of question, light as the inward drift of coastal moisture on an overcast Scottish evening: how much did all *that* cost?

Elinore Crum is very, very angry.

Since Agent Solo's vaporising weapon for humans was still in development, it was not possible for Elinore to obliterate the man on her right. She had wished to do so from the moment of introduction.

"Hi, honey," the man had said, rising from the table when a waitress ushered them to it. "At last! Gorgeous as ever." He spoke right over Elinore's head as if she were another waitress. He patted Melba on the bottom as he kissed her, then pulled out her chair for her and kissed the top of her head before seating himself. Elinore stood stock still for a second or two, before marching around the table to the only other chair.

Between cooing and billing at each other, the man and Melba managed to give some instructions to the waitress, who wrote everything down with a stony face. Then she looked directly at Elinore and smiled kindly, saying, "And can I bring anything special for you, miss? Orange juice, maybe, or something else?" Her pencil remained poised over her pad. Melba flapped her hand and started to speak, but Elinore was too quick. A tiny tongue of fire seemed to be flickering in her middle, pricking her into action.

"Can I please have a big glass of Ribena?" she asked.

"Of course, pet. Right away." She snapped the band on her notebook and turned on her heel.

"Ri-bena, huh?" said the man. "Never heard of it. Don't like orange juice?" He was finally addressing Elinore, who stared at him and said nothing. Miss Agnes Pound, she knew, would have condemned his deplorable ignorance of the courtesies of introduction. And how *dare* he pat her mother's bottom in full view like that?

"So, Elaine – I'm Dwayne. Real pleased to meet you. Your mom's been telling me all kinds of great stuff about you." He shot his arm across the table, obviously meaning her to shake his hand, but Elinore fixed her eyes on his big, chunky, shiny watch and sat on her hands.

"I'm not Elaine. I'm Elinore," she said.

"Gee!" Dwayne slammed his forehead with a hand. "Sorry, kid. Mind if I call you Elly? So, here we are, all friends at last. Great to meet you, kid. We'll have a toast when that slowpoke waitress gets round to bringing us something to drink. Ri-bena, huh? Is that what all the kids like here? Wee-eell, Miss Elly, I'd say you might get a new favourite just as soon as you taste some fresh Florida orange juice." He half-turned his head to Melba and gave her a slow-motion wink while executing a bizarre grimace with one side of his mouth.

"Oh, *Dwayne*! Oh, you're priceless! *Too* funny – but don't frighten her, darling!" Melba practically screamed in hilarity, which made respectable heads shoot up and turn all around them.

"I am not an Elly. I am Elinore," said Elinore.

"Uhh-hh . . . OK," said Dwayne. He drummed his fingers on the table and behind his aviator glasses his eyes went all over the place before resting on Melba. "Hey, gorgeous!" he said, grinning. "Oooh!" went Melba, wriggling and giggling in her seat. Just then, the waitress returned with a laden trolley and Elinore was able to maintain her silence for quite a while as the tea things were set around. The waitress placed at Elinore's right hand the biggest glass of Ribena she could have hoped for. "Here you are, miss. Will that be enough for you to start with?"

"Yes, thank you very much," said Elinore. "It's just what I wanted." The drink was a deep ruby glow against the white linen tablecloth, and Elinore was thankful for the sight of it alone: something beautiful to focus on for the duration of this incomprehensible occasion. For, beyond the tall glass of Ribena, a distressing object lay on the table. It was a cowboy hat with repoussé silver embellishments around the twin peaks of its crown. Elinore did not want to see it. She had the eeriest sensation that, if she looked at it for two seconds too long, this piece of cowhide (or hide of whatever kind from that wild animal-infested part of the globe) might fly right across the table and slap itself over her face. She would be smothered while Melba and Dwayne made eyes at each other, heedless of her death throes.

"So, Elly – Elly-*nore*: how's life for a country kid in the city? The not-so-big city!" More laughter from both adult quarters. "Looking forward to vacation? Got her signed up for any summer camps, Melba?"

"Camps?" said Melba, momentarily forgetting not to furrow her brow.

"*What?*" said Elinore.

"Elinore's terribly creative, you know. She can keep herself amused with bits of paper for *hours* on end!" declared Melba. "And books. Such an independent little person. We'd – I never have to worry about Elinore being bored."

By now, the tiny flickering flame inside Elinore had grown. It was more like a campfire warming an explorer forced to bivouac in strange, hostile territory. Taking a long, fortifying draught of Ribena, she decided to confront the lurking danger of Dwayne head on.

"What do you do? Are you going to stay in Scotland forever? And why are you wearing a cowboy hat in Edinburgh?" She wanted to ask why he wore gold jewellery around his neck, but held that question in reserve.

Dwayne looked taken aback. "Uhh . . . I'm in oil, and I, uhh, troubleshoot things. You know: go around and sort out the stuff that beats all the other guys. And my hat is, uhh, it's just what I wear. Like my boots. Never thought about it. D'you like it? Here, try it on, why don't you? A Stetson always makes a girl look kinda cute!"

"Oh, Dwayne – let me! Me first!" Melba leaned across the table and snatched the hat from Dwayne's hand, which was above Elinore's head.

Elinore recoiled and froze as the horrid hat passed so close to her face that she could smell it, Aramis and all. Melba plonked it over her shining blonde helmet and squealed as it covered most of her face. She tipped it right back and, eyes shining, drawled, "Howdy, pardner! I just rode into your town. Think I'll fit with the locals?"

Dwayne roared with laughter and clapped his leathery hands long and loudly. Those seated around them were jolted and offended. "Oh, baby!" cried Dwayne. "Can't wait to get you home to Dallas!"

Elinore's heart seemed to have leaped into her throat and was beating rapidly there like a prisoner demanding release. She was utterly mortified. What if Susanna had happened to be present in *that* hotel dining room too?

Their waitress put an end to her immediate torment. She handed Dwayne a slip of paper and said, "Beg pardon, sir, but here's that telephone call you were expecting. The caller is still on the line."

Dwayne cleared his throat, sat up straight and frowned at the name on the paper. "Head honcho – must be calling from home at this hour. Gotta go." He strode off, exuding the self-importance of big business, and Elinore watched his pointy-toed, chased-leather tan boots cross the carpet. She saw that their heels were the same height as those of her mother's lowest-heeled shoes; her mother owned no flat shoes. This horseless interloper from the Wild West was *in* her life now, along with the Caltrops. Her heart was still knocking about in the wrong place, and she felt breathless, but she was not going to confine her suspicions a moment longer.

"Mummy, why do I have to talk to that man? Is he the new Hector? *Are you going to get married?*" She kept her voice low in case this notion got loose on the air around them and made everyone in the room laugh.

Melba looked affronted. "Please do not refer to Dwayne as *that man*," she began, much too loudly for Elinore's comfort, and then stopped. She frowned again, signifying both extreme mental effort and a subject so heavy that it outweighed all concern for the vulnerable smoothness of her brow. Elinore waited. Her tummy grumbled audibly. She was very hungry, but all the talk and all her nerves had sidelined the food in front of her. She took two sandwiches and began to eat, watching Melba's face all the time. Finally, glibness and glorious visions of Melba's future resumed their usual joint operations in Melba's brain.

"Now listen, Elinore – this is an *opportunity*. We mustn't let those slip away in life. Shakespeare said something about that, I think, but never mind, your teachers can tell you exactly what. Teaching you is not *my* job. My job is to look after *us*, and Dwayne knows all about the hard time I have with that. He's a terribly *generous* man – just look at this delicious tea, for a start, and have you said a word of thanks to him yet? – and that's very, very, *very* important if I'm going to have a hope of – if we are going to have a – a – *happy life*."

Elinore folded her arms and stared at Melba. "I was really happy in Criven and I had fun all the time with my friends. I *liked* it. It was my *home*. Why can't we go back there and be the same? And I don't need any Hector. It's better without him. I want a pony instead, like Julie Fairgrieve."

"Good gracious, child! What earthly use is a pony when you can have a gift horse instead? Stop being difficult or people will see that you're spoilt and think I'm a bad mother. You have no idea how important this opportunity is. Don't you want to be happy in a nice house and do nice things like this all the time?"

"But I lived in a nice house in Criven. I miss *everything* in Criven *all* the time! If you want to live in a big house, you could go back there and be nice to Mr Finnie instead of *him*, and live in the manse. And I know a man called Tom who's got a super house, it's even bigger than the manse, and he's the kindest man in the world and he's all alone like Mr Finnie, and he wants a wife too. *He* would say you're beautiful too. Everyone thinks you're beautiful. Why can't you just be beautiful in Criven? *Why* do we have to live here with those ugly old Caltrops? *Why* are you making me be nice to that man? He looks stupid and he does stupid things in front of people. *That's bad manners!* It's very bad and everybody will think it's bad. You mustn't do that if you're a proper grown-up. So *there!*"

Melba's cheeks were pinkly hot, which Dwayne would doubtless have seen as gorgeous while not noticing her narrowed eyes and set mouth. "Reaa-lly . . ." she said. "What an incredibly ungrateful child I've been harbouring. I can hardly believe my ears. Now listen: I am your mother and you have to do what I say. It's as simple as that. If you're going to be a horrid little girl who is rude to someone who wants to treat you like his own child and take care of your poor struggling mama, you will have to suffer the consequences. Do you understand? What if Dwayne buys a pony for you?"

"Where? Is he going to take us back to Criven? I'm not going anywhere else with him."

"Well, if you insist on being a nasty, ungrateful little so-and-so, you shan't be going anywhere at all. I mean it!"

Elinore could not understand this threat. "What do you mean? Mummy, are you going to America with him? Are you going to run away and leave me with the Caltrops? When? Tell me!" Alarm tugged at her tummy and tinged her voice. Melba said nothing. She smiled instead, a cat-in-charge-of-the-cream sort of smile.

Dwayne reappeared, also smiling. "All fixed," he announced. "Sorry, been gone too long from you ladies. Went to the little boy's room too. Damn taps. You Scotch must have asbestos hands or something. Two taps, one for boiling, one for freezing, no mixer. A guy could end up in hospital!" He sat down and piled his plate with a selection of baked goods. "Hey, look at all this good stuff still sitting here. Come on, kiddo, eat up! That's what we're here for." He applied himself to a rock cake for a few seconds, and then spoke with his mouth full and crumbs on his moustache. Elinore wanted Miss Agnes Pound to rise from her grave and scream at him for at least two major transgressions. She felt like screaming herself, but took a big slice of Dundee cake instead.

"What did you say, darling?" enquired Melba sweetly.

"Summer camps. Just wondered what you got set up for Elly-nore."

"Oh. Well. I rather think Scotland doesn't *do* summer camps. Weather, you know. And midges – *plagues* of midges! They can make you feel miserable at any age, believe me." Dwayne looked mystified. Midges could have been plague-bearing vectors for all he knew. Elinore decided to prod him.

"Some of my friends *at home* go to Pony Club camp in the holidays. I'd go with them if I had a pony. Or I'd go pony-trekking. I've always wanted to do that. Do you ride too? Is that why you wear the cowboy things?"

"You mean horseback riding? No, can't say I do." Dwayne looked hard at Elinore as if something about her had just struck him. "So, uh, you like animals?"

"Yes. I like all kinds of animals. I want to *go home* so I can have animals of my own – more than one kind, perhaps."

Dwayne was still staring at her. "You like cats too?"

"They're all right. I love dogs and horses most of all. I want a puppy. I don't think they like cats much, especially when they grow into dogs. But when they chase cats it's fun to watch. Mummy *promised* me I could have a puppy later, or two, so it could have company – but then we moved." She risked a small but intense scowl in Melba's direction.

Dwayne pulled out a handkerchief and mopped his brow. He gulped some tea.

"Sweetheart," he asked Melba, with peculiar emphasis, "do – you – like – cats? *Love* cats?" Now he was staring at her too, and if a sickness was in his eyes it was not that of love.

"Oh, Dwayne, what an *interesting* question." Melba paused. Something was suddenly out of kilter in this man's air, triggering her self-interest into rapid assessment of possible danger. Melba's sensitivity was acute, but only insofar as how she was perceived by those important to her immediate needs. If Dwayne were to have a heart attack in the next five minutes, it would be a lesser evil than seeing Dwayne's estimation of her desirability dwindle because she had said something to upset him. He was divorced. Had the love and tending of cats filled a sad domestic void? Would Dwayne expect her to shower daily devotion on him *and* a feline horde? Or was he, like her, prey to sneezing and watering eyes if a single cat wandered by? That would be ideal – but how could she tell? Behind the whizzing calculations of her unilateral emotional intelligence, a tiny bell of memory was ringing at the word "cats". But it was a far-off sound, like that of an ambulance racing to someone else's emergency.

"Cats – yes, well, one certainly can't say like mother, like daughter when it comes to Elinore and her animals." Little laugh. Dwayne was not laughing. "You know, I have never given the love of cats any thought."

Elinore's mouth was full of sandwich, or she would have corrected that statement instantly.

"But I don't think cats and *clothes* mix, do you? I think animal hairs of any kind should be kept well away from clothes. And upholstery. And you should never let a cat anywhere near curtains. Someone I knew had a dreadful experience with cats and curtains. Three cats. They got a scare and ran up her brand-new silk curtains and *hung* there! The curtains were utterly shredded. *Ruined.* If that happened to me, I'd simply *die.* I do like to keep a nice home, you know. Cats *may* have their place in certain homes, but as a conscientious housekeeper I have to say that one ought to be careful with them. Don't you agree, darling?"

She opened her eyes as wide as she could. Dwayne was still looking at her, but he was nodding and his hand was reaching for another rock cake. Melba congratulated herself. It was so important to keep a man reassured on matters of domestic comfort, as she recalled having read somewhere. She had answered his question acceptably while revealing nothing at all about her feelings for cats. In truth, if they all vanished from the earth in an instant, it would mean nothing to her. Except for the big cats: they should be spared to ensure a continued supply of pelts for the luxuriant furs that one day, one day soon, she would own.

Elinore had had enough of all this. If her mother wished to natter on and tell fibs about cats being more or less acceptable in her house, so be it. The satchel by her chair reminded her of the unwritten letter to Tom. At this rate, Usha's letter would reach him days before hers, and what if the postmen went on strike again, as they had done a little while ago? What if they started that again tonight? These days, society was crumbling and anything could happen out of the blue, according to grown-ups' conversations she had overheard. Her letter would never reach Tom and then he would think her manners were awful. Landing on his doorstep with a wolf would then be awkward, to say the least.

"Mummy, I have homework," she announced. "And I still have to go to school tomorrow. I can't stay up late."

Dwayne looked at her approvingly. "That's good, kiddo. You're a star student, aren't you?"

"I'm not a student, I'm a pupil. I'm still at school." Foundered on a minor point of transatlantic vocabulary, that was the end of Dwayne's conversation with Elinore. "Excuse me," she said, and got up without reference to her destination, just as Miss Agnes Pound had instructed her to behave, to find the ladies' loos.

In the foyer, she asked the receptionist where to go. "I like your boots," said the girl. "I could do with a pair like that."

"Thank you," said Elinore. "I got them in Jenners."

"Oh, I'll have to take a look," said the girl. "Very nice. Now, can you find your way to the ladies?"

Elinore was cheered by this kind of attention. Her second compliment in one afternoon! In the loo, she wondered if her mother would now start saying things like "the little girls' room". Dwayne's potential for embarrassing Elinore in public could be endless. She tried to imagine him in the company of Arabella or Tom. This made her furious and sent her tummy whirling. She spent a long time washing her hands, partly because she liked the rose scent of the soap and partly because she was trying to work out exactly why such an idea made her furious. She decided it had something to do with that other occasion in a hotel, when a girl called Susanna had seen her wearing shabby cast-offs in the company of a mother who was talking far too loudly and attracting the wrong kind of attention. If Dwayne became the new Hector, people like Arabella and Tom might judge her as somebody she was not. They might give up on her. The real Elinore would be invisible, just as if Dwayne's evil hat had well and truly smothered her.

What on earth could she do about Dwayne? It was another mission for Agent Solo. But Agent Solo already had enough on her plate with the Caltrops. Elinore sighed. If only she could climb back into Sir Walter Scott's spaceship and escape the lot of them.

In the dining room, Dwayne had pulled his chair close to Melba's. They were holding hands and talking in low, urgent tones.

"Honey, I never had kids. And I'm not getting any younger. I'm kinda hoping we can live the life I've been working for. Meeting you has taken the shine off the job, that's for sure. I just want to quit and kick back while I've still got the you-know-what."

"Oh, poor darling Dwayne! You mustn't fret. We might not have summer camps here, but we do have our own great tradition of sending children away to school. For nearly the whole year! Isn't that clever? Yes, yes, I know – not just a pretty face. You have no idea!"

12

Rain continued to fall throughout the day after Elinore's introduction to Dwayne McMonagle. She took it as a bad omen in that respect, and consequently glowered all through breakfast, and scowled whenever Melba spoke. Strangely, Melba did not reprimand her, although once again Elinore felt her mother's eyes upon her in an unfamiliar way. Was Melba returning like for like in the matter of black looks? No, that could not be, decided Elinore, for she had never been the object of Melba's sustained attention.

Big, unanswered questions about that ridiculous Dwayne were now in the air. Elinore could feel them floating above her head, disturbing her, and she was not going to let Melba evade them. She had been unable to pin anything down in the taxi back to No. 17 the previous night, because Dwayne had accompanied them (as far as Elinore could tell, simply for the opportunity to sit on the same seat with a giggling Melba and clutch at her while the taxi bowled along). She did not demand an answer before bedtime because tackling Melba took persistence, and therefore time, and her unwritten letter to Tom was very pressing.

Through being out for tea, Elinore had been spared contact with the Caltrops since Mr Patel had dared to send his voice through their telephone. From their looks, Elinore knew that now she had been labelled impossibly bad. She half expected to be given a bowl of gruel and nothing else, as if she were a workhouse brat. The air of the morning room was heavy with unspoken censure, complementing the wet gloom outside.

On the way to school, Elinore put her Basildon Bond blue envelope into a pillar-box with great relief. Arabella's gift of stamps had made that part simple. She was particularly pleased with the many brightly coloured, graphic forms of emphasis she had worked into the text (sadly, impossible to reproduce here), and hoped that Tom would spot their resemblance to elements of the paisley shawl. Labouring over them had called to mind monks producing illuminated texts in freezing, candlelit cells. She was part of a tradition, then. As the evening drew on and she was still working, she had twiddled the knob of her revived radio and discovered something called Radio Luxembourg, which promised much livelier company than the shades of long-dead monks.

> Dear Tom,
>
> I am writing to thank you for <u>**LOTS**</u> of things! I am sorry that I could not send this letter right away, which would have been proper. I had to find nice paper for it first. BUT I have been thanking you in my head all the time anyway. Here is my list of thanks.
>
> <u>**No. 1**</u> Thank you for inviting me to your house!
>
> <u>**No. 2**</u> Thank you for letting me bring Usha with me!
>
> <u>**No. 3**</u> Thank you for letting us run around anywhere and explore!
>
> <u>**No. 4**</u> Thank you for showing us everything in your lovely old house, which is completely the best house I have ever been in!
>
> <u>**No. 5**</u> Thank you for the stories about the people from olden days.
>
> <u>**No. 6**</u> THANK YOU for the BEAUTIFUL presents you gave me! I will tell you what I think about the presents once I have finished this list, in case I forget any thanks.

<u>No. 7</u> Thank you for writing a real letter to me! I like letters a lot. Now I have two special ones because Arabella sent me one from a place called Castle Welkinlaw.

*I got a **HUGE** surprise when I opened the parcel. The paintings and the shawl are the most special things in my whole life and I promise I will look after them <u>very carefully indeed.</u> I would like to learn about the pictures. The little men riding down the hill are quite friendly to look at when I am going to sleep. I don't know why the Three Wise Men don't have any crowns or special clothes. It is interesting! The angel and the lady are much nicer than Sunday school stories. I <u>might</u> listen to that angel, especially because he is on the ground in a painting and not flying around in the sky. Sometimes I make up a story about what he is telling her! But only a little story because I keep falling asleep.*

I keep the shawl in my clothes drawers when I am not looking at it. It feels nice to leave it on the bed at night. It makes me feel like a lady who lives in a house where everyone is rich and famous. Really and truly it is like a GARDEN!!! I am so amazed that you gave me it.

Usha is very excited about the present you gave her, but she won't tell me about it before she shows me it. I will see it this weekend.

That is all I have to tell you right now. I wish I could visit your house every weekend. Actually Squair is a very nice place too. If I can't go back to Criven, I think I would like to live in Squair and have a dog like Boris.
**** **T H A N K   Y O U!!!** ****

Yours sincerely,
Elinore Crum

At Aikenhead Primary School, the pupils were even noisier than usual and restive in their eagerness to get to the end of term. One more pointless day until they were done with school for eight weeks, which stretched forth as a blissful eternity. The disturbance of the missionary's visit only fuelled this atmosphere. Elinore sat on a bench in the gym hall, as bored as everyone else with Mr Phil Curglaff's slides of his endeavours in Africa and his earnest speech about the great benefit that every Aikenhead pupil could generate by supporting him. He underscored this with a begging sort of prayer before his slide show and a prayer of thanks, more or less, after the collection of all the coins that their good wee hearts had found for him.

Elinore's boredom was different: it was infused with scorn for the missionary's reasoning. All those children in the slides, with their wide, hopeful smiles and huge, shining eyes – they needed *Jack and Jill* books to help them learn to read! Not *Bibles*! Not hundreds and hundreds of pages of tiny, fiddly text that sounded like nothing anyone ever said or wrote in the 20th century! She refused to believe for one moment that a deluge of bibles could help these children escape hunger and poverty.

Moreover, she disliked Mr Curglaff on sight. Had he presented the most intelligent, reasoned and moving case possible for funding any charity, it would have made no difference. He was a slimy person who kept massaging and rubbing his hands together as if they were slithery with oil. His hair was even oilier than Dwayne's. Dandruff speckled his black suit, which carried a whiff of stale cigarette smoke, and his shoes were insufficiently polished. Even if Elinore had been prepared to believe that the dirt on them was the dust of Africa, these shoes would have ruined his credibility. Miss Agnes Pound stated clearly that neglected footwear was too widely and readily regarded as evidence of low, ill-bred character to excuse under any circumstances. Had she been a dog, Elinore would have growled at him. Taking from her satchel the envelope containing the Caltrops' donation, she removed two coins of the lowest denomination and put the rest in her purse (which had a satisfying bulge to it now, even after the purchase of paper and batteries).

Agent Solo would later shred the envelope and dispose of it in a bus stop litterbin on the way home. For once, the internal judge of her badness was entirely silent. Mr Curglaff was bad and that was that. Besides, no one would ever know what she had done, least of all any child in Africa. *So there.* Someday, she would find a proper way of meeting those huge, hungry hopeful eyes with generosity.

As she went to bed that night, she looked at the *Annunciation* and wondered what that angel would have made of the missionary Curglaff. Then, thinking of her birthday the following day, she said aloud, "Dear Mr Gabriel –" no, that did *not* sound right. "Dear Sir Gabriel" – he did look noble and anyway Miss Agnes Pound had not included archangels in the chapter covering Correct Forms of Address – "if you know that something special is going to happen to me when I am ten years old, please give me a clue tomorrow, when it's my birthday. Or in a week. Or in a month if you need more time to send the clue. Thank you *very* much."

It was a sort of prayer, she supposed, but mundane enough to be unlike any that a Caltrop or Curglaff might utter, and so that was all right, despite going against the grain of her personal philosophy concerning heavenly beings. Some people believed the Virgin Mary could accomplish all sorts of miracles, but, even if Elinore had been one of them, Mary was looking far too flustered in this picture for Elinore to want to address her. *Not listening*, as Tom had pointed out. Just like old Miss Cruickshank in Criven, when two tomcats came face to face in her garden and tore into each other in front of her. She had dropped her knitting, thrown up her hands and started screaming, "Help, help, help me!" Elinore, who happened to be there because she liked to visit Miss Cruickshank's pretty garden with the stream running through it, tried in vain to tell her that the cats were not interested in clawing at *her*. She would not listen.

The more Elinore looked at the *Annunciation*, this deceptively straightforward scene, the more she enjoyed it. It was – *elegant*. No doubt a religious person would say that was the wrong word to use about this painting, because it was the same word that people used for three earthly deities inhabiting Elinore Crum's Pantheon of glamour: Jackie Onassis, Princess Grace of Monaco and Audrey Hepburn. Well, so what? Until she could discuss the painting with Tom, it would remain for her a work of great elegance.

On June 30th, she awoke to a fine blue sky and happy birds. That was a good start. She went down to breakfast. Mr Caltrop read aloud his snippets from the newspaper and Elinore learned that something called Holyrood Week had begun. The Queen and the Duke of Edinburgh were *here* – in the same city as Elinore Crum and quite likely eating porridge and boiled eggs in their palace only streets away. This was invigorating news, unquestionably a good omen of the first class.

For a little while, everything else was as usual. The same looks of dissatisfaction directed at her by Melba; the same scrutiny of her mouthfuls by Mrs Caltrop; the same munching and slurping, squeaking of toast on plate, scrunching of eggshell under knife and trickling of tea from a spout. Clearly, the Caltrops were not going to acknowledge her birthday, and Elinore was glad of that, whatever the reason. A present from them would be laden with some kind of obligation and designed to make her a better, nicer child; she was sure of it. As for parental recognition of this special day – well, Hector was definitely dead and in the guts of a bear. She did not believe that her direct address to Sir Gabriel would result in delivery of a gift from the afterlife, and she did not want it, for Hector had never given her anything she liked or could even recall. And Melba had never remembered the exact day of Elinore's birthday. One problem was its closeness to her own in August: only five or six *weeks* lay between them. Melba's expectations of abundant recognition of her own special date multiplied daily with the passing of June. In Elinore's most distant memories lay a few pretty cards and small delights that had come out of brown-paper parcels with stamps on them. But that was before certain telephone calls and tears and tantrums, and long, loud exchanges between Hector and

Melba. Elinore knew it had something to do with the mysterious absence in her life of grandparents. As Elinore grew older, Melba would only brush her questions away with "Later – you are far too young to understand."

When the doorbell rang and Mrs Caltrop went to see what the postman could not deliver through the letterbox, Elinore had no reason to lift her gaze from the toast on her plate. She was pondering the comparative horrors of fatal inoculants. Agent Solo was proposing injection of the Caltrops' food with one. Typhoid fever was attractive, and cholera could surely carry off a Caltrop as effectively here as in India (she was thinking of the parents of all those poor orphaned colonial children in old stories). It would be a delight to inflict bubonic plague on the Caltrops (the black pustules being an appealing feature), but she knew enough history to acknowledge that confining an outbreak to No. 17 would be difficult. Apart from Mr Curglaff, she had no wish to remove anyone else from Edinburgh's populace. Dwayne was a problematic recipient because he would infect Melba as she lay weeping over his deathbed. Agent Solo put him in a special category for the time being. It was labelled Fate Undecided.

Elinore was greatly surprised, then, when Mrs Caltrop reappeared with two envelopes and announced, "These are addressed to Elinore Crum and I had to sign for them." Ignoring Elinore, she looked at Melba with her eyebrows raised, as if the Royal Mail had committed an impropriety.

"It's that woman, isn't it, giving you things again," said Melba.

"I don't know what you mean."

Melba sighed. "She's very impertinent, very *rude*, to think I don't know how to dress my own child."

"Quite," said Mrs Caltrop. "Larding a child with all that frivolity can bring no good."

"You can't send clothes in an *envelope*!" Logic and justice stung Elinore into a very loud reply, the only one she could think of on the spot.

"Don't shout!" snapped Melba. "Your manners have certainly deteriorated with all this gadding around."

Mrs Caltrop started to add to this condemnation, but Elinore leapt from her chair and ran upstairs.

It had never occurred to her that Arabella might do anything more to acknowledge her birthday. She found that Arabella and Tom had each sent her a birthday card and a 10-shilling note. *Twenty shillings!* Elinore Crum was now in possession of one whole pound in addition to her coins.

She took her purse from her satchel. She ought to be leaving for school immediately – but not with all that money. Anything could happen, with rough boys running amok on the last day of term, and the ominous, muttering cliques of girls who might just decide to go for her at last before she disappeared. The purse went in a drawer, below all her knickers. She rushed to clean her teeth, lace up her shoes and run downstairs and out of the house before anyone could ask her what the postman had brought.

School broke up one hour early, and Elinore fled, running for the sheer pleasure of knowing that Aikenhead would not exist for many weeks. Then she slowed to an amble, since arriving at No. 17 one hour early was not going to give her any extra birthday joy. She would change into her denims and go out in the sunshine. She could compose letters of thanks to Tom and Arabella in her head while exploring another street or two.

When she rang the doorbell, Mr Caltrop let her in. He looked at her in a doleful, grumpy way, and hesitated just enough to give the impression that he would prefer to leave her on the doorstep. He was clutching his newspaper, into which he tended to fade, to become one with the stories of local worthies and the political uproar or scandal of the day; whatever dynamo powered him was dependent on church meetings or services, and defence of his horticultural territory. Lately he had been much exercised by the decision of the Methodist Church to allow women to be full ministers. He disappeared into the morning room without uttering a word. Mrs

Caltrop was talking on the telephone. Her voice dropped to a mutter and she turned her back as Elinore went upstairs.

On her bed lay a flat package carelessly wrapped in white tissue paper, with bits of sellotape holding it together. On top was a sheet of Basildon Bond writing paper that had clearly been taken from Elinore's table, and written on with one of her pencils, since she could see that her materials had been disturbed: *Happy Birthday from Mummy.*

Inside was a shoulder bag far superior to any cotton one turned out by a Greek factory. This one was woven silk. Like the vase in the Balmerinoch Hotel, it was patterned with red dragons, and also with flowers in greens, ochres and reds on a gold ground. The interior was a screaming scarlet and had a little zippered compartment on either side. The strap was a tightly woven rope of black silk. The top of the bag folded over like the V of an envelope and closed with a braided toggle and loop. Elinore was ecstatic, and so eager to fill it with Agent Solo's essentials that she never noticed the dust, perhaps from face powder, inside the bag, or a rubbed patch on one side, or the loose, snagged threads. For Melba to have remembered on the very day, and to have produced the one thing that was top priority for Elinore – and in such unimagined, sumptuous form – was simply a miracle.

"All right," said Elinore to Sir Gabriel. "I think this is a big clue. And the extra money is a monster clue. I think you're telling me that I'm going to have a super-duper time now that I'm ten. Thank you very, very much!" She kept looking at him, biting her lower lip and frowning as she debated the rightness of another request that had come to mind. It was so tempting! The results of the first one had been so swift. It was irresistible.

"Please, Sir Gabriel," she whispered, "make the Caltrops disappear forever. I mean, let me go home to my own home and never, ever, *ever* see them again. Except I'd like to see Usha again, and she has to live in Edinburgh. So, maybe you could just make something happen to them." She went very close to the picture and dropped her voice even further. "Like what happened to Hector." The details of the desired removal were not as important as permanence.

When she was all ready to go out, she listened at the top of the stairs. Mrs Caltrop was still on the telephone. When the conversation ended and Mrs Caltrop went into the morning room, Elinore crept as quickly as she could downstairs and out of the front door. At the gate, she heard the door open and Mrs Caltrop's voice, but looking back was out of the question. She ran as fast as she could until she was safely round a corner. Mrs Caltrop would never come running in pursuit. Elinore knew that instinctively, without ever having heard the phrase "loss of dignity."

She made for the churchyard where she had waited for Usha. So many interesting things had happened since then that it seemed to be a long time ago, but less than a fortnight had passed. She followed the bounds of the church, looking for interesting streets, and took one that led downhill in a long curve. She liked going where she could not see an end. This led her to a broad, busy road, like a main road through a town, with lots of shops, some big, some small, on either side. Pleased with this variety, she meandered along and looked in every window, patting her beautiful bag every so often just for the feel of it, and the knowledge that all her essentials were safely in one place on her person. When she came to the Olde Luckenbooth Gift Shoppe, she stopped. The window was crammed, with little regard for stylish display, and all the more intriguing for that. Elinore took several minutes to peer at every delightful item before deciding to go inside. She patted the bag again. Yes, Elinore Crum had every right to inspect the wares more closely: she had money to spend.

Twenty minutes later, she came out carrying a paper bag. Inside was a small box in midnight blue velvet overlain with gold thread in a diamond pattern. Inside the box were note cards and matching envelopes; each card showed a different watercolour painting of a native Scottish plant or flower. On Elinore's face was a smile so wide that she felt her mouth stretching as if it would never go back to normal. She had found the note cards on a half-price sale table. She had got a bargain, which meant saving money! She could also convey her thanks to Arabella and Tom in a *beautiful* way (that was important), and very properly. She could do the same for Julie Fairgrieve, and tell her how special it was to have a tranny all of her own. Miss Agnes Pound herself would have been happy to send these cards. Finally, a velvet box was the perfect place for small treasures. If she ever had a necklace, she would keep it in there.

Now she was eager to return to No. 17 and get on with the job of composition. What an amazing birthday she was having! It was supercalifragilisticexpialidocious, all right. She made up a little song as she climbed the long curving street back to the church. Each verse described a gruesome fate befalling the Caltrops, and it was hugely satisfying.

Mrs Caltrop let her into the house and said that Melba would not be home for tea, having telephoned to say that she was dining out with a friend. Mrs Caltrop sounded angry as she gave this news, and she looked angry as she stared at the bag in Elinore's hand.

"Where have you been? What do you have there?"

"Presents," said Elinore without thinking, or rather, thinking of the notecards as presents to send her friends.

"What? Who else is giving you things? Have you been in that dirty Hindu shop again?"

"Mr Patel's shop is *not* dirty! And I can go where I want!"

She made to push past, but the woman seized her arm and gripped it. "Owww!" shrieked Elinore, in equal parts pain, fury and horror at being touched by a Caltrop. Mrs Caltrop bent down until her bad breath was hot on Elinore's face and hissed, "You are a very bad, spoilt child and the Lord is trying to save you from a life of sin." Her grip on Elinore's arm tightened and she gave it a hard shake that hurt the shoulder.

"You can go without tea until your mother returns and we have discussed your rudeness *and* this running around on the streets and meeting undesirables."

Mrs Caltrop straightened up and let go Elinore's arm. She turned on her heel and went towards the kitchen. Elinore fled upstairs. She had to sit down on her bed, for she was shaking. She unbuttoned her blouse and tried to inspect her arm and shoulder, which were both hurting. Finger-mark bruising was already beginning to show.

Hours later, Melba let herself into the house. In a pleasant, warming haze induced by wine, fantastical visions of the future and the scent of imminent success, she crept up the stairs and into her room. Bed . . . She would not even wash her face. Everything could wait until morning.

The bundle of clothes on her bed sat up and demanded otherwise.

"Mummy – are you going to run away with that man? You *have* to tell me right now."

"Elinore, get out of my room this instant. This isn't the moment for talking about anything. And what's this – you've eaten all my biscuits!" It was true: Elinore had been glad to give up another revolting Caltrop meal, but the packet of digestive biscuits on Melba's dressing table was another matter.

"She said I couldn't have anything to eat. I was starving. And she hurt my arm, it's all bruised. And I'm not going out of here until you *tell* me. You never tell me anything."

Melba's head was spinning. Ah, the unfairness of life! So much for her to cope with at one time. She plopped onto the bed. Any outlandish tales of the Caltrops could be ignored, but she must keep the business of Dwayne, her ship to freedom, on an even keel.

"Dwayne has some wonderful plans for a family holiday. They take a little time to work out, that's all. Now go on, back to your own bed."

"But I don't want a holiday with Dwayne! He isn't my *family*. And if you leave me behind, I'll just run away too. I'll never stay in this house. Why can't I go and stay in Criven? Why don't you ask Mrs Fairgrieve if I can stay with Julie?"

"We are not talking about leaving you anywhere." Truth was certainly more malleable after a few drinks. "Anyway, Dwayne is going away next week, all the way back to America. You'll see, I'll still be here. We're just – getting to know each other. Now let me into my own bed. I have to work tomorrow and you have to go to school."

"No, I don't. It's summer holidays now."

"Oh. Well, I know you can amuse yourself perfectly well wherever you are." This reminded Melba of something. "But before you go, how about some gratitude for that lovely birthday present I left on your bed?"

"I like it a lot, and thank you very much," said Elinore. She slid off the bed, trailed out of the room and down the corridor. Melba locked her bedroom door and went to bed. Her last thought before sleeping was a hopeful one, a wish that more American tourists would lose things right outside Grisella's Gowns, for her to chance upon and give a new home, and save her the bother and expense of a birthday present. Especially things like bags containing expensive cosmetics.

A whole day went by before Elinore could let Sir Gabriel be on view once more. Her disappointment and sense of being hugely let down by him made her turn the *Annunciation* to the wall. She had lost confidence in his supposed hints of a stellar year to come. If only Mrs Caltrop had not seized her and hurt her arm; if only Melba had been more reassuring about Dwayne's place in the scheme of things. Her birthday would not have been sullied and she would not have the uncomfortable feeling of walking through dangerous swampland where man-eating creatures lurked.

This feeling was heightened by the arrival of Mrs Wattie, whose Tuesday and Friday duties had been completed within school hours until now. Elinore was in her room, writing her letters of thanks to Tom, Arabella and Julie, when the roar of an upright vacuum cleaner broke into her peace. She ignored it until it grew louder and closer. When she looked out into the corridor, a squat woman in a blue nylon housecoat was shoving a Hoover around. She had short dark hair that was too black to be natural, and a worn, tea-coloured face with deep lines around dark, hooded eyes. Her mouth was the opposite of Mrs Caltrop's: thin to the point of disappearing when set hard, as it was now. She stared at Elinore, silently and inscrutably, and pushed the Hoover closer towards Elinore's door. Elinore hesitated in her doorway while the Hoover roared on until, after a few seconds of this stand-off, Mrs Wattie cut the power and demanded, "Will ye let me get on wi' it or no'?"

It seemed that she wanted into Elinore's room. Feeling confused but not wanting to be anywhere near this noise and apparent hostility from a new source, Elinore hastily gathered together her writing things and went out to sit on the lawn. She stayed there well after she had finished writing, lying flat on the grass until she was certain that Mrs Wattie was gone from her bedroom and bathroom. When she returned, the room had a stale smell that she had noticed before on other so-called cleaning days. It was a mystery: did cleaner floors always equal dirty air? Her bathroom door was open and Domestos tainted the air from that direction. It was time to get out of the place. She put three of Arabella's first-class stamps on the envelopes and went off to post them, her Chinese bag slung across her chest. Then she carried on towards MacAlpine Place.

The ladies at the charity shop were the same two who had put the Laura Ashley dress aside for her. They greeted her as if she were an old friend, and asked if she was going to look for a garden party dress. "It's the season, you know. All the fine folk will be at Holyrood today for the Royal garden party."

Elinore was smitten with desire to see something of this spectacle. It would be a delight to see these fine folk all dressed up and going into a palace. No doubt the Queen herself would be hidden away, only seen by her guests, but still, every other sight would be fuel for daydreams about being invited herself one day.

"Is it far away? Could I walk there?"

The ladies laughed, but not unkindly, and explained that the bus was a better idea, or rather two or three buses. Did Elinore not have a grown-up who could go with her? No? Och, that was too bad, she'd just have to make do with looking for a nice dress that she could wear when she was invited next year.

Elinore spent so long in the charity shop that she forgot all about lunchtime until the ladies took out their sandwiches. The funny thing about having so much money was her reluctance to spend it. She had to think a great deal about everything she looked at, and in the end she decided to return for a second look at the several items that interested her. She said goodbye and went to visit Mr Patel. He sold things she could eat, and she was ravenous. Her tummy had never felt so empty.

Three male customers were at Mr Patel's counter, and the little shop was full of prognostication and cast-iron assertions about politics, punctuated by "mark my words" and "believe me." The men all seemed to approve of the new Prime Minister, but not the giving of the vote to eighteen year-olds. The young were a danger in any sphere, it seemed. Elinore was not interested and looked at comics while she waited for Mr Patel's attention, but she did wonder when she would be old enough to appear inherently dangerous in the eyes of more people than the Caltrops. The discussion moved on to a place called Derry, or Londonderry, which was confusing because it was actually one place and nowhere near London. Any talk of social upheaval that included riots and soldiers in the streets of her own land did make Elinore pay attention. It was unnerving, because it immediately connected to her barebones knowledge of the Russian Revolution. This centred mainly on sepia photographs of the Romanov family, who haunted her imagination. It was too easy to imagine their lovely white dresses, and Prince Alexei's sailor suit, all drenched in blood. She buried her head in the latest *Princess Tina* until Mr Patel greeted her.

She bought a bag of peanuts and raisins and a bag of salt-and-vinegar crisps. Mr Patel said that he was going to close the shop early to enable him to see Usha in her school concert. "She sings in the choir and next year she will choose a musical instrument to play – maybe two," he said proudly.

"Gosh," said Elinore. "She'll have to practise all the time. I hope she still wants to play with me then."

Mr Patel looked horrified at this concern. "Oh, my goodness, yes! Usha will be your lifelong friend!" he exclaimed. "What a pity that you don't go to the same school." Suddenly he threw up his hands in contrition. "Elinore! Please excuse me. I should have asked you straight away: will you not come to the concert with us? Mrs Patel and I will be walking there. We will go in two hours precisely. I am so sorry we didn't ask you sooner."

Elinore was stunned. Was this Sir Gabriel's doing? It was a chance to see inside a real girls' school, to sit there and watch a performance as if she belonged to one of *those* families. But all those eyes, the scrutiny of the entire Ina Blackadder School . . . She would have to rush off immediately and change into a skirt, and comb her hair, and rush back to the shop. She had no conception of how long any of this might take, and the lack of a watch did not help. She only knew that she must *rush* along those streets – again.

"Oh, yes, please! But I have to go and put on my good clothes. I'll run as fast as I can and I promise I won't be late! Please, please wait for me if you're going and you see me running back."

She was out of the door before Mr Patel could say anything more, and pelting towards Dunallan Crescent. Just beyond MacAlpine Place, she saw a small figure in a pale blue suit, who was talking over a garden gate to another lady. The sun shone on the snow-white hair of the blue figure and made her bejewelled combs twinkle. It was Lady Groule. She turned at the sound of Elinore's feet and peered through huge sunglasses that made two startling black holes on her small, refined face.

"Ah – Miss Elinore Crum! What a pleasant surprise. What fire are you rushing to?"

Elinore stopped, out of breath. She opened her mouth and started to speak, but without any warning the world spun around her. Her voice sounded tiny and faraway in her own ears and her legs jellified. She could not control any of this. Then the spinning world turned completely black and she fell down.

13

Lady Groule observes with keen interest the child lying on her friend's sofa. She is also concerned about her own huge black sunglasses. These are now on top of her small head, as worn by models and jetsetters pictured in *Vogue*, and make her look like a beetle in a Hardy Amies suit.

"It might have been shock at the sight of me," she muses aloud. "She was running flat out until I said hello and then she was flat *out*. Alice says that two giant black holes are alarming for people who expect little twinkly eyes in an old lady's face. But then, daughters-in-law do say what they like these days, or think they can, don't they?"

Lady Groule's eyes do not twinkle so much as spark and glint in the manner of sun on Arctic snow or of brilliant-cut diamonds (also known as ice). This is not to say that they are cold, merely that, like Arabella Cheyne's eyes, they cut deeply through surfaces and miss nothing. Lady Groule is attuned to whatever is just below plain sight, whether scandal or human potential. What is already known is not terribly interesting to her, unless it has significance as a clue to whatever line of enquiry she is pursuing. ("Significant" is a favourite word of hers.) Lady Groule scents peculiarity in the unconscious Elinore Crum and it is irresistible. If they were dark instead of blue, her eyes would be those of a terrier bred to dig and dig and dig until its quarry is unearthed.

"I doubt it was shock," says Celia Chisholm, laying a blanket over Elinore and a hand on her forehead. "The running was the problem, I think. It's hot outside, but she isn't feverish. She was holding those" – Celia points to the bags of peanuts and crisps – "and she's as thin as a rake. It's past lunchtime. She's about ten, I'd say, and all children are bottomless pits at that age, for good reason. They need more food than a grown man. She simply ran out of vim. Does she come from the kind of home where children eat crisps instead of solid meals?"

Celia is practical. Her husband is a retired surgeon, her two brothers are doctors and her father was the administrator of a famous hospital. During the war, she devoted extraordinary effort and organisational talent to the Women's Voluntary Service Mobile Canteens, Rest Centres and Housewives Service, but above all as a Food Leader. Her three hearty sons (doctors, of course) are able to work excruciatingly long hours in hospitals or (when they want fun) hurl themselves about on a rugby pitch or up and down mountains, all because Celia fed them proper meals at the appropriate hours when they were boys. Celia deplores the modern tendency to snack on packets of rubbish.

Lady Groule, who avoids cooking anything and whose idea of a snack is a gin and tonic, is forced to accept her friend's assessment.

"I know next to nothing about her, except that she's a friend of Usha Patel's – a very new friend. We met in the shop, but I had to dash off. Now, Celia, what am I going to *do*? The concert starts in one and a half hours precisely." Lady Groule is already dressed for the occasion. She happened to be conversing with Celia Chisholm at the crucial moment only because she had included the return of a borrowed book (a deliciously indiscreet memoir that mentions a mutual friend) in her afternoon constitutional, her little walk around the neighbourhood that is so often unexpectedly revealing.

Celia is also a member of the Ina Blackadder Old Girls' Association, but she has no patience for school concerts and no intention of accompanying her friend. "You're going to go off and enjoy yourself – nothing to worry about. I doubt very much that she's concussed. I'll get some Horlicks into her as soon as she comes round, and a nice thick sandwich or two."

Elinore heard muffled voices before the blackness began to fade and her eyes opened wide. Sunlight was filling the broad bay window of Celia's sitting room at that moment, hitting her straight in the face and making her wince. She closed her eyes again. She must get up – there was an urgent reason, she had just overheard it, and it was slipping away – but she felt sick and shivery despite the blanket that covered her.

"Elinore, can you hear me?" asked an unfamiliar voice. She raised her hand. "Are you hurting anywhere?" She opened her eyes and forced them to stay open, turning her head to avoid the light and finding Lady Groule's alert face instead. Then another lady bent over her and asked again if she was hurting.

"No," answered Elinore. "Why would I be hurting?"

"You were running down the street and you fainted," said the lady. "You fell right down on the pavement."

Then everything flew back into place in Elinore's head and she struggled to sit up. "I've got to go!" she cried. "I'm going to the concert. I'll be late and the Patels will go without me and I'll miss it!"

"Nonsense!" said Lady Groule, clapping her hands together as if to dismiss this fear instantly. "Fate has dropped you into my care and I'm going to the concert too. This is Mrs Chisholm. She knows everything about hurt children and she will decide if you're all right to be on your feet. We can walk there together if she approves."

"But I *can't!*" Elinore clenched her fists and then pushed the blanket aside. "I need to put on my good clothes first. I don't want all those girls to see me like this. They've got *uniforms.*" Without warning, something rose up in her throat and in her eyes, and her face seemed to swell. She was crying. She never, ever cried, but she was crying now. Lady Groule and Celia exchanged looks, and Lady Groule edged her chair closer to the sofa. She knew exactly what feminine insecurity had spawned this panic.

"My dear gel, let me see if I understand. You are wearing very nice clothes, just as you were wearing very nice boots when we first met. But you would feel more *at home* at the concert if you looked a little more like the other gels there – yes?"

Elinore nodded dumbly, overcome with emotion. What would be worse: losing the chance to visit a real girls' school, upsetting the Patels by failing to appear or sitting in her denims, sandshoes and jumper amid hundreds of impeccable uniformed girls? And what if Usha wanted to introduce her there and then to Susanna, whom she was anxious to impress above all others? It was a dreadful moment in the life of Elinore Crum.

"Where do you live, Elinore?" asked Celia.

"Dunallan Crescent. But I was going to put on my good clothes and run back so I could go with Mr and Mrs Patel."

The ladies exchanged another look, and Lady Groule clapped her hands again. "We can beat the clock!" she said, and hoisted her handbag. "Everything *I* need is in here. Now, Elinore, you shall go to the concert, but you must do *exactly* what Mrs Chisholm tells you, because she is an expert in the care and feeding of delicate young things. We can't have you sliding under the chairs in the middle of a performance, can we?"

Celia was already on her way to the kitchen.

"I shall ring for a taxi while Celia feeds you," continued Lady Groule. "We'll go straight from Dunallan Crescent to the school. The taxi will wait while you change. Why don't you save time and wash your face now? Here, take my comb too. Down the hallway, second door on the left."

Cold water, a hair comb, a mug of Horlicks, a sandwich straight from heaven (and another which Celia had wrapped to let Elinore eat in the taxi), and above all release from the jaws of despair – all combined to work a small miracle on Elinore. Nevertheless, as Lady Groule was hustling her down the garden path to the waiting taxi, Elinore felt new consternation. Whatever must that lovely Mrs Chisholm think of her? How could she say thank you properly? And she had *cried!* It was only late afternoon. Hours and hours of this bizarre day lay ahead yet, beyond her control and rife with upsetting possibilities.

Hours and hours to come, thought Lady Groule, ripe with opportunities to *take the lid off things* (a favourite phrase of hers). This Elinore Crum was a mystery: intelligent, polite, well-spoken, well dressed (and determined to uphold standards in that department – that was significant), and related to someone who knew the Balmerinochs and Squair. But not exactly happy, apparently; not an Ina Blackadder pupil (why ever not?); not long established in Edinburgh; and not even properly fed, according to Celia. The element of child protection added strong spice to this latest human-interest drama in Lady Groule's life.

The taxi was driven by a large, red-faced man, whom Lady Groule greeted as an old friend.

"George, you will have to excuse Elinore's sandwich. If she doesn't eat it, she might well faint, which would be considerably more awkward for you than a few crumbs."

George seemed to find this hilarious and roared with laughter, making his red cheeks even redder. He promised to get them to the school as if on wings, and asked whether he should help carry anything out of the house they were going to stop at first.

"Thank you, but no – unless Elinore faints with excitement and we have to go in and carry her out!" George roared again, Lady

Groule cackled and Elinore managed a weak smile. She felt safe with this ancient lady and a taxi driver as big as a bull. This day *might* yet turn out all right.

At No. 17, Lady Groule got out of the taxi with her. "I can't let your parents think I'm kidnapping you, can I?"

"Mummy's still at work and I don't have a father. He's dead. This is the Caltrops' house."

Lady Groule thrilled with eagerness at this cast-iron evidence of family melodrama. She added a little of her own before Mr Caltrop answered the ring of the doorbell, simply by abandoning the etiquette of face-to-face conversation and moving her alarming black shades from the top of her head down to her nose. She sensed that implicit rudeness might be advantageous here.

"Good afternoon. Mr Caltrop, I presume? I am Lady Groule – here is my card." Mr Caltrop's mouth fell open. Zinnia, Lady Groule of Meggat, he read. A respectable address not far off, a telephone number – how could this possibly be one of the undesirables with whom Elinore had been consorting? He wished Roberta were at his side instead of chairing a meeting, for titles were exceedingly important to her and she knew the right way to address anyone.

Lady Groule liked to see this discomfiture, and did not even wait for him to introduce himself. "Might I sit down inside? We're on our way to a concert and Elinore needs to change first." She put a foot firmly on the brass strip that lay under the front door, and this energized Mr Caltrop.

"Indeed, indeed!" he exclaimed, and held out his hand. "Kenneth Caltrop. Roberta – my wife – Mrs Caltrop is out. Most unfortunate. It's one of her missionary meetings."

Lady Groule smiled, inclined her head, ignored his outstretched hand and walked straight into the hall, where she sat on the only chair, put her sunglasses on top of her head again and looked around. It was doubly dark after the brightness outside, and after Celia Chisholm's floor-to-ceiling pastel decor, and the air was stuffy and stale after Mrs Wattie's ministrations with the Hoover. Ugh, she thought, eyeing one of Mrs Caltrop's mushroom hats on the hallstand.

"I understand Elinore lives here," she said to Mr Caltrop, who was looming over her. No manners, she thought; it makes no difference that Elinore will be down in a trice, he ought to have shown me into a room, and I could have sniffed out something significant.

"Yes, indeed! Elinore and her mother needed a safe haven after the terrible loss of the man of their house. A shocking thing. But the good Lord guided them to us, and we're glad to do the Lord's bidding and offer them shelter. Especially for the sake of the child, you know. Running loose and wild with one parent gone forever and the other out at work – oh, we cannot underestimate the devilish temptations of delinquency these days, can we?"

Dear God, thought Lady Groule, the man's a holy roller. I don't like this one bit. But she could now ignore Mr Caltrop because Elinore was running downstairs.

"Very smart, Elinore. The whiteness of your blouse will dazzle everyone present." With that, she pulled her sunglasses down onto her nose. Now she could barely see even the outline of Mr Caltrop, but that was beside the point. Intimidating the man was the point. She rose, took Elinore's arm and said, "Goodbye. Do remember to give my card to your wife. It's highly unlikely, but we *might* have some ancient connection in common."

As they hurried towards the taxi, Elinore did not hear the front door close and felt Mr Caltrop's eyes on them. Lady Groule proclaimed "*Ghastly!*" without lowering her normal voice, which carried well in any direction.

George revved the taxi's engine and they were off. They sped past MacAlpine Place and Elinore was suddenly aghast. "Oh, no! The Patels! What if they waited for me? What if I made them late?"

Lady Groule patted her knee. "All taken care of. I told Celia Chisholm to ring them and explain. She's utterly reliable, I promise you. Now do calm yourself, and put everyone else out of your head.

It's time for some fun!" She forbore to say that she had been having fun ever since Elinore had revived, and that she was going to have a great deal more as she winkled the story of this child out of the local woodwork. *Someone* must know the name of Caltrop. Ugh!

George was having fun too. He always did when he drove Lady Groule, and did his utmost to oblige when the taxi company relayed her requests for his services. He relished her withering backseat commentary on current affairs, and especially on the local affairs she espied from the taxi window. If only the world had advanced to the point where people could carry their very own phones, whether walking down the street or driving a taxi – anywhere and everywhere. He wouldn't miss a single opportunity for fun or business then. This wasn't the first time Lady Groule had asked him to step on it, and he liked a bit of speed. He hurtled down the last street, to the head of a T-junction where the Ina Blackadder School for Girls spread itself along four substantial Victorian houses linked by annexes. Cars were crawling all around in competition for parking space, and the school's main entrance was thronged with parents and other relations of pupils, and many girls in uniform. Elinore's heart leaped. She was here by right: she was a guest, invited twice over, no less. People *wanted* her to be there! Sir Gabriel might not have been wrong after all. If this evening did turn out to be fun, she would turn the *Annunciation* around as soon as she returned to her room, and have another think about the omens of her new year.

Perhaps some cosmic influence was enlivening the Edinburgh air that evening, encouraging upsets and uncertainties, omens and portents, to come flitting around like bats. When Mrs Caltrop arrived home, well satisfied with her firm chairing of that day's meeting (in particular the extinguishing of one Miss Dalmeny during a crucial exchange), Mr Caltrop rushed at her in agitation. He was waving his newspaper and talking about a lady, and so naturally she assumed that the Church in England or even the Kirk in Scotland had made the news again with another ill-advised gesture towards equality for women. Then he rushed back into the morning room and came back with a visiting card, which he thrust at her while she was still hanging up her hat and coat.

"What are we to make of this?" he cried. "The rules never said anything about consorting with *titled* strangers, let alone admitting them to the house."

Mrs Caltrop stared at the rows of engraved print on the card. "*Who* left this?" she demanded. "This person has nothing to do with the church or any of my meetings."

"The *child* brought her here! On their way to a concert, she said. A concert! What have we let into this house, Roberta? First it's Indians ringing us up for social reasons, and now it's aristocrats, the very incarnation of dissolute self-indulgence. No thought but hedonism!"

"*In* this house? I simply do not understand. The Crums are not to bring people into this house. I made that perfectly clear, did I not? *Were you entertaining her,* Kenneth – this Lady Groule?" Beneath the implicit reprimand, Mrs Caltrop's social aspirations churned and boiled, raising a froth of acute disappointment that her duties had denied her the chance to welcome a titled lady into her own home.

Before Mr Caltrop could answer, the telephone rang.

"Hello, Mrs C!" came Melba's breezy voice. "Just letting you know that I shan't be home for tea. But Elinore will be. I'm out all by myself tonight!" Little giggle.

"Elinore might *not* be here," said Mrs Caltrop. "She has gone to a concert, it seems, in the company of a woman we have never met. I was not present when the pair of them came to this house, and so that is all I can tell you. I find this casual, careless attitude to the decorum of our home very distressing, Melba. Did I not make it clear that you must discuss visitors with Mr Caltrop and me well in advance? Every home must have its rules, or it would not be a home – it would degenerate! I *will not* have that!"

"Oh, well, if she's with a woman it must be all right," said Melba, "although we don't want another Arabella Cheyne, do we? One is quite enough for an entire family. Now I must dash, we're run off our feet here. 'Bye!"

Mrs Caltrop's hand shook as she replaced the receiver. The unexplained and the undisciplined were sending tremors through the foundations of No. 17 Dunallan Crescent. This seismic shuddering must be halted before it developed beyond her control.

Some hours later, Melba and Dwayne sat in a cocktail bar. They too were feeling the future rock their present, but they were enjoying the sensation and encouraging it, as if they were on a fairground ride. Dwayne was overjoyed to discover that Melba had a valid passport. This was entirely due to Hector, whose flights of fancy had once involved his wife and child to the extent that they were prepared for emigration to another country (a country that was never finally decided upon, let alone advised of the Crum family's intended arrival as would-be citizens). Dwayne had strung out his troubleshooting in Scotland for as long as his employers would accept, and in forty-eight hours he would be back in Dallas. In one week, Melba would be there too, for what Dwayne insisted on calling the vacation of a lifetime. Words were not his strong point, but everything else he said that evening made his meaning abundantly clear: the vacation would inaugurate the lifetime of a new conjugal unit, Dwayne and Melba McMonagle. Sure, she'd have to go back to Scotland to wind things up and deal with the kid, but then the world, or Dallas-Fort Worth at least, would be their oyster. The Green Card business would be a snap. Thus, infatuation had all unknowing met female ambition, and every obstacle was cursorily acknowledged, if that, and dismissed in rapture and wilful blindness, including the matter of cats.

"So, uh, you don't think Elly-nore needs a kitty to make her feel at home when she's around? Keep her company while we're out on the town? She was talking about a puppy, remember? Or two. Hell, I don't know what kids want."

Cats *again*, thought Melba, wary of these dangerously opaque references from an otherwise direct man. Did he love or hate the little beasts? If it was love, dependency or downright addiction, where did that leave her? Oh, it was far too much to *think* about! The important thing, the *only* thing, was to get her feet on American soil at someone else's expense. His cute little rancher, whatever kind of house that was, might be heaving with cats, but no doubt she could parlay red-nosed, watery-eyed sneezing fits into such guilt and concern in Dwayne (for *her*, not the bloody cats) that it could only strengthen her position.

"You mustn't bother yourself about Elinore, darling. I keep telling you, she more or less looks after herself, thanks to my careful upbringing of her. Once we settle where she's going to be at school, she'll hardly ever be in the house. And when she can't be at school, why, you can help me learn all about summer camps and Easter camps and Christmas camps too, if they have such a thing in your wonderful country. So many exciting new things to learn about, Dwayne! I admit, sometimes it's a teeny-weeny bit scary. Remember, I was just a widow, living a quiet life with my child, and not even in little old Edinburgh as you call it . . ."

One thing that Melba had already learnt was how easily Dwayne's attention could be moved away from potential trouble spots and back onto herself, where it belonged.

At the Ina Blackadder School, Elinore was learning too.

First, she discovered that the pupils all around her were wearing navy skirts with box pleats, just like her own new navy skirt. She belonged.

Second, before, during and after the concert, she was either seated or standing next to that *grande dame* Lady Groule, apparently the most important woman in the room after the headmistress. By virtue of this proximity, people expected an introduction. "This is Miss Elinore Crum," Lady Groule would say on each such occasion, "who is new to Edinburgh and might be attending the school." This was such an intoxicating idea, and yet so completely out of the question without a genuine, first-class miracle, that Elinore could only let the lovely words be repeated without question or demur, and smile at the middle-aged and elderly ladies who told her how happy she would be there, just as they had been.

Elinore made her third discovery at the very end, after all the choral singing, the duets, the piano solos, the orchestral renderings of well-loved and frequently abused pieces, the poetry and drama recitals, and after she had clapped until her hands stung and the headmistress had made a rousing speech about the infinite potential of these young ladies, and the orderly rows of seating had dissolved into a hubbub of girls and their families. After all this, Elinore felt a tug on her sleeve and turned to find Usha, Mr and Mrs Patel and Susanna. Lady Groule and the elder Patels immediately began reviewing every highlight of the concert (that is to say, those parts in which Usha had figured). Usha herself was not interested in any of that: she was astonished to see Elinore. Giving her a little push, she said, "Elinore Crum, meet Susanna Berg. My two best friends!" She stood there beaming, as if she had done something very clever.

"Hello," said Elinore. "It's nice to meet you properly."

Susanna said nothing at all for a few seconds. Her eyes darted from Usha to Elinore and back to Usha. Elinore felt sudden alarm: what new form of judgement was this?

"Oh, Susanna, you're *silly!*" cried Usha. "You can't speak unless you open your *mouth*."

Susanna rolled her eyes, and finally spoke in a mumble. "It's all right for you. You don't have to wear these things. I keep biting my tongue and I don't even sound like me. I'm still *learning* to speak, so *there*."

Elinore had never seen so much metal in a person's mouth as the elaborate braces on Susanna's top and bottom teeth. She said the first thing that came to mind. "Golly – how can you eat? How can you clean your teeth?"

Susanna gave a huge sigh. "I'm actually *starving*. No Mars bars, no toffee, no dates, no crunchy biscuits. Same with lots of other food. I have to clean my teeth for *hours* every night, because stuff gets stuck in the wires even though Mummy just feeds me mush." She fiddled with her hair for a moment and then said to Elinore, "I've seen you already. At the hotel. Then you came past our house, but I couldn't say anything because I just got them put in and I couldn't speak properly. It was really, really embarrassing. Sorry for not saying hello to you. I really wanted to."

"Oh, that's – all right," said Elinore, who could scarcely believe that she was the object of this gracious apology.

Usha filled the space again. "Where's Daniel and your parents?" she asked Susanna.

"Oh, they couldn't come. They had to go to the Queen's party at Holyrood, and you can't take children there, so Daniel stayed with Fredy. He didn't want to come here anyway. And Fredy wanted to watch something on TV. She says it helps her English."

"Did your mother get a new dress for meeting the Queen? I want to see it!" Turning to Elinore, Usha continued, "You should see Mrs Berg's dresses – they are *sooo* beautiful! Like flowers. She always lets me see her new ones."

Susanna gave Usha a little shove. "You think everything nice is like flowers! You've got them on the brain. One day your head will turn into a *tulip* or something."

Usha giggled and shoved Susanna back. "No, I'll be a rose and you'll be a potato, 'cause you like eating them so much!"

Elinore still had no words. Blackadder girls were human like her but they clearly lived in a different universe. Their parents went to meet the Queen and they were entirely nonchalant about it. This occasion was turning into something out of *Dr Who*. Was George's taxi really a Tardis? Was Lady Groule an alien?

Then Susanna said, "You can see her dress tomorrow, but only if you bring Elinore over so we can do things. Can you come then?" she asked Elinore directly. "You can stay all day. Mummy says she might have to do some shopping. She does really boring shopping, but we can stay in the bookshop. The manager lets us because we do it all the time – Usha and me. Daniel sometimes comes too, but we don't have to bother about him. He just stays where the Corgi Toys are because he collects them. And Mummy *has* to get me a new book every single time! I don't use my pocket money – I make her buy them!" She grinned at Elinore, and her impossible braces caught the light, emphasising the likelihood of alien nature. Aliens who could *make* their mothers buy things for them – an incredible concept. "Do you like books?" Susanna asked her.

"Yes, she does," Usha answered for her. "And you've got to see what her friend Tom gave me when we went there. He's got a real library. But I don't want to carry anything to your house, so you have to come to mine first. We can all meet at my house first."

"Where do you live?" Susanna asked Elinore.

Crash! The parallel universe inhabited by Bergs and Blackadder girls collided with Elinore's own universe: the one ruled by Caltrops, where other girls were forbidden to visit. And she would never want Susanna to see her miserable bedroom anyway. In that moment, she understood that she was the alien. She had to throw this line of enquiry off. She must pretend that the other girls were like the foxhounds who ran across the Criven fields and hills, and who could quite easily go tearing away on a completely false scent that led the hunt nowhere it wanted to be and certainly not to any fox.

"Dunallan Crescent," she answered, quickly adding in the same breath, "Who are Daniel and Fredy?"

"Daniel's my brother – he's seven. He's really called Jonathan, but he hates it and he won't speak to you if you call him that. Fredy's the au pair. Her proper name is Frederikke with two Ks and she's from Denmark. I don't know how old she is. I don't think she's exactly *old* but she's got huge bosoms like old Miss Cartwright – doesn't she?" Susanna dug Usha in the ribs and the pair of them fell about in a laughing fit. Elinore waited, smiling in a sort of desperation, for she had no idea what an oh-pear was, and why it should come from Denmark, and she was *not* going to ask.

"But she's really, really nice, and she makes super food for us," continued Susanna. "So you *have* to stay all day tomorrow, for lunch and tea and everything. Promise?"

"Yes," said Elinore.

The after-concert socialising eventually wound up, and Elinore found herself on the street with Lady Groule, the Patels and Susanna, all ambling comfortably in the direction of MacAlpine Place. Only in Criven had she ever gone about in such a sociable group, and in that small place six children would count as a crowd. But this group included three grown-ups, and twice they overtook and stopped to chat with acquaintances of Lady Groule who had also been to the concert. Once again, Lady Groule introduced Elinore as someone who might soon belong to the Ina Blackadder School. This walking was most enjoyable, and such talking was still heady music to Elinore's ears, but the rest of her was growing nervous. Dunallan Crescent was still quite a way off, but Susanna's home was so close to it that with every turn of the street came the possibility that she might want to accompany Elinore all the way to No. 17. She seemed to be an easy, open-natured girl, which was very pleasant but also very difficult for Elinore.

The Patels insisted on walking Lady Groule home, which was a flat in a terraced house in a quiet street with a central garden surrounded by railings.

"Shall we have tea next week? You three gels are all on holiday now, so it shouldn't be too difficult. Wednesdays are out: that's my hairdressing day. Usha, you can be the lady-in-waiting in this instance and take care of the organising – I'll expect your call very soon."

When she was installed in her armchair, with her feet up and a nice drink in hand, Lady Groule picked up the telephone and rang Celia Chisholm. She recounted her brief experience of No. 17 Dunallan Crescent with relish.

"Caltrop," she said. "I don't know the name at all, do you? I'm convinced they feed that poor child psalms three times a day, and the house certainly goes with that sort of person – perfectly hideous and dreary. But it's a puzzle, because she's so well turned out. Those nice boots from *Jenners*, and perfectly neat and prim tonight, as was proper. But I don't want to unnerve her with quizzing. I can probe in subtle ways when she comes to tea." Lady Groule raised her glass and took a refreshing swallow. Celia was silent. "Celia, are you still there?"

"Yes," said Celia. "Just thinking. That name – Caltrop. No one I *know*, and I'm sure I didn't hear it from Alistair, but still . . . Just a minute." Celia put down the telephone and Lady Groule knew that she had gone to her husband's study, where Mr Chisholm would be poring over his stamp collection. When Celia picked up the telephone again, it was to say that Arthur had never heard the name of Caltrop before in social, medical or golfing circles. "But what about forenames?" she asked Lady Groule.

"Hmm . . . He said Kenneth, and – and . . . Oh dear." She took another swig. "Ruby or Rosamund or Rosa – something like that. Rubella. Yes, Rubella sounds right."

"No, no, that's a disease. You're not up to scratch tonight, Zinnia. What's in that glass of yours?"

"Oh, put it down to excitement. I haven't had a decent mystery to poke around in for ages, and it must be going to my head. I'll tell you that name as soon as I remember it, or as soon as I get it from the child herself."

At that moment, the child herself was being quizzed at another tea table, in ways that were far from subtle.

After escaping any immediate risk of Susanna's curiosity extending to No. 17 (simply because Susanna had announced that she was starving and must go straight home for a great big tea), Elinore had rung for admittance in the usual way. Mrs Caltrop opened the door. Her lips and teeth were arranged in that manner so evocative to Elinore of carnivores.

"Elinore. So, here you are then, after your concert. What a busy day you seem to have had. You can tell us all about it over tea."

Elinore was aware that Mrs Caltrop was striving to display whatever she understood to be niceness with a smile. This was disconcerting.

A place had been laid for her at the table, but not for Melba.

"Where's Mummy?"

"She will be dining out tonight. Now, here are fish fingers for you. You like those, don't you?"

Elinore saw two soggy fish fingers on her plate, and four on each of the Caltrops' plates. Not having eaten them before at No. 17, she had not been given the opportunity to indicate whether she liked them, and in any case her preferences were completely unimportant in the context of food. This sudden attention to them was more than disconcerting; it was alarming. Melba's absence bothered her too.

"*When* will Mummy be back?"

"Late. Very late, no doubt. But we would like to know about *your* social occasion. Do tell us what kind of concert it was."

"A school concert. I went to the Ina Blackadder School to see my friend – my *friends*. One of them is in the school choir."

Mrs Caltrop's eyes showed shock, disbelief and anger; her mouth contracted into the familiar pursing of disapproval. She stared at Elinore for a moment before speaking.

"I see. And who *invited* you to a school that you do not attend?"

Elinore stared back. She was not going to lie. "Mr Patel asked me to go with them, to see my friend Usha. And Lady Groule took me with her, after I – met her again. I met her before in Mr Patel's shop."

The social complexities thus revealed turned Mrs Caltrop's head into a pressure cooker. Her cheeks bloomed into carmine dahlias as she strove to keep hold of all manner of control.

"I see. Patel. The man who rang here. So you continue to associate with them, despite –" She checked herself and took another tack. "It strikes me that Lady Groule is not the kind of person to buy from such a place. I am very surprised. And, above all, I am surprised that she should want to know *you*."

"Mr Patel introduced me to her. She's Usha's godmother, sort of, I think." Elinore was not going to use the word "fairy" in front of Mrs Caltrop.

Mr Caltrop had been frowning and staring as Elinore spoke, and now he and his wife exchanged looks of disquiet.

"Elinore, I cannot separate fact from fancy in any of this. I *shall*, eventually, but for the moment I must know one thing. Why did you bring Lady Groule to this house?"

"Because I had to put on my good skirt and blouse. You have to dress properly if you're going to a concert or anywhere. Arabella said so. She told *you* that when she wanted a wardrobe for my clothes."

Mrs Caltrop could not argue with that, but clarity was still eluding her. "But you have not told me *why* she had to accompany you."

"Because we were going to be *late* if I had to run here and run back! We came in a taxi."

"Ah. You were at Lady Groule's house, and she kindly called here en route. I made it clear that you were never to bring people here without permission, and I *am* displeased about this, but Lady Groule is an exception and we can always make her properly welcome the next time she accompanies you home. You ought to ring first, you know. We shan't talk about visiting the Indians any more, but I am sure Lady Groule would let you use the telephone when you visit *her*. Now, will you have some bread and butter?" Mrs Caltrop's mouth rearranged itself again; she was still striving for mastery of these peculiar circumstances, still grasping for a leash that would yank these running dogs to heel.

Elinore was exasperated. These questions were stupid, Mrs Caltrop was stupid too, and having food thrust at her like this was so out of character that it was bizarre. She sensed that Mrs Caltrop wanted to know something more, but Elinore had supplied almost every detail except that of her fainting fit. "I wasn't *at* her house, and I wasn't at the Patels either, and we were in a big hurry. We were at another lady's house. She's called Mrs Celia Chisholm and she makes *super* sandwiches. She went to school with Lady Groule – they told me. They went to the Ina Blackadder School. I don't know any more about anything." Elinore scowled at Mrs Caltrop. She felt oddly safe in doing that, but nevertheless she had no intention of prolonging this nonsensical interrogation. "I'm going upstairs now."

She rose from the table and left the room as quickly as she could without running, not noticing, therefore, that Mrs Caltrop's mouth was still hanging open at this mention of an old girl from her own school. Neither did she hear the exchange that followed.

"Do you not know these ladies, Roberta, if you were at school with them?" enquired Mr Caltrop. "It might do no harm for us to know them too, since the child is already on good terms, it seems."

"Oh, be *quiet!*" snapped Mrs Caltrop. "Keep your ideas to yourself." One of the names mentioned by Elinore had brought an echo, not a pretty one, out of a place in her past. She silenced it by getting up and rushing into the kitchen.

Now Mr Caltrop's mouth fell open too, and his head swivelled as he looked around the tea table. The absence of the usual people in their usual chairs seemed to disorient him as much as his wife's uncharacteristic outburst.

Melba returned to No. 17 at an hour well before the Caltrops' bedtime. She had already decided to tell them about her little vacation, for it might do no harm to hint at an imminent permanent departure. The sooner she could leave, the less money she would have to fork out in those irksome *little contributions*.

When she opened the front door, she heard the sound of the wireless from the morning room. She marched in there and found Mr Caltrop ensconced in his armchair, alone and half asleep over his newspaper. He jumped in alarm when Melba said hello, and clutched the arms of his chair. Below his lower lip were two large brown smudges that Melba thought made him look ridiculous, if not mad. She would not broach any topic with him.

"Is Roberta in the kitchen, Mr C? I must have a chat with her."

"The poor woman is ill. She's taken to her bed."

"*What?* Is it contagious? I mustn't, *mustn't* catch anything. This is a *terribly* important week for me!" Melba's alarm was genuine.

"I can't say exactly what it is, but the doctor isn't needed. She calls it a migraine. We have to keep the house quiet and not have people coming and going until she feels better."

"Oh, thank goodness – a migraine is nothing at all. And I'm always quiet as a mouse, aren't I, and I never bring people in, do I?"

Mr Caltrop's lower lip shook, which made the brown smudges – it must be food, thought Melba – even more noticeable, and he looked distressed as he replied.

"But the child is bringing people here – most unexpected characters! She is entering into social circles the like of which we cannot fathom."

"People? Really? Oh, I shouldn't bother about it, Mr C. She *is* quite independent, you know. If she's making friends, it's a good thing, because other people will feed her now and then. I'm sure Roberta will see the practicality of letting her form her own little circle of playmates. I'm off to bed now. Goodnight, Mr C!"

"But – but these people are not – one does not *play* with a titled lady. And then there are *the others*. We are greatly vexed. I assure you, Elinore will find proper playmates only at Sunday school. We must enfold her in the care of the Kirk without delay!"

Melba was gone from the room before the words "titled lady" had come out; they might have halted her. On the other hand, they might not, given her near complete absence of interest in Elinore's doings unless they immediately affected her. Not until she was upstairs did the existence of playmates for Elinore suddenly present itself as something that could be managed so that it affected her in useful ways. She must talk to Dwayne as soon as possible. Damn! If only the men in white coats would hurry up and invent phones that people could use under the bedclothes. Phones with a sort of silent ring so that no one else – especially mangy old complainers with migraines – would ever know when conspiracy was afoot.

14

It is Saturday morning. At breakfast tables all over Edinburgh, plans for the enjoyment of a second consecutive fine day are being aired and stitched together. Everyone looks woeful and voices the same warning: we must make the most of this, it'll be gone tomorrow, you know; aye, that's right. Embedded in the local DNA (at least since the 1550s) is the acceptance that fair weather will inevitably be followed by foul. The greater the pleasure taken under clement skies, the swifter and more dismal the retribution.

At No. 17, Elinore has turned the *Annunciation* the right way around in acknowledgement of Sir Gabriel's possible hand in the provision of good omens for her tenth year. She is wondering how the Queen, in her palace down the road, will spend this summer day after eating her porridge and walking corgis in the park. Elinore has seen pictures of Holyroodhouse, which is open to the public when the Queen is elsewhere. It looks unusually accessible for a palace, nestled in its trees and lawns below Arthur's Seat, which anyone can climb for a view of a royal residence, and neighbour to ordinary streets lined by houses of all sizes and kinds of ownership. Elinore very much wishes that she could visit this palace, and even more that she could *see* the Queen herself, who for once is so dizzyingly close. But today she will visit Susanna, whose parents were promenading at a royal garden party only yesterday. It is the next best thing under the circumstances, and exciting enough on its own.

First, though, she is going to Usha's house. Into her Oriental bag go all essentials: the list of problem words to show Usha; her pocket-money purse; a new Biro; a handkerchief; and some pieces of paper for important things like telephone numbers. She has got through another breakfast at the Caltrop table and is wearing the right clothes for the day. The blood of John Knox does not flow in her veins, and she is ready and eager for whatever good and interesting things might fall from the sunny skies. In answer to certain questions, she has told a big fib about settling down with her paint set, and consequently she manages to run out of the house before anyone can detain her.

Elinore had never before been in a home that revolved around the life of one child. She saw the pride in Mr and Mrs Patel, because that was on the surface, but not the depth of hope and carefully concealed parental anxieties that were forming a kind of cargo for that child to carry for the rest of her life. As Usha's friend, Elinore was immediately elevated and enveloped by eager attention. It was disconcerting at first, and she felt shy. Attention, especially the coddling kind, had not figured in her life, and attention these days mostly came from the Caltrops and always for the wrong reasons. When she arrived at the shop, Mr Patel put a "Closed for 5 minutes" sign on the door and swept her upstairs as if she were a personage from Holyroodhouse. Mrs Patel plied her with water, orange squash and Ribena in case she was dehydrated, and biscuits, two kinds, in case she was famished. Elinore was surprised that her walking around should cause so much concern for her wellbeing, but happy to let the sweet tastes erase the memory of breakfast. The Patels thanked her again for joining them at the concert and recapped all the highlights. Then Mr Patel returned to his counter and Mrs Patel resumed her cooking and cleaning. Elinore saw that she was hardly shy at all in her own home.

This home was a compact flat: a small, narrow kitchen, a bathroom, a sitting room, two bedrooms, a broom cupboard or two, and an L-shaped hallway. The ceilings were high, however, and the sash windows just as large as those at No. 17. Usha's room had pale blue floral wallpaper and net curtains edged with a deep frill. A pink bedspread covered the divan bed, piled with cushions in varied colours and patterns, but mostly floral. On top of the cushions lay a plump teddy bear, wearing a blue velvet bow tie; on the bedside table was a little terracotta pot from which sprouted a few inches of greenery.

Usha made introductions. "This is Blue Peter" – the bear – "and that's Lily" – the plant. "She isn't a lily, she's an orange pip that I grew by myself, but I like the name Lily. And I called him Blue Peter because of *Blue Peter* on the TV, and he came with that tie, so I think he needs a blue name. Do you watch *Blue Peter* too?"

Elinore was too occupied in looking around at another girl's bedroom to answer. They were side by side on the bed, which was against one long wall of the room, because they had nowhere else to sit. A desk took up most of the opposite wall, a real one with drawers on both sides and a kneehole, into which was pushed a chair with three cushions stacked on the seat. This left mere inches between bed and desk. To the left of the desk was a small wardrobe. Above the desk was a long shelf nearly filled with books. Elinore envied this set-up. It was so cosy. If she had such a desk, she would sit there from dawn to dusk on rainy days, absorbed in endless projects. More books stood neatly on the desk between hefty bookends sculpted to look like owls in a pale, banded stone. Elinore coveted them instantly, and got up from the bed to stroke their rounded heads. The stone was smooth and cool.

"I *love* your owls. I wish I had proper bookends like that."

"They're from Lady Groule, for my birthday this year. They're made of onyx, and they belonged to her husband. He's dead, but he used to be important. She said she doesn't like any birds unless they're dead on a dinner plate. She's funny sometimes." Usha giggled and sprawled on the bed, hugging Blue Peter. "When's your birthday?"

Elinore was busy admiring and touching the Anglepoise lamp on the desk – you could bend it right over your books! – and she didn't catch the question.

"What?"

"Your birthday – when is it? Mine's on the 10th of March and guess what, Susanna's is on the 6th. We're almost twins, and we always have a great big party together at her house."

"I just had my birthday. It's on June the 30th."

"Gosh! That's only – the day before yesterday. You never *told* us. Why not?" Usha sounded puzzled and aggrieved.

Elinore was puzzled too. "Why would I tell anyone?"

"So we could do nice things for you, silly. A birthday is a special day. Everyone has to be very good to you all day long. It's what my Mummy and Daddy say, so it's the rule." She laughed again. "Did you get nice presents?"

"I got this bag from Mummy." She was still reluctant to admit to Arabella's birthday shopping spree as responsible for everything she wore. "And Arabella took Mummy and me out to a hotel, and when we went to see Tom, that was a treat from her. And then she and Tom sent me 10-shilling notes for pocket money."

Usha shrieked and bounced off the bed. "*I forgot!* The present from Tom. I keep it safe in here." She pulled open the deepest desk drawer and took out a large, red velvet-wrapped rectangular object. "I got Mummy to give me this cushion cover to keep it in, in case the corners get bashed. Looooook! I'm going to learn every single plant by heart."

"It" comprised three weighty books, companion volumes by a Reginald Nutbeam: *Wild Flora of Field and Forest*, *Wild Flora of Heath and Headland* and *Wild Flora of Moor and Marsh*. "There are beautiful pictures all the way through and they've got a surprise in them. You have to look extra-super carefully and see if you can find it – no, actually you *don't*, because it's right in front of your nose."

"But there's loads and loads of pictures. Do I have to look at every single one? Do I get a clue?"

"No! You don't get any clues and you don't need them anyway, 'cause you've already seen the surprise. You could just look at one picture and see it right away. I'm not telling you a single thing. That's too easy."

"But that's not fair! You know all about plants and things and I only know some things."

"The surprise isn't *about* plants, silly. Go on, look! It's easy-peasy." Usha sat on the edge of the bed, grinning and bouncing in excitement. Her hand was nowhere near her mouth. Elinore thought it was funny how her shy friend could be so vivacious amid familiarity; she might even turn out to be a bossy-boots. She would probably be a teacher one day.

Just then, Susanna appeared in the doorway, and Usha shrieked again. "Look! I'm showing Elinore the present I got from her friend Tom. Come and see." The three of them sat on the bed, backs against cushions ranged along the wall, legs stuck out straight in front. Elinore liked this position for two reasons: it was lovely and comfortable, and it allowed her to admire another pair of her new socks (no one wore outdoor shoes in the Patel flat) and be glad about them. How easy and simple it was to join in when you didn't have to worry about things like holes in your socks.

"We have to go to my house soon," Susanna told them. "We're going to get our hair cut – Daniel and me – and Mummy says you can go too, but we mustn't be late for lunch."

"We can't go until Elinore finds the surprise," said Usha.

"Can I look for it too?" asked Susanna.

"You won't know what to look for, but Elinore does, she saw it already. Oh, no! I let out a clue. You've *got* to get it now." Usha dug Elinore in the ribs.

Elinore began to scrutinise the frontispiece of one book, dividing it into imaginary quadrants as if she were playing a game of Spot the Difference. When she got to the lower right corner of the lower right quadrant, she whooped in recognition of the artist's signature: Quentin Greenlees.

"It's the man who painted the magic bathroom! It's the brother of the governess – isn't it? I remember his name because it had a colour in it."

"*Yes!*" shouted Usha, clapping her hands.

"What are you going on about?" asked Susanna, screwing up her face. "*What* magic bathroom? That's crazy."

They told her the story, and Susanna said that she wanted to see the magic bathroom for herself and all the other wonders of Squair that Usha had already described to her. "Do you think I could go there with you some time?" she asked Elinore. "I like old places a lot."

Elinore swelled inside with the sheer warmth of acceptance. *This* was magic. One minute she had been standing on the street, beyond the pale of Susanna's world, looking different in all the wrong ways; the next minute, Susanna herself was asking a favour of her – a favour that only Elinore could grant.

"Oh, yes," said Elinore. "Let's all go together. I think Tom would be really pleased. He kept saying he was sad because no one went to visit him. And he likes showing off all the old things in his house. It's like a museum."

She had no idea how this visit could be accomplished, but she decided to ask Tom and Arabella about it. And Sir Gabriel, for good measure: no Basildon Bond or postage required there.

Then they got off the bed, put Mr Nutbeam's great works back into the cushion cover and set off for Susanna's house. Usha asked Elinore what Tom had given her, and Elinore promised to bring her own presents next time. She had forgotten all about sharing the excitement of the lovely things, but no matter: "next time" was already being arranged and that was wonderful to contemplate.

"I brought something else, though," she told Usha. "Tom sent me a letter and I don't know some of the words because they aren't English. Maybe you could help me with them."

"He sent me a letter too. Mummy and Daddy read it. They said he was a great gentleman. I just think he's funny. And Arabella's funny too. You're lucky. I don't have any funny aunts and uncles."

Susanna said she definitely wanted to meet Tom and Arabella if they were funny. "I like funny people. As long as they're just funny-ha-ha and not funny-peculiar. That's scary."

"Lady Groule is definitely funny," said Usha. "She always makes Daddy laugh. She wants us to go to tea next week, remember. I have to tell her when. So, when are we going? She said not Wednesday and I can't go tomorrow because I have tutoring."

"Let's go on Tuesday. Daddy's taking Daniel and me swimming on Monday. He promised! Do you like swimming, Elinore?"

"I don't know how to swim. But I like rivers, and I really want to go to the seaside."

At the Berg house, they went around to the rear because, Susanna told them, Mrs Berg was in the middle of painting the front vestibule. A small boy shot out of the back door, waving a model car in either hand and making zooming noises, which he did not interrupt for one second while eyeing the three girls, especially Elinore. He ran off across the garden, which was larger than the Caltrop's and nothing at all like that place of regimented growth, and disappeared into a shrubbery.

"That's Daniel," Susanna said, otherwise ignoring him.

The kitchen was a big, bright room with a pine table in the middle, and another table, six chairs and a huge sideboard at one end. A girl was standing at the counter by the sink, chopping vegetables. Her short hair was so fair it was almost white, and she was the tallest girl, or woman, that Elinore had ever seen.

"Hi, Fredy, this is Elinore. She's my new best friend. Are we going to have lunch now? I'm *quite* hungry. And Usha and Elinore are staying for lunch too. Elinore, this is Frederikke from Denmark, but everyone calls her Fredy."

"Hello, Elinore, I'm pleased to meet you, and hello to you too, Usha," said Fredy. Her eyes were very blue in her tanned face, and she wore a striped T-shirt and bellbottom jeans. Elinore thought she looked amazing, like a model in Melba's fashion magazines. "You are having chicken risotto for lunch. Come back in twenty minutes, OK?"

Susanna wrinkled her nose. "Oh, phooey!" she said. "We had that last night."

"That's why you are having it for lunch today," Fredy told her. "I made a lot of it because your mother said you might bring friends to eat here." Elinore still had no idea what an oh-pear was, but this one had a lovely accent. She wished she could walk into this kitchen at the end of every day.

"Phooey!" said Susanna again. "Elinore, do you like risotto?"

"*Phooey?* Sounds like another of those words you found in a comic, Susanna." A mild voice made them turn around. "Hello, Usha, how are you?" A smiling woman in jeans and a man's shirt, brown-haired like Susanna, held out her hand to Elinore. "Hello, I don't think we've met before. I'm Susanna's mother. Are you at school with her?"

"This is Elinore Crum and she doesn't go to our school," butted in Susanna. "But she's my new best friend, and Usha's, and we're all going to stay here for the whole day, for tea too."

"That's just fine, but be ready for lunch, hands washed, at the table. You've got to jump in the car straight after that – haircuts, remember? We're going to be on time, *this* time! Elinore, do your parents know you're here? If I'm taking you around the town, I think I should tell them, especially since they don't know me at all. What's your phone number?"

Elinore froze. Worlds were colliding again. She did not want the Caltrops intruding on her glorious day even marginally, and if Mrs Caltrop were feeling particularly evil a telephone call might turn out horribly. She might offend Mrs Berg, who would then eject Elinore from her home immediately.

"Um – my mother's at work. It's called Grisella's Gowns, but I don't know the phone number."

"Oh, not to worry, I'll look it up."

One part of Elinore wanted to hover by Mrs Berg while she rang Melba; the other part wanted to shut out all connection with the world of No. 17 Dunallan Crescent. Susanna eliminated choice by rushing her upstairs. "Come and see my room!"

Elinore knew envy was a bad, traitorous feeling, but she could not resist the tide that swept over her on entering a square room, as large as Melba's, painted pale yellow. The ceiling was white, the doors and woodwork were white, and the sun poured through an undefended window where looped-back curtains shouted gleefully in a language of giant yellow, blue and green poppies. Prints of stylised animals hung in rows on the walls. Two twin beds each had their own side table and lamp, and were covered in white bedspreads edged in the same fabric as the curtains. Between the beds was a little bookcase. Another, much bigger one, stuffed with books, stood by the window, close to a wicker chair. Cushions of all sizes, some as long as Elinore, were piled on the floor around the chair, and *Princess Tina* comics overflowed from a wooden greengrocer's box. Another box held a mess of *National Geographic* and other glossy magazines. Susanna had a desk in white-painted wood like the other pieces in the room, and an Anglepoise lamp too, and a big dictionary. Clearly, Usha and Susanna faced the same expectations when it came to homework.

They flopped onto the cushions by the window and looked at Susanna's newest book, an illustrated history of fashion. "Granny and Grandpa Silber gave me a book token for my birthday, but I lost it for ages, and I didn't get it back until Fredy moved my desk when she was vacuuming, so I just got the book now. I haven't read it all yet. I think I'm going to be a fashion designer when I grow up."

"But you keep saying you're going to paint pictures like your mother does," said Usha.

"Well, maybe I could do both. Elinore, what are you going to be?"

Elinore's eyes were skittering around the fascinations of this heavenly room. She had not been paying much attention to Susanna's new book or to what the others were saying.

"What?"

"What are you going to be when you grow up?"

No one had ever troubled to ask Elinore this before. The closest that she had come to the question was her statement that she would like to do Arabella's job. But Arabella's job was beyond Elinore's powers of description at that moment.

"Well . . . I don't know yet. I like painting and drawing, and reading. I'd like to make houses with lots of lovely rooms in them."

"Elinore just had her birthday," said Usha. "It was the day before yesterday and she never told me."

"Didn't you have a party or anything?" asked Susanna, surprised. "Usha and I have a huge party, because our birthdays are almost together and we have the same friends at school. We have *two* cakes! And guess what, this year we had special *Danish* ones! With fruit on top. Fredy made them. They were super-duper."

"And she sang the birthday song from Denmark," reminded Usha. "I know! Let's ask her to sing it for Elinore."

"Yes, and maybe we could have another party for Elinore. I *love* parties!"

"Me too. I want to wear my party dress again before I get too big for it. Mummy says I'm going to split the seams soon."

Susanna spread her hands wide and made a ripping noise. "Ha-ha, you're going to pop out of it like a big baby out of a mummy's tummy. It might happen at a *party!* With *boys* there!" She and Usha screamed at this notion and fell about on the cushions, laughing their heads off.

Elinore sat upright, silent in a welter of feelings. Part of her felt as though it were locked away in the Caltrops' house, a world that was incommunicable to these girls; another part felt as though she had escaped that world and miraculously joined this one, never to return to No. 17. Knots of dichotomy began to tie themselves and tighten in her tummy. She stared at the weave of her new denims. Her lovely new clothes had got her this far, which was a considerable distance, but neither they nor Miss Agnes Pound's *Book of Charm & Essential Etiquette* offered instructions for correct behaviour in the face of open doors and generosity that she could never reciprocate.

The bedroom door opened and Daniel marched in to stand over them. "You have to come down right now or you won't get any food!"

"Go away, you can't come in here!" yelled Susanna.

"Yes, I can, if Mummy tells me and she did *so* tell me." He stuck out his tongue and made a rude noise at Susanna before running out.

"He's a pest, he *wrecks* my room. He's Dennis the Menace! Do you like the *Beano*, Elinore? You can have all my old copies if you want. Mummy says I can't keep huge piles of paper in my room, and Usha doesn't want them."

"No, I don't, 'cause I can read comics for free," chortled Usha.

Elinore sat in the front seat of Mrs Berg's car. When they found out that she had seen next to nothing of Edinburgh, everyone said she must sit there for the best view and Mrs Berg would tell her the names of places. It also enabled Mrs Berg to ask Elinore questions about her life and present home: quiet, careful questions not heard by Susanna, Usha and Daniel as they giggled and squabbled on the back seat. It was hard to evade Mrs Berg's sharp attention, Elinore realised; a little bit of Arabella was in this woman. But she seemed to be a very nice mother, and so Elinore decided to open her mouth somewhat about No. 17 and life in general. Besides, after two generous helpings of that delicious thing called risotto, full of chicken chunks, she was feeling more relaxed. In the absence of Arabella and secret pudding from the Balmerinoch, she was hungrier every day now. It seemed to make her more nervous and Agent Solo's activities more irregular and cautious.

Elinore had never been in a hairdressing salon before. Criven did not possess one, and Melba did not feel it was necessary to pay a hairdresser to do for Elinore what she could do with kitchen scissors. Elinore had grown up in the belief that those born with gleaming blonde helmets or tumbling, silky tresses *must* go to hairdressers, just as babies needed milk and she must go to school, and that this did not apply to people with strong, untidy, unpretty hair like hers. Mrs Berg did not know about this belief, but within half an hour she had managed to obliterate it.

Salon Z was all things to all heads of hair. It gave the blue-rinsed ladies exactly what they expected, week in, week out; it also gave the hip, the cool and the trendy exactly what they craved, those visions that veered this way and that according to decree by arbiters of youthful fashion. Mrs Berg was none of those things, but she had been a client of Mr Zuccarelli's from well before his epiphany about the need for all-inclusive hairstyling and the resulting transformation of his establishment. She saw no reason to change, especially since prices had remained reasonable and children's heads were surprisingly well cared for here. Mr Zuccarelli's philosophy was simple: treat every small, white-caped figure in the chair exactly like an adult regardless of age (minus the usual therapeutic and confessional conversation service offered by all hairdressers worth their salt) and thus keep pace with their sense of self-importance as it matures into the adult kind. Mr Zuccarelli possessed no self-importance and endless cheerfulness. He adored a challenge. No clients removed themselves from Mr Zuccarelli's care unless they died or moved to London.

When the Bergs entered, a commotion of welcome ensued. Usha was no stranger either, having accompanied Susanna and Jonny on several previous occasions. After the usual jokes about cutting the long, glossy black plait that she had no intention of shortening, she sat down in the reception area and delved into the magazines scattered around while Susanna and Daniel were led to the basins. Elinore's attention was drawn to the framed black and white photographs of famous heads, lovely or handsome, arranged on the walls. There was Audrey Hepburn – she knew *that* face and hair. And there was a much younger Audrey Hepburn, with a fringe, and there was the fringe again, in three different iterations. There was a blonde with huge, panda eyes and a sort of half fringe. Elinore stood and looked, cocking her head, considering, wishing. Her hair was always a problem and sometimes an embarrassment. She would swap heads with Usha or Susanna in a heartbeat. Arabella had not mentioned this problem during the Cinderella shopping trip, let alone presented a solution; therefore, Elinore concluded, the solution must not exist, or at least not in the present. She might start wearing hats, pretty or trendy, when she was a teenager.

"You would look wonderful in a fringe, dear," an unfamiliar voice said softly behind her. Elinore turned to find a lady smiling at her. "Remember, your hair is part of the house where you keep all your dreams. You have lots of dreams, don't you? And hair is like clothes – your clothes are charming, by the way" – she made a sweeping gesture with one hand – "and clothes tell stories about us to the whole world. Why don't you give yourself a fringe, dear? It could make life quite extraordinarily *exciting* for you!"

"Here's your change, Mrs Marlock," said the girl behind the reception desk. "And would you like to make another appointment before you go?"

"I think I'll wait a little, thank you. Life has been quite unpredictable lately and I hate cancelling at the last moment. Goodbye for now!"

Mrs Berg overheard this advice and saw its effect on Elinore, who had turned to study the fringed beauties again. Mrs Berg's mildness was deceptive. It concealed an irrepressible spontaneity and energy for creating and beautifying. She might stay up until after midnight three nights in a row to start or finish a painting, and then get up at four o'clock on the following summer morning because inspiration was also prodding her to paint the vestibule the colour of ripe apricots. Life was short: why wait to get started on anything? She was also a mother and a doctor's wife, and her brief conversation with Melba Crum had done nothing to dispel her sense that something was amiss in the care of Elinore. She needed cheering up for a start! And what on earth was that Melba using on the child's hair?

"Elinore, *I* think a fringe would be just perfect on you too. How about it? Usha, don't you think Elinore would look smashing with a fringe like that?"

"Yes! Go on, Elinore. Then you'd look nice for your birthday party."

"Oh, when's your birthday?" asked Mrs Berg.

"I had it already," said Elinore.

"Yes, but you didn't have a party," said Usha. "Mrs Berg, Elinore never told us she had a birthday. It was the day before yesterday. Susanna and I want to have a party for her."

Mrs Berg had heard enough. "Fine! The party starts right now. Come on, Elinore." Elinore stood rooted to the spot in disbelief and uncertainty: all this *attention* from people she had barely met. Mrs Berg took her by the hand and led her firmly to Mr Zuccarelli. She knew he adored a challenge.

First came a discussion, primarily between Mrs Berg and Mr Zuccarelli, since Elinore was too unpractised in expressing her own preferences to contribute more than "Yes" and "I *think* so" a few times. Susanna added excited, encouraging interjections as soon as she saw what was going on. Then came washing by an apprentice with firm hands: head back over the basin, shampoo smelling of oranges and lemons, something called conditioner smelling of flowers, head swathed in a towel as if she were turbaned. A white cape was placed over her with a flourish, so that Elinore, Susanna and Jonny were equals as they sat in a row at the back of the salon. Elinore felt excitement displacing her earlier feelings. Daniel, seated next to her, surprised her by speaking directly to her. "I don't like all the water on my head", he said, which explained the spray bottle in the hands of the young man cutting his hair.

Next came Mr Zuccarelli, ready to treat this new client like junior royalty. He waved his scissors and comb, his moustache quivered and his eyes shone at the prospect of transforming Elinore Crum. He looked every inch the archetypal Italian maestro of ladies' hairstyling, although he had been born only as far away as Haddington (his father, a former prisoner of war who had married and remained in Scotland, was the real thing). Snip, snip, snip. Elinore's hair began to fall, some of it on her face, but she dared not move a muscle. She thought of pictures of the Queen at her coronation, also in a white robe, and holding heavy, precious things in each hand while men of the church made her into a proper queen. What if the Queen had had a terrible itch on her nose just then? What if her scalp had prickled? What if she had had a sneezing fit? How would a massive crown stay on her head then, if she couldn't use her hands? What a thought.

Finally, Mr Zuccarelli waved a hairdryer over her head, but only briefly. What good was his mastery if a young girl could not make her own hair look presentable with no more than a brush and comb? And that was what Elinore desperately wanted to know as she stared at an entirely new head in the mirror. Her hair was smooth and soft to the touch all over. It was fab, super, super-duper, amazing, marvellous, absolutely lovely, said everyone. It is a miracle, said Elinore to herself.

"Many happy returns, Elinore!" said Mrs Berg. "A new you for a new year of your life." She clapped.

"Happy birthday to you, happy birthday to you," Susanna began to sing. The whole salon joined in and cheered at the end. Elinore was still sitting in her chair in front of the mirror, and she could see herself blushing. It was all so wonderful that it was almost frightening, because it made her want to cry, and she could not understand this.

"I wish I had my camera," said Mrs Berg. Mr Zuccarelli rushed to the reception desk and returned with a Polaroid camera. He took and printed two photographs, one for Mrs Berg and one for Elinore. On the way out, Mrs Berg had final, murmured words with Mr Zuccarelli. Yes, *of course*, if the young lady happened to appear with Susanna and Daniel in future, in the care of Frederikke the *au pair*, her haircut would be included in the bill sent to Mrs Berg.

"Here are your birthday presents from all of us Bergs, Elinore," said Mrs Berg, handing her a paper bag with Salon Zuccarelli printed on it. Inside were bottles of shampoo and conditioner, a bright yellow plastic hairbrush and a matching comb with wide teeth. "Ask me what you do with them when we get home."

"Thank you very, very much indeed," said Elinore, tormented as usual by the inadequacy of her words. It was an Arabella day all over again.

Mrs Berg still had to do her boring shopping.

"What are you getting?" asked Susanna.

"Handkerchiefs and navy blue socks for your father, cotton wool, calamine lotion, yellow thread and some haddock," replied Mrs Berg.

"See? I said it was always boring shopping," Susanna told Elinore. "But we're going to look at books!"

Elinore was overjoyed, especially when she found that the bookshop also had a large stationery department. With her pocket money, she bought a spiral-bound notebook and a real address book with alphabetic tabs. The shelves and shelves of books were so tantalising and engrossing that Mrs Berg returned far too soon for her liking. Oh, the *smell* of all those crisp new books . . .

Susanna argued with her mother over a purchase.

"I can't decide, so I'll just have to get both."

"Sorry, that's not on, Susanna. One book only or wait and think about it until next time. Or use your own pocket money."

"But *why* –"

"No arguments! Make up your mind while I go and drag Daniel away from his wee cars."

Mrs Berg is very good about laying down the law, thought Elinore, because she doesn't get red in the face or start yelling. It made the idea of creeping into the Berg family even more attractive.

"Will Daddy be home for tea?" asked Susanna when they were all in the car again. "I want Elinore to meet him."

"Yes, he will, if no one falls down dead or has a heart attack." Mrs Berg did not believe in sparing her children the fact of death's tendency to arrive with no warning, as unpredictable as Dr Berg's working hours.

"Does he have to drive around a lot to see sick people?" asked Elinore. She was thinking of Dr Elliott in Criven, a man who never seemed to sleep. He drove for miles and miles through the hills to farms and cottages, at all hours, in all weathers. His surgery comprised a couple of rooms in the house he had lived in for the past forty years. Elinore tried to imagine Dr Elliott running up and down the towers near Aikenhead Primary School, and failed; he was too old. With so many houses and towers, Edinburgh must have thousands and thousands of middling-young doctors.

"No, he just drives to the hospital," replied Susanna. "He mends people's hearts there. But he can mend lots of other bits too."

Elinore sat stroking her amazing new hair, wondering what it must be like to have a heart that needed mending. People were always dying of broken hearts in stories. Mrs Berg watched her from the corner of her eye, and decided that her husband's profession was entirely ignorant of certain heart-related ailments.

15

Melba Crum, who knows nothing at all about Dallas, Texas that has not dropped from Dwayne McMonagle's lips, has already transplanted herself there in all ways but the corporeal. Her beautiful face and body give dwindling, lacklustre attention to Grisella's customers. In their girdles, corsets and solidly constructed, full-coverage brassieres, they stand plaintively before her in fitting rooms, dithering between gowns that offer glamour and those that will do just fine for a fancy occasion but are not too – well, you know, *showy*. It would not do to look like a plate of fish on that fancy occasion, and maybe catch the eye of the photographer from *Scottish Field* in a manner never intended by the woman inside the dress.

In Melba's mind's eye, Dallas is awash with glamour. It has to be: it is in America. She is counting days and hours until she steps off the plane at the North Texas Regional Airport and plunges unhesitatingly, in a baptismal manner, into whatever rites of conversion in becoming American are presented to her. It is Saturday afternoon. Today no longer counts in this waiting and counting, especially at four o'clock and with the happy prospect of some suitcase packing this evening. (Another Saturday night out with Dwayne would have been happier, but he is in a hotel bar somewhere on a business associates' night out, which qualifies as unavoidable work.) That leaves a mere two days until she departs very early from Waverley Station on Tuesday 5th of July, for London and Heathrow Airport.

Grisella is not pleased that her new salesgirl is about to vanish for two weeks, and she suspects what Melba already takes for granted: that Melba's return to Edinburgh will be as brief as possible and unlikely to include hours spent in Grisella's shop. On the other hand, Melba goes about in a dwalm all day now. No more enthusiasm for turning gowns into groats! Grisella regrets this change, for lately plenty of customers have suddenly found themselves walking out of the shop with the very bit of expensive glamour, tissue-wrapped in a bag, that they would have eschewed without benefit of Melba's fits of enthusiasm. Grisella's Gowns does not accept returns and will only exchange for a different size of the same item within two days, and so Melba's attentions can be profitable. And she is showy, in just the right way for a dress shop. Grisella sighs, and over in a corner Melba sighs too. She is thinking of Elinore, and how best to persuade the Caltrops that being responsible for the child over two whole weeks during school holidays would be a very small thing, really. After all, Elinore was so besotted with her books and paints, so *independent* – why did she have to keep reminding people of that when it was so *obvious*? – that it was hard to think of any possible problem. And now Elinore spends time with friends, apparently, which means everyone has even less of Elinore to bother about.

When Melba returned to Dunallan Crescent that evening, it appeared that the Caltrops might hold different views on this subject. She had barely removed her key from the lock when Mrs Caltrop charged through the hall to inform her that the child had been gone the whole day, leaving no word of her whereabouts, and were Kenneth and she supposed to be responsible for any mishap?

"Oh, terribly sorry, Mrs C, it's all my fault!" trilled Melba. (How odd those last three words sounded to her own ears: she simply could not recall ever having uttered them before.) "A woman rang me and we were so rushed that I completely forgot to tell you. She's been out with a friend all day long."

"Friend? What woman?" demanded Mrs Caltrop, craving anything that she might work into an excuse for initiating contact with Lady Groule.

"The friend's mother. I forget the name, but I think it began with a P." Mrs Caltrop tutted in disappointment and irritation. "No, it was a B – yes, Burke. Or something like that. Mrs Burke. They live around the corner, do you know them? She said Elinore was going to go out with them and stay for lunch and tea."

"But why would this Mrs Burke not call me? *I* am the one who puts a square meal in front of the child three times a day."

Melba stared at Mrs Caltrop, trying to discern the logic in this. And I'm the one who pays your *little contributions*, you horrid old cow, she thought.

"I cannot have food going to waste because the child will not remember her responsibilities," insisted Mrs Caltrop.

"I *quite* understand, Mrs C, but Elinore thinks *I'm* responsible for giving her permission to stay out because I'm her mother. You see, if she knew that you were really her *guardian*, which is just the same thing, isn't it, she would tell the other mothers to ring you, wouldn't she, and that's just what I've been wanting to talk to you about, only you were in bed with a headache and I couldn't possibly have disturbed you then, could I?"

"Guardian?" Mrs Caltrop's head went up and her nostrils flared at the scent of control.

"Guardians – Mr Caltrop too, of course, under the circumstances. Now let's sit down and have a little talk, shall we?"

Very soon, Melba was congratulating herself. It was remarkable how easily the Caltrops (or rather, Mrs Caltrop, since her husband was a mere cypher, a nought in the sum of No. 17) had swallowed the prospect of a fortnight's sole responsibility for Elinore, how keen they were to be her guardians – yes, she could tell they *liked* that word. They appreciated the benefits of not only allowing but encouraging Elinore to run around with friends whose mothers were happy to feed another child and keep it under watch all day long. She could hardly wait to tell Dwayne! The first part of her plan had gone swimmingly: her brilliant plan of leaving Elinore in Edinburgh indefinitely, with the Caltrops. A fortnight was just practising for the future. Oh, she was so darned clever, just as Dwayne kept telling her! And because he was such a terribly important businessman, an *executive*, he would instantly recognise and applaud her wisdom in saving on boarding school fees. Elinore could simply carry on at whatever school she was already attending.

Melba's wide blue eyes were blind, of course, to the ways in which the admirable conveniences of her abandoning were dovetailing with Roberta Caltrop's aspirations, thwarted as these had been by the loss in 1947 of her previous habitat and elevated status. She was blind to Mrs Caltrop's relish for the divine task of rescuing a child from perdition in two weeks flat and the ensuing admiration of the whole church. This unexpected responsibility was more than acceptable: it was sweet, like the Caltrops' bedtime chocolates and other unguessed-at treats.

When Elinore returned to No. 17 later, the state of accord between Melba and Mrs Caltrop brought out a strangely pacific attitude towards her. She was ready to be reprimanded for running out in the morning; it did not happen. Mrs Caltrop was clearly trying to interrogate her while being nice about it. Although Elinore had escaped another tasteless, off-putting meal at the Caltrop table, thanks to a scrumptious one at Susanna's, she was surprised to be invited to sit down and tell everyone about her doings while they poured tea.

"How near is the Burke's house?" asked Mrs Caltrop, already calculating the advantage of a neighbourhood lunch and tea service for the child.

"They aren't the Burkes, they're the Bergs," replied Elinore. "B, E, R, G."

This stimulated Mr Caltrop into speech. "And what kind of a name is that? They must be from some other part of the world."

"No, they aren't from anywhere, they're just Scottish. They have two grannies and a grandpa here."

"And what does the father do for a living?"

"He's a doctor in a hospital."

"Well, that is very good to know," said Mrs Caltrop, heartened by this respectability. She had feared more of the shopkeeper caste or similar.

After a few more minutes, Elinore had had enough of being questioned about her day. From experience, she did not expect Melba to show any interest in the people with whom she had spent it, but turning up with a wonderful new haircut surely deserved some glancing acknowledgement.

"Mummy, do you like my new hair? You haven't said anything."

"Hair? Yes, super, I can't think why you never wanted it cut properly like that before. But then, little girls always want to look like their friends, don't they, and now you're so at home here, you've got a whole *street* of friends to copy, it seems!" The grown-ups laughed at this. Elinore was baffled.

"But I've only got two friends and their hair is different from mine," she protested. "Well, maybe I've got more than two, but Lady Groule's hair is all white, and she's really old, so that doesn't count."

Melba's mind had drifted towards her wardrobe by this point and the rest of her began to follow, lured by the pleasure of choosing clothes for her holiday (which she reminded herself to call a vacation). Lady Groule's name carried no charge for her, and old, white-haired women could not possibly be interesting. But Mrs Caltrop sat up, electrified, and intensified her niceness.

"Lady Groule – is that not the same Lady who called here while I was out yesterday?"

"Yes, and we're going to tea with her on Tuesday."

"We?"

"Susanna and Usha and me."

Melba was no longer in the room. Mrs Caltrop took control. She sprang up and went to the writing desk. She sat down, took out paper and an envelope, and placed in front of herself Lady Groule's card, which had been left in a prominent place for all eyes to fall on it (but sadly only Mrs Wattie's had yet done so). She wrote in silence, covering both sides of the paper. When she had finished, Mrs Caltrop sealed the letter inside the envelope and came to bend over Elinore, staring closely at her and holding the envelope high. Elinore saw Lady Groule's name on the outside.

"I am entrusting this communication to you and you *must not neglect it*. You must give it to Lady Groule when she entertains you on Tuesday. Do you understand?" Elinore nodded and leaned sideways in her chair, trying to avoid Mrs Caltrop's breath; it was as fearsome as her gaze. Mrs Caltrop bent closer. "If you lose this letter or forget to hand it over, I will know immediately, and I warn you, there will be consequences." She straightened up. "Consequences!" she repeated, making the S's hiss and thrusting the envelope at Elinore. Elinore felt alarmed, puzzled and vexed. She wanted to keep the Caltrops out of her doings and well away from her new friends as much as she possibly could. This letter felt like an invasion.

"Yes," she said, in answer to everything and nothing. She took the envelope and left the room.

While cleaning her teeth that night, Elinore looked at herself in the spotted, streaked mirror above the basin and decided that now she looked interesting, if not pretty. She also thought she looked more intelligent. Her eyes looked bigger and her cheekbones wider and higher. She tried smiling at herself, tentatively. She did not think Audrey Hepburn would have looked exactly like that when young, but no matter: she, Elinore Crum, was ten and she was new. It was super! She grinned widely. Supercalifragilisticexpialidocious!

In bed, she felt tired, but Jumpin' Jack Flash was back in her head and keeping her from sleep, throwing the day's experiences around in random pictures and fragments of speech – and smells, the aromas of food in the Berg kitchen and the perfumed chemicals of Salon Zuccarelli. Zuccarelli, Zuccarelli – you could make a little song with a name like that. It was printed on the bag of hair things that Mrs Berg had given her. Elinore decided that in her new notebook she must start a new list, to record interesting names of people, and Zuccarelli could be number one. She got out of bed to fetch her shoulder bag and turn on the overhead light. If only she had an Anglepoise lamp like Usha and Susanna.

Mr Zuccarelli's Polaroid of her was lying in the bottom of the bag. A few more of those and she could have sent one each to Arabella, Tom and Julie Fairgrieve in Criven. She was ten, she was new! She remembered asking Sir Gabriel for good omens about her tenth year, thanked him aloud once more, and then felt guilty about giving him so much attention at the expense of the homely little men in the other picture. She did not want them to feel neglected, especially in this ugly room. All of them, but especially the flustered Virgin Mary (being a lady and so naturally inclined to liking pretty things, she presumed) would feel much happier above Usha's desk or on Susanna's yellow walls. She took both pictures off the chest of drawers and went back to bed, setting them flat in front of her so that they could all work together on writing things down.

The addresses and telephone numbers of Susanna and Usha were already in place, and she had written in Lady Groule's name too; she could also put in Mrs Chisholm, once Lady Groule gave her the particulars. Dr Berg had noticed her collecting this information. He approved of it, telling her that it was an excellent habit to start young; friends and even family could disappear, he said. He was a very smiling man, and quite loud compared with Mrs Berg – no, not *loud* (Tom Balmerinoch was louder), and definitely not shouting like Hector, just happy to cause uproar at the table. Yes, that was it: he made everyone else loud because he liked to tease them and with a perfectly straight face say outrageous things that might be jokes or might not. Daniel was quite different in the presence of his father: he gabbled away and once or twice told everyone else to listen to him. Mrs Berg, however, never let anyone get away with bad manners, not even Dr Berg. Returning to No. 17 after the carefree, egalitarian hubbub of this teatime had been like walking into a wall of stuffy, stale-smelling quietness. But it was not quietness of the kind that pervaded the Dower House at Squair; Elinore had no word for the Caltropian kind that pressed down on her like a heavy felt hood.

Jumpin' Jack Flash had retired for the night by the time her writing was finished. She lay down, but with both pictures still in front of her, standing on her tummy, so that she could converse with all the characters. It had suddenly struck her that the little men, or at any rate the three of them that were the Magi, were only lacking a C in their name to become something else altogether, perhaps as powerful as Sir Gabriel. Appearances could be deceiving. Look at Elinore Crum! She would never have guessed that such an interesting-looking girl had been under that tiresome, messy hair all along. Her last thoughts and words before sleep were about the day to come.

"Dear Sir Gabriel and Magic Men: today was super-duper and I really, really hope it will be like that tomorrow too. Yours sincerely, me."

At breakfast on that Sunday morning, Melba gulped her tea, nibbled some toast and gave herself hiccups by bolting her boiled egg. Then she ran upstairs, for this was Dwayne's last full day in Scotland and she was not going to waste a minute of it. After her little talk with Mrs Caltrop, she had consigned Elinore to the equivalent of the Empty Quarter in her mind; a useful place. All was well now and all manner of Elinore business would be well.

The Caltrops were readying themselves for church. Mrs Caltrop was already projecting one week hence, when she would expect Elinore to accompany them. That it could not happen on this Sunday was a sore loss, but it would be prudent to wait until Melba was several thousand miles beyond the child's range of appeal, and anyway she was sure that much could be accomplished in the intervening week.

"Now, Elinore," she began in her nasty-nice voice (as Elinore had labelled it), "you will be busy with your friends, will you not, while we are at church?"

"Yes," said Elinore, "all day. Just like yesterday."

"And what church do they go to? A doctor is a pillar of the community."

Elinore thought of the big stone pillars inside Criven church and could not see any connection with the amiable Dr Berg. "I don't know where they go."

"But will you go with them? That is an important matter, and something I would expect you to tell me." It had occurred to both Caltrops that the foreign name might indicate popish leanings.

Nonplussed, Elinore could not reply at first. Nothing of the sort had entered her head, but perhaps she would indeed be expected to go with the Bergs and join in, much as she had been taken along to Salon Zuccarelli. Worry began to tinge the day. What about her clothes? She would have to wear a skirt and good shoes to church, and she could not possibly play in those. But if she went to Susanna's house right away, she might have time to find out about church and run back to change at No. 17 first. It would be terrible to let down the Bergs by not looking proper. More dashing around along streets! Even the thought of it was tiring. And what about the key she did not have, to let herself in if the Caltrops had already departed for their church?

"I don't know," was the only answer she could think of. She went upstairs, gathered her things together and left the house, more worried than excited, and forgetting again to take her gifts from Tom to show everyone.

Susanna was rolling around on the lawn, playing with her big, plump cat. The front door was open, and Elinore could see Mrs Berg on a stepladder; she waved a brush at Elinore and called out a hello. Susanna jumped up and cried, "Oh, *here* you are! I'm in a bad mood, but you'll make me feel better, won't you? My mouth hurts. My whole head hurts. *Owwwww!*" She squealed and the cat jumped in alarm. "Silly Fatso!" laughed Susanna, but then she sighed and flopped back onto the lawn. "It *hurts*, really it does. I've got rubber bands in there, or maybe they're steel, and I have to keep going to the dentist so he can make them tighter. Owwwww," she repeated, but this time it was a moan.

It sounded like torture to Elinore, and she doubted whether she could do anything to make Susanna feel better. Melba's sore heads and bad moods always received the same treatment, bed rest or shopping for clothes, both of which effectively shut out Elinore. "Do you want to go to bed?" she asked, feeling duty bound to do so.

"*Bed?* Why? I'm not *sick*. And Usha's going to be here in the afternoon, so we'll be doing lots of things, and you and I can do lots of things too until she comes. Do you want to help me sort out my comics and magazines? Mummy says I've *got* to do it today or she'll give them all to Daddy to take to the hospital. She means it, she always does!"

Elinore saw her moment and seized it. "But don't you have to go to church, or Sunday school, or anything . . ." She faltered, seeing Susanna's look of surprise.

"*We* don't go to church. I think my Granny and Grandpa Silber go sometimes, but it isn't a church, it's called a synagogue. And they don't go on a Sunday. But we never go to anything. Do you have to go? That's boring!"

Elinore's worry fled, to be instantly replaced by curiosity. "What's a synagogue? How do you spell it?" She reached for her bag and took out her notebook and pen.

Susanna told her she was funny, but spelled out the word anyway. "I know I'm right because Daddy wrote it down for me and it's in my dictionary. Come on, you can look if you don't believe me and then we can do my comics."

They met Dr Berg in the hall, carrying a mug of coffee in one hand and a file folder in the other.

"Daddy, Elinore got a new word from me: synagogue. She wrote it down. She's always writing things down."

"Excellent, excellent – didn't I say that already? It's called attention to detail. Keep it up, Elinore, and you'll make a fine medical student." He gave Elinore a huge wink and disappeared into his study. Elinore stood still, surprised and warmed by this lofty praise.

"Come *on*, don't pay any attention to him! We've got lots and lots to do." Susanna grabbed her arm and pulled her upstairs.

By the end of her hours in the Bergs' domestic embrace, Elinore had concluded that this family was exactly like those depicted in magazine advertisements. Two parents, one girl, one boy, all fair of face, light of hair and properly dressed; Mrs Berg even looked nice in her old painting clothes with her hair scraped back under a kerchief. Just as in the magazines, everyone was happy and smiling, and every room in their house was beautiful. The walls were mostly white, and held so many old and modern pictures of so many different kinds – even in the bathrooms and the kitchen! – that Elinore thought she could spend a whole day just looking at them. It occurred to her that Mrs Berg would be the best person to help her with the Italian words from her two pictures. As for Mrs Berg's own paintings, they were like some of Elinore's dreams: they did not always tell a clear story, and some of them told no story at all that she could discern among the shapes and washes of colour, but their vibrancy drew her eye and made her pause whenever Susanna said, "Mummy did that one." Elinore had asked her to point them out; it was an amazing thing to have an artist for a mother, she thought, and one day Mrs Berg's paintings might be famous, and seen in books and museums. She decided that these pictures looked better and brighter when you saw them from the far side of a room, which probably explained why the staircase and half-landing were lined only with photographs of people, in black and white or sepia. Some were of Susanna and Daniel as infants.

"These people are my grannies and grandpas, and these ones are my Korngold cousins, and that's a sort of cousin too, but he is a Hertzmann, and that's my Aunt Jane, Mummy's big sister. She lives in London, and guess what, we're going to visit her at Christmas. Have you ever been to London?"

"Is your mother really called Mimi?" Elinore had overheard Dr Berg call her that. "It's so pretty."

"Her real name is Naomi. She puts Naomi Silber on her paintings, because she was making them before she met Daddy. She's going to have her own shop for pictures one day, and she's going to call it The Silver Mountain Gallery, which is what you get when you put Silber and Berg together – it's really clever, isn't it? Granny Silber's *always* talking about it with her."

Elinore's eyes ran over this further evidence of Susanna's full and perfect life: grandparents, aunts, uncles, cousins and more. She envisioned a host of Bergs, Silbers and other delightfully named families populating similar charming, spacious houses up and down the land. Clearly, misfortune had no place in the entire history of this family: no ravening beasts bringing sudden death to a parent, no forced departure from a beloved home, no exile in the land of Caltrops. They could not possibly be so welcoming and cheerful otherwise. Questions about the surnames were on the tip of her tongue – for instance, why did everyone have a special name, maybe with colours in it and not something ordinary, like Crum or Fairgrieve or Elliott? – but Susanna was off again with one of her own.

"What's your mother called? I saw her in the hotel with you. Her clothes were really bright! I like that kind of pink sometimes, but yellow's my favourite, at least, right now it is."

"She's called Melba. She likes clothes more than anything." The question of names was suddenly displaced by something more important to Elinore. "Is your mother really going to show us the dress she wore to meet the Queen?"

When Usha arrived after lunch, this showing took place in the Berg parents' bedroom, where the dress was laid out on the bed for them to see and even touch (but only after they had washed their hands within earshot of Mrs Berg). It was a sleeveless sheath in apricot silk, with a narrow belt of exquisitely embroidered flowers in ivory and deeper shades of apricot, and tiny green leaves. It was paired with a loose, open coat in the same silk, and a finely woven straw hat with a wide brim over which spilled a creamy mass of chiffon roses. At once, they all said the silk was the same colour as the newly painted vestibule.

"I know," said Mrs Berg. "I wanted to start painting a wall that colour as soon as I saw the dress in the shop. That's what you call inspiration." Elinore remembered lying on the floor of her mother's bedroom at No. 17 and dreaming up a house of her own, with, amazingly, an apricot-coloured entrance hall. Was that inspiration too?

Usha said she wanted to take the hat home, so that she could have roses on her head whenever she wanted.

Susanna rolled her eyes and told Usha she was a nitwit. "Susanna!" said her mother sharply. "People have been wearing flowers on their heads for centuries. They are *not* nitwits." She put the hat on Usha's head, and it dropped down to cover her eyes. "Yes, looks fab – I'll make sure I leave it to you in my will, dear."

Elinore had a pressing question. "Why did the Queen want to meet you? Did you do something special?"

"Well, we didn't actually *meet* her. There are hundreds of people there, you know, all over the lawns, and she can't get around to saying hello to every single one. But we had a good view of her, and the Duke of Edinburgh too, and I was just there for the view after all. My husband's the one who got the invitation, for all his hard work at the hospital, and a couple of other reasons, I suppose – he's been busy with some charity committees. Someone tells the Queen if you've been doing good things in the community, and then you get an invitation. It's the Queen's way of saying thank you very much. But I'm just the wife, just a painter! Once I'm famous, maybe she'll send me my very own invitation."

"Do the ladies have to curtsey if they meet her? Do the men bow down low?"

"I think some ladies did, some didn't. It isn't like meeting Queen Victoria! Could be something to do with their arthritis. Or they might have forgotten to practise, like me. Imagine if I'd fallen over in front of her! I don't want to be on the front page of *The Scotsman* for that."

Susanna and Usha thought this was screamingly funny, and Mrs Berg had to chase them out of her bedroom before they would stop practising their falling-over curtseys across the carpet.

"Thank you very much for showing me your dress," said Elinore. "It's really beautiful and I loved the hat too. I think you'll look just like the Queen when you put them on."

"Why, thank you, Elinore, that's made my day. Makes me feel better about spending all my pocket money on one outfit. I'm skint now. No more fancy dresses until I sell another painting."

Painting for pocket money? What a perfectly wonderful job to have. As good as Arabella's, thought Elinore, and not at all mysterious or difficult to describe to other people. But Arabella liked beautiful clothes too, she was Elinore's aunt, unquestionably amazing and as real as Susanna's Aunt Jane on the staircase wall. *She* could be safely introduced to Mrs Berg.

"My Aunt Arabella does things with paintings too. She doesn't paint them, but she looks at them in people's houses and moves them around. She's staying in a castle right now and they have lots and lots of old pictures for her to look at. She wrote me a letter about it."

Mrs Berg was all ears. "Really? I must hear more about this lady. What's her last name? Cheyne . . . Arabella Cheyne . . ." She wrinkled her brow. "I don't know where I've heard that before, but I'm pretty sure I have. Perhaps I'll get a chance to meet her someday."

As she lay in bed that night, replaying Sunday's enjoyments, Elinore decided that she needed a diary. She had seen a red one on Usha's desk. It had a flap with a lock, a tiny key, a loop for holding a pen, and the word DIARY stamped in gilt block capitals on the front. So many pleasant, interesting things were happening to her all of a sudden that her memory might not have room for them all, and things could be pushed out for good. Further, if she wrote down the details, it might help her to make up her mind about a vital question: should she ride her imaginary wolf (after it had efficiently mauled both Caltrops) to a new home in the Bergs' house or in Tom's? They were such very different places, and yet she felt as though she belonged in both. She liked being in Usha's cosy flat too, but it had no extra room for her, let alone a wolf.

Given the nature of magic (she presumed), it was possible that one day she could, like Alice, suddenly whiz through one of those magazine advertisements with the perfect families to find herself in the Berg family forever. Susanna had given her so many old magazines that she had plenty of material for a swift start on that kind of experiment. But magazine magic might not be able to transport her to Squair, for Tom and his house were both so messy that they could never be in an advertisement. Another possibility presented itself just as she was falling asleep: what about a house where, like Usha, she would be the only child, the sole object of everyone's care and attention? That would be the way of things if she lived at the Dower House in care of Tom. But perhaps she was going to make another new friend soon who could be a doorway to precisely those circumstances, and the magic experiments could take a different turn into a Wonderland of bright, tidy rooms and the usual number of two adults, each as lovely as Tom. Who knew what Sir Gabriel and the Magic Men might come up with for her tenth year if she asked them politely? They were doing awfully well so far.

Monday morning, however, brought only upset and alarm to Elinore. It began at breakfast, when Mr Caltrop relayed two pieces of news from his newspaper. First, Holyrood Week was over, and the Queen would depart that day. Elinore felt inexplicably downcast by this, as though Her Majesty's proximity had somehow influenced the previous few days benignly. No chance sighting of her could possibly happen now.

"She had a fine day for the garden party this year," observed Mr Caltrop. "That's two in a row. The Lord might bless her with a third just when we attend."

This was not a joke, and neither was Mrs Caltrop's response.

"I am fairly confident that we will be invited to Holyroodhouse next year. Remember, our names will be put forward by not one but two bodies. Edinburgh cannot have many with that distinction."

Elinore heard this with disbelief. She could understand that the Queen would want to say thank you to a doctor who could mend people's hearts and other bits, but in Elinore's view the Caltrops led a pointless existence, productive of nothing except rules and disgusting meals. What could they possibly do in a church that might equal the cleverness of cutting people open, mending the sick bits and sewing them up again? Furthermore, they were simply too evil to deserve royal recognition. She was impelled to convey this incredulity.

"Dr Berg went to the garden party, and Mrs Berg went with him. I saw the invitation, and I saw Mrs Berg's special dress too. And her hat. You have to do something *special* to get invited. She told me."

Mrs Caltrop radiated her own incredulity, thickly coated with loathing, at Elinore. It was her supreme desire to be noticed by Holyroodhouse in this manner, and publicly, indisputably honoured. Was she expected to believe that these latest acquaintances of the child had arrived on the guest list before her? That these people, who might not be Indian or Pakistani but whose name was still suspiciously foreign, had even been permitted to set foot on the royal lawns? She remembered asking Elinore to provide a certain detail that would be crucial in putting these Bergs into the right category. She ignored the inflammatory idea of their attendance at Holyroodhouse, and said to Elinore, "You were to tell me what church these people go to. Well?"

"They don't go to any church, ever."

"Non-believers! A prime cause of the undermining of society," exclaimed Mr Caltrop.

"So – they deny the existence of our God?" asked Mrs Caltrop.

"I don't know. They didn't say anything about God. Susanna just told me that her Granny and Grandpa Silber go to a synagogue sometimes, but I don't really know anything about what that is. I just got the word from Susanna." Elinore spoke as she thought on the matter: until she bothered to find out more, and only if the subject were interesting enough, a synagogue was an architectural construct, different from church mainly in the way that a cinema was different from a theatre, for example.

No munching, scraping sounds punctuated the silence that blanketed the breakfast table. Mrs Caltrop's gaze took on a deeper aspect of loathing for Elinore, and yet part of her rejoiced. Her task as the child's saviour was becoming more urgent and praiseworthy with every passing day. She could already taste her triumph in its accomplishment. She would not neglect to tell everyone at church about the pariahs whose company Elinore had been keeping.

"In *this* neighbourhood?" croaked Mr Caltrop.

"I don't know where it is. I said, they don't go to it," said Elinore, confused.

Mr Caltrop's mouth dropped open, his head sank into his shoulders and he put up his newspaper again. It was the only way he could immediately think of to express his concern. Mrs Caltrop leaned across the table and fixed Elinore with the kind of look that in another creature would have hypnotised rabbits. "Do you not have *any* notion of what kind of –" she began.

Melba flounced into the room and seated herself, apparently in a much better mood than was usual on a Monday morning. "*Good morning, Mrs C., Mr C.!*" She reached abruptly for the toast rack and knocked Mr Caltrop's newspaper back into his face just as he lowered it to look at her. "Oops! So sorry! Any exciting news that I ought to know about?"

Mr Caltrop cleared his throat and put the paper back up. Only three seconds later, he cleared his throat again and announced, "The Balmerinoch Hotel – that has a familiar ring to it. Why might that be, Roberta?"

"Oh – that's the place where *that woman* took us for lunch! I told you all about it, I'm sure I did, and that's where you've heard the name," said Melba. "Dreadful mess. Workmen banging away in every corner. And we saw the plain Jane who owns it: no wonder the place is so peculiar. The *nerve* of that Arabella! She could just as easily have taken us to the Caledonian."

"There will be a lot more workmen in the place, I fear, for the paper says a water main has burst and flooded it, along with the neighbours. The electrics are badly affected too. It's had to close, and they don't know if the damage can be put right before the Festival. Indeed, that's only a month away!"

"Jolly good!" laughed Melba. "It must be divine punishment for being a rotten hotel and taking advantage of people, wouldn't you say, Mrs C.? With any luck, they'll have fire in the attics next, and disease amongst the guests as soon as they reopen. Flood, fire, pestilence, what does that leave? Now, excuse me, it's been awfully entertaining, but I must dash, duty calls and all that." She took another piece of toast and scampered out of the room and upstairs.

Perfidy and Schadenfreude were the words that Elinore wanted as she ran after her mother, but she had yet to encounter them. As she burst into Melba's room without knocking, she yelled, "You're horrible! You mustn't say those things about Arabella and Clova. They're very good people, and if you say bad things about them it means that *you're* the bad one. So there!"

Melba was standing over one of the several piles of clothing in the room, holding a dress up in front of herself. She lowered it and looked at Elinore: at a small, skinny, flushed, scowling creature with clenched fists, a hairstyle courtesy of a woman she had never met and clothes given by another, at whom she had just sneered. This human being appeared abruptly alien and incomprehensible in terms of its supposed connection to her. Her old revulsion at the very word "childbirth" reared up in her and she shuddered, which Elinore saw and took as meant at her. It was, of course. Finally and consciously, Melba had reached the end of her notion that a child would be a good thing to have (much as any other object of the moment's desire had been regarded, roughly ten years ago). A child was certainly no longer a useful thing, now that this one's existence had done the job of dressing her for Dwayne as a nobly struggling widowed mother. It was redundant; its continued presence was in danger of becoming an obstacle. Melba acknowledged this mental terminus for exactly half a second before switching permanently and irrevocably onto her new onward route through life.

"Ree-ally? Your new friends haven't done anything to improve your manners. One more word about how bad I am, or Mr and Mrs Caltrop, and you'll suffer the consequences."

Consequences, thought Elinore, there's that word again – what's going to happen to me? She scowled even more and clenched her fists all the harder. "I don't care!" she cried. It was the only brave response she could think of. "I *like* my friends."

"Go away and let them spoil you rotten, then. Go on, shoo-shoo! I'm on my way to work and I don't have time for you and your disgusting behaviour."

Elinore turned for the door, and saw two open suitcases, their lids propped against the wall. Each had a pile of garments and sundries beside it and some folded items already inside.

"You're going away, aren't you? You never *said*. Are you going to America with Dwayne? Why didn't you tell me? When are you coming back?"

Melba took Elinore by the shoulders and pushed her out onto the landing.

"I told you last week. It's a holiday and you could have come too – remember? – but that's permanently out of the question now, since you're so ungrateful and rude. I'm going tomorrow and I'll be back in two weeks."

A little thrill ran through Melba as she said this. *I might not . . .* The power of choice was intoxicating.

"You're leaving me with *them*. I'm not staying here on my own, I'm *not*! You have to take me back to Criven! You *have* to!"

"Get *out!*"

The bedroom door slammed shut in Elinore's face, and she heard the key, the key that her own door did not possess, turn in the lock.

"What is the meaning of this noise? It's disgraceful at this time of the morning – at any time, do you hear?"

Mrs Caltrop was standing halfway up the stairs, her head angled to glare upwards at Elinore.

"Nothing," said Elinore, turning towards her room.

She sat on her bed, feeling a strange wobbliness in her legs. Two weeks. Without a calendar to pin it down, this stretch of time became fluid and hazy. Elinore did not have one. Perhaps Mr Patel sold calendars too. She would find out soon, for she was due to spend the day with Usha while Susanna visited her grandmother in Pitlochry. She made sure her shoulder bag contained the essentials for another day out with friends, and once again took herself out of the house as quickly and quietly as possible.

Mr Patel was apologetic: calendars were not part of his stock, and in any case, he explained, in any shop, they would all have been sold by the end of January, not to reappear in shops until December. Consequently, Elinore and Usha seated themselves on Usha's bed and used crayons to construct a calendar showing the fortnight from Tuesday 5th to Tuesday 19th July. Tuesday 12th was coloured orange to mark the halfway point. Elinore stared at the little boxes, which she would tick every day. She could not understand why she felt so apprehensive at Melba's departure, since her absence signified no gaping loss of attention or assistance. In fact, if Elinore had been left to stay with any one of her new friends – in Susanna's yellow bedroom, for example – two whole weeks without Melba would have been endless fun. It must be those Caltrops, thought Elinore, I just hate them and they're making me nervous.

"You're sad, aren't you?" asked Usha. "I'd be sad if my Mum went away for two weeks."

"Well . . ."

"But I bet she brings you back a super present from America. And maybe you could go there for a holiday too, if she goes again."

"I don't *want* to go there! And I don't want to go anywhere in the whole world with that man. He's so – stupid. He smells funny. And he's got bad manners."

The big question, the one that any girl might ask under such circumstances, hung unspoken between them: what if Melba and Dwayne got married? Usha was too polite and too sympathetic to her friend's visible unhappiness to ask it; Elinore was too scared that voicing it might turn it into reality.

"Let's go to that church and make daisy chains," said Elinore.

"Yes – and we could take something to read."

They secluded themselves in a hot, sunny corner between tall gravestones, with a tartan rug all the latest comics and a couple of books. It felt rather daring to be there (after all, Edinburgh was not Criven), but no one appeared, let alone challenged them. At first, Elinore sank into the sensory pleasure of being out in the sun with stories, on grass that was not under the rule of Caltrops; but the stories were all about girls whose lives were normal – two parents, siblings, a home or boarding school that never moved or changed, and adventures that were comfortingly resolved by the end of every story – and the contrast between that realm and her own worked on her and increased her apprehension. Nothing she read gave her any clues as to the management of evil Caltrops or ugly, bad-mannered suitors who had the power to whisk Melba away to another country. She began to feel as if a weight were pressing on her, and then she felt hungry too, very hungry, as if her insides were dropping out of her feet. They were to return to

Mrs Patel for lunch at noon, but that was still forty minutes away, according to the church clock, and Elinore could not bring herself to be impolite and ask for food before the correct moment. Suddenly, to her horror, she felt like bursting into tears. It was like being on Mrs Chisholm's sofa all over again. She lay down flat on the rug and put an arm over her eyes, determined not to give herself away as a cry-baby this time.

Her tummy had other ideas.

"You're hungry!" giggled Usha. "Your tummy's shouting."

"Sorry," said Elinore, with her face turned away.

"Why? It's not rude to be hungry. Come on, let's go home. I want to eat something too."

"Will your mother mind?"

"No – why would she mind? If she isn't finished cooking, she'll just give us nuts and raisins for a snack. She lets me eat those any time, but not crisps and sweeties."

Elinore rubbed her eyes vigorously and sat up, gathering the comics together.

"This is a nice place to sit if you don't have a garden," said Usha. "I never came here before. Ooh, what's wrong with your eyes? Are they hurting?"

"No, just – itchy," lied Elinore. "Something got into them." She rubbed them again.

"Come on, you can use my special eye stuff at home. It's called Optrex and it makes the redness go away when I read too much."

Mrs Patel heaped food on Elinore in the form of a fragrant, spicy stew that Elinore thought made the Caltrop version of stew only fit for pig swill. (She knew all about pig swill: she had even helped tip some of it into a trough at a Criven farm.) Her energy and spirits climbed with every spoonful, and soon she was proposing a visit to the charity shop down the street. Usha said she had never been inside it.

"Gosh, if I lived in your house I would go there all the time," said Elinore. "It's got treasures. You might find some more old books about flowers."

Usha bounced out of her seat. "Let's go!"

Elinore found a treasure that afternoon. It was a worn, cloth-bound book with thick, soft pages and colour plates, called *The Book of Edinburgh for Young People*. An embroidered, monogrammed bookmark with a tassel led her to page eight, where she saw a paragraph underlined in pencil:

> *And everywhere you go you can read history: not written in books, but in stones, which to my mind is far more interesting; and remember, Edinburgh will never be to you the enchanted city she is to many people until you have learned to do this for yourselves.*

Convinced that the bookmark and pencilling were signals from a young person of long ago who was speaking directly to her, Elinore felt thrilled. She also felt a sense of responsibility as the recipient of this message. It was like receiving a coded communication for Agent Solo. She must study this book very carefully to crack the code and extract the secret.

16

Much later that day, after Mrs Patel's hospitality had enabled her to miss another Caltrop tea-time, Elinore was getting ready for bed when her world began to fragment a little more. This was signalled by a bumping sound that she might have missed altogether if her door had been closed, if she had not been going from bathroom to bedroom at the right moment. At first, her desire to avoid the Caltrops was stronger than her curiosity, and the bumping stopped after half a minute anyway. But when it was repeated, and accompanied by cursing in her mother's voice, she went to investigate. Melba was halfway down the stairs, manoeuvring one of her suitcases from step to step in front of her.

"Mummy, you said you weren't going away until tomorrow!" shouted Elinore from the landing. "Why aren't you *telling* me anything?"

"Oh, be *quiet*, Elinore. Stop that shouting. I *am* going away tomorrow, but I need to get these ready for the taxi now."

"When?"

"When what? I wish you would go back to your room and stay there. Your questions are only hindering me."

Elinore ran down the stairs until she was one step above Melba. "*When* are you going away tomorrow?"

"Half past seven," replied Melba, naming a time that was a full hour and a half later than the moment at which her taxi was due to arrive at the front door. It already felt like a glorious start to her holiday – oops! vay-cation – to run out of No. 17 and avoid the nuisance of Elinore, and, with luck, the Caltrops. All three of them were now in her Empty Quarter. She was already flying in the mid-Atlantic air.

"I don't have a clock," said Elinore. "You have to come and tell me in case I'm asleep."

"All *right*. Now go back upstairs and stop bothering me."

Slowly, Elinore returned to the company of *The Book of Edinburgh for Young People,* her notebooks, Sir Gabriel and the Magic Men, and the BBC, all of which were on her bed and ready to be picked up in that order for enjoyment or special consultation. Her legs felt wobbly again. She banged her head seven times on the pillow to ensure that she would awaken at exactly seven o'clock in the morning (it was what some people did, successfully, in stories). Part of her wanted to leave the bedroom door open too, but another part wanted to keep it firmly closed against hostile observation by Caltrops, and that part won. Picking up the Edinburgh book, she began to read it with all the attention she could muster under the circumstances. This was immediately rewarded by discovering something on a flyleaf she had overlooked. It was a name pencilled in careful primary-school letters: Miss Helena Albacyr. Uncertainty over pronunciation of Albacyr could not dim her delight in a lovely-sounding foreign name, a *mysterious* name; it was also quite possibly the name of the reader who had left a bookmark and underlining for her to find. She added it to her name list there and then, after Zuccarelli. On page four, which was really only the second page, she was excited to read what seemed to be another message:

> *Wherever you go in the streets you are sure to see groups of boys and girls carrying big straps of schoolbooks, and numbers of grave-looking, black-coated men, whom you are safe to put down as doctors, or lawyers, or clergymen, or teachers.*

Yes! It had been just like that for her. She had seen those other children, uniformed ones, going to school, and she had already met one doctor, Susanna's father. Was it Elizabeth W. Grierson, the book's author, who was speaking to her now, or was it that long-ago young person, possibly Helena Albacyr? Now it felt even more like a responsibility to read carefully and look for clues. The book claimed her fully, at least as far as page eight. There she found the name of Sir Walter Scott, who could be no less than a lifelong friend to her after she had travelled in his spaceship. The author called him "that Prince of Story-tellers". Elinore said this aloud: it sounded very fine, and she repeated it before changing it to "Miss Elinore Crum, that Princess of Story-tellers", which had suddenly come to her as a delightful title for a possible job when she was grown up. Anything was possible now that she had a new and perfect hairstyle. She laid down the book, imagining her life as this Princess, who would naturally receive garden party invitations from the Queen, and it was all so soothing that she fell asleep in seconds, with the overhead bulb still sending its low-wattage, cheerless light down onto her.

By now, Elinore's body used ample helpings of food to help it sleep, since that was also essential for growth. A lunch and tea from Mrs Patel, then, resulted in oblivion that continued until quarter past seven on that Tuesday morning. Well before she reached the foot of the stairs, Elinore saw that no suitcases were standing in the hall, and heard only the usual Caltrop sounds for that time of day. Her mother's bedroom door was standing wide open. Elinore sat down heavily on the bottom step, disbelieving and very upset. *Why* was it all right for a grown-up to tell her an enormous fib, but not the other way around?

Mrs Caltrop's leaden tread sounded in the hall, and Elinore shrank back against the banister rails. Mrs Caltrop was making for the telephone, and so discovered Elinore more or less at her feet.

"Why are you not dressed?" she demanded. "Breakfast will be served in minutes. We will discuss your day then."

"My day?"

"Yes – your tea with Lady Groule, and other activities. Get dressed immediately, or you will be too late for any breakfast."

Mrs Caltrop picked up the telephone receiver and stared at Elinore with raised eyebrows, clearly waiting for her to return upstairs before she spoke to anyone.

Elinore stood in front of her wardrobe, her tummy in knots, her legs still weak and her throat heavy with a lump. She whispered instructions to Agent Solo as a means of keeping these upsets at bay. Another problem was right in front of her: what to wear to afternoon tea with a capital-L Lady, when she would be out and about with Susanna and Usha for hours before that? It was the same dilemma that had plagued her on Sunday. She decided to dress once again for playing and see what happened.

At the breakfast table, Mrs Caltrop reminded her of the envelope she was to hand to Lady Groule. "You will show it to me as you leave, to prove that you have not forgotten to take it with you."

Agent Solo was advising Elinore to avoid saying yes to Mrs Caltrop whenever possible. Elinore agreed with Agent Solo that saying nothing made her feel less like a small animal giving in to a large, dangerous one. She kept her eyes on her piece of toast, which she was cutting into quarters.

But Mrs Caltrop was now asking a direct question. "Will you be in the homes of your friends until it is time to call on Lady Groule? Will they feed you?"

Please, please, please feed me, thought Elinore fervently. "I always have very *nice* meals at my friends' houses," she replied. It was not a yes, and it was the truth; therefore, it was a good answer. She kept her eyes on her toast and did not see the expression on Mrs Caltrop's face. The organising of Elinore's day continued.

"Regardless, I want you to be out of here this morning. Mrs Wattie will be here earlier than usual to start the spring cleaning, and you must not be underfoot."

Elinore felt panic rising. Out, out – everyone wanted her out of the way, but how early would certain friendly doors be open to her? She could not recall any advice in the *Book of Charm & Essential Etiquette* for would-be early-morning callers, and she suspected it simply was not done.

In her room, she decided to wait until Mrs Wattie's appearance actually forced her to leave. She had plenty to do. She took out the brown paper in which Sir Gabriel and the Magic Men had been presented to her, and wrapped them up again. Inspired by the reverence of a red velvet cushion cover as protection for Usha's Reginald Nutbeam books, she took the greyed, threadbare slip off the lumpy, feather-spilling object that served as her pillow and put the precious paisley shawl into it. The usual essentials went into her bag, and the letter for Lady Groule. Then she went into Melba's room.

Uppermost in Elinore's mind was the hope that Melba had left behind some packets of biscuits or other snacks. She closed the door so that no one would see her behaving like a thief – no, *not* a thief: this was Agent Solo in action! – and searched the room. It was as characteristically untidy and garment-strewn as if Melba were due back that very afternoon. In a dressing-table drawer, Elinore found two boxes of Black Magic chocolates and two notes to Melba from Dwayne – disgusting, soppy words that she blushed to read. The top box was empty, but the one below it still held four chocolates. Heartened by this success, Agent Solo subjected every part of the dressing table and all the rubbish on top of it to her Super X-ray-Eye search. The dressing table had never received so much attention since the day of its acquisition by the Caltrops. It had a cowed, mute look about it, as if Mrs Caltrop had punished it for years for its sin of being made with an inherent welcome of perfume, prettiness and powder puffs, not to mention an eagerness to do justice to aspiring beauties in its mirror.

Agent Solo turned to the wardrobe next. She was on the trail of Melba's shoe-cleaning kit, which she correctly assumed Melba would have left behind, for would Dwayne not have lots of polish in his own house for his silly pointy-toed, high-heeled boots? Although Dwayne was responsible for Melba's departure, Elinore felt better thinking about him at that moment than about anything else, because scorn and ridicule were easier to express than fear and apprehension. She found the shoe-cleaning kit under a bed, and returned to her room to use it and eat the four chocolates.

With shoe-polish, it would be easy to maintain her new footwear to the standard laid down by Miss Agnes Pound.

> *"The cleanliness, suppleness and shine of leather must concern a lady as much as they do a gentleman, reflective as they are of every other part of one's self-presentation and, ultimately, of character (see Chapter 2). An old toothbrush will serve as an excellent tool for keeping the welts clean, and should be used vigorously before the application of any polish. Do not neglect the soles. Clean them with a damp cloth and apply polish regularly."*

Elinore's new clothes were another worry. How to launder them and keep them looking new in Melba's absence? Melba was only bothered about the standards of her own clothing, of course, but at least (prompted by Elinore) she had included Elinore's underwear, socks and so on in the twice-weekly wash that Mrs Caltrop had stipulated as the Crum laundry allowance: one day for towels and bed-linen, the other for clothing. But what about the other lovely new clothes? How was she to keep her blouses in a state fit for attending a concert at short notice, or meeting an important Somebody, if not the Queen? It had not escaped Elinore's notice that white sheets, towels, tablecloths and so on in the Caltrop household were not actually *white*. She could not bear to hand over her precious snowy blouse to a process that might reduce it to something like the pathetic towels and bedlinen she had to use. Her underwear and white socks were just as vulnerable. Above all, the idea of putting her clothes in the hands of Mrs Caltrop felt terrifying, like putting herself at risk of destruction. Elinore decided to ask Sir Gabriel and the Magic Men for advice later on. Meanwhile, she had time to fill. She picked up the Edinburgh book again, to learn more about the intriguing sights and experiences that were right here, all around her, and yet beyond her reach as long as she was in the clutches of the Caltrops.

Behind her closed door, Elinore was unaware of Mrs Wattie's arrival. The order of battle against one winter's accumulated dust and grime began in Melba's room. Mrs Caltrop's disapproval of Melba meant that spring-cleaning there was restricted to throwing all personal items littering the floor onto the beds, vacuuming the carpet and mopping the linoleum. Mrs Wattie finished that in record time and dragged her vacuum cleaner along the landing towards Elinore's two rooms. Elinore heard this and ran out.

"I'm sorry, I didn't know you were here. I'm going out now."

Mrs Wattie looked sour and offended. "Nae need to run. I'll no' bite."

"Mrs Caltrop said I had to stay out of your way."

Mrs Wattie barked a short, mirthless laugh that ended in a smoker's hack and muttered something that Elinore did not catch. She left the Hoover standing there and went back to the main landing, to pick up buckets, cloths, a mop and other cleaning things. These she dropped with a clatter on the bathroom floor, before turning to Elinore and pointing at her bedroom. "Stay in there if ye want while I redd oot this place. Makes nae difference." Then she marched back to the landing again to pick up a short stepladder, which she set up below the bathroom skylight. Elinore watched and waited, hesitating because it seemed rude to turn her back on

Mrs Wattie and simply go off, despite the woman's complete lack of interest in her presence.

Mrs Wattie climbed onto the stepladder and began to slap a wet cloth against the skylight. Elinore waited a few more seconds before saying what seemed to be correct. "Thank you very much for making my bathroom clean."

Mrs Wattie's cloth stopped moving. She turned her head and looked down on Elinore from her extra height. Her eyes were inscrutable pits. She rolled them upwards and said very clearly, "*You're* thanking me? God gie us grace!" in a tone that seemed to drip loathing on the whole world, including, and perhaps especially, Elinore Crum. Elinore turned and left. It was all beyond her comprehension, and in any case she had been told to take herself out, out, out.

She ran all the way to Susanna's house, unsure whether it was too early to go there but so desperate to be inside it that she would risk a social misstep. In her head, it had become a kind of fortress where Caltrops and Watties could not reach her.

The front door was open and Mrs Berg was busy again in the vestibule, washing the tiled floor on her hands and knees.

"Good morning, Elinore!" she called. "Susanna's waiting for you – just go round the back. She's been talking about nothing else this morning."

Long before it was time to visit Lady Groule, Susanna and Usha had reassured Elinore that playing clothes were actually the perfect thing to wear to tea with this particular capital-L Lady.

"She makes us work! We get on our hands and knees, because she can't do that any more, and she says we're better at it than Mrs Digby, 'cause we're small," said Susanna.

"Yes, she says we're really good at scrabbling," added Usha.

Elinore was mystified. "Why does she make you play Scrabble on your hands and knees?"

Susanna and Usha screeched at this. "No, silly-billy, not that kind of Scrabble!" said Susanna. "She calls it scrabbling like mice, because we go in cupboards and under tables and wee places, and we get stuff out for her, lots and lots of stuff that she wants to show us. She can't do all that bending, and she says Mrs Digby isn't very good at it either – not as good as *we* are."

"You'll see, it's lots of fun," said Usha. "It's better than TV if you like history and old things and beautiful dresses. It's like books coming to life!"

"Does Mrs Digby stay in her house too? Is she her friend?"

"She is the housekeeper, but not like Fredy. She doesn't live in Lady Groule's house."

"It isn't a house, it's a flat," said Usha. "But not like my flat."

Zinnia, Lady Groule of Meggat was the widow of a baronet, Sir Ronald, who had been Somebody in Law; in other words, something of an institution in Edinburgh. Glasgow had its Tobacco Lords, and Edinburgh its Law Lords. She had loved Ronnie very much, but not his beloved Meggat, in the county of Angus. This was now in the hands of her eldest son, the new baronet, and his wife, who were strenuously, ingeniously coaxing income out of the ancestral house and lands in ways that Sir Ronald would neither have imagined nor countenanced. None of that was of the slightest importance to Lady Groule these days. As long as Alastair and Alice were happy, and could provide her with a reliably heated bedroom and bathroom on her infrequent visits, and properly cooked meals from that *dungeon* of a kitchen that used to give her such nightmares, Meggat took up no space whatsoever in her present thoughts. Her natural setting was exactly where she had been born and where she lived now, in a pleasant Edinburgh street with old friends and ever-new entertainments on tap, and shops to supply whatever one wanted (no muddy Land Rover required to reach them), and trains on the doorstep to whiz one down to London when something a little grander was in order. And plenty of gossip. And *things that happened.*

Her flat comprised the first and second floors of a medium-sized terraced house. It would have been quite spacious had not all four floors constituted the Groules' town house for about forty years previously, steadily accumulating and very infrequently shedding contents. Decades of Zinnia's *marvellous* clothes and shoes, the sort of thing one could not possibly get rid of; decades of Ronnie's suits and robes and shoes and books, the sort of thing one put off, fondly and helplessly, getting rid of; and such a quantity of photograph albums, letters, books, magazines, theatre programmes, memoirs, music, china, silver, linen and miscellaneous memorabilia that she could not possibly estimate it, especially since she now had only the vaguest idea of what might be stuffed where. That was the trouble with a continually enjoyable, eternally interesting life that was full of memories worth keeping and frequently sharing.

Lately, however, she had come to congratulate herself on having the wisdom to hoard the evidence of her fascinating life in this way (quite overlooking the fact that intention and planning had never once influenced the result). She had begun to be *interesting* to the young. Some wheel of time had turned sufficiently to focus young eyes on figures and fashions from a past that was like the day before yesterday to Lady Groule. Gels were interested in her old clothes; young men were intrigued to hear that she had known So-and-So and Such-and-Such quite well while they were in power, and had little tales to tell of them that had never been told until now. Lady Groule *liked* young people. She was convinced that their company kept one youthful, and that this company should be increased every year as one aged, just like whatever the stuff was that that ridiculous Barbara Cartland was touting these days. Furthermore, without ever bothering to think much about it, let alone express it as a personal philosophy, she had come to see herself as a kind of service to the young. She had always lived enjoyably and well. Her children were happy, healthy and industrious, just as her husband had been until his comfortable death, whisky in hand, in his favourite armchair after a day's pheasant shooting at

Meggat. Why not indulge in a little pushing and prodding, some string-pulling and ear-tickling – some fun, in other words – to ensure that certain others also had the chance to live enjoyably and well, especially when their intelligence and other virtues deserved it? Fate was always putting such individuals in front of her, she would say, forgetting her own inquisitiveness, her relish of human drama and her readiness to enter into immediate, often intimate conversation with anyone who caught her attention.

Thus had Fate introduced Lady Groule to Usha Patel and then to Elinore Crum. They sat now at her table, with Susanna Berg, as upright in their chairs and precise in their manners as if they were little Edwardians – charming gels! Susanna had brought lemon tarts baked by her grandmother in Pitlochry, for all to share and with plenty left over just for Lady Groule. Usha had given her a bag of mixed nuts flavoured with some spice known only to Mrs Patel, and it was understood that Lady Groule would *not* dole these out, for she found them addictively satisfying and perfect for nibbling on in the middle of the night. The mysterious Elinore Crum had brought an envelope addressed in an unfamiliar hand, an exquisite antique shawl and two pictures just to show her, which gratified Lady Groule; she liked to be acknowledged and respected as a connoisseur.

Elinore was suffering such agonies of nerves that she could barely eat. They had sprung up in her even before leaving Susanna's house to walk to Lady Groule's flat, when she saw that Mrs Berg and Mrs Patel had each given their daughters a little something in honour of their hostess. She took Usha aside and tried to explain why she, Elinore, must rush to Mr Patel's shop immediately and find something to give Lady Groule too; to avoid disgrace, in other words.

Usha wrinkled her brow and asked, "Why? She doesn't need anything."

"But you've got something for her, and Susanna. She'll think I'm rude and horrible, and she won't ask me back ever again!"

"Elinore, you're silly!" Usha wagged a finger at her; just like a teacher, Elinore thought. "These things aren't from us, they're from my Mummy and Dad and Susanna's granny, the one called Granny Berg. Lady Groule knows her."

"But you don't understand, it's proper to bring something, and I don't *have* anything!"

"Yes, you do: the shawl Tom gave you. She knows all about old clothes – you wait and see. And you could take your pictures too. She's *always* showing us pictures, all kinds, and some of them look a bit like your ones. Honestly, if you show her things like that, she'll like it a lot."

That turned out to be true, but still, Elinore felt empty-handed and deficient in manners.

The next alarm rang for her when she handed over the letter and realised that she had run off from No. 17 without showing it to Mrs Caltrop as instructed. "*Consequences!*" hissed in her ears.

"Oh, good, I didn't get any post this morning," said Lady Groule. "I wonder who's thinking of me? Thank you, Elinore, I'll open it as soon as I've poured tea." She laid it by her plate.

And then, the worst thing of all . . . Barely had the girls seated themselves and spread the monogrammed linen tea napkins on their knees when the telephone rang.

"Do excuse me," said Lady Groule. She picked up the receiver. "Zinnia Groule here. Yes, that is so – Lady Groule. Yes, there – is – only – *one* Lady Groule here." She rolled her eyes at the girls and they giggled. "A letter? And who are you, pray? Caltrop. Roberta." She sat up, alert, and her eyes fastened on Elinore and stayed there. Prickly hands gripped Elinore's insides and tightened. "No, that name is not familiar to me. Oh, I see. Yes, yes, I do recall now." Elinore could hear a tiny, tinny version of Mrs Caltrop's voice going on and on. "No, I have *not* read the letter yet, Mrs Caltrop, because this is my at home afternoon and I was on the point of offering tea to my visitors when you rang. Lesser things must wait. Presumably this letter is not to inform me that Elinore is unwell and cannot join us for tea, because she is seated here in front of me. Yes, I *might possibly* ring you later, sometime later, I can't say when just now because I *am* busy, as I've explained, and it does not appear to be an emergency demanding my immediate attention." More noise from Mrs Caltrop. Lady Groule held the receiver away from her ear and looked at it with distaste. Susanna and Usha covered their mouths and shook with giggles, and Elinore's mouth opened in astonishment. "Yes, Mrs Caltrop, thank you for repeating that. Now I really must go and give my undivided attention to my visitors. Thank you. *Goodbye.*" Her eyes narrowed into icy slits and that last word carried an arctic freeze. She put down the receiver almost firmly enough to qualify as slamming it, and took a deep breath.

Then she turned to the girls and said, "Elinore, I hear your mother has gone to America. I have been there, you know." She poured tea for them all, and rattled off a story about a visit to New York and the absolutely incredible department stores there, and the immense apartment buildings that were ranged, street after street, like the biggest castles one could possibly imagine around a great big park filled with trees, and all so luxurious that not even an emperor of old could have imagined their comforts and conveniences, or could have traded his empire's gold and jewels for them. Especially those *fabulous* bathrooms with scalding hot water and central heating around the clock.

After this story, during which the girls had sampled Mrs Digby's dainty sandwiches and home baking, she casually picked up the Caltrop woman's letter and slit the envelope without interrupting the flow of another story, about an American who came to Scotland years ago and thought he could wear the kilt properly, and who tried and *tried* to buy Meggat from her husband. Without appearing to do so, she managed to watch Elinore, read the letter, urge food on the girls and start a completely different story about travelling on the Continent. She knew that Elinore was watching her and trying to discern her reaction as Mrs Caltrop's words thudded off the page and into her comprehension.

Dear Lady Groule,

I must beg your leave for my unavoidable absence from home when you called Friday last. My Committee duties are many and I am greatly in demand at certain times. Fortunately, only within Edinburgh at present, but of course we must be prepared to go where the Lord in his wisdom sends us, must we not?

However, my reason for sending you this letter is to advise you of my status and my husband's as Guardians of the child Elinore Crum. Her mother appointed us as such on the eve of her departure for America. We are therefore completely responsible for her health until Mrs Crum's return later this month; that is to say, for her moral wellbeing above all. We have of late been considerably disturbed at evidence of her proclivities for undesirable company, and I feel I must warn you of this straight away. To worsen the dangers, Elinore displays alarming and increasing tendencies towards secretiveness, obstinacy, rudeness, general disagreeableness, fabrication and fantasy. As Guardians, Mr Caltrop and I are naturally much exercised by this, and we are most anxious to furnish Elinore with examples of The Right Way to Live, <u>particularly</u> with respect to our Church.

I am sure you will understand our concern for Elinore and our desire to improve her lot, not only for the present, but also for her future, insufficiently founded as that is on the Sands of Indulgence instead of the Rocks of Discipline. She has been allowed an astonishing degree of latitude, especially after losing her father. (I should be delighted to discuss with you <u>in person</u> that tragic occurrence, the reason for our extending the mercy of shelter to mother and child.) I fear her mother will not have the strength to be a steadfast disciplinarian. Elinore's need for the <u>strongest</u> of guiding hands is <u>great</u>. Furthermore, she has lived until now in complete deprivation of the mitigating and ameliorating *influence of God's forgiveness. I cannot tell you how much we fear for her if she is not enfolded firmly and promptly into the bosom of the Lord.*

In light of this urgent need (which, I am confident, you will apprehend instantly as being of the gravest kind), I promise to communicate with you frequently, and to apprise you <u>without delay</u> of any troubling circumstance concerning Elinore, that is to say, arising from her wilfulness. Naturally I trust that you will act in the same manner with us, her devoted Guardians. Please do not hesitate to call on us again, and to telephone at any time! The Lord has doubtless brought us together for no less than the enactment of Good and the divine deliverance of at least one of the Young – a lamb, already straying and close to lost! – from the scourge of Juvenile Delinquency that in this age, in this very city, imperils us <u>all</u>.

I remain, most assuredly and sincerely,
Your earnest Associate in the Exercise of Care for a Child,
Roberta Caltrop

17

The day had been warm, and scents of flowers and mown grass floated around Elinore as she made her way through peaceful, garden-lined streets towards Dunallan Crescent. On one side of the pavement, girls in pastel-coloured shorts and T-shirts jumped around chalked hopscotch squares; on the other, a father was trying to convince a small boy that the ground would not swallow him if he took the training wheels off his bicycle. Birds flitted through the shrubs and trees, singing their song of late afternoon and already looking for the right branch or hollow to hold them overnight. The gauzy, golden light changed its angle bit by bit, lengthening shadows and making the remaining sunshine seem even warmer in contrast. Elinore felt cold and confused.

She was cold because she was nervous, and because she felt lonely and adrift, having just left the unique warmth of teatime at Lady Groule's, which was rather like having tea in a miniature museum open by invitation only. It was the Groule Museum of a Life Well-lived and Loved. It was the past, a small-p past that was all about Lady Groule and what she liked to call her adventures or experiences. The Dower House at Squair, on the other hand, held the capital-P Past. It was full of all Scotland and even the world over centuries, and many people's views of both. Tom had told her why: a boy once lived there who collected whatever intrigued him;

he never left Squair but the world came to his doorstep and left behind the history of everything, for people like Elinore to find. Thus Elinore comprehended the similarities and differences between the two homes.

Elinore was nervous because she knew that something unpleasant would come at her as soon as she stepped inside No. 17. High up against her chest, she carried her only armour: one of Lady Groule's shopping bags, containing not only her two framed pictures and the shawl, but also a large, heavy shoebox filled with postcards.

She was confused because Lady Groule had been confusing. As far as Elinore could tell, she had not warmed to Mrs Caltrop; even Susanna and Usha had discerned that, and giggled, and on the street afterwards had practised imitating that *"Goodbye!"*, which sounded like a goodbye for ever and ever. But Lady Groule had said not one word about the letter. Worse, from the moment she had begun reading it, her expression had turned coldly ferocious, and that look had thereafter landed on Elinore every so often until the visit ended. It was much more disturbing than the look that Melba had lately bestowed on Elinore. And yet, she had been the soul of kindness and gaiety in her actions and conversation, and had shown genuine pleasure and appreciation (so Elinore felt) when looking at the antique shawl and the pictures – especially the *Annunciation*.

"Leonardo!" she had cried, lifting the picture up and peering at it. "I have *seen* this, in the Uffizi Gallery in Florence. Now there's a memory! I was wearing a superb *tailleur* that day, silk, of course – and an archangel would wear nothing less than silk too, don't you agree? – *in that very red*, that, ah, ruby – no, perhaps more of a garnet, or Venetian red. Anyway, there I was in my silk and there was Archangel Gabriel in his, and I must say we caused rather a stir for as long as we appeared together!"

That was how Elinore came to be clutching a shoebox full of postcards, which were either reproductions of the great paintings that the Groules had viewed on their Continental jaunts or views of the galleries and museums housing these works.

"Coincidence is a blessing," Lady Groule had said. "It saves me from having to think too much. I came across this box all by myself, you know, just the other day. Such fun to go through it, but I shan't do that again for another generation and I'll be dead by then, so what to do with all these pretty pictures now? My fireplaces are stopped up and I don't want to put them in the bin. The bin men would not appreciate them if I left them on top of it. So, I left the box sitting on that table over there, waiting for inspiration, and along came Miss Elinore Crum, *aficionado* of great art!"

Aficionado? Elinore could wait no longer, despite Lady Groule's confusing facial expressions. "Is that word Italian?" she asked, and took her notebook out of her bag. "Could you please spell it for me and tell me what it means?"

Lady Groule obliged, and repeated the word in her best Italian manner. Elinore wrote it down and looked at her list of the other words and names that had come with the two paintings. "Could you please help me with these ones too? I don't know how to say Italian words."

Again, Lady Groule obliged, and with gusto, but after that, although she lavished the same attention and courtesy on Elinore as on the other girls, her fierce look became fiercer and also rather frowning, as if she had a terrible headache. It was all at odds with her instant approval of Elinore's notebook habit, although she did not echo Dr Berg's vision of a medical career for Elinore. "I am impressed, Elinore. You will either be a writer or a detective, and perhaps even *both* in the form of a new Conan Doyle!"

"What's that?" asked Susanna.

"*Who*, not *what*, dear gel," replied Lady Groule, "Sir Arthur Conan Doyle, creator of the great Sherlock Holmes. The *greatest* detective. If you haven't discovered him yet, you will. Conan Doyle was an Edinburgh man, and the Ina Blackadder School won't let you out without making sure you know *that*."

Elinore was pleased to hear that writer or detective had been added to doctor as a possible career. It was a nice change from being told off and warned about *consequences*.

The threat of these filled her with apprehension as she walked up to the front door of No. 17, rang for admittance, and waited. And waited, and then waited with a different kind of anxiety because she needed to pee.

Mrs Caltrop opened the door a crack and said, "Go to the back door. That is the only door you will use from now on." She closed the door.

Elinore ran around to the back door, which was still locked. Mrs Caltrop made her wait another minute. She was desperate when she was finally let in, and said, "Excuse me, I have to go in here," bolting into the dark little lavatory before Mrs Caltrop could stop her.

When she came out, Mrs Caltrop was standing with folded arms. Even in the dim kitchen, Elinore could see the dangerous red flowers flaming on her cheeks. "To the morning room!" she ordered.

The table was set for tea, with only two places. Mr Caltrop sat there, looking almost as angry as his wife: he was fidgety and impatient to start gobbling the food already piled on his plate.

"You will not have any tea tonight, Elinore. Let me be quite clear: this is not only because you have just had it elsewhere, which would be a perfectly good reason on another day, but above all because you disobeyed me this morning."

She paused, clearly expecting Elinore to query this. Elinore said nothing.

"You ran away despite my instructions *and* my reminder about showing me the letter to Lady Groule before you left. I had to ring her to ensure that she had received it."

"You didn't have to. I didn't forget it, and anyway I'm going for tea again next week, and I could have taken it then, or tomorrow or any time."

"Be quiet! This insolent answering back will stop or you will feel the consequences!"

"I'm not, I'm explaining –"

Mrs Caltrop took a step forward, raised her hand and bent over Elinore. "Don't think that because you're associating with the *ladies* of this world you have any importance whatsoever, Elinore Crum. God is the only Lord and he is judging you at this very moment."

"Indeed he is," chimed in Mr Caltrop. "His verdict on you at this moment will stay with you unto the day of your last breath, Elinore Crum!"

"God has given you into our care for your own good, and I will ensure that he is not disappointed in the result!" continued Mrs Caltrop. "Now, did Lady Groule read my letter straight away?"

"Yes."

"And what did she *say*, what did she *do* with it?"

"Nothing. She just put it in a drawer."

"*Nothing?* Did she not give you any message for me? What are those things you are carrying? *Have you been stealing?* Is there anything in there for me?"

"No, they're all mine, I took some things to show her and she gave me some old postcards. She gave us sandwiches and scones and lots of cakes and things, and little sausage rolls that were really good. I had a lovely time and she never said anything at all about you." It was true, and Elinore badly wanted to prove to this Caltrop that she had been fully, genuinely welcomed by Lady Groule.

"*Lies!*" screamed Mrs Caltrop. "I will teach you not to give me your wicked little fictions! Go to your room and do not appear again until tomorrow morning."

Elinore sat on her bed, holding the box of postcards tightly against her, and staring at Sir Gabriel and the Magic Men, whom she had returned to their place on the chest of drawers. Her faith in the good omens that they had apparently engineered to mark her tenth birthday was severely shaken; it was all too easy to worry that she did not actually meet their standards, that some badness in her actions must now be weighing against her. Perhaps it was because she had stolen the money meant for the missionary Curglaff.

What if some other angel, more of a policeman type, or even God himself, had informed Mrs Caltrop about *that*? *"Have you been stealing?"* It was an absurd, unjust, baffling accusation, but it would keep ringing in her head. She felt sick.

And then there was Lady Groule's judgement of her. Mrs Caltrop *must* have written something to make the way she looked at Elinore contradict so markedly her gestures as a hostess. It occurred then to Elinore that Lady Groule was just possibly another Caltrop in camouflage. Now she felt very sick indeed, and utterly let down. It was all dreadfully confusing and nerve-wracking, and she had no one to ask about it except Usha and Susanna. But Caltrops did not inhabit their perfect, happy worlds, and trying to explain, Elinore knew, was beyond her. She could not, would not begin that.

If only she were back in Criven, where everyone had been kind and normal; where she had never felt nervous except once, when she saw that a bull was in the same field that she happened to be crossing. How could somewhere so close be so far, far away? It was like looking at a scene through the wrong end of binoculars. All the bits of her life were dislocating themselves, even Melba.

Elinore wanted to cry, but if Mrs Caltrop burst into her room while she was crying, it would make her feel even more frightened. She went into her bathroom, washed her face and got ready for bed. The bathroom, her bedroom and the short corridor that bounded these spaces, the ones that were deemed good enough for her to use, showed little evidence of Mrs Wattie's redding out, save a persistent whiff of Ajax, Windolene and Domestos combined. It seemed to have stuck to her towels and bedclothes. In Elinore's mind, it made bars around her. She sat up in bed and began to look at Lady Groule's postcards. In a few minutes, she was halfway into another realm, and wishing she had a magnifying glass just like one of those she had seen at the Dower House. Every single postcard was crammed with detail, and every single one was magic.

At that very moment, Lady Groule had magic on her mind too. In one hand was a gin and tonic, in the other, the telephone receiver.

"I tell you, Celia, if I had a magic wand I'd wave it and spirit the poor child right out of that house instantly! Every time I looked at her, I felt quite *murderous*. And I couldn't ask her anything, couldn't get her confidence, because the other gels were sitting there. It wouldn't have been at all right, would it?"

"Dear me," said Celia Chisholm. "Well, are you going to read out this letter to me? I'm all agog now, but I can't pop over and see it for myself because I've got my curlers in."

"I can hardly bring myself to repeat that vile woman's utter twaddle. I don't even want to touch the thing. One moment."

She went to the tea table, which had not been cleared, and took the sugar tongs from their bowl. Then she opened the drawer in the telephone table, extracted the letter with the tongs and began to read it aloud over the telephone. She really needed a third hand for the glass of gin to help her get through it.

"*Your earnest Associate in the Exercise of Care for a Child* – oh, it's absolutely nauseating!" she concluded.

"Her first name – what's this harridan called?"

"Sorry, I thought I told you. It's Roberta."

An intake of breath from the Chisholm end, then silence.

"Celia? Celia, are you there?"

"Yes. Just – remembering. Now look, Zinnia, I don't have a magic wand either, but you and I have got work to do. Elinore shouldn't be anywhere near that character. Can I tell you a bit of a story?"

"My dear, I'm all ears! But let me top up this glass first."

"Not too much! I want your head completely clear. You'll be putting it together with mine so we can come up with something practical. I don't think rescue is too strong a word."

"Golly!" said Lady Groule, sitting up straight, thrilled to her bone marrow. This was why one simply had to live in town. *Something was happening.*

18

Abraded nerves will wreck sleep at any age. The nightmares and imaginings they can produce, however, are ten times as potent in the young. On Wednesday morning, Elinore's eyes opened too early and she was sure that she had been awake and fending off monsters all night long. She pulled back her curtains to let the dawn help banish them, and returned to her tense huddling in bed as light brought colour to the gardens of Dunallan Crescent.

Her first coherent thought was of Melba. Where was Melba waking up today? In a fancy bedroom in a super-modern house, like the ones on American television shows? Now that Melba was really and truly in the real America, Elinore felt that she belonged there, like all beautiful and special people. Melba was beautiful, and she was special because she was so beautiful. She belonged in America as a bird belonged in a tree or in the sky, a fish in the sea, a bear in Alaska. Being neither beautiful nor special, Elinore knew that she could not expect to belong there, not *really*, and all the more so because she did not want to go there.

This line of reasoning led her to the sudden sense that her mother would not return – at least, not for any longer than a bird would alight before taking to the air again. She had gone to the right place for a Melba. The right place for an Elinore was either

Criven, now unreachable, or somewhere yet unknown to her. In between lay a blank, an indefinite present and future dominated by Caltrops. This new understanding of her life made her tummy screw itself up and her heart leap into her throat and bang around, which was quite scary, because she knew it belonged much further down in her chest. But it stayed in her throat and refused to return to the right place.

She thought of Dr Berg, who knew all about people's hearts, and that made her want to be in Susanna's house as soon as possible. "Come back tomorrow morning!" Susanna had said as they parted after Lady Groule's tea. She had not said come at nine o'clock, or ten or any other time. A desperate fear assailed Elinore now: if she did not get to the Berg house early enough, she might not be allowed to leave No. 17 at all. She jumped out of bed and began to dress. To make quite sure of the time, she turned on her radio.

Elinore was not aware of the advantages that Mrs Caltrop perceived in allowing her to continue visiting friends. Two were obvious: first, someone else was spending money and time on feeding the child, and second, the child was Mrs Caltrop's only apparent route to familiarity with Lady Groule. The third advantage was more subtle and delicious to Mrs Caltrop: what she allowed, she could also forbid, and all visits would cease if Elinore did not toe the planned line of control. So much disciplining to accomplish within two weeks! That was why she too had got up early, prompted by a different kind of excitement, and why she appeared on the landing at exactly the moment that Elinore reached the stairs. In her grey dressing gown and slippers, and with her steel-wool hair flattened by a hairnet, Mrs Caltrop looked like a bulky rat, and her eyes gleamed at the sight of Elinore as a rat's would at the sight of something tasty on the floor.

"Good morning, Elinore. You appear to be all ready to go out. But you will have breakfast first, of course. Then you can tell me just where you are going today, and whether you are likely to spend time with Lady Groule."

After her screeching, accusatory dismissal of Elinore twelve hours previously, this was an astonishing little speech, and so was the nasty-nice smile that followed it. Elinore, frozen at the top of the stairs, said nothing. Yes, she had been about to leave: to be gone long before another Caltrop breakfast, to walk around and around the neighbourhood, turning on her radio (in her bag) now and then to check the time until the morning was advanced enough for the Berg household to be ready for visitors. Going hungry until lunchtime would have been nothing at all.

Elinore did not know what to say. Mrs Caltrop's eyes stayed on her, while her eyebrows rose and she continued to grimace in her unique misrepresentation of charm until, abruptly, she pushed past Elinore and went downstairs. Without turning her head, she said, "I expect you to appear for breakfast at the usual time."

I don't know what to *do* any more, thought Elinore. Her heart had jammed itself up in her throat again and she felt shaky, in fright at Mrs Caltrop's sudden appearance and in anxiety and disappointment at her failure to get out of the house unchallenged. She returned to her bedroom, took the radio out of her bag and tuned in to Radio One, a link to the normal world. Tony Blackburn was cracking jokes on his Breakfast Show. He read a letter from a listener who wanted to thank him for playing a particular song that had cheered her up and changed her life at a bad moment. "And thank *you*, Elinore in Sutton Coldfield, for taking the time to tell me that. All right, let's spin that magic again for all you happy people!"

Elinore? Magic? It was a secret message. It had to be. But it was hardly anything to go on, just Tony Blackburn saying thank you. Elinore could not think of a single song that might work happy magic on her. Then she remembered how Lady Groule's box of postcards had achieved just that the previous night. She must send proper thanks to Lady Groule right now. *That* was what Tony Blackburn was trying to tell her. Elinore got out her blue velvet box of notecards. She could not afford to slip up in the matter of politeness with a person – a capital-L Lady! – who could look so ferocious.

She already had quite enough ferocity to manage within this home that was not a home.

Over breakfast, Mrs Caltrop announced that Elinore would be introduced to the church on Saturday afternoon, at an annual social event for families, before attending Sunday school the next morning.

"But I don't go to Sunday school. Mummy said I didn't have to, a long time ago. Before Hector went away."

Mr Caltrop stopped eating and his mouth stayed open, a sure sign that this was a gravely serious moment.

"You will start going this Sunday," said Mrs Caltrop in a strangely placid tone given the subject. "We are your guardians now, and we are duty bound to act in your best interests. And you will continue to go after your mother has returned. I know she will be happy to see our care of you continue in that manner." Her thick lips stretched into a smile and she leaned forward. "And I am sure *you* will be happy to give up to Jesus a portion of your play time every week. You will meet many other little girls at Sunday school, from good *Christian* families. If you disobey, your play time will cease forthwith and your liberty will be curtailed in other ways."

"But I don't have to . . ." Elinore's protest trailed off. The plain meaning under Mrs Caltrop's pomposity had sunk in. She dropped her head and concentrated on the toast. Agent Solo was nowhere within range, but Elinore had not forgotten her instruction to avoid saying yes at certain moments. This was a terrifying moment.

"As for today, you will not be having lunch and tea here, will you?"

"No. I like eating with my friends."

"So I have noticed," said Mrs Caltrop, still smiling in the way that Elinore imagined the most dangerous snake in the world would smile, or a crocodile, an alligator or a shark. She was sure that each of those creatures would also have breath that smelled exactly like Mrs Caltrop's.

Elinore arrived at the Bergs' house just as Mrs Berg was helping Daniel into a taxi.

"Mummy's going on the train," said Susanna. "She's going to Glasgow to visit a friend, and she took Daniel because her friend's got a boy he can play with. I wish she would leave him behind in Glasgow! She says I have to do jobs for Fredy today and start learning to be a good housekeeper or she won't bring me back any treats."

Elinore pointed to a pile of bedlinen on Susanna's bedroom floor. "Is that a job?"

"Yes, it's called strip the bed. Now I have to carry it all down to the washing machine. Whew. What a life. I got that from the *Dandy*. W-H-E-W. Whheeewww! I can say that one a lot, but if I say what a life, Mummy gets a look on her face and tells me to stop it. But she's away! Tee-hee, tee-hee! You see that one in all the comics, don't you?"

"Thank you, Susanna," said Fredy as she received the pile in the kitchen. "Now you take all these clean things upstairs, and later I will show you how to make the bed properly. First you come back down here and we fold the things in this basket and put them away neat and tidy."

Susanna pulled a face and sighed. "But Elinore's here and jobs are really boring for *her*!"

"No, they're not, honestly," said Elinore quickly. "I like it. It feels nice when everything's clean." She meant in the Berg and Patel households, which did not smell of Domestos.

Elinore thought it was time to learn about housekeeping too, and she stayed in the kitchen while Susanna stomped upstairs with the fresh bedlinen.

"Fredy, what can you do if you don't have a washing machine to keep everything clean?"

Fredy looked surprised, and then laughed. "You ask someone to buy you one straight away! How could I wash all the sheets and towels in this house without a machine? They would need another Fredy just for that!"

Elinore tried to stop her enquiry being derailed. "But if you just don't have one, and you have to wash your clothes, what can you do? It's very bad to wear dirty clothes, isn't it? Could you put them in the bath?"

"Oh no, not the bath! We don't need to live in the old ways, like our grandmothers. You could go to a place called a laundrette, where you have to pay. But you don't have to worry about these things, Elinore. That's for grown-ups. You are always nice and clean, and you just give the clothes to your mother when they're dirty, and she puts them in the machine, yes? Unless your mother also has an *au pair*!" She laughed again.

"I don't actually know what that word is."

"It's French, but you hear it everywhere you go. It looks like this." She took the telephone notepad and wrote down *au pair*. "It means a person who comes from a different country to help in the house and look after the children too." Elinore read the written word, which obviously had nothing to do with fruit. "So, I am a Danish girl who works in Scotland, and my job has a French name. Next year I might go to America. I have a friend there."

"Elinore's mummy is in America," said Susanna, hoisting herself onto the kitchen table and swinging her legs energetically.

"Really? What city is she in, Elinore? It's a huge country," said Fredy. "My friend lives in Portland, which is so far away it's almost in Hawaii."

Elinore had never heard of either place, and wondered why Melba had not given her a piece of paper with her holiday address on it. It would have looked good in her address book.

"I don't know where she is," she confessed.

"Well, you can tell me when you start getting postcards from her. When is she coming home?"

Elinore's homemade calendar was still in her bag, and she pulled it out to show them.

"Whew! That's a lot of days," said Susanna. "Do you miss her lots and lots?"

This question was completely unanswerable. Elinore avoided it by staring fixedly into the laundry basket on the table, from which Fredy was taking line-dried towels and folding them, and then picking out a towel and doing the same.

"Elinore, stop! You're doing a *job!*" cried Susanna. "Fredy will just give you more and more and then we'll have to work all day long even when Usha comes. What a life!"

Fredy said nothing, but she looked at Elinore and began to wonder. When she was not spending her summers exploring cultures via other people's kitchens, children and laundry routines, she was a student of literature and philosophy at Aarhus University, and she had been thinking of switching to psychology. Reading between the lines, interpretation of the unsaid as much as of the words, and dredging up the real message all came naturally to her; academia had only honed this. "What *can* you do if you don't have a washing machine . . .?" *Can* rather than *do* in this context implied that help was needed. And why mention a bathtub as an alternative to a washing machine? She sensed complexities, and that it might be appropriate to encourage the unsaid to reveal more of itself.

Usha rang while Elinore was using one of the Berg's bathrooms and thinking how lovely it must be to look at pictures on the walls while lying in a bath (a hot, deep bath, of course). Usha would be along after lunch, Susanna reported, because she had to help Mrs Patel with chores in the morning. Elinore thought it was funny that Susanna should accept that arrangement as normal while grumbling about the chores doled out by Fredy.

For their next job of the morning, Fredy sat them down outside the back door with colanders, bowls and a big bag of peas to shell. They sang along to Radio One while they worked. If this is learning housekeeping, it's fun, thought Elinore. The sun grew hotter and they took off their jumpers. Elinore was happy to show off a yellow T-shirt that she had only worn once before; she knew it was definitely not ready for the washing machine yet. Fredy could see both girls when she stood at the kitchen sink. She had a particularly good view of Elinore's upper right arm, where bruising stood out on her pale skin: five livid finger marks, Fredy was sure of it. This was the unsaid revealing itself forcefully in any language, and it was also a complexity, a dark one that Fredy would have preferred not to encounter on a child's body.

When she returned to No. 17 that evening, Elinore went straight to the back door. Mr Caltrop was peering at a flower bed. He looked at Elinore without a word and then bent his head over the plants again. Elinore turned the knob of the door, assuming that it was unlocked because Mr Caltrop was only ten feet away from it, but she was wrong.

"Please can you let me in?" she asked him, but he merely shook his head in refusal, sighed and moved along to another flower bed. Elinore was dumbfounded. Fortunately, this time she was not in desperate need of peeing. She pressed the doorbell and waited. Mrs Caltrop appeared after a minute or two.

"You will have had your tea, of course, but regardless I will expect you downstairs in half an hour," she told Elinore. "We must discuss our day tomorrow, when visitors will be here."

Elinore felt very tired. On her way back to No. 17, knowing that she would not be given any more food that day, she had planned to curl up on her bed, organize the art postcards into subject groups and try not to think about what Mrs Caltrop might say next. Moreover, tomorrow already contained an important event that she had arranged with Fredy and absolutely must not miss: Elinore Crum's private laundry hour.

Fredy had chosen a moment when Susanna and Usha were distracted by their own chatter to ask Elinore, quietly and simply, "Would you like me to wash some clothes for you tomorrow? You bring them straight to me, as early as you can so we make them dry, OK? You put them all in this bag." She put a rolled-up plastic bag into Elinore's hand. Elinore was stunned. Her mouth opened in the automatic thank you, but Fredy put a finger to her lips and shook her head, smiling. "Go and put this bag in your pretty Chinese one right away," she whispered.

Now Elinore looked at Sir Gabriel and the Magic Men. "Please, please, please help me get my clothes to Fredy tomorrow so she can make them all nice and clean. Thank you very much indeed." She still felt grievously let down by the way their good omens had developed, or failed to, but surely clean clothing was a safe thing to request humbly, and well within the capacities of super-magic beings.

When Elinore entered the morning room, Mrs Caltrop did not invite her to sit down, and so she stood with her hands behind her back, nails digging into palms, while learning about the visitors who were coming to meet her tomorrow.

"You will appreciate that we are doing this for *you*," said Mrs Caltrop. "We are bringing good folk into our home specifically to welcome you into our fold. On Saturday and Sunday, you will meet many more, and tomorrow's occasion will be a helpful introduction." And would give Mr and Mrs Caltrop an extra opportunity to burnish their credentials as saviours of the lost and misguided. "The little Begbie girls will be coming with their parents, and Mrs McKendrick will bring her son."

"Are they the same age as me?" asked Elinore.

"That is irrelevant. Sunday school is about the joy of following Jesus, which has nothing to do with age. These children are all Christians in the Protestant faith, and that is all that should concern you. You will be here at half-past one and ready to greet them at two o'clock. I expect you to be clean and neat. Do you have any further questions?"

"No."

"Good. However, I have one more thing to tell you. If you allow your wilfulness and bad character to spoil the goodness of this occasion in the slightest degree, the consequences will be severe. *Severe.* Do you understand?"

Elinore nodded in lieu of the yes that she did not want to say. When she was in her room again, she saw that her fingernails had dug deep red marks into her palms.

Thursday morning was bright, but only in a fitful way. Clouds were massing over the hills beyond the city. Elinore awoke early again. Her first thought was of the laundry she must take to the Berg house – discreetly. It was a private matter between Fredy and her, and possibly Mrs Berg; she wanted to avoid questions from Susanna and Usha for as long as possible, and above all from Mrs Caltrop. It made her feel bad to be suspected of stealing every time Mrs Caltrop saw her with a bag in hand, and to be reminded of the money she had decided not to give Mr Curglaff.

If only she could fly out of a window. If she could fly, she would escape the Caltrops completely. On the other hand, a magic carpet would be better than wings, because it could transport all her treasures, which, strangely, had increased as her life had become more and more fragmented and frightening. Pictures in frames; an antique shawl; hundreds of fascinating postcards; five books; a Chinese silk bag; pocket money, birthday money and all the little things one could buy with that; luxurious scented soaps; brand new shoes and clothes – what next? Still, as she put her dirty laundry into Fredy's plastic bag, Elinore thought that having nice things in a hostile environment could be a problem. If you did not have them, they could not be confiscated or stolen, you would not be suspected of stealing them, and you would not have the worry of trying to keep them clean and proper all by yourself. It was a puzzle, all right, because the nice things meant she could be the equal of Usha and Susanna, and accept invitations from Lady Groule to tea and concerts. They also provided solace and their own kind of magic, and she could not imagine leaving them behind.

She lifted the bag of laundry: *so* big and heavy, she thought. It was neither, in fact, but it could not be concealed in her shoulder bag and that automatically made it large and problematic in Elinore's eyes. Bothered, she sat on her bed and looked at it. She felt tired already and it was only morning. A clock chimed: she would have to go down to breakfast soon.

Her radio had been playing all this time, bringing smiley Tony Blackburn into her room. All the disc jockeys sounded smiley all the time, but Tony Blackburn was the smiliest of all. It must be because everything in his life was perfect, and perhaps she would sound like that all the time if she had a life like his. But perhaps all DJs ended up being happy automatically, even if their lives were not perfect, just because they played pop music all the time. It was the most smiley music in the world, even when singers were moaning soppy things about love. Pop music made you want to dance. It could cheer people up at difficult times – look at that other Elinore in Sutton Coldfield!

As Elinore pondered the bag of laundry and the convenience of a magic carpet, Tony Blackburn announced the next song, *Up the Ladder to the Roof* by The Supremes. Elinore loved this song. By now, it had been nearly three months in the charts, and she had been hearing it since the day she had first turned on her little radio. Words in pop songs were usually indistinct and often mystifying and bizarre when they could be deciphered, but not in this case.

Come with me
And we shall run across the sky
And illuminate the night
Oh-oh-oh, I will try and guide you
To better times and brighter days

Don't be afraid
Come up the ladder to the roof
Where we can see heaven much better
Come up the ladder to the roof . . .

The next song was *Down the Dustpipe* by Status Quo, which was always gibberish to Elinore. Why a dustpipe and not a drainpipe? Roofs, ladders, drainpipes . . . It was funny how some songs went together. Roofs, ladders, drainpipes . . . People were always shinning up and down drainpipes in stories, especially when they wanted to escape. Elinore did not think she could manage that, but Agent Solo looked out of the bedroom and boxroom windows anyway, just in case she suddenly needed a useful drainpipe. Then Agent Solo had an idea that could be turned into action immediately.

The boxroom window overlooked the back of the house, and it was almost at the gable end, far from the kitchen and scullery windows. If Elinore dropped her full laundry bag out of the window, it would land on a patch of soil with no tell-tale flowers to squash. She could retrieve it when she left the house, and no one would see her. She was now expected to use the back door anyway.

❧

Mrs Berg listened to Fredy's observations about Elinore, and said that they only sharpened her own sense that something was amiss. She thought it best to apply discretion as long as the situation was unclear, and to leave Fredy in the role of intermediary since Elinore seemed to trust her. Consequently, Susanna was being kept busy upstairs with another housekeeping lesson when Elinore arrived that day, and Mrs Berg refused to let her down tools until the job was properly completed. Fredy quickly sorted Elinore's laundry, set the washing machine in motion for its first load and told her she would take care of everything. She did not ask why the bottom of the plastic bag was smeared with earth.

"I have to go before half past one today," said Elinore.

"It might not all be ready then. If it isn't, you can come back and pick it up this evening. Some things I would also like to iron for you, and you could have those tomorrow, OK?"

Elinore could hardly believe she was receiving all this help. Keeping clothes nice was so easy this way – just press a few buttons! – and she had full confidence that Fredy's laundering would keep white things white. But the day's obstacles and hazards were far from surmounted or dodged. She kept checking the time, afraid that she would enjoy herself too much and forget all about the visiting church people, thus bringing *severe consequences* down upon her head.

Her socks and underwear were slightly damp but otherwise all ready for her at a quarter past one. Mrs Berg popped her head around the kitchen door. "Will we see you for tea tonight, Elinore? Six o'clock? We're having bangers and mash – hope you like that!"

"Yes, I do. I would really like to come back."

"Good. We won't be here tomorrow night, you see – in fact, we won't be back until Sunday evening. We're going to stay with Granny Berg in Pitlochry."

"Oh." Elinore felt as if something holding her up had collapsed. Then she remembered Usha, whose father never took her anywhere, and grasped the straw of that haven.

Fredy told her that she would be going with the Bergs. They had bought her a ticket to see one of her favourite plays at the Pitlochry Festival Theatre, and then she was going to have a day off to visit Perth, Dunkeld and Scone Palace.

"If I was staying behind, you could come here and have tea with me, which would be very nice," said Fredy, giving Elinore's arm a friendly little squeeze (making sure it was the arm without the bruises). "So, tomorrow all your clothes will be dry, and ironed too, and just come for them before half past ten, OK? We leave then."

"All right," said Elinore. "I hope you have a very nice time. I didn't know there was another palace in Scotland."

"Yes, absolutely. I love all these places. Have you been to the castle here, and Holyrood Palace? No? Oh well, maybe we can go together, because they are amazing and they have so much for one Danish girl to see, she has to go twice!"

※

The hour of Elinore's introduction to the church was upon her. Mr and Mrs Begbie arrived first. Mr Begbie was almost as tall as Mr Caltrop, and lanky; the trouser legs of his brown suit flapped as he walked, and his jacket did the same around other parts. He wore a blue V-neck pullover over a white shirt with a huge, strangling collar, and a knitted tie in a blue that did not match the sweater. He had gingery hair, a gingery-red moustache, a blotched, boiled-lobster hue to his face, and an Adam's apple that appeared to be in perpetual bobbing motion, which made Elinore feel ill whenever she looked at him; she tried not to.

Mrs Begbie was short. In another female, a heathen follower of fashion, her looks could have been enhanced with appropriate cosmetics and a sympathetic hairstyle, not to mention clothes that actually fitted; the result would then have been described as pert and youthful. As it was, she would have blended well into most Eastern Bloc female populations. She wore a mottled lavender and grey Crimplene suit that ignored the female form other than to let her calves appear below the tubular skirt. The legs ended in shiny, black vinyl low-heeled shoes with an incongruous oversized buckle on the toe. Elinore, who was keeping her gaze cast down for several good reasons, saw that the buckle was plastic, and that its gold colour was flaking off. Mummy would never, ever put her feet in shoes like that, she thought. Neither would Melba have put on brick-toned foundation. On Mrs Begbie, it met her pallid neck in a hard-edged tidemark.

Myra, Sharon and Sheila Begbie were arrayed in homemade frocks that were not quite party ones, but still too fancy for school. They were not quite fashionable either, with their puffed shoulders and full nylon skirts stiffened by a petticoat layer, and they were all exactly the same style but in different colours. Myra wore prussic acid blue, Sharon sulphur yellow and Sheila absinthe green. Each girl had dark hair cut in an exact copy of their mother's nondescript chop. Each had putty-like faces moulded into exactly the same silent, suspicious dislike directed at Elinore.

The Begbie family was still milling like poisonous liquorice allsorts in the hallway of No. 17 when Mrs McKendrick arrived with her son Malcolm. Anxious to avoid any form of contact with this Caltropian cohort, Elinore moved backwards up the stairs as far as the third step. She saw Malcolm looking at her with an open mouth and wide, stricken eyes. He was bigger than Elinore, perhaps even older, but he too moved backwards from the press of people until he was half concealed by his mother's raincoat. He kept his worried, half-shocked gaze on Elinore all the time. He's *scared* of me, she thought, astounded that anyone welcomed into the Caltrop house should be scared of her.

Mrs McKendrick could hardly be parted from her beige raincoat. "The wireless said thunder before evening," she said, and repeated it thirty seconds later as if to stress the wisdom of keeping a raincoat on indoors. Her A-line navy blue shift dress reminded Elinore of Mrs Wattie's housecoat, the main difference being some tatty lace at the neck. Her tights sagged at the ankles and she wore flat porridge-coloured slip-on shoes. When Mrs McKendrick removed her floral headscarf (with another comment about the forthcoming thunderstorm), Elinore saw mid-length ashy hair, parted in the middle and left hanging straight. The woman had not a trace of colour on her face. Lipstick might have been unwise, however, for it would have drawn attention to her appalling teeth.

Mrs Caltrop herded them all into the sitting room. The guests appeared to be a little awed by the furnishings and general tone of the room, and many were the iterations of "Very nice, Mrs Caltrop" and "Very fine, I must say" and "Oh my, this is quite the grand room, Mrs Caltrop." Lady Groule's card had been put on the mantelpiece, dead centre against the dome of the torsion pendulum clock with the golden balls. Each visitor sidled up for a good sideways look at it, without letting on that they were looking at it, just as Mrs Caltrop had hoped and known they would. They all admired the clock, which no longer kept time.

(It is important to note here that the visitors were not addressing Mrs Caltrop by her first name at that point: they were not friends of hers, or even social equals. Mrs Caltrop had plucked them unerringly from the pews of church regulars, partly because of their children and partly – mostly – because of the ease with which they could be impressed by the Caltrops and the pleasure that that would afford the latter.)

Elinore dragged her heels until Mrs Caltrop grabbed her shoulder (ten times harder than Mummy, thought Elinore, wincing) and pushed her into the centre of the room. Everyone stared at her expectantly and unsmilingly. Mrs Begbie licked her lips. Malcolm McKendrick looked as if he might burst into tears.

"I am very pleased to introduce you to the newest member of our congregation and Sunday school – Elinore Crum."

The prussic acid blue Begbie girl and the sulphur yellow one tittered. The absinthe green one looked at her sisters and then did the same. Mrs Begbie smiled affectionately at them and said, "Hush now, girlies."

"Elinore is a stranger to Edinburgh, and to all the joys of the church," continued Mrs Caltrop. "She has been with us for some weeks now, and we have come to understand her great need for the friendship of girls and boys whose feet are set firmly and joyously on the path of righteousness. The path that we have been chosen to lead her along!"

"Amen to tha'," said Mr Begbie, in a strong Glaswegian accent that made his voice sound as though it were coming through a clogged drain.

"Amen, amen, amen" said Mrs McKendrick, Mrs Begbie and Mr Caltrop.

"Now, we are going to have some tea and of course a chance to get to know Elinore."

"Can I give you a hand with the tea, Mrs Caltrop?" asked Mrs Begbie.

"That would be appreciated," said Mrs Caltrop. "And do please call me Roberta."

"I'll just stay put with Malcolm, if you don't mind," said Mrs McKendrick. "This is a big day for him, you know." She paused and looked anxiously at Malcolm, before adding in a stage whisper, "It's been only six months." Malcolm buried his face in his mother's armpit and began to bawl. "There, there, pet. No bogeymen here. Elinore's just a nice wee girl your own age, and you know what, she's just like you! Her daddy's gone to heaven too."

"Six months – you don't say!" said Mr Begbie. "You'd think it was yesterday." He turned to Mr Caltrop and the two men leaned forward in their chairs and talked in low, intense tones with much head-shaking.

Despite her indignation and discomfort at being displayed in this way, under a great big fib – anyone would think she *wanted* to go to Sunday school! – Elinore's curiosity was aroused by Malcolm McKendrick's daddy in heaven. If that boy is just like me, she reasoned, his daddy got eaten by something too, maybe another bear, maybe even in Alaska – maybe his daddy knew Hector! She would be just nice enough to Malcolm to find out.

"Excuse me," she began.

"Do you have any dollies?" interrupted a sharp little voice at her elbow.

The youngest Begbie, the green one, was standing beside her, still unsmiling.

"No, I don't. I've never had any dolls." Elinore could not bring herself to utter *dollies*.

"Why not?"

"Only babies play with dolls."

The green Begbie's mouth opened and stayed open, in distress.

"I am not a baby!" she wailed, still standing there.

"Are you calling our Sheila a baby?" demanded the prussic acid blue Begbie, hands on hips.

"No, I'm not. I just told her why I don't have any dolls."

"Why not?"

"Because they're stupid and I hate them." Elinore took a breath. She wanted to summon nine hungry grizzly bears and lock them in this room with the nine humans tormenting her today. Instead, she added, "And only babies play with dolls." It was the truth, and so it was a good answer.

"You are so calling us babies!" cried the blue Begbie.

"Yes, you are so!" echoed the yellow one. "And dollies are not stupid!"

The green one wailed more loudly, and Malcolm McKendrick cried, "Muuuummm . . ." into his mother's armpit. Mrs McKendrick put both arms around him and crooned, "There, there now, poor wee man." The two men leaned closer to shut out the noise and completely ignored its generators. Elinore felt a weird triumph, which lasted about two seconds.

"*What* is the meaning of this, Elinore?" rapped out Mrs Caltrop as she wheeled in a tea trolley, followed by Mrs Begbie.

"I don't know. I just said I didn't have any dolls."

Mrs Begbie bustled to her youngest, the absinthe green Sheila, and hoisted her onto her knees. Myra and Sharon clustered by her legs. All three girls stuck their fingers in their mouths and began to suck energetically, while sending Elinore looks of pure hatred.

Mrs Caltrop was breathing heavily and her cheeks were growing lurid flowers. She bent over Elinore and hissed, "Did I not warn you? Did I not say how severe the consequences would be if you dared to show the bad side of your character to this gathering?"

Elinore stayed mute and kept her eyes on the carpet.

"My wee man's just raring to talk to Elinore, you know!" said Mrs McKendrick, who appeared unaware of any upset beyond Malcolm's shaking body. "Will you not come and sit down here and tell us all about yourself, pet?" She patted the patch of sofa beside her and looked hopefully at Elinore. Mrs Caltrop pushed her in that direction, and she went. She sat down beside Malcolm and folded her arms, waiting for him to remove his head from his mother's body.

The tea that Mrs Caltrop then laid out was supposed to be special, because it offered not one but two flavours of jam (the very cheapest kind, but served with silver spoons), Battenberg cake, and a choice of egg mayonnaise sandwiches or mustard cress ones, both on white bread with no crusts.

"Well, these dainty wee things are Holyrood style and no mistake, Roberta," said Mrs Begbie, referring to the sandwiches.

"Some people are saying brown bread is the thing, but I just don't see Malcolm eating that," said Mrs McKendrick.

"A plain white pan loaf is to be preferred for all uses," pronounced Mrs Caltrop.

Elinore had no appetite at all. She was going to enjoy bangers and mash later with the Bergs, anyway. This was simply an ordeal to get through. She focused on Malcolm, who, she felt, was far less a danger than the chemical triplets, and decided to be helpful.

"Hello, how are you?" she asked.

"Fine," came a very small voice.

"I'm in Primary Four at school. What class are you in?"

"Primary Four too."

"Are you the same age as me? I'm ten now."

"Yes, I'm ten. I'll be eleven in a wee while."

Mrs McKendrick beamed at Elinore in approval. "See? I knew you two would get on like a house on fire."

Elinore plodded through some more questions. It meant she could ignore the Begbies for now, but she did think Malcolm was a great big baby. She wanted to find out what had happened to his father, though. When Mrs McKendrick was deeply involved in the discussion of preparations for Saturday's church social event, she edged along the sofa to Malcolm.

"Malcolm, do you know what happened to my daddy?"

Malcolm shook his head.

"Do you want me to tell you? I could make it into a story for you."

Malcolm nodded, but then shook his head. "I don't like story books."

Elinore swallowed her astonishment and undiluted scorn. "I'm going to *tell* you the story right now. But you have to sit up properly or it won't work."

Malcolm sat up. His mother felt this, stopped talking and looked around. "My! These two have hit it off and no mistake. Malcolm and you are best pals already, Elinore. You're doing the work of Jesus on my poor wee man and you haven't even got to Sunday school yet. I'm most impressed, Roberta."

Mrs Caltrop preened. "Guardianship is a great responsibility, but I think I can safely say that all the evidence shows we are shouldering it just as the Lord would want us to."

Mr Caltrop interrupted. "Iain and I are going to inspect the garden. Would the ladies like to accompany us?"

"Oh, yes, that would be very nice, and we should do it right now before that thunderstorm," said Mrs McKendrick. "Roberta, I'll just get my coat and scarf, if you don't mind."

The entire group began to meander around the garden, on which the sun had ceased to shine, although the air was hot and humid. Now Mr Caltrop was in charge of the entertainment, and he boomed away about the dangers of dogs, cats and delinquents. Elinore dawdled and kept Malcolm back, beginning to spin a tale about a man who sailed away to a far-off land that was very, very cold. That was almost all she knew about Alaska, but her embellishments were convincing enough to hold Malcolm rapt and completely physically separate from his mother. She drew the slender thread of the tale out and out until finally she stood still and asked Malcolm, "So what do you think happened next? Go on, guess what happened to *my* daddy."

Malcolm stopped walking too. "Do I have to make a guess?" he asked.

"Yes – that's what I said!" Elinore was almost beside herself with impatience at this boy who really and truly was a big baby.

"Oh – I have to think about it."

"Why not just guess?"

"Guess what?" demanded a Begbie voice. "Are you telling secrets? You're not supposed to tell secrets about people. It's *bad*."

All three Begbie girls had circled around to end up behind Elinore and Malcolm. "It's not a secret, it's a story," said Elinore. "I'm telling Malcolm a story."

"You didn't tell *us* the story," the eldest Begbie accused Elinore. "Why not? Why aren't you being nice to us too?"

Several answers to that came readily to Elinore, but she stayed silent, and tried to make her lip curl contemptuously (she had read about that skill in more than one book, and had been trying to master it for some time).

"Girlies!" came Mrs Begbie's voice. "You play out here for a wee while longer, with Malcolm and Elinore. We're going inside to have a talk."

"If you need to come in, you can use this door and Elinore will show you where to go," said Mrs Caltrop. "Elinore, you are in charge of our young guests, and I expect the utmost in courtesy from you. Remember the rules about the Anderson shelter, the washing line props and the flowerbeds!"

Elinore's insides churned with anger, frustration and a niggling worry that this torture might go on for so many more hours that she would miss bangers and mash with the Bergs. How was sh*e* supposed to *play* in this garden with these idiots?

"I don't want girls' games," said Malcolm, startling Elinore. "I was hearing a story and you stopped it." He pointed at the Begbie girls, and Elinore could see that he was getting upset again, but for a completely different reason. He wanted a story. She seized the moment. She was the storyteller, the only one.

"And I'm not going to play silly games either!" she shouted. "I'm going to tell the story all over again, and you can listen too. You have to go away if you don't want to hear it, and I don't care where you go!" She sat down cross-legged on the grass, folded her arms and glared at them in the nastiest way possible. Malcolm immediately sat down right in front of her.

"I don't like you!" said Sheila Begbie. "I'm not going to sit down." Myra and Sharon, however, plopped themselves on the grass.

"If you say anything bad, Jesus will tell God and he will come down and strike you," said Myra.

"That's right," said Sharon. "We get that in Sunday school, so it's the truth."

Elinore wondered fleetingly where Sir Gabriel might stand on any of that, and then got on with the retelling of her story. It was going rather well – not a single interruption – until a piece of absinthe green nylon flashed across the grass and dived between Myra and Sharon.

"There's *bad* girls here!" it howled. "I want my Mum!"

Sheila Begbie had gone away as Elinore had commanded, had gone around the corner of the house and come face to face with two strangers: a girl with shiny steel teeth and a dark-skinned girl, the darkest person that Sheila had ever encountered at such close quarters. Now the two strangers appeared on the lawn, a little hesitantly because no one had ever before run away crying from them at first hello.

"Elinore! We heard you out here, so we didn't knock on the door. Can you come to tea at five o'clock, not six o'clock? Mummy said we had to come and ask you."

Worlds collided. Calving icebergs caused a tsunami on an oriental shore; glaciers rumbled and scored their passage across vast landscapes and mountain ranges in hours instead of millennia; tectonic plates slid and heaved along fault lines the length of continents; and Elinore Crum froze in shock and horror at the titanic consequences to be unleashed by the arrival of these two visitors.

"Who're you, scaring my wee sister?" roared Myra Begbie, scrambling to her feet. "You can't come in here!"

"Why not?" asked Susanna. "This is Elinore's garden and we're her best friends, so we can come here if we want to." But she looked taken aback.

"You have to go inside now – go *on!*" said Elinore, desperately trying to shove three Begbies and Malcolm towards the back door. Sheila was still howling.

"Don't you tell me what to do!" Myra slapped Elinore's hand away, and Sharon immediately slapped Elinore too. "You're bad! If you play with Pakis, Jesus won't like you, 'cause Pakis and darkies are really bad people, and you'll get bad germs off them too. My Mum and Dad say so."

"Yes! My Mum and Dad are going to tell you off! They're going to make you cry!" said Sharon in glee.

"*Shut up!*" screamed Elinore at the top of her lungs. She put a hand each on Myra and Sharon and pushed with all her might. They both fell down sprawling on the grass and the screaming was indescribable. Malcolm ran to the back door and cowered on the step, whimpering and covering his face with both hands.

Susanna and Usha stood still, bewildered by this reception and frightened enough to hold hands. Elinore started to speak to them, but all that came out was "Please . . ." before she too burst into tears and covered her face in utter shame.

Usha sprang to her side. "Elinore, don't cry! Elinore, it's all right, we'll look after you, we're your best friends!" She took Elinore's arm and tugged her, instinctively wanting to remove her from this scene.

Susanna took Elinore's other arm. "Just come with us! Come on! We can tell Daddy if these girls are hurting you and he'll come and sort them out – he will, promise!" She too tugged gently at Elinore.

"Let that girl go!" roared Mrs Caltrop from the back door. Then she strode across the grass, pulled Usha and Susanna away from Elinore and began to rage at them, fully aware that Mr Caltrop, Mr and Mrs Begbie and Mrs McKendrick had all rushed out behind her, to console their offspring and provide a venomously approving audience for the grandest display to date of Roberta Caltrop's devotion to the faith.

"I *know* who you are! I *know* you have been leading Elinore astray into your wicked, evil, profane beliefs and your dirty alien faiths. God knows that too. He sees into your hearts! He sees all your thoughts and your evil plans for tempting this girl off the one path that will lead her to salvation, all your nasty deceptions in the name of friendship. How dare you presume to think of yourselves as friends of this Christian girl? You, a Jew and you, a Hindu! How dare you come here and think you will push yourselves into this sacred home, where we do God's work from dawn to dusk?" She shook the girls so hard that they cried out, and that was the last straw for Elinore.

She hurled herself at Mrs Caltrop, kicking, hitting, scratching, punching and screaming, "Stop it, stop it, stop it!" over and over. A hand tried to clamp over her mouth, and she bit down on it and clenched her teeth as hard as she could. The hand sprang away and then two hands grabbed her by the neck and almost lifted her off the ground while pushing her towards the back door.

"Get out of this garden!" she heard Mrs Caltrop say, keeping her turned away from Susanna and Usha. "Get out and never come back, do you hear? If you ever try to lure Elinore off the Christian path again, I will set the police on you!"

"Susanna! Usha!" screamed Elinore. "I'm sorry, I'm sorry –" She was bundled inside the back door, and then Mrs Caltrop hauled her up the stairs to her room, pushed her inside it and banged the door closed. It had no key, but the door to Elinore's short corridor did, and Mrs Caltrop turned it.

19

Disaster has swallowed up Elinore Crum and secreted her in a prison-like space, for imminent digestion by the Caltrops. She curls up on her bed, weeping, and beyond her window the skies let loose the classic prelude and accompaniment to catastrophe, whether real or imagined: thunder, lightning and a torrent of rain.

A dramatic alignment of meteorology and incident affects other individuals on this evening, and no doubt an astrologer could mine these events for significant interrelated planetary influences. Of significance to the story of Elinore Crum is how these smaller cogs mesh to become one large cog, an accident of timing that will turn her future decisively in one direction.

For Zinnia, Lady Groule of Meggat, the storm becomes an irritation, a thing that inconsiderately blows in to disturb the way she usually deals with a visit to Meggat. She is to be a guest at the dinner party on Saturday night in honour of Alastair's birthday, and she expects to be picked up on Friday evening and driven there by another guest. The same guest is to drive her back to Edinburgh early on Sunday afternoon. Convenience and comfort will rule, and she will not be exposed to Meggat's many unique discomforts for any longer than propriety demands in the case of a family celebration.

On Thursday night, the helpful guest barrels into a pile-up just off the rain-shrouded Forth Road Bridge and is taken away for a weekend in hospital. Alastair tells his mother not to worry: he will pick her up instead on Friday morning, after an early appointment with a lawyer in Edinburgh. It will be in the Land Rover, he says: Alice's little car is kaput, and anyway it is useless in the rain, the heavy rain that is forecast to last throughout Saturday. "The Land Rover," he says cheerfully, "is just the thing!"

Yes, thinks Lady Groule sourly, the thing guaranteed to ruin my weekend. Alastair's decrepit, bone-shaking Land Rover will jounce her around on a hard, grubby seat in unbearable noise and uncontrollable draughts for almost two hours, all under pouring rain.

"And do you also propose to return me to my home by that vehicle?" she asks.

"Oh, haven't thought that far ahead yet," says Alastair. "Busy times, very busy. But you know we love having you here – just stay and enjoy yourself as long as you want!"

Dr Beeching's axe has fallen on the county of Angus too, and Meggat is consequently so far from the nearest railway station that everyone for many miles around is dependent on the car, or the Land Rover. Lady Groule is quite unable to reach Waverley Station unaided.

Lady Groule sighs. If she cannot be in Italy or France or at the Goring Hotel on a filthy wet weekend, she would like above all to stay at home, not stuck in the marsh of familial busyness, deep among the dreich and dolorous hills. And now she will lose all the Friday hours she had planned to devote to her joint investigation with Celia into the circumstances of Elinore Crum. She picks up Elinore's note of thanks, delivered this morning. The pretty card, the first-class stamp and above all the attention to courtesy by a child who (Celia says) must be enduring some form of torment add to the conundrum and mystery. She sighs again.

Several streets away from Lady Groule's cosy, cluttered, lamp-lit rooms, arrangements at the Berg household have also been tossed about by the weather. Dr Berg has stepped out from between two parked cars on a rainy street and been knocked over by a speeding motorcyclist. More accurately, he has been bruised all down his left side, and his left shoulder, arm and wrist feel dodgy; he has taken himself off for X-rays. Teatime has been pushed aside as Mrs Berg rushes off to meet him at the infirmary. Susanna appears, running along the street just as Mrs Berg is reversing into it from her driveway. The clouds have burst, Susanna's face and hair are wet, and she shrieks and covers her head with her hands at the sound of a thunderclap. Mrs Berg knows that her daughter is unreasonably afraid of thunder and lightning, and is unsurprised to see her face covered with tears as well as rain. "Get inside right away and change out of those wet things," she orders. "I'll be back with Daddy as soon as I can. Fredy will tell you all about it."

Daniel is crying because he has overheard enough to think that a big car has run over his daddy and flattened him like Tom and Jerry on the cartoons. Understandable, thinks Fredy. She assumes that Susanna has rushed in weeping copiously for roughly the same reason, plus thunder, and is shivering because she is wet. She consoles and puts right in accordance with those assumptions, and so Elinore Crum is completely forgotten by Fredy and Mrs Berg, along with the bangers and mash.

Over in MacAlpine Place, another accidental drama is being enacted, and this time it is a matter of life and death rather than bumps and bruises. Mr Patel goes to look out of his shop door at the drenching rain, hoping that the street drains will carry all the water away from his door as they are supposed to do. He sees a zigzag of lightning, which he judges to be quite far off, and an odd mound on the pavement opposite, which annoys him because it is likely to be a bag of rubbish that someone has deliberately dumped. Yet another example of the laziness and uncivil tendencies that seem to characterise the age he lives in now. But then he sees a shoe, and he realises that a trouser leg is above it. He rushes out of the shop and discovers that the mound is an elderly gentleman who appears to be unconscious. Mr Patel is a small man: he cannot carry this fallen body over to his shop, but he must do something, and no one else is in sight. He runs back and calls for Mrs Patel. When they reach the man on the pavement, they find a passer-by, a young woman with a child, hovering in the same state of anxiety over this stranger. Mr Patel sends his wife back to the shop to call for an ambulance; then he takes the man's shoulders and the woman takes his feet, and together they stumble across the street and into the shop. They lay him on the floor. Mrs Patel brings towels, blankets and a pillow and runs back upstairs for a hot water bottle. It seems a long, long time before they hear the ambulance, although only a few minutes have actually elapsed between Mrs Patel's call and the arrival of those who can save this man's life. But wait: the ambulance men say that their haste would have been in vain if Mr Patel had not got to the stranger first.

Just as they rush off noisily, a police car draws up, and two officers go into the shop to take down particulars of the incident. The woman who helped Mr Patel is still there, and her little boy starts to cry, unnerved by all this bewildering action and large men in uniforms dominating the small space where he has been parked in a corner. Then Usha Patel runs frantically into the shop. She has seen an ambulance drive away at top speed, and here is her father being questioned by police. A child is crying, the shop floor is strewn with familiar towels and blankets, and her mother is nowhere to be seen. It is too much of a shock for Usha, who has been shaken to the core both literally and figuratively by Mrs Caltrop. Everything spins, her hearing goes and she slumps onto the floor. The policemen are alarmed and want to get on their radio and call for another ambulance. But Mr and Mrs Patel know that Usha has fainted before when she has overdone some effort, and they think she will be all right. One policeman carries her upstairs to the flat, and the other continues to gather details of what Mr Patel saw and did in the rain.

At the Balmerinoch Hotel, Clova is surrounded by upheaval and the ever-present subject of drains instead of paying guests. She looks out at the unremitting downpour. Water from below, water from above . . . "Enough!" she mutters, and goes to ring a friend. She wants a hot bath and a bed in ordered surroundings, and not a single plumber, engineer or other kind of workman within sight or sound.

Within the old, thick walls of the Dower House at Squair, all is gloom and dark by four o'clock in the afternoon as the rain dims even further what daylight can creep in through the old, small windows. Tom Balmerinoch rubs his hands in pleasure. Rain is conducive to contemplation, concentration and then intense bursts of activity. He sits down to plan an uninterrupted downpour of words onto paper.

The thunder and lightning died away after a while, but the rain fell all night long and into the morning. Radio One and other BBC voices kept Elinore connected to the normal world and the passage of time. She fell asleep on top of her bed for a while, and when she awoke the radio informed her that it was a quarter to eleven at night. She understood then that she was going to be left alone until morning. She washed her face, cleaned her teeth and drank some water from the tap, thankful that Mrs Caltrop had not locked her into a place with no access to a bathroom. Then she went to bed, after turning the pictures of Sir Gabriel and the Magic Men around so that she was not being looked at by beings to whom she had apparently been a grievous disappointment. What other reason could there be for such a reversal of good omens?

When morning came, she dressed, and remembered the clean laundry that was waiting for her at Susanna's house. The Bergs would save her! They would come looking for her when she did not return for her clothes! And then the gut-wrenching memory and shame of Mrs Caltrop's hideous words flooded her mind and drowned that hope. The Bergs would never want to see her again. Elinore put her hands over her ears and wept, trying for the umpteenth time not to hear and see the unforgivable treatment of her friends. She went back to sit on top of her bed, and wondered whether the Caltrops were intending to starve her.

At the usual breakfast hour, Elinore heard the door to the landing open and then close, and the key turn again. A tray had been left on the floor, with a boiled egg and one piece of toast. The sight of it made her feel like a dog in a kennel. She ate, and then put the tray on the floor outside her room.

Agent Solo intervened and said it was time to make a list of the people who could possibly rescue her if she could only get a message to them. The Patels were not included: like the Bergs, they would never want to see her again. Arabella – yes, but she was very far away in Northumberland. Lady Groule – yes, even if she had been looking ferocious, and especially if George the taxi driver was at her side. Clova – yes, because she would stand no nonsense from the Caltrops. Tom – yes. Mrs Chisholm – yes, but she had no address or telephone number for her. That was the sum total of possible rescuers, and none could be alerted without a telephone. Without wings, she could not leave through a window and run away to the nearest sanctuary. The drainpipes were inconveniently placed for any secret agent and the windows too high for jumping.

Elinore could only wait and hope that her wishes might reach one of these people. If only Sir Walter Scott's monument spaceship could land in the garden . . . What fun to fly off with Maida and him, and look down on Mr Caltrop, a smashed Anderson shelter and several completely flattened flowerbeds.

She returned to reading *The Book of Edinburgh for Young People*. Perhaps the ghost of Helena Albacyr was watching her read the book that had once been hers. Arabella did not seem to think much of ghosts, but according to some stories they could be helpful. "Dear Helena," muttered Elinore, "please use your ghost power to scare the Caltrops to death and get me out of here. Or go to Arabella or Tom or someone and tell them I am locked up. Thank you very much."

She had already reached Chapter III, 'Edinburgh in the Time of the Stuarts', but she leafed back to the previous chapter to reread the description of King David receiving supernatural help when attacked by *"an immense white stag, which speedily pinned both the King and his horse to the ground with its antlers"*:

Escape from death seemed hopeless, as the Monarch had only a short hunting sword with him; but suddenly a little silver cloud appeared, out of which came a hand, which placed in that of the sorely pressed King a miraculous cross or "Rood", which was composed of some wonderfully brilliant substance.

Terrified by its lustre, the stag fled, and the King slowly and thoughtfully retraced his steps to the Castle.

That night, when he was asleep, Saint Andrew, the patron Saint of Scotland, appeared to him, and commanded him to build a monastery on the exact spot where he had been so miraculously delivered from deadly peril.

No, at second glance, this story could not offer hope or inspiration to Elinore Crum. Neither royal nor inherently saintly, and seemingly bad enough to trigger increasingly awful events, she could not expect help of this nature. Besides, the author of the book was far from convinced herself of the tale's veracity:

It is a pretty story . . . although there is much in it that we cannot quite believe.

The ghost of Helena Albacyr was a better bet. She must have been foreign with a name like that, which somehow brought to mind Ali Baba and abracadabra. She must have had magic in her, and she *must* still be hanging around somewhere! Elinore carried on reading, in the hope that ghostly Helena must feel her desperate longing for escape. On and on fell the rain outside. Her hunger grew and grew. *The Book of Edinburgh for Young People* aggravated it with descriptions such as the following:

> *. . . you can fancy with what delight Andrew, or Donald, or Wat would open it, for inside there would be . . . a stock of homemade scones, and a cheese, and perhaps a pat of butter . . .*

> *These two little vessels . . . come from the other end of the Mediterranean Sea . . . and the boxes which the active Greek sailors are lifting out of the hold, contain delicious dried fruits – figs, currants, raisins and spices.*

> *. . . at last it begins to dawn on you that, if you do not hurry off and catch the car, you will be late, and the hot buttered scones will be cold.*

The hot buttered scones did it. Elinore put down the book and cried and cried, for a home of her own where everything and everyone was warm, including the welcome at the beginning and end of the day, every day, and people like the Caltrops and Dwayne McMonagle and the Begbie girls would have no place except in horror stories. She cried because she never cried and now she could not stop. She curled up on the bed and cried until her throat ached from the spasms, and her face was swollen, and that is exactly the sight that greeted the agent of her release some time later.

The door to the landing opened with a crash and footsteps hammered down the corridor to Elinore's door. A clattering sound announced that the breakfast tray was being kicked aside. The door was flung back to reveal a figure Elinore recognised, despite a startling change that had come over it. The figure let loose a burst of profanity which cannot be translated accurately here, and stamped in to stand over the bed, eyes black and blazing with fury. Elinore stared up at her, as shocked as if Helena Albacyr herself had wafted through the keyhole. It was Mrs Wattie.

Mrs Wattie looked taller, because one end of her was in fashionable shoes with platform heels and the other end was now a trendy hairstyle, newly dyed jet black, backcombed and lacquered with hairspray to add hitherto undreamed of volume. Between these two points was a great deal of cosmetic artistry on a canvas of Sunkissed Beige Fluid Foundation; a scarlet dress with giant aqua flowers, puffed sleeves and shoulders; and a chain belt of enormous gold links alternating with what looked like diamond-studded sovereigns. Her perfume was Unforgettable by Avon, and it filled the room. She pointed at Elinore and issued a command.

"Up now! Ye'll be oot o' this house as fast as I can get ye oot. But ye need tae eat first."

Mrs Wattie hustled Elinore downstairs to the kitchen, where she put a hunk of cheddar and a knife onto one plate, heaped digestive biscuits onto another, and pressed Elinore into a chair at the kitchen table. "Eat up!" She produced a bottle of orange squash from the depths of a low cupboard. Then she ran out of the room, and, after some slamming of cupboard doors from the morning room, returned with an armful of chocolate bars and several kinds of fancy biscuits.

"I ken a' their wee secrets," she said, with the darkest look imaginable.

Elinore was eating and drinking, but she was shaking too, and her eyes kept darting to each door of the kitchen. Seeing this, Mrs Wattie sat down beside her and laid a hand on her arm.

"Now, Elinore, you listen tae me. We hae to get ye oot o' here an' intae another hoose like greased lightnin'."

"What?"

"We need tae get ye tae a friend's hoose afore yon pair o' unspeakables come in the door. Ye've got friends roon' aboot here, I ken that. That auld skinflint was always talkin' about the meals ye were nae eatin' here, for one thing. You tell me whaur they live an' I'll tak ye ower there."

She sat back, folded her arms and, for the first time ever, smiled at Elinore. It was a wicked smile in vivid scarlet. Elinore stopped eating, put her head down on the table and began to cry all over again.

"I don't have any friends any more," she sobbed. "She was cruel to them and they ran away. Everyone's very angry with me, and I can't go to their houses ever again."

"Ye mean she went for yer wee friends an a'? A' right – ye're comin' hame wi' me for the noo."

Mrs Wattie sprang up and rummaged in a cupboard by the back door. She took out several shopping bags and two laundry baskets. "Now you go back upstairs and put a' yer clothes in these. The auld cow's got plenty more if ye need them – an' then we're puttin' it on the magic carpet!"

Seeing Elinore's mystified expression, she repeated herself. "Aye, magic carpet – an' dinna ask me to explain now. I need tae get on the blower."

Elinore went halfway up the stairs and stopped. She could go further only if Mrs Wattie went with her, for it was too terrifying to be alone anywhere in this house in case it swallowed her up again. She crouched on a step and listened to Mrs Wattie giving orders over the telephone.

"It's yer ma!" she barked when someone answered. "Get yersel' back up here right now, fast as ye can. I'm a' ready, an' so is a wee passenger. She's got some bags an' she's comin' home wi' us for a wee while. Nae questions, jist step on it!" She hung up and followed Elinore.

In her room, Elinore realised that flight would endanger her beloved treasures. "What about my books and everything? *They'll* get them if I leave them behind."

"Ye're no' leavin' anythin' behind," replied Mrs Wattie, who seemed to have six arms at that moment. Elinore's clothes and shoes were packed in a trice, the framed pictures laid carefully between them. Her books went back in the box in which they had arrived, and her various treasures in another one. And that was it, give or take two or three more bags. Quickly, they carried the lot downstairs and outside, to the very gates of No. 17.

Elinore felt panicky. "How do you know they're not coming back soon? What if they come along the street? How long –"

Mrs Wattie waved her candyfloss-pink nails dismissively. "Ssssh, dinna work yersel' up, there's nae need. Ah tell ye, they're *not* comin' the noo, an' if they did, we'd be doon the street screamin' blue murder an' I'd hae the polis on them. *I'm* the one wi' the power now! *I'm* the one tae push *them* aroon' an' shove their own disgustin' medicine doon their auld gullets!"

A brand-new Ford Capri, blue with a black roof, roared up and braked abruptly. A young man jumped out and ran around to the boxes and bags.

"You strippin' the place o' the family silver, Ma?"

"Haud yer cheek, or that car's back whaur it came from afore ye know it. Come on, get these things loaded in! This is Elinore, our wee passenger, an' she wants away lickety-split. Elinore, this great lump is my son Kevin. You go in the back. Nae bad for a magic carpet, eh?"

Elinore scrambled into the back seat, and in seconds Kevin had filled up the rest of the space with all her belongings. Her heart was pounding and she felt as though she would burst into tears again. Then the engine revved, the car sped out of Dunallan Crescent and Elinore Crum was finally flying on a magic carpet.

"Say bye-bye tae yon hoose o' the livin' dead! Ye'll nae need tae see the inside o' it again," said Mrs Wattie.

20

From Dunallan Crescent, they drove down the slopes of Edinburgh to a much older neighbourhood, where soot-blackened tenements rose like elongated castles on both sides of the streets, many of which were paved with setts. In one of these, a heavy front door opened from the street into a dark stone passageway, at the end of which was the Watties' flat. It looked onto a drying green, not directly accessible from the street, and shadowed on all four sides by a further six storeys of tenement.

Mrs Wattie plumped up the cushions on a couch and told Elinore to make herself comfortable while she made tea. "I need tae wet ma whistle afore I get on the blower. I canna believe there's nane o' yer friends who'd gie ye shelter in a storm. We jist hae tae ask. I'd hae ye here for as lang as need be, but it's awfy sma', that's the problem, what wi' my husband an' twa boys bigger'n he is an' nae spare room."

Elinore sat upright, dazed and nervous but increasingly aware that she was beyond the reach of the Caltrops in this place. Outside was Kevin, who appeared to relish his role as guard. He had opened the tenement door for his mother, but then had gone back to his new car parked on the street, announcing, "They can come if they want! I'll flatten 'em, an' so will Mike." He jerked his head to indicate another hulking young man strolling up. "We're busy on the car for as long as you want."

Opposite Elinore was a mantelpiece, from which an ornate clock looked down at her. The clock face was set in a Louis XV style waisted rosewood case inlaid with floral marquetry; brass mounts twirled and curled around the edges, rising to a little brass twig with leaves and a flower on the very top. It ticked loudly and a gong struck every hour and half-hour. This clock was the most eye-catching object in the Wattie living room, and completely incongruous, but Elinore's gaze would have remained fixed on it even if it had been a plastic and chrome bedside alarm clock from Boots.

"I don't think they're coming to get me – not now," she said to Mrs Wattie, who was settling herself down on the couch with her tea.

"Comin' *here* to get ye? The idea!" huffed Mrs Wattie. "Have ye no' heard that a man's home is his castle? This is oor castle an' no mistake, an' yon pair o' deplorables couldna even find it, let alone get past Kevin oot there." She cackled and nudged Elinore with her elbow. "Yer bodyguard, Princess Elinore! He'll no' budge frae that car until a' yer wee things are oot o' it. Any excuse tae stand there polishin' it."

Elinore's gaze returned to the clock. She could see that Friday afternoon was ticking by, but time was behaving strangely. It still felt like Thursday, and Thursday felt like an ocean in which she might drown if she stopped swimming.

"D'ye like my clock?" asked Mrs Wattie. "A gift frae a gentleman, that was, a very, very fine man. That henpecked auld Caltrop couldna haud a candle tae him."

"I think it's a lovely clock. Do you have to dust it every day? Lady Groule has things like that and when we went for tea she said the fiddly bits were terrible dust traps."

"Aye, they are, an' that's why I got given this one. I used tae clean the hoose o' that gentleman, in the New Town it was, an' he collected clocks – French ones, he said, an' this one's French, he showed me how ye can tell. An' it's auld: made in the year of his birth, he said, which wis 1886. He hated seein' dust on those clocks, an' he said I kept them clean better'n anyone. This one wis my favourite. See that wee rose on top? That's why. Anyway, he died, an' he left me this clock in his will. Flabbergasted, I was. Makes a difference to a hoose when there's one nice thing in it, ken whit I mean? It's a sight better than they flyin' ducks on the wall ower there. Not that that husban' o' mine sees anythin' in it, or that great lump Kevin. Anyway, *I* say my guid-mornin' and my guid-night tae that clock every single day, an' if it keeps me healthy an' happy, it's naebody's business but my ane!"

"I know about that," said Elinore. "Nice things make you feel happy. Tom gave me some lovely things and they made my room feel really special. And Arabella gave me all my new clothes, and if you have new clothes you feel really, *really* special – like a royal person!"

"Tell me aboot it!" said Mrs Wattie. She put down her teacup and rubbed her hands, grinning like a black-eyed, scarlet-mouthed monkey. "Do I hae a story for you! But I canna get started on that afore I dae all that talkin' on the phone. We need tae find ye a bed for the night, Princess Elinore. Can we start wi' this Ladyship ye jist mentioned?" Mrs Wattie told Elinore she had recognised the name of Lady Groule from the card that Mrs Caltrop had been moving around as an exhibit of her social standing. "I kent fine whit she wis at: it was aye under my duster in a new place!"

So began the task of telephoning certain people in Elinore's address book. Lady Groule, of course, was long gone to Meggat. At the Balmerinoch Hotel, a workman answered and said that the owner was away for at least two days. Elinore did not have Mrs Chisholm's address, and so Mrs Wattie could not find her in the telephone book. Finally, she tried Tom, letting it ring and ring after Elinore said that the telephone was in the middle of a very big house. Tom answered after the fourteenth ring.

"Is this Mr Tom Balmerinoch? My name is Mrs Irene Wattie, and I'm callin' you about Elinore – aye, that wee Elinore in Edinburgh.

Aye, she's right here beside me. She's tellin' me to call you because we had tae get her oot o' that hoose afore those Caltrops did some damage. Or afore I did some damage tae them!" Tom's voice burbled through the receiver for a moment. "Aye, that's right. No, her mother's awa' wi' her fancy man in America. Aye – alone! Locked up, if ye must know." Tom's burbling became a squawk. "That's right, Mr Balmerinoch. I took her awa' oot o' there pronto, but I canna keep her in my wee tenement glory-hole, there's nae room, nae spare bed. Can ye come –" Tom interrupted and squawked again for a bit. "Och, that's grand! All right, then, d'ye hae a piece o' paper for my address?" Mrs Wattie recited her address and telephone number, and only then turned to Elinore.

"A' fixed up. He's comin' here to pick ye up as soon as he can. D'ye want a wee word now?"

"Hello, Tom," said Elinore.

"Elinore! I am *beside* myself over this news! I'm coming to take you to Squair, is that all right? Can you hang on until I appear? I think you are in the hands of an angel, whoever she is, but I won't ask you all the questions I *must* ask, not just now, I'll get some petrol in the car and I'll be off straight away, will you manage, will you *hang on*?" He stopped and drew breath.

"I'm fine, Tom. Please come soon." Elinore burst into tears again as soon as she put down the telephone.

"Ach, ye're still in shock, and nae wonder," said Mrs Wattie, patting her with a bejewelled hand. "Now sit doon here while I get some mair food into ye. Horlicks – that's the thing. An' then I'll tell ye a story. D'ye want tae know why I'm a' dressed up like a plate o' fish an' no' guddlin' aroon' wi' a lavvy brush?" She fluffed her hair and stuck out a foot, admiring the platform-heeled shoes.

Elinore nodded. Horlicks and a story were comprehensible, a tiny island of comfort in this ocean where she was still swimming.

"Right-o." Mrs Wattie began her story as she moved about the kitchen end of the living room, heating milk for the Horlicks.

"D'ye ken what Premium Bonds is? Weel, nivver mind. My sister Elsie's had a win big enough tae mak ye swoon, an' she's got no husband, nor children, a' it's jist us twa girls left now – so she's sharin' it fifty-fifty wi' me!"

Mrs Wattie's glee was intense and uncontainable. She waved her milk-stirring spoon at Elinore to emphasise the extent of her unheralded power and status.

"They Caltrops – I could buy their hoose right oot frae under their feet! Ye'd nivver hae guessed, would ye, that last day I was there? Aye, I kent then, but I didna say anythin' 'cause I didna hae the dosh in ma hands. I was jist bidin' my time til today. But ye ken, I was ready tae strangle them that day – it's hard tae be a wee yes-wifie when ye know ye can wipe the floor wi' people like that, orderin' ye aroon' an' tellin' ye to thank yer maker every hoor o' the day. See, I knew they twa auld corbies'd be awa today. They told me I had to get the key frae under a pot in the garden an' let mysel' in. An' I had it a' planned! Aye, I'd come, but I'd come late an' no' do a hand's turn. I'd sit doon in Lady Muck's ane chair an' wait for her. I wanted the pleasure o' throwin' her miserable wee packet o' money and prayers back in her sour face. Ye'll no' see me again this side o' hell or heaven, ye toffee-nosed auld gits – *that* was the goodbye I had a' planned! Oh, an' I was goin' tae say goodbye to you too, Elinore, an' wish ye a' the best."

"*Me?*" Elinore was still reconciling the memory of the hostility radiated by Mrs Wattie only days ago with this new and highly active concern for her safety.

"Why not? D'ye think I was blind to whit was goin' on? I've got eyes. Now your own ma was blind: she wis all up in the air wi' her fancy man. I coulda seen that for mysel', even if the auld bizzom hadna told me to keep my eyes peeled for signs that she'd got a fallen woman under her roof. Not that I'd tell her anythin', mind you, but it was fair entertainin', like a story oot o' the *Sunday Post*. See, your ma's nivver goin' tae be doon an' beaten – your ma's like one o' those rubber duckies in a wean's bath. She'll be the right way up an' lucky wi' a fancy man a' her life, but you're no' her, and you're a wean. Ye need ither eyes on you, since yer ma's got nae eyes an' nae heid for ye at a', in my humble opinion. Ye've nivver asked me tae mak a phone call tae America, have ye? It's no impossible! D'ye even ken whaur she is ower there? Did she *tell* ye?"

Mrs Wattie plunked the mug of Horlicks into Elinore's hand and stood, head cocked, eyebrows raised, while Elinore considered her mother's place in this. She shook her head. It was the only way she could answer these questions, for the whole business of Melba was a complexity that her brain could not accommodate at that moment. She shut it out.

"So, we jist do whit we can," continued Mrs Wattie. "Now whaur was I? Oh, aye. I get there – an' that magic carpet got me there lickety-split too, nae bus for me the day, ha-ha! – I get there an' I let mysel' into the hoose an' first thing I see is – whaur's my bag?" She jumped up to fetch a scarlet leather handbag, and took out of it a note. Elinore recognised Mrs Caltrop's handwriting and her tummy screwed itself up.

"Mrs Wattie," read Mrs Wattie in a highly affected parody of Mrs Caltrop. "The child is confined to her rooms as a consequence of her dangerous, destructive behaviour and wilful disobedience. This is a very serious situation. The door to her quarters is locked. You may open it to put in a tray with some bread and butter, but that is the only contact you should have with her. Please ensure that door is locked again. I will deal with her when I return this afternoon."

Mrs Wattie folded up the paper and put it back in her handbag. "That's evidence," she said, tapping the bag. "That's a' I need tae get the polis to start stickin' their noses in her business."

Elinore hunched herself into the corner of the couch and drew up her legs. Mrs Caltrop's description of her punishment made her feel shivery. What if Mrs Wattie had not appeared? Mrs Wattie looked at her in concern. "Ye're nae ower the shock yet." She left the room and came back with a blanket. "You keep warm an' if ye want more Horlicks it's on tap, a'right? Now whaur was I wi' my story? Oh, aye – dollin' oorsels up. First thing Elsie an' I did, we were off tae Jenners and such like for our new clothes. Got my hair done at that place– Zook-somethin', Zooker, ach well, where a' the smart set go. We're no' done yet, believe me."

From her kitchen cupboards, Mrs Wattie took a cake tin and a biscuit tin. She took out a package of cream cheese from the refrigerator and smacked her lips. She would enjoy this previous luxury as an everyday staple now, she announced, before cutting the block of cheese in two and putting half on a plate, beside a pile of crackers and a massive wedge of Dundee cake. She handed the plate to Elinore, settled back into the couch and began to expand on her vision of the abundantly provisioned and furnished new life that she and her sister Elsie had already started creating, courtesy of a lucky Premium Bond number.

Quickly, Elinore discovered the pleasure of helping someone else spend money. She could offer no useful ideas about holiday destinations, except to say that the Eiffel Tower looked fascinating and no, she did not think Disneyland would be quite right for her ("Wait til ye meet Gordon, my youngest – it's a' he can talk aboot!" said Mrs Wattie), but houses were quite another matter. Mrs Wattie invited her to contribute bright ideas for fitting out the new seaside home that was the most important item on the Wattie family's giant shopping list. The Dundee cake and Horlicks did their job, and soon Elinore was feeling cosy and relaxed. She forgot about the passage of time until the French clock struck three.

"Is Tom late?" she asked.

"I canna say, 'cause I dinna ken exactly whaur he's comin' frae, but if it's East Lothian he's got a bit o' traffic to deal with, roadworks maybe. You watch that clock: I'll lay money on it he'll be here afore the half-hour's oot."

They continued with their grand envisioning until the sound of loud voices and a banging door broke in. Elinore looked at the clock.

"See? Ten past three. Jist as I said." Mrs Wattie nudged her again with her elbow before getting up to greet Tom, whom Kevin was escorting in.

Tom looked shattered, as though he, not Elinore, had been that day's escapee. His hair sprang up even more wildly than Elinore remembered; beads of sweat were on his brow, his jacket collar was half up, half down, his shirt adrift from his trousers and his mouth open as he breathed heavily. Greasy black smudges dotted his trousers and one arm of his jacket. "Elinore!" he exclaimed, and knelt down in front of her, putting his hands on her shoulders and turning her this way and that, as if some part of her might be missing. "This is *terrible!* Are you sure you're all right? Mrs Wattie, is she really all right?"

"I *am* all right," said Elinore. "I'm all right *now*."

"Aye, she is, because she's got a good wee heid on those shoulders," said Mrs Wattie. "Come in, Mr Balmerinoch, you're the one that needs attention now. Are you thirsty? Did you hae trouble getting here?"

"Tom – it's Tom, please, Mrs Wattie, and yes, I'd be grateful for a glass of water, or two. I got held up with roadworks outside Dalkeith, and I had trouble *before* I set off, with that car of mine, and trouble with it *after*. I just hope it gets us back to Squair. I'm, ah, not very clever with cars."

"I am," said Kevin. "Can I hae a look at it?"

"Delighted," said Tom, handing him the keys.

Mrs Wattie made him sit down and drink his water. Elinore could not stop smiling, for Tom's presence right here in Edinburgh seemed to put the seal on the immediate past for her. Even without a wolf to carry her there, she would be at Squair within an hour or two, safe in another world altogether.

Tom was looking at the mantel clock with interest. "That's a very fine clock, Mrs Wattie. Is it French, by chance?"

"Well, now – whit a treat to hae a man in this hoose who appreciates my clock!" She puffed up with pride and pleasure, and told the story of the clock's acquisition all over again. Tom became rather excited.

"Your old gentleman, was he called Arthur Ormiston – Professor, or maybe Dr Ormiston, a Doctor of Letters?"

"He was!" cried Mrs Wattie. "Did ye ken him?"

"Only very slightly, but I admired his writings a great deal, and I still do. He was a friend of a friend, and I was once in his house. He certainly did have many clocks. I don't know how he could study and write day after day in the middle of all that ticking and chiming and clanging."

"Oh, aye, you're right – the racket! I mind once . . ." They were off and away, two hounds running joyfully on the scent of reminiscence. Elinore marvelled at how people discovered they had connections with other people, interesting ones; her life was nothing like that. She was just Elinore Crum. Momentarily out of the conversation and the limelight, she was suddenly overcome by tiredness. Her limbs felt like spaghetti, and her neck could not keep her head from drooping.

Kevin came in again and announced that Tom's car was running fine for now, and they had a rather one-sided technical discussion about engine oil. Then Tom stood up. "Well, it's high time we were out of your way, Mrs Wattie," he said.

"It's Irene," she said. "If ye call me the other, I jist hear that auld cow Caltrop. Kevin! You take Elinore to Tom's car so she can show you how she likes her things put away in it." With her back to Elinore, she grimaced and gesticulated at Kevin, enough for him to understand that he was to remove and distract Elinore.

"Right, then," he said. "Elinore, do you ken where you put the bags in a bug?

"No – what bug? A bug is a germ, isn't it?" she said, feeling sleepy and fuzzy-headed.

"Not this bug. Come on oot an' see."

While Mrs Wattie gave Tom graphic revelations about life at No. 17 Dunallan Crescent, Kevin led Elinore to a dusty, dirty, yellow Volkswagen Beetle. "OK, where's the boot?"

"In the back," said Elinore. "Where it always is."

"Wrong!" He pulled open the back of the Beetle and Elinore saw an engine. "That's funny," she said. "What about the front?"

"Right! We're puttin' some o' your things in there. Anything fragile? You sure my ma didn't run awa' wi' all their fancy china?"

Elinore looked around as Kevin fitted everything that was hers into the Beetle. She saw a long stretch of undulating green at the end of the street. "What's over there?" she asked, pointing.

"A park. Then it's Holyrood."

"The palace where the Queen stays?"

"Aye. We're cheek by jowl wi' Her Majesty doon here. She just hasn't got aroon' to invitin' us in yet."

"You mean you could just go for a walk down there and see the palace?"

"Aye – have you not been down to see it? Want a wee whiz aroon' the sights afore you go – in *my* car?"

Elinore's fear of chance discovery fought with her longing to see Holyroodhouse at close quarters, and the allure of royalty won.

"I'd really, really like that, if nobody minds."

"Ach, no, Ma's dyin' to talk the ear off your friend Tom. I'll just tell them, and you get in the car with Mike – in the front seat so you get a good view."

Elinore thought she could always duck down if she saw the Caltrops, and then again, Mike was even bigger than Kevin – and then suddenly the Caltrops evaporated, and so did her sleepy tiredness. "This is so exciting!" she said.

"If you say so," said Mike. "We jist live here, an' it's a' the same auld stones to us."

When Tom and Elinore finally left for Squair, addresses and telephone numbers were exchanged all over again, and Tom wrung

Mrs Wattie's hand in fervent gratitude. "No one else in the world could have done what you did for Elinore today," he said.

Mrs Wattie was clearly pleased with this compliment, but not about to let it go to her coiffured head.

"Ach, it was nothin'. I tell you, I've waited lang enough to get my own back on that Lady Muck for treatin' me like – well, nivver mind. Soon as I saw I could lift Elinore oot frae under their noses like I was the flamin' angel o' mercy, there was no holdin' me back." She smiled another of her radiantly wicked smiles and added, "An' I'm no' done yet!"

The last thing Mrs Wattie did for Elinore that day was to envelop her in a hug, an aura of Unforgettable and assurances that Elinore would always know where to find her. "We'll be flittin' afore this year's out. Sandy an' I'll be sittin' doon next week wi' one of those estate agents – see what it takes to move oot o' here a' thegither an' see if he can retire early. His heart's nae that guid, an' I dinna want him disappearin' jist when the fun starts."

The yellow Beetle was called Lady Jane Wilde, said Tom, because of her temperament and tendency to go her own distinctive way. "She was the mother of Oscar Wilde with an E, whom you will meet in due course. I have to tell you what she's called in case you think I'm mad when I'm talking to her. Dialogue encourages her to keep going. I don't think Kevin Wattie would agree, though."

As they drove to Squair, Tom repeated something Mrs Wattie had said. "Like the flaming angel of mercy! She really was, wasn't she? Especially in that marvellous red dress. She would have struck down the Caltrops with her handbag instead of a flaming sword."

Elinore had a different idea. "Do you think she could be a secret agent too?"

"Most emphatically *yes*," replied Tom. "It's all there! Working in disguise, waiting a long time for the right moment to act (that's called being a mole, by the way), undercover operations, neutralising the enemy operatives *highly* effectively, a network of fellow agents ready to leap into action too, flashy high-speed cars for escaping, well, *one* car, certainly not this one – let's see, what else, oh yes, a safe house, a debriefing session – that's what I've just had. Yes, Mrs Wattie is absolutely a top agent. What shall we call her? Agent Irene? Agent W?"

"How about – Agent Solo?"

"Perfect! Agent Solo it is."

They were driving along the coastal road just then, within sight of Tantallon Castle. The late afternoon sun deepened the orange-red of its stones and the black of its shadowed embrasures. It did not look as menacing a place, full of violent echoes from history, as Elinore recalled from her previous sight of it. On the contrary, it appeared more as a guardian of her new life. Once past this castle, she would be beyond the reach of the Caltrops for ever and ever. Now she could happily leave Agent Solo behind too. Someone else, with far greater powers than she could possibly summon, had already taken over that role and was combatting evil with the utmost energy.

21

Sleepiness blanketed Elinore even before Lady Jane pulled up in front of the Dower House. She stumbled a little on getting out of the car, and Tom flapped around as if she were made of porcelain.

"Are you feverish? Do you have a headache, a tummy ache or any other kind of ache? All this excitement! It must be very bad for you – look what it's doing to me. I think you should lie down somewhere quiet while I bash around and sort out certain things. I must chase all the spiders and mice out of your bedroom for a start."

"I could help."

"I'm sure you'd be like Genghis Khan with the spiders and the mice, but if you're exhausted and you fall downstairs because your eyes are closed, and break your neck or something like that, I'd be responsible. I'd have to run away and join the Legionnaires or hurl myself to my death from the roof, out of shame."

"I don't want you to do that," yawned Elinore.

Tom led her to a sofa in the dim, silent drawing room. It had three straight, upright sides like separate flaps on a cardboard box, and these were joined at the corners by heavy braid wrapped around finials. With plenty of cushions and plaid rugs, this Knole sofa quickly became the perfect conveyance to sleep.

In stories, characters sometimes awake not knowing where they are at first. Elinore had always wondered how this could be, but that is precisely how she felt when her eyes opened some time later. She was in a shadowy, high-ceilinged room full of strange furnishings and indistinct objects on the walls: speckled mirrors and portraits of men in tall wigs and ladies in low-cut dresses. Persian carpets lay on bare wooden floors. At the far end, a panelled door was slightly ajar, and some light, not daylight, shone from the passage beyond it. At first, she heard nothing; then her ears picked out the gentle sound of wind in trees just outside the windows. Was she back in Criven, then, where that sound had been the melody of all her days and nights? Her fingers felt velvet and brocade, and the rough wool of the tartan rugs around her; a musty, dusty smell filled her nostrils. Gradually the picture of the immediate past fell into place. She was at the Dower House in Squair.

The clock in the square entrance hall bonged as she passed it, and just as before it made her jump. She peered at the clock face: half past six! If she was in a story, it was almost a Sleeping Beauty one.

After her ears ceased ringing from the noise of the clock, Elinore discerned a voice. She followed it along the passage that she knew would end in the kitchens. There she came upon Tom, seated at the table and writing by lamplight. Paper, some covered in handwriting, some in typescript, surrounded him, and he was muttering to himself. Not noticing Elinore in the murky shades beyond the kitchen entrance, he suddenly threw up his arms and cried, "Enough! I've heard all I need, you lackey – you contemptible dog." Silence. "You cur! Hmm. Better." He scribbled anew.

"Excuse me, Tom, can I come in?" asked Elinore, not sure what she might be disturbing.

Tom looked up, startled. "Elinore! Good heavens. Forgive me, please. I thought I'd just take a quick look at this while you were resting, and – and – Good Lord! Look at the time." He jumped up and rubbed his head vigorously with both hands, making a fresh disaster of his hair. "It's tea time! Or dinner time. What a rotten host I am. All right, we must eat, and drink, and above all make you comfortable. You don't look like a girl who's *terribly* scared of mice, if I may say so, which will make it all very easy. Now – food."

He pulled open the door of a refrigerator that was at least a quarter of a century old. Elinore held her breath, remembering what Arabella had said about the dangers of Tom's cooking.

"Hmmm . . . well . . ." He closed the door quickly.

"Elinore, we are going to dine out. Is it raining again?" He went through the scullery and opened the back door. "Damp but not wet, no wellington boots needed, but you might want a coat or something to keep you warm. Follow me! I have the perfect solution until you unpack."

Within two minutes, they were walking out of the Dower House towards the village green. The evening was a little cool, and over her shoulders Elinore wore a tweed jacket of Tom's. It reached her knees but it felt like a good joke to go around in it, no arms showing, rather like a Dalek from *Doctor Who*. "Where are we going?" she asked, for once not worrying about whether she was properly dressed.

"The best place in which to celebrate your escape."

They walked right across the village green and entered the Skirving Arms Hotel.

"Tom! Good to see you. And a guest too – good evening, miss, welcome to the Skirving Arms." A short, balding man held out his hand to Elinore as if she were a capital-L lady, and she struggled to shake it without letting the Dalek jacket fall to the floor.

"Elinore, this is Peter, our host. Peter, this is Miss Elinore Crum. She's staying here for the time being – little bit of a family emergency, people all at sixes and sevens, you understand the kind of thing."

"Yes, indeed, and anything we can do, you just tell us. We can always help to keep a young lady well fed." Peter winked at Elinore and she wondered whether he too had heard stories about Tom's cooking. "Come and seat yourselves by the window."

The Skirving Arms struck Elinore as a very comfortable place. She was happy to be in a hotel again. If I'm very rich when I grow up, she thought, I'll spend a lot of time going to hotels all around the country, and I'll make a list of the ones I like best so that I can tell everyone to go there.

"I like this place," she told Tom. "Thank you very much for bringing me."

"You'll like the food too. Here's the menu – choose anything you want. You need to build yourself up, Mrs Wattie says, and I'll believe anything that woman tells me. *Amazing.*" He shook his head in admiration.

"Clova makes good food at her hotel too. I've been there twice."

"Oh, yes, Arabella mentioned that." Tom suddenly struck his forehead and looked horrified.

"Arabella! Good Lord – she doesn't know where you are, Elinore. She doesn't know *anything* yet, does she?"

"No, I don't *think* so. Mrs Wattie doesn't know her. Nobody knows her in Edinburgh."

Tom gave a short, dry laugh. "Well, that's not *quite* so, my dear – but as you mean it, that's correct, she knows no one who will tell her to what planet Elinore Crum has vanished. But what if she suddenly wants to talk to you? The Caltrops could spin any yarn if she were to call there. She says she has *responsibilities* for you! She'll have my head on a platter if she thinks *I'm* not looking after you responsibly!" Elinore was surprised to hear of all this responsibility for her. "We must ring her straight away after dinner. If we can, that is – she's like an otter or a seal, always poking her head up somewhere that's nowhere near where you last saw or heard of her. One day, someone will invent a telephone that people can carry all the time, wherever they go, and only then will we know where Arabella Cheyne really is at any moment."

"But she might just turn it off, and then people couldn't talk to her anyway."

"Yes, very likely, knowing her – that's an astute observation. Do you, ah, happen to know where she is?"

"She told me: Castle Welkinlaw in Northumberland. I wrote it all down in my address book."

"I see. Decorating dungeons, is she? Oh, here's Peter to take our orders: let's talk about food instead of Arabella and her peculiar doings."

Fish and chips, followed by apple pie and custard, had a remarkable effect on Elinore. Her legs began to skip as she trotted back to the Dower House. Adventure, that experience so readily encountered by perfectly ordinary children in stories, had finally caught up with her. She was also eager to tell Arabella about her escape.

"All right, let's get on with it," Tom said, flexing his arms and wiggling his wrists as if about to pick up an awkward load instead of dialling the number of Castle Welkinlaw.

"Ah, good evening – Mrs Anskett, I believe? I'm a friend of Arabella Cheyne, and I hear she is staying with you. Could I possibly have a word with her? Yes – Tom Balmerinoch, calling from Squair. Thank you."

When Arabella came on the line, Tom threw back his shoulders and said, "Arabella, don't interrupt until I've finished, or I'll put the phone down. Elinore is here – Elinore is *staying* here. We have rescued Elinore from the appalling Caltrops and she must never, ever return. Elinore is therefore at the Dower House for as long as – as long as, um, Elinore wishes to be here."

A staccato enquiry leaked from the receiver.

"We? A lady and I. No, no, I don't believe you know her, but a terrific character, and an angel, an absolute *angel*. We can talk about her later." Tom smirked, as if very satisfied about something, and mystified Elinore by raising his left hand in a thumbs-up gesture. "The important thing is that Elinore is *here*, and completely safe. Yes, right here." He held the receiver out to Elinore.

"First things first, Elinore," said Arabella. "Is that man looking after you properly? What have you had to *eat*?"

"He's very good at looking after me," Elinore assured her. "We went to a hotel for dinner, and it was scrumptious. And he says I have to have a nice hot bath tonight, so I sleep properly and don't have nightmares. *And* he cleaned the mice out of my bedroom – he says he did."

"So far, so good," said Arabella. "Now listen! Breakfasts made by Tom are acceptable as long as he serves you porridge, cornflakes, toast, boiled eggs, that sort of thing *only*. If there's any milk, give it a good sniff *before* you pour it, is that clear? Anything that comes out of a packet or tin is also acceptable, as long as he only has to put it on a plate, or heat it up or add water – *water only*. Cheese and biscuits are fine. Apart from that, I have told him that you are to eat at the hotel, and I don't care how many times the pair of you go there as long as it keeps you alive and perfectly healthy until the hour of your departure. Is that understood, Elinore? And one more thing: *wash your hands before you eat*. Tom is not the only risk. He is happy to share his home with legions of mice who are spreading disease day and night."

After a few more injunctions of this kind, Arabella said she would speak to Tom again. The ensuing discussion seemed to be more serious, for Tom's triumphant air began to deflate and he sighed a couple of times. "All right, all right," he said finally. "When? And how?" More noise from Arabella, a long silence during which Tom whistled and told Elinore that she was talking to the Ansketts, and then Arabella returned and asked for Elinore.

Without the slightest preamble, she changed the course of Elinore's life.

"Elinore, would you like to come down to Welkinlaw and give me a hand? Be my assistant? I think you'd be rather good at it."

"You mean – come to *stay* in the castle?"

"Precisely. And then, when our work is complete, in a week or so, I'd say, you can come back north with me. Come for a good long holiday. If you *want* to, of course."

Elinore's mouth fell open. She could not think of a single thing to say. Tom seized the receiver from her. "Arabella, you're being outrageous as usual, I can tell by the look on Elinore's face. It's *much* too much for Elinore to think about at the end of a very peculiar day. Or two days. We'll talk about it tomorrow. No, no, no, *no* more. Good*night!*" He replaced the receiver very firmly.

"Ridiculous woman," he said to Elinore, waving both hands in the air. "All that flap over my ability to provide the basic necessities for you, and then she practically *kidnaps* you. *Announces* her intention of doing so, at any rate. Impossible woman. I think you've had quite enough alarums and excursions crammed into one day, don't you? Come on! Bath time. Let me explain the quirks of the bathroom taps. Then it's bedtime."

In a small bedroom where the floor sloped this way and that, Elinore climbed into a bed that was comfortingly similar to the one she had left behind in Criven. The mattress, however, was horsehair (Tom had said) and a handmade patchwork quilt covered her. The same musty smell that she had noticed in the drawing room was even stronger here, and dust was layered everywhere, making her sneeze, but it was still much better than air that smelled of Domestos and Ajax. At first, the unfamiliar sounds of a very old house settling its timbers for the night kept her awake. She left the bedside lamp on until her eyelids began to droop, looking around the room and marvelling. She could barely comprehend that this single day had begun in misery at No. 17 and ended here, in a fairytale house full of mice and whispers. Just before sleep overtook her, she heard Arabella's voice in her head: "A good long holiday." She, Elinore Crum, was turning into one of those children in stories, the ones who went on long summer holidays, *proper* holidays (Elinore had never been on anything remotely like a holiday) in places like Cornwall or the Lake District and promptly fell into mysteries and adventures. "A-*maz*-ing," murmured Elinore Crum to herself. "I could really be someone in a story..."

22

Breakfast the next morning was perfectly acceptable and safe to eat, as far as Elinore could tell, and Tom made a pile of toast for her with a toaster that was even older than the fridge. Its thick black cord was so frayed that it looked fringed. He read *The Scotsman* as he ate, occasionally reading aloud entertaining snippets. But Elinore spotted for herself the one item of news that truly did interest her, as she scanned the page facing her as Tom sat reading opposite.

"Fake missionary arrested for charity con." Below this column heading was an unmistakable photograph of the missionary Curglaff. Elinore craned across the table to read the small print description of this man's misdemeanours, and his downfall thanks to a suspicious, sharp-eyed teacher in one of the schools he had visited. Her heart leaped in joy at this news. She was still craning and reading when Tom lowered the paper. "Found something fascinating?" he asked, and she told him everything about her brief association with a real thief.

Tom was full of admiration. "You *are* astute – didn't I say that last night? You should be proud of yourself."

"So, I'm really not a bad person, am I? Even if I did keep some of the money?"

Tom snorted. "You are a *wise* person. How would you have felt if you had given him all of it, now that you know he's a con man? He was only going to use it to feather his own nest." Then Tom became insistent, like Arabella with all her do-this-but-not-that talk on the telephone.

"Elinore, pay attention! This man Curglaff is a signpost for the rest of your life. Even if the only thing telling you to beware is a tiny, tiny little voice in your insides, you must listen to it."

"A voice in my tummy?"

"Yes, give or take a few inches. Your insides always tell the truth. The world is chock full of people showing themselves off as good, when actually they are bad in a thousand ways."

"The Caltrops said I was bad because I didn't want to go to Sunday school. But I don't believe in all the Jesus stuff, about him loving all the children in the world and the good people being the ones who're just like him."

"The Caltrops' idea of badness is pernicious rubbish, and you're an independent thinker. Be proud of it!"

"I think it's all a big fib, because the Jesus people are nasty to the people who are different from them. *They* don't love *them*. So they're telling fibs, and that's bad. Isn't it?"

"Yes, it is. You have just described one of our sad world's most besetting evils."

"What's besetting? Is it like upsetting?"

"Yes, but much stronger. It means like a plague, a torment, and that would be pretty upsetting. You could wish that the Caltrops were beset with – well, what kind of plague *do* we wish on them, hmm?"

The conversation became outrageous after that.

Tom said they would lunch at the Skirving Arms at noon, and Elinore could do whatever she liked until then. "I'm going to bash on with my, um, my project. I've got lots of new ideas all of a sudden. It must be the enlivening effect of this conversation."

"What's your project? Is it what you were doing last night?"

"Yes, but it's a secret. I'll tell you only if you promise not to tell Arabella or anyone else."

"Promise! Cross my heart and hope to die!"

Tom shuddered. "No, no, not necessary. All right – I'm writing a story. A book. It's about a man who solves mysteries and finds lost things and unmasks bad people – people who are even nastier than that man Curglaff."

"Gosh! That's clever."

"Have you heard of Sherlock Holmes?"

"Yes, Lady Groule told me – she told Usha and Susanna and me."

Tom, who had been leaning his elbows on the table, snapped upright in astonishment. "Lady *Groule*? Did I hear you aright? Groule of Meggat? How on earth did you come to meet that female Machiavelli?"

"What's that?"

"Oh, ah, we'll do that word later. But please explain about Lady Groule. I knew her a long time ago, when I was about your age."

Elinore told him the entire story of her acquaintance with Lady Groule. As she did, the events of a mere four days ago, and her worry and shame over Mrs Caltrop's treatment of her friends, assailed her afresh. She sat twisting her hands, head bowed as she spoke, until Tom interrupted.

"Elinore, don't you think you ought to tell your friends where you are? They might think the Caltrops have eaten you up."

"I think they'll just hate me. Their parents will think I'm bad because – it's all because of *me* that *she* was screaming and calling them horrible names."

"*Not* true, but I don't expect you to believe that immediately. It's been too much of a shock. But look, how about ringing up Lady Groule? She'll talk to your friends' parents. I know that woman! You'd have to chain and gag her to stop her. I can ring her for you.

It's my responsibility to help you over this social hurdle, Elinore, because I am your *de facto* guardian."

"What's *de facto*?"

"It's Latin for in fact, in reality. It means that at this moment I am your guardian willy-nilly, because I was the only suitable person at the end of a telephone at the crucial moment. All right, that's settled. I'll ring her later, when I can be sure that even that *grande dame* will be out of her bed. And we will have to talk to Arabella again. *She* is a relation, and I am not, meaning that she is really your guardian now."

"*They* said they were my guardians now. *She* said Mummy told them that." Elinore had suddenly decided to see how long she could converse without once uttering the name Caltrop. "Does that mean they can be my guardians forever? Do I have to keep hiding from them even if Mummy comes back?"

Tom stared at her. "Even *if* your mother . . .?" he began in a questioning tone. Then he stopped and leaned across the table. "Elinore, listen very carefully. The Caltrops will never be allowed anywhere near you ever again. If your mother wishes to argue over who is best placed to look after you, she may do so, with Arabella and with me. But I am a lawyer and I have to say that, given the evidence, your mother would not win that argument." He sat back, looking solemn, which was an entirely new look as far as Elinore was concerned.

"Oh," was all she said. She did not want to think about her mother at all, especially in connection with the future. Without any thought of Melba, the present and the immediate future was peculiar and full of change, but it was exciting, and she had encountered nothing but kindness since the moment Mrs Wattie had appeared like the flaming angel of mercy. As soon as she added Melba, however, present and future became a jelly of uncertainty under her feet. She therefore put Melba in the same place in her head as the Caltrops, behind a door.

"Tom, how long can I stay here? Do I have to go soon? I mean, I think it would be fun to stay in the castle, but I just *came* here. It's fun here too."

Tom pulled a face. "Fun for me too, having such an entertaining house guest. Got to make use of the old place, you know. Did I tell you and Usha how *I* came to live here? No? All right, that's a story for later. But back to the present – I'm sorry, I ought to have said that Arabella rang early, before you were up, and it's all decided. You'll be off on Monday, the day after tomorrow. Mr Carr is coming to collect you. He's the factor at Welkinlaw, the man who takes care of everything. But he comes from up around here, and he's just been to his mother's funeral. Very convenient of her to die when she did."

"Oh," said Elinore again. She looked around the breakfast table, which in truth had been well laid with plenty of food, and then asked, "Do you think I can come back some time?"

"Of course!" cried Tom, waving his hands in the air. "And you'll have Usha along too, won't you? And your other friend, what's her name?"

"Susanna," said Elinore in a whisper. A lump in her throat had jumped up from nowhere, and she was afraid she would cry.

"Yes, Susanna, Susanna and Usha – the friends you're going to get in touch with *very* soon with a bit of help from Zinnia Groule. All will right itself, Elinore. Trust me! I'm a lawyer! Now I must get down to my other work. If you want to draw or paint, you can keep me company."

In the dining room, the long table held the same piles of paper that Elinore had seen the night before, and two typewriters sat amid them. Tom patted the smaller one, which was the most modern-looking item that Elinore had seen so far in the Dower House. "Lovely thing. My fingers fly on it – well, they try. And it's portable, so I can carry it around and work wherever I want." On the opposite side of the table sat an older, bulkier typewriter. Elinore was immediately intrigued. Her fingers stretched out towards the keys.

"Could I try typing a little bit on this one?"

"Of course. Here, you put the paper in like this." With just enough information to enable the keys to strike the ribbon, the paper to roll up or down and the carriage to return, Elinore had the basic tools for making the words in her head look like words in a book.

"I think I could make a story too."

"Why not? We'll both get to work and see what we can achieve by lunchtime."

"But I don't know *exactly* what I'm going to write about. I might have to *think* about it all day."

"Rubbish! Your imagination is bursting out of your ears. You invented Agent Solo, didn't you? You just need a name for a character and then you'll be off, like an express train."

"Is that what happened to you?"

"Yes, and you could do exactly the same if I show you where and how. But remember, it's top secret."

They went into the small library with the faded rose-pink wing chair. "I had *half* an idea, a long time ago, but no name. Then I came in here one day, looking for a guide to the stars in the night sky, and I found my character completely by accident. He was on the same shelf as the book of stars."

Tom took down a volume bound in oxblood leather with a title stamped in gold: *Mercurius Davidicus. Charles I. Oxford 1634*. He turned some pages with great care, showing Elinore the heavy black letters and illustrations. "This book is from the time of King Charles I, the one who had his head chopped off by Oliver Cromwell."

Elinore drew breath in awe and gazed reverently at this artefact.

"As soon as I saw the title," continued Tom, "the letters rearranged themselves and I had the name of my character instantly. And then I had the *whole* idea for my story: Davidicus Mercury, hunter of the lost! Solver of mysteries, and not only of the criminal kind! He lives in Edinburgh, by the way, around the turn of the century. Plenty of allusion to Mercury and Hermes too, and excuse me if I blow my trumpet about the cleverness of that. He works *intuitively* – that voice in the guts, Elinore, that voice in the guts! It's high time we had a notable *Scottish* sleuth, don't you think?"

Elinore thought that it sounded most impressive, even if partly incomprehensible.

"Anyway, the point is that you can do it too. Just roam around these shelves and see if a name jumps out at you. Pull out any of the books – see, you can stand on that stool if you want. Then let your imagination do the rest."

But Elinore's imagination had already run away with this idea.

"But I've got one already! I found a name for a story!" She ran to fetch *The Book of Edinburgh for Young People* from its box in her bedroom.

"Helena Albacyr," said Tom, looking at the flyleaf. "Al-ba-keer? Al-ba-seer? Spanish or French, I'd say. What an exotic find! Perhaps Helena was descended from survivors of the Armada – some ships are supposed to have been wrecked on Scottish rocks, you know. Perhaps she had no Scottish blood at all! It's entirely in your hands, Elinore: you can write *anything* you like about her. Even if she's still alive as an ancient old crone, she'll never know or care."

"I'm going to write a ghost story!"

Tom started her off with a pad of lined paper. "The more you type, the faster you wear out the ribbon. So, it's a good idea to write a draft first. You can make all the mistakes and changes you like without using up the ribbon."

Then she retreated to the wing chair in the little library. By the time Tom called her for lunch at the Skirving Arms, she was able to tell him that her story was halfway to completion.

"Excellent! Here's another tip: once you have written The End, take fresh paper and write out the whole story all over again. That's called a second draft."

"Why not type it on the typewriter?"

"Because as soon as you start, you will see things you want to change or add or cut out altogether – believe me, you *will!*

Remember, the more you do with a pencil and eraser, the longer your typewriter ribbon will last."

"Can't you just buy a new one when it runs out?"

"Of course, but here's the thing: the ribbon always runs out when you've forgotten to buy a replacement."

The weather forecast had announced a return to sunshine and rising temperatures. After lunch, they moved their paper, pens and pencils out to the table on the drying green, and Elinore set to with renewed passion. They were interrupted, however, when Boris came ambling around the corner of the house. He was followed by his owner, Mrs Forsyth, who wished to invite them to dinner. She had noticed Tom going by with his young visitor. Tom accepted with delight. Elinore wondered if Mrs Forsyth was another person who knew that Tom's cooking was dangerous.

She finished her first draft quite quickly, and announced that she was going to start the second one immediately. So far, it had been just like the process of writing out a rough copy of a special letter.

"Will I have the pleasure of reading your story before you leave?" asked Tom.

"I'll *try* to finish it for you. It's got a lot of things in it and I think I'll be very slow at typing."

"I think you'll be a lot faster than I was in the beginning. My fingers aren't the right size, or they don't connect with my brain in the right ways."

"Have you been writing other stories?"

Tom looked startled. "What makes you say that?"

"I just wondered. You're so fast at writing. You use up a lot of paper but you don't crumple it up and throw it all over the room like Hector did."

"Hmmm . . . you are as observant as Davidicus Mercury himself. I might have to put you in the story as a young assistant. But no, no, I've never ever written a book in my life before, or a single short story, never even *thought* of such a thing, and that's why we must keep it a secret, because I'm sure everyone will poke fun at me for trying. And someone might steal my idea!"

Elinore was pleased to hear that she might inhabit a story in this way. Assistant to Arabella, assistant to Davidicus Mercury! It was like being grown up. At the same time, her insides were telling her quietly but unmistakably that Tom had just told her a fib. It was as plain as day to her, somehow, that he was already a real writer. She wanted to laugh and remind him about his serious advice concerning her tummy as the place of truth, but she decided that would be rude, and might make him feel upset. She put his reply in a new place in her head: Things to Keep an Eye On.

The Forsyth's house was full of books. The grown-ups talked about the books they were reading, the plays and films they had just seen and the programmes they had heard on the radio. Tom did not say anything about the story he was writing, and of course Elinore was sworn to secrecy. But he talked about his new portable typewriter, which he called an Olivetti, and told the Forsyths that Elinore was working hard to complete her first story. They applauded and said they hoped they might have a chance to read it, because they were always keen on discovering new authors.

Altogether, it was a cosy evening, especially because the table was lit with candles. Elinore thought this was a beautiful sight, but she was glad to be a twentieth-century girl who did not have to read by candlelight. Her bedroom might have a floor with camel humps under the bare boards, a horsehair mattress and tons of dust, but it also had a lamp on a bedside table, which Elinore could turn on and off just by reaching out a hand. By the time she and Tom returned to the Dower House, twilight was settling in and she was yawning. To curl up under the patchwork quilt and read *The Book of Edinburgh for Young People* in comfort and good light was luxury, especially knowing that she did not need to get up, go all the way to the door to switch off the ceiling light, and find her way back to bed in the dark without stepping on a mouse.

Her portion of the world felt manageable and considerably safer in the glow of that lamp.

※

"We forgot to talk to Lady Groule yesterday," Tom said at breakfast the next morning, "but it might be too early just now. She might be one of those very grand ladies who never grace the day until noon, especially on a Sunday. Remind me at lunchtime."

The adventures of Davidicus Mercury and Helena Albacyr filled their creators' minds for the rest of the morning. Elinore was so anxious to show herself worthy of a typewriter ribbon that she wrote out a third draft. Then she was satisfied, and would have begun pecking out the story immediately had Tom not said that it was time for lunch.

"What about Lady Groule?" asked Elinore. "You said to remind you."

"I did. But let's eat first. You can have a big glass of that red stuff you like so much, and I'll have a big glass of some other red stuff. It's called fortification."

Lady Groule was having a glass of something clear. It was definitely medicinal at that moment, and traditional, in the sense that she always required it to help her shed the irk and boredom of Meggat and settle back into her home comforts. She was already seated in her armchair by the telephone, writing a list of the calls she must make (Celia's name was at the top), when it rang. She looked at it, wishing for an invention that would display a name, or a number at least, in case she preferred to be not at home to any particular caller.

"Zinnia Groule here."

"Lady Groule – good afternoon. I'm Tom Balmerinoch, a name you might not recall, but I'm sure you'll remember my parents, Thomas and Dorothea, at –"

"Good *heavens!* A voice from the past. A Balmerinoch! Yes, I *certainly* remember a boy, and they only had one so it must have been you. Your knees were always in a ghastly mess, and your hair and your fingernails were unspeakable. and you were always busy with something complicated. I remember all that because you were late to the table every time, and your father would not have anything served until you'd appeared – to embarrass you into good behaviour, he said. I can't say it worked! But it did make me remember you because I was always kept waiting when I was ravenous, and I used to curse you under my breath. Now, what *was* your name?"

"It's Tom. And I must tell you why I'm ringing up out of the blue, it's rather important –"

"This is very curious, you know, because I happened to meet a charming young gel who knows a Balmerinoch who lives at Squair. Is that you?"

"It is indeed, Lady Groule, and I believe we are talking about the same young lady – Miss Elinore Crum. She is beside me as I speak."

"What?" cried Lady Groule. "Elinore Crum is at Squair? Not in Edinburgh? Are you quite sure we are talking about the same gel? *Is she all right?*"

A short, muffled exchange followed at the Dower House end, and then Lady Groule heard Elinore say hello, and that she was indeed at Squair.

"Thank God!" exclaimed Lady Groule. "This is simply the best news I have had for days and *days.* Elinore, we have been *dreadfully* concerned about you. Are you *quite* all right?"

"I'm fine, honestly," replied Elinore, greatly reassured by this warmly emotional response. She added quickly, in case new warnings about Tom's cooking were to follow, "And Tom is very good at looking after me. We go to the hotel for lovely food all the time."

"Food? Oh, my dear, that doesn't matter at all, as long as you're being fed enough for your age and I'm sure you are if there's a grown man around – they're always wondering about the next meal. No, no, your safety is the important thing. Elinore, I really think you should stay at Squair – stay precisely where you are. Don't go *anywhere*, do you hear me? Now, do let me have a word with whatever his name was – yes, Thomas. And Elinore – you *must* stay there."

Mystified, Elinore handed the receiver to Tom. The life-threatening contents of Tom's kitchen were clearly of no concern to Lady Groule, but she sounded as if she might blow up like a pressure cooker if she knew that Elinore was about to depart for Northumberland.

After five minutes of sitting in one of the tall-backed sagging chairs that flanked the hall table on which rested the Dower House's sole telephone, and watching Tom listen to Lady Groule in full spate, Elinore decided that her time would be better spent on her story. She went to the dining room and inserted a sheet of paper into the older typewriter. She began to press keys. This produced a clacking sound that was disturbingly loud to her ears, especially in a high-ceilinged, wooden-floored room like this. It must be terrible to be a secretary, she thought, making that din all day long. But the clacking keys were producing black typescript on a white page: a stark, thrilling sight. She forgot about everything else in her laborious transformation of handwriting into the next best thing to a page from a proper book.

Tom did not come into the dining room for another quarter of an hour. He made to sit down beside her, but sprang away to another chair when she cried, "You mustn't look! It's a surprise and anyway it isn't finished."

"Are you getting on all right with the shift key? And how about punctuation marks?"

"Oh – I'm not sure, but it doesn't matter because I want to read it out loud to you, and I know where all the special bits are meant to go."

"A literary recital in my own home? What a pity you have to leave so soon. Think of the entertainments we could have. Mr and Mrs Forsyth would come, and Boris, if he was very good, and a few other likeminded souls I know here, and we'd sit by candlelight in the library. But that would ruin your eyesight and then I'd be in trouble with Arabella. Bigger trouble than usual."

Tom cleared his throat and then started off in a serious vein.

"Now listen, Elinore. Lady G. is going to do exactly what I told you she would – ring the parents of Susanna and Usha right away. And she is very, very glad to do it." He cleared his throat again and continued in a different voice: "Elinore Crum is a wonderful gel, an extraordinary young lady, and a very good friend to Susanna and Usha, and we all think the world of her. Tell her she mustn't worry about anything, because *I* am in charge now." Tom raised his eyebrows in a questioning way and in his normal voice said, "Any more worries about your friends, then, Elinore Crum? If so, you must pack them up and send them to Lady G. and she'll obliterate them for you. But they can't stay here any longer. I refuse to give them house room."

Elinore blushed but could not help a little smile, which spread into a big one.

"If Arabella weren't carrying you off so soon," added Tom, "I'd ring those parents myself and have them bring down Susanna and Usha to see you here. Then we could have a party!"

"Oh!" exclaimed Elinore, in some agitation at the thought of such a deliriously happy occasion floating past her like a cloud, unable to become solid reality because of timing. "Please, *please* can I come back some day, and please could we talk about a party again, that kind of party? Mrs Berg's got lovely dresses for parties. She showed me one. She met the Queen in it, at a garden party. And Mrs Patel wears saris. She looks like a queen from India!"

"My word, what exalted circles you move in, Miss Crum," said Tom. "D'you think my shabby old house is good enough? Of course you can come back to Squair – *will* come back. And we'll get all the friends you want to come along too. This house isn't going anywhere, unless it falls down around my ears, and I am working to prevent that, you know. It just doesn't look at present as though I'm doing anything."

"Maybe it needs Arabella's house medicine. She is Mary Poppins for houses."

"What or who on earth is *that?*"

Elinore did her best to explain, and Tom did his best to keep a perfectly straight face. In the end, they agreed that Elinore would learn a great deal more as Arabella's official assistant, and then she could tell Tom all about it. Then Tom rose and gathered up some blank sheets of paper and a pen.

"All right, back to work," he said. "I've got a letter to write, and you have a magnum opus to finish PDQ."

"What's that?"

"Magnum opus is Latin for great work."

"I know. I read it once and I looked it up in my dictionary. I meant the other one, the PDQ."

"P for pretty, D for damn, Q for quick. You must not go around saying that until you are at least 21 years old, and if Arabella hears you say it you will be banned from visiting this house. You've been warned."

Tom took himself off to the garden, where he wrote a very long letter. Elinore would have been surprised to know that this effort was motivated by the desire to be helpful to Arabella, with whom he was always arguing, it seemed. But Tom had decided that Arabella must know promptly what Lady Groule had imparted to him, and that it would do Elinore no good at all to overhear any of it. Besides, as a lawyer, he had also decided that a carbon copy of this letter would be wise, so that he would not have to rely on his memory should the need for corroboration arise. Tom sighed. He would never have typed it in front of Elinore anyway, but carbon paper was messy and fiddly, and worse when used with handwriting. If only he could press something on a typewriter that would make an instant, exact copy; if only typewriters had memory banks.

. . . but she is as sharp as a fox and no one should be fooled by any hyperbole. Her friend Celia Chisholm must have all her wits about her too, or ZG wouldn't have any time for her. They all went to the same school, but were in different forms, didn't know each other and ZG had already left before any rumours started.

Roberta Leitch, as she was then, was a boarder, since her family was in India. She sucked up to teachers but was a bully to other girls – worse, in fact. The kind of thing that grows into cult of personality. Lust for power. She made younger or shyer girls do what she wanted, and she had her followers. Her idea of fun (one of them) was to start a rumour about another girl and encourage its spread <u>and</u> its mutation into something vicious. But she was clever and sneaky enough to avoid having anything pinned on her. Celia says the word was that teachers loathed her but couldn't get rid of her and, to make matters worse, some relation of hers had made a sizable donation to the school library.

She – RL – was always trumpeting about that, for she was a snob into the bargain. So, there she was, a little horror from day one at the Ina Blackadder School.

But it got worse as she got older. Theft (hushed up thanks to another large and timely donation from the same Leitch relation); experiments with alcohol and cigarettes; come-hither behaviour at school dances and any other occasions involving Henderson College boys – and all the time exerting her peculiar influence over the vulnerable, and leading them astray. Shoplifting was another problem. She liked to steal fancy dresses and jewellery. The school didn't know about that, but the other girls did, especially the ones in her dorm who had to watch her parading around in her stolen finery.

Then a girl died, and Roberta was implicated. She and two other girls (younger, of course) had sneaked out of school one night and gone to a dance hall. They drank themselves silly, and one girl went off with a chap in his car – <u>encouraged by Roberta</u>, that was the thing. The other girl was witness to that. Roberta herself was rapidly drunk and out of control, and no one knows what she really got up to that night, because the other girl got frightened and scuttled off back to the school.

The next morning, Roberta was nowhere to be found in the school, but the police were on the doorstep with news of a drunk driver who had killed his passenger in a terrible crash. Roberta was eventually reported to be in a hotel, after word was put out that she was not only missing but also wanted for questioning by police. When she did reappear at the school, it was under strict isolation in the sick bay until she was carted off by someone who made sure that she was put on a boat back to India.

The reason that Celia Chisholm knows all the details, despite the school's best efforts at controlling scandal, is pure accident. Her mother was friendly with the sister of the school matron, and one day this woman called on mama while Celia was at home, sick with the flu, and supposedly in bed. But Celia crept downstairs and overheard plenty. Later, she asked her mother outright to tell her everything, and that's why we've ended up with this valuable information right now. Incidentally, the extraordinary woman who rescued Elinore left me in no doubt about her suspicions of alcohol use by Roberta Caltrop, and she was certainly in the best position to note its evidence.

[Note to reader: Tom Balmerinoch's desire to inform Arabella about the background to Elinore's sudden arrival at Squair does not extend to informing her of the identity of the aforementioned "extraordinary woman." In fact, as he writes those words, he relishes the idea of causing certain feelings to arise in Arabella as a result.]

Here is the <u>crucial</u> thing, though. What do you know about Elinore's parents? Celia's mother told her that the school ended up convinced that Roberta Leitch was mentally and emotionally unstable. Apparently, her brother most definitely was cuckoo, and the talk was of a family tendency. Is Roberta not related to Elinore's father's side? From what you've told me of him, he was a first-class delusionist. And as for the mother – well, your label of "pathological selfishness" is a start.

Elinore is great company, and I'll be sorry to see her go, but frankly, I'm relieved that she will very soon be safe behind the walls of Castle Welkinlaw and with a good few utterly sane adults around. Roberta Caltrop can't get at her now, but who knows what the mother will try when she comes back from her dalliance in Dallas? (Sorry! Couldn't resist it.) Note: Elinore says "if" not "when" in that respect. Interesting.

This is far from the first time I've heard of individuals using religion as a screen for their absolutely rotten goings-on, and no doubt you too can name a few. We can only speculate at the mental convolutions that could turn a scandalous Leitch into a churchified Caltrop. Elinore has had a lucky escape. I am not sure what damage might have been done. We must keep our eyes open, without making too much of a fuss, if I may offer my humble male opinion. She is at present completely absorbed in writing a story, and that's probably a healthy sign. Do you know any doctors? She seems rather too thin, and my eyes might be deceiving me but I think a bruise or two might bear looking at. There might be more.

23

THE STORY OF MISS HELENA ALBACYR AND THE GHOSTS
by Miss Elinore Crum

*O*nce upon a time, a girl called Helena lived in Edinburgh, which is the capital city of Scotland. She was very beautiful with long, long, long fair hair. She had big brown eyes like a deer, and her eyelashes were so long they tickled her cheeks, which were quite pink, like roses. She had very long legs. This was a good thing, because she liked running around and climbing everywhere. But it was not easy to do that when Helena lived. It was the time when girls and ladies were not allowed to wear trousers. Not even when they were riding horses or bicycles! But Helena climbed trees and dykes and places with lots of rocks anyway in her skirt.

She had a dog called Pirate who ran about everywhere with her. He was called that because the hair on his head was all black around one of his eyes like a pirate's patch. The rest of him was white. Sometimes he rolled around in the mud and then he was NOT white any more. Helena's mother got very angry with him then. She always said, "You are a dirty dog! You must have a bath before you come in or you will make my beautiful carpets dirty too!" Helena's mother was called Mrs Albacyr.

Pirate loved sleeping on Helena's bed. Mrs Albacyr did not agree with this at all. Neither did the maid agree with this, because she was the one who had to do all the sweeping and dusting and every day she said Pirate left his hairs everywhere. She could not sweep them up with a vacuum cleaner, because they were not invented yet. But Mr Albacyr did not mind Pirate, not even when he was dirty or naughty. You see, Mr Albacyr was the one who had the idea of giving him to Helena. It was a very big surprise for her! He shouted Happy Birthday and woke her up and made the puppy Pirate run into her bedroom! But Mrs Albacyr did not agree with that idea. She gave Helena a very pretty dress with roses and ribbons for her birthday that day and she said, "DO NOT let that animal tear it with his claws and teeth!"

One day it was time for Helena's next birthday. She was going to be ten. She decided to have some special fun on that day all by herself and she decided to keep it secret from everyone. Her birthday happened on a Wednesday, which means that she was supposed to go to school. But she did not! Instead she went to Princes Street all by herself and climbed up the Sir Walter Scott Monument to the very, very top. She wished that Pirate was with her. Then she heard a dog barking far, far below on the ground. She looked over the edge. It was Pirate! "OH! He followed me!" said Helena. Then a truly horrible thing happened. A man came along and tried to drag Pirate away to steal him. Helena shouted, "Leave my dog alone!" But she was too high up and only pigeons heard her. She was very angry and very upset and she forgot to be careful. She leaned over the edge and the wind got in her long, long, long hair and pulled her right over into the sky! But Helena was not a pigeon, so she could not fly. She fell all the way to the ground and made a terrible THUMP!!! Everybody was screaming. Pirate was howling and barking, which is like crying if you are a dog.

Then Helena turned into a ghost. She knew she was one because Sir Walter Scott was dead, so he was a ghost too and he came along straight away. "Little girl, please do not cry. I will help you be a happy ghost," he said. "I want my dog Pirate," said the ghost of Helena. "Oh, do not worry," Sir Walter said. He was a very kind ghost indeed. He patted Helena on her head and he said, "Pirate is going to die of a broken heart anyway, because he loves you so much. He will be a ghost dog and you will both live happily ever after."

Helena asked Sir Walter a very important question. She said, "What am I going to do now? Do I have to go to school if I am a ghost?" Sir Walter said, "NO! Ghosts do NOT have to go to school. Nobody makes ghosts do anything. You can do ANYTHING YOU WANT."

Helena said, "All right, I am going to live in a lovely big house in the country by a river. Pirate can run around and get wet and dirty every single day. My house will have magic carpets that clean themselves. Or no carpets at all. Every day I will have hot buttered scones for tea and Pirate can eat some too. I will have a pony and I will wear jodhpurs like a boy when I ride it, not a silly skirt. Also, I would like to visit Edinburgh and meet other ghosts such as,

Queen Margaret, the wife of King Malcolm
Mary Queen of Scots, but NOT if her head is cut off in case I feel sick
Queen Magdalene
Queen Jane
Lady Sophia Lindsay
And Pirate wants to meet Greyfriars Bobby.

Also, I really, really want to visit Holyrood Palace so I can see where kings and queens live when they come here, and Edinburgh Castle because I have never been there and it looks EXTRAORDINARY. I want to go all over those places and see EVERYTHING. When I am inside them, I would quite like to practise going through walls and doors. Then I could visit Buckingham Palace and Windsor Castle and Balmoral Castle and nobody would see me. Not even the Queen!!!

"Good idea," said Sir Walter Scott. Then he said, "I will come to your house in my monument, which is really a spaceship, you know, and I will fly you to visit all those other ghosts. Your dog Pirate can come too and play with my dog Maida. She always flies with me. We can fly away to any royal places anywhere as long as they are in England and Scotland, I mean Great Britain, because my monument is not made for flying a long way over the sea. You have to ask another ghost if you want to go to foreign countries. The ones who came from those places can do it."

"All right. I will ask Queen Margaret because she came from Hungary and Mary Queen of Scots because she stayed in France first you know", Helena said. Sir Walter said, "Yes, I know all about her. I will also tell you if I meet other ghosts with the right kind of monument for flying."

Then the ghost of Helena Albacyr lived happily ever after. Mr and Mrs Albacyr were very sad in the beginning, but then they had twins so everything was all right again in their house. The maid was happy because she liked babies much better than dogs. That was because babies have no hair, but actually she was all wrong because babies are MUCH more dirty and messy than dogs! You have to watch out for Helena when she is flying around visiting the other ghosts who are quite famous. If you give her a wave she will visit you too! She will never do anything bad in your house and her dog Pirate will never make anything dirty because actually ghost dogs are always clean.

THE END

Elinore thought that Tom was the perfect listener. His attention never strayed and he reacted with shock or pleasure at all the right places in her story. When she had finished reading it, he clapped long and hard, and said, "Brilliant! Unique! Full of drama and pathos! And very, ah, how shall I say, *intelligent*. Yes, that's it: intelligent! I'm feeling unintelligent at this moment, because some of the, ah, ghosts you mention are completely unknown to me. Have you really been learning about them at school?"

"No, they're in my *Book of Edinburgh for Young People*. I mean, Helena Albacyr's book. I didn't know about them all before I read that."

"You're a scholar, Elinore Crum! Did Scotland really have queens called Magdalene and Jane? I thought they were all Margarets or Marys. And what was special about Lady Sophia Somebody?"

"Um, well . . . Queen Magdalene was only a queen for 40 days, so people probably forget to put her in books, and she came from France. Oh, no! I forgot! I forgot to put her in the other bit of the story, where she could fly Helena over the sea to France because she came from there. And Queen Margaret came from Hungary – I forgot to put her in that bit too. That's *two* mistakes." Her face fell.

"No, no, not mistakes, just omissions. All you do is add their names in the right place. So, why did Helena want to meet Lady Whatsit, and Queen Jane?"

"Because they were very clever and brave. Lady Sophia Lindsay got a man out of prison by dressing him up like a servant, and they were almost caught by the guard. I *love* stories like that! And Queen Jane got her son out of Edinburgh Castle by putting him in a thing called an ark, and then they carried it on a mule and put it on a ship. The little prince was inside it all the time!"

"Good Lord. I've been reading *all the wrong books*." Tom passed a hand over his eyes and looked mortified. "I must educate myself forthwith. Now, back to your story. It's splendid, Elinore, and I want a copy. It deserves a place in my library."

"Really and truly?" said Elinore.

"Really and truly. It also deserves more of an audience. Mr and Mrs Forsyth should have the pleasure of hearing it. Don't you remember how interested they were the other night, when they heard you were writing one? Go and call on them, story in hand, and they will beg you to read it aloud, which you do beautifully, by the way. And then come back here. Remember, I want a copy before you go! One of us has to type it out again."

"I love typing! But maybe you should do it this time. You could make it perfect. I don't think this one is *really* perfect."

"All right. I can type it quite quickly on my Olivetti, and you can have that copy, and I'll keep the original."

"Why? You should have the perfect one if you're going to put it in the library with proper stories."

"Oh no, you should have it. You'll want to show it to other people, I guarantee. Arabella for one, and the Welkinlaw people. You're an author! People will be *interested!*"

"Really and truly?"

"Utterly and absolutely. And another thing: originals are valuable. You're going to be famous one day, and your very first piece of typescript will then be worth thousands and thousands of pounds. I can sell it and pay for a new roof on the Dower House. And some new drains, and, let's see – oh, new electrics, *definitely*. All thanks to the Bank of Elinore Crum. I can see it now."

"*What?*" Elinore didn't know what to make of this, but she had to laugh at the outlandish idea of her being famous. "That's ri-*dic*-ul-ous!"

Marching up to the Forsyths' front door and announcing herself as a visiting author almost overwhelmed Elinore with shyness, but she trusted Tom enough to set off through the gates of the Dower House and along the road. The late afternoon sun shone full on her, the air was soft and warm, and Squair seemed almost to sparkle around her. It was such a pretty place, and so peaceful that every singing bird could be heard as a soloist. But where are the children, wondered Elinore. It suddenly occurred to her that she had seen or heard none.

She had no need to summon her nerves to knock on the Forsyth's front door, for Mrs Forsyth was inspecting flower heads in her front garden. "Ah, Elinore!" she greeted her visitor, almost as if she had been expecting her. "How are you? I hear you're going to leave us tomorrow. It's been a pleasure to see at least one young person around the village, you know."

"Where do the other children go and play?"

"My dear, we don't have any! Not since the primary school closed two years ago. The families kept moving away, you see, and the retired people kept coming instead. Now the old school is being turned into a pottery, which is nice enough, but a school keeps a village alive, I always say. I hope you'll be back for a visit before long."

"I hope so too. I really like staying here. But I don't know when I can come, exactly. I don't really know a lot right now."

"But before you go, will we have a chance to hear the story you were writing? We're very keen on new young writers!"

With relief and pride, Elinore showed her the typescript. "You could read it or I could read it out loud, like I did for Tom. It isn't *perfect* yet. If you read it, you'll see the bits I forgot."

"Oh, well, if you're offering us a reading, that's what we want. Entertainment! Why don't you and Tom come over here for supper and then we can all hear it together?"

Elinore ran back to the Dower House with this invitation, as pleased as Punch.

"What did I tell you?" said Tom. "Now, give me that paper you've been clutching and I'll whiz off a copy in my very best imitation of a secretary. You sit there and tell me about any bits that you want to alter – *before* I type them, please!"

When he had finished, Elinore thought her story looked even more like something straight out of a book. This made her want to write more stories, and type them, of course. She wanted to stay right where she was and carry on living *this* kind of life. Everything felt at home here: her mind, her body and most certainly all her books and other treasures. She sighed, and put her head and her arms down on the table.

"Are you collapsing from exhaustion, Miss Crum? All this mind-bending, back-breaking work of composing to a deadline and typing and watching me type?"

Elinore smiled, but did not laugh. "I was just thinking. I was thinking – it would be good if I didn't have to go away. I just want to have a place that doesn't move around all the time. And where all the people are nice all the time."

"Hmm . . ." said Tom. After a few seconds, during which Elinore's eyes traced the flame and whorl of the woodgrain next to her nose, he added, "I'm most honoured to hear that you like this old place so much, Elinore. And you certainly fit into it as if you'd been born here. You haven't shrieked at a mouse once. It's a terribly unsettling time for you, yes, but you must remember that, from now on, anywhere you leave – anywhere that you *like* – is somewhere that you *can* return to. You only have to ask." At the back of Tom's mind rose the shadow of Melba Crum and a tangle of legalities, but he mentally spat in their direction and carried on. "Who knows, you might be back here for a whole summer holiday next year!"

"But I don't know where I'm going to be after the summer holidays are over *this* time. It's a bit scary."

"Completely understandable. We, ah, don't have answers to some questions just yet. But Arabella and I won't let anything bad happen to you – that's a promise." As he said that, Tom was struck by Elinore's silence concerning her mother and the character whom Mrs Wattie had referred to as a "fancy man frae America." That silence signified much more than expressions of apprehension, he decided; but he would not probe. He would gather evidence from other sources instead. "You're far from the end of the holidays just yet. A lot of good things can happen in a short time, believe me. We just can't see around corners, that's the trouble."

Elinore lifted her head. "Do you really have corners in time? If you go around one, could you go backwards or forwards?"

Tom covered his eyes and groaned. "Please! You make my old brain work too hard. You're asking the kind of question that the most famous physicists in the world are wrestling with. You're so alarmingly bright, you're blinding me."

"What's a physicist?"

The telephone rang and Tom jumped up. "A scientist who studies physics," he called over his shoulder as he went out of the room. This did not much help Elinore, and she reached for the huge dictionary whose permanent home at present was the dining-room table. She had barely made headway in the F pages when Tom came back.

"Sorry, physics starts with the PH ffffff, not the F ffffff, " he said. "P-h-y – you'll get the rest. That was Mrs Anskett. Listen, Elinore, she sounds delightful, and she's terribly excited about having you to stay. She was ringing to say she's been in touch with Mr Carr and everything is in order for him to collect you tomorrow, at about five o'clock. She wanted to know exactly what you liked to eat, so that she could be sure to get in all the right things – that's highly reassuring, in my opinion. Makes me look like the worst host in the land. *And* – now this is top secret and you mustn't let on I told you, cross your heart and hope to die?"

"Yes, promise, cross my heart and hope to die!" breathed Elinore, agog.

"Mrs Anskett is going to make you a birthday cake. She found out all about you from Arabella, and of course Arabella knows you had a birthday but no cake, no party, and that's just not on when one is ten, is it?"

Elinore could only look at Tom, astonished. It was as if some holes in her life were being filled in beautifully while others were yawning like chasms.

"It's a *surprise* cake, Elinore – d'you understand? When it appears in front of you, you have to be *surprised*, or I'll be in hot water. I'm only telling you now because I think you need to know that you're off to stay with jolly good people, and so far we've only had Arabella's word on that. Now you've got mine! I'm a lawyer, remember? Trust me! Lawyers know all about people and their ways." He wagged a finger at Elinore and closed one eye in a protracted wink. She giggled, as much in relief at this news as at the sight of him.

"I promise. I'll write and tell you what kind of cake it is. I could send you a piece too!"

Tom smacked his lips and rubbed his hands. "Excellent idea. I need brain food too, or Davidicus Mercury will never come to life. Now, speaking of food, we are expected at the Forsyths shortly. I'm going to wash and change. When that clock in the hall strikes again, we'll be off."

Mr and Mrs Forsyth applauded *The Story of Miss Helena Albacyr and the Ghosts* as heartily as Tom, but their comments and questions about its content were slightly different.

"I'm most intrigued by Sir Walter Scott's place of honour in this tale," remarked Mr Forsyth. "Portraying his monument as a spaceship is highly original. I can't think of any writers who are using our local landmarks, indeed, our *national* ones, with such, ah verve and wit. Can you, dear?" "No, I can't," replied Mrs Forsyth. "They could learn from this. And Elinore, you clearly know about Sir Walter. I didn't know he had a dog called Maida."

"It was in a book," said Elinore. "But I haven't read any of his stories yet. I've got one called *The Heart of Midlothian*. It's a very old book, and the words are tiny. There's a *lot* of words."

The Forsyths hastened to assure her that her learning would not suffer if Scott's works had to wait several years for her full attention. "But you would enjoy visiting his house at any age," said Mr Forsyth. "Abbotsford. A glorious place. Have you been there?"

"No, I don't know where it is," replied Elinore.

"Close enough for a picnic!" cried Mrs Forsyth. "You'll just have to come back on a fine day, Elinore, and we'll all go."

"But tell me, how did the idea of the flying monument come to you? Was it just the sight of it in Princes Street?" asked Mr Forsyth.

"Um, no – I dreamed it. When I saw it, I didn't think it looked like a spaceship, but in my dream it was all ready to go up. I flew all over Scotland in it."

"A young Coleridge!" exclaimed Mrs Forsyth, clasping her hands in delight.

"There is *no* opium in the Dower House," said Tom firmly. Everyone laughed and Elinore was mystified. Then Mr Forsyth, who was a clinical psychologist, became serious. He sat up straight and his eyebrows shot up too. "My word. This is fascinating. Do you feel up to describing your dream?" Everyone leaned forward, waiting on her words.

Elinore was bemused at this attention, but she was happy to oblige with a detailed account.

"Prophetic!" said Mrs Forsyth, who was quite a romantic. "I'm convinced of it."

"Possibly," said Mr Forsyth, whose experience was full of anecdotal evidence of such phenomena, which, as a professional, he could not be seen to support unreservedly and without some crisply rational, objective explanation.

"But don't you remember the woman we met at that dinner a while ago?" asked Mrs Forsyth. "What was her name? The one we overheard interpreting a dream for that sad-looking man. Remember how he kept quiet until she was finished, and then he told her that what she said was exactly what had come to pass in his life? No one else in the room knew until then that he'd started divorce proceedings. And then she did the same for someone else there, but they were huddled in a corner, and I couldn't listen." She sounded disappointed about that.

"You weren't supposed to," chuckled Mr Forsyth. "But I do remember her. Marsh, March – Marchmont?"

"No, that wasn't it," said Mrs Forsyth.

"Marlock?" asked Tom.

"Yes!" said both Forsyths at once. "Do you know her well?" added Mrs Forsyth, with a certain eagerness.

"Oh no, not at all. I had a similar encounter with her *years* ago. She made everyone laugh by stating loudly and categorically that I was going to be a successful author and that my name would be in lights! Me! As I said, it was years ago, and I haven't written a single word of purple prose, not even of the palest lavender. Perhaps she was having an off day, or the stars weren't aligned just so. I've written screeds and screeds, but everyone knows that legal briefs never reach the West End stage, let alone Hollywood!" Laughter all around. It was agreed that Elinore was the true star in waiting among them. Tom, you are a big fibber, thought Elinore. But this fibbing was all right because it was about his secret book and it was really a very good joke. Besides, she felt she could trust him in matters that were no joke at all.

"Well, if I meet someone like that, I will ask them about my dream," she said. "And a lady did tell me once that I would have an exciting life. She said I should cut my hair in a fringe and it would happen."

Now Mrs Forsyth was sitting up, alert. "Oh, my! And where did you meet her?"

"At the hairdresser's. I *did* get a fringe – the one I've got right now." Elinore stopped, and turned to Tom. "Do you think she was telling the truth? I mean, some things did happen to me afterwards, and then I came here, and now I'm going to stay in a castle, and then I'm going to stay with Arabella for my holidays. But I don't know what kind of exciting she meant. I didn't like *all* of it!"

Tom hummed and hawed, out of his depth, and Mrs Forsyth came to the rescue. "Tell us about Arabella, dear. Where does she live?"

"I don't know exactly where, just in the Highlands. She lives in a farmhouse on top of a hill."

"Really . . ." said Mrs Forsyth, contemplating Elinore's description of her northward flight in Sir Walter Scott's spaceship.

24

Overnight, the weather turned, and Elinore awoke to drizzle and drifting mist. She had not slept well. In darkness, the skittering worries and wonderings in her head were echoed by rapid scratching and pattering all around her, and particularly under the bed. Whenever she switched on her bedside lamp, all sound ceased; it resumed within seconds of switching the lamp off. In the end, she left it on and turned on her side, to fall asleep again while studying the birds, fruits and other intricacies of a William Morris fire screen.

The damp grey morning joined with her tiredness to make her feel tremulous in the face of another departure and the unknown that lay beyond that. Arabella was fine (even if she was a witch), going to stay in a castle was fine, Mrs Anskett and a birthday cake *sounded* fine – but leaving the Dower House, the prettiness and peace of Squair, and the kindness in everyone she had encountered there was bringing back every emotion that had accompanied her removal from Criven. And after Criven had come . . . Elinore shivered.

"Elinore! Telephone!" Tom's voice came faintly upstairs. She ran down, still tugging on her yellow sweater. It was good to have bright clothes for days like this. Tom handed her the receiver and went off to the kitchen, whistling.

Lady Groule had been busy, efficient and voluble. For Elinore, the first result of this was the sound of Usha saying, "Hello, Elinore, it's *me*! Me, Usha. Are you all right? I wish you were here and so does Susanna!"

The happy burbling that followed this went on and on, until suddenly Elinore felt sick, and the natural gloom of the hall took on a strange, swimming greyness that obscured the chairs, the table and the portraits. Usha's voice faded, and so did the strength in Elinore's legs.

"Usha, I have to stop now. Sorry. But I can phone you . . ."

She did not hear Usha's reply, because she had to drop the receiver onto the cradle and sit down immediately. The chair seemed to swallow her up and her surroundings disappeared into greyness even faster. The next thing she saw were Tom's shoes. He was pushing her head and shoulders down, and urging her to breathe deeply. She did, and eventually the greyness went away, but she still felt sick.

"Elinore! Can you hear me? Can you stand up and get to the kitchen?" asked Tom.

At the kitchen table, she sat and shivered as Tom rushed around, heating water and toasting bread and forgetting about it, but eventually putting a hot chocolate drink in front of her and a pile of buttered, burnt toast, quickly followed by scrambled eggs.

"Bacon coming up next!" cried Tom. "Not up to hotel standard, and should be served *with* the eggs. Awfully sorry! Please don't beat me for it." He put on a scared face and made his teeth chatter, and Elinore managed a smile. The hot chocolate was magic stuff, she thought. She had last tasted it in Criven, although not in her own home.

"Ah, a smile. You will live. Has this happened to you before?"

"Yes, once when I was running. When I stopped, I fell down, but Lady Groule was there, and a lady called Mrs Chisholm. They took me into Mrs Chisholm's house."

"And did they feed you?"

"Oh, yes. They said I needed it. Is that what I need now to make it go away?"

"Yes. *It* is called fainting, and I think you really needed breakfast before all that chattering with Usha, and the surprise of it. All right, here's the bacon. Hmm, I think I'll have a second breakfast. Keep my strength up for all the day's excitements. Tell me, how is your friend with the lovely name, Usssshhha?"

"She said she was missing me. And Susanna is too. You were right."

"Naturally," said Tom. "Now eat up. I'll bet you any amount that Susanna will call you too, very soon, and you'll want to stay upright for that, won't you?"

"I can bet. I've got pocket money."

"Lucky you. I won't have any pocket money until you're famous and I can sell your manuscript."

"But you might get famous with your story about Mr Mercury."

"Might. You never know."

"It's a good secret. It's funny when everyone's talking about writing things and you say you never write anything."

"Well, it's funny for us, because we made it a secret, and you're very good indeed at keeping it with a straight face. Saving *my* face. As I said, you could be Davidicus Mercury's assistant." Tom put bacon between toast and made a thick sandwich. Then, in between bites and chewing, and with much hand waving, he returned to the matter of Elinore's insides.

"*But* remember this, Elinore – pay attention! – if someone says you have to keep a secret and you don't agree with that idea, just as Mrs Albacyr and her maid didn't agree with the idea of dogs, haha! – if you don't feel good about it in your insides, you must find the right kind of grown-up and tell them. *Must* tell them."

"Even if it breaks the secret?"

"Yes. That doesn't matter a jot if your insides think it's all wrong to keep it."

"How do I know the right person to tell?"

"You will. And you can always tell me. I'm a lawyer, remember? I'll set you right! Now promise you'll remember that. Cross your heart etc., etc. – don't bother with the rest, it's too gruesome."

"Cross my heart. Promise."

The ring of the telephone echoed along the stone-flagged passage from the hall, and Tom rose, taking the last of his bacon sandwich with him. He returned without it, and waving both hands.

"What did I tell you? *What* did I just tell you about good things coming around the corner? Go on, run along and talk to your friend Susanna."

Much talking between grown-ups, between Lady Groule and the Bergs and the Patels (or rather Mr Patel, since his wife was so far from talkative), had taken place before Susanna and Usha were able to speak to Elinore. Fredy's observation of a child's bare arm was now shockingly significant, and Mrs Berg was chastising herself. After the grown-ups had delved into the circumstances of the preceding Thursday and Friday (and some time before that), they realised that they must ask the two girls for the truth of what had upset them so badly on the afternoon of the thunderstorm. Eventually, it came out that they had been frightened by wickedness, not weather.

This left the Caltrops. Mrs Berg did not hesitate there. She went straight to No. 17 Dunallan Crescent and rang at the front door, and then at the back when no one came. It was Sunday evening then. At first, she assumed that they might possibly be away "churching", as she put it. On Monday morning, she returned early enough to have interrupted breakfast, but No. 17 remained shut up and silent at her ringing. The grown-ups conferred further and agreed to keep an eye out for any signs of the Caltrops' return, or that of Melba Crum. They would then decide what approach to take. At that point, they allowed their daughters to ring Elinore at the number given them by Lady Groule.

Mrs Berg and Fredy were very anxious about Elinore. After Susanna had spent at least ten minutes reassuring Elinore of her undying friendship and that she was perfectly well and happy, Mrs Berg took the telephone from her, and, with interjections from Fredy, banished forever Elinore's dread of judgement and rejection by the Berg family. Then Mrs Berg spoke to Tom.

"As I've already told Elinore," he said, "I think we must have a garden party next year. I understand you're accustomed to the Holyroodhouse kind, but I *beg* you to consider joining us, *en famille*, at Squair, if your crowded social calendar permits."

Elinore could hear a peal of laughter from Mrs Berg's end. After a little more talk, Tom put the telephone down, folded his arms and looked triumphantly at Elinore.

"There! What did I tell you? Nothing for you to worry about. Lovely people. I'm sure Usha's parents are too. Does everyone know you're off to stay in a castle now? I bet Susanna and Usha have never done *that*."

By the time Elinore and Tom were walking to the Skirving Arms for lunch, the drizzle had stopped and the sun was slanting through the mist and low cloud. The ruined castle looked picturesque, even dreamlike; the colours of flowers and shrubs in the gardens around the green glowed vividly against soaked, muted foliage; and Elinore's sadness about leaving it all was tempered by rising curiosity about Welkinlaw. The excitement of Susanna and Usha at the very idea of going to stay in a castle had been infectious.

Tom insisted on her choosing roast beef, and told the waitress to make sure that plenty of it was put on Elinore's plate. "This girl is growing too fast for her energy to keep up!" he declared.

"Then I'll see you both get enough for a working man," said their waitress. "And what about all the trimmings? Same there?"

"Exactly the same, especially the Yorkshire pud. And we'll each have a big plate of minestrone soup first, please."

"Och, it's just like feeding my dad, and he's a keeper, out all day long."

Elinore looked around the dining room. A wet, cool Monday was almost a guarantee that no tourists would appear. Two late middle-aged ladies were at one table, but they looked local, and they called the waitress by her first name. Sitting all by himself by a window, however, and staring out in deep thought at the village green, was a man who appeared to be foreign. As long as he was preoccupied with the scenery, Elinore could look him over carefully, noting each detail that marked him as different.

The waitress brought their soup, and every time she raised the spoon to her mouth, Elinore peered and added another clue.

"What's wrong with the soup, Elinore?"

"Nothing. I like it. Why?"

"Every time you take some, you frown. You look as though you're forcing it down your throat."

"No, I'm *watching!*" In a whisper, she explained. Tom was seated opposite her, and could not easily see the man at the window table.

"Hmm, interesting. What clues have you spotted?" Tom was whispering now too, and he did not turn to look. Elinore was pleased. This was proper secret agent behaviour.

"Umm . . . he's got a big gold ring. And a watch with a gold strap. It was shining when he looked at the time."

"All right. That rules him out as, say, a gamekeeper, like our waitress's father, or a farmer. But it's not enough to mark him as foreign. He could be a retired gentleman who's moved here from Edinburgh, or even London. Perhaps he's all on his own like me and likes to eat here because he forgets to fill up his fridge and doesn't much enjoy cooking anyway. Next?"

"His hair is a little bit long, and it's all grey. But he looks really clean, not like a hippy. He doesn't have any hair on his face. His skin is sort of normal colour and he doesn't look really *old*. He's got glasses, and they're *round* and they're *gold* too." Elinore had seen plenty of children and adults wearing round spectacles before now, but, apart from Tom's tortoise-shell rimmed ones, only the flesh-pink kind that came courtesy of the National Health Service.

Tom leaned closer. "Good observation," he said, "but still, if Davidicus Mercury were relying on your description so far, he'd say it wasn't enough to identify this man as foreign right off the bat. What else do you see?"

Please keep looking out of the window, Elinore said to herself as she scrutinised the man again. He was still thinking hard, apparently, as he viewed Squair drying and steaming slightly under the strengthening sunlight, and tapping his fingers on a couple of books that lay on his table.

"He's wearing a white shirt with yellow stripes, the stripes are quite thin, and a brown waistcoat that isn't made of cloth – I think it's the kind of unshiny leather you make shoes out of, but I can't remember the name."

"Suede?"

"Yes. I can't see any more until he gets up."

"What about a tie?"

"No, he's got a scarf. It looks like a big handkerchief with a pattern. And he's got books on the table, but he isn't looking at them. He just looks through the window. If he lived here, he probably wouldn't stare at it like that, because he'd know all about it and it would be a bit boring."

"Intriguing," said Tom. "Well, this is what Davidicus Mercury would say: he'd look at all those clues, he'd put them all together, and he'd say, the sum is greater than the parts. Guess what that means?"

Oh, no, not *sums*, thought Elinore, I just want to be a spy. She shrugged.

"It means that your intuition, the voice in your insides, is telling you that all the little things you see add up to make this man a very likely foreigner, even if the little things by themselves don't prove anything. Got it?"

"Ye-e-s," said Elinore.

Just then, the waitress brought an entrée to the man's table, and he asked her a question.

"Oh yes, delivered fresh every day," she replied, in a voice much louder and clearer than the man's. "Straight off the boat at Newhaven. Have you not been there yet? Newhaven fisher village, very historic. You'd likely find plenty for your camera."

"He *is* a foreigner!" hissed Elinore. "He doesn't know about Newhaven. I do! I read about it in my Edinburgh book. There was a picture of a lady called a fishwife from Newhaven. I bet he's eating *fish*." She sat back, folded her arms and grinned at Tom, vindicated. "I was right! Let's ask her where he's from, or we could ask Peter."

"No, we will not. That's cheating. We might still find out more with patient observation."

"Huh! You make *my* brain work too hard."

"Serves you right," said Tom, and thumbed his nose at her. She thumbed hers back, and collapsed into giggles. The man at the window table looked up and smiled, and Elinore blushed. Their roast beef arrived. It took Elinore a long time to eat everything on her laden plate, and her watchfulness waned as she concentrated on demolishing the helpings of foods she loved. Peas always took a lot of chasing. When she looked up again, the man was rising from his chair as if to leave. She saw blue denim jeans, slightly flared, and suede desert boots, and then he was gone from the dining room.

"Now what?" she asked Tom, after reporting those details.

"*Now* you can ask someone."

"But you said –"

"I said we *might* find out more. We didn't, so it isn't cheating now."

"Huh."

Their waitress told them he was Mr Fisher, from Canada, who was very keen on photography.

"See?" cried Elinore. "I was right! He *is* foreign. Isn't Canada where America is?"

"In a manner of speaking, but don't ever say that to a Canadian. They are next door to America but different from Americans, even if they sound alike – some of them."

"You mean like Scotland and England?"

"Perhaps. I'm far from knowledgeable about dominions."

"What's that?"

"What Canada is, if it still is. Now, what pudding are you going to have?"

On their way back to the Dower House, they spotted Mr Fisher looking at the exterior of the doocot next to the castle. A square canvas bag was slung over his shoulder, a camera was in his hand, and he was wearing a light jacket with many pockets and something like a bush hat.

"No, not Scottish, not British," said Tom. "Not dressed like that here. You were right. Good work! You are hereby formally appointed assistant to Davidicus Mercury."

"Gosh! Now I have two really important jobs."

"What's the other one?

"I'm going to be Arabella's assistant too, to help with the house medicine. In the castle!"

Elinore capered along the street in celebration at being in such demand, and Tom wondered how he might keep her in that frame of mind, at least until she had to get in a car and be driven away to yet another temporary lodging.

Elinore had next to no packing to do. Tom brought down all her bags and boxes to the hall, and, remembering what she had seen in the Berg household, she said she would strip her bed and make a laundry pile.

"How gracious of you," said Tom, surprised at this sign of a more structured domestic life than he had presumed to have existed for Elinore.

"Where's the washing machine?"

"I don't have one yet. It's on my great big shopping list of new things. I pay someone in the village to do all my laundry.

"You need lots of new things here. You should see Mrs Berg's kitchen."

"I can imagine. Space-age compared with mine, yes? Now, if you're all ready for Mr Carr, you can do whatever you like for the next few hours."

"I think I want to say goodbye again to Mrs Forsyth. I really liked her food."

Boris greeted her in the garden, but Mrs Forsyth did not come to the door when Elinore rang, and she saw that their car was not in its usual place. She went back through the abundant garden, sniffing all the flowers along the path. When she raised her head from the huge roses by the gate, she saw Mr Fisher walking slowly along the road in her direction, looking this way and that.

"Hello, there," he greeted her, smiling in recognition.

"Hello."

"Am I on the right road for the village school?"

"No, this road doesn't go there. But anyway, it isn't a real school, because there aren't any children here now."

"No *children*? None at all? And where do you go to school, miss?"

Elinore was thrown by this simple, obvious question. In an instant, she felt as though she were hanging over space. Where on earth *would* she go to school next? Her mouth opened and closed, and Mr Fisher waited politely. "Edinburgh," she said in the end.

He nodded. "Well, I'd like to see the old school anyway, so maybe you can point me in the right direction. And d'you know which route I'd take to see the big old house that's supposed to be around here? Is there a footpath to it or a proper road?" He pronounced "route" as "rout", to Elinore's fascination.

"I'm staying in an old house. It's big and it's hundreds of years old. You just go along this road." She pointed.

"Really? That sounds just the place I'm after. Would your folks mind if I came along and had a look, maybe took a few shots?" He lifted the camera slung around his neck.

Folks. Were they parents? "It's not my house, it's Tom's, and you could come and ask him."

"Why, thank you. I'll just follow along then. And may I ask your name? I'm Jack Fisher."

"My name is Elinore Crum, and Tom is Tom Balmerinoch."

Mr Fisher grinned and shook his head. "I'll see that name in print before I attempt it."

The entrance gates of the Dower House stopped Mr Fisher in his tracks. "*Wow!*" He craned and bent and knelt, moved backwards, forwards and sideways and took many shots. "Pineapples! Incredible!" he said, pointing his camera at the ornamented tops of the gate pillars. Elinore looked up with interest. She had always meant to ask Tom what the wind-worn blobs were meant to be, but now it was clear, even if the reason for topping Scottish pillars with fancy fruits was not.

She left him in the courtyard, gazing around in awe and excitement, and ran indoors.

"Tom! Tom! Where are you?"

A muffled shout from the dining room. She burst in and jigged around, waving her arms in exactly Tom's manner, in triumph at having secured for full examination the object of their earlier curiosity.

"I've got Mr Fisher from Canada. He's here. I *brought* him here. He was looking for a big old house, so it must be this one. We can find out all about him now!"

Tom laid down some papers, took off his spectacles, polished them on his shirt, put them back on and looked at Elinore in astonishment. "Encouraging the young entry is one thing, but what am I turning you into? Elinore, you're supposed to *observe*, not capture for the purpose of interrogation! Come on, then. We must entertain Mr Fisher from Canada."

Jack, as he insisted on being called, was enthralled with the Dower House, and profuse in his gratitude for being invited to explore it. However, after some discussion, it turned out that he was really looking for the closed-up mansion over the hill. His grandmother, long dead, had been in service in her youth, before marriage and emigration to Canada, and he believed that she had worked at Squair House. He had never bothered much about his antecedents and Scottish background, but, as he put it, now was the time to fill in some gaps.

"So, how do I get from here to there? I've got a hire car at the hotel. Can I get really close, maybe even inside?"

Tom shook his head. "It's completely boarded up, and the main gates are padlocked . . ." He tailed off, looking at Elinore. "But your local guide here can lead you to a splendid vantage point – in fact, the best for a photographer, because it's the only high ground for some distance that overlooks the house and policies. It sits in country that's rather like a saucer, you see."

Elinore jumped up. "I know where to go! I can show you everything!"

"My lucky day," said Jack. "One more question: is it going to rain again today? I'm not sure I brought the right clothes for Scotland in July." He pointed to his suede desert boots.

"Come with me," said Tom. "This house came with more boots of all kinds than I've ever bothered to count."

As Jack and Elinore crossed the rough domain of moles that passed for a lawn at the Dower House, Tom watched them, or rather Elinore. She was striding along in her wellington boots, pointing this way and that, and he could hear her listing all the sights that in her opinion were worthy of a photographer's attention. It crossed his mind that for a child, a girl, to go off through woods and fields with more or less a completely strange male adult – a *foreigner*, no less – was exactly the kind of thing that responsible adults warned children against and told them never, ever to do under any circumstances. "Quite right," he said to himself. Why then had he sent Elinore off so readily? Because gut instinct had prompted and approved it; because it allowed her an outlet for her engaging enthusiasm and to offer her little bit of local knowledge as something genuinely, immediately useful in the world; and above all because this unexpected excitement would keep her spirits high right up to departure. If he had just put on his own boots and taken Jack up the hill, Elinore would have simply been a child trailing along in the wake of two men talking. He would have been forced to keep an eye on his watch too. While he remained in the house to greet Mr Carr, the pair could spend as long as they liked on this unexpected adventure.

The shadow of Melba, the parent in the eyes of the law, rose again at the back of his mind.

He told it to do something impossible to itself, and added, "Your pathological self-absorption wholly disqualifies you from further intervention."

Jack Fisher was standing not far inside the densely overgrown wood, turning around and around on the spot, wondering if enchantment was a real thing and whether he had stumbled into it. The glimmer of light on and through leaves, the mossy statues and traces of paths made his hands shake with excitement and fumble over lenses and settings. He *had* to get this right.

"I know all the paths in here," Elinore told him. "I went all over them with my friend. You can see lots of these statues and things if you want me to show you. And some of the trees are special, Tom says, but I don't really know about that. But we can look for them! I can show you!"

"Please and thank you," said Jack, which Elinore thought was quaint. "This is – this whole place is unbelievable. Lead on!"

After a good half hour, they reached the wrought-iron gate in the Dower House boundary wall. Jack photographed it closed, they wrenched it open, he took more shots from both sides and they started up the sloping field. But after a few strides, he stopped.

"Elinore, would you mind going back down there to the gate? I've just had this great idea."

He posed her in the open gate, looking out and up the field, looking through the bars of the closed gate and finally he told her to run through the gate with her arms raised, while he captured the image from behind. Elinore felt a little shy at being the sole object of this kind of attention, which she associated with magazines and very pretty people. But it was fun! Jack was grinning all over his face, and he pumped his arm in the air after the last shot, saying, "Yes! That'll floor 'em. Real meaningful stuff."

As they climbed towards the crest of the field, he told Elinore that he belonged to an amateur photography club back home. He was planning to blow everyone else out of the water, as he put it, when it was time to display his Scottish pictures at the next members' show. "And I'll make sure you get copies of every single one – well, not the duds – every single one with you in it. I'll send them. And you just let me know if you want me to take some more pictures, okay? I'm at your service. This is a *huge* favour, taking me all the way up here. Huge."

"It's fun!" said Elinore. "I like old places a lot, and it's fun to show them to people. Do you just have new houses in Canada? Tom says Canada is next door to America, and I've seen pictures of America and programmes on television. It looks like *everybody* lives in modern houses there."

"Well . . . we've got our historic places for sure, but that doesn't necessarily mean old, and I can tell *your* idea of old is way, way older than what we're used to. How old are you?"

"Ten and a little bit. Almost a fortnight," said Elinore.

"Okay, maybe you could think of it like this. Scotland is like a person who's older than the oldest person you've ever met, and Canada is still just a kid, like a person your age, when you compare them."

"Gosh . . ." Elinore's mind was working as hard as her legs. What an interesting way of looking at places, or things. She would have to experiment with it.

Just before they reached the crest of the hill, the sun broke fully through. When Jack Fisher set eyes on Squair House for the first time, it was bathed in light and the scene was sharp and clear for miles around. He stood as if in shock, and all he uttered for some minutes was, "Oh, Jesus . . ."

Oh, no, not another one, thought Elinore. She had thought him much too nice to be another religious person, and neither did he seem to be the same thing as that awful Dwayne man, even if he did come from the country next door.

Matthew Carr was driving his employer's car, a creature beloved by both men. This car was known as the Bristol, because that was the name of the manufacturer. Neither Matthew Carr nor Henry Anskett would have demeaned it by giving it a female name, as Tom had done with his Volkswagen. Like sea captains, though, they always said "she" and never "it."

Once a year, Henry Anskett drove the Bristol to Edinburgh so that it could undergo the equivalent of an annual medical examination. His wife, Marigold, went too and they timed it to coincide with some shopping, a play, a film, catching up with friends, and so on. This year was different, because Matthew's aged mother had stumbled up to death's door and was expected to pass through it in less than a week.

"You must take all the time you need," Henry Anskett told Matthew. "Take the Bristol for her check-up and do the thing in dignity while you're at it." He meant the funeral. "Good timing: you can kill two birds with –"

"Stop, Henry!" said his wife. "How can you be so *thoughtless*?"

"But I don't *think*," said Henry, injured. "These things simply come out, you know."

"No, I don't know," said Marigold. "I never make puns, and thank goodness for that."

"My apologies, Matthew. As I was saying, the Bristol is at your disposal. I'll just call the garage and tell them you'll be dropping her off next week. At your convenience, of course, once you know the day of the funeral. You must *drive* to the funeral – you can't get on a bus for that."

Then came Arabella Cheyne's request. "Something peculiar has happened and I am now in charge of a ten-year-old girl," she announced in her usual way. "Can she come down here and stay until I'm finished? Her manners are excellent, she loves dogs and anywhere very old, and she's well used to cold beds, that sort of thing. She's at Squair, between Edinburgh and Berwick."

"Oh, my dear, she must come immediately!" exclaimed Marigold, who had always longed for a daughter. "For as long as necessary! How will she get here?"

"Yes, yes, get her down here of course," echoed Henry. "And Matthew can bring her. Carr for carriage and handling of children!" He beamed, caught Marigold's eye and coughed.

Matthew arrived in Squair on the stroke of five o'clock, partly because he was a punctual man, and partly because he would never have driven fast enough to arrive too early. He left that sort of risk to Mr Anskett. His job was to treat the Bristol as if she were the Gold State Coach. When he drove through the gates of the Dower House (sagging gates, rusted hinges, mortar on pillars sorely in need of repointing), he saw a disgraceful-looking Volkswagen Beetle, two men and a skinny child in wellington boots. They were standing on the weedy gravel in front of the entrance to a dilapidated house, looking up; one of the men raised a camera.

"Oh, aye – looking out for the next bit to fall off?" said Matthew under his breath. His factor's eye had taken in everything in an instant. He straightened his tie and got out of the car, presenting himself not so much as Matthew Carr but as Welkinlaw itself, the acme of good and prudent management.

Elinore saw a short, barrel-like man emerging from a shining blue car that was quite unlike any she had seen before. He wore a checked shirt, plain dark green tie, very hairy greenish tweed jacket, khaki trousers and brogues that looked like conkers. Under a tweed cap, his cheeks were red from winter days spent outdoors. It was hard to say how old he was, but that was always a problem with grown-ups. His vehicle was very far from a Land Rover or muddied estate car, but in every other respect he was a familiar sight from Criven.

"Jesus!" said Jack Fisher to Tom. "I don't believe this place! What kind of car is *that*?"

"No idea, but it's a museum piece. Mr Carr! Hello. I'm Tom Balmerinoch." They shook hands. "You're spot on time, and we're all ready for you. This is your passenger, Elinore. Very kind indeed of you to give her a lift. I've had a look at the map, and it's clear that she couldn't get to Welkinlaw by any other means except helicopter."

"Aye, that's the state of things now the railway's gone. Good afternoon, miss."

Matthew Carr stuck out his hand for Elinore to shake as if she were another grown up. She saw him glance down at her feet, and she knew at once that, although he might say nothing, she should not get into that extraordinary vehicle wearing wellington boots or indeed anything with a trace of dirt on it. While the men talked, she went indoors and rummaged for her suede boots in one of her boxes stacked in the hall. Then she rushed upstairs for a last visit to the magic bathroom. She used one of Tom's combs to tidy her hair, took the corner of a towel and wetted it to rub off a smudge where a leafy branch had caught her cheek, and checked jumper and trousers for other traces of her latest adventure. It would not be a good start at Welkinlaw if she carried bits of sticky willy on herself into the car and left them to put their little hooks into the next passenger.

All three men were still in the courtyard, their attention on the car. Matthew was explaining her pedigree, especially for the benefit of Jack, who was enraptured.

"Bristol 403 1953," he announced. "Year of Her Majesty's coronation. She went all over Scotland that first year, with the pair of them." Matthew patted the bonnet of the car, thus confusing Jack about the identity of "her". "Hand built in Bristol. Same company that built our planes in the war: Blenheim, Bolingbroke, Beaufighter, Buckingham, Brigand and Buckmaster." He rattled off this list so fast that Jack lost the names, but he said "Wow", anyway and lifted his camera. "May I? The interior?"

"Be my guest," said Matthew, and he opened all four doors of the car and the boot and the bonnet as if he were a top salesman. "Fresh from her going-over, what we do every year, you know – up in Edinburgh. Mr Anskett takes her up to the same mechanics himself, but I had the privilege this time. Most enjoyable, I must say. A fine outing. Mind you, Carr's my name and cars are what I like – some of them."

Elinore remembered the funeral of Mr Carr's mother. He did not appear to be cast low by grief. She was glad, but not for his sake: she wanted some cheerful company if she must leave Squair.

With help from Jack, Tom began to carry out Elinore's belongings, most of which fitted in the boot. Matthew spread a plaid rug tenderly on the back seat and placed the remaining few bags on top of it. The car's seats were in soft, pale, buttery leather and all the edges were piped in a contrasting blue rolled leather that matched the exterior paintwork.

"Now then, Elinore, you sit up front with me and see all of where we're going. You want the best view of the castle when we come on it. I hear you like a bit of history. We'll see plenty of that between here and there."

Elinore wondered who had bothered to tell him about her unimportant interests and make them a matter worth mentioning at the start of her journey. Added to the other signs, it boded well. Still, when the moment came to get into the front seat and have the safety belt adjusted tightly across her, she felt completely lost and unable to speak as Tom looked down at her. He held up his hand and ticked things off on his fingers.

"Elinore, I want you to remember three things. Number one, you can come back here at any time in your life. Number two, pay attention to your insides. Number three, I should like another ghost story, please, as soon as you're inspired to write one. Mr Carr, is Welkinlaw home to any ghosts?"

"Well, now," said Matthew, "that depends on the eyes that might be looking for them. If you're a young sprig like Elinore here, you'll have sharper sight, won't you?"

Jack Fisher shook Elinore's hand and thanked her for being a fine guide through the wood and up the hill. "You wait: I'll be sending you some great photos! Some real winners!"

Matthew started the engine. "Just a minute!" exclaimed Tom, and he ran indoors. He came back with an envelope and handed it to Matthew, who looked at the name, nodded and put it safely in his inside pocket. And then they were off, with much waving. This is a car for a princess, thought Elinore. In front of her was so much polished walnut that it was like being in a room with fine furniture. A princess would not be a cry-baby. She took a handkerchief from her oriental silk bag, blew her nose and very quickly wiped her eyes.

"Well, now," said Matthew, "we're off to England! Have you been across the border much, Elinore?"

"No, never. But I used to live close to it, in a place called Criven. At least, everyone said it was close and you could see English names on the signposts."

"Criven? Oh, aye, I know that name from signs too. Bit off the main road, isn't it? As for the border, you wouldn't know there was one if no one put up a sign. And we're not that far in at Welkinlaw. You might get all the way there and think you're back where you started. Not Squair, mind. More like Criven thereabout. Do they keep sheep around there or is it dairy herds?"

"Actually, there are lots of sheep and they're Cheviots."

"Well, now!" (Here Elinore realised that this phrase was part of Matthew, like a leg or an arm.) "Not everyone can name the breed they're looking at, even if they did grow up in the middle of 'em."

"They have *some* cows too, but not a lot. The brown and white ones called Ayrshires."

Matthew nodded. "Ayrshires they are."

"And Mr MacMillan had a bull called Sharley. I mean, that wasn't his *name*, it was the kind of bull he was. He was a white colour that looked a bit pink. He was *really huge* and quite fierce. That was what Mr MacMillan said. David MacMillan was in my class at school and he said his father was very strict about not letting everybody go near the bull – only some of the men, and only if he was with them."

Matthew whistled in surprise at this accurate description of a Charolais bull. "Very knowledgeable *you* are! Thinking of going into my line of work when you're older? What else do they have in Criven, then? Do hounds ever meet there? You'd have the Jedforest, the Lauderdale, the Buccleuch, the Border Hunt – all those packs nearby and a lot of open galloping country, wouldn't you say?"

With gusto, Elinore took up her favourite subject: the topography, natural history and denizens of Criven, both two- and four-footed. This conversation lasted until Matthew asked if the village also had a fish and chip shop.

"No," said Elinore. "I really like fish and chips, but I hardly ever got them. You have to go somewhere like Galashiels for that.

"Well, now, it's past tea time by this clock, which is *never* wrong" (he tapped the clock on the walnut dashboard) "and you're in for a treat. Your aunt *and* Mrs Anskett told me you weren't to go hungry on any account. I said, right then, we'll be stopping for a proper meal and I know just the place. We're coming up to the town now. My cousin's wife's brother went into business here the other month. We'll turn left at the first crossroads, and you keep your eyes peeled for the Café Splendido. That's Italian, that name. My cousin's wife's Italian, or her dad is at any rate."

Elinore spotted the café at once. It had a white sign with red swirling letters and the final 'O' of the name was a stylised sun. She decided that it looked very nice and that now she was feeling definitely not sad. Matthew parked the car right in front of the café window. Before they had even entered the bright red and white interior, the aromas coming out made her decide that now she was definitely cheerful.

From behind the counter, a small, black-haired woman cried, "Oh, you got here!" and came out to shake hands. "Maria, meet Miss Elinore Crum, who's on her way to Welkinlaw. She likes her fish and chips – she's just told me that. Elinore, this is Maria, my cousin's wife's sister. And here's her brother, the businessman himself."

A man came out from the kitchen, wearing the loose white uniform of a cook, and more handshaking and explanations followed. Maria insisted they look at the full menu before plumping for fish and chips. She seated them at a window table, where Matthew's eyes moved incessantly to and from the parked car. He had removed his tweed cap for the first time since Elinore had met him, and she saw that he was nearly bald; she could not help thinking that his head was like the smooth, curved bodywork of the Bristol.

In the end, they did choose fish and chips. While Maria stood and chatted with Matthew about the funeral of his mother, Elinore looked around and noted every detail, from the red and white checked tablecloths and the chrome-edged chairs with shiny red seats, to the pictures of Italian landmarks on the red walls, the plastic daisies in little vases on each table, and the display case full of confectionery that looked *amazing*, especially the cake stand piled high with chocolate eclairs simply bulging with whipped cream. Elinore preferred to avoid cream, which too easily made her feel sick, but she loved the way it made foods look rich and special. This place was a treat just to look at.

"Thank you very, very much for taking me here, Mr Carr," she said. "It's the nicest café I've ever been in."

"Well, now, I'm glad to hear that and we'll pass it on to Maria and Tony. And you've not even had a bite of their food yet! But let's have no more of this Mr Carr business, Miss Elinore. It's Matthew to you, especially since you'll be stopping at Welkinlaw for a bit. We don't stand on ceremony there. Very fine people, Mr and Mrs Anskett, very correct when need be, but not a bit of side on 'em, and that's fine wi' me. Can't say the same for all their neighbours, mind.

Hoi!" He suddenly half-rose and rapped on the window. Startled, a passing boy moved away from the Bristol.

"No one so much as breathes on that car," said Matthew.

Maria put plates of steaming, thickly battered fish and big, fat chips in front of them, and a cruet of vinegar, HP sauce, tomato ketchup and mustard. Elinore saw that her plate held just as much as Matthew's.

"Don't you worry if it's a wee bit too much for you," Maria told her. "We'll just wrap it up for a snack you can eat on the way."

"Over my dead body! There's never a crumb of food allowed in my car," declared Matthew, shaking salt and vinegar vigorously all over his fish and chips. "We'll take our time here. Elinore wants to taste your fancy food too, Maria." He jerked his head at the confectionery display. Elinore smiled. She had begun to think that this short, round man was just as nice as Tom in his own way, even if, as a driver, he did make her just a *little* nervous, because his legs simply did not look long enough for his feet to touch the pedals – the brake pedal in particular. Their speed had been sedate, but, more and more, Elinore was imagining the Bristol as a creature that wanted to plunge ahead and gallop unchecked. She knew it was silly to worry, but this powerful, gliding car was transmitting a personality that she associated with the wildest of horses.

She went to use the lavatory, which was in a little corridor between the kitchen and the serving counter. Over the clatter of pots and the hiss of frying, she caught the familiar sounds of Radio One, and recognised the song that started playing. She had last heard it in her miserable bedroom at No. 17. "*All right now, baby, it's a-all right now.*" The group was called Free. The lavatory had a mirror, and she took a comb from her bag, straightened her fringe and made her hair look neat around her ears. This would be her last chance for tidying herself before meeting Arabella and yet more new people. Her reflection showed exactly the same Elinore Crum who had been locked up by Mrs Caltrop; but how could that be, when so much had happened to her since then? She must be different, somehow.

When she came out, the song was still playing. *"All right now . . ."* She *was* all right, at least just now. Perhaps that was why she looked the same: she was just – all right. Good things were happening, and she was on the road to even more. The song was another magic message, she concluded.

"Well, now," said Matthew, when she sat down again, "how about one of those éclairs? You go and choose whatever takes your fancy."

Before they left, he flourished a banknote at Maria and told her that she must keep the change. Arabella had given it to him, with instructions to feed up Elinore and take the same care of himself en route, and not to return with any money left over.

They were still in Scotland, Matthew informed Elinore as she buckled her safety belt once more, but not for much longer. The inherent drama of the landscape was heightened at this hour, as the dropping sun threw deep shadow across hills and enriched every natural colour. As they drove through Hawick, she remembered being taken there once or twice when Hector had been alive and present, and in particular a sculpture in the town centre.

"I saw that horse statue before! I *love* it," she exclaimed as they passed the 1514 Memorial.

"Aye, that's a very fine work," agreed Matthew. "Stirs the soul. D'you know how it came to be? There's two stories in that. First one is the battle, t'other one is the father and son who carved it."

These stories were brief, but being historical and so rooted in Matthew's own background, which spanned both sides of the border, they inevitably led to more, and questions from Elinore. The cadence of his speech, the comfort of the gliding car and a growing sense of security combined with a full tummy to make Elinore relax and eventually doze. With great surprise, she suddenly realised that the car had stopped, and that Matthew was pointing ahead and saying, "Look now – there's Welkinlaw! Thought I'd stop here and let you see how grand it is. See how it drops down sheer to the river?

Only on the one side, though, that's the thing. If you didn't see this view first, doubtless you'd come up on the rest of it and think that's no castle, it's just a big old house. We go down there and round a bit and come up through those trees to the right, see? There's a proper avenue, very fine timber, smooth going all the way. Nothing rough for the Bristol, let me tell you!"

"Gosh," murmured Elinore, still dozy. "It looks . . ."

"Not far to go from here. All right, now?"

"All right now," said Elinore.

25

More than the baronial scale of the place, more than the profusion of fearsome antique weaponry on the first walls she saw, and more even than a life-size portrait of a gentleman who was unquestionably a king, staring down at her from among the pikes, halberds, battle-axes and broadswords – more than all that and some other evidence of a well-used castle, Elinore was immediately awed and abashed by her welcome. She could not believe that she was quite worthy of it.

Arabella was nowhere to be seen at that moment. As the Bristol pulled up under a substantial portico, a woman ran down the steps and opened the passenger door. Elinore, still fumbling with her safety belt and shoulder bag, found herself looking straight into the face of someone who was clearly thrilled at the sight of *her*. She had grey hair, and might possibly have been a grandmother; beyond that, she bore not a shred of similarity to Mrs Caltrop. Instead of a mushroom hat and clothes like porridge, she wore a heathery sweater with a floral scarf at the neck; a cardigan the colour of stormy sea; and a tweed skirt that mixed both hues. Her lipstick emphasised her smile, and her hair looked as if it saw rollers every day. She smelled of lavender.

"*Elinore!* Welcome! We are *so* excited to meet you at last. How are you? Has Matthew looked after you – oh, silly question, of course he has. But you must be tired, and hungry and thirsty, and longing to sit down and rest. Come in, come in!"

"She's been in the Bristol, Mrs Anskett – she's very well rested! And we did stop just as you ordered," Matthew told her.

"Oh, yes, of course, I just meant that Elinore will be longing to sit in something that isn't *moving*, it does make a difference. Now Henry *is* coming to help with luggage, while I take Elinore in and look after her, and Matthew, in case Henry has already forgotten, as usual, please tell him that Elinore will be in the Little Primrose Room – not the big one, the *little* one, and all you have to do is leave everything in the passage outside the room, because it is a little tight, and I'm going to help Elinore put everything away as soon as I've taken care of her." She held out both hands to Elinore, who was still sitting in the car, astonished at all this pouring over her like warm bathwater. "Now come in, dear. We're all ready for you, and Henry is just as excited as I am. I don't know where he's got to. Something to do with a dog, I should think. Are you happy with dogs, Elinore? Ours are wonderful, and they'll be excited to see you too, but you must shout if they bother you. Yes, that's right, dear, up the steps and indoors, and we'll have you settled in no time!"

With one arm around Elinore's shoulders and the other under an elbow, as if Elinore were a little, tottering old lady, Marigold Anskett took Elinore up the steps, past a massive wooden door that was studded with nails as though it belonged in a storybook castle, through a vestibule piled with stuff (Elinore had no time to discern exactly what) and into the enormous hall. A tall man in shabby brown corduroys, a dun-coloured jacket and navy sweater strode in from a passage on the left, and threw open his arms at the sight of Elinore.

"Ah! Our guest, at last. Welcome, Elinore, welcome. Was it a good journey down? Were you comfortable in the car? Glad I could send it for you – damn good thing about that funeral, wasn't it?" He had very clear blue eyes and almost the same ruddiness as Matthew, but far more hair, at least on the sides of his head. He looked as if he laughed as often as he could.

"Henry, *please*! That's shocking. Elinore is young and she has barely stepped over the threshold. Elinore, I do apologise. I never know what's going to come out of his mouth." Mrs Anskett was still holding Elinore and she clutched a little more tightly as she said this.

"Oh, lord, in trouble again," said Henry, holding out his hand. Elinore shook it, finally managing to say some words of her own.

"Hello, Mr Anskett. I had a lovely time in the car, and thank you very, very much for letting me come here."

Mrs Anskett let go of Elinore and threw up her hands, as she and Mr Anskett both spoke at once.

"Just call me Henry, Elinore. We're never on parade here."

"It's Marigold, dear, Marigold, *please*! And you mustn't talk about *letting* you come here! We're thrilled to bits that you *could* come."

Matthew brought in some of Elinore's luggage, and Henry went out for more.

"That Primrose Room's whereabouts . . ." Matthew said with a questioning look at Mrs Anskett. His foot was on the bottom step of the biggest, broadest staircase that Elinore had ever seen, which took up most of the right wall of the hall.

"Turn left at the top, along the landing almost to the turn and it's the second door from last on the left. I think I left it open to air the room. Elinore, let me show you the nearest loo while we leave them to it. If I were you, I'd be simply desperate by now!"

"Is Arabella here?"

"Oh, yes! She's communing with the stones. She said she'd be along as soon as the message had stopped coming through. Henry says that when Arabella's here it's like being back in wartime intelligence. I think it's terribly funny, because of course we used to say then that walls have ears, but now Arabella says *we* have to listen to the *walls*, or rather, she does the listening. She *is* marvellous, isn't she? Here's the loo, one of them, anyway. Can you find your way back or shall I wait?"

Elinore assured Marigold that she would have no trouble making one turn and walking straight along a passage back to the hall.

She heard Arabella before she saw her.

"The young don't get hypothermia, Marigold. At least, not indoors in mid-July. I'm sure Elinore will survive the night with all you've done so far."

Arabella was standing with Marigold by the vast, blackened fireplace, which could have held them both, upright. In one hand was a pad of lined paper covered with handwriting, and the unopened envelope that Tom had given Matthew; in the other a mug. When she saw Elinore, she smiled broadly and exclaimed, "Elinore! It's true, then: Tom did not kill you with his cooking. I'm so glad."

"Good gracious!" cried Marigold. "What on earth has this poor child been subjected to?"

"Plenty," said Arabella, "and she can tell us all about it later. Elinore, Marigold wants to show you your room and help you unpack. I'm just going to carry on with something rather important. See you later!" She vanished down the passage by which Elinore had returned and that led, eventually, to the kitchens. She made another mug of tea and sat down to read Tom's letter.

Marigold was showing Elinore the softness and cosiness of the striped flannel sheets on the bed, and the two hot water bottles waiting to be filled, and which of the blankets folded over the foot of the bed were, in her opinion, the warmest, and how the window opened in case Elinore should want more fresh air at night than was already supplied by the draughts that would come in anyway, courtesy of the old, loose wooden frames.

"The big question, Elinore dear, is whether you might need a radiator, which I can wheel in this instant. You aren't used to the air of Welkinlaw. Lots of people say it's just the same inside as out, isn't that funny? I can't bear to think that you might not be comfortable while you're here, especially after the dreadful – the *dis*comforts you've been enduring."

Marigold screwed up her face in distress at the thought of Elinore's immediate past, and clasped her hands like a Madonna. Elinore, who had been standing in the middle of a long, narrow, very high-ceilinged room that had immediately pleased her, suddenly sat down on the bed. Once again, her legs had gone wobbly with no warning, and it was as if all the energy in the rest of her had drained out of them in two seconds. But worst of all were the tears that she simply could not contain, despite the clenched fists at her mouth and eyes squeezed shut. She bowed her head, mortified. It was not only because the tears were there at all, but also because they were spilling over in response to sheer kindness, which made no sense at all. Without a doubt, she must be puzzling and offending Marigold, who would never believe now that Elinore Crum had been Miss Agnes Pound's best student ever.

Marigold sat down next to her, and the next thing Elinore knew, as she ground her fists harder against her face, was that she was being enveloped in something called a hug. She had read about hugs too, but, like summer holidays in Cornwall and thrilling adventures, they had hitherto been the experience of other children.

❧

They did not eat a proper dinner that night, because at Welkinlaw it had already taken place, while Elinore was enjoying fish and chips in the Café Splendido. The Ansketts liked their days to begin and end early. But they always enjoyed something light before bed, and for that Elinore joined them on the evening of her arrival.

Marigold led her down through the hall, along passages and up another flight of stairs. Once again, she had an arm around Elinore and was guiding her with the utmost consideration. Elinore had recovered somewhat. She knew that her melting into wobbliness and tears had been no disgrace in Marigold's eyes (quite the opposite), and she knew that she was on the way to tea; this was important, because food did appear to be medicine for the wobbliness.

They arrived at a room that was oddly low-ceilinged, considering the other spaces she had seen so far. One end of this room was a low, long casement window with a broad sill, full of geraniums and other potted plants; below it, the tufted cushion of a window seat stretched the full length of the window. As Elinore entered, the sun was well down to the right and throwing its low beams across a dramatic landscape. Being from Criven, she was used to the spread of bare hills with isolated patches of evergreen forestry; however, these uplands seemed wilder and craggier to her eye, and even the sky looked more spacious.

Marigold put toasted cheese and tomato sandwiches in front of Elinore, and told her to help herself to the fruit cake, the malt loaf and anything else on the table that might take her fancy. A sideboard held an electric kettle, a toaster, a hot plate, jugs and thermos flasks and an array of jars, bottles and tins, from which Marigold produced a mug of Horlicks for Elinore. "One of my great favourites," she said, "and very settling at all times."

The most settling thing for Elinore were the three dogs who lay stretched out on the hearthrug at Henry's feet as he read a newspaper. They got up and rushed over when Elinore came in with Marigold, tails going furiously, noses sniffing and twitching in excited examination of this new thing in the room. One was a liver and white spaniel (whether cocker or springer, she was unsure); one was a black Labrador; and one was just like Boris from Squair. Henry introduced them.

The Labrador was Sir Geoffroye, otherwise known as Geoff. "He's the only living creature in this family with a title. Ours got lost along the way. A real Sir Geoffroye did live here, though. He had appalling warlike habits, by all accounts, but Geoff does not. Geoff!" Henry got the dog's attention and pointed to Elinore. "Just put your hand out to him, Elinore. Paw, Geoff!" Geoff lifted one paw for Elinore to take. She shook it gently and Geoff wagged his tail.

The spaniel was Polly, and the Boris-like dog was Joe. "He has a long, pompous name on his pedigree, but that's no use in the field, is it, old boy?" Joe laid his head on Henry's knee just as Elinore had seen Boris do with Tom and the Forsyths.

"I know a dog who looks exactly the same as Joe," she said. "Is he a Clumber spaniel?"

"Yes, he is! Marigold, did you hear that? Elinore knew Joe was a Clumber. They're sadly uncommon nowadays."

Marigold clasped her hands again in emotion. "My dear! Arabella said you were extraordinary, and this is proof. Henry makes other people guess what kind of dog Joe is, and they *never* know. Only one person did, and do you know, he wasn't a shooting man, he'd come to look at the pictures. Joe's a fine Victorian, he said, or was it Edwardian? I'm not exactly sure what he meant."

"Out of fashion," said Henry. "Ridiculous business, dogs going in and out of fashion as if they were hemlines."

Elinore began to eat her sandwiches, and Henry switched on an old black and white television in readiness for the evening news. Its reception was poor, and he rose again from his armchair to fiddle with the aerial and some cord that trailed and looped among the tallest geraniums on the windowsill.

"I still don't think that's good for my plants, Henry," said Marigold.

"I've never broken off a single leaf."

"No, dear, you weren't listening when I explained last time. I said that the electrical current might be harming them."

Henry guffawed. "*What* current? We don't even have enough for a half-decent picture."

"I must ask Arabella," said Marigold. "You know, Elinore, she has an answer for everything."

"Is she still listening to the walls?" asked Elinore.

"Possibly, or having a bath. I'm not sure if one does both at the same time."

Elinore had been surprised to hear that Arabella had pronounced her as extraordinary. It also gave her a twinge of nerves. She might not measure up as assistant to a kind of witch, and the evidence was piling up that Arabella *was* a kind of witch, if not a witch-queen. It must be more demanding than being assistant to anyone else, except perhaps the Queen.

As if on cue to these thoughts, Arabella entered the room, carrying on a tray a bowl, a mug and a plate.

"Elinore, how nice to see you. I thought you might have disappeared to bed. How are you? Settling in all right?"

"Yes. I love my bedroom, and the dogs." Elinore looked for them. Geoff and Joe were on the hearthrug, and Polly was curled up on the window seat next to a black cat that Elinore had not noticed in the room before. "Oh – a cat! I didn't see it."

"That's Puss," said Marigold. "She was probably asleep under newspapers in that big basket by the fire – one of her favourite spots. We still haven't found the right name for her after two years. She loves Polly, and it's mutual, but not the other two. And she's an absolute demon with mice."

"Shouldn't that be demoness?" said Arabella. "Elinore, you must be very used to mice after Squair. Did they keep you awake?"

"Good heavens!" said Marigold. "The things Elinore has been through!"

You have no idea, thought Arabella, recalling Tom's letter.

"Elinore, if you are very, very tired, you must sleep in as long as you like tomorrow morning," continued Marigold, with a hand on Elinore's arm. "You have nothing at all special to get up for."

"Yes, she does!" said Arabella. "Elinore is my new assistant – correction, the *only* assistant I have ever employed. We've got work to do tomorrow. Furthermore, I've had a message, and we need to talk about it tomorrow."

Marigold jumped up from her chair. "Henry! Henry, did you hear Arabella? She's had a message! Is Welkinlaw really talking to you, Arabella?"

Henry had dozed off to the lullaby of a BBC newsreader. "Ehrrm – what? A message. Excellent news." His eyes closed again.

"Welkinlaw has talked to me from the moment I arrived," said Arabella, "but I meant a different kind of message. A thoroughly modern one. It amounts to the same thing, though. Life is all about communication, and all life is energy, and everything is energy communicating with itself."

With that gnomic summation, Arabella applied herself to the porridge in her bowl; prunes and chunks of other dried fruits were mixed through it and on top was a drift of chopped walnuts. A large slab of pale, crumbly cheese rested on the plate. The mug gave off lemon-and-tea scented wisps of steam.

"Dear me," said Marigold, "that sounds like the hobby of someone I knew. She used to talk about the energies of life communicating through an Ouija board. I must admit, I find that sort of thing quite off-putting. It's like finding people in my house whom I haven't invited."

"Ouija boards have nothing to do with my work and I have nothing to do with them. *Nothing*."

"What a relief," said Marigold. "I wouldn't want Elinore to be mixed up in *that*. Now, look, she's yawning! Let me take you up, dear. This room is miles away from everything, but it's south facing and warm, and it's the only one where the television seems to work, so we do end up here in the evenings."

"Good night, Elinore," said Arabella. "No need to jump up at the crack of dawn. I think you've had rather a full day. Sleep it off!"

In the Little Primrose Room, Elinore lay propped against two pillows. She wanted to survey her latest landing place and relish its comforts, although she was losing the struggle to keep her eyes open. She could hardly believe that the day now ending in an

English castle had begun in a house in Scotland, and that in between she had met a man from Canada; been driven for miles and miles –almost right past Criven – in a car fit for royalty; eaten fish and chips in an Italian restaurant; and finally had landed in the cossetting arms of a lady called Marigold, who was as lovely as her name and who, like this castle, might have been taken straight from the pages of a storybook.

It was instantly obvious why most of her belongings were still piled outside in the passage. Elinore's room was much larger than Usha Patel's, but so filled with large pieces of furniture that it ended up being almost as small and constricted. However, this meant that it felt cosy to Elinore. The walls were papered in a cream and white stripe, echoed in the cream, green and yellow Regency striped fabric of the floor to ceiling curtains. Her narrow bed was really an upholstered daybed, reminding her of the Knole sofa at the Dower House; its enclosing fabric sides intensified her feeling of being swaddled in comfort, and the greater comfort of knowing that the people here had actually wanted her to come. She was beginning to revel in this attention instead of feeling embarrassed because she could not possibly be worth the effort. Some of her clothes were hanging in a towering wardrobe at the foot of the bed; all had been scrutinised by Marigold and some had been whisked away for laundering. She had lapsed into tears again when it finally dawned on her that some of her clothes were still at the Berg house, because Fredy had wished to iron them. How many days had it been since she had smuggled her bag of dirty clothes to Fredy? It was a long, long time ago – but no, not really. She tried to count the days backwards and fell asleep instantly.

26

The Ansketts blend into the colours of their own land. Drystone walls, weathered fences, lichen, rocky escarpments, bare hillsides, patches of woodland, tracts of forest and blustery skies where crows and inland-scouting gulls wheel endlessly. Their castle has grown out of this place and they are its creatures, as the woodworm, the beetle, the rodent, the weed that takes hold on a sill and forces itself through a window jamb, the little brown fungus in the corner of a scullery, and the blooming mould on interior walls are all its creatures too. It is all timeless and unchanging and all threatened. Weather can do sudden, terrible damage; three cold seasons of the year and too many soaking days in summer for century after century have ground away at Welkinlaw's endurance, its projection of power and imperviousness.

The newspapers, the wireless and, most recently, the small screen in the corner, which transmits grainy black and white images from events in far-off places that have nothing to do with Welkinlaw, ceaselessly bring reminders that now everything is connecting with everything and everywhere else at greater speed, inexorably. The Ansketts are kindly, worried, courteous, responsible people who live frugally on the edges of these dim, cold, stupendously overcrowded rooms, many of them shuttered and covered with dustsheets. Their few luxuries are characterised by the car they bought long ago, in the decade when someone was telling them that they had never had it so good.

Elinore Crum is happy because she feels protected here. The Caltrops could not get in, and Melba would not want to come in, for Welkinlaw holds nothing she needs and much that she detests and despises. The Dower House at Squair was full of things that Elinore could pick up and wonder at, a place where women and girls had left their decorative mark and a boy had begun collecting and never stopped. It was a sort of living picture book full of captivating stories, a drowsy, mothy museum of curiosities, and Elinore would have stayed there gladly, infinitely; but Welkinlaw is even better because it is impregnable. In her mind's eye, she still sees the view that Matthew Carr pointed out, of massive, sheer walls dropping down and down. She joins it with the memory of approaching the castle by a long, long avenue, and these things represent what, so far, she likes most about being here. It is that no one can arrive at Welkinlaw to take her by surprise and no one can get in unless they are let in. She can never be shut up again as long as she can shut herself up within Welkinlaw. If only I could stay *here*, a voice in her head says as her eyes begin to open on her first morning in a castle.

Elinore had slept very soundly indeed, in silence broken only by the wind whistling through windows now and then. Despite the shabbiness, she was inclined to think that this castle might be too grand for mice, for she had not heard a single scratch or rustle. She found her way to and from the bathroom shown to her previously by Marigold. (Rooms in current use were all strangely distant from each other, as if stranded by an ebb in the tide of daily use, and reached by many turns and stairs.) Toiletries that she had already seen in Arabella's bathroom at the Balmerinoch Hotel were clustered there on a shelf. Dressed and ready for anything, she examined the Little Primrose Room, where nothing at all was little except the globes and millefiori paperweights lined up on the mantelpiece. She kept her head cricked to one side until she had read the title on the spine of every single book crammed into the bookcase; lifted the lid of a chest at the foot of her bed, wherein lay blankets, quilts, mysterious brown paper packages sealed with red wax, and bundles of fabric rolled up and tied with dressmaker's binding tape; tipped the cheval glass to the angle that best showed her from head to toe; inspected every picture on the wall (two large, three medium and fourteen small ones); and almost turned the key in the door that led into the adjoining and presumably Big Primrose Room. She stopped because she was not sure where Arabella or anyone else might be sleeping.

The draught from the window carried in a shout and a few short, sharp whistles. When Elinore strained over the broad, rather high stone sill, she saw Henry Anskett out with his dogs. He was walking in a sloping, parklike ground dotted with trees, and she realised that her bedroom overlooked the front of the house. As Matthew had outlined to her, Welkinlaw had two faces, and this was the deceptive, country house side that concealed the character of the much older castle. The spaniel, Polly, was charging off into the distance, towards the beginning of the avenue, but Henry and the other two dogs had turned back towards the house. In the absence of a clock, this was a good sign that she could go downstairs to the big hall and expect someone to come along and tell her what would happen and where to go next, especially where breakfast was concerned.

As she went out into the passage, her eyes fell on a particular box. She thought her homemade calendar might be in it. The calendar would help her pin recent events to particular days, and would also show the date of Melba's supposed return. Unfathomable complexities would be set in train then, one way or another, but at least she could count how many days were left during which she might justifiably never think about it at all. She found the calendar and saw that Melba had been gone for exactly one week on that very day. One week left, then.

Elinore also found the typescript of her ghost story. Then she remembered the poem at the very front of *The Book of Edinburgh for*

Young People. Its language was flowery and old-fashioned, but she liked the sound and feel of it nevertheless, and she had meant to copy it out for learning by heart. It seemed to belong with her ghost story too, although she was not sure why. Where was that book? She moved the box that she had just opened. Below it was one she had never seen before. Glued onto it was an old label showing Tom's name and address. The box was tied up very securely with string, but Elinore sat down on the floor and patiently untied the knots. Inside was the typewriter she had used to type her story, and a letter.

> *Dear Elinore:*
>
> *Please use this to write more stories of all kinds! It is now <u>all yours</u>. I look forward to receiving copies of each story. Arabella can help you buy new ribbons when you need them. I believe she knows how to use one of these machines too, which will be useful when you want to be an Advanced Typist. Unlike yours truly!*
>
> *With my very best wishes and in hope that you will visit the Dower House again SOON, I remain,*
>
> *Your most devoted reader,*
> *Tom B.*

Elinore was still sitting on the floor by her baggage when Marigold came upstairs.

"Good morning, Elinore! Did you sleep well? Are you ready for breakfast?"

Elinore looked up at this kindly woman and decided to share her excitement. "I've got a typewriter! I didn't know I had it until right now. It's Tom's and he gave it to me."

"Really? Do you know how to use it? May I see?" Marigold knelt down beside Elinore and looked into the box. "Oh, how that takes me back! I took a secretarial course when I was young, and I had to sit for hours at machines exactly like that, with a dozen other girls, all bashing away in a room with a low, sloping ceiling. The racket! I thought I'd go deaf! And is this all your work, dear? I must say, it looks very proficient!"

Marigold picked up the typescript of Elinore's story.

"I made up the story, and I did type it the first time, but Tom typed that one for me," said Elinore. "I didn't know how to use a typewriter before he showed me. I didn't know he was going to give it to me. It's amazing!"

Marigold clasped the story to her breast. "Elinore, you must read this to us. If you want to, of course. I'm sure it's *wonderful*. It would be lovely entertainment, just like the old days, and such a nice change from that horrid television."

"All right," said Elinore. "It's the first one I've ever written, but I think I've got ideas for some more."

"How thrilling! Now, come down for breakfast and eat lots, because your brain needs food and I'm not sure that you've been getting enough for all your parts lately."

They met Arabella in the hall, perched on the padded leather top of the brass fender that fronted the fireplace. She was writing on a lined pad. Her hair was pulled back into a pony tail and she was wearing a navy sweater, bellbottom jeans and sandshoes. Elinore wondered how old someone had to be before they could no longer dress like a teenager; Arabella *must* be old, and she still looked like Queen Elizabeth I, but perhaps Elizabeth had once looked like a teenager too.

They all went along the passage to the kitchens. There, in the main kitchen, Henry was drinking from a large mug while reading the *Farmers Weekly*. Marigold ran around collecting things from various distant corners to put on the table. It was a cavernous space, compared with the kitchen at the Dower House, and furnished with dressers, cupboards and sideboards of the same massive scale. The most impressive item was an enormous blackened range that took up most of one wall; it was covered in dust and piled with old newspapers, pieces of cardboard and other things that looked combustible. Marigold began cooking on an Aga. One of its lower ovens was open, and Elinore saw the black and white face and chest of Puss inside.

Eventually, breakfast was on the table and, as they began to eat, Arabella announced that she was going to tell them about the message she had received. "No, don't stop eating," she commanded, as Marigold immediately laid down her toast and looked earnest and expectant.

Henry put up his hand as if he were at school. "Ahem – am I needed this morning? The Dunfeshies will be here in an hour."

"Not at all," said Arabella, "as long as I'm allowed to do what I want without any arguing from you after I've done it. Now, let's get on with this discussion before Welkinlaw begs for our attention again with some expensive prank."

"My dear, how can you possibly call it a prank when all the lights go out upstairs *and* in the dining room and the library, a piece of ceiling falls down into a bathtub *and* the kitchen sink drain backs up just as Mrs Kightley is trying to produce dinner for the Birds? It was one of the worst nights of my life," said Marigold.

"Ah, the Birds – a fine brace of Americans!" chortled Henry. "The wife did chirp rather, didn't she? I thought they showed a decent sense of humour, all things considered."

Elinore, who knew what a brace of partridge or pheasant looked like, thought this was terribly funny, and chortled too. Henry winked at her, Marigold sighed and Arabella said, "Let me ask you: did these incidents affect the Birds directly and adversely? Did the plaster fall into *their* bathtub? Did they sprain ankles or lose expensive jewellery in the dark? Did they find their dinner to be inedible?"

"Dinner was splendid," said Henry. "Mrs Kightley's beef. The Birds were thrilled about dining entirely by candlelight – don't you remember, Marigold? Romance. *Ro*-mance. That was the word they kept using. And little Mrs Bird was chirping madly because her husband kept saying how gorgeous she was in candlelight. Very odd."

"The effect of novelty on Americans. Candlelight is merely a tiresome necessity to you. But what about the rest of it?"

"Well, the plaster fell in *our* bathtub," said Marigold. "Mrs Kightley was able to use a scullery sink. And all the switches worked in the Birds' bedroom and bathroom. Isn't that strange, now that you mention it? We gave them a couple of candles for finding their way around on the stairs and landing, and they wanted to buy the silver holders! As souvenirs of an enchanting evening, they said."

"A charming story," said Arabella, "and exactly what I expected. After some time spent contemplating at dreamholes in the lesser used parts of Welkinlaw –"

"Dreamholes? How other-worldly! Do we really have them, whatever they are?" Marigold was clasping her hands in her Madonna pose again.

"I'm not sure I want them in my house," said Henry. "You said no voodoo, Arabella."

"No voodoo, Henry. Dreamholes are slits in the wall for light, air and defence."

"Oh, yes. We do have plenty of those at the very top of the house."

"As I was *trying* to say," said Arabella, "I've been listening to what Welkinlaw has to tell us, and yesterday I had a letter, a reply from someone whom I'd asked to do a bit of digging in New York. Under the circumstances, the two messages marry up perfectly, if you'll excuse the pun."

"New York and Welkinlaw? The only thing that might connect those two poles is Oliver," said Henry. "*Might* connect," he added, with a gloomy sigh.

"*Will* connect," said Arabella, looking supremely smug. "Especially if I have a hand in it, and I do. This girlfriend of his – what do you know about her?"

Henry and Marigold looked at each other.

"She's called Mary and she's – a lovely girl," said Marigold. "With simple tastes. Oliver says so. That's all he says, except that he won't even think of bringing her home here until we've smartened up Welkinlaw. But Welkinlaw was *never* smart or grand, and neither are we. We're not *Chatsworth!*" she ended on a wail.

"Oliver's girl is called Merry, not Mary. It's short for Mercedes. She is as plain as a pikestaff and the sweetest-natured, best-mannered girlfriend in all of New York State, my informant tells me," resumed Arabella. "Loves dogs and children. Legs like fence posts, enjoys hiking and making things in a kitchen."

"Well – why on earth can't Oliver bring her here straight away, then?" asked Henry. "It sounds as though she wouldn't mind that we're not at all grand or smart. I think she'd fit in splendidly. And what a name! A girl called Mercedes would appreciate the Bristol."

"And she likes to cook! A nice, old-fashioned sort, if you ask me," said Marigold.

"I said, she likes making *things* in a kitchen. Mercedes has a special kitchen where she mixes up face products for ladies who don't want to grow old."

"What an interesting hobby," said Marigold.

Arabella took a lavishly illustrated, full-colour brochure from an airmail envelope and handed it to her.

Waxwing Eternal Beauty Inc.
Let your beautiful self take flight
and soar above the ravages of time!
Waxwing products combine the riches of Nature
and the skill of Science.
Exquisitely packaged for your convenience,
these unique cremes and lotions will pamper your skin
into lasting youthfulness.
Come fly with Waxwing into a beautiful future!

"A waxwing is a bird," said Henry. "Comes over here in the winter. Plump little thing. Likes berries."

"That's Mercedes," said Arabella. "Her Berry Bomb Facial Rejuvenator sells out as soon as it lands in the shops – only the most exclusive shops, by the way. And she *is* plump."

"How clever to think up a little business for herself. Isn't that what's called a cottage industry? She'd have plenty of space to play with her pots and potions here," said Marigold, waving a hand at the surrounding scullery warren. "Do they actually work, the things she makes?"

Arabella shrugged. "No idea. I only know that enough people seem to *think* they do for Waxwing Inc. to have made several millions of dollars last year."

"*What?*" Elinore thought both Ansketts might fall from their chairs in shock.

Arabella shrugged again. "No surprise, really. She has business in her veins. She is Mercedes Wax, the only child of Edgar Wax IV, and heiress to a fortune that would make your eyes bulge and Welkinlaw's timbers shiver."

As if to underline this, a clang-splash came from one of the back rooms. Marigold jumped up.

"The bucket! The one I put on a stool under that leaking pipe. How could it fall over?"

"*Sit*, Marigold, please. That's just Welkinlaw communicating, as I'm trying *so* hard to explain," said Arabella.

"I must get something clear in my head," said Henry. "Is, ah, Miss Wax, is she in love with Oliver because she's very rich and he's in banking? And is Oliver in love with her money or her? Yes, Marigold, I know you don't like to hear such things, and we did bring Oliver up not to be a cad, but I must see how the ground lies there. And if that's a pun, I apologise. Ansketts don't marry for money. One shouldn't." He took Marigold's hand and they smiled at each other. Elinore felt a deep pang and wished that she could adopt them as parents immediately.

"Oliver and Mercedes are deeply, immovably, inextricably and genuinely in love with each other," stated Arabella, flapping some typed sheets of airmail paper as she spoke. "It's right here, from my trusted source. Every gossip columnist and person on the New York Social Register knows it. It's just one of those things."

"Oh, I used to *adore* that song!" said Marigold. "And those lines – 'Just one of those fabulous flights / A trip to the moon on gossamer wings / Just one of those things.'"

At that very moment, a small bird flew straight in through the open top half of the sash window, and whirred around the kitchen. Marigold shrieked, but looked as if she might burst with pleasure. "There! It's a sign, it has to be, a good omen. A *lovely* omen about Oliver and Mary, er, Merry. It must be a waxwing!"

"If you like," said Arabella. "That song is about having a fling. Oliver and Mercedes are meant to be glued together forever, preferably right here."

Henry got up and opened a door to the back courtyard. The little bird shot out. "A sparrow," he said. "You won't see a waxwing in July. Arabella, my dear, this is all very startling and fascinating, but I still don't see how it will stop Welkinlaw from falling down around us. And we're no closer to getting Oliver to bring his girlfriend home and settle down. I'm a farmer! Omens and portents might have worked for my distant forefathers, but I need solid ground under my feet."

"Let me continue," said Arabella calmly. "All Wax girls marry men with castles. They don't go after titles so much, but they do like castles. Something to do with the first Edgar Wax and his beginnings in a Lancashire hovel. Perhaps the girls see it as their duty to add lustre to the family name."

Henry laughed. "Ha-ha, very good, Arabella! Giving the family name a good *waxing* and polishing, eh? Have they ever married any Poles, or Frenchmen for their chateaux? I was just thinking of a joke I heard once about a French polisher. Silly joke. All right, Marigold, I shan't repeat it."

"What you've said is quite silly enough," said Marigold. "Poor Arabella's trying to be serious."

"Well, I don't need to try, I *am* a deeply serious person. Where was I? The Waxes and their castle-hunting female offspring. Yes, they have an extraordinary record of bagging castles – see for yourself, they're all in Debrett's and Burke's. Mercedes Wax needs a castle too, and she is truly eager to see Welkinlaw. I believe if she came here she'd want to settle in and make it her home. She loves Oliver and Oliver has got a castle. She could go off and buy one, I suppose, but that isn't the same, is it? It wouldn't have *heart*. Oliver is the problem. Frankly, he's inherited your dithering. Marigold, don't look at me like that. He doesn't want to spend the rest of his life being a banker in New York, but he's scared he'll lose the love of his life if he reveals this chaotic, crumbling pile as their future home. That's why you've got to help Welkinlaw make the best possible impression. The house has been quite clear that it wants new blood and excitement, and it all ties up beautifully, as you are about to hear."

Henry looked at a pendulum clock on the wall, whose loud tick had underscored the drama of this meeting of the Old and New Worlds. "Will I hear very soon? I must get out and make sure everything is in order for the Dunfeshies, and give a hand with them."

"Your Dunfeshies are part of the lure, Henry. The word is that Mercedes Wax is experimenting with a new product line, the Cleopatra Collection. Nothing to do with the milk of asses: she's after ewes' milk."

Henry's face was a study. "Good God! Dunfeshie ewe's milk is famously rich and creamy. Some people in Scotland are making cheese with it from a 12th century recipe – it was in the *Farmers Weekly*. But I only bought them to improve the flock we've got already. They'll do very well on this grazing. Handsome creatures too, if that means anything. Black tails, and horns on both rams and ewes. And they don't need to be dehorned."

"Oh, how lovely," said Arabella. "Mercedes Wax will be smitten. Which brings me to Welkinlaw itself. Your house desperately wants more people in it. It's bored. Fed up. Depressed, actually, because its existence has become pointless, pretty much since the end of armed conflict between neighbours. It's losing its strength and its looks. Try and put yourself in its place – Henry, don't look at me like that. Please try to stretch your mind as well as your ears. Welkinlaw has been standing here year after year, looking noble and all that, trying to impress people with merlons and murder holes, and wishing its portcullis hadn't been walled up. The last outstandingly useful thing it did was to house a lot of evacuees during the war. It's *bored!* It wants to lead a colourful, interesting, unpredictable life. This place really hummed in past times, and it misses that."

"But whenever people come here, it misbehaves. My nerves, Arabella . . . The night of the Birds really was the last straw. And they were only here because they knew Oliver, they'd been very kind to him when he first went to New York. I kept thinking of what they might tell him. What if it kills someone? Oliver will disown us!"

"It will only kill you, never a visitor," said Arabella. "Can't you see? Every time something nasty happens when people visit, *you* are the ones affected. Visitors seem to think they've had a marvellous time. When Welkinlaw is obstreperous, it's a cry for understanding. For help! It's taken me a little while for the pattern to become clear, but it's unmistakable.

"It will bankrupt me in the end," said Henry. "I can't keep selling land to pay for repairs after its fits of bad temper."

"You must be ingenious and open-minded if you are to keep the roof in place and stay on, at least until Oliver and Mercedes move in. Pulling up the drawbridge and laying in siege supplies is no longer an option for keeping progress at bay."

The Ansketts were discomposed, but finally paying attention.

"You speak as if Oliver is definitely returning, Miss Wax is coming too as his fiancée, and Welkinlaw is going to be put to rights in no time with liberal doses of cash. But Oliver isn't rich, and, since we are no longer in the 15th century, her money doesn't automatically belong to my son and heir," said Henry.

"They will spend it together on what they love and desire. Does it make any difference whose money stops the leaks, as long as Ansketts still own Welkinlaw and can afford to keep it up? The Wax girls go after castles they can *live* in. What's the point in owning a ruin? You can't invite all your smart friends to stay. You can't promise yourself a decent hot bath every night. You can't be photographed looking soignée in the drawing room you've just redone, and then send the picture to *Town & Country*."

"What's that?" asked Maigold.

"Not *Country Life*, but nice and shiny all the same," said Arabella. "Now come on. The time for talking is over. I am leaving on Sunday and we have a mountain of tasks to dynamite before then."

"*Dynamite?*" Both Ansketts looked frightened.

"Dynamite," said Arabella. "How can you get something out of the way by climbing over it or trudging around it? Blow it up and be done with it! Come on! Spit-spot!"

Arabella looked at Elinore and winked, slowly and very deliberately. Throughout this discussion, Elinore had been silent except to ask for things like marmalade to be passed to her across the broad table. But she had been attentive, her head swivelling from one speaker to another. She had come to some conclusions.

First, Arabella Cheyne was unquestionably a witch, and a bossy one. Elinore had the feeling that the more people Arabella could order about all at once, the happier she would be. Perhaps her father and grandfather had been military men. Spending the rest of her summer holidays under the same roof as a bossy witch might not be easy, but Elinore knew that she would be safe there. She still wanted to stay exactly where she was, though, in the vicinity of cossetting Marigold.

This led to Elinore's second conclusion, namely that Oliver Anskett must be a very stupid boy, or man, to not want to come home. And come home from *America* too, the land of *Dwayne*. Ugh. She hoped that everything would turn out happily for Welkinlaw and that the Ansketts could stop worrying soon, but, really and truly, Oliver did not deserve such nice parents and to live in a castle. She, Elinore Crum, deserved that, because if this were her home she would fall in love with it instead of a husband, and she would stay in it forever and ever.

Her third conclusion was that, sadly, this was not going to happen, just as Melba was never going to fall in love with Mr Finnie and marry him, so enabling Elinore to stay in Criven. Neither was Melba ever going to meet Tom Balmerinoch and fall in love with him, to the same result. Elinore was now assistant to Arabella Cheyne, and her mother was in America with a man whom she probably did want to marry. Elinore was on her own, on an adventure. In adventure stories, children always found in the end the treasure, the answer to the mystery, the thing that had been stolen, the key to the door of the room, the truth about the ghost, the way back when they were lost. The expected meetings or reunions took place unfailingly at the appropriate points in the story. She could only assume that she and her boxes would stop moving around soon, that she would come to rest in one place that was really, really nice, preferably a mixture of Criven, the Berg household, the Dower House and Welkinlaw, and with Mrs Patel close enough to invite her frequently to eat delicious, spicy dishes that made her feel warm inside like nothing else. And with a hotel nearby for times when the person in charge of the house did not feel like cooking.

When she had finished ordering her universe thus, she repeated her second conclusion to herself, in her head. "Oliver Anskett is definitely the stupidest boy in the world."

As if he were party to some of these thoughts, Henry addressed her. "Elinore, how about some fresh air? Would you like to come along and watch the sheep arriving? Oliver used to be my shadow when he was your age."

Elinore sent another mental raspberry in the direction of Oliver Anskett, banker in New York, and got up eagerly from the table.

"Look for the dust clouds if you want to find Marigold and me when you come back in," called Arabella as Henry and Elinore went out.

It was a beautiful, sunny day. They walked along a winding drive that led first to a large stable yard and then farther on to what Henry called Home Farm. Elinore was entranced by it all: so much to explore! More so than in Squair or even Criven. Here she would have untrammelled liberty, for already she could see that Welkinlaw perched high amid miles and miles of moor and grass.

Matthew Carr was busy in a field at the edge of Home Farm when they walked up. With two men, he was adjusting the gates of a large pen in readiness for the new flock. When he saw Elinore, he grinned and said, "Well, now! It's Miss Elinore. I have to keep an eye on her, you know. She's a clever one and she'll be after my job if I'm not careful. Knows all about Cheviots and Charolais bulls and lord knows what. Know what's coming in here today, Elinore?"

"Yes, I do" she replied without hesitating. "Dunfeshie sheep. They have black tails and horns, even the ewes, but you don't have to dehorn them."

Matthew's jaw dropped, and his two helpers laughed out loud at him, even though he was their boss. The boss of them all, Henry Anskett, put his hand to his mouth and cleared his throat. "As you can see, our guest has settled in here *very* quickly," he told the other men.

The sheep arrived in a float, and rushed down the ramp into the pen like a woolly, baa-ing tide. The four men busied themselves checking over each one for anything out of order after the long journey, especially in their legs. On the door of the float's cab, Elinore saw printed an address in Aberdeenshire, and with a start she realised that these sheep must have come all the way from roughly where Arabella lived. Her next destination, in other words. The driver was speaking to Matthew in an accent that was new to her ears. If all the sheep are like that up there, she thought, that's one thing I'll know already.

Everyone looked as though they would be preoccupied with sheep for a while, and Elinore wandered off to look inside the steadings. She heard a dog bark and followed the sound, making for the entrance to a small yard. She could see a cottage or two at its far end. As soon as she entered the yard, she froze. A police car was parked there. Her legs turned to jelly and her heart leaped up into her throat as she edged backwards, away from discovery by someone who had surely been sent to track her down. Everything Tom had told her to remember vanished from memory, and that space was filled by fear. She had escaped from the Caltrops and she had run away without telling Melba. Or it was something to do with the money she had donated to herself instead of the missionary Curglaff. Whatever it was, it was *something to do with her,* and being bad. She must get herself safely inside the castle. She heard Henry calling her name and ran shakily back to the sheep pen.

He was standing by a Land Rover. "Can you find your way back to the house, Elinore? I'd like to go off with Matthew and look at a few things. Keep straight along that road and you'll come to the very door we started from. Don't let those ladies blow up the whole house with their dynamiting!"

Elinore nodded and set off at a walk, but only until the Land Rover had disappeared in the other direction. Then she ran, and kept going until she reached the back premises of the house. She felt like crying. The beautiful morning had darkened all around her.

27

Elinore pushed the heavy door closed and waited for a few seconds. She could hear her heart pounding in her ears and her own rapid breathing, but no car engine and certainly no police siren. She walked into the kitchen where she had breakfasted earlier, and saw a woman stoking the Aga with logs. When the woman turned around and noticed Elinore, she nodded and said, "Good day to you," without the least surprise, as if Elinore were long known and in the habit of wandering into her kitchen.

She was a tall, hefty woman, taller even than Henry Anskett. Greying black hair was scraped into a large bun on the back of her head and the whole lot secured by a hairnet. Marmoreal white skin, her height, build and ponderous way of moving made her like a statue come to life or one of the massive dressers turned human. Over a blouse and skirt, she wore a totally incongruous ruffle-edged apron that was the most colourful object Elinore had seen in Welkinlaw so far: a whimsical pattern of petals in pinks, oranges and yellows, against which green stick figures capered. Their heads were flowers with smiley faces.

"Fine day now, isn't it?" the woman continued. "Bit overcast earlier, but I knew it'd burn off." She sounded like Matthew Carr, but even more Northumbrian. Elinore liked the inflexions and rhythm of the speech. "You're Elinore, surely? I'm Jane Kightley. Mrs Kightley, they call me, but you can call me whatever you like. They always say they don't stand on ceremony here, and that's true, but they do mind their manners, and you can't say that for all, can you?"

Elinore remembered that Matthew had made a similar comment. She decided to mind her manners too. "Hello, Mrs Kightley." She was on the point of asking where Marigold and Arabella might be, but the noise of a vehicle made her freeze again. Worse, it was quickly followed by a loud knock on the door and a man's voice calling, "Hallooooo! Anyone about?"

Once again, Mrs Kightley showed no surprise or any other reaction, beyond calling, "In here, Fred."

Elinore was so seized by fear that for a second or two she saw the postman's uniform as that of a policeman. She stood rooted until Mrs Kightley said, "Fred, this is Elinore, who's here for a day or two. Elinore, this is Fred, who brings our post and takes away whatever I think he's worth in the way of a biscuit or two."

"And a cuppa!" cried Fred. "Never less than a welcome at Welkinlaw, that's what I say." He put a pile of mail on the kitchen table, took off his cap, rubbed his head vigorously, sat down and grinned at Elinore. His thick, straw-coloured hair stood on end, his face was very red and his eyes very blue. Altogether, he looked on fire and as vivid as Mrs Burdon's apron.

"How d'you do, Elinore? Come far to visit us, have you?"

"I came from Squair, which is near Edinburgh. Mr Carr brought me."

"Matthew was up at his ma's funeral," Mrs Kightley told Fred. "Went up in that old car that Mr Anskett's so fond of."

"That old car?" Fred looked as shocked as he sounded. "*Old car?* That's a rare piece of British engineering. A thing of beauty that will never age. I hope Mr Anskett never hears you say that, Jane Kightley." He turned to Elinore. "And if you come down all the way here in such a fine machine, I envy you."

"How come all you Rowles boys were born with engines on the brain? All of you driving around all day long too: vans, cars, lorries, trains and whatnot. All the same."

"Aye, an' all of us after a cup of tea and bite of cake on the way," said Fred. "Talking of which, where's the bite that goes wi' this, Jane?" She handed him a plate with two biscuits on it. "Thank you kindly."

He addressed Elinore again. "If you see a police car round here, Elinore, that's my brother Eric, most likely on his way to our gran's or parked outside. He's come for a cuppa, just like me. You tell him, hallo from Fred! Our gran lives on the Home Farm, just down the way there. I do call in on her myself, when there's something to deliver – naught today, though – but that's my job, an' no one can say boo to me for it."

"Eric'll lose his car an' be stuck down the police station if he's not careful," said Mrs Kightley. "It's not his job to be visiting his gran on official time and petrol, is it? Mind you, he's a good boy to be doing it. You won't catch me telling on him."

Elinore sat down at the table and braced herself to ask a question. The right answer would stop her heart from banging around in her throat and her tummy from screwing itself into knots.

"I saw a police car this morning, when I went to the Home Farm with Henry," she said. "Do you think that was your brother?"

"Aye, t'was! No other reason for police to come up here, is there?"

Elinore stayed silent. Fred and Mrs Kightley exchanged a few more comments on local goings-on, and then Fred took his leave, wishing Elinore a fine stay for as long as she was at Welkinlaw. All this time, Mrs Kightley had been moving around the kitchen, putting things away and taking other things out, encouraging the Aga to burn more fiercely and piling vegetables on the draining board by the sink. She did not so much walk as roll, as if she were on castors, and she did a lot of that, for the kitchen was a microcosm of Welkinlaw the castle: everything was at considerable distance from everything else.

"Do you know where Marigold is, and my aunt?" asked Elinore.

"They were talking about clearing out one of the old nursery bedrooms. You're in that Little Primrose one, aren't you? Well, if you go past that and round the turn and up the steps, only about six of 'em, so you won't mistake it for the stairs that come down this way, you go up there and you'll find 'em. And if you can leave this lot on the tray on the round table in the big hall as you go, I'll thank you kindly." She handed Elinore the letters brought by Fred. "You come back down here whenever you want a bite yourself, Elinore. A proper one, not what I give that Fred. He's done all his growing, but you haven't, and you're a bit peaky looking. Which reminds me: you can tell them that they'll be eating in an hour, on the hour."

When Elinore found them, Arabella and Marigold were sitting on the floor by the open door of a room. They were wearing old shirts and slacks, and rubber gloves lay on the floor beside them. Elinore remembered the wardrobe cleaning at No. 17 (a day that seemed very far off now) and Arabella's pronouncement that gloves would enable one to tackle any job. They did not appear to have had that effect on Marigold. As Elinore came along, Marigold was saying with surprising firmness, "No, no more! I've made up my mind. I can't believe it's taken me so long. You should have told me outright, Arabella."

"Oh, there's a time for everything," said Arabella. "Hello, Elinore. Marigold is having an epiphany. I think it's because of all the revelations that came with breakfast today."

Marigold smiled at Elinore, but continued voicing her thoughts. "We simply shouldn't be here. We've been taking it for granted that we'd carry on living here in some corner of the house when Oliver finally came home, but that's no good. Welkinlaw doesn't want us hanging about inside, does it?"

"Correct. It does not," said Arabella. "I couldn't really tell you to get out of your own house, though, could I? These things take time. I did warn you at the beginning that you'd start to clear out your own heads along with all the rubbish that Ansketts have been piling up in these rooms. It's inevitable if you ask me in to help. New thinking, Marigold! Viewing the universe from a new perspective! Now you're ready to join the likes of Galileo and Isaac Newton, and Darwin. You're evolving. Where *do* you want to live?"

"In the old stable block," replied Marigold promptly. "I did think about it a few years ago, when so many pipes burst in that awful winter. It was just after someone asked Henry if he was interested in selling up – someone who wanted to make Welkinlaw into a sort of hotel, except he called it a retreat. He *was* odd! Dressed all in white with a ponytail. Henry didn't take to him and told him to go away before he'd even got to the money bit. But then I thought, what if the right person did take it off our hands? Where would we go? And I had the idea of converting the old stables. I could see it all: not too big, not too small, a modern kitchen, window boxes, pretty curtains . . ."

"Perfect," said Arabella. "Meanwhile, where does that leave us with a gloomy, messy, misbehaving castle that's pining for its blood-and-thunder glory days and a son who's expecting you to do something about it?"

"I haven't got that far in my head yet," sighed Marigold. "Perhaps we should have some tea. It might warm up my enthusiasm for getting on with this room. Then it will be lunch time. I'm sure I'll feel more active after lunch."

They went up to the sitting room with the long window, and Marigold made tea after going down another passage to fill the kettle from a bathroom hand basin that was slightly closer than the kitchen. Elinore stroked Puss, who was sunbathing on the window seat, and wished again that she could stay here, at least until that stupid boy Oliver came home and his lovely parents went to live in the stables. She had no opinion on Mercedes Wax, since a lady who mixed up sheep's milk for other ladies to plaster on their faces was beyond her comprehension. Marigold began to open the post she had picked up in the big hall, and briefly the room was quiet save for the ticking of a clock and the rustle of paper as Arabella looked idly at a two-day old newspaper. Then Marigold shrieked and thrust a letter at Arabella.

"Tell me if I'm dreaming! It's fate, or destiny, or witchcraft – or is it you, Arabella? How could *this* possibly have come along right at *this* moment?"

Arabella scanned the letter. "Well, yes, it does have something to do with me."

"I knew it! I've never known anyone like you for knowing people. You *know* this man, don't you? But I can't imagine how you arranged for me to see the light precisely half an hour before seeing that letter."

"I didn't do that and I've never heard of Eldritch Films UK. All I did was find the reason for the ruinously expensive and occasionally embarrassing bad behaviour of your house and show you how it related to the foot-dragging of your son and heir and his paragon of a girlfriend. And I started you off on cleaning out cupboards and whole rooms, and deciding which ancestral visages were pleasant and worthy of wall space and which were not, and I got very exasperated with your dithering, and Henry's, whenever you had to make a decision. I have done nothing whatsoever beyond that."

"You had someone in New York send you a report on Mercedes Wax."

"That has nothing at all to do with any of this, and certainly not with Eldritch Films UK. Marigold, *you* are responsible for this piece of unearthly good fortune. You and Henry. You both decided to do something about a situation where everyone was frustrated, and you put on your rubber gloves and got down to work alongside me. Things changed as a result. Welkinlaw felt that it was being taken seriously, that people actually wanted to listen to it – and things changed again. Just because you can't *see* something doesn't mean that it isn't happening somewhere!"

"Well – I suppose so, but I still don't understand how all that stirring the dust has led to this." Marigold brandished the letter from Eldritch Films UK, which Elinore was by now longing to read.

"To believe in the things you can see and touch is no belief at all, but to believe in the unseen is a triumph and a blessing," said Arabella. "I didn't come up with that, Abraham Lincoln did. But I do keep telling you that life is all about communication, and all life is energy, and everything is energy communicating with itself. Haven't you come round to believing that yet?"

"I might if I understood it," said Marigold.

"Oh, never mind. Let's just rejoice, shall we, and start planning that charming new dwelling you're going to create over the stables."

Elinore was desperate to know what was in the letter, and she could not resist asking, "Is it a good letter or a bad one?" In the stories she read, letters could change lives. They brought dreadful news that made people swoon or drop dead, or exhilarating news of a huge fortune that rightfully belonged to the impoverished hero, or glad news that the soldier beloved by the heroine was not dead at all but wounded and pining for word from her, and so on and so forth.

"Elinore, I apologise," exclaimed Arabella. "I forgot you were with us. You must read it for yourself. After all, you are my assistant. May I, Marigold?"

Arabella handed the letter to Elinore, and the two women began to discuss how many individual rooms the Ansketts should incorporate into the stable block conversion. Elinore read the letter, read it all over again to make sure she understood everything, and read it a third time just for the pleasure of feeling like a grown-up. The news it contained was so incredibly good that it outdid any epistolary episodes in any story she had ever read.

> *Dear Mr and Mrs Anskett:*
>
> *Allow me to introduce myself before I explain the reason for my writing to you. I am Marcus Lanner, Founder, Chairman, Managing Director, Executive Director, Chief Executive Officer, Chief Financial Officer and Owner of Eldritch Films UK.*

Over the past five years, my company has gained a sterling reputation as a leading producer of spine-chillers and hair-raisers; that is to say, works of art in the cinematic genre. Our success has allowed us to collaborate with some of the most talented literary stars of the past decade.

You may be familiar with the name of John Passwater, whose 'Bloodied Web' trilogy was awarded last year's Violet Swillan Prize. I am proud to tell you that we have commissioned a series of six original screenplays from Mr Passwater. Each film will feature an actual historical setting in the British Isles, and a plot that draws on the richness and variety of British tales and legends of the supernatural. Each film will be shot entirely on location for maximum authenticity and impact.

The Location Scouting Department of Eldritch Films UK has identified Welkinlaw Castle as an ideal location for our purpose. Further, it appears to harmonise perfectly with the descriptions of settings in two of Mr Passwater's screenplays. (Mr Passwater is known to place great emphasis on the atmospheric significance of setting.)

Of course, our rating of Welkinlaw Castle is so far based only on views of the exterior and on one illustrated article (Country Life, 1920) showing the interior. I am most eager to learn whether you would consent to allowing a team from our Location Scouting Department to tour the interior. Further, if you are agreeable to allowing filming to proceed within and around Welkinlaw Castle, I should like to know at your earliest convenience whether the Castle contains any large or very large items of furniture that you would consent to having:

(a) painted blood red or pitch black and left in situ at close of filming;

or

(b) painted as above and subsequently purchased by Eldritch Films UK and removed for future use as props.

Finally, Eldritch Films UK would naturally pay you a substantial sum for the use of your castle in this way. The usual process is to pay an agreed amount in advance, with a separate deposit made solely to cover any accidental damage to the property. The balance of the payment is made at the close of filming, according to how many days were in the end spent on the property. Incidentally, our Painting & Carpentry Department and our Plumbing & Electrical Department will be on location for the duration of each film, and we are entirely agreeable to putting them at your disposal for minor repairs and touch-ups at no charge, regardless of whether they might have been necessitated by our activities. We pride ourselves on the care and attention we lavish on our location owners.

I greatly look forward to receiving your reply to my enquiry, and I trust that you will understand not only my excitement at having discovered Welkinlaw Castle, but also my eagerness to move quickly towards a decision as to whether Eldritch Films UK can use the property as I have described.

Please do not hesitate to telephone me at the number shown on this letter, should you wish to discuss my proposal in a more immediate fashion.

I remain,

*Yours faithfully,
Marcus W. Lanner MBE*

"He's got a Medal of the British Empire," said Elinore when she had finished reading. "That means he met the Queen, didn't he? Because he's clever and he did something really good?"

Marigold spluttered into her tea, and Arabella said, "We can agree that one of those statements is correct. He could only have received his MBE at Buckingham Palace, from the very hands of the Queen."

"I think his films must have a lot to do with ghosts," continued Elinore. "I know what hair-raising means. If you see a ghost, your hair *always* stands up. Is he going to come here and try and find them, and make a film about it?"

"He doesn't need Welkinlaw's real ghosts. He's arranged a quantity of unreal ones in advance, according to that letter, and he'll populate the place with them," replied Arabella.

Elinore looked doubtful. "How can you have real ghosts and unreal ones? It's a bit confusing."

Arabella smacked her forehead. "You're absolutely right! That's why I need an assistant, to keep me from talking nonsense. I'll leave you to define whether a ghost is real or unreal, and how that applies to ghosts in films and stories."

"I wrote a ghost story when I was at Squair," said Elinore.

"I've seen it – beautifully typed up, too," said Marigold. "But I haven't read it, and Elinore, you did say you would read it aloud. Let's do that after dinner tonight, shall we?"

"Entirely fitting, given this letter and your epiphany," said Arabella. "I can't wait to see Henry's face when you start telling him about a new home in the stable block and a film company coming to paint his furniture blood red."

Faintly, very faintly, a hollow clang reached their ears.

"Oh, hark – Mrs Kightley must have lunch ready for us," said Marigold. "If Henry appears, not a word about *any* of this! We'll seize our moment later, when he doesn't have sheep on the brain."

"Is that like counting sheep when you can't sleep?" asked Elinore.

"No, unfortunately. Sheep are one of those things that keep Henry awake and distracted. We want him to be peaceful. Slumberous, wouldn't you say, Arabella?"

"Yes," said Arabella. "You are learning, Marigold, even though you say you're not. Communication is everything and timing is everything in communication."

Elinore did not think she was close to fully understanding, let alone learning, Arabella's ideas about how the world worked, but so far that had not disqualified her from the job of assistant. She decided she was going to think instead about a new ghost story set in a castle. She would have to pay attention to the details of Welkinlaw, because it did not sound as though she was going to end up in another castle during the remainder of her summer holidays.

In the kitchen, Mrs Kightley was still moving around incessantly like furniture on castors, but with slightly increased speed. The reason was the Aga, specifically its sudden mystifying cooperation with her efforts to produce heat.

"Listen to that!" she told Mrs Anskett when they walked in. "It's fair roaring up the flue. Never in all my time here have I heard that, and I'm not wasting it. I'll be stopping here longer today, so I can do some baking and boil up some more stock while I'm at it. No point in having a freezer wi' naught in it. And what about your dinner? Might as well get on wi' that too so you have a chance of something hot without turning on the electric. Tomorrow's set to be fine and warmer than today, according to the wireless, so I can finish up the washing then. You never know, the washing machine might take a turn and behave itself too."

"I'm so grateful, Mrs Kightley," said Marigold. "All the extra hours you've been putting in have made all the difference. It's freed me up to get on with this clearing out while Arabella is here. I'm afraid it just doesn't go on the same when she isn't here."

They ate freshly-made leek and potato soup and cold rabbit pie with carrots and cauliflower. Mrs Kightley put enormous portions in front of Elinore. Henry did not appear until they were starting on a Bakewell tart with custard. He was excited about his Dunfeshies, and kept rubbing his hands and saying he had had an idea or two, but would not tell them just yet.

"Well, dear, if you won't tell us about these ideas of yours, stop dangling them in front of us. We've got plenty of our own to discuss!

Elinore was looking around the kitchen as she sat eating, and beyond to what could be seen of the scullery warren. She had had an idea too: a story about a hungry ghost, and she would set it in a kitchen exactly like this one. How to start? She recalled Tom's advice about finding the right name first, and wondered where Welkinlaw's library was. It must have one, she felt, and she would like to spend time in it anyway, just for the pleasure of looking at lots of old books.

"Elinore, what would you like to do this afternoon?" asked Marigold, after Henry had gone off on more farm business. "Arabella and I will carry on with that horrible dusty room. Of course, you can help, but it might be very boring."

"Is there a library in this house?"

"Let me show you right now."

The library was close enough to the big hall for Elinore to see that she could easily find her way to and from it. It was dark when they entered, because the tall windows were concealed not only by heavy velvet curtains but also by wooden shutters, which Marigold opened.

"Heavens! I suppose we haven't been in here for a while. Oh, yes, I remember: not since the night of the Birds. We shut up the windows like that to keep the cold out."

Left on her own in a dusty room with hundreds of old books on shelves that went from floor to ceiling – and the ceiling was very high indeed – Elinore was deeply content. Above the fireplace was another full-size portrait of a gentleman, but, unlike the one in the hall, it did not show any overt signs of monarchy. In fact, Elinore thought he looked remarkably like Fred the postman in 18th century dress. Other pictures were dark, muddy landscapes framed in such a way that there was more heavy gilded wood and plaster than oil painting. She wasted no time on them, or anything else except the books. To her delight, this library had two mahogany ladders on a brass rail that allowed her to examine the topmost shelves. She pushed them around – the squeaking was enough to rouse a ghost – and climbed up and down them a few times. After an hour or so, when it was obvious that she could spend a whole day in this room and still not know the insides of every book, she came to a shelf that appeared to be dedicated to the diaries and memoirs of travellers and explorers. Between a Colonel This (the Sudan) and a Captain That (Burma) was the name Daisy Melmurdo and the title *My Journal of Travels Within & Without*. Elinore pulled out the green leather-bound volume and turned to the first page of the Prologue.

> *This memoir begins in the year of my fourteenth birthday,*
> *a most trying period of confinement that extended until*
> *after my sixteenth. Indeed, I felt at times a prisoner!*

"Amaaazing!" said Elinore softly (it was that kind of room). She wanted to start reading immediately, but out in the sunlight, very little of which came into the library. She went through the big hall and out of the castle by the front door, and across the sloping lawn that was really a park, to where she remembered seeing a bench that had been constructed in a circle around a huge copper beech tree. After a few minutes, Polly the spaniel trotted up and flopped down to stretch out at her feet, followed by Puss, who did exactly the same. Apart from the ever-present wind in the leaves, and the sounds of birds, Elinore heard nothing but the imagined sound of Daisy Melmurdo's voice, and she was deeply content. The castle might be in a bad mood much of the time, but this spot under the spreading branches, with the light filtered by maroon leaves, was at that moment the most peaceful place in the world.

Some hours later, the Ansketts, Arabella and Elinore were eating dinner at a round table in the big hall, which could have held a banquet table in addition to all the furnishings that already encumbered it. The big hall was closer to the kitchens than was the dining room, explained Marigold to Elinore, which is why they ate in the kitchen, the distant south-facing sitting room or the hall, unless they had the kind of guests who expected to be treated like royalty.

"Or expect us to live like royalty," said Henry. "Generally, we never *invite* people like that. They land on us for other reasons."

"But the Queen might very well enjoy dinner in a smallish room with a television for company instead of people who have to call her ma'am," observed Arabella. "We just don't know about it."

"A boiled egg and the six o'clock news, that sort of thing?" said Henry. "I should think the news would be continually depressing if one were a monarch with no power to order subjects to show common sense and decency towards each other. And nothing but strikes, strikes, strikes these days. I'm not going to watch the news tonight. The dockers are going to strike soon, I'm convinced, and there will be a lot of talk about that, and the rest of it will be sports. Golf tournaments in Scotland. Not my cup of tea."

"I wonder how long Britain could continue brewing tea if the dockers don't allow any more in," said Arabella.

"Bananas are a *much* more serious matter than tea, under the circumstances," said Marigold. "I adore bananas. And what about oranges? Oh, this is too much like talk of rationing and things like bananas disappearing for years on end. I'd rather talk of something *completely* different." She took a deep breath, placed both hands on the table, and said, "Henry, are you feeling comfortable?"

"Yes, of course, my dear," said Henry. "Dinner was excellent. The Dunfeshies are happy and healthy, and I'm looking forward to ferreting around in the library. I've got an idea or two that I want to read up on. And then I think I'll write a letter to *Farmers Weekly*. No television, no golf, no strikes this evening. Is there pudding, by the way?"

"Yes, there is, and it's a surprise. Henry, I have to tell you that *I* am going on strike," said Marigold.

Henry looked puzzled. "Ah – is that the surprise? What does striking have to do with pudding?"

"Nothing whatsoever! Please *listen*, instead of being as you are with the electric current and my geraniums. *I* am striking. I am not going to wrestle any longer with a castle that doesn't want me – us – in any of its corners any longer. I want to make a comfortable, happy new house in the old stables, and I want Oliver and Mercedes to come here very soon and do whatever they think is right for the place. We must put our efforts into moving out instead of hanging on and hoping, and trying not to be messy, and clearing up after generations of other messy people. We're going about it the wrong way! Tell Oliver that we are vacating the premises and that he must stop imagining himself in some romantic melodrama. Tell him to bring Mercedes Wax here without delay. You could write to him tonight instead of to *Farmers Weekly*. Again!"

A fizzing, crackling sound made them all look up at the lamps placed on either end of the mantelpiece. They flickered briefly and then went from dim to bright in an instant. The ivory silk shades glowed, making every fly spot from the past forty years blackly visible. Arabella smiled and gave Elinore another of her slow, deliberate winks. Elinore was holding her breath. From what had been said earlier, she had expected Marigold to announce this exciting new plan later, when Henry and his dogs were all dozing in front of the BBC news; but that was before television had been pushed off the evening's entertainments by Henry himself.

Henry was still looking at Marigold in bemusement, and so she seized the moment and carried on, quite aware that her declarations had already been the most surprising thing he had ever heard from her.

"We've had a letter from a man who makes films. He wants to pay us lots of money to come here with all his departments of this and that and make Welkinlaw into, well, a film star, I suppose."

A shriek came from the direction of the kitchens, loud enough to carry along all the twists and turns of the intervening passages.

"It must be Mrs Kightley, but she *never* raises her voice," said Marigold. "She's incapable of surprise, not even when Oliver sent her that astonishing apron from New York."

"Let me investigate," said Arabella. "Do carry on surprising Henry."

"All right," said Marigold. "Are you still listening, Henry? I want you to tell me if we have any items of furniture you absolutely cannot be parted from. The man who wants to put Welkinlaw in films also wants to paint the furniture and take it away, some of it at any rate. I mean, he wants to *buy* it, Henry, which is shockingly good news, and really, I'd like to give him a free hand. And then you must make decisions about the pictures. It ought to be fairly simple, after all the clever people who've come to look at things here, don't you agree?"

Marigold had faced Henry with an inescapable truth. All the specialists from all the best auction houses in Edinburgh and London, and even a handful of academics who knew everything there was to know about English portraiture and landscapes – all those who had negotiated Welkinlaw's dark thickets of looming furniture, and had shone lights on the fronts and backs of joyless, dingy pictures, had reached exactly the same conclusion. Welkinlaw, they had proclaimed, was remarkable and possibly unique in all of England for its striking absence of anything remotely valuable or beautiful. Even the monarch in the hall was dismissed as unimportant, a dreadful copy of a poor copy of an original in a stately home in Berkshire, an original that was already suspect because it bore evidence of three different hands.

"Um, well . . ." began Henry. "One must put something on the walls. D'you think you and Arabella could weed out some nice landscapes – no, forget that, there's a perfectly good landscape outside. Sporting scenes, then, and farming ones. Don't we have some still-lifes with piles of game birds, a gun or two, and some good-looking dogs? Very skilful, I've always thought, even if the birds are not in flight. I'll take whatever we can fit in of those. Sheep, must have sheep, and cattle in a park are always pleasing – and did I mention, there was a piece in *Farmers Weekly* the other month about a painting of a bull, a polled British White, that went to auction, painting, not bull, and it fetched tens of thousands of pounds!"

Now it was Marigold's turn to look bemused. "Henry, what are you saying? Are you giving me carte-blanche to deal with the pictures? What is this *fitting-in* we have to do? What about the ancestors? They aren't *my* ancestors, so I do have to ask you about them."

"I should have thought it was obvious, my dear. The ancestors belong here, not in the stables. Why would I take a single one with me? Their pictures are all huge, and they'd crowd out my agricultural scenes and game birds. Someone else can look at the ancestors day and night. Oliver can! They all look so accusing, as if one is letting them down. And that haughty, cross-eyed fellow with the crown is the worst. He's making me more dyspeptic and irritable the older I get, and there's no escaping the bugger."

"Henry! Language! Elinore!" said Marigold in an agonised stage whisper. Elinore tried her best not to laugh and only just succeeded. Marigold was half out of her chair, agitated by her determination to pin Henry down.

"Henry, you sound as if you approve of my idea of a new home. Please stop waffling about animals and ancestors, and tell me!"

"Of course I approve. I'm merely asking you to make sure that certain things come with us and that we have enough wall space in our charming new home to fit them in. Life moves on! Isn't that the saying? Well, I suppose a couple of old fogeys can move too, to let the new blood in. As long as they keep the roof on and fill up the place with lots of little Ansketts. Is there anything else I need to know, or may I go and fiddle about with my own ideas now?"

"Ohhhhhh!" cried Marigold, and sank back on to her chair. She looked stunned, but Elinore assumed that she was happy, apart from being called an old fogey, because Henry seemed to be saying that he was all right about moving into the stables. Arabella reappeared then and sat down.

"Mrs Kightley has fled," she announced. "All the lights in the kitchens and sculleries, the ones that haven't worked for years, came on at once. It gave her a shock. Her face was wet with perspiration – is that a landmark, or a record or something?"

"How odd. She's unshockable, and she always wanted more light down there. We tried," said Marigold.

"You'd be shocked too if you saw what was in the corners – that was what she kept saying, but she didn't describe it and I'm not interested in looking. She's gone home to give Mr Kightley his tea, which sounds very sane, so I think she'll recover."

"Reminds me of a book I read, a farming story. People kept talking about something nasty in the woodshed, but I don't recall finding out exactly what it was," said Henry. He rose from the table and said he was going off to consult some books that he knew his grandfather had added to the library. He paused to tell Marigold that he should want to take quite a lot of books to the stables, and so would she please ensure that a proper space was made for them. "I don't hold with books in the lavatories, although I know some people stack them high in there." He went off, whistling, until Marigold called after him.

"Henry, the pudding – the surprise. Two surprises, actually."

"Oh, yes, pudding," said Henry, and returned to the table. Marigold whispered to Arabella, who disappeared again in the direction of the kitchens. After a few minutes, during which Marigold repeated her need for watertight confirmation from Henry that he was content to follow her plan of action, and Henry nodded and said, "Absolutely, dear, one hundred per cent. Yes, red or black paint, I don't care, they can paint whatever we don't want or take it away. Yes, isn't it marvellous that the experts told us we have firewood, because then we shan't make a mistake and get rid of something special, hmmm, what, yes, I *do* have ideas too . . ." and so on, Arabella returned.

She was carrying a silver tray, on which rested a large birthday cake with a white silk ribbon around it and ten candles blazing.

"Happy birthday, Elinore!" They clapped loudly, and then sang Happy Birthday to her. Elinore was struck dumb. It did not matter that Tom had let on that this cake was being baked for her. It was so big and so sumptuous in its decoration – white chocolate roses on dark chocolate icing – that she would have been speechless with surprise anyway. Moreover, she had no memory of candles on any of her previous birthdays, and Melba would never bring cake into the house in case it ended up in her mouth and ruined her figure.

"The evening's entertainment is not over," said Marigold. "Elinore has written a story and she's going to read it aloud to us later."

"Jolly good!" said Henry. "Much better than strikers and golf. Have you written many stories, my dear? We could have one every evening, at least until the news is worth listening to."

"A delightful prospect, if we were staying on," said Arabella. " But I trust Oliver and Mercedes will find a nice room for Elinore, so that she can visit Welkinlaw in the future."

Marigold immediately clasped her hands and looked saintly. "Of course they will! And Elinore can stay with us too, in the spare bedroom or two that I plan to have. You must come for holidays, dear, and bring plenty of stories in your suitcase."

"Aha! Holidays," said Henry. "May I present one of my ideas? I want to go off with the Bristol and tour the Continent. I want to look for the old, forgotten sheep breeds and bring some back to Welkinlaw and experiment with crosses. My grandfather was interested in that sort of thing, and my father, but a couple of wars got in the way. I'd be more than happy to look at high-yield, super-rich milk producers if it helps Miss Wax settle in. Who knows, she might want to make Welkinlaw sheep's milk cheese too."

"The Bristol? What about me?" said Marigold. "The Bristol doesn't speak French."

"You too, dear."

"I would really like to come back here for my holidays, so I could write stories about the castle," said Elinore. In the spirit of the day, her discovery of Daisy Melmurdo's memoir had given her new ideas too, which were changing her reasons for wanting to stay in a castle. They were now more to do with imagination than protection; the word inspiration had entered her thinking, if not her vocabulary.

28

Another high, windy place – that was how Elinore imagined Airt, from what little she had been told, and she had very few other impressions of it in her head. She knew from her books that Balmoral Castle was somewhere among the same hills. Airt began to pepper Arabella's talk as they were departing from Welkinlaw, and it appeared on the labels that she made for certain boxes.

> Miss Elinore Crum
> c/o A. Cheyne
> Fhairlach, by Mains of Airt
> Boddo Bridge
> Aberdeenshire

These boxes held Elinore's books, her typewriter and the bulk of her other belongings. Henry was pleased to see that she had discovered something to her taste on his shelves of ancestral volumes, and told her that she must keep Daisy Melmurdo's memoir. He had no idea how it came to be there, since Melmurdo was not a family name. Elinore was still meandering through the first of Daisy's prolix descriptions, but even if she had finished reading the book, she would not have packed it away. Daisy was a new friend and must travel in her oriental silk bag.

On the Friday after her Monday evening arrival at Welkinlaw, a carrier collected Elinore's boxes for delivery to Arabella's home. Arabella and Elinore would travel by train from Edinburgh to Aberdeen. On the Saturday afternoon, they drove away in Arabella's hired car. Mrs Kightley had made a batch of parkins as a farewell gift, and their gingery, treacly aroma filled the car. The day was hot, and the car windows stayed down even after Elinore and Arabella had stopped waving to Henry and Marigold, who stood with the three dogs on the front steps. Elinore still judged the absent Oliver to be a stupid, selfish and silly boy, but, if it turned out that he was happy to let Elinore stay in his castle in future, she would raise her estimation of him, somewhat. She wanted to see the place after Oliver and Mercedes had cleaned it up and redecorated it, which at present was unimaginable.

They retraced some of Elinore's journey with Matthew Carr. Before they left, Arabella explained that it would not be possible to detour through Criven or call on Tom at the Dower House, for she had to be in Edinburgh in good time for attending to some business that evening. Elinore was relieved. She had spent weeks and weeks wishing to be returned to Criven, and she would talk about the place to anyone who cared to listen, but visiting it again was another matter. The feeling of not knowing where she was going after her holidays weighed on her, and she knew that if she met any of her Criven friends or glimpsed the cottage where she had lived, or even the school or the river, it would only make that feeling worse.

Leaving Welkinlaw had not been as unsettling as leaving Squair. First, they were on their way to a night at the Balmerinoch Hotel, which had recovered from its flooding and reopened. That was a familiar destination, and Elinore was excited about having a room all to herself, and going down to dinner all dressed up. Second, she was leaving in the company of Arabella, and she had to admit that having an Elizabeth Tudor witch for an aunt was becoming more fascinating and less potentially nerve-wracking (although still peculiar and unpredictable) with every day that passed. For a start, Arabella, like Tom, had left Elinore in no doubt that she would have defenders should anyone try to take her away. Elinore had said something in the kitchen at Welkinlaw that caused Arabella to take her aside and point to a vat-like stockpot that Mrs Kightley had just heaved onto a shelf. "Do you see that pot? If anyone even thinks of coming along and snatching you for any reason, I shall personally pour boiling oil on them. And I have a pot just as big as that at home."

Third, that home of Arabella's was beginning to be alluring. Welkinlaw had given her even more space than Squair for running around outdoors, but one and a half days of her stay had seen limiting rain and squalls. Moreover, she had spent much time indoors, exploring room after room, and helping Arabella and Marigold do the mucking out, as Arabella called their work. Indoor exploring also allowed her to indulge and enlarge her various ideas about how to accomplish time travel (the return kind only – she had no wish to be stuck in Welkinlaw's bloody past). Now she wanted to be out and roaming under the sun, with plenty of rivers and hills at her disposal. The Highlands were also comfortably far from Edinburgh, adding to her sense of freedom expanding.

As soon as they reached the outskirts of Edinburgh, Elinore fell silent. Despite all assurances, a part of her remained stubbornly on guard against Caltrops, and something else, a nameless, troubling shadow. She relaxed as soon as she was in the Balmerinoch, however, and settling into yet another new room. This one had its own little bathroom, and altogether it was the most spick and span, perfectly put together space she had seen since being in Arabella's room down the corridor, on the day of the great shopping spree in Jenners.

Arabella had told her to go down to the hotel sitting room when she was ready. When she walked in, two small figures and two tall ones jumped from their chairs and yelled "Surprise!" before running across the room to make a fuss of her. This meeting was the business for which Arabella had said she must arrive on time: the business of ensuring Elinore was ready to go out with Fredy, Susanna and Usha to see a film, while Arabella and Mrs Berg sat down and talked over tea.

Mrs Berg handed over a bag containing the laundered clothes that Elinore had been unable to collect; all were ironed and some even starched. Arabella smiled. "Thank you. She's all together now, one might say. Her clothes mean a great deal to her."

"They're very good clothes for a child who's been so ill-treated. I recognised all the labels. It's the oddest situation I've ever come across," said Mrs Berg. "What will happen to her? And what can the mother be thinking of?"

"The mother doesn't think," said Arabella. "Which may well be to our advantage in the end. All I know is that Elinore will never return to her so-called care if I have anything to do with it. The same applies to the Caltrops, even if the mother does go on living with them in Dunallan Crescent, which I doubt."

"Oh, them. Let me tell you the latest."

Mrs Berg had returned a couple of times to No. 17 to ring and knock, before Lady Groule had passed on to her another vital piece of information from Celia Chisholm. An old school-friend of Celia's had rung her with a juicy piece of gossip. Out shopping in St Andrews, the friend had been elbowed off the pavement and into the car-filled street by a striding, muttering woman who was dishevelled but nevertheless clothed in respectable tweediness. "Be careful! Stop that or you'll hurt someone," the friend admonished the woman.

The woman let loose a volley of nastiness, pushing her face too close to Celia's friend, and, even more strangely, condemning her to the fires of eternal damnation for abandoning proper Christian meekness in a public place. The friend had no choice but to look closely at the thick-lipped, florid, frothing features of this aggressive stranger, and it dawned on her that she had seen all this before, many years before. Then a man ran up and took the woman by the arm – "but half-scared, you know, as if she was going to eat him alive, no mistaking it – a look far worse than hen-pecked!"—and said, "Roberta! Roberta, come away, you must come away now." The friend knew at once that she was looking at Roberta Leitch, who had been in the form above her at the Ina Blackadder School, and she decided that she would "come away" too, and put plenty of pavement between herself and someone who had once made school life miserable for her. Her haste was speeded by the fumes of strong drink that Roberta had breathed over her.

It did not end there. A disturbance took place at the edge of the hallowed Old Course, and it was reported that a raving woman, followed by a pleading man (both of advanced years) had had to be removed for disturbing the peace and being a public nuisance, especially with respect to the woman's aggressive behaviour towards any female whom she saw as indecent, immoral and (bizarrely) inebriated. Alcohol consumption was cited as a contributing factor.

"My, my," said Arabella. "And have you continued to check their house?"

"Certainly," said Mrs Berg. "They are inside now, I can tell, but they don't answer the door, and I have better things to do than keep watch for when they might sneak out. I simply yelled at them through their letterbox – front and back, for good measure – and told them that if they ever so much as spoke to any child I knew, ever again, I would set the police on them for cruelty to children. I think that's about as much as we can do now, isn't it? They're stark raving mad – or she is. The main thing is that Elinore is well out of their clutches."

"Yes," said Arabella. "The Caltrops are history as far as we're concerned. But they will linger in Elinore's head, sadly, and we still don't know what exactly will happen once the mother returns. She might decide that her daughter is the dearest thing on this earth to her, and take it into her head to pursue Tom Balmerinoch and me as kidnappers. But he's a lawyer, and I – well, let's just say I have my own resources."

※

That night, the lingering images in Elinore's head were of the splendiferous musical spectacle that she and her friends had watched. Instead of Caltrops, she had a theme song popping up whenever she thought she might sleep.

Hello, Dolly,
Well, hello, Dolly,
It's so nice to have you back where you belong
You're looking swell, Dolly,
We can tell, Dolly,
You're still glowin', you're still crowin'
You're still goin' strong.

That song would make anyone happy, Elinore thought. And Barbra Streisand was *absolutely incredible*. She had never seen anyone singing and dancing like that. Her head was full of colour and song and the swirl of Hollywood costume art. Her head was also resting on a monogrammed pillow in a pretty room in a hotel. Altogether, it felt like halfway to being a princess, even though she had no palace and not even a picture of the next room she would go to sleep in. I could be a *lost* princess, she thought. I really and truly could be in an *adventure*.

※

Waverley Station was the kind of place where adventures began. Elinore had only a few dim memories of being on a train, and none of this vast, crowded, echoing, glass-roofed expanse of platforms through which trains came and went, or stood and rumbled in ascending and descending bursts of sound, and disembodied voices garbled the names of destinations from top to bottom and side to side of Britain.

She sat opposite Arabella in a compartment, glued to the window. As the train pulled out of Waverley, she saw the black rock base of the castle on one side and the sloping lawns of Princes Street Gardens on the other. Sir Walter Scott's monument was at the top of the slope, she knew, but too far up for her to see. The ornate Ross Fountain made her gasp. She liked fountains: they had a touch of magic about them. She wished she could have stood by it and made a wish. Really, she had seen nothing of Edinburgh. If it had not been for the *Book of Edinburgh for Young People*, she would have learned nothing either, but the book had also stirred the desire to see it all for herself.

> *And everywhere you go you can read history: not written in books, but in stones, which to my mind is far more interesting; and remember, Edinburgh will never be to you the enchanted city she is to many people until you have learned to do this for yourselves.*

"Will I ever come back here?" she asked suddenly. "I never saw the Castle. I want to climb Sir Water Scott's monument, and see the Greyfriars Bobby fountain, and go inside the palace . . . and all that."

She turned back to the window as the train came to a stop at Haymarket.

"Yes, you will," replied Arabella. "We *can* reverse this journey. We can get on a train in Aberdeen and be here in a couple of hours. Monuments don't move, remember. They'll still be here when you can be here too."

"I'd like to see all the things I read about in the book I found. The one that used to belong to Helena Albacyr."

"Ah, yes – Helena. And Helena's book. Finding a name in a book and making up a story about that person shows great imagination. I hope you'll exercise it again soon."

"Oh, yes, I will. I've already got a new person for a story and she's called Daisy. But it wasn't *really* my idea. It was Tom's. He told me to go and find a name and wait for the story." Elinore stopped, remembering that Davidicus Mercury must remain hidden until he was a book.

"*Tom* said that?"

"Yes, and he told me how to say Helena's last name two different ways. He said it was French or Spanish. And he said I could write anything I wanted about her even if she was still alive, because she would just be an old crone now and she'd never find out that I turned her into a ghost anyway."

"Tom said *that*?" What an odd look on her face, thought Elinore. "I see. Tom is also creative, then. One would never have guessed."

Elinore clamped her mouth more firmly on Tom's great literary secret.

As the train ran along the coastlines of Fife, Angus, Kincardineshire and finally Aberdeenshire, Elinore saw plenty of sea and rock to make up for never having been that close to them in her life before. When she finally stepped down onto the platform at Aberdeen, she caught a salty tang on draughts that gusted into the station from one end. The station was another glass-roofed structure, but much smaller than Waverley and not nearly as dark. Outside, the day was bright and warm under a blue sky, as it had been when they got out of their taxi at Waverley Station, but to Elinore the air felt quite different from that of Edinburgh. Arabella walked across the car park to a most surprising vehicle.

"Meet Bumphrey," she said. "Cars are usually female to their owners, but this one would be offended by a girl's name and probably stall in resentment. He was a present from a grateful client, just when I needed a new car."

Bumphrey was grey and very far from new. Neither was he rare and valuable in the manner of the Bristol, even though he was at least fifteen years older. He was smaller too, but his boot was capacious and their luggage was quickly stowed. As Arabella drove away from the station, she said, "It isn't going to be bumpy like this *all* the way! The streets here have setts, like cobbles, and Bumphrey's suspension is a bit like old knickers – the elastic's gone." Elinore had no trouble understanding that.

The hard bouncing underneath her subsided when they reached the wide, smooth main streets of Aberdeen. She saw at once that this city was not blackened like Edinburgh. The buildings were in a silvery granite that shone in that clear light, and the sense of airy spaciousness was enhanced by the quiet Sunday streets. Very quickly, they were out of the city and travelling past fields and farms, and then the hills became higher and the patches of wood and forest more frequent and expansive. Bumphrey was well behaved enough, but Elinore wished that his rather low, narrow windows were much bigger, to allow her a good look at this new scenery. Arabella constantly pointed out landmarks and named the villages and towns that they passed through. Elinore saw that the granite of buildings could be a faded pink in colour too, echoing the stretches of heathery ground. The elements of countryside around her were at once the same as those of Criven and completely different; the colours were the same, yet different. Everything was new and interesting yet familiar enough to be reassuring. Her spirits were rising and rising. She forgot all about her homemade calendar with the words "Mummy comes back" in the box for Tuesday 19th July, as she looked at the passing sights. This part of the world might offer even more fun than Criven or Welkinlaw. She remembered Matthew Carr asking her about Criven, and his comment on the open galloping country there. Galloping horses would just break their legs here, she thought, but I could climb *everywhere*.

"Do you have foxes here?" she asked.

"Yes, plenty. If you look out of your bedroom window and see lights moving around at night where there aren't any roads, it will be farmers shooting foxes. Lots of places for them to hide in the craggy places where the mountains start."

"Are there real mountains here too?"

"*Very* real mountains. You'll be looking at a famous one every time you open and close your curtains."

They turned off the main route from Aberdeen and crossed the River Dee on a broad, high bridge that took the road into a village that was built around a square. "Nearly there now," said Arabella. "This is Boddo Bridge, and you could scoot down here on a bicycle. But you wouldn't be scooting up again that easily – oh, no!"

Just beyond where the last houses of the village petered out, Arabella turned onto a narrow road that wound and dipped, but overall kept rising. Bumphrey groaned and strained, and Arabella urged him on by calling him impolite names. "All that luggage is a new experience for the old thing," said Arabella. "Not to mention all those great big parkins that Mrs Kightley gave us." They passed a few houses, one small farm and a much larger one that lay below them on flat land by a river.

"That's Mains of Airt, where the Lindsays live," said Arabella. "You'll meet the Lindsay boys very quickly. They seem to know when something new is in the vicinity without a word being spoken."

Then the road made a sharp turn and rose even more steeply. After a few hundred yards it ended by the side of a white-painted house on the level top of the hill, where Bumphrey came to a stop.

"Watch the wind doesn't knock you over when you get out," said Arabella.

Elinore got out and stood still. A light breeze ruffled the leaves of the few trees clustered on the far side of the house, and her hair; it was refreshing after the confines of the car. A curlew's bubbling cry was the only other thing to greet her. She looked doubtfully at Arabella, who said, "Oh, how pleasant, we can make it to the house without being flattened this time. But just wait! The wind will come."

On very old maps, the house was once marked as An Fhaire Aileach. Time whittled the name to Fhairaileach, and even further to Fhairlach but could not alter its ancient meaning of 'the airy lookout'. From where the metalled Airt road ended abruptly at a gate in a drystone dyke, a stony track wandered away across undulating moorland of rough, tussocky grass mixed with patches of heather and dotted by scanty clusters of pines. From the windows of Fhairlach, Arabella could see all comers, whether by moor or road. She detested unexpected visitors unless they were her neighbours.

Elinore saw an L-shaped house, whitewashed with black-painted woodwork, whose upper dormer windows made it look as if it were keeping watch over the southern approach. Its position at the ending of the fields also gave it the sense of guarding the moorland beyond, which spread to the horizon. Behind the house was a steading and some other outbuildings, whose granite was rough and free of whitewash. The front door was in the middle of the short part of the L, beyond an open porch with two broad steps up to it. The carrier had left Elinore's boxes under cover there.

"We'll bother with boxes and baggage later," said Arabella, unlocking the door. "Let's see what my gnomes have been up to in the kitchen, shall we?"

Gnomes. But of course, it was the home of a witch, her lair on the top of a hill. With no neighbours to poke their noses into her business, a witch could live as she pleased up here with any kind of creature as domestic help. Elinore braced herself for a cauldron in front of a fire and bits of dead animals hanging around, like the crows and weasels she had seen nailed to a gamekeeper's gibbet near Criven. But when she stepped inside, her first words were, "It's like a snowy day in here!"

"My blank canvas," said Arabella. "Halfway point to perfection in this house."

Every wall and ceiling within sight was pure white. The walls were absolutely bare. A box of tools stood on the bottom step of the staircase, reminding Elinore of the Balmerinoch. The hall had no windows, but open doors on either side showed white rooms into which the light poured freely. The floors were bare wood with not a scrap of carpet. Every sound echoed. Elinore stood still for a moment, just looking. The absence of obvious witches' accoutrements was a relief, but this empty whiteness was a shock in a different way. It made her acutely conscious that her old life in Criven was now even farther away, and that she had come here for a brief time, a few weeks, that did not connect to a future. She was in a strange, empty space all of her own.

In the kitchen, Arabella was opening the refrigerator and lifting the covers of some dishes on the countertop while humming to herself. "Excellent, excellent. The gnomes have made a fine supper for us, and brought in breakfast things too. We'll go shopping tomorrow. Oh, wait – where's the pudding? No pudding. I wonder if the junior gnomes ate it all up."

She went out into the hall and picked up the telephone. Elinore sat down on a hall chair and listened, even though Miss Agnes Pound would have frowned on that. Half of her accepted that it was entirely natural for a witch to have a few gnomes about the place, and half of her was uncertain.

"Hello, Vera, how are you?" said Arabella. Elinore heard something loud come back along the line. "Yes, we've just arrived, and everything's lovely, as usual, thank you very much. I was wondering, bearing in mind that I have a guest, if the pudding was going to arrive later, since I see no sign of it in the kitchen."

A squawk came down the line. "Yes, I mean no pudding at all," said Arabella. "Rhubarb crumble with a jug of custard, if I recall . . ." An even louder squawking came, followed by silence, while Arabella hummed and smiled. Then Vera (what was the right term for a she-gnome, wondered Elinore, and could it really be called Vera?) returned and was very voluble for a good minute. "Wonderful!" said Arabella. "I'll just pop out when I hear it." Vera said something else, to which Arabella replied, "Don't worry, only the dead or the stone deaf could fail to hear it. Many thanks, Vera – oh, don't worry about it! I always say you've got Happy, Sleepy, Bashful and Dopey in your kitchen, four fine hungry gnomes" (she winked at Elinore) "or have I got it wrong, are they the dwarves? Anyway, accidents happen. Bye-bye."

"I was right," said Arabella. "A junior gnome ate our pudding, but more rhubarb crumble and custard will arrive fairly soon. When you hear a sort of roaring, growling noise, just go out to where Bumphrey is parked and you can receive the delivery."

"*Me?*" said Elinore. "You mean – meet the gnome?"

"Why not? You're going to eat the pudding, so you might as well see how it gets here. Now, would you like to see your bedroom?"

They went up the stairs – clump, clump, clump on the bare wood – and everything was white here too, made even brighter by the sunlight coming down through two big skylights. Arabella pointed up at them. "My very first task when I came here: secure the roof and let more light in. We don't have leaks and drips falling into buckets at Fhairlach, and after Welkinlaw I'm sure you're glad to hear that."

At a half landing where the stair turned, she pointed through an open door. "My study and bedroom, and my own bathroom around the corner." Elinore glimpsed furniture, pictures on the walls and carpets on waxed, shining floorboards. She wondered where Arabella might keep a book of spells.

On the landing, which had more tool boxes and piled-up materials, she opened the door that was straight ahead. "Your very own bathroom."

After the white of snow, Elinore was startled by the deep coral colour of the bathroom walls. Everything else in the bathroom, which was empty except for the porcelain fittings, was white. "It looks nice and hot in here."

"Good. Any bathroom in Scotland should at least *look* hot." She opened a door in the coral-coloured wall and took out towels and a bath mat from an airing cupboard.

Then she opened a closed door to the right of the bathroom and ushered Elinore into another white space. A dormer window, uncurtained, was filled with blue sky. The floors were the same uncovered wood as elsewhere, except for a white woven rug by the single bed, which was covered by a dark blue bedspread embroidered with large white leaves and flowers; it reminded Elinore of the dress Susanna was wearing when she first saw her, in the dining room of the Balmerinoch Hotel. Opposite the bed was a pine bookcase with three deep shelves and two glass doors, and a white-painted rattan chair. On either side of the bookcase were tall built-in cupboards. Otherwise, the room was empty. It was warm, thanks to the sun, and smelled of fresh paint. Arabella opened the window wide.

"This bedroom is the only one that's finished apart from my own. The floors are still being sanded and finished in the other two. What do you think?"

"Can I bring all my things in here? Can I put my books in the bookcase?"

"Everything. Right away. And we'll find a reading lamp and other essentials, and put up curtains."

"*Gosh!*" Elinore stood in the middle of the floor and turned around, before going to the window. The view made her feel like a bird. On the right of the road up to the house, steep fields rose to shimmering birch woods; on the left, the fields dropped down equally steeply. Purplish-green hills swelled beyond the fields on every side, growing wider and higher towards the horizon. Trees were everywhere, and the landscape was threaded with drystone dykes. An uneven glint marked the course of a river that she had seen from the car, down on the flatter fields where the big farm was.

She turned to Arabella, who was standing with her arms folded. "It's super. It's the most special room I've ever stayed in."

"What? Even more special than a bedroom in a castle?"

"Well, it was a very *interesting* room there, but I didn't have my books and things in it, so it wasn't *special* like this."

A whining, growling sound reached them through the open window. It grew louder, punctuated by sharp bangs like gunfire. Without bothering to look out, Arabella said, "Gnome coming. Will you go out and get the pudding, please, Elinore? I'm going to finish equipping your bathroom."

Wishing that the heavy front door had glass in it, Elinore opened it very slowly and kept her body behind it. The noise had stopped and no gnome was in sight. She tiptoed out to the porch and looked over to Bumphrey. Beyond the stonewall that separated the road end from the garden, she heard something, and then a head and shoulders popped up from behind the wall and she started. Whatever it was had on goggles that were too big for its face and an odd leather cap with dangling straps on either side. The part of the face that could be seen was covered in freckles. "Hiya!" it called out, and then all of it came through the gate in the wall. It was a boy, a little older than her. Grinning madly under the goggles, he marched up to the porch and handed her two heavy bags. "Here's the pudding. You got oors, 'cause we ate the one that was for here, my brothers an' me. It was guid!"

His goggled eyes fell on Elinore's boxes in the porch, and he squinted to read the labels. "Are you Elinore Crum? Are you here to stay?"

"Yes, I am and I'm here for my holidays."

"Any books in there?"

"*All* my books. Do you like books?"

"Oh, aye! D'you hae any Biggles?"

"What?"

"Biggles! Flying ace! I've got eight an' I'm efter all o' them. The man that wrote them's deid, but he wrote a fair lot when he wasn't. Okay, I'm off now. See ya!" He turned and ran with arms outstretched to the gate.

"What's your name?" called Elinore, following him.

"Ginger! Fit else would it be?" Now Elinore saw that he had arrived on some kind of a motorbike, a lightweight, mud-spattered one. He started it up and the whining, growling noise resumed. "Vaarrrrrooom!" he yelled and then was gone down the road, bent low over the handlebars, elbows sticking out like wings.

Elinore carried the bags into the kitchen, where Arabella was putting a casserole dish into the oven of an electric cooker.

"Here's the pudding. The gnome was called Ginger and I think he wants to be a racing driver."

"He wants to be a pilot. Was he wearing those goggles and an old flying cap?"

"Yes, and he talked about something to do with flying called Biggles. What's that?"

"Only Ginger can tell you about Biggles. He's one of the Lindsay boys from Mains of Airt. His proper name is Keith, but only his mother and father call him that now, and even they might have to give up soon because he's quite deaf to it."

"Like me and Ermine. I hate it."

"Quite right. An ermine is the stoat in winter white. I can't imagine that you'd want to be named after a stoat, even if its fur is pretty."

"Stoats steal eggs and eat little birds."

"They do. They're opportunistic predators." A woman called Ermine was at the forefront of Arabella's mind as she spoke, but this was not the moment to introduce Crum family history of which Elinore was blessedly ignorant.

While their dinner was heating, they unloaded Bumphrey and carried all Elinore's belongings into her room. Arabella walked around with a tape measure and called out items to Elinore, who wrote them down as a neat list. Curtains, bedside table, lamp, chest of drawers, desk, chair, lamp for desk. "Cushions – plenty of cushions. After books, cushions make a room. Cushions are *very* important, Elinore."

"Do I really get a desk?"

"Of course. You can't put your typewriter on the floor, can you? Well, you could, but I don't think it would improve your typing."

They ate dinner at a pine table in the kitchen, by a window that looked over the moor and surrounding hills. Elinore ate slowly, partly because the shepherd's pie and everything else was tasty, and partly because she was absorbing this new landscape too. The colours were changing by the moment as the sun dropped and shadows lengthened. The hills seemed to grow higher, and it was all majestic. No wonder kings and queens liked to take their holidays up here. The Queen had been at Holyroodhouse and now she was at Balmoral, down the road again from Elinore Crum, who had got out of bed in one place and by the next bedtime had ended up miles and miles away in another place. Criven to Edinburgh, Edinburgh to Squair, Squair to Welkinlaw, Welkinlaw to Edinburgh, Edinburgh to Airt. Made into a list like that, her travels sounded quite adventurous.

"Is the food all right? Your fork is moving ve-e-ery slowly to your mouth," said Arabella.

"I was just thinking that I'm seeing a lot of places now. I keep going to new ones."

"And some are better than others, aren't they? Well, I trust you'll think this one is all right, because I must say I'm looking forward to having an assistant. Have you ever stacked wood?"

"What kind of wood?"

"The kind that goes in that Rayburn. When we use that, we can cook and get hot water for nothing, and light fires in the downstairs rooms. It's free because the wood is lying all around, and I just collect it and saw it up. I'm going to start my winter log pile now, and you can help if you want. I saw it and you stack it up neatly. I'll give you a big pair of gloves."

"Because if I wear gloves I can do any job?"

Arabella smiled in a satisfied way. "Correct. You are very quick, Elinore Crum. You are *definitely* the right assistant for me."

29

Melba Crum views the grime and greyness of Waverley Station with distaste. She has elevated herself so far above and beyond Edinburgh that her foot quivers as it touches the station platform. Only a brief alighting in this blackened old cage, she promises herself, as brief as I can possibly make it.

Outside Waverley, it is as fine a July day as Edinburgh can possibly produce. Melba shivers in the taxi. The sun is not shining from a Texan sky and so must be a lesser kind. At No. 17 Dunallan Crescent, she opens the front door with her own key and drags her suitcase up the steps. She feels suffocated as soon as she takes two steps into the hall. Odour of cooked cabbage, no air-conditioning and it is all so ugly and *brown*. Melba now associates with brown in strictly limited contexts: Italian or French leather handbags, all-over suntans, the upholstery of certain cars (certain *automobiles*), fine cigars held in bronzed, manly hands and the like.

The Caltrops come charging along to investigate this abrupt, unheralded ingress.

"What is the meaning of this?" demands Mrs Caltrop.

"Of what?" asks Melba. "I have returned, exactly as and when I said I would."

"You said the 20th. That is tomorrow."

"Really? How odd. Well, it can't make any difference to you, can it? Or did you let my *lovely* bedroom to a new lodger? Is some girl up there right now, stuffing undies into a suitcase? Or is it a *male* lodger, Mrs Caltrop?" Melba lets out a peal of laughter, which is slightly manic even to her own ears.

Mrs Caltrop says nothing. She and Mr Caltrop stand in the hall and watch as Melba heaves her suitcase up the stairs. Melba flings open her bedroom door, shoves the suitcase in and slams the door shut. She looks around the room in a kind of disgusted disbelief. After some desultory taking out and putting back in of suitcase contents, she remembers that she has a child, still presumably where she left it. She rummages in the suitcase and pulls out a plush stuffed animal toy, a Texas Longhorn; the perfect gift for a child who persists in hanging around muddy farms. She also pulls out a tissue-wrapped object that Dwayne has insisted on her taking; the perfect gift for a cute little girl, he said, after giving her a different kind of gift for the *cutest* big girl.

Melba combs her hair and sprays on plenty of something by Chanel, which has replaced the Ô de Lancôme. She picks up the Texas Longhorn and the tissue-wrapped object, and marches along to Elinore's room. She can see that the door is open before she reaches it, and she calls out, "Surprise! Guess what I've got for you!" (She only does this because that is what Dwayne did every time he was away from her for more than an hour, and she cannot seem to come up with any other greeting.)

The door is wide open and every vestige of Elinore has vanished. It takes a little time for this to register with Melba, and then she looks in the bathroom next door. Hardly any evidence of Elinore was ever in there, but it too has gone.

Melba goes back to Elinore's room and leans against the doorframe, considering. If the child has gone from this house, lock, stock and barrel (as Dwayne would say), and no one has bothered to inform her, it cannot be as the result of misadventure. The police have not tracked her down in Dallas to deliver ghastly, inconvenient news. The Caltrops have not uttered a word about Elinore. Therefore, nothing actually bad can have befallen Elinore. Something she read in a magazine – a true story! – creeps into her mind: something about a mother and daughter in a 19th century Paris hotel, breaking their journey from India; sudden illness of the mother, the rushing out of the daughter to obtain a prescription, the daughter's return to find no trace of her mother and denials all round that the woman had ever entered the hotel with her. It had been plague, hushed up to the utmost. Melba remembers the Caltrops' very strong associations with India.

She steps smartly away from contact with the door, and returns to her own room, with a hand over her nose just to be safe. After about five seconds in there, she reaches the same conclusion as before. Since no one has *bothered* her about the child, and since no plague notice is affixed to the front door, or any door, the reason for this disappearance must ultimately have nothing to do with her, and so she need not bother about it either. Much more important to turn it to her advantage without delay. Suddenly blithe, Melba goes downstairs and corners the Caltrops in their den, the morning room. They are sitting in their wing chairs with hands folded, exactly as if they are waiting for her.

"Well, what a surprise – no Elinore!" says Melba. "Do you know where she's off to, with all her books and bits and bobs?"

"She had the temerity to vanish while we were out at a church function. It is all the doing of that woman," replies Mrs Caltrop, who is careful not to specify which woman.

"Oh! That horrid Arabella," says Melba, feeling a sudden lightness, as if jet lag had never happened, as if she were already tripping off a return flight to Dallas. "Awful meddling creature. So, she's taken Elinore off, has she? And no doubt Elinore herself had a great deal to do with it, with all her complaining and wanting this and that – such an ungrateful little so-and-so. Well! That makes everything *terribly* simple, doesn't it?"

Melba feels that she can crank up some radiance now, and flashes a winning smile. She remains standing and tells the Caltrops that her own disappearance from Edinburgh will now be underway, rather more quickly than she had expected thanks to Elinore's having gone first. "*So* convenient! No school arrangements to bother about, no guardian responsibilities for you, no – anything!"

Melba runs upstairs feeling lighter and lighter, pushes everything she has taken out of her suitcase back into it and closes it. She finds a bag under the bed and tosses a few more remnants of her old life into that, and then runs to the top of the stairs.

"Oh, Roberta! I need a taxi – would you mind awfully? If you ring now, it will be here by the time I get my luggage down to the door."

And that, essentially, is how Melba Crum ended up at the Caledonian Hotel, making a reverse charge transatlantic telephone call to Dallas, and Mr and Mrs Caltrop ended up with a plush Texas Longhorn toy and a beribboned ceramic heart that declared, "Someone in Texas loves ya!"

30

The days of Elinore Crum's present and immediate future are no longer delineated on a hand-drawn series of boxes. "Mummy comes back" has come and gone, rather as lunar phases and the feast days of saints have also passed without disturbing life at Fhairlach. Her handmade calendar has gone into the pile of paper destined for kindling. Arabella has opened one of her many cupboards and taken out several full-colour calendars, still in their wrappers, that she received at Christmas, and she fans them out to let Elinore choose. *Cottage Gardens of England. Splendour of Snowdonia. London Parks and Promenades. Devon Delights. King Arthur's Country. Shakespeare's Land. Ancient Glories* (cathedrals). *Our Ancient Glory* (castles). *Man's Best Friend* (dogs). *Man's Greatest Friend* (horses). *Castles of Mar.*

Elinore picks *Castles of Mar.* (Arabella puts all the other calendars aside for donation to the school in Boddo Bridge, where the littlest children will cut them up with small, old, blunt-ended scissors and squeeze crusty glue from rubber-tipped pots over the resulting scraps. In her abhorrence of piles of the redundant, she is a frequent donor of art materials for infants.) *Castles of Mar* states in text that it portrays a mere twelve of the three hundred and fifty castles within Aberdeenshire. This astonishing figure is further evidence that Elinore has landed in what she privately calls a fairy-tale country. If she had been more inclined to Sunday school, she might have named it Eden or paradise. On the map, Aberdeenshire is a minuscule space in a tiny country at the top of an island that itself is peculiarly small, given its history of reaching around the world to claim vast lands and populations as its own. On the ground, the county feels like a huge, mysterious country, with craggy heights around which roads unfurl endlessly and split into yet more byways into the trees or across the moors, or great vistas of hill and farmland suddenly opening up around a bend. Aberdeenshire *must* be a small place, she has seen it on the map, and yet the scale of it defies this reality. Every destination seems to be a long way off when they go by road, even though Arabella is a driver who never dawdles. Elinore believes that the innumerable winding back roads and tracks must lead eventually to forgotten or even secret places in the hills, and that the mountains and moors must have magic properties understood by long-ago people, but not by those who now clamber over them in brightly-hued nylon. She dreams of making discoveries in that realm. The place is full of briskly-moving watercourses, some very big and known all over the world for what they offer anglers, others mere burns. Edging this county and its neighbours in a long curve is the sea, which is a story and a magic all by itself.

Crowning it all (for Elinore) is the presence in this faery land of Balmoral, the Queen's summer home. Books and magazines inform her that the royal family's affection for this place is as deep and broad as the River Dee itself. Apparently, the Queen goes around and about the Highlands more freely than she is able to do elsewhere in her kingdom. This notion is like a sprinkling of glittering dust over the whole county, and above all the very part of it in which Elinore is staying. "I stay on Royal Deeside," she says to herself now and then. (She wants to say "I *live*", but the future beyond the first forty or so boxes on her new calendar is a void, and she worries about offending something, somewhere by presuming to *live* in a place when she is only meant to be passing through.) It is impossible to forget where she is, since every local shopping trip, however humble the need, means being confronted with extensive array of merchandise claiming to represent Royal Deeside. Elinore loves it all. It keeps the fairy dust suspended and shimmering in the air, at least for as many weeks as the royal family is trundling discreetly around in dark green Land Rovers on the same narrow roads that she uses.

The *Castles of Mar* calendar goes up on the wall above Elinore's desk, a pine table, on which rests her typewriter. It is yet another example of choice offered by Arabella, who has not so much allowed Elinore to pick furniture and decoration as made her entirely responsible for the comfort and look of her blank slate of a room. Mary Poppins had a carpetbag. Arabella Cheyne has outbuildings and cupboards. These storage spaces are the counterpoint to the mostly blank walls and sparsely-furnished or empty rooms within the house at Fhairlach, which are that way in deference to Arabella's pursuit of perfection. Once each phase of the renovation work has finished and the dust and commotion have been cleared away, Arabella will unpack, arrange and hang, and rearrange, and get up at midnight to rearrange again at the urge of a passing inspiration. She likes to savour perfection in the light of dawn. The rooms will speak to her, she says, once they are revived and refreshed, and they will tell her exactly what painting should be hung above what table, and so on.

Meanwhile, everything on Elinore's bedroom list is supplied by the contents of the Fhairlach treasure troves, including fabric which Arabella takes to a sewing machine and brings back as a pair of curtains. Elinore has personally inspected and chosen every item. It is one of the most satisfying – no, *the* most satisfying thing she can remember doing, except perhaps for composing her ghost story. The paisley shawl from the Dower House is attached to a special rod and hung all by itself in her bathroom as a true work of art. Its colours look even more vibrant against the coral walls, and make the bathroom feel even warmer. Sir Gabriel and the Magic Men go up in her bedroom, and Elinore feels she has done right by them: they always deserved a freshly painted wall. They have company too, in the form of an oil painting of a Delft jug that holds an exuberant bunch of ox-eye daisies; the jug sits on a white-painted garden table. The picture radiates summery freshness, and reminds her of Susanna's bedroom and making a daisy chain for Usha. *Her* room is perfect, she thinks, and the austerity of the rest of the under-furnished house no longer strikes her as odd. Its freshness is enlivening and she can bring any friend to it with pride.

By the end of Elinore's second week at Fhairlach, the number of people around her whom she could confidently count as friends had reached eight, and those were only her peers, roughly speaking. She had begun to construct a post-Criven order of the universe, in which Arabella and Tom reigned jointly in the place of the sun, orbited by certain grown-ups: Mr and Mrs Patel, Dr and Mrs Berg, Lady Groule, Mrs Wattie, Henry and Marigold, and lately Mr and Mrs Lindsay at Mains of Airt and Mr and Mrs Patterson down the road. Other grown-ups were gradually populating a sort of surrounding constellation. This universe was finite and flat, designed to swivel and reveal another order in which Susanna and Usha were at the top; her new friends came below them and were dotted around in space with no order of rank, much as they lived along the Airt road: the four Lindsay boys, Louise Patterson and her twin brothers Mike and Andy, and Johnny Lamont.

The Lindsays had not a gnome among them. Elinore found this out the day after her arrival, when she and Arabella called in at Mains of Airt on their way to the Boddo Bridge shops. Vera was Mrs Lindsay, who had acted on Arabella's request to bring up dinner and breakfast all ready to eat before they arrived; she was in the habit of doing this. Happy, Sleepy, Bashful and Dopey were her sons Keith (Ginger), Wee Rob, Jim and Bruce; Mr Lindsay was the big, original Rob. They were a loud and cheerful lot, and Mr Lindsay, a burly man, was loudest of all. The barking and yelling of short, sharp names echoed around the house, steadings and yard all day long, as Lindsays ran about demanding each other's attention and Mr Lindsay demanded speed, more speed and improved attention to particulars on the part of his sons. His three collies were Moss, Mac and Jess, and their names blew around too in the general hail of monosyllables. The longest name in the place belonged to the Aberdeen Angus bull, who was called Schiehallion Imperial Gladiator, but only on the paper of his pedigree. "Yon's Glad," said Ginger, waving dismissively at the massive, glowering black beast. "Short for Gladys, 'cause he's as saft as butter. My mum got the name aff the TV."

Ginger shared a bedroom with Wee Rob and it housed a towering, toppling collection of comics, annuals, adventure story books and works of reference; ninety percent of the latter were out of date by at least two or three generations. Elinore was invited to view this library in depth, and she quickly found out the reason for Ginger's adoptive name. Obsessed with flying and determined to join the RAF, he had found a literary hero in Biggles, the pilot adventurer; he had also found the red-haired Ginger Hebblethwaite, a youngster who defied his father and ran away to become a pilot and joined Biggles' trusty team. All the male Lindsays had red in their hair, but Keith had the most, and he became Ginger overnight. To Elinore, he repeated his desire to buy every Biggles book, and his sorrow that Captain W.E. Johns was dead and beyond producing more than the almost one hundred titles in existence; and then he said she could borrow, one at a time, the eight he possessed.

Ginger took her further along the road to the Patterson house, an old manse, and knocked on the back door. When Mrs Patterson opened it, he said, "Hiya, Mrs Patterson, here's Elinore from Fhairlach," as if she were a delivery, and immediately scooted around the corner of the house to where other boys were audibly busy with something.

"Hello, Elinore, nice to meet you," said Mrs Patterson, who was dark-haired and tanned, wore bright pink lipstick and sounded English. "Come in, and I'll get Louise."

Louise? Ginger had only mentioned the names Mike and Andy in association with this house, along with a warning about the strong likelihood of ghoulies in the small church and graveyard next to the manse. Elinore followed Mrs Patterson through a large, untidy kitchen into a large, cluttered hall and waited while she went halfway up a staircase that had little heaps of clothing on most steps and called, "Louise! If you're up there, come down and meet a new friend."

A thud came from somewhere downstairs. A door in the hall opened and a tall, willowy girl with very long blonde hair came out. "I'm sorting out all that music Miss Dysart gave me," she told her mother, and then to Elinore, "Hi." She leaned against the doorjamb and smiled.

"Ginger brought Elinore along," said Mrs Patterson. "She's up at Fhairlach with Arabella. OK, I'll leave you two to it." She disappeared into the kitchen.

"Is your name Elinore Cheyne, like Arabella?" asked Louise, who was still leaning sideways against the door.

"No, I'm Elinore Crum. But she's sort of my aunt."

"Crum?" This seemed to activate Louise out of her languidness, and she stood upright. "Do you know Avril Abernethy? Are you going to go to our school?"

"Um, no," replied Elinore, in answer only to the first question. She wanted the conversation to move away immediately from the subject of her future.

"You have to meet Avril! She's called Biscuit, because of her name, and you could be Crumb because of yours. Crumb and Biscuit! Or Crummy! It's brilliant!"

Unable to link either of Avril Abernethy's names with biscuits, Elinore said nothing, but that did not matter because Louise was switched on now. "Names are *so* funny! Do you know about Engelbert Humperdinck, the real one?"

"The one on the radio?"

"No, *he's* not real. Really and truly. I just found out. Come and see." Louise went back into a sitting room that was dominated by a grand piano. Part of the floor and the seats of some armchairs were covered by sheet music, bound albums and stacks of LPs.

"Someone just gave all these to me," she explained, waving a hand. After proving to Elinore by means of a record of the opera *Hansel and Gretel* that Engelbert Humperdinck was really a 19th century German composer, Louise swerved into pop music and asked her what her favourite Radio One show was. Before Elinore could answer, she said, "Come upstairs and see my record player! And I got a new transistor for my birthday. When's your birthday?" That was that for the next two hours.

No one introduced Elinore to Johnny Lamont. After their first accidental meeting, she remembered overhearing Mike and Andy Patterson mention a Johnny whose tree house they were going to look at, but no one in her new circle had mentioned a Lamont house and a person of her own age in it.

On the Saturday afternoon after her arrival, Elinore was walking up the road to Fhairlach. She was talking to herself, counting off on her fingers all the topics and names of new places and people that she wanted to include in letters to Tom, Lady Groule, Susanna, Usha and the Ansketts. She also wanted to send a postcard of a castle, preferably Balmoral, to Mrs Wattie, and the same to Matthew Carr. This was going to be a big job and she wanted to start it right away. But not this evening: she had a date with secret agents in the sitting room at Mains of Airt, where the first episode of an eagerly-awaited espionage drama was going to air on television. The absence of television at Fhairlach was no great miss, thanks to the Lindsays and the Pattersons. She stopped walking: spy programmes constituted yet another topic of burning interest, but she had run out of fingers. "Drat, drat and double drat!" she said loudly.

"That's Dick Dastardly," came a small voice from the trees to her right.

Gnome, thought Elinore, and her tummy jumped. She looked up and down the birch-covered slope until she saw a boy sitting cross-legged at the foot of a tree. He blended with his surroundings as if he were a hen pheasant or a rabbit. As soon as she had caught his eye, he said, "I like Wacky Races too. Sometimes I call my dog Muttley."

"Where's your dog?"

"At home. I don't take her everywhere because she's a bit old." The boy got up and walked down through the trees to the road. He was smaller than Elinore, pale with dark shadows under his eyes, and slight compared with the Lindsay or Patterson boys. Under fine, mousey-brown hair, his face was the most serious-looking face that Elinore had ever seen on a boy, but not in a swotty way; more as though it had forgotten how to smile.

"My name's Elinore. What's yours?"

"Johnny. I know who you are – I know you're at Fhairlach. I saw you. Where did you come from?"

"Um – I was in Edinburgh. I'm here for my holidays." Elinore started walking up the road again, mainly to move away from the subject of her destination after the holidays. Johnny fell into step beside her and pinned the talk inescapably to Edinburgh.

"Have you been to the Camera Obscura? Or the Observatory? Or the Museum? I think I'd like to live in a museum. I'm going to Edinburgh University after I've been to school – I *think* I'm going, anyway. They've got a botanic garden in Edinburgh – have you been to it? You can see trees and things from *all over* the world." He stopped walking and looked at Elinore as if to confirm her appreciation of this information.

Elinore thought he was quite odd, but she could not dismiss him as a daftie. He knew about Edinburgh landmarks that she had only experienced in the pages of a book. Instead of no to everything, she said, "I've got a friend who lives near Edinburgh and he's got a whole wood in his garden. It's like a jungle and he told me it's got trees from other countries. And I've got another friend who loves trees and plants. She goes to the Botanic Garden."

Johnny looked at her in a straight way, no trace of a smile, and then he said, "I like trees and I like stars, but I don't know which ones I like the best. Did you know the trees are just stars on the ground? It's the same wi' the dandelions an' the wee daisies. They're the ones that fell oot o' the sky. It's gey windy up here, you know."

Elinore had no immediate answer to this. They rounded the last bend before Fhairlach came into view, and Johnny stopped walking again. "You could see a *lot* of stars up here," he said, pointing at the house. "You see the most when there aren't any lights roon' aboot. I like this place."

"I like it too," said Elinore. "I do see stars, but I don't know what they're called. I just know the moon." She felt stupid as soon as she had said that: who was the daftie now, talking as if the moon was hard to tell from any other light in the sky?

But Johnny just nodded, and said, "People think you're mental if you like to look at the moon. But I want a telescope. I could look at *a'thing* then, and nobody could say *a'thing* aboot it."

Elinore giggled, until she saw that Johnny was still serious. He turned away with a wave and said, "I have to go home now. See you."

"All right," said Elinore. Instead of going straight down the road, Johnny scrambled over a drystone dyke and set off down a field towards the shallow river that ran past Mains of Airt. Elinore suddenly thought of Biggles flying through the night sky, and shouted after him, "Do you know Ginger Lindsay?"

Johnny turned and waved, which could have meant anything. Elinore watched him walking down the sloping field until he disappeared from view.

"I just met a boy who likes trees and stars and the moon," Elinore told Arabella. "I think he's very clever, but really, he's quite odd too."

"Not if he likes planets and talks about them," said Arabella, who was reorganising her kitchen crockery cupboards. "Perhaps he's going to be another Patrick Moore. You'll see him on television and remember the day you met him. Now, talking of meeting people, will you be accompanying me to church tomorrow?"

Elinore's head spun. Never once had Arabella indicated that she was in favour of anything except avoidance of church, which, under the circumstances, was a relief and an enormous reassurance to Elinore.

Arabella carried on talking as she moved blue and white bowls from one shelf to another. "There's a fair chance you'll meet the children of the new minister. The church is the little one next to the Patterson's house. It hasn't been used for a while, because they couldn't find a minister to take on the job. He has to do three other churches, you know, and they're all in the back of beyond, so I expect we'll see him once a month. Better than nothing if it keeps the doors open. Anyway, I hear he's got a wife and some girls. What do you think?" She closed the cupboard doors and turned around. "Elinore, what a face! One would think you'd been sucking lemons."

"Do I *have* to go? You never ever *said* anything about going to church."

"Quite right, I didn't, and no, you don't have to go. I just thought you might be interested in some new faces, especially if they're about your age. The manse they live in isn't far off the Airt road end."

Instantly, the Begbie sisters came into Elinore's mind, and she recoiled from the idea of meeting any more children steeped in the word of God. On the other hand, she had to get to the bottom of this extremely upsetting revelation about Arabella. She stuck her hands in the pockets of her trousers and began.

"I thought you *weren't* religious," she said, "so *why* are you going to church?"

Arabella chuckled in a wicked, wicked way. "Oh, I'm very, *very* far from religious. I'm going to show my face in that wee old church down there because it's the only place where the Airt people get together as a community. If it closes its doors forever because no one ever turns up, we all lose something, even if we can't tell a hymnbook from a haddock. And that, I assure you, is the extent of my hypocrisy with respect to churchgoing."

"What's hypocrisy?"

"Going to church because you want people to think you're a fine, upstanding Christian and you might as well show off a new hat while you're at it. Some people go around doing terrible things and still show up in church even if they don't believe in God, because they do believe that just sitting in a pew will make them goody-goodies in the eyes of the world. They are called hypocrites. It's being two-faced."

Light dawned on Elinore. "Mrs Wattie said Mrs Caltrop was a two-faced auld bizzom. Is that a hypocrite?"

"That is an excellent definition of a female hypocrite. Who is Mrs Wattie?"

"She rescued me from the Caltrops when they were out. She was their cleaning lady, but then she got a lot of money, so she could run away from the Caltrops too. But I think she was going to go back and tell them off for being horrible evil people."

"And for being hypocrites. Indeed. Fascinating. Now I know who this mysterious lady is, the one whom Tom was hinting at so coyly. If you feel like it, we must sit down some day so you can tell me exactly how this astonishing rescue was carried out. But first, let's settle the church business. If you want to stay and amuse yourself here, that's fine; if you want to come with me, put on something better than trousers and comb your hair, and that will be fine too. I have a feeling all the Lindsays will be there, and the Pattersons. Perhaps even the boy you just met. What's his name?"

"Johnny. He didn't say his last name."

"Was he a wan, serious-looking boy, a bit thin and small?"

"Um, yes. What's wan?"

"Looking tired and pale, and not very well."

"He looked like that."

"Then his last name is Lamont, and he's the son of the gamekeeper who lives at Burnside of Airt, which is below here. Talking of the moon – do you like this?"

Arabella held out a shallow bowl, one of the scores of mismatched blue and white pieces in her cupboards. She had no such thing as a dinner service or a full set of anything that looked the same, whether for four, six, eight or more places. Eating with Arabella was a visual adventure in blue and white. Flying in the face of her austere adherence to the slow, patient building of perfection in empty white rooms, she called her plethora of blue and white china patterns the perfection of serendipity. This meant that whatever she found by chance in a charity shop or someone's attic or an antique shop or a foreign city would automatically be perfect when brought home and added to her collection. The bowl she showed Elinore had a simple depiction of a white hare standing upright at a large mortar and pestle. Around the outer edge, leaping hares were interspersed by the blocky characters of an oriental language.

"Is it Chinese, like my bag?" asked Elinore.

"No, Japanese. It shows the jade-white hare who lives on the moon. He could be a rabbit – it doesn't make any difference to the story. He's grinding the elixir of immortality."

"I know what elixir means. It's one of my favourite words because I like the sound of it. Immortal means you live forever."

"Correct. When I look at this bowl now, I think of Mercedes Wax mixing up stuff for ladies who want immortal beauty. Do you want to put it in your room?"

"Gosh, a hare in the moon! I really like that idea. I wonder if Johnny Lamont knows about *that*. I could show him if he ever comes here."

"Exactly. And if you see him at church tomorrow, you can tell him about it."

"All right, I'll *think* about going . . ."

By the time Elinore rose from her pew in Airt Church the next day and followed Arabella out, she was halfway to admitting that the past three-quarters of an hour had not been an unendurable waste of time that must never be repeated. First, everyone she knew, and at least half a dozen she did not, were in attendance too, hatted (except for Mrs Patterson, who played the organ) and suited and generally spruced up. If she had not gone, she would have been the odd one out.

Second, Mr Imrie, the new minister, and his family were quite unlike other associates of the pulpit whom she had met. He appeared to be much happier to stand out of his pulpit and chat with every person who came in, regardless of age, and introduce his family: wife and three girls, all of whom to Elinore looked like cream puffs. They had brownish-blonde fluffy hair, blue eyes and a rosy, happy look. They favoured pink and pastel blue in their dress, and ribbons in their hair; Mrs Imrie wore a hat with a floral ribbon around the crown. Mr Imrie himself was not quite a cream puff, being tall and spectacled, but he had lots of fair, wavy hair, and he smiled and laughed as much as the four other Imries. He shook Elinore's hand vigorously, as if she were a grown-up, and said, "Hello, what a pleasure to meet you – may I ask your name? Elinore. Rachel, Rachel – this is Elinore, who looks as if she might be in your class when school starts." He took his second youngest cream puff by the elbow, and she promptly put out her own hand, saying, "Hello! Pleased to meet you!" and beamed at Elinore. She was wearing a striped shift dress and white openwork sandals, both of which Elinore admired. It was occurring to Elinore that perhaps the unspeakable Begbies and McKendricks might have come from a religious planet not inhabited by people like the Imries.

The service was very short. Mr Imrie's sermon did not mention heaven, and Elinore could not recall later if he had even mentioned the word God, except in the Lord's Prayer and one other succinct effort of his own. His concern was the here and now, and the happiness and health of everyone whose home had Airt in the address.

He expressed his fervent hope that he could contribute something worthwhile to local wellbeing. And then Mr Imrie returned to the door to thank everyone even more enthusiastically than before (he repeated every name correctly too) and tell them how much he hoped to see them all in the same place three Sundays hence.

Elinore saw Ginger kicking stones down the path to the road, until Mrs Lindsay told him to stop scuffing his good shoes. He stuck his hands in his pockets and rocked backwards and forwards on his heels instead, grinning at Elinore. She went up to him and asked if he knew a boy called Johnny Lamont.

"Oh, aye."

"So, what's he like?"

"OK. He's aye spoutin' something. When they do a quiz at school, you mak sure to get him on your team, but he's no' a teacher's pet. Maybe he's a bother to them wi' a' his questions."

"Who?" said Andy, coming within earshot.

"Johnny Lamont," said Elinore. "You never told me he lives here too, but I met him yesterday."

Ginger and Andy looked at each other. Ginger dropped his head and started nudging stones again. "He can't always come over," said Andy. "And then he gets here and he says he has to go home again just when you're getting going with something. Mum's always trying to get him to stay for tea."

"It's his ma," said Ginger, still looking down at his feet. "She's near deid. That's what our Mum says."

"Mine too," said Andy, who also began shuffling his feet.

"Ginger! You coming over to our house?" came a shout from Mike Patterson, who was running across the grass that separated the church from the old manse.

"Aye! But not in this get-up, or Mum'll skin me. I'll be back in a wee minute. Seeya later too, Elinore!" He was off, and Andy too, as if they were running away from more questions.

"Elinore! Don't go away!" It was Louise, with the Imrie girls in tow. "This is Rebecca, Rachel and Ruth, and this is Elinore. She *loves* music too. We're all going to my house, are you coming? Mummy says we can have a picnic outside instead of proper lunch, and she'll take everyone home in the car afterwards."

The Imrie girls smiled at Elinore, and they all set off for the old manse.

"Do you live next door to here?" one of the girls asked Elinore. Louise answered in her stead.

"No, Elinore lives up the hill. You should see her room! It's *so* beautiful, and it's *so* clean and tidy. I'm a messy pig."

All the Imrie girls giggled nicely at this, and the youngest, Ruth, said, "Mummy says I'm a messy wee piglet!"

"Me too," chorused Rachel and Rebecca. "But it's hard when you've got lots of books and you've just flitted," added Rebecca. "I want a new bookcase for my birthday, a great big one."

A fellow bookworm. Elinore put aside all reservations about religiosity.

"All right, I'll come too," she said. "I can write all my letters later."

"Oh, do you have penfriends too?" asked Rebecca eagerly. She appeared to be a little older than Elinore.

"No. What are they?"

"People you write to who live in different countries, and they write back. I've got five. You can see all the letters I've got when you come to my house. I was keeping them in a chocolate box, but I've got so many now I need a new box. The stamps are really interesting, but I don't collect stamps, I just keep them all in case *Blue Peter* wants them."

"Me too," said Rachel and Ruth at once. "We save *everything* for Blue Peter."

Elinore studied these newcomers covertly. They might be cream puffs to look at, but their filling seemed to include brains too. They had also supplanted her as newcomers: *she* was a local now, being introduced as if she had lived here all along. So far, giving up nearly an hour of her precious Sunday to sit in the dispiriting stone interior of Airt Church and breathe that peculiar musty, chill air had been *interesting* at least. She was almost ready to concede that Arabella had been right about that.

31

The deeper the tentative roots, the farther the reach of the wings. It was an irony of which Elinore was unaware as she sat at her desk and wrote letters and postcards to many people. She only knew that the more at home she became at Fhairlach and around Airt, the greater her desire to share the place with her friends elsewhere.

She pictured a delivery system that made use of Airt's most abundant natural resource. From the window of her upstairs room in a house on the top of a hill in the north of the country (not too far, as the crow flew, from the very top of island Britain), she would throw her letters and postcards onto the wind, and they would at once sprout wings and fly to each address, distance no object. On the other hand, she fancied that the wind might also carry word to Susanna and Usha of Elinore's daily pleasure in new friends – so many in such a tiny, strung-out place in the hills! – and make them feel neglected and forgotten. It was a point of honour, therefore, to write at least once a week and reply promptly. Rebecca Imrie had shown her the chocolate box bulging with the fruits of pen-friendship, but Elinore did not want to add any more correspondence just yet. At the back of her mind was the knowledge that she did not *live* at Fhairlach, regardless of what other people said or thought; she had been brought there to stay until something happened. The future was still like one of Arabella's white, empty rooms. To introduce herself to a penfriend would require explanations and descriptions. As Rebecca had enthusiastically explained, that was the point of it all: to learn about other countries and ways of living through the humdrum details of another person's life. The school, family, holidays-in-Spain-or-at-the-seaside, dogs-cats-and-ponies, Christmas-tree-and-Easter-egg, exam-passing and parent-directed stuff which had never filled Elinore's life anyway. She had no intention of inventing it.

In their weekly flurries of letters coming and going, Rebecca and Elinore were both dependent on a vital link, a person whose arrival was far more important than that of Santa Claus. Mr Aitken the postie was the one to wait for eagerly and impatiently, and he came six mornings a week. On the seventh morning, he went to church in Boddo Bridge, and on the seventh afternoon he inspected his garden and beehives minutely and allowed himself a period of inactivity on a bench, where he read a newspaper, smoked his pipe and greeted every passer-by over the wall. Mr Aitken's flowerbeds were dazzling in summer, and his vegetable and fruit patch a cornucopia. Elinore had seen the heavy-headed blooms, the giant jewels of strawberry and raspberry, and massive green things she could not name, crammed into a small garden where all trace of lawn had been dug up; she had heard the bees droning from one pollen lode to another. An inchoate connection took root in her mind between Mr Aitken, the bees, the glories of his garden and the bulging postbags that he drove around for many, many miles in his red van. He became synonymous with growth and harvest, helping Elinore tend her garden of friends.

Naturally, he knew every single person and their business. After the Imries had moved into the manse, he was quick to tell Rebecca that her penfriend hobby was admirable and doing a fair bit to keep him employed. Having seen Elinore in the company of the Imrie girls a few times in passing, it was natural for him to think that the airmail letter he handed her one Saturday morning meant that Elinore had taken up the same hobby, especially as he had already delivered a number of letters personally addressed to her in girlish hands.

"Aye, I'll be needing a bag just for you young ladies' post, that's what it's coming to," he said, waving the letter at Elinore. "Then they'll need to gie me a bigger van. Aye, I can see it now. You just carry on makkin' your friends a' aroon the globe and maybe I'll even get a bigger pension oot o' it. Bye-bye til Monday, then, Elinore."

Elinore did not recognise the handwriting on the envelope, and saw no return address on the back. The postmark was blurred, especially over the stamp, which was small and nondescript. Her first thought was that Rebecca must have arranged a penfriend for her as a surprise. She decided to prolong the intrigue and take it with her unopened to Louise's house, where she could read it aloud. She and Rebecca were going to spend the morning there, supposedly helping Louise clean out her bedroom. Mrs Patterson had promised to redecorate it, but only if Louise would sort out her possessions once and for all. The big old manse was untidy from top to bottom, and full of half-finished tasks that had been dropped in favour of bursts of inspiration or simply out of boredom. The Patterson parents were both musical (Mr Patterson owned two record shops), and Mrs Patterson was busy writing words and music for a Christmas show. Creativity took precedence over cleaning, and the drifts of possessions in Louise's bedroom would have gone on accumulating and being shoved from one corner to another if Louise had not been struck with envy at the sight of Elinore's room. Louise had lured her friends into helping by saying she might want to give away some books, records and bric-a-brac.

Mr Aitken had also handed Elinore a bundle of post for Arabella. She left this on the kitchen table, where Arabella liked to open letters while drinking tea. Then she called goodbye from the foot of the stairs. Arabella was walking around and standing in each corner of a bedroom, listening. The floorboards had been finished and it was time to learn just what the revived, refreshed room really wanted to have in it.

Half an hour later, Arabella was reading a letter that had been addressed to her, but not written for her.

> *Dear Elinore,*
> *I hope you're having lovely hols in Scotland! I'm having a lovely time in Dallas but I don't think you would like it AT ALL!* [This bit was particularly clever, Melba had thought.]
> *Not to worry. We shan't be coming to drag you away from the back of beyond anytime soon.* [A useful Americanism, although it did not exactly mean 'never', as Melba had employed it.]
> *It's so hot here you wouldn't believe it and it's so humid I have to do my hair every single day. <u>Such</u> a lot of work. In fact I am in the beauty salon right now. With air conditioning, I can sit here in comfort and have my tootsies taken care of and drop you a line at the same time. Then I'm going to have a little snooze while my fingernails are done and then I can post this to you on the way home. Dwayne and I are going out to dinner tonight with his boss at an Italian restaurant! Isn't that exciting? I still don't know what dress I'm going to wear because I have SO many lovely new ones thanks to Dwayne. I told you he was a very nice man, didn't I?* [Melba could not resist that.] *And guess what he's going to buy me for my birthday this year? A brand new car all of my own! I haven't decided what colour I want yet, but I think white with cherry red seats would be very smart. I want a convertible, which means that I can drive around with the top down on sunny days and it's always sunny here, not like dreary old Scotland! Isn't that the most marvellous birthday gift? Lucky me!*
> *I must stop here because it's time for my manicure now. Toodle-oo! Be good! Don't argue or be obstinate because it*

might upset Arabella and I don't think she is quite so nice and forgiving as the Caltrops. And be good at school.

Bye-bye!
Mummy

Arabella sipped her tea and pondered the Christian precept of unconditional love towards all, particularly those who do harm, and the concept of karma, which, although not yet part of fashionable discourse in Scotland, was not unknown to her. It was pleasant to contemplate a variety of appalling fates and reincarnations for Melba Crum. Then she went upstairs to the small room, something between an alcove and an anteroom, that was between the half landing and her bedroom. It was her study, as opposed to her workroom downstairs. Here was a desk and another telephone, and her address books. She took out the one she kept for anyone who mattered to her in Airt, and dialled the number of the headmaster of Boddo Bridge School. His number had been added to her book very recently.

"Good afternoon, Mr Duthie, this is Arabella Cheyne at Fhairlach. I hope I'm not disturbing you. I'm calling to confirm that Elinore *will* be starting school at the end of the holidays. You can put me down as her guardian. Yes, I am a relation, but to what precise degree I have yet to work out. Families can be so very complex, can't they? Yes, *quite* right, we can sort out the fiddle-faddle later on, the only thing that matters is Elinore's wellbeing and education. Patterson? Do you mean Louise and her brothers? Yes, just down the road, and in fact Elinore is there right now. She'll be thrilled to know she's starting in the same class as Louise. Yes, it *is* a great relief to me too, and thank you so much for smoothing the way. Goodbye!"

Arabella put the letter from Melba into one of her desk drawers, and returned to the business of furnishing the bedroom that she was about to elevate from emptiness to comfort. Something was advising her to put this job ahead of completing the dining room, which had been number one on the agenda until six o'clock that morning. It was the same form of early-morning advisory that had led her to semi-furnish Elinore's room before leaving for Welkinlaw, and, long before that, to look closely into the bit of family gossip that had come her way about a young child having gone to stay with the Caltrops in Edinburgh. Nevertheless, her mind continued to work on two tracks, like a well-schooled dressage horse (another form of perfection she admired).

The letter was for Elinore, but addressed to her: did that mean that another letter had been addressed to Elinore, but written to her? Double or single bed? Twin beds? Elinore had run off perfectly happily without mentioning any letter from Melba. Twin divan beds could be pushed together if necessary. Elinore would have opened a letter from Melba on the spot. The small sandalwood chest was coming to mind, and where was that armchair in a striped chintz with the same colour as the wood? Mr Aitken liked to hand Elinore her own letters as a kind of separate delivery; he would not have bundled her post with Arabella's. Chest of drawers – the tall rosewood one with brass corners and fittings? Why was this room taking on a rather masculine feel? What would be best in the long run: letting Elinore read the letter and thereby making no attempt to buffer its careless yet ingenious cruelty, or telling Elinore that Melba had written to her, Arabella, to say that Fhairlach would be a better home, all things considered, for as long as Elinore wished? Carved sandalwood, campaign furniture, stripes – all right, this room *was* expressing itself in decidedly masculine tones, so no dainty bedside tables, how about those two large rattan boxes with mahogany lids – hmm, now we're edging into the colonial. Perhaps the letter should be left to ferment overnight. Brass reading lamps, no silk shades. No doubt the early-morning advisory would then present something for her to act on. Enough solid brown, even if it was wood: a Persian rug on the floor, where was that hunting rug, wonderful mounted bowmen on an ivory ground. Yes, better to wait for clarity. Or would a kilim be better – the Turkish one with broad stripes, echoing the armchair pattern? And it might be an idea to have a quiet word with Mr Aitken *before* Elinore rushed at him hungering for letters, which would be difficult: all letters from America regardless of addressee to be put straight into Arabella's hands.

Enough! That was a deluge of furnishings, compared with her usual practice of one item a day for days or weeks. Something was up. She would bring everything into the room and leave it to absorb them until it was ready to consider other additions. A week or two, a month – a room must be listened to and never rushed in the matter of perfection. The telephone rang, as if to signal formally that this period of mulling was over.

☙

"Do you want any of my dolls?" asked Louise, showing Elinore a jumbled mass of pink plastic limbs in a laundry basket."

"I don't like dolls," said Elinore, who could not understand the attraction of such repellent objects.

"All right, you can look at these ornaments instead, 'cause I don't want any of them."

Elinore saw a recumbent unicorn, white china with a shiny gold horn, looking very lost among jewellery boxes that resembled little grand pianos, and musical boxes that were round or square, all bejewelled and velvet lined, doubling as jewellery boxes. "I like that unicorn. Why don't you want it?"

"I just don't. My granny gave me all that stuff and I don't like *her* very much. She's always nagging me about practising piano and doing everything perfectly. She says I'll turn into a tomboy and then I'll be sorry later. Mummy makes me tie up my hair and wear a dress when I go to see her." Louise screwed up her face. "My other granny isn't like that. She sends me great big birthday cakes in the post!"

"What?" said Elinore. "Proper birthday cakes? How come they don't get all smashed up?" She was thinking of Marigold Anskett's gorgeous chocolate confection.

"Because they've got icing all over. Daddy says you need a road drill to get into the soft part. I hate the icing, but the cake inside is nice. Do you like feeding birds? I give all the icing to the birds, because my birthday's in winter. Mike and Andy get birthday cakes like that, but they eat them all up and Ginger always helps them."

"You mean they get their cakes in the post too?"

"Yes. You can send *anything* in the post. Even animals, I think."

Elinore decided to ask Mr Aitken what exactly could be delivered in his red van. This reminded her of the letter in the back pocket of her trousers, and she pulled it out. "When's Rebecca coming? I want to show her this."

"I think she'll be slow, because she's coming on her bike this time. Is it a penfriend?"

"I don't know. I didn't ask for one, but I think maybe Rebecca got me one. I was going to show it to her and see if she could guess who sent it."

"Why not show me? Rebecca's a slowcoach on her bike and she might not get here for ages and ages." It was true. The Imrie cream puffs, although never less than willing to join in, were not as hardy or active as the others. Louise looked languid and willowy, but her long legs pushed her bicycle rapidly up and down the Airt road, and she could outrun Ginger Lindsay easily.

"All right."

Elinore's tummy went into a spasm as she recognised Melba's handwriting, which had not been on the envelope – the envelope that was clearly addressed to her, despite the salutation and contents of the letter. "It's from my –" she began to say, and stopped.

"Is it from one of *your* grannies?" asked Louise. "You never tell us about anyone except your Aunt Arabella."

Elinore did not reply.

Dear Arabella,

How terribly kind of you to scoop up Elinore. My life is frantically busy now, and I will soon have lots of new responsibilities as Mrs Dwayne McMonagle, so it's a great relief not to have to worry about her. I'm sure she's deliriously happy to be wearing wellingtons again for most of every day.

Please feel free to do anything you like with her. I know I have some papers somewhere, birth certificate, that kind of thing, which I'll send on as soon as I find them. Dallas is such a whirl of a place to be that my poor little head has been spinning for weeks!

About the birth certificate. I really, <u>really</u> want you and Elinore to feel happy about a future together, at least until she's old enough to make her own way in the world. It might help to make her more <u>yours</u> if I tell you she isn't mine. Or Hector's for that matter. I don't know whose child she is! A foundling – isn't that the right name? Anyway, she was left on a doorstep, ours actually, and it was during Hector's existential period or transcendental – so confusing, and he's been dead so long now, two or three <u>years</u>, that all these scientific words have just vanished from my poor head. The point is he absolutely had to escape from Society and so we went to a cottage in some awful glen in Perthshire straight after the wedding. A croft. It was terribly romantic at first, but then not so.

I really don't know how it got there, the baby that is, because we'd gone off for a picnic and there it was when we got back. I was overjoyed! The answer to a prayer! You see, I really really thought a baby would be a lovely thing to have, quite a lot of fun actually, I <u>was</u> only just 16 after all, and everyone says it's so good for a marriage. But Hector simply wasn't keen on the idea, and he kept saying I couldn't have *a baby because I'd lose my figure. But a baby on the doorstep takes care of that, doesn't it? And a few other things. Once I knew all about the disgusting things I'd escaped, truly a fate worse than death, I wouldn't have anything to do with it <u>ever</u> and it was <u>such</u> a relief that a ready-made baby had come along.*

At first Hector wanted me to put it back, even though he couldn't say where <u>exactly</u> to put it back, but the very next week he had a letter from his horrid mama, telling him about Ermine Crum's will, and naturally he changed his mind in five minutes! Who wouldn't? The rest was quite easy. No one in the family had seen me for simply ages, and I just stayed out of sight for a while. And then we moved to Criven anyway, so it didn't matter.

As soon as I heard that you'd taken Elinore to stay with you (and by the way Mrs Caltrop gave me a piece of paper with your address on it, at least, I hope this is your address, because she said she got it from a man called Tom something), I remembered a delightful saying I've learned in Dallas. It's called "<u>passing the goodness along</u>". (I do LOVE Texans!) I thought to myself, if I just tell Arabella everything right now, she won't feel the slightest bit worried or guilty about having Elinore all to herself, and then we can all be happy. And I'll be passing the goodness along too! It seems that Elinore just pops up where people want her to be.

Must stop now, because it's time for my manicure. I'm being introduced to Dwayne's boss and his wife at dinner tonight! Dwayne says I'm a huge asset, especially because I'm English. Isn't that sweet?

Do write if you have anything to say.

Best wishes,
Melba

It was the sixth morning of August. The sun had burned off the early mist hours ago and the air was already warm. The garden was alive with birdsong under a blue, blue sky. Mrs Patterson sat at the grand piano by an open window, one hand holding a pencil over a music manuscript sheet, the other trying out keys and chords. She was so intent that at first she heard no commotion upstairs. But the commotion moved downstairs into the hall, outside the closed door of the sitting room, and gradually she attuned to it as something other than expressions of girlish joy over trinkets and pop star posters. She put down the pencil and went to investigate.

"Louise! You can't be cleaning your room if you're making that racket down here," she said. Then she saw Elinore huddled on the bottom step of the stairs; her face was white and teary. "Elinore, are you sick?"

"No, she isn't, she just got upset, and I'm trying to *help* her, and she won't *let* me," cried Louise, hopping in exasperation. "She wants to go home, but she just got here, and Rebecca isn't even here yet. She's being like Johnny Lamont!"

"Enough, Louise!" said Mrs Patterson sharply. "I don't want to hear that about Johnny again." She crouched down by Elinore, and realised that her eyes were dilated and her breathing rapid. A mental list of sudden-onset, highly communicable diseases of childhood immediately presented itself. "Elinore, if you're sick, you have to tell me so we can get you home and call the doctor. Have you got a pain somewhere?"

Elinore nodded mutely, and Louise burst out in impatience, "Mummy, she was reading a letter and she got all *upset!* That's not being *sick!*"

Finally, Mrs Patterson saw the blue, white and red corners of an airmail envelope poking from Elinore's clenched fist. "Oh, my word – have you had bad news, Elinore?" Elinore nodded again, and, slightly shocked, Mrs Patterson was on the point of asking who on earth it was who could have broken the bad news to a child that way. But she restrained her curiosity and stood up. "All right. I think you need to tell Arabella, and if you don't feel well enough to walk up the road, I'll run you up there in the car, quick as a wink."

This jolted Elinore out of her huddled state. She was being a nuisance, she had been crying and she was going to cry again if she could not keep it in, she was ruining a day of fun for Louise and Rebecca, and now Mrs Patterson had to leave her piano work to drive her home. It was too much and everyone would be fed up with her in the end. She stood up very quickly and said, "I can walk, I'm fine, honestly. I'm sorry, I didn't mean . . ." Her words sounded tiny and far off in her own ears; then nausea suddenly rose as a darkening grey mist came down, and she fainted onto the hall floor.

When Elinore came to, her first sensation was of time having slipped, sending her back in Edinburgh to lie again on a strange sofa with anxious faces hovering above. Edinburgh. Caltrops. People who pushed her around and locked her up. She had to escape. Gradually, the restraining hands and soothing voices matched themselves to faces with reassuring names: Arabella, tucking a blanket around her, and Mrs Patterson, about to place another wrung-out cold facecloth on Elinore's right cheekbone, which was throbbing painfully.

"Ah, you're with us again, Elinore," said Arabella. "And Dr Simpson will be here any minute too."

"What happened to me?"

Arabella's eyes met those of Mrs Patterson. "You had a shock and you fainted, which is a perfectly natural reaction."

"Especially when it's a big, nasty shock," said Mrs Patterson, who was still dumbfounded at the contents of the letter she had read.

"Yes, exactly. And you hit your cheek on the newel post. Do you remember what you were doing before you fainted?"

"Um . . . I was in Louise's room. She said I could have a unicorn."

"Yes! I want you to have it! Unicorns are magic, so it'll help you get better quickly," came a shaky, sniffly voice from elsewhere in the room.

"Please, please get better soon, Elinore," came another trembling voice. Louise and Rebecca were squashed together in an armchair in miserable support of each other; Louise was chewing the ends of her very long hair and Rebecca was attacking a fingernail.

Elinore lay silent, puzzling over the full-stop role of the unicorn in her memory. What came afterwards? A letter. Something in the letter that was unbelievable, incredible, but nevertheless capable of jumping out and punching her in the stomach. At once, she stopped trying to think backwards or forwards.

Dr Simpson arrived. Mrs Patterson shooed the girls out of their armchair and closed the door on Arabella and Elinore. As he bent over her, Dr Simpson reminded Elinore of Henry Anskett's spaniel Polly (even though his head could have done with a lot of Polly's hair), because he had large, alert brown eyes and quick, precise movements, and he was cheerful; if he had possessed a tail, it would have wagged. In fact, he appeared delighted to have had to rush from his home to an unconscious child on a Saturday morning. He opened a big black case that was most ingeniously filled, Elinore thought, with essential medical supplies, and proceeded to examine a great deal more than her forehead. He inspected her arms and even rolled up her trousers to inspect her shins; this resulted in a satisfied "Hmmm!" (A bird flushed, perhaps, if he had been a spaniel.) A few murmured questions and answers went between him and Arabella, and then he asked Elinore about other fainting episodes, her appetite and whether she ran around a lot every day or felt tired, and so on. He took a syringe from his ingenious black case and drew blood from Elinore; she kept her head turned away and it was not that bad. Finally, he took her hand and patted it, saying it was a pleasure to meet her and that he would look forward to seeing her again in his surgery very soon. When he left the room with Arabella, Louise and Rebecca came tiptoeing in with tragic expressions, as if Elinore were a young Victorian heroine about to expire of consumption on this very sofa.

Elinore felt she must reassure them.

"I'm not *dying*," she said. "Honestly! Dr Simpson says he'll see me very soon, so I'm not going to turn into a ghost. And anyway, you said you were giving me that magic unicorn."

Louise and Rebecca burst into tears.

In the absence of a sofa at Fhairlach, Elinore lay on her own bed, propped on three pillows. A painful lump was still swelling and spreading on her cheek.

Clump, clump, clump on the bare staircase. Arabella was bringing up a tray with something resembling a late lunch for them both.

"Do you know what a dumb waiter is?" Arabella asked as she pushed the bedroom door open with a foot. "It is not a mute person who serves food."

Elinore thought about it. "A robot waiter?"

"Close, remarkably close. A dumb waiter is a little lift for things like this tray. If I were rich and more ingenious, I might have installed one in this house. My sister has two of them, one for laundry and one for food. But then, her kitchen is in the basement and her dining room on the second floor or is it the third? She has people running around after her, so I suppose she needs the dumb waiters to keep them from getting fed up with carrying things up and down the house all day, because then they'd go on strike or run away to work for someone else. Personally, I'd run away from her after half a day."

"What's her name? What kind of house does she live in?"

"Her name is Elspeth and she lives in one of those grand terraced houses in London. Tall, white, with a portico as big as a bedroom. Elspeth isn't like me. She's even grander than her house and she disapproves of me. My philosophies will never blend nicely with her dining room or her drawing room, no matter how many different decorators she hires."

"If she's your sister, does that mean she's my – my . . ." Elinore fell silent and looked out of the window.

"Yes, it does. We *are* your relations, Elinore. The correct term is adoptive, but you don't need to bother with that, they are just *yours*. You have a fair number of them besides Elspeth and me. None of them has anything in common with a Caltrop." She set down the tray and pulled the white wicker chair over to the bed. "Or a Crum," she added, seating herself. "Now, let's eat, and have a talk about what's what. Mmm, potted hough and oatcakes! And these are beef and tomato sandwiches. Just what Dr Simpson would order for you."

Elinore managed a smile. "That's funny, Mrs Chisholm gave me the same kind of sandwiches when I fainted outside her house."

"Sensible woman. You didn't end up with concussion then, did you?"

"No, I didn't hit my head."

"Well, you don't have it now either. What you do have is mostly shock from a nasty whack to the soul." Arabella took a large bite of potted hough on oatcake and said "Mmmm" again.

Elinore lay back on her pillows and treated Arabella to one of her frowns. "Is that what Dr Simpson said?" She touched her expanding cheekbone carefully. "*She* said things about my soul. Is it in my face or in my head?"

"It is everywhere and nowhere in you all at once. It is invisible, and yet its existence is attested to by thousands of years of philosophy. Dr Simpson is most unlikely to mention the word soul in any diagnosis, but he's a good doctor and he'll know at once when a soul is ailing or wounded, even if his kind of medicine doesn't necessarily bring a cure. Elinore, don't look at me like that, I feel like a criminal in the dock. If you were a judge in robes and wig, you'd be terrifying. Here, eat this sandwich. Then you can't glare at me."

Elinore smiled again, broadly this time. "Sometimes I don't know what you're talking about."

"I'm nourishing your brain. Beef sandwiches can only do so much. Back to your soul: if you mean that Caltrop woman was talking about your soul, just take it for granted that anything coming out of her mouth was perverted nonsense. No one has any business saying things about your soul unless they're nice things. Mr Imrie might very well talk about the soul, and you may listen to him. You might find some useful nuggets of principle in his talk."

"I don't want a soul if it makes me religious."

"I wouldn't either. The business of the soul is to help you find the things you love in life and to be as happy as you possibly can be. Happy, Elinore! Are you happy right now, at this moment?"

Elinore's smile vanished and her head dropped. She clenched her fists, knowing that she could start crying again too easily.

"No, of course not – because you've had a big shock and it hurt you. That's what I meant by a whack to the soul. You're very good with words. Can you tell me exactly what it was in that letter that hurt you? Was it one thing or two things or more? This is where we have to start, to make you feel better, and that's what Dr Simpson says too." Arabella leaned forward intently.

"Well . . ." said Elinore, still not looking up. Her voice trembled but she got the words out. "If Mummy and Hector didn't have me, if they just found me, I don't know who I am. I'm not anything. I don't know where I'm *from*. I don't know where I'm *supposed* to be."

"Yes, I understand. Are you upset that you're not in America with Melba and Dwayne?" Arabella had vowed that she would never again use any term denoting "mother" to Elinore where Melba was concerned.

Elinore raised her head sharply. "No! I don't want to go there *ever*. I was scared they were going to come and get me and take me away. And I hate that man, he's stupid. I never want people to think he's my –" Her brows drew together again.

"Aha! Your soul is talking. All that was hanging over you, wasn't it? It's gone now – pouff! It will not happen, and I will never, never let it happen, and neither will other people who care about you. You can trust that absolutely."

"Tom said that. He used to say to trust him because he was a lawyer. He said it quite a lot."

Arabella half rose from her chair and her eyebrows rose too. "Tom said *what*? Balderdash!" She sat down again. "Actually, only half of it is balderdash. Pay attention, Elinore: you can trust Tom one hundred per cent *except* for his cooking or his kitchen, but *not* because he's a lawyer. I can't have you growing up thinking that every lawyer is trustworthy. But we can deal with that later. I'll make sure you have plenty of Dickens and Trollope to read, and other fine tutors in human nature, including the nature of lawyers. Now, where were we? Another sandwich for you? We're out of Ribena, sorry, but try this. It's called tonic water. Most people drink it only with alcohol, which means they miss a fine drink for all hours and occasions. All right, back to your soul. Would you say that your soul is hurting because you've found out that you don't come from the place or the people you thought you came from?"

"Yes."

"Where do you *like* to be?"

"Here. I just want to keep staying here. I mean, I want to *live* here."

"Thank goodness for that. This *is* your home now: this house, and Airt, and a lot more besides. And no one can remove you unless you want to be removed. Does that make you feel better?"

"Oh, yes. But I still don't know where I *came* from. Maybe someone is looking for me, and they'll never know I'm here."

"But if you stay in one place for a good while, I mean right here, at least until you're grown up, they're more likely to find you, aren't they?"

Elinore agreed. Arabella was talking sense, despite the gobbledegook bits. She tried expressing more of her new worries.

"I know I've got a home, but I don't have a story any more. I wish I had a story like someone who's royal. Like Princess Anne. *She* knows who she is because it's all written down in history books and she lives in the same place where all her ancestors lived. She's got her own *story*."

"Ah, I see. The kind of story that has ancestors in it, and places. A castle or two, perhaps?"

"Yes, because even if Princess Anne goes away from Buckingham Palace, she goes to her *own* places, like Balmoral. Everyone else in her family went there. I just want to be in a proper story of my own with all the things that don't keep moving around. And then everyone will know who I am and I won't have to keep *explaining*. I hate explaining. I hate it when normal people ask me things, like Susanna and Usha. And Louise."

"Might I suggest borrowing a story until you find one of your own? You have a proper home right here; you also have proper relations in their own homes, such as that sister of mine in London. Those are all yours – you simply haven't met any of them yet except me. Did you have relations, grandparents and aunts and uncles and so on, when you stayed with Hector and Melba? And I *don't* mean those unspeakable people in Edinburgh."

"No. I asked Mummy why not, but she didn't want to tell me. My friends in Criven had them."

"So, you haven't really lost a story, have you? You were all by yourself anyway, even if you were with Hector and Melba. I think you're actually in a story of your own right now: you're a princess who was kidnapped and put to sleep, and now you've woken up and you don't know what's what."

Elinore's head came up and she looked at Arabella. "Really . . . ?"

"All the best magic and mystery stories have a lost person, don't they? Or a mysterious absence of parents. They always turn out well in the end. Who knows what kind of ancestors you might have? Meanwhile, you've got a perfectly respectable story to be going on with while you're at school and making new friends. You're starting afresh. You can tell people whatever you want, whatever makes you feel comfortable. You live with your Aunt Arabella at Fhairlach because . . ." Arabella shrugged. "The rest is up to you. You can tell them the truth or say Hector and Melba were both eaten by the same bear, or they went exploring together and fell off the edge of a mountain or they went east and got thrown into a pit of man-eating tigers – anything you like. Mrs Patterson and Dr Simpson know what Melba said in that letter, but no one else does, and they will never breathe a word unless you give them permission. You can tell Louise and Rebecca that you got a shock when you read that Melba was going to get married again. *You* are the author of Elinore Crum's story, Elinore Crum!"

"Gosh . . ." said Elinore. She looked out of the window again. Only the very tops of a couple of hills were visible from her bed, and all the rest was sky. "So, I could just say that I live here because I didn't want to go to America with Mummy, and I don't have to say anything about Hector. I don't really remember him anyway."

What a blessing, and what a pity Texas is not known for its grizzly bears, thought Arabella, but perhaps a kindly deity will arrange for Melba to meet a rattlesnake, or fall down an oil well.

"And I could talk about aunts and uncles and other people if you tell me how many I've got," continued Elinore.

"A legion of them. We can visit them, and one or two might very well decide to visit us, especially when they hear that an interesting young lady who writes ghost stories is now in residence. So, tell me, is your soul feeling rather better now, even if it has no precise place in your body?"

"A bit better. But I still have a big question, about who I really belonged to. And I have another big question, about why they didn't want me."

"Unfortunately, I don't possess the right kind of magic for finding answers to those questions. We must wait and see, and leave the door open for them – the answers, I mean. But I think it's important not to let the questions become bigger than you are, though."

"What do you mean?"

"Well, if you think about who and why too much, it might stop you being happy here and now. If you start worrying about it, you should talk about it or go and do something you love doing."

"I love doing lots of things."

"I know. What do you feel like doing for the rest of this afternoon? No running around, no tiring yourself out."

Elinore's eyes wandered around her room. "Can I have a duster for my new unicorn? He's quite dirty and he should be shiny. And I want to finish the Biggles book that Ginger lent me, so I can get another one from him. I don't feel like reading about Daisy right now. She just goes round visiting people's houses. Oh! The spy programme! I was going to watch it with the Lindsays tonight. Can I still go?"

"Hmmm, a spy programme . . . does that qualify as medicine for the soul?"

"Yes, yes, it does! It's really exciting. And the spies go to interesting places in the world. I don't want to miss any bits. I think I'm fine now." Elinore swung her legs off the bed and stood up.

"The miracle of a good beef sandwich," said Arabella. "All right, I'll walk down to the farm with you, and I'll pick you up afterwards in the Land Rover. One walk is enough today, I think.

༄

Later, Arabella summoned Elinore to the dining room for further instruction about the soul. The dining room doubled as a library, and one entire wall was covered with floor to ceiling bookshelves – white, of course. It held a round table but no chairs, for Arabella had yet to find half a dozen in the perfect style and she had no intention of giving a dinner party anyway. Elinore came in and saw a large book on the table open at a full page, full colour illustration.

"Eeww, what's *that*? Is it a ghoulie?"

"It's one artist's idea of a man whose soul is hurting. I wondered if it could be a picture of what you felt like today."

Elinore considered. "Um, yes. It's like he wants to scream but he can't get it out. It was like that for me, and I couldn't tell Louise what was wrong. Did he get a big shock too?"

"More or less. It's a world-famous picture and it's called *The Scream*, funnily enough."

"Gosh! I guessed!"

"Indeed. Utter brilliance, as I keep telling you. Now listen, if ever you know you feel like the man in that picture, it means that your soul has had a whack. You mustn't keep it inside like that man. I can't have you ending up with a face like his. You'll scare the living daylights out of everyone, Mr Aitken will be too frightened to deliver the post and I'll end up with a bad reputation throughout the county."

Elinore giggled. "I know. You said I had to tell somebody or do something that's fun."

"Correct. Do both. And will you remember this picture?"

"Oh, yes, I will. It's called *The Scream* and it's *horrible*. When are we going to walk down to the farm?"

Arabella allowed herself a small portion of congratulations on her handling of a unique emergency. She did have a philosophy for child-rearing, but until now it had been just that: a philosophy untested in practice, a theory based on observation, a gut feeling that dogs and children alike would thrive under the same conditions. A stable home free of neurotic humans; plenty of good plain food, exercise and fresh air; appropriate rules for ensuring civil behaviour at all times; neither coddling nor beating; and unlimited opportunity to learn new things. She had observed the cleverest dogs of her friends, their mastery of new tricks and their delight in performing the same, and being assured that they were good boys or girls, quite the dearest and most wonderful creatures in creation. It is time for empirical research now, thought Arabella. Her Mary Poppins role in the world had until this month been unique, largely inexplicable and nothing to do with children. This sudden expansion of it took her into territory that was a mass of roads well used by regular Mary Poppinses, but never before trodden by her.

※

In Dallas meanwhile, the future Melba McMonagle was beginning another crammed day of leisure and beautification (the two being frequently combined by virtue of lengthy salon appointments in the prone position). Her nails were a matter of urgency, for the lacquer on one had chipped. When she arrived at the salon, she found that the manicurist assigned to her was the same girl who had kindly taken care of her letters on her last appointment: putting a folded letter in each envelope as instructed, addressing the envelope Melba had forgotten to write before leaving home and sealing them both, while Melba lay back, oblivious, her fingernails wet with fresh lacquer. It was *so* important to do *nothing* with the fingers just after a manicure.

That week-old memory evaporated in seconds into the fumes of nail polish and remover, and Elinore herself was finally put in the Empty Quarter for good.

32

By the time of Elinore's appointment with Dr Simpson, her cheek was the colour of a thundery sky and the lump and the pain were both steadily diminishing. Dr Simpson was more concerned with the quality of her blood. He asked her about nosebleeds. Yes, she had had some annoying trickles, and one gushing one at the Dower House, but since they had fortunately always occurred at a time when she could lean over a sink or use a handkerchief, and she had kept her clothes free of stains, she had quickly forgotten about them. Tom had forgotten to mention the gushing one in his letter to Arabella.

Now Dr Simpson appeared to be satisfied. After another and more thorough examination, during which he pointed out a proliferation of tiny red dots on her legs and arms (so tiny and widespread that Elinore had never noticed them), and on other parts that she could not see, he talked about things called platelets and then the results of her blood tests. His diagnosis was anaemia.

"You're growing fast, and we have to keep an eye on you, or you'll use up all your fuel too quickly. Do you like roast beef?" he asked.

"Yes, I do. It's one of my *most* favourite things."

"Good. Your aunt will be making sure you have plenty of it, to help put the iron back into your blood. You need an extra tiger in your tank!"

"Gosh! Do you mean I need two tigers?"

"Two of the biggest tigers you can find."

After leaving the surgery, Arabella drove to Coullmar, a proper town with much more of everything than Boddo Bridge. Elinore was under the impression that they were going to do household shopping in the big Co-op there, and as they walked along the High Street Arabella said nothing about any other errands. But without warning, she opened the door of a shop selling nothing but bicycles and ushered Elinore inside.

"Can you ride a bicycle?"

"Yes, I learned in Criven. I got on my friend's bike and she helped me."

"Excellent. You won't have any trouble trying out one of these, will you?"

"*Me?*" A bicycle of her own had never been more than a dream.

"Yes, you. All those Pattersons and Lindsays seem to have wheels as well as legs, and even if we do put two tigers in your tank you'll have trouble keeping up with them without a bicycle. No, *don't* faint here, Elinore! It's better to stay upright for the good surprises in life."

After the purchase of a bicycle in two-toned blue with silver accents, Elinore wheeled it to where Arabella had parked her noisy rattletrap Land Rover with its patched, sagging canvas on the back. This was another gift from a client and even more of a boneshaker than Bumphrey, but Arabella was satisfied that it would get her through the worst of another winter or two. By then, the floors and other essential, expensive interior work by tradesmen at Fhairlach would all be finished, and she would consider buying a newer vehicle if one had not come her way by other means. They hoisted the beautiful, shiny bicycle into the back of the Land Rover. Elinore was still ecstatic. "I can't believe it! I can't believe it! It's really all mine!

Arabella, are we going straight home after the shopping? What if someone steals it when we're in the Co-op? I have to guard it!"

"All right, Miss Two-Tigers, you guard it and I'll shop."

She was sitting half-turned in the passenger seat, running her eyes over every part of the bicycle, when a fluting voice spoke through the rolled-down window almost in her ear.

"Excuse me, is Arabella Cheyne nearby? This is her Land Rover, is it not?"

Elinore jerked around and found herself face to face with the upper part of a tall, rather large woman. It was a dull, windy day, threatening rain, and she was wearing an unbuttoned mackintosh over a loose, patterned shift that reminded Elinore of Susanna's bedroom curtains. Her hair was brownish with grey all through it, under a bandeau, and she had violet blue eyes in a pleasant face that smiled encouragingly at Elinore.

"Yes, it is, and she's in the Co-op."

"Oh, I won't bother her then. I know she likes to shop at top speed, and no dilly-dallying! I'm Mrs Blent. Would you mind telling her that something very special has arrived at my house and I'm not quite sure what to do with it? She can come along any time – right now, if she wants. I've just been to the post office and I'm on my way home."

"We're going home too," said Elinore, thinking of her bicycle.

"Are you staying with her? She's been away and I've been away too, so we must catch up with each other over tea."

Not today, said Elinore firmly to herself, but out loud she said, "Arabella Cheyne is my aunt and I live with her now." How easily that ran off her tongue. Suddenly she remembered her ugly, bruised cheek and put up her hand to cover it.

Mrs Blent's face shone and beamed at this news.

"How *wonderful!* That *is* exciting, *very* exciting. What is your name, dear?"

"Elinore."

"How pretty. Elinore, thank you for passing on my message to Arabella. How lucky you are to live with her. It must be great fun.

Lovely to meet you, dear. Bye-bye." Mrs Blent gave a little wave and carried on along the High Street. Elinore saw that her shoes were bright pink, like Mrs Patterson's lipstick.

For lack of anyone else with whom to pass the time, Elinore began a *sotto voce* monologue with herself as audience. "I am Elinore Crum and I live on Royal Deeside, with a witch. I am really a lost princess."

What came next? No, what came *before*?

"I was flying through the air to my castle and I fell off. Fell off, um . . . my unicorn. I landed in Scotland and I turned into a baby. No! A wicked queen locked me up and then *she* turned me into a baby. And then she got bored with me and threw me out of the sky when she was flying around. On a black cloud. Some people found me and decided to keep me. But then they changed their minds and left me somewhere too, when I was a girl. Then a witch came along and said to the girl, oh, you can be my assistant. You can live in my house and I will teach you all my magic. But you need two tigers in your tank because you have to be strong if you are going to grow up into a witch like me. You must eat roast beef with roast potatoes and Yorkshire pudding and peas, with gravy, *every single* day! The doctor will look at your blood and see if you are strong as iron. And you have to ride a bike until you learn how to fly on a unicorn again. The girl asked the witch, what if my mother and father – what if the king and queen find out where I am and come along, and want me to be a princess again?"

Elinore paused. An idea had popped up out of nowhere, an idea so obvious and sensible and yet so thrilling that she bounced as much as the thin, hard Land Rover seat would allow. I can do that, she thought, and I can do it *soon*. Then she continued composing the alternative story of her life.

"The witch said, well, you can go away with them if you really want to . . ." Elinore paused again. The idea of leaving Fhairlach and Arabella, even in fiction, was instantly painful. In fact, it made a lump in her throat, bigger than the lump on her cheek, and made her eyes prick. That part of the story, the king and queen searching for their princess and finding her in Airt, would take some working out. Everyone had to be happy in the end. (Except the Caltrops.) She would turn her thrilling idea into action and not think about what might happen next and, anyway, she had too many happy things to think about right now. She turned around in her seat to look at her bicycle again, and wonder whether, like Bumphrey, it should have a name. A fast name. The Blue Racer... The Blue Tiger. That sounded just like something out of Biggles. Elinore Crum and the Adventure of the Blue Tiger. Miss Two-Tigers and the Blue Tiger. Yes! "Hurry up, hurry up, Arabella, I want to go home right now, before it rains."

When Arabella returned with laden baskets, she said, "One more stop: the butcher's, for all that red meat your tigers are raring to devour."

"A lady called Mrs Blent said hello. She wants you to go and see something special in her house."

"Well, we're here now, we might as well do that. And then to the butcher's."

"But what about my bike? It's going to rain and I'm *dying* to ride it."

"I think you'll survive another hour or so. Ailsa Blent always has delicious home baking on offer. Are your tigers strictly carnivorous?"

"What's that?"

"Eats nothing but meat. Wouldn't touch cake."

"We-e-ell..."

The town of Coullmar was much admired by Albert, Prince Consort during his lifetime. Even before Queen Victoria and he had first alighted there, on one of their earliest exploratory jaunts by carriage through the countryside surrounding Balmoral, it had been known for the health-giving waters of Wells of Coullmar, a hamlet on one of the steep hills encircling the town on three sides. The fourth side was open to the River Dee. The royal pair took their ease there on two further occasions, allowing Prince Albert to rhapsodise fully over the fresh, piney air and the charmingly Bavarian essence of Coullmar's beauty; to attest to the superior quality of the water (even ordering bottles and casks of it to be delivered to Balmoral); and, not least, to place Coullmar in felicitous kinship through natural and manmade beauty and a quirk of spelling with the town of Colmar in Alsace. It mattered not that the beauties of Colmar were markedly different and far from Bavarian. Prince Albert's whimsical joining of the two place names was more than enough reason for droves of Victorians to make it a fashionable watering place, a Highland Malvern, above all in the months when their monarch was in residence at Balmoral. Thereafter, it became a desirable retirement spot for colonial servants. Streets of handsome villas and spacious bungalows soon filled the land between river and hills, with porches, verandahs and conservatories aplenty in which one might sit and reminisce about the fresh, piney air of various hill stations. In India, Malaya and Ceylon, they had lived in houses called Fairhaven, Rosebrae, The Laurels and Albert Lodge. Now they lived in houses called Simla, Nainital, Penang Hill and Nuwara. It was good that in all generations they had a monarchy as a kind of sheet anchor, for their hearts were always adrift in the other place wherever they were in the world.

Ailsa Blent, a widow, lived at Mussoorie Lodge in Osborne Road. She was from Stirling, and Mr Blent had been an Inverness native, but they had never thought of changing the name of their house. It had always been called Mussoorie Lodge. Her husband had been a bank manager in life, and in death he inhabited an oil painting in the hall of his earthly home. Ailsa Blent had painted it. After Arabella had listened to this house and moved a great deal of Balmoralia out of it in the first year of Ailsa's widowhood, Ailsa had given up her competent but unremarkable portrait painting for flower studies and dreamy landscapes that were beginning to sell rather well. The daisies in the Delft jug on the white garden table, in Elinore's bedroom, were her work. A greeting card company was going to reproduce two winter scenes for Christmas this year. She signed all her works Bluebell, on account of her violet eyes and Bell having been her maiden name.

When Elinore walked up the garden path at Mussoorie Lodge, she was expecting the front door to open onto something like No. 17 Dunallan Crescent. Instead, she was invited into a chintz-filled, ornamented interior in which every room was painted in a different pastel hue, with ceilings, cornices and woodwork all in white. Lots of lamps with fringed silk shades stood on little draped tables, and much of the furniture was Louis this or that in gilded ivory-painted wood. It was softly bright and cushiony, feminine and floral like Ailsa's paintings. Ailsa floated happily in light, loose clothing from room to room and in and out of her studio like cumulus on the move. She never permed her hair now, and her twinsets and pleated tartan skirts were long gone to the Oxfam shop in Aberdeen. It was all the doing of Arabella Cheyne.

Ailsa Blent led them into the dining room and pointed to a dustsheet-covered rectangle propped against the back of a chair.

"I have – I *had* – an aunt or cousin at some distant remove from me, in Edinburgh, in Randolph Crescent, you know, and oh my goodness, she thought herself a grand kind of woman!"

Arabella winked at Elinore. "We have one of those in our family, don't we? In fact, I was just telling Elinore about her."

"Well, this one was a hundred odd when she died, and to be honest, I'd forgotten all about her long since. But she remembered me, because of some portraits of mine she'd seen in somebody else's house. She never had children but she did have a husband, and there was no lack of comforts, for he was from Glasgow money – shipbuilding or bits for ships, that kind of business, you understand. I did have a letter from a lawyer, telling me that I was mentioned in her will, but with no details. These affairs take such a time to settle, don't they? I had one more letter, saying that I was to receive some Wedgwood and a painting – and then *this* arrived."

She lifted off the dustsheet, and Elinore found herself looking straight into the eyes of a pale, dark-haired girl with a fringed bob, a faraway yet serious expression and a delicate white froth of a muslin dress. A watery-blue silk sash was tied high around the dress, falling over the lilac cushions of a chair rather like one of Ailsa's bergères, and contrasting with the deeper shade of a posy of violets held in the girl's clasped hands. Elinore was riveted, unconsciously holding her breath. She was looking into the eyes of her double, even of similar age; the longer she looked, the more she felt that this girl was also her double in personality. Overall, she had the air of a true princess.

Arabella bent low towards the painting, which, although mounted in a handsome giltwood frame, was incomplete in the background and parts of the dress. "A date but no signature. 1920 something. How odd. But it looks like a Ferdinand Lascoe, don't you think? I've seen his work before, in some exalted settings. Ailsa, this can't possibly be your ancient relation, the period's all wrong. She would have been middle-aged by then."

"Oh, indeed, and she was blonde, a real Viking in looks. She had her own portraits, and I've seen plenty of photographs of her in her heyday too. I have no idea where this came from or who the sitter might be. I never saw it in that house in Randolph Crescent."

Elinore was silently indignant. Two lost princesses were *here* in Ailsa Blent's dining room, and yet Ailsa and Arabella had not fallen over in astonishment at this strikingly obvious phenomenon. Disgruntled, Elinore sat down on the floor, in case the embroidered seat covers of the Blent dining chairs were not for the likes of her corduroy trousers. Outside, the rain finally came on, and heavy drops spattered the dining room window. The room lost some of its pastel radiance (it was the palest of green). Ailsa shivered. "Let me get tea right away. Then we can sit down and talk comfortably." She wafted out of the room.

Arabella turned to Elinore and said, "Seeing this girl's hairstyle reminds me: we must make an appointment to get your hair cut, or your fringe will be over your nose. She looks a bit like you, doesn't she?"

Still sitting on the floor, Elinore folded her arms and said, "I think she's *exactly* like me and she could be in my family – my *real* family. See? I really could be a princess! Can't we talk to the man who painted her and find out all about her?"

"We don't know if Ferdinand Lascoe did paint her, and we can't ask him because he died a few years ago. Let's hear what Ailsa says first."

Over tea and rock cakes, Ailsa explained that she had thought of Arabella as soon as she had realised, very quickly, that she did not want to keep the portrait.

"I don't know why, it just doesn't seem to belong here, even though it's very beautiful and accomplished. And you always, *always* say, Arabella, that if it doesn't feel right it must be improved or removed."

"I do," said Arabella, smiling in a satisfied way. "How gratifying that at least one person remembers what I tell them."

"Oh, my dear, you saved my life after Duncan died, how could I forget?" Ailsa waved her hands in protestation at such a thought.

"I only saved your house from any more years of looking like the head office and main branch of a bank, not that I mean any disrespect to your dear husband. I listened to what it said – fortunately, only its accent was French, and very few of the words – and then you blossomed and did all the rest yourself."

"Well, as far as I'm concerned you saved my life. And my house is so perfectly me that here I am turning up my nose at an exquisite work of art because it doesn't feel *me* enough to keep. Yet it seems all wrong to send it off to Milne's or Christies. I'd feel I was abandoning an orphan, and after all, she did land on my doorstep like a foundling!"

Ailsa give a little laugh. Elinore started at this mention of doorsteps and babies in the same breath, and bent her head over her rock cake on a gilt-edged, floral plate and frowned furiously. That princess in the portrait really and truly should belong to her, Elinore Crum. They were doubles! It was a clue to her own mystery and it was being ignored! She was becoming exasperated at the blindness of these grown-ups, especially Arabella, who was normally so sensible.

"If I were you, I'd start off at the Aberdeen Art Gallery," said Arabella. "There's bound to be some expert there who can at least point you to another expert if they can't identify the artist right away. You never know, they might be glad to receive it as a gift for their collection, once provenance is established. Public display in a fine space like that would be just right for her, I feel."

"Of course! How obvious. I knew you'd have a solution, Arabella. Isn't she wonderful, Elinore? You're going to have such a marvellous, marvellous time with her at Fhairlach."

Arabella and Elinore ran down the garden path and flung themselves into the Land Rover to avoid being soaked. Arabella stopped at the butcher's shop and then they were off on the road home. As they rounded the bend at Mains of Airt, she hit the brakes as a small figure, the same indistinguishable grey colour as the tarmac, the rain and the dykes on either side, tumbled across straight in front of the Land Rover, slipped and fell on the verge.

Arabella jumped out and ran across. As she helped the figure up, Elinore could see that it was Johnny Lamont. In the fortnight between her first encounter with him and the day of drama at the Patterson house, she had seen him roaming a few times, but always in the distance. He had either waved to her and continued on his way or not noticed her at all, or pretended not to notice her. She had a feeling that he probably saw everything, wherever he was. Now he was drenched, without even an anorak, and Arabella was trying to coax him into the back of the Land Rover. He sounded as if he was protesting. Elinore's curiosity pushed her out into the rain to join them.

"But she won't know where I am! She's at the window and she won't see me coming, then she'll get all upset, and my dad's not home. I have to go!"

"Johnny, listen to me. Your leg is hurt and you're going to make it worse if you go down that steep field when it's all wet and slippery. And then you have to get over the burn, which will be deep with this rain. I'm not letting you do that. I can drive you home right now if you don't want to come up to our house first."

"It'll take too *long* on the road," cried Johnny, in a voice of despair. Elinore looked at him in alarm: yes, he was crying, the rain could not camouflage it.

"Johnny, have you ever been in a car going from here to your house?" asked Arabella. Elinore looked at her in amazement: it was horrible standing in this rain, and Arabella's long hair was a straggling mess, but she might have been standing inside Ailsa Blent's dining room, she was so calm.

Johnny shook his head; he was crying harder now, and shivering. "If you haven't done it, you don't know how fast it is, do you?" continued Arabella. "I can get you there so fast you wouldn't believe it. If you go down the field, you could have a fall and not get there at all. Then what will your mother do? She can't go out and look for you, can she?"

She opened the back flap of the Land Rover and, without waiting for any sign from Johnny, lifted him straight up into the vehicle like another bag of shopping. He hunched right over on the little bench on the side, staring at the blue bicycle as if it were from space. Arabella reversed slowly until she could turn in the Mains of Airt road end, and then they were chugging and bouncing back along the way they had just come. The Land Rover was hard on the ears, the interior was all steamed up, and the bends in the road made their swaying progress feel a little dangerous to Elinore, but Arabella looked serene, and so Elinore decided she would be too.

Once they were on the main road, she had no idea where they were going, but after about ten minutes Arabella turned off onto a track that made the jouncing even worse until they reached a small house and outbuildings right at the foot of a hillside, and stopped. Elinore's ears rang, for now the only sound was the rain.

"You stay in here, Elinore," said Arabella, as she got out to help Johnny down. But he was already out and stumbling to a door, which he opened and went through without closing behind him. Arabella followed him inside and the door closed.

Elinore rubbed the windshield and her window. This was apparently a day of surprise and mystery, and hours were left before bedtime to fill with more of the same. She could see no clues to Johnny's distress in the exterior of this house, although nothing about it looked happy or particularly cared for. Tall larch trees dripped and swayed their boughs around it. The hill behind it was dark and so high that she had to bend down and crane her neck to see its top through the windshield, and then she realised that it might be her hill, the one on which Fhairlach stood. She felt very glad that her home was up there in that radiant white house, and not down here in a place that suddenly reminded her of imprisonment by Mrs Caltrop. It had rained heavily then too. Perhaps the weather had its own scheme for strange events in the lives of people.

Arabella reappeared and got into the Land Rover. "Whew, what a day," she said, and then they were off again. "Your bicycle has travelled miles already and you haven't even ridden it," was her next comment.

"What about Johnny?" asked Elinore, all agog. "Is he all right? Is his mother in that house?"

Arabella sighed, which was unusual for her, and said, "I think we should talk about Johnny when we're not being deafened. And the more we talk, the more these damned windows will steam up. Try not to breathe, Elinore!" She turned her head and gave Elinore her slowest, most exaggerated wink yet.

33

The rain let up after an hour, but dark clouds hovered still and the sun showed no sign of appearing for the rest of the day. Arabella set up her ironing board and ironed to the accompaniment of Radio 4. Then she put bones from the butcher's shop into a huge pot and began turning them into stock for soup. She was very good at making soup, and certain puddings, but she could not be bothered with cakes, pastry and anything that involved a rolling pin, rising yeast, precisely-weighed quantities or what she termed fiddle-faddle. When the stock came to simmering point, she put the lid of the pot on firmly and disappeared into her workroom. This was next to the sitting room, which in turn was opposite the dining room. It was lined with shelving and cupboards, all full of bolts of silk in gorgeous colours, other sumptuous fabrics, plain cotton and linen, and bags and boxes of ribbons, beads and other trimmings. A table with a sewing machine stood at the window, and another, bigger table in the middle of the room. When Elinore had asked Arabella what she made in this Aladdin's cave of colour and texture, Arabella would say only that her lips were sealed at present. Sometimes, if she went to the bathroom in the middle of the night, Elinore could hear the sewing machine whirring away behind the closed door of the workroom, and, faintly, the BBC World Service.

Meanwhile, Elinore had put aside the idea of trying out her new bicycle and immediately making it wet and muddy. She was busy with other business. This was partly the usual letter-writing to Susanna and Usha, and partly an unusual request for assistance. It did not matter if Arabella saw the address on the envelope of the latter, for she would only approve, but she must not see the contents because these mentioned the doings of the great and wise Davidicus Mercury, whose existence was yet to be revealed to the world.

Dear Tom,

I hope you are very well and happy and writing lots of adventures for Mr Mercury in your garden! I mean, only when the sun shines! Today I got very wet and so did Arabella, because we were helping a boy called Johnny Lamont. I think I told you about him already. I have only met him once properly and today was no good for talking because Arabella almost ran over him in the Land Rover! She made him get in and we took him to his house, which is not in a very nice place, but it might be nicer when the sun is shining there. My friends say his mother is dying, but I don't know about that. Anyway, Arabella says she will tell me all about it later. She is busy right now.

GUESS WHAT?????!!!!!!

I HAVE A BICYCLE!!!

Arabella got it for me today. Actually a lot of things happened today, not just Johnny Lamont. First I went to see Dr Simpson, who is in Boddo Bridge. He told me I needed TWO tigers in my tank! He said they had to be the biggest ones. Also, I have got aneemia. I don't know if that is spelled right because I can't find it in my dictionary at the "ane" bit.

Then we went to Coullmar and I got my beautiful, wonderful bicycle, which is blue with silver bits. I am calling it the Blue Tiger. I thought we were going home so that I could ride it, but then a woman called Ailsa wanted Arabella to go to her house, so we did that and then it rained so I haven't even got on it yet.

SECRET! TOP SECRET! EXTRA SECRET!

Arabella said she told you straight away about the letter from Mummy in America and so I don't need to say anything about that. I am going to live at Fhairlach for ever, which is VERY VERY GOOD INDEED! But it is NOT good that I was a baby left behind somewhere and nobody knows anything about me. I would still like to know what my story is. I am not in a ghost story! I had a good idea about this. Could you please ask Mr Mercury to hunt for the people who left me behind, because you said he was the Hunter for lost things and <u>real people.</u> It is <u>really, really, really important.</u>

The lady called Ailsa showed me a painting of a girl which was quite old. Arabella said it was from nineteen twenty something. SHE is ME! Truly, honestly, cross my heart and hope to die. She looks exactly like me. I said it was a big clue but no one else talked about that, so it was very ANNOYING. They want to put it in the art gallery. Maybe it is a painting of my real grandmother or another lady in my real family. I want it! She looks just like a Princess! THAT is why it is important too. I don't want to run away from here and live in a castle but if I have a king and a queen who are looking for me I think I should know about it. They need to know about me too so we can find each other. PLEASE can you tell Mr Mercury he should look at the painting too in case he knows who the girl is? No one knows who painted it, Arabella says.

I don't have anything else to tell you just now, but Arabella says she will tell me about Johnny Lamont's mother tonight when we are sitting down for tea. It is another mystery! I can write another letter to you about that.

Now I have to do some other things. Please say hello to Boris and Mr and Mrs Forsyth! I have not written another ghost story yet. My next one is still going to be about Daisy, but I am tired of reading her book. She talks about being ill and lying down a lot, and she goes round and round the countryside to different houses but she does not do ANYTHING exciting. Instead I am reading Biggles books that my friend Ginger Lindsay is lending me. They are excellent. I think you should read them too.

Lots of love from
Elinore xxxxxxxx
PS Please tell me what Mr Mercury says very soon!

As she signed her name with one of her current and ever-expanding flourishes, Elinore remembered another mystery. This one was for Arabella, however. She went downstairs.

Arabella was laying out vividly hued tropical print fabrics on the centre table in her workroom, alongside others in contrasting plain colours and some coils of ribbon, the smooth, shiny satin kind.

"What are you going to do with all these?"

"Aha. Time will reveal all, but not this afternoon. In two days' time, perhaps."

"They're so-o bright, they make my eyes jump," said Elinore, looking at the detail of each print. "I like that one best." She leaned over a length of crimson patterned with outsize leaves and fronds in green and white, and boughs on which colourful little figures perched. They wore balloon trousers, voluminous shirts, waistcoats and the kind of upturned-toe slippers that she had seen in illustrations of Arabian fairy tales. On their heads were fur-trimmed conical hats. Each figure was exactly the same. Elinore looked more closely. They seemed to have huge whiskers around their face – no, it was a ruff of fur. "They're monkeys," she said. "I thought they were little men. But they look like Johnny."

"They do," said Arabella. "But tell me why you see them like that."

"It's their eyes. They don't have sad faces, but their eyes are a bit like black holes, and so are Johnny's, and he does look sad. And he's got a little face. Actually, he's quite little all over. I wonder how old he is."

"About as old as you," said Arabella, "although he seems to weigh nothing. If he wanted to be a jockey, he'd be just right."

"He wants to go to university in Edinburgh. He told me."

"Well, if he's saying now that he wants to learn, he'll go far – I hope. I like the sound of his questioning mind."

"I've got a question in my mind too. I want to know about Ermine Crum, because it's my name, and I hate it, and it was in that letter. Why am I named after a *stoat*? You said an ermine was a stoat, didn't you?"

"I did. I will tell you about Ermine Crum, if you wouldn't mind helping me with a little job."

Arabella went to a cupboard and took out a six-inch square box. "Tip these out and look for all the beads that match the red and the green in that fabric, and the blue of the monkey's waistcoat. Make three piles of those colours on the lid and put the rest back in the box."

This was a spur of the moment directive. Arabella's dog-based philosophy of child rearing informed her that if something slightly uncomfortable and potentially troubling had to be carried out at one end of the creature, a distraction should be provided at the other end. She had also seen this employed on certain horses, when a twitch would be put on the nose before the farrier picked up a hind hoof. The coming revelation about the nature of Hector and Melba could affect a sensitive child in any number of unpredictable ways.

"Beee-eau-tiful!" breathed Elinore, as she made a sparkling stream fall across the heavy canvas covering the table top. "This is fun! You can start the story now."

"All right. There was once a horrid child called Ermine. She was spoiled rotten from birth and she grew up to be even worse as a woman. She managed to find herself a husband, but they had no children. When her husband died in a train crash, she inherited the entire fortune from his business and all his property, which was considerable. Then Ermine let the whole family know that she would bequeath this fortune to a girl *if* the parents called her Ermine. They would have to christen the child that, not just change the name."

"I know what comes next! They called *me* Ermine because they wanted the money!" Then Elinore frowned. "But they never had any money. They just talked about it *all* the time. What happened to the money they got from Ermine?"

"They never got a penny of it. When Ermine died, she left just enough cash in the bank to cover her funeral, a wake with plenty of whisky, and a few other things you need when you're dead. Nothing else. She didn't even have a house to leave to anyone because she'd already sold it and gone to live in a fancy hotel where there was no shortage of staff to wait on her. She spent the rest of her money on having a splendid time. She sailed around on cruise ships and went to Paris for her clothes, and she never wore the same thing more than once a month. She also gave a lot of money to some charities when she was still alive. I don't think she gave two hoots about abandoned cats and dogs, and maltreated donkeys in Cairo or orphans anywhere. But she did care a lot about seeing her name and picture in the newspapers, and being invited to dinners and balls with titled people, and all that sort of attention."

Elinore looked up again, and paused in her sorting. "You were talking about that before."

"Was I? I don't know a single living person like Ermine Crum."

"No, you were talking about going to church, about people who go because they like other people to see them doing it. I know! I know what Ermine Crum was: a two-faced bizzom!" Elinore shouted this in glee. "What about all the other people who had babies? Was I the only one called Ermine?"

"Yes, that's how it turned out. No one wanted to have anything to do with such a scheme. It would be very embarrassing, don't you think, to know that people were saying, oh, look at that child, her parents called her Ermine only because they knew it would make them rich."

"I think other people would say the parents weren't caring about their child, because they didn't care what the child thought about being called Ermine. No one asked *me* if I *wanted* to be called that."

"Exactly. Ermine had the last laugh in the end and all the attention was on her, just as she liked. Now you know." Arabella held her breath, wondering what pitfall of child psychology might presently yawn at her feet as a result of this revelation.

"That was an *excellent* story! Do you know any more? I haven't finished my job yet."

Arabella exhaled. "I don't have one on the tip of my tongue, but give me time and I might find some more skeletons in the family cupboard."

Elinore looked gleeful again. "Oh, yes, skeletons *please*. You could tell me about all the old places you go to, like Welkinlaw, even though you said you don't talk to ghosts. Or you could just make something up. Really and truly, I think you are *quite good* at stories, Arabella."

"Thank you, I am deeply honoured. But I don't have your talent as a storyteller. I could never have written about Helena and the ghosts. And anyway, I believe truth is always stranger than fiction. Real life has the strangest stories of all."

"Well, perhaps . . . I just love reading all kinds of stories. It makes me feel good."

"Then you must keep reading all kinds of stories. It's one of the best things in the whole world for making you feel good."

"I have another question about my name. Why do you think I was called Elinore?"

"Perhaps you were named after Elinor Glyn, who was famous for the stories she wrote, or perhaps you were named after Elinor Dashwood in a *very* good story called *Sense and Sensibility*. And there was a queen called Eleanor of Aquitaine."

"A Queen Eleanor . . ." said Elinore thoughtfully, still sorting beads with both hands. "But I like the name Elinor Dashwood a lot. Elinor Dashwood, Elinor Dashwood. I wish I was called that."

Arabella allowed herself another portion of congratulations. Dogs and children – just the same in the end. Straightforward communication in all matters. She went to the kitchen to check her simmering soup stock. Wet days were so good for cooking and housework, dramatic intervention on behalf of a soaked, despairing small boy notwithstanding.

"Arabella, I have another big question for you." Elinore was right at her elbow.

"If you startle me like that again, I might fall headfirst into the pot and drown. What is the question?"

"Can I please change my name? My whole name except Elinore? Can I do that before I go to school in Boddo?"

"What an interesting idea."

"I don't understand why I have to have names I don't like. I think grown-ups should ask the children what they want to be called, or else it isn't fair, is it? And if you write a book, you can call the people in it anything you want. Why can't I call myself anything I want? *And* you *said* –" Elinore took a breath and Arabella held hers – "you *said* I could tell people anything I wanted about myself, or what happened to Hector and Mummy. You said I could make my own story. So, I want to make a new name because I hate Ermine and now I hate Crum too."

Dogs. Children. Freewill. Identity. Arabella acknowledged the weak links in her philosophy.

"*And* I don't want to be called Crummy. It's horrible! It's like being called Ermine. *Please*, Arabella! I want to go to school with a new name." Elinore folded her arms and aimed her best glower at Arabella.

"Who on earth calls you Crummy?"

"No one, but Louise keeps talking about a girl called Avril Abernethy, who's called Biscuit, and she said Avril would call me Crummy when I go to school and then everyone else would too. I don't understand, and I don't want it, so there."

"Ah. I see. Well, let's deal with Abernethy first. It is a type of biscuit much favoured by elderly people, who think it's good for the digestion. Do you understand now?"

"Yes, and it's still stupid and I'm not going to be a Crummy."

Arabella put the lid on the stock pot. It seemed an apt metaphor for what was simmering in Elinore's consciousness, what concepts of self she was extracting from the meaty bones and marrow of life.

"I couldn't possibly disagree with any of these points, so I suggest you make a start on finding a new name for yourself."

"*What?* Right now? Before tea?"

"Why not? Go and find lots of names and start making a list of the ones you like. Or take bits of one and mix it up with another and make a new one. Or jumble up the letters and make something entirely new. The world of names is all your oyster with which to make a pearl."

Now that has a fine ring to it, if I say so myself, thought Arabella. Elinore's frown reappeared. "Sometimes you're just havering," she said.

"Who taught you that useful word?"

"Mr Lindsay. It's what he says to Mrs Lindsay when she says he has to do something and he says he doesn't have to."

"I'm crushed. I thought I was being incredibly helpful."

"Oh, yes, you are, really you are! I'm going to start my list right now! Thank you very, very much!"

She rushed from the kitchen and went upstairs, but only halfway. "Arabella!"

"No yelling here, please! This is not Mains of Airt."

Clump, clump, clump down the stairs. The addition of one small, highly active figure to the austere interior of Fhairlach had required a new consideration of noise by Arabella, and revised priorities for purchasing things such as stair carpet.

"What did you say about jumbling up letters?"

"Bring paper and pencil and I will show you."

Within ten minutes, Elinore's mind was reeling over a discovery so *amazing* that it needed a better adjective. *Unbelievable.*

Arabella had told her to write out Helena Albacyr's full name as a string of letters with no spaces. "See if you can find letters in there to make up the name Arabella. Cross them out as you find them."

"I did it!" said Elinore after few seconds, relishing this new game. "That's really interesting."

"Now see if you can turn the left-over letters into another name. Any name. You could take each letter in turn and try starting a word with it."

Presently, Elinore looked up in disbelief. "Arabella..." Then she looked down again at her six-letter trial words, only one of which was a name for use in the world she knew: Cheyne. She frowned in an accusatory way.

"I don't *understand*. How did you *know* your name was inside Helena Albacyr? Is that magic? You keep saying you're not magic, but I don't know..."

"No, I am not magic. But I am Helena Albacyr and her *Book of Edinburgh for Young People* was my book. Or rather, I am Arabella Cheyne and that was my book. One day I decided I wanted to be someone else too, and so I invented Helena."

"Ohhh... Really and truly, cross your heart and hope to die, it was your book?"

"Since you've got that hanging-judge look on your face again, I'll prove it, if you care to fetch it."

Two minutes later, she said, "Please turn to the chapter on Edinburgh soldiers and find the page that's missing a piece, as if a giant mouse has bitten a chunk out of it."

"It's here. Next to page 81. Gosh..."

"Now go the very front of the book, and find the list of illustrations. You'll see a word at the top: frontispiece."

"I know what it means: the picture at the front, before all the others."

"And can you find one? No, you can't, because it's been missing for years and years. If it had been there, you would have seen a picture of a soldier on a grey horse. What does it say about the frontispiece in the list?"

"A Scots Grey in the King's Park."

"Now do you believe it was my book?"

"Yes, all right. But I found it in Edinburgh, in that shop we went to. How did it get there?"

"That could be a very long story, and then we'd never have any tea tonight. Let's just say that my mother was having a big clear-out, and she cleared out some things of mine, which was very naughty of her."

"You clear out things all the time."

"I consult their owners first."

"Umm . . . I can give you back the book if you're missing it a lot. You can put it with your other books and I could still look at it. It belongs to you, doesn't it?"

"How kind-hearted of you, Elinore. I appreciate the offer, truly I do. But this book belongs one hundred per cent to you. Now, will you set the table, please? I can see that your brain will be working overtime tonight, and it must be properly fed at the regular times."

"I still think it's magic. It was your book and I found it. It has to be magic! Maybe another witch stole it from you and she dropped it when she was flying about, *and* it fell on Edinburgh, and someone found it and gave it to the shop."

"It was coincidence. Something extraordinary happened to bring the book and you together with no obvious reason. Why not call it magic, if you want to? But, excuse me – what's this about *another* witch? Surely I'm not the first witch?"

"Um, yes, you are. But not a bad one. You're definitely a good witch. Can you wrinkle your nose like Samantha?"

"Who on earth is Samantha?"

"*What?* How come you don't know about *Bewitched?* I think you really need a television. Never mind, I can tell you *all* about Samantha. But you *have* to pay attention!"

෴

That night, the myriad possibilities for being herself whirled around in Elinore's head and would not let her sleep. It was Jumpin' Jack Flash at his most frenetic.

She turned on her radio and found Radio Luxembourg. The songs she had been listening to all summer were still coming over the air. Then she turned it off, because she wanted to concentrate on her list of names; until she said each one aloud, she could not quite get the measure of it. On the page, unvoiced, they were like clothes on hangers, waiting to be given life by a body.

Finding all parts of a new, perfect name could be a project of months, not the few weeks that remained before the start of school. She had made one decision already: Elinore could remain as her everyday name, for she had no quarrel with it. That left a surname and a middle name.

She could use Arabella's surname until she found the right one. That was Arabella's suggestion too. "Elinore Cheyne" sounded fine, and moreover it was an Aberdeenshire name, although the origin was French; it meant oak plantation. Elinore liked it for all those reasons. She also liked its ability to negate the nickname of Crummy.

For a middle name, she wanted a historical one, or that of a literary heroine. Arabella had reeled off a list of books for her to investigate for that purpose, so many that Biggles might have to be put aside for a long time. The world of Biggles did not include heroines as far as she could see. It was a very exciting kind of exploration, and Arabella said it was also the best exercise for her brain.

She turned on her radio and tuned in to Radio 4, in case some appealing names came floating out. New and interesting ones came floating out every single day. She switched off her bedside lamp and began to doze, half-listening to BBC talk, thinking of all the new ideas she had encountered since morning. When she had got into the Land Rover with Arabella, it was supposedly for a simple drive to see Dr Simpson and then shop in the Co-op. *Anything* could happen in a single day. She switched on the lamp again and looked at two of her pictures.

"Dear Sir Gabriel and Magic Men," she murmured. "I don't want any more things to happen if they aren't good. I don't want any more bad surprises. I only want the ones like getting a new bike and finding out I can have a new name. Thank you very much."

Her last thought before sleeping was that coincidence was definitely magic. It made sense. Arabella, being a witch, should know better than to think otherwise.

In her workroom downstairs, Arabella was busy with the three tropical print fabric lengths she had selected earlier, and listening to a concert on Radio 3. As her hands worked and Johann Sebastian Bach played, her mind was free to collate the latest findings of her empirical research and consider their significance with respect to her original dogs-and-children philosophy. For example, what might be the canine equivalent of "But you *said*"? Remembering that a juicy bone had been buried in a flower bed? Who could fault a dog for digging it up again months later and ruining the tender, blooming flowers?

"But I don't *understand*" had no apparent counterpart in dogs. Dogs never demanded clarification with respect to themselves. They trotted along in line with expectations or went off and did things behind one's back if they wanted to make a point.

Arabella's main satisfaction in this exercise was the addition of a new idea to her philosophy. In fact, it might well be an entirely new and discrete philosophy which did not include any four-legged creatures. Literary fiction, she had decided, was a marvellous opiate for children of all ages. It had no obvious side effects and incalculable benefits for later life when taken regularly and liberally at Elinore's age.

34

Free as any bird over Fhairlach, Elinore swooped down the hill on the Blue Tiger, around the bend and all the way to the Pattersons' house in less time than she could have imagined. The sensation was so intoxicating that she simply kept going past the end of their drive. How quickly could she reach the other manse, where the Imries lived, on the main road? She would find out. As she alternately pedalled and coasted, for it was mostly downhill, she realised that without a wristwatch she would be unable to boast about her speed in getting anywhere. She would have to look at a clock on departure and arrival.

The Imries gave her and the Blue Tiger a gratifying reception. After a drink of juice, she turned around and went home. The first quarter of the journey was only mildly strenuous, but eventually she re-encountered each exhilarating downhill stretch in reverse, and had to get off now and then. But that was all right too, for she was walking along a particularly lovely part of the road and she could look closely at everything she had previously seen only through car windows. The sun had reappeared with vigour and all around the wet ground was glinting and singing as it dried. Curlews sang their bubbling song out of sight and the wind made the trees sparkle. Elinore felt as happy as a birthday balloon blown up to bursting point.

For some hundred yards before the old manse, the road flattened, and so she was able to pedal very fast up to Louise's front door. After showing off the Blue Tiger there, she did the same at Mains of Airt. When Mrs Lindsay saw the basket on the handlebars, she put into it half a dozen eggs and said that Elinore would be very useful now.

It was no use pretending that she could get herself up the last and steepest hill to Fhairlach by pedal power. It would take a lot of time and increments of standing on the pedals and pushing to reach even half-way, and Arabella had quoted Dr Simpson in giving strict warnings about overdoing it.

"But I'm fine now. My nose doesn't bleed and I'm not going to faint any more. I just know it."

"No, you don't know it, and I'm the boss, so you have to pay attention or I'll demote you from assistant to skivvy. No heroics on the bicycle and come home *before* you feel ravenous."

After lunch, Elinore dusted her bookcase, arranged its contents with even greater precision, and sat down to write a letter of thanks to Lady Groule, who had found more vintage postcards from her travels and sent them to her. Then Arabella told her to jump in Bumphrey immediately because she was going down to Boddo for a haircut.

"But you said that would be on Friday. You *said* I could do what I wanted today."

"Friday has become today. Mrs Forbes' daughter has had a baby before it was due, and she's going to Aberdeen to give a hand. Come on! Spit-spot!"

Boddo Bridge had a tiny barber's shop next door to the chemist, but no hairdressing establishment for ladies. Instead, Mrs Forbes, who had the right kind of scissors and experience from before her retirement, did the job by special appointment. She took her scissors, combs, clips and useful hand mirror to a select number of kitchens and living rooms in the village, and outlying clients came to her house. She had been trimming Arabella's hair for a long time, an undemanding task. When she met Elinore, her eyes lit up at the chance to maintain what she called a proper hairstyle.

"It's just the thing for you, dearie," she told Elinore. "Reminds me of days long past, when all the girls had bobbed hair, and the ladies. You look at pictures of the Queen Mother from then – she's got her fringe too. Aye, how time flees awa . . ."

"I know she had a fringe," said Elinore. "I've got some books with old pictures of her. She was called Elizabeth Bowes-Lyon, and she lived in Scotland. Then she was a duchess, but she didn't have a fringe when she was a queen."

"My, you're a quick one!" exclaimed Mrs Forbes. "And *you'll* be looking like a wee princess when I'm done. You've got the face for it. No doubt you'll be a fine-looking quine in hats when you're older!"

Elinore thought this was nice of Mrs Forbes, but she was still aggrieved that Arabella and Ailsa Blent had been blind to her as the instantly recognisable twin of the princess in the mysterious portrait. Other routes to becoming even tenuously royal were limited. Much as she would have loved to move into Balmoral, it was unlikely to happen as a result of discovering that she was related to the Queen Mother. Anyway, Fhairlach was an excellent place to live, and it only got better and better. But if she had a name like Elizabeth Bowes-Lyon, that would be the icing on the cake. Everyone would know who she was and where she came from. A name, a name, the right name . . .

"Lovely hair!" said Arabella, when she reappeared to collect Elinore. "You look a proper little flapper."

"Huh," said Elinore, even more aggrieved at this *lèse-majesté*. "That's silly, whatever it means. I've got a princess style. And a duchess style too. Mrs Forbes said it was, so there. Do you think Elizabeth is a good name for me?"

"Any name is good if you like it and it feels exactly like you."

"It's very historical, isn't it?"

"Yes, shiploads of history in Elizabeth."

"I wonder what Mrs Blent's princess is called . . ."

The following day was the 11th of August, and already the hours of light in Airt's latitude were contracting: a steady loss of minutes and seconds from either end, unnoticed as it was happening. Arabella's woodpile was undergoing a steady increase in anticipation of suddenly cool nights. It was time to have the chimneys cleaned before everyone else in Airt and Boddo Bridge had the same idea.

Frank Timm, chimney sweep and ironmonger, came up the hill in his van, knocked on the front door and was admitted by a young girl whom he was not expecting to see and did not know. No, that is not quite true.

He had been driving slowly along the Airt road in sunshine and heat. His van window was wound down, and he enjoyed the feel of the sun and air on his bare arm, and the way the leaves shimmered and flickered on the birch trees. Frank liked sun and heat a great deal. The only trouble with elemental pleasures, though, was their tendency to transport him back to his youth, when they had been readily enjoyed and assumed to be forever available. It was not his nature to dwell on what was irretrievably lost, or what might have been, especially since he was so content with the life he had. He was bothered that such involuntary lapses into nostalgia were becoming more frequent. Perhaps he was merely getting old. He knew from all his visits to the fireplaces, Rayburns and Agas of the elderly that he must inevitably cross a line in time when his youth would start to become more easily and vividly recalled than the previous week. This knowledge was underscored whenever a customer came into his ironmonger's shop and asked for parts or even whole items that, sadly, he could no longer obtain for them. The world was becoming too quick at deciding that many things were out of date, in Frank's view. He disliked plastic and he loathed shoddy merchandise. Long, long before planned obsolescence became a phrase that had filtered down even into the consciousness of housewives, Frank had sensed this new, regrettable way of the world. Perhaps it was another reason for his recent tendency to be drawn back through the summers of his youth.

Today, he had been remembering a silent film about a group of young Berliners. On a day like this, they went picnicking and boating, and really that was all there had been to the film. *Menschen am Sonntag.* People on Sunday, as unpretentious as its title. At the time, though, it had been a hit; people called it a work of genius. What a novelty to see amateurs portraying young characters with jobs and lives the same as those they would return to after the cameras stopped rolling. Their joking and arguing echoed your own; you knew how it felt to be working at that age and longing for the next Sunday to arrive, to bring you a few more carefree hours of enchantment. Frank had never before recalled this inconsequential detail of his youth. It was vivid, and that bothered him, in light of those meandering elderly minds he encountered nowadays.

So it was that, when Elinore opened the door to him, he was startled enough by the sight of her to slip into a greeting from the language of his youth.

"*Guten Tag*," he said, struck by a face that was playing tricks on him. It belonged in the era of that film; in even older memories of roaming, playing children, himself one of them. It was the hair, of course: dark, bobbed, cut very cleanly and short, with a straight fringe. Without the fringe, she would have looked like the dark-haired actress in *Menschen am Sonntag*, which would have been an even more disconcerting coincidence. But the hair was also working with green, almond-shaped eyes and high cheekbones to make something indefinable that separated the child from the locality of Airt.

Elinore frowned, uncertain. "Are you Mr Timm?" she asked, seeing the van behind him.

"That's me. Is Miss Cheyne at home?"

"Yes, but she's busy, and she said I could let you in and show you all the fireplaces." After *Mary Poppins* and *The Water Babies*, Elinore could not miss watching a chimney sweep at work.

Only the flue and chimney of the Rayburn needed a full cleaning. The fireplaces in dining room and sitting room had been scoured out and their chimneys thoroughly cleaned of very old soot before Arabella had even ripped off the layers of wallpaper on the surrounding walls. She had never lit a fire in either of them since, and that had been a few years ago. Still, it was important to check for birds' nests or even dead birds, anything that could fall unseen into a chimney and block it. This winter was going to be different, Arabella had decided. A Christmas tree would go up, neighbours would be entertained by the side of a roaring fire, or she and Elinore might even invite them all to a proper party.

Elinore relayed these details to Frank Timm as she watched him work with his rods and brushes in the dining room. "I'm already looking forward to Christmas," she said, "even though it's still summer. I love Christmas trees!"

Frank grinned. "What is the girl or boy who doesn't want Christmas to come? All that good food too. Do you like the marzipan on the Christmas cake?"

"Oh, yes!" said Elinore. "I love it. It's much nicer than hard icing."

"I agree. When I was your age, I was living near the city where they make the best marzipan in the world. Do you know where Germany is?"

"Um, over the sea. Next to Switzerland. I know about Switzerland, because I've got a story about it, called *Heidi*."

"Ah – the same Heidi as my daughter's Heidi, I'm sure. Yes, over the North Sea. Then you go around into the Baltic Sea, to Lübeck. You tell Miss Cheyne to buy only Lübecker marzipan when she makes your Christmas cake."

"*She* won't make the cake! She says it's too fiddly-faddly and she'll just make a big mess of it."

"Oh, no, no, that's no good. What's a kitchen without cakes? What does she cook on that Rayburn I keep so clean for her?"

"Well, she's always making soup, and she's good at that."

"Soup!" Frank shook his head in sorrow at this.

Arabella's voice came faintly from the back of the house, and Elinore ran off.

Returning, she said, "Mr Timm –"

"I'm Frank, please. And what's your name?"

"It's Elinore. Arabella says to tell you she isn't hiding, she's coming through soon. Um, how come you have an English name if you're from Germany? Tim is short for Timothy, which is English. And Frank is English too. Or Scottish."

"In Germany, Timms are just Timms – last name, with two Ms. In Germany, I was Franz-Joachim, but Frank is better for Scotland, no? But I keep my last name to tell myself where I come from, and the same for my children. A name is like a tree in the ground."

"Gosh," said Elinore, "that's interesting. I'm looking for a new name too."

"And where are you from, if I may ask?" It was still hard not to see Elinore as a figure who had slipped in time and place.

"Oh, I'm just Scottish."

Arabella walked into the room. "Hello, Frank, how is Moira these days? I haven't been in your shop for ages."

"Thank you, she's very well. I'm just thinking that I should ask her to make one of her special Christmas cakes for this young lady here."

"Then Moira will have a friend for life. Can I write a cheque for you now?" He named a figure and she went to fetch her chequebook.

"Is your wife from Germany too? Does she make special German cakes?" asked Elinore, thinking of Fredy and the Danish birthday cake that fate had prevented her from experiencing.

"No, Moira is from here. If someone gives her a recipe, she will make anything from anywhere, as long as she can find the right ingredients. My daughter Frances is like that too."

"Frances . . . that's pretty. Did you call her that because you're Frank?"

"That's right, and because I was Franz. My son is George because my father was Georg. You see?"

Elinore was silent for a moment. "Do you get homesick, like Heidi did? Homesick for Germany?"

Frank busied himself for a moment. With the uprising of some memories, like Moira's bread yeast that would rise and rise until punched down, and the sharpness of this child from both sides of time, his ordinary day had become different. Was a little nostalgia the same as homesickness? What to say? "Then I would be in an interesting condition," he began.

Arabella reappeared with the cheque. "No, surely not, Frank? To be in an interesting condition is a roundabout way of saying a woman is going to have a child."

Frank chuckled. "Ach, what a language! Nothing exactly what you think it is. You can put your foot in the ditch every time you open your mouth. I was telling Elinore about the place where I was young, which was by Lübeck. Now it's on the wrong side of the border. Not a place for me any more."

"Isn't Lübeck the city with the roofs like witches' hats?"

"Witches' hats? On *buildings*?" said Elinore.

"Yes, the Holstentor," said Frank. "That's Lübeck."

When he left shortly afterwards, Frank reminded Elinore to find herself a new name that would be like a tree in the ground. "A name for where you come from and a name for where you decide to stay. Then your whole name has roots."

Later, Frank Timm wondered what he might find if he visited Lübeck, now right on the East German border. People travelled overseas so readily these days, pushed by nothing stronger than pleasure and curiosity. It would make a change from the usual holiday at Carnoustie.

Elinore was wondering about the same place. A city famed for marzipan where buildings had witches' hats for roofs must definitely have magic in it. It would be fun to visit one day. Arabella said she had never been there, but Elinore was not so sure about that. As far as she was concerned now, old, peculiar places all had an Arabella look or sound.

She fell asleep while listening to Radio 4, to the BBC voices that still soothed as they had done in Edinburgh. Hours later, she awoke to the last strains of a lilting, swaying piece of music. Then came a measured voice reading something called the Shipping Forecast.

. . . easterly or northeasterly three or four. Fair. Moderate with fog patches . . . Forties, Cromarty, Forth, Tyne, Dogger. East or southeast backing northeast four or five. Occasional thundery rain. Moderate with fog patches . . . German Bight. Variable three, becoming south or southeast four or five . . . Humber, Thames, Dover, Wight, Portland. Southeast veering southwest four or five, occasional six. Thundery rain then squally showers . . . Biscay . . . Trafalgar . . . Finisterre . . . Sole . . . Lundy. Southeasterly becoming cyclonic, then westerly four or five, occasionally six later. Thundery rain . . . Fastnet . . . thundery showers . . . Irish Sea . . . Shannon . . . Rockall . . . Malin . . . Hebrides, Bailey, Fair Isle, Faeroes . . . Southeast Iceland. Northeasterly three or four, occasionally five. Fair, moderate with fog patches."

In the darkness, Elinore saw herself as if from above. Her bed was on an island in a sea, and all around were winds, rain and forceful weather, rising and falling in strength, and whirling around the island in circles, like the rings around Saturn on her map of the planets. Ships and fishing boats were out there. She was safe in her bed, no matter what storms might batter the island. This was an attractive, comforting picture, and it also reminded her of Frank Timm's advice about finding a name, since trees needed deep roots to withstand storms; that was plain to any country child who had seen sad giants on the ground, their roots sticking up in the air in a circular, earthy tangle.

She came from Criven but now she was in Airt. Cheyne was her Airt name, and it meant oaks. King Charles II had hidden in an oak tree, and oaks had strong, deep roots. Cheyne, therefore, was the perfect surname for a lost princess. Elinore was her Criven name, the one by which all her friends knew her, and Arabella had mentioned a few famous Elinors or Eleanors too; that was all to the good and she liked it, so her forename could stay too. The only name she needed was a middle one, a name that was completely hers. It could be a secret if she wanted, but not the kind of secret that Ermine had been. It was *ridiculous* that parents should have the right to slap names on children as they pleased!

※

"Today is the Glorious Twelfth of August," said Arabella at breakfast.

"No, it isn't. It's cloudy and the sun's just a little wee circle."

"That may be, but for all the gentlemen who are preparing to stand in shooting butts for most of the day" – she waved her hand at the moor stretching far beyond the rear of Fhairlach – "this is the glorious start of the grouse season."

"Do I have to stay off the moor?"

"You'll be fine on the track, and you can go anywhere you want on a Sunday. Otherwise, you should wait a while before you go off on one of your wide explorations."

"I haven't gone up there very much yet. Johnny Lamont does. I could go with him, but I never see him. You were going to tell me about his mother – you *said* so, but you forgot."

Elinore folded her arms, leaned back in her chair and looked expectant.

"Hmm, did I? You'll find out something today, because you're going to take her a present on my behalf."

Elinore sat up with a jerk.

"Why me?"

"Because I'm busy, and after all, you *are* my assistant – aren't you?" No winking. Arabella appeared to be serious. "All you have to do is knock on the door and hand Mrs Lamont a parcel. Tell her it's from me, say goodbye and come home."

"But – aren't you going to drive me there and wait? I don't like that place."

"Drive you? What on earth for? Go down through the fields just as Johnny does, cross the river, bear right through some trees and you'll see it. You could cycle there, but it would take much longer in the end."

"Will I get germs from Mrs Lamont?"

"No, you will not. She was very ill some time ago, and again this spring, but it wasn't the kind of illness you could catch. Everyone seems to think she's dying, but I wonder about that. She might be just like you were, when your soul got whacked. If you see Johnny down there too, remember this: he's very scared that she might be carried off to hospital when he's away out, and that she might never come back. It happened once before, the first time she was taken ill. He was at school, and no one remembered to tell him. When the school bus dropped him off, the house was empty and he didn't see his father for hours. Can you imagine that? So, he never likes to be away from the house for long, and Mrs Lamont has become very dependent on him for company and all sorts of help. She has stopped going out, you see."

"Out of the *house?*" Elinore was horrified.

"Out to the village or even to her own road end. I wouldn't be surprised if she hardly goes out for air and light. She needs a little uplift, Elinore, and you're the one to deliver it. And if you do that, you'll do something for Johnny and his father too. It's very, very hard on Mr Lamont, and he does his best, but you know, a keeper is out on the hill all day and every day, and this is his busiest time of year. His employer will want to show many good days out for all his guests and the other guns who've paid for the privilege."

Wearing her wellington boots, Elinore set off. A lightweight bag was slung across her chest, and in it was an envelope and a soft, square shape wrapped in brown paper. Despite some trepidation over the unknown, Elinore liked the feeling that she had been entrusted with a real job of some importance. The day was still dull, but the sun was slowly clearing a space, and she only bothered about rain now if she was on her Blue Tiger. She could not bear the thought of a speck of rust on that gleaming chrome.

The route to Johnny's house was as simple and quick as Arabella had promised, and the stony little river was fun to wade across. On the opposite bank, the grass was short, springy and speckled with daisies, almost like a rough lawn; Elinore saw a huddle of sheep some distance off, and guessed that they kept it cropped like that. It would be a good picnic spot, with the water gurgling and chuckling away. She thought of *The Wind in the Willows*, even though she knew that this place was completely unlike the riverbank of Ratty, Mole and Otter. For a start, a burn was not a river, and here this water was very close to being no more than a burn.

Through a dark, hushed stand of conifers she went, and there was the gable end of Johnny's house, a few hundred yards away. No sign of life showed in the house, the outbuildings or the kennels with their barred enclosures. Her heart beat a little faster as she went towards the front door, deliberately not looking at any window in case she caught sight of a ghostly white face staring out at her.

"Elinore."

She knew it was Johnny's voice, but jumped in shock nevertheless. He was coming up behind her.

"Are you coming to see me?" He looked and sounded puzzled.

"You *scared* me! No, I'm not here to see you. Arabella said I had to give this to your mother." She patted the bag and the brown paper rustled.

Johnny looked at her in that straight way of his, silently, and then walked around to the rear of the house, turning once to make sure that Elinore was following. She saw that he was limping slightly. He opened the back door and went in without giving any sign that Elinore should do the same, and so she waited on the doorstep, looking through a scullery to a kitchen. They were dim and dreary rooms, and she would not have entered them unbidden anyway, even if Miss Agnes Pound had not instructed her never to march over any threshold before a proper invitation had been issued. She heard voices, murmurs that sank into whispers.

Then a woman came through the kitchen, clutching a shapeless blue cardigan around herself. She was a taller version of Johnny, except even paler, if that were possible, and her fine, light brown hair was shoulder length. She was trying to smile, although that seemed to be almost too great an effort and went nowhere near her eyes, which had dark, bluish shadows under them. The arm, wrist and hand that she held out to Elinore looked so thin, and were trembling so visibly, that Elinore was too alarmed to take the hand and shake it in the firm, outgoing manner decreed by Miss Pound (who had a special contempt for limp handshakes).

"Hello, Elinore. Johnny's been telling me about you. Did you walk all the way down here this time?"

She's got a pretty voice, was Elinore's first thought. "Yes, I did, and it was really quick. I brought you this from my Aunt Arabella, and a parcel." She handed over the envelope and extricated the mysterious brown-paper parcel from her shoulder bag. Arabella had refused to tell her what was inside, saying only that Mrs Lamont's eyes must be the first to see it. Mrs Lamont's eyes widened and she took half a step backwards, as if the parcel were a threat. "Oh . . . that's – what a surprise."

"I can carry it inside for you," said Elinore, still holding out the parcel to her. Johnny inserted himself into the doorway beside his mother, and then Elinore heard a clack of claws on linoleum. The sunken face of an ancient yellow Labrador pushed between their legs and stared at her too. Suddenly she could not stop a grin breaking out. It was like offering food to shy, wild animals! Or was *she* the wild animal? Without thinking, she said, "It's all right, honestly! There's nothing scary inside – not from us."

Mrs Lamont let out a minute sound that might have been a laugh, and a smile that went a little higher towards her eyes. Johnny looked up at her sharply. She took the parcel carefully in both hands. "You're a very kind girl to bring this to me, Elinore. Will you tell Miss Cheyne . . ." She frowned, as if the right words would not stay put in her head. "Tell her it was a kind thought indeed and much appreciated. I'll open it up right away. Johnny, are you going to keep Elinore company back up the hill?"

She moved backwards, lifted a hand and turned away into the house. Elinore had suddenly had enough. She wanted to run back to the daisy-strewn grass by the river. "Goodbye," she called, and walked quickly away without waiting for Johnny to decide what he was doing. Reaching the conifers, she broke into a trot, which turned into a leaping run, meant to be the gallop of a horse, as soon as her feet touched the springy turf of open ground. The multitude of daisies at her feet prompted an outbreak of a favourite song: "Daisy, Daisy, give me your answer do . . ."

The sun had pushed the clouds back quite a bit, and a shaft of light was hitting the top of the sloping field ahead of her. If I go up there very fast, she thought, I could step on that piece of light. It might be magic! I might go up into the sky! She took off at a run. Halfway up the field, she had a thought that was truly *amazing*. She paused briefly to catch her breath and look out over the landscape. Was that Johnny and his dog coming through the trees? No, she would not wait, she would run on and share her amazing thought with Arabella.

"Arabella! Guess what I was thinking?"

Arabella put a finger to her lips and shook her head. She was standing in the hall, telephone receiver at her ear. Elinore had already taken off her boots, which were forbidden within the house. She went quietly upstairs with exaggerated, high-stepping action, every inch the cartoon Pink Panther.

In her bedroom, she surveyed the growing number of enjoyable tasks awaiting her. Her name lists must be reorganised alphabetically. Daisy Melmurdo was crying out to be turned into a ghost and sent on an adventure that could then be typed up after the requisite number of drafts. She must send Tom another letter, just to tell him the incredible story of the true identity of Helena Albacyr. The wild flowers in the vase that Arabella had given her needed fresh water, and some were wilting. That could be job number one because it was easy. She took the vase into the bathroom and started singing

"Daisy, Daisy" again. Daisy was a pretty name too, but it would not go on her list, because it did not feel as if it belonged to her.

At that moment, she had her second great thought of the day. A brilliant idea! She hoped that Arabella would agree. It was *so* exciting! Arabella was still talking. Elinore became the Pink Panther again to go downstairs and into the kitchen. It was time for lunch. Who on earth could be on the telephone?

"I'll tell you that once I've heard your assistant's report on the errand of mercy," said Arabella a few minutes later.

After Elinore had done this in great detail, Arabella thanked her and said that she was being promoted to apprentice with immediate effect. "Does that mean you'll tell me what was in the parcel?" asked Elinore.

"A cushion. I made Mrs Lamont a cushion in that material you liked best, with the monkeys."

"That's all? Why couldn't I see it?"

"Because it had magic in it, and it had to stay wrapped up to keep the magic inside until Mrs Lamont got it. Since you believe I'm a witch, and you're now my apprentice, you'll just have to accept that explanation. Besides, my cushion magic is only in test phase at present."

"Arabella!" Elinore put her hands on her hips and tried to scowl. Then she remembered her great big important thoughts and aired them.

Number one: "If I don't have any parents, or grandparents or anything like that, it isn't a bad thing at all, it's actually a good thing, isn't it, because I don't have anyone to stop me going around and doing what *I* want to do. I mean, I've got you, but you don't bother me, at least, not very much. If I had a mother like Mrs Lamont, I couldn't do *anything*. If I couldn't go outside for as long as I wanted, I'd go *mad!* And I wouldn't be living here if I had parents, would I? I really, really love my bedroom, and I love this house too, even if it is empty. Well, it has *some* furniture, but actually, this house is an *igloo!* Are you going to get a stair carpet soon? I'm right, aren't I? It's good not to have any parents because they can't boss me around. And Louise says her grandmother is a pain in the be-hind because she never stops telling her what to do."

Number two: "I don't need a middle name, do I? Why not have no middle name? Is there a law about having middle names, or do you get them when you're christened in the church? Anyway, if I don't have a proper middle name, I can have any one I like and just keep changing it if I want a new one and no one needs to know unless I tell them. So, I can just go to school and be Elinore Cheyne, can't I, and it will be fine, won't it?"

Arabella maintained an attentive but neutral expression in the face of this outpouring of admirable logic.

"I applaud all of that unreservedly," she said in response. "Here is another idea: when you write a story, you can call yourself anything you like. A new author for each story – it's called a pen name. Why let the characters in the story have all the fun with names?"

Elinore's face suffused with joy and she clapped her hands. "Yes! I've got loads of names already. Gosh! This is really exciting, isn't it?"

Arabella nodded solemnly and allowed herself another, larger portion of self-congratulation at this seismic juncture in a person's life. Then the discussion leaped abruptly from philosophy to practicality.

"Who was talking to you on the phone for so long? You said you don't like it when people go on and on like that. Was it an important person?"

Refusing to divulge the workings of cushion magic was one thing; refusing to identify telephone callers was another, and might lead Elinore to begin conjuring suspicions of transatlantic negotiations over her status. Dogs and children, straightforward communication at all times: this element of her philosophy was perfectly sound, Arabella believed.

"Yes, it was. Before I tell you, you must promise to keep secret her name and anything I say about her. One hundred per cent secret, Elinore. Not a squeak of a hint to anyone. Can you do that?"

Given Elinore's faithful guarding of the secret of Davidicus Mercury, her look of deep scorn was understandable "Of course I can! I'm not a *baby!*"

"All right, Apprentice, we have a new client. Have you heard of Athena Dancey?"

"Oh, yes, she's famous! She's in the spy programme I'm watching. She's Juliette, the spy who makes people nervous, because they don't really know what side she's on. Was she really talking to you?"

"Yes, she needs some help. She wants me to find out why one of her houses is making her feel so miserable."

"When are you going to see her?"

"That hasn't been decided yet." Arabella had never had to consider the needs of an apprentice before, let alone a ten-year-old one.

"Did you know she comes from Heggie?"

"No, really? How did you learn this extraordinary fact?"

"Mrs Lindsay told me. Mr Lindsay and all the boys said she was havering. They said that no one like her ever came from a wee fisher place like Heggie, but it was in Mrs Lindsay's *Woman's Own*, and she showed them, so they had to shut up and say sorry."

"Quite right too. But listen, Apprentice – your lips are sealed, aren't they? Not a word to any Lindsay or anyone else. Athena Dancey is very famous, but she's entitled to as much privacy as the rest of us. We cannot have *Woman's Own* snooping around her because you've let something slip."

"Arabella! I *told* you, I'm not a baby. I can be a secret agent too. I'm *full* of secrets! Um, when will lunch be ready? My tummy is not full and it's making a terrible noise. I have a question: do you think tummy noises wouldn't be so loud if we had carpets everywhere?"

From Athena Dancey, epitome of contemporary glamour, to tummy noises via the Banffshire coastal village of Heggie in mere seconds. Arabella felt slightly off centre.

Mr Aitken came to deliver a parcel, a cardboard box wrapped in brown paper. It was not a small box: he used both hands to lift it from the van and place it in Elinore's.

"Fit like the day, Elinore? Any stamped letters for me to tak awa doon? Here's a surprise for you – mind, it's heavy." Mr Aitken sighed dramatically. "That's just what I need: a fair few parcels to fill up the van a' the year roon. Keep us a' in business and get me that new van. Bye-bye now!"

The parcel was addressed to Elinore Crum. She was tired of seeing that name; she must write to everyone very soon and tell them that she was Elinore Cheyne for good. She took a pair of kitchen scissors and opened it up. Inside, the box was tightly wadded with balls of newspaper, on top of which lay a sealed envelope marked, in Tom's handwriting, *TOP SECRET! For the eyes of EC ONLY!* Elinore was glad that Arabella was out in the old steading, dragging furniture around.

In the middle of the wadded newspaper were two framed black and white photographs. One, rather mystical, showed Elinore half-turned on a path through the jungly wood at the Dower House; she was looking directly at the camera. The other showed her in motion, arms outstretched and inches off the ground, as she bounded through the wrought-iron gate between the wood and the sloping field, going from dark into light. Between the two pictures was a letter from Jack Fisher and an envelope containing many more shots of herself, Tom, the Dower House and gardens, and the poor battered Squair House. Some were in colour, some in black and white, and all were crisply detailed to a degree that delighted Elinore. It was the next best thing to being there.

> *Dear Elinore:*
> *As promised, here are some memories of my afternoon in the village of Squair. I hope you like the two of you that I've had framed. They both won prizes in my camera club's*

> annual show! This was a big thrill for me because I've never won anything before in that show.
>
> My visit with you and Tom was the highlight of my whole time in Scotland. If you hadn't come along just when you did, it would never have happened! What I want to do now is invite you to stay with my family if and when you ever come to Canada. We'll show you a great time – that's a promise. You've got my address and phone number right here on this letter. I'm enclosing a couple of family photos so you can see what we look like! One or two of the grandchildren are about your age.
>
> Wishing you all the best, Elinore, and with thanks for helping me be a prize-winner,
>
> Jack

Elinore was ecstatic. Not only because of the wonderful photographs, but also because she had received an invitation to visit another country. She looked at Jack's address: where exactly was Vancouver, and what did BC mean if it was not part of an ancient date?

Then Elinore opened Tom's letter.

> My dear Elinore,
>
> This will be a very brief letter because I want to take Jack Fisher's parcel to the post office and send it on to you without delay.
>
> Marvellous photos of you! No wonder they won prizes (he wrote to me too and told me all about it).
>
> Davidicus Mercury has instructed me to tell you that he will be honoured to investigate on your behalf. He has opened a file on the case; it is labelled
>
> CRUM, ELINORE: Foundling Seeks Clues.
>
> Mr Mercury says that it will take him some time to gather information and get to work on this investigation,

> because he has several others on the go at present. He asks you to be <u>reasonably</u> patient!
> I must run off to the PO now.
> Your loyal friend and advisor,
> Tom

Elinore took out the box of notecards she had bought in Edinburgh. They were just the right size for a short note to all her friends (and Davidicus Mercury), telling them that she was now to be addressed as Elinore Cheyne. To Tom, however, she wrote a letter, because she must also tell him that Helena Albacyr was none other than Arabella. Jack Fisher, she decided, deserved something much better than print alone.

"Can I send something like shortbread to Canada?" she asked Arabella. "Something that comes in a tin with Royal Deeside on it?"

"Shortbread might be reduced to crumbs if it's hurled across the Atlantic. But yes, we'll buy the biggest tin of Royal Deeside something we can find, and he can share it with all those grandchildren."

Arabella hung the two framed photographs where Elinore could see them from her bed.

The next day was a Saturday. In the early evening, Elinore joined the Lindsays in front of their television. Watching spies slither around corners and race through streets, and trying to guess the next moves of each side, was thrilling enough. Now she had the pleasurable sensation of watching a famous actress play an equally famous spy while she, Elinore, was guarding a secret about her. *Unbelievable!* Elinore inched closer to the screen; she liked to sit on the floor. She wanted to scrutinise Athena Dancey, and hear every syllable spoken by her character, the politically ambiguous Juliette.

Juliette had become the subject of a cryptic exchange between two ancient spymasters meeting in the middle of a park in some continental city.

"What are you asking for? What favour do you think I owe you now?" rasped one.

"We need a legend for a girl," croaked the other. A few bars of the series' theme music trickled over the scene as the men turned from each other and walked away into the mist, muffled in Homburg hats, scarves and overcoats.

It turned out that Juliette required yet another false identity before she crossed a certain border; evidence of a life that she had never lived must be put together meticulously, so that her false identity would withstand stringent examination by the enemy.

A legend for a girl. *A legend for a girl.* The phrase rang in Elinore's head, even as she continued watching the drama. I want that, she thought, I want a legend for myself.

As she walked homeward up the steep hill, she considered the nature of this legend. No, she did not yearn for another identity. She was Elinore Cheyne of Fhairlach and that was very fine. But why not have a real life *and* a legend? A legend belonged to the past, and her past was a mystery. Why not fill in that blank with a story of her own making? No one need know about it, except the great Davidicus Mercury, who might welcome some of her ideas as possible clues.

"Ve neet a legent for a gel," she said to herself, in imitation of the spymaster, who had sounded a little like Frank Timm.

Why not make up a legend for the future too? If it contained enough magic, it might come true. In her legendary future, she would visit the city of marzipan where roofs were like witches' hats. She would visit Vancouver in British Columbia, which was just a dot on an atlas page at present, but nevertheless a dot on the immense Pacific Ocean, all the way on the other side of the world – and she did have an invitation. She would go to Switzerland too and explore Heidi's Alpen landscape.

Would she be a spy? She was not sure about that. Spies were always hiding, and no one could explore if they were meant to be hiding. She would be an adventurer instead of a spy, then. Men had managed to land on the moon, and so Elinore Cheyne could surely get on an aeroplane one day and fly to fascinating places on planet Earth. *Anything* could happen!

The next morning, she accompanied Arabella to church without demur. She was now prepared to endure this hour or so out of loyalty to the Imries, the cream-puff family who were unfailingly kind and happy to see her, even as she made it clear in subtle and not-so-subtle ways that Elinore Cheyne was absolutely not religious. No one could tell that she was spinning an amazing legend in her head while letting Mr Imrie's nuggets of wisdom, as Arabella called them, slide in one ear and out of the other.

That afternoon, instead of playing with Louise or rummaging in Ginger's seemingly endless collection of dog-eared comics and books, she helped Arabella with some furnishing and picture hanging. The first piece to be put in place was a very large Victorian oil painting of a stag and several hinds in a misty, heathery landscape at sunrise. Fortunately, it had no frame, or Elinore would never have been able to hold up one end while Arabella nudged the cord onto the hooks in the wall. When they stood back to see how it looked on the back wall of the kitchen, where the pine table and chairs stood, Elinore crowed with delight.

"It's like another window! It's just like here!" The sole window in the kitchen looked out across the shallow valley in which lay the Mains and Burnside of Airt, towards the hills that rolled away into the Cairngorms. The heather was now in full bloom, and the stunning spectacle of purples and pinks washing over many hundreds of undulating acres showed that the artist had not exaggerated. "I think it's *beautiful*."

"The *Lord of Morven* will be relieved to hear it."

"Who's that?"

"This stag. Imagine how you'd feel if you were taken from your home and thrown into a junk shop because you were inconveniently large and no longer fashionable. No doubt that's what happened to him: the owner died and the house was cleared."

The longer Elinore looked into the large eyes of the stag, the more expressive they appeared to her. He was a supremely noble creature. He deserved to be safe in the kitchen at Fhairlach, with a view to the very hills he had once claimed as his own.

"But how do you know he's a lord, and what's Morven?"

"A plaque was on the frame when I bought it, with the artist's name and the title of the picture. The frame was hideous, and all cracked, so I chopped it up with my kindling axe." She went up to the painting and tapped on a feature of its background. "That's Morven. If you set off along the track out there, across the moor and over quite a few miles, you'd reach it, and then you could climb to the top. We might do that one summer, once those tigers in your tank are all fit and fired up, and your legs are longer."

"Is it a mountain or a hill? It looks a bit small in the picture."

"I think it's a hill that some people call a mountain. It's all very technical, to do with height above sea level. All I care about is whether I can get to the top of a high place and what the view is like once I'm up there. And the history of the place, and the legends."

"Legends? You mean legends to do with the Morven that we can walk to?"

"I mean in general. Aberdeenshire has as many legends as deer on the hoof. I have no idea if any of them concern Morven, but we can find out. That reminds me: we should get you a ticket for the library in Coullmar."

"We've got a library in the dining room."

"That won't satisfy *you* forever. It has no Biggles in it for a start, and I'm not a librarian. Librarians are encyclopaedias on legs. They can show you exactly which books will tell you what you want to know, including local legends. Compared with a librarian, I know nothing. All right, let's go back to the pictures and choose one for the dining room, shall we, now that you've mentioned it?"

"But you knew about the witches' hats on the buildings where Frank Timm came from."

"Believe it or not, once upon a time I too was a schoolgirl. I had geography lessons. I had to learn about the Hanseatic League, which was a group of northern cities, including Edinburgh, all trading with each other hundreds of years ago. Lübeck, the city Frank was talking about, was the chief city in the league, and naturally I saw pictures of it. I have a photographic memory and so from that day to this those pictures are still in my head."

"Oh . . . all right," said Elinore. This explanation was far too prosaic for her liking. Arabella's knowledge of the witches' hats of Lübeck must be for reasons of magic, and that was that.

Some minutes later, Elinore asked another question.

"Can Morven be my middle name, if I want to have one after all? I like the way it sounds."

"Why not? Elinore Morven Cheyne. Yes, that does have a fine ring to it. It sounds as though you grew out of these hills like a rowan tree."

"That's what Frank said. I mean, we were talking about names and he said names should be like trees in the ground. That's why he's got a name from here and a name from Germany."

"How very, very wise."

"So, I have a Criven name and an Airt name, and if Morven is my middle name it could be my, um . . ."

"Your Scottish name."

"Oh. But I don't know if I'm really Scottish. What if I came from a country over the sea? I could even come from *Switzerland!* Or even *Germany!* Or *France!* Or where Radio Luxembourg comes from."

"You mean, your natural parents, one of them or both, could have come from over the sea. But what if they were both as Scottish as Mr and Mrs Lindsay? You were found in Perthshire, remember, and that joins on to Aberdeenshire.

"Oh."

"And here's another thought, Miss Elinore Morven Cheyne" – Elinore grinned at the sound of this – "where does your heart live? What did you say when I asked if you wanted to go to America too?"

"I said *no,* I wanted to be *here.* I love being here most of all. What do you mean, where does my heart live? My heart's inside me."

"It's another way of saying, where do you love to live."

"Ohhhh, I *see . . .* "

"And once upon a time you loved to live in Criven, and never wanted to go away from it, didn't you? You would have plonked yourself down quite happily in Squair too."

"Yes! I *love* both those places."

"So, everywhere you really love happens to be in Scotland. It might be that your heart belongs in Scotland. And if your heart belongs in a place, so do you. It doesn't matter where in the world someone is born or comes from: if they live in a place they love, where they feel absolutely at home, it's their place too. It belongs to them just as much as to anyone whose family was there from the year dot."

"Ohhh, I *see . . .*"

"Look at Frank Timm. He had no choice in coming here, because he was taken prisoner in the war and sent to the camp that used to be between Boddo Bridge and Coullmar. He had to go out every day and work on the farms. When the war was over, he decided not to go back to Germany. Nothing was the same there any longer. He had lost nearly all of his family and his hometown was in the Russian zone, which you will learn about later. But he had other reasons. He saved the lives of two children one day, which made him a local hero, and then he met Moira and they fell in love – and he realised that he had fallen in love with the place too. He told me that this place made him feel warm in his heart after everything awful that had happened to him because of the war. So, you see, Frank Timm has just as much right to say this is *my* place as you or me, or the Lindsays, or the Queen and all her family in Balmoral Castle."

"Because his heart wants to live here too?"

"Precisely. It doesn't matter that he only came here a few years ago and couldn't speak English. He loves the place, he always does right by it and he considers himself one of the people who've always been in it, and so it's his place just as much as the Queen's. This is what he said to me one day: 'When your heart goes out to join the land, you know you are in the right place.'"

Silence. They were in a long, narrow room, almost like a walk-in cupboard, at the back of the house, where Arabella's many framed pictures were carefully stored under dustsheets and blankets. It was not a room for two people. Elinore sat down cross-legged in the doorway, chin in hands, and watched as Arabella moved pictures from side to side, unwrapped some completely and hummed and hawed over others.

She is thinking, thought Arabella.

I think I'm having another big thought, said Elinore to herself. Just because I don't know who my real parents were doesn't mean that I'm from somewhere else. Maybe that girl in Ailsa Blent's picture is Scottish! But you can't have Scottish princesses nowadays because Scotland never had a queen after Mary got her head chopped off, and I really, *really* want that girl to be a real princess because she is *me*. Drat, drat and double-drat! *But* I can still be a lost princess in my legend. A lost Scottish princess. I can be – *Princess Morven*. And no one can stop me! Not even the Queen!

Elinore felt as if a warm pink glow had descended on her, and this was reflected in the beatific smile that lit up her face. For once, Arabella missed that, her own face being close to a picture in an inconvenient corner. Elinore's big thought continued to expand. I could be an adventurer-princess. I could do *amazing* things. I might save people too and be a hero like Frank – oh, what did he do?

"Arabella, how did Frank save two children? You said he did."

"I think you should ask Frank to tell you. It's his story after all, and it sounds as though you two enjoy talking about life. Ask him to show you the special trees he's been planting. And his special benches."

※

Elinore Cheyne, formerly Crum and also known to herself as Princess Morven of Scotland, half-wakens some seconds after midnight. The friendly BBC voices sent her to sleep hours ago, and too quickly for her to turn off her transistor radio. The lilting waltz is playing again. Hearing it before her eyes have opened turns it into the sound of a dream called Sailing By.

"*And now the Shipping Forecast issued by the Met Office on behalf of the Maritime and Coastguard Agency at double-oh fifteen today. The general synopsis at nineteen hundred. Low one hundred and sixty miles west of Shannon...*"

No, she is not dreaming. She has fallen into another kind of lullaby, however, and this one is more effective than any other.

"*Forties. West backing southwest three or four. Showers later. Moderate or good. Cromarty. Southerly becoming variable three or four. Showers later. Moderate or good. Forth, Tyne. South or southwest three or four. Showers. Moderate or good.*"

Long before the first drumroll of God Save the Queen signals goodnight to all other midnight listeners, it carries her away.

"*Dogger. Southwesterly three or four. Showers. Moderate or good... Hebrides. Easterly veering southerly three or four. Rain or showers. Moderate or good. Bailey. Variable, mainly east or northeast, three or four. Occasional rain, moderate with fog patches.*"

The princess of no known parentage and slightly foreign features sleeps at the top of her hill in the north of a smallish island with as ancient and long-recorded history as hers is young and full of blanks. She is oblivious of the report on the state of the seas, which trickles out of her open window.

"*Fair Isle. Variable becoming easterly three or less. Occasional rain. Moderate or good.*"

It goes out across the moor, the hills and forests and into the sky. It weaves itself with stars and fog, with wind and squalls of rain, into a celestial net strung for the safety of mariners, and perhaps for that of a lost princess too.

"Faroes, Southeast Iceland. Variable becoming easterly three or four. Occasional rain. Moderate with fog patches becoming good."

After the ships and fishing boats receive their midnight weather story, the whole island sails on in time towards the dawn of another paragraph in its own story. It is a tiny vessel carrying countless hopeful passengers, each one with a cabin trunk holding a soul and secret dreams of rooted happiness.

For a girl of no history and the desire to make her own legend, "fog patches becoming good" is a cheering forecast.

35

Thomas Balmerinoch arranges his papers on the long mahogany dining table, clears his throat, adjusts his spectacles, rubs his hands and begins writing. Not, however, the story that will introduce Davidicus Mercury to the literary world; that manuscript remains piled at the farthest end of the table. Tonight, Sorcha Belmonti is at work. Publishers in London are awaiting her latest fictional romance, which is one hot, breathless chapter away from its conclusion. Miss Belmonti's publishers are breathless too, for her four books in print have garnered successively greater sales and attention.

The enigma of Miss Belmonti herself only piques this rising interest. She adamantly refuses to give interviews and communicates solely via her agent. No one is allowed to know anything about her, save that Sorcha is a Gaelic name meaning 'light' or 'brightness'. Some claim that she is therefore Irish; others posit a Scottish-Italian background. Everyone agrees that her novels instantly captivate female readers, from the young (that is to say, those of the young old enough to be allowed to read them) to the elderly. Women are seen clutching Sorcha Belmonti paperbacks everywhere now, on buses, trains and the tube; on park benches during lunch hours; in canteens, kitchens and staff rooms from one end of the country to the other. They take refuge from daily tedium in the mesmerising

Belmonti world, in which endings are unfailingly happy and frequently ecstatic. The male characters in this world are hugely compelling, because, unusually for the genre, they defy stereotyping and are presented with such insight into the male brain, such *generosity of understanding* (to steal the words of one reviewer), that it is as if they had come from the brain of a man.

Sorcha Belmonti is impatient this evening. She wants to be done with book number five. One reason is that the sooner she is paid for it, the sooner she can put a new roof on her crumbling old house. Tradesmen have been coming and going for weeks, leaving estimates and priorities of work. The woodworm and rot in the timbers must be routed forever, the slates must be replaced, and the chimneypieces remortared and strengthened, all in an exercise of near military precision before the fine days of late summer and autumn dissolve into early winter. This operation must come first to safeguard all future interior or exterior work, decree the tradesmen.

Another reason for Sorcha's impatience is her excitement over a new plot that has come to hand in the most unexpected way. She hungers to get on with it. Her agent has the same desire, fuelled by the sudden interest shown by an American film company in turning book number three or four, or perhaps a mishmash of the two, into box office lucre. If the Americans were offered a previously unpublished story, a Sorcha Belmonti exclusive, how much more might they be willing to pay? It is the stuff of dreams and drama; in other words, straight out of a Belmonti plot.

Sorcha will employ her usual array of dazzling locations and diverse, mostly well-dressed characters – White Russians, aristocratic emigrés of non-existent middle European duchies, polo-playing Argentinians, Greek shipping magnates (one's imagination has no limit where Greek shipping magnates are concerned) and so on – in other words, all that could be considered appropriate for the discovery of a lost princess who had been abandoned as a foundling.

Nevertheless, no Belmonti romance forgets Everyman, or rather, Everywoman. Where do the dreams and drama lie if not in the progress (tortuous, of course) from Woolworths to Harry Winston, to coin a phrase? How else can Everywoman be made to feel that deliverance to a rich, radiant life might conceivably come along for her too? This lost princess, therefore, will be found in the grittier parts of some city; she too will watch the clock on the wall of an oppressive workplace and spend countless hours on stuffy, overcrowded buses trundling through rainy streets – when she can afford the bus fare, that is. On the other hand, she could be a farmer's daughter, toiling in byre and field. Oh, yes! Sorcha Belmonti will have men in suits slavering for the rights to film *this* story! Then she can afford to deal with the walls and ceilings of her house, and annihilate those damned mice in the process.

Sorcha has decided that she will allow Tom Balmerinoch to use this plot too. He and that Davidicus Mercury character can stay in Scotland and run around looking for clues in heather and on doorsteps in the back of beyond. They want to do justice to the foundling within *reality*, they say. Well, they would, wouldn't they, as a detective and a lawyer in cahoots? Let them get on with it. She is in the business of transcending reality.

Arabella Cheyne, busy at her own table many miles to the north, would never describe her own business in such highfaluting terms. House medicine is good enough, and so too is her Mary Poppins soubriquet. If cushion magic proves its efficacy, she will continue to refer to it as such. Those for whom the cushions are a gift will not be told about the magic.

Tonight, she is assembling the materials for two more cushions; the outer materials, that is. The inner ones, some intangible, require daylight and considerable care. Her intuition is sharpest in the morning. Arabella cannot afford a repetition of events, years ago, when certain of her skills were integrated into gorgeous handmade skirts that wreaked havoc among the ladies of Edinburgh – the kind of havoc that Sorcha Belmonti might well have turned into fiction. Some of it was even stranger than fiction. No harm was done; quite the contrary, in fact, but still, with Morningside matrons running amok in unforgettable ways, a discreet vanishing from the scene and a polite refusal to create any more garments had been the wisest choice.

Some of us will carry secrets forever, thinks Arabella, or at least for as long as our gifts to our fellow men remain inexplicable by science.

※

Below Fhairlach, at Burnside of Airt, Johnny Lamont and his father are adjusting cautiously and sceptically to an inexplicable change in Mrs Lamont. She has been smiling, and the smiles have reached her eyes. In the shadowy sitting room at the front of the house, a gift from a neighbour, whom Mr Lamont knows only by sight as Miss Cheyne of Fhairlach and in a few brief passings at that, sits on the couch by the window. Its vivid crimson is almost shocking in that room. Whenever light catches the blue waistcoats worn by the little pantalooned tree-climbing creatures portrayed all over this cushion, it strikes a spark of blue fire from a tiny jewel sewn on each one. Mr Lamont notices the tree-climbing creatures when his wife shows him the cushion.

"That's Johnny to the life," he says, pointing. "In a tree too."

"Aye, a wee monkey with great big eyes," says Mrs Lamont, and she not only smiles but laughs too, which is a shock to her husband.

Later, he notices small changes in the sitting room, where Mrs Lamont spends a great part of each day on a couch by the window. The cushion sits there, radiating colour and warmth, but not amid any of the clutter that has come to pile up on the couch around Mrs Lamont. Things have been put away, folded, straightened and so on. The table next to the couch has been cleared and dusted – yes, it must have been dusted, or else how could the wood show a faint, unfamiliar sheen? Mr Lamont looks around for more signs of sudden improvement and surreptitiously crosses his fingers, hoping that this odd lightness of being will not vanish on the stroke of midnight.

At the Aberdeen Art Gallery, a junior assistant under-curator is finally leaving her office after more than an hour of self-imposed overtime. The reason is the recent arrival of a donation to the Gallery's permanent collection – or rather, a proposed donation. The portrait of a young girl is beautiful, highly accomplished and completely in the manner of the great Ferdinand Lascoe, but it is unsigned. The Gallery cannot exhibit it as a Lascoe until authenticity and provenance are established beyond doubt, and that will take time. Experts in London and elsewhere must be consulted, for a start.

The junior assistant under-curator has fallen in love with the painting. She cannot resist spending a few minutes in the gallery library before going home, following a thread of enquiry that she has not mentioned to any colleague. The few minutes extend, and she finds it necessary to take notes, and pull out more books, and then she becomes too absorbed to notice the clock on the wall. Noises made by cleaners starting their work finally break the spell. The very junior staff member puts on her coat and gives the girl with the fringe and the bunch of violets one last glance. Someday, someone might invent a mechanism that would enable this picture to be circulated instantly among the experts and be compared with images of other work by Ferdinand Lascoe. Such an invention, allowing all available images and information to show on a screen at the touch of one's fingers, would not obviate diligent research and meticulous examination by experts, but it would certainly speed the process up. Another one of her idle fancies that she will keep to herself, at least until the BBC puts it on *Tomorrow's World*.

What a pity the portrait cannot be displayed in the atrium of the gallery, with a sign asking all who enter, "Have you seen this girl before? Please tell us where!" It makes sense to her, because anything that generates the likelihood of positive coincidence makes sense to her, but she will never suggest it. People already make enough fun of her liking for paperback mysteries.

The junior assistant under-curator switches off the light and sets off for her home in Kingswells. She goes by bus, and she never goes anywhere without a paperback. As she pulls the latest Sorcha Belmonti from her bag, its cover displaying the usual full-colour assemblage of glamourous people and places, she sighs again over the unknown girl in the unverified portrait. She cannot understand why people always say that truth is stranger than fiction, while frequently dismissing the use of coincidence in fiction as far-fetched. Ridiculous! Sorcha Belmonti is a mystery herself, and so who can ever say how much real life might be in those stories? She thinks of the notes she made in the library and smiles in a satisfied way. Anything could happen, anything at all.

IN GRATITUDE

I have never before sent a story out into the world. Some people might be able to do that unaided, but I am not one of them. A story that turns into a book needs a cover, one that speaks in its own way, and for that I am very fortunate to have been introduced to Jonathan Cruickshank. His accolades include those of Scottish Landscape Photographer of the Year (John Muir Wild Places section); Scottish Nature Photographer of the Year (Urban section); and Historic Scotland Competition winner (2016). While exploring Jonathan's work, I found not only the right image for this book's cover, but also one so right for the sequel to *A Legend for a Girl* that it crystallised my vague title and triggered many new ideas (I am now writing that sequel).

I am also indebted to Duncan Ball, Information Specialist of the Met Office in Exeter, for providing records of particular Shipping Forecasts and patiently answering all my sometimes-confused enquiries. From my earliest childhood thoughts about such things, the weather of the British Isles and round about seemed to carry endless stories, or even to be a story in itself. It is a quirk of the imagination that has never left me. The Shipping Forecast stirs emotions that I cannot even name. The Met Office is a national treasure, in particular its Digital Library and Archive. When I discovered it, I had to stop myself roaming there, because my head went into the clouds and hours of writing time were endangered.

The mysterious painting of a young girl is also important to the story, and it exists in reality as the finished portrait of Marguerite de Gramont, painted in 1928 by Philip de László. I was meandering online, looking for a portrait of a lady in a blue dress, when I found it. Instantly, Elinore's story changed in my head. Within half a minute, I was thinking of a sequel. If you wish to see the portrait of Marguerite de Gramont, visit the website of the Philip de László Catalogue Raisonné (http://www.delaszlocatalogueraisonne.com/). The Catalogue is the immense, costly work of The de László Archive Trust, which is striving to trace, photograph and publish the more than 4,000 works that de László produced over fifty years. The Trust depends on sponsorship, above all for commissioning photography; it might trace a long-lost jewel of the de László oeuvre, but it cannot publish a photograph of it without the paid assistance of a professional photographer.

Every creative person finds their own fuel, and the beauty, superb artistry and inherent stories of de László paintings work for me. The story of Philip de László is fascinating in itself, especially when his work is understood as a uniquely important record of a period of British and European history. I believe that such efforts to record fine art and make it freely visible online to anyone, anywhere, deserve respect and support. Neither artistic heritage nor beauty is invulnerable. A donation to The de László Archive Trust is a way of helping to keep this work going, for everyone's benefit. I am indebted to Katherine Field, Senior Editor, for her courtesy and swift replies to all my questions.

Coincidence runs through this story as freely as, in my experience, it does in life.

Some years ago, I was walking through Cheltenham, minding my own business – shoe repair, dentist, that sort of thing – when my future decided to have a word with me. It placed a woman in the middle of a wide, crowded pedestrian thoroughfare, made her point at me with outstretched arm, and roar, "*You* have a book in you, my lady! You have a story to tell."

It was the time of the autumn horse fair, an important destination for gypsies in the southwest. This gypsy had clearly made me her business. I turned back and listened to what she had to say, for I did indeed have a book in me, or at least the hope of one. Whether she was foretelling *A Legend for a Girl* or one that I have yet to write, I will never know. She spoke with astonishing knowledge of my life, but said no more about books.

She was the loudest but neither the first nor the last person to urge me to write; nor was she the most persistent. My dear and special friend Rosemary Brown of Zürich takes that honour. In the absence of gypsies popping up during some very difficult times over the next 20 years to remind me of my destiny, "The Other Rosemary" offered me her friendship, unique wisdom and unstinting kindness. She is an accomplished professional astrologer, whose insight gave me answers about myself that had been entirely lacking until I came to know her by chance in 1996. Rosemary pressed me unceasingly to write, to pick up and work with the tools that she so clearly saw I had been given. Years later, she employed her other professional side as copy-editor and proof-reader of this book – twice. It is now 2017 and we still have not met! Another story . . .

From Rosemary Brown, I gained my first real understanding of the inseparable nature of mind, body and universe, and the role of our creative impulses in that matrix. In this regard, I also thank Stephanie Austin of Port Townsend, Washington. My growing understanding and questioning led me in turn to three remarkable practitioners in Vancouver, BC, whose input helped me manage and overcome certain health concerns so that I could get on with the job of writing this first book and finishing it. In the order of my discovering them, they are:

- Melisa Dzamastagic DO(UK) M(Ost) Med, BAppSc
- Mahsa Ahmadi, Dip. DTCM, R.Ac., C.SMA
- Susan Lee Woodward, Medical Intuitive

Each is a magician in her own way, and they all deserve immeasurable credit for my completing this first book.

My sister Lisanne has always been my best friend and the soul of generosity. When I needed to become a hermit and concentrate on this story alone, she and Den let me retreat for some winter months to Edward's Tower at their home in France. I became the red-eyed, woolly-hatted "Creature in the Tower", subject to outbreaks of angst, but I did accomplish what I set out to do. Lisanne laundered, cooked and shopped for me, and lent an ear to my maunderings; she also sat down and listened when I demanded a more critical audience than somnolent dogs and a cat. (I should say that I intentionally wrote *A Legend for a Girl* to be read aloud.) If you have a mind to run away for similar reasons, look up Domaine de Leygue. It is utterly peaceful, a fine place for hermits.

Yes, I ran away to France, and I left behind Mr Wonderful. Oh, the patience, kindness and goodheartedness of this man! The rest of the world knows him as Colin, my fiancé and partner. They have no idea that he is also my unlikely but invaluable muse. When Mr Wonderful met me, I was not quite what I have become. His passion for antique stoves notwithstanding, he deserves great admiration for putting up with me now, a self-fuelling furnace of blazing ideas for countless stories and ever-growing determination to write as many of them as possible. I take full responsibility for the domestic discomfort and sheer inconvenience arising in the wake of that determination – when you have to write, you *have* to write – and I thank him with all my heart and soul.

Finally, I must go back to the very beginning of my own story and thank my mother, Anne Chalmers, for being the polar opposite of Melba Crum. I was superbly fed (my mother was always the best cook I knew), very well clothed to meet any weather that rural

Scotland threw at me (she even sewed beautifully tailored dresses and jackets for me), and ensured that I was surrounded by the world's finest music from such an early age that I could not help but grow up with a curiosity about the lives of all great artists. And how Melba Crum would have recoiled in distaste from my mother's insistence on the virtues of fresh air and exercise, especially if that involved accompanying one's children outdoors in all seasons! I am infinitely fortunate for these reasons and countless others.

Rosemary Delnavine
May 2017

ABOUT THE AUTHOR

Rosemary Delnavine grew up in Scotland. Television had been invented but was not always in her home, and the Internet had not even reached the sci-fi pages of her comics. She could read and write long before school age and was expected to amuse herself under all circumstances, especially in isolated, hilly places.

She disliked eleven of her thirteen schools and was often admonished for daydreaming. Apart from books, her formative pleasures were the countryside, horses, dogs, and Lego bricks; the latter inspired her earliest choice of profession, to be an architect. [This is not what she became.]

Until recently, she was an administrative assistant at a pediatric medical research centre. She has had other occupations, most of them unsuitable.

She lives at present in Vancouver, British Columbia, but her inspiration remains rooted in the British Isles, and in Scotland above all. *A Legend for a Girl*, her debut novel, is the first in a planned series.

Printed in Great Britain
by Amazon